I had a very famous director call me and ask if I'd be interested in writing a new screenplay of *Moby Dick*. "Sure thing," I said.

"One change," he said. "We want you to write it from the point of view of the whale."

David Mamet, 'L.A. Homes'

…the patient who is presented in the supervisory session is a fiction…

Thomas Ogden, *Rediscovering Psychoanalysis*

THE PARRY AND THE LUNGE

DAVID MATHEW

First Montag Press E-Book and Paperback Original Edition February 2018

Montag Press
ISBN: 978-1-940233-50-5
Cover art ©2018 Daniel Serra
Design © 2018 Rick Febré
Author photo © 2014 Jonathan Jewell

Montag Press Team:
Project Editor – Charlie Franco
Managing Director – Charlie Franco

A Montag Press Book
www.montagpress.com
Montag Press
1066 47th Ave. Unit #9
Oakland CA 94601 USA

Montag Press, the burning book with the hatchet cover, the skewed word mark and the portrayal of the long-suffering fireman mascot are trademarks of Montag Press.

Printed & Digitally Originated in the United States of America
10 9 8 7 6 5 4 3 2 1

Dedicated to Jackie & Lola

THE PARRY
AND THE LUNGE

DAVID MATHEW

PROLOGUE

Wouldn't it be nice if the dead *stayed* dead?

It breaks your heart, death, but at least you should be able to gather comfort from the fact that the end means the end. They are not coming back to haunt you. It's a reassuring feeling, I would argue, or at least it ought to be. But…

Some nights I go looking for him; other nights *he* finds *me*, even if I don't want to be found. His presence – his reappearance in the gloom – is a drug. Nothing but. I withdraw for as long as I can, but I know I'll repine if I'm without him for very long. And then I'll hurt.

Stephen knows this too. Tonight he makes contact as I'm heating up loblolly for my evening meal.

'I killed someone before I had my first kiss,' he tells me.

'I don't want to know any more,' I reply.

'I want to tell you. I need to tell you.'

The feeling of being diluted – diluted as thin as my gruel – is remanent from his most recent communication. From the ones before that as well.

If I could, I would slam down the phone. I would sit in the dirty silence; try my best to earn back my strength. Even sleep. But Stephen will not let me go; it doesn't matter what I do because it's always been my fault from the start. I wanted him when he didn't want me.

Now, there is no twelve-step programme.

I'm hooked; I'm on the line.

'Tell me about who you killed,' I say quietly.

Stephen will not stay dead, no matter what anyone else wants or believes.

This is more Stephen's story than mine, I should say. Then again, what do *I* know?

Part One: The Parry

Nature gave us one tongue and two ears so we could hear twice as much as we speak.
Epictetus

In an alternative theory, the illusion is not the result of discrete sampling but instead of perceptual rivalry between appropriately activated and spuriously activated motion detectors... We propose, that a motion aftereffect is superimposed on the moving stimulus, sporadically allowing motion detectors for the reverse direction to dominate perception.
Keith A. Kline and David M. Eagleman, 'Evidence against the temporal subsampling account of illusory motion reversal'

The influence of civilizations hung over the border like a cloud.
Jack Kerouac, *Lonesome Traveller*

Eyesite

I.

1.

Hannah's favourite joke is about Hell.

A man arrives at the gates of Hell and is met by a demon who informs him he's got three choices for his eternal punishment. 'You can see what the punishments are, but once you've chosen there's no going back on your decision,' the demon informs him. So the man opens the first of three doors. Inside, for as far as the eye can see, there is fire, and millions of naked men and women shovelling hot coals and being prodded by devils with burning pokers. The man slams the door shut. 'Okay,' says the demon; 'are you sure?' The man is sure. He opens the second door, and as far as the eye can see there is ice, with millions of naked people screaming inside it and scratching at it. Again, the man slams the door. The demon asks him if he's certain, and again the man stresses he's certain. He opens the third door. As far as the eye can see, there are millions of naked people, all standing up to their waists in shit, but drinking cups of coffee and chatting pleasantly. Well, I don't like coffee much, the man thinks, and the smell of shit is something I'll have to get used to, but it's better than the first two punishments. 'I'll take the shit,' the man says to the demon. The demon asks him if he's thought it through properly, repeating the fact that once he's confirmed this alternative, this is what he'll face until the end of time. 'I'll take the shit,' the man reiterates, nodding confidently. The next thing he knows, he is naked, surrounded by nudity, with a cappuccino in his hand, and up to his hips in stinking ordure. This won't be so bad, he thinks. Then a voice booms out: 'Okay, people, your coffee break's over. Get back to your headstands.'

This joke reminds Hannah of her choices in romantic partners.

2.

During times between periods of welcome male attention – these times often containing periods of *un*welcome male attention – Hannah turns her affection to the inanimate and the inane. One of her pet loves is stairs: ascending them. When she stands at the foot of a staircase she might not smile exactly, but she feels momentarily blessed at the thought of what she is about to do, and she runs up the flight pell-mell, counting each stair. Asked once by one of her female friends why stairs were so interesting, Hannah replied enigmatically, not fully understanding the response herself: 'Why do we even try to reach the sky at all?'

3.

Hannah's most recent romantic partner is a man named Toby.

Toby is thirty-nine, fattish, oafish, professional; he runs a friendly team in a telesales department of a local newspaper, in charge of advertising space for the Sales and Services section. The job is enough to maintain his interest in novelty neckties and good ingredients for adventurous recipes every night, with a bottle of pricey French red to accompany the meal. He is not looking for companionship when Hannah bulldozes into his life with all the subtlety of a British sitcom...

Hannah's first flirtation was to crash into his car, and from there it was a case of eyes meeting across an insurance claim.

As they swapped addresses in the supermarket car park, Toby noticed Hannah's fruity perfume or body mist, and Hannah noticed a chevron of shave-abrased skin on his right cheek. They both trusted the mild fondnesses of their initial impressions. On parting, Hannah reiterated 'Sorry' – not certain if she meant for the accident or for the fact she was walking away.

She walked back to her car, some eight or nine lanes from Toby's Citroen, pushing her half-laden trolley. It was this very trolley that she had used to collide with the man's vehicle. Fate was present: the reversing car, the chesty gust of wind, the lapse of concentration (Hannah was thinking about work), and the shopping trolley with its one dodgy wheel that dragged it in a lurch to the left. A surprising amount of paintwork damage, really; neat as an appendix scar.

Hannah's second flirtation was to stop beating about the bush and wasting time. In a supermarket car park, where the average speed is approximately ten miles an hour, Hannah was going ten percent over the unofficial limit when she asserted her right on the road to the main exit, thereby ignoring the car pulling onto the same road from her left.

Toby and Hannah didn't bother arguing about whose right of way it was (it was Hannah's), and they even had a laugh as they said things like 'One each then' and 'No need to do the addresses again, I suppose'. Minor damages to both vehicles; the insurance companies would compensate. Individually, each of them celebrated the day's turn of events by returning to the workplace feeling high and sweet. Toby obtained her phone number from Directory Enquiries and called her two days later, having the collision to fall back on if there seemed to be no other topic of conversation to hand.

The relationship is dead fourteen months later.

4.

Sam is the diary that Hannah never writes. Unknown to the subject, Sam is not the *only* diary that Hannah never writes, but Sam is the minute-taker of Hannah's life: the official, approved biographer – the lovelorn cleric.

'You'll never guess what happened this morning. I started to dream again.'

'Oh dear.'

'I had a dream about two airplanes,' Hannah continues. 'The sky was perfect, and there was a jumbo jet being pestered by a biplane – the kind in the First World War? The ones with two wings…'

'All planes have two wings, Hannah…'

'Two *sets* of wings…'

'Or they'd fly around in circles.'

'Two *sets* of wings, I said!'

Sam smiles teasingly. Hannah can hear this down the line.

'I'm aware of the concept of a biplane, darling.'

'Well, this one could move like a wasp; it kept getting closer to the jet then backing away.'

'Am I going to need to get my cup of green tea from the other room?' Sam asks. There is the sound of keys being tapped.

'I'll be quick. Why, what else are you doing this morning?'

'Giving myself a hernia moving boxes. Unless you've got a better idea.'

'Sounds like you're typing.'

'Just a thank-you threat to Mike.'

Hannah nods her head in understanding. 'Maintenance payment's arrived then?'

'Yeah. With the usual spleen.'

Sam's ex-husband Mike will honour the agreement of providing maintenance to his children, but only on the condition that he accompanies each cheque with a letter containing fulsome and vociferous abuse, aimed at his ex-wife. These accusations and reproof arrive on letter-headed notepaper from the lumber business Mike co-owns. At the bottom of the sheet, where three addresses are printed, Mike usually remembers to circle the address for Head Office.

'You're a bitch?' Hannah ventures.

'Along those lines,' Sam replies. 'He's going back into blood country.'

Hannah takes this in her stride, but it wasn't always this way. The first time Sam mentioned that Mike had composed that month's lambast in blood, all five of the friends had been shocked. It was Annette who had said, after a pause, 'How do you know it was his own?'

'So what are you writing back?' Hannah asks.

Sam clears her throat. '"Dear Mike, Thank you for the cheque, as always. Next time could you write a longer letter? I do love to hear from you. With love and best wishes…"'

'Not bad. Try to convince him to make it a short story.'

'A novel would be good…'

'So what are these boxes you're humping?'

'Just some junk; some old clothes. I'll give 'em to the charity shop.'

'Do you want a hand?'

A diary knows when it's wanted and when it's needed. It's only a blink past six-thirty in the morning, and it was the diary who made the call.

'What are *you* going to do today?' Sam asks.

'I'm about to get ready to go to work.'

'How far have you got?'

'Teeth brushed.'

'Stop right there. Call in sick. I have something to make our day. We're going to get castrated. My treat. And you can tell me all about your dream. I promise I'll try to stay awake.'

5.

Toby was Hannah's palate-cleanser. Their time together led to a period of realignment of her perspectives. Once and for all, she studied her fallopial vital statistics: she finally decided she didn't want a child. At one point, Sam had proffered one of her wise sayings. 'All emotion is like water. Even love. You can take sustenance from it or you can drown in it.' Hannah's problem had been that neither of the options was true for her. From which she'd concluded that she didn't love Toby – she felt neither nourished, nor overwhelmed – and that must have meant that she didn't love him.

These days she worked in Research, and Toby was gone.
But was he *gone?*

The unctuous nature of what remained of his hair; the perpetuated over-kindness, his true feelings, say, over the weekly forgetting of the rubbish collection, and his sore joints. These aspects tended to linger, but in a nice way – like a kite flying overhead.

She thinks about Toby as she abandons her study – temporarily – of perioperative fasting, and climbs into heavy winterware and makes a move towards the place where Sam has suggested they meet up. 'There's no such thing,' Sam once said, 'as Memory Lane. Or Memory Autobahn. Memory Freeway. What we're talking about is Memory *County.* Memory *State*: the size of Montana.' Hannah had used the Internet to look up the size of Montana: it's the size of England. But she focused in on a sorghum field to the south of a town called Kallispell. And there he was – Toby – in the dirt and bustle, her favourite little scarecrow for some time, grinning crookedly. Smiling with stitches.

6.

Castration is how Sam phrases it: the painful loss of the necessary items – as a result of a past wrongdoing, perhaps. In *her* case... Sam enjoys castrating herself of money. She earns a lot; but she doesn't enjoy her ex-husband's contributions, other than as token victories. So she spends them willy-nilly, enjoying herself every step of the way.

'Hi.' She greets Hannah with pursed lips and tilted head. The rendezvous is a bus stop in the gut of the Milton Keynes Shopping Centre.

Kiss.

'I need a suit,' Sam informs Hannah.

'Why?'

'Because I have the money to buy one.'

7.

The dream that Hannah relays is as fresh as an Italian salad. In it, a biplane tests the patience of a jumbo jet. It niggles like an insect. It manoeuvres so that its wings bracket the left wing of the jet. Then the plane twists. It breaks the jet's wing off.

'Well, I think we can see a possible interpretation of that,' says Sam.

'You sound like you're about to lecture.'

'You're a ballbuster, Hannah. Ballbusting's what that dream's all about.'

Hannah laughs. 'Now how did I know you were gonna turn this around to sex.'

'I didn't say sex. I said ballbusting.'

'...Well, don't make me *beg*.'

'The space between the biplane's wings: that's the vagina.

The jumbo jet's wing is the phallus… You were breaking his dick off. Simple.'

Hannah remains amused. '*Whose* dick off? Toby's?' she says as they leave, burdened by bags, a boutique. Hannah has bought nothing.

'Mankind's. That dream was a revenger's tragedy, babe. Choose: Chinese or Indian or pizza. My treat.'

'Why don't we try that new Japanese place? By the bank.'

'Smoking or more smoking,' the boy asks, his expression professionally *tight*; his almond-shaped eyes a belt-buckle silver. With the small body pressed so compactly into a tiny black waistcoat, and with his hair gelled neatly into a widow's peak sharp as a chevron, the waiter gives both women the impression he's been dressed by his mother for the school photograph.

'Did you say *more smoking?*'

'Yeah yeah, upstair more smoking,' is the crisp reply. 'You won?'

'Yes, please,' Sam answers.

As the waiter performs a twirl as dainty as that of any ballerina, Hannah whispers, 'We don't even smoke anymore!'

'I know. I just wanna see what *more* smoking entails.'

'I didn't think smoking was allowed *anywhere* in public anymore.'

'And smoking *what*,' says Sam, 'is what I'd like to know.'

'It's not a hash bar, Sam!'

Overburdened by purchases, the women climb the stairs in rhythm with the shifting of the waiter's pert rump. Hannah feels a sense of openness and lightness in her head.

The restaurant is called Profit. Although the room is far from cavernous, only three tables are occupied, each by one man and one woman, in suits.

'Leave bag there you won. No one steal.'

The invitation comes as a relief. Next to a hat-stand the women place their belongings and are ushered to a table set for a party of seven. Both say thank you. As they get themselves settled, the waiter returns with two menus the size of coffee tables. The font size of the print thereon is microscopic.

'No wonder they all squint,' Sam mutters

'Racist.'

'Yeah right...Am I *reading* this correctly?'

'Oops. See what you mean, Sam. Look, do you want to leave? I had no idea it was so expensive. Sorry.'

'I'm not talking about the prices. Under Appetizers: Lipstick Tuna...What's that?'

'No idea. Oh look: in the Puds: Sneezy Girl Ice Cream. That sounds pretty amazing.'

'Sounds pretty *nasal* you mean. Pork Magique I can understand, I suppose. Not very Japanese, though, is it? I'd sue the translators.'

'You really would.'

'And where's all this *smoking* we were promised?' Sam continues.

'Seriously: do you want to go?'

'No way! I want to try the whole thing *a la carte*. Nary a noodle to be seen.'

'No: the Mains: look. Noodle Blue Rinse. Whatever that might imagine itself to be.'

Sam reads on. '*Pump Action* Noodles? Noodle *Surprise*? Surprise being, I bet, they bring you a cauliflower and a tuning fork. Bizarre.'

The friends spot the next one simultaneously, and bark out in unison:

'*Noodle Fellatio!*'

And that's it: they start laughing properly, in the way that only close friends can, or will allow themselves to. Sam says, 'I'm having *that*. No question.'

'What could they've been *trying* to say, I wonder.'

'Or I might have the Chicken Cha-Cha-Cha, I've changed my mind.'

The waiter is with them again, this time carrying a palm-sized e-book and a toothpick. 'Anything to drink first?'

Hannah and Sam turn to the next page. Here, the drink offerings are more reassuringly tame: recognized brands of lager and pop. For the first time, Sam pays real attention to the pricing system, almost praying for a misprint: she nurses a cartoonified, italicized bugbear for marked-up tariffs on drinks in restaurants.

'Is that true? Eighteen pounds for a chardonnay?'

'Yes, madam.'

'And that's a *glass* of chardonnay. You don't…leave the bottle or anything?'

'No, madam.'

'Do you squeeze and ferment each grape individually?' Sam asks.

'Yes, madam.'

'Pardon?' says Hannah.

'One grape at a time, sweet Jesus.'

Sam says, 'We'll wake up in a second. It's not as if I can even tell a good wine from a bad wine, anyway!'

'So a chardonnay for you, madam? And madam?' – turning to Hannah, who adds:

'We're really not in Kansas anymore.'

'Kansas?' asks the waiter. 'You won Kansas?'

'What is it?' Hannah wants to know.

'Cocktail.'

'I see. What's in it? No, don't tell me; I'll have a Kansas, and my friend'll have…' Consulting the relevant gobbets on the menu. '…a Sacred Bruise.'

'Good choice.' The waiter taps at his e-book with the toothpick; for a second he waits for the Order Received sign to flash up. 'Ready your Starters yet?'

Sam is first. 'Beef Mozzarella Hoedown,' she says.

Hannah adds, 'Cabbage Lowlife.'

In the end, neither opting for the Fellatio, the women complete their requests; they fold shut their coffee table menus and recommence their blathering.

'Why *seven* set places?' says Hannah, referring to their table. 'What's *seven*?'

'Lucky for some.' Sam shrugs.

'Seven's not a lucky number in Japanese,' Hannah answers. 'What were you talking about? Photographs?'

'I can't remember.'

8.

No one expects to be the victim of violence…

High above the sand, Hannah felt like a distinguished citizen. She was riding a camel, emptying her mind, as her covered shoulders baked in the early afternoon sun protecting the Pyramids. The guide was a five-foot prune in what appeared to be four hundredweight of bed linen; he held the camel's reins, but Hannah scarcely noticed him. Her attention was spread across the deep blue sky; the moment was perfect.

Or nearly. When Sam called from behind – 'Do you think we can get them to gallop?' – it shattered the glass that Hannah had forged around her senses.

Hannah reminded herself it was Sam's holiday too.

In one of the tombs, Sam had discussed her desire for a sexual encounter. Something about the proximity, she'd said, of hot, dead air; she felt in the mood. Hannah had told her she was weird; but she'd been grateful for that conversation. Although it had taken the women a mere half a minute to descend the slope beneath the Pyramid, Hannah had felt far from comfortable. Claustrophobia clawed at her face like a gritty breeze. At least Sam's desideratum to blow a native in the space of his forefathers had taken her mind off the sensation that she and her friend were trapped, pretending to appreciate hieroglyphics they didn't understand. She'd looked forward to getting back to natural heat.

Now, even this relief had been obliterated. More than ever before, Hannah realized what a solitary Mummy Bear she was. Even the desert, it seemed, wasn't vast enough.

The descent from the camels' backs was fun. The animals bent awkwardly, soothing their stomachs on the scorched earth, relieved of their burdens. Sam paid the guides.

'How much did you give them?' Hannah asked.

'Fifty Egyptian.'

'That's *well* over the odds!'

'It's what they asked for!'

'Well of course they did. They saw us coming. You never heard of haggling?'

'It's undignified. Lighten up, Han. They might feed their families for a week on that.'

'Good Samaritan to the last,' said Hannah.

Sam was concerned. 'Why, didn't you enjoy it?'

'I loved it,' Hannah lied nicely through a smile. 'Are you getting hungry?'

'Yes. Let's get some postcards first. They're better than photos.'

They walked away from the camel guides, in the direction of a shed-sized wooden box that seemed, from the collection of unattended tables outside, to be a good place to pay over the odds once more – this time for bottled water. 'Drink first,' Hannah suggested. 'The pretty boys with the postcards will find us easily enough.'

'I want one with green teeth,' said Sam. 'For the authentic peasant experience.'

They laughed, and Hannah called her a racist. One of the tables – white plastic, leaning slightly, warped – was where Sam and Hannah perched. Sam took the opportunity to finger a tooth at the back of her mouth. 'Still hurting?' Hannah asked.

'The painkillers are working, but yeah – still a bit.'

'Shouldn't you wash your hands first?'

'Why?'

'Because we've just been on camels! They have fleas.'

'Yum yum.'

Hannah laughed again. 'I'll remember that line for your obituary, shall I?'

'Give it to Dorothy.'

While watching other holidaymakers potter around the ruins in the near distance, Hannah and Sam fell silent. Sam took a travel book from her bag and read. Hannah asked for water from a young boy who arrived to serve them, carrying a battered metal tray. The tray was as shiny as a newly-minted coin; it caught the light and speared a ray at Hannah's shades.

'I wonder if the Elders approve,' she said, rolling a cigarette.

Sam looked up. 'Pardon? Can I have a pinch of tobacco?'

Somewhere behind their backs – towards the road along which the coach had brought them here – a drill was biting into stonework or earth; it made a noise like a car faltering before the ignition kicked in.

'In their beds beneath the ground,' she said. 'Do they approve of the money-making?'

'Tourism?'

'Yeah. I wonder what the dead think.'

'They think: hey, I'm hungry. My stomach feels like my throat's been cut.'

'Maybe they feed on our energy down there.'

'Yes, maybe. You sure it was your regular toothpaste you had this morning, Han?'

'Here's the water… *Shukran.*' To the boy, who had returned bearing sweating bottles, Hannah handed out a ten-pound note; it was dirty and as thin as an old cobweb.

'*Afwan.*'

Although they sat there less than twenty minutes, the women noted a young man carrying a parrot whose legs were strapped to his arms, who begged for seed money; another hoped for funds for school books; a third with no goal, no destination clearly stated, or possibly even in mind. The parrot looked fat enough, grumpy too, but Sam still fed it the equivalent of twenty English pounds.

'You're going to run out of money,' said Hannah.

Sam cleared her throat of smoke. 'Not till Hell freezes over. Which in *this* heat seems unlikely.' She flicked her ash inexpertly in an ashtray emblazoned with an image of Ra.

'It certainly is hot,' Hannah allowed.

In the end they didn't eat. They finished their bottled water, agreed to haggle over postcard prices, then boarded the coach back to the Zamalek district of Cairo, hell bent on a shower and a gin. Not necessarily in that order. Sam placed the travel guide on the lowered tray in front of her. As the engine shook the vehicle into compliance, they chatted. There was a lot of noise. All the passengers waited for the last of those with valid tickets to return from the tombs, the relics, from the jigsaw puzzle of rocks – the anagrammed city.

Because no one expects to be the victim of violence.

The thief boarded the coach with no more than a ticket check and a probable approximation (by the driver) of the last time the man had washed. The man stank.

Like eggs popping free from a pregnant turtle, coaches left the Pyramids in swift succession. The journey from there to Zamalek – and the hotel – is twenty minutes, allowing good to so-so traffic conditions. But in Cairo there are no such things as good to so-so traffic conditions, which is why forty minutes had been timetabled.

Terrorism works most effectively in the first ten percent or the last ten percent of a journey. Hana the thief opted for the former, standing up in seat 14B with a cry. Watched by the entire contingent of the trip, the thief moved in a crabwalk. He carried a gun – a Beretta. His expression was passive.

'I want your wallets and purses, please,' he said in perfect English.

9.

'There are bills,' Sam opines, smiling thinly, 'that when they come, the mega-rich of this world – the *really* rich – must look upon with some sort of disdain. Do you know what I mean? Those who think ostentatious is a synonym for good.'

'So?' asks Hannah, at length.

'This isn't one of those kind of bills. This is *truly* exorbitant.'

'How much?'

'With a tip? About three hundred.'

'For *lunch*? You can't afford this on your own…'

'Yes I can.'

'Well all right, you can. But it's immoral. It wasn't *that* good.'

'Yes it was, don't lie. You were purring like a kitten the whole way through, so don't protest you weren't.'

'All right, I won't, but even so…'

Sam holds up her hands. 'My treat, I said; my treat it'll be.'

'You sure?'

'Sure as shit falls off a shovel, my dear.'

Hannah frowns. 'Forget about morality for a moment, can that bill even be *correct*? What's the damage before you add the tip?'

'Two twenty,' Sam answers, her smile expanding.

'What's so funny?'

'You're gonna love this…'

'Go on then. Why are you not letting me see the bill?' Hannah's voice has dropped in timbre and in volume. 'What does it say?'

'Do the Maths. Two hundred and twenty,' Sam entices, nodding.

'Plus ten percent tip,' says Hannah with confidence, the cartoon light-bulb glowing white above her head, 'does not add up to three ton.'

'Right!'

'Even with a *twenty* percent tip! What have they added on?'

'Ready? This is special. I quote: *A no argue something for service:* twenty five quid. It's a peach, don't you think?'

'It's a *cheek* is what I think. They can fuck their tip!'

Sam starts laughing. 'Wait till you hear about the extras!'

'Let's talk about that two-twenty in the first place. How did we get *there?*'

Sam is laughing herself raw by this point. 'I'm gonna need the toilet in a minute.'

Not so amused, Hannah turns her head to one side, exhales hotly, and mutters that Sam had better not: there'll probably be a charge for the loo roll.

Sam regards the bill once more. 'There is an' all.'

'You're jesting. Give it here.' With which she lobster-pinches the slip of thick paper from between Sam's fingertips. Her eyes move quickly. 'They are taking the piss.'

'Literally! And we *pay* them to take it!'

Hannah remains disgusted. 'Two pounds for a pee!'

'She's probably on minimum wage,' Sam counters.

'I've already paid her!'

Everything has been itemized. *Door service; no-squeak stairway* – 'Well, that's not bloody true for a starter!' complains Hannah – much to Sam's further amusement – right down to the soap used in the washroom, the clean utensils ('clean *utensils?*' Hannah barks; 'should we have offered to eat with our fingers?'), before, many lines lower on the paper, delivering the *coup de grace:* the bill itself. 'They are billing us… five pounds… for writing us a *bill.*'

'I know!' Sam is all but hysterical.

'This is a crime,' Hannah tells her. 'I'm not paying for this.'

'You're not paying for anything.'

'You know what I mean. Stop laughing, will you? It's getting on my nerves.'

While removing her purse from her handbag, Sam manages to go a long way in doing just that. Tears in her eyes. 'Can't remember laughing like that for a long time.'

'It's a crime, Sam. Be reasonable.'

'I *am* being reasonable. Getting *angry* is unreasonable. And if it *is* a crime, it's a beautiful one, you can't deny that: the perfect caper.'

Sensing her own defeat on the matter, Hannah sighs, wishing silently they had smoked – smoked whatever – and offered such scant resistance to the robbery as she could muster. 'You are not giving them a fifty quid tip, Sam. I forbid it.'

'You're right. I'm upping it to a flat hundred. This is the best chuckle I've had since Mike went into A&E with a burst appendix.'

Hannah glances around. 'Where's our waiter? I want out. Atmosphere of a casino...'

Sam waits before replying. 'Classier than that,' she replies. 'Should I call him?'

'Better not. He might expect a blowjob for attending our table,' says Hannah.

'He might just get one,' Sam replies. 'I wonder how much they charge for *that.*'

10.

At the thief's request the coach moved through traffic.

Hannah and Sam were seated in 17A and B. Nearest the window, Hannah was in A. Abhorring the treatment to which she and her fellow passengers were being treated, she wanted to stretch out a leg and trip the thief up. Regardless of the fact that the gun might go off. Beyond a perforated eardrum or shattered skull, what harm could it do?

'Swap seats with me,' she said.

'Don't be stupid. He just wants money.'

Hannah looked up at the coach's ceiling. A portal, about a metre squared, was open by a fist-sized crack: to keep a modicum of fresh air — hot but nonetheless fresh — circulating while the engine was dormant. The driver had forgotten to close it again before leaving the site. While experiencing Sam's disapproval levelled squarely at the underside of her left jaw, Hannah maintained her stare at this vent. It seemed like a logical choice: to escape.

She leaned towards her homophonic namesake, proffering a fistful of Egyptian pound notes. Only her mind and not her mouth said 'Choke on it,' but it was ordered loud enough, apparently, for the thief to swallow some sort of titanium meatball.

'There's no need to be rude, madam,' Hana said to Hannah.

'I agree. Get a job for your drug habit.'

The man made a theatrical gesture of shaking his shoulders. Not in misunderstanding: no. Rather, in an open gesture, a rotten-food-in-fridge-door disgust, he said clearly, 'There are no drugs in my life.'

Hannah hit him.

From where she was trapped by the window, she was unable to get much strength, sense of accurate direction, or even malice into the punch; but it connected. Hannah's fist brushed the end of the thief's chin, causing, if not pain, then certainly distressed surprise. The man stepped back. Hannah felt panicked: horror and incredulity jostled in her system. Where she'd risen her backside from the chair in order to execute the lunge she now sat back down. Her pulse twittered.

The thief pointed the gun at the bridge of her nose. Both Sam and Hannah, and others beside, noted that the end of the weapon was fluctuating a centimetre or two to either side of rock-solid stability. The thief had been shaken by this insurrection.

Seconds tottered past. No one spoke. The coach had been delivered into the eye of a storm, where a fragile type of calm co-existed with violent possibilities. Hannah's *eyesite* at this moment consisted solely of the darkened nostril of the Beretta, lined up to her forehead's worry lines. She could even imagine a red electronic bead on her skin, projected in warning from the weapon; and it was at this moment she realized she would neither apologize nor acknowledge her tormentor. Though it took guts and courage, Hannah turned away from Hana; she focused on the outdoor cafes, their diners and drinkers on parade, it seemed, sipping from small cups or smoking apple tobacco from water pipes, as if they themselves – the customers – were on sale to the highest bidder; juice bars thrived; outside cluttered emporiums, postcard and clay camel vendors plied trade, cars parped and rattled.

Hannah laughed; she couldn't help herself. Was the coach still moving because the driver was in cahoots with the thief? Would they divvy up the rewards somewhere tonight? This afternoon? Such idle speculation, though mistimed, was encouraging, and Hannah was grateful for it as some sort of bodily distraction. In this spirit of ludicrous calm, she tried to slow her heart rate – or at least to soften the tattoo.

'Madam? You wrong me,' the thief said. 'You may have your money back if it means losing it leads to an assault on my person.'

Hannah found the man's blend of hubris and hypocrisy quite suffocating. It was enough to tear her away from what she could see through the window: all those people, doing what she herself had done for hours, exploring and following one another's trails like army ants. Girding herself for the challenge, and feeling the raw emotion radiating from Sam's body, Hannah returned to the weapon, which by now was shaking more wildly in its owner's grip. She was both afraid of and felt pity for the gun. But not its wielder, whose other hand clutched the pound notes that had been exchanged.

'Take it back,' said the thief, leaning in.

'I don't want it. Buy some heroin.'

'You insult me. Take it back – or I'll shoot you as I would a lame mule.'

'And how would that be?'

Sam found her voice, but all she could offer was an admonitory '*Hannah…*'

'Out of shame? That you've let it go so long a wounded animal? *Fuck* your money.'

The thief frowned at this death of logic. 'But it's *your* money, madam,' he protested.

'It's tainted,' Hannah told him. 'Do you know what that

word means? *Poisoned.*'

The man opened his mouth; he was about to retort, either with judicial discourse, or with spleenish invective – or perhaps he would snort mucus into the back of his throat, the better to spit a ball of hatred at his white-skinned enemy.

None of these options did he get a chance to achieve. The knee delivered decisively into the man's groin took care of that: *Sam's* knee. In one nippy motion, unbelievable to both women afterward, Sam had risen from her seat, knocked the thief's gun-holding arm to one side with both her hands clasped into a single fist – the trigger clicked – and planted her right knee in his bollocks with good force.

The thief bent at the waist, his cry of complaint like a badly-hit note on a clarinet. Falling backwards down the aisle, it was as though he'd been caught in the mouth of a vacuum; the coach's apparent airlessness matching his own. He was sucked down the aisle in the direction of the driver. But the trigger had *clicked.* There had been no concentrated crack or detonation; there was no blasted hole in the coach's ceiling. The gun wasn't loaded. And from the second of this understanding, the thief had no chance. Weakened already by Sam's effort to geld him, he was prey to the perching Johnny-Come-Latelies and back seat have-a-go heroes, now finding their latent lusts for honest fair play, into restraining the stinking waste of a life with bare knuckle force and ire on their sides.

After a few seconds the thief stopped struggling. Anchored stomach down on the coach floor by the knees and elbows of others, he wrenched his chin up to get a look at Sam and Hannah. Like everyone else was, they were standing in their seats. The coach felt fuller this way; for the first time it must have seemed so obvious to everyone quite *how outnumbered* this thief had been from the very beginning. But the thief didn't care about his odds, not now he'd lost. He only required the audience of the two friends, whom he addressed – 'Madam?' and then to Hannah, 'Madam?' – in a still voice voided of emotion.

'One day I will find you both,' he told them with crystal clarity. 'My name is Hana.'

II.

1.

Fingers thick with oil and perspiration, Doc Marten-booted feet up and crossed at the ankles on a desk fully cluttered with paperwork, unpaid bills in taupe envelopes, and a credit card franker, with a worried brow slowly relaxing into a contented expression of warm calm, brew in one hairy-knuckled fist and a roll-up smoke in the other, he, Lord of all he surveys, is Roy. And lo, he saw that it was good. Roy was happy.

At Bible Street Cars it is the end of the working day, and it has been a most productive nine-hour shift. Roy exhales in the direction of a broken-arsed Mondeo, while contemplating the gentle pleasure of a journey-home pint at The Leper. He has a *pica* for strong lager and lime.

Thus decided, he uncrosses his ankles, swings his feet to the floor, and stands up to a collection of creaks in his bones. He yawns proportionately into the high wide spaces of his place of work. The garage is vast. Busy, too, there are plenty of cars waiting, in various states of repair and disrepair. Some for which Roy silently expresses hope, some despair. There is a lot to work on, and that's just the way he likes it. In a celebratory mood, then, he ignites his final cigarette of the day, and in his head he recites the priority list for tomorrow – the running order based on promises he's doled out and ease of customer satisfaction. He always leaves brake jobs till last if he can help it: they're the trickiest little cunts on God's earth.

Hello? What's this? Footsteps on the driveway outside. The sound is unexpected and peculiar. No one *walks* to Bible Street Cars – or not many people do anyway, not unless the vehicle they've deposited for his safe care is their only conceivable means of transport. The set-up is no walking business, either from Leighton Buzzard *or* Stanbridge – and certainly not so close to the end of the day. Roy closes his eyes; he sips the air through clamped teeth. *Dear oh dear*, he recognizes the amateurish error he's made; he has left open the double doors through which his customers drive their vehicles in need of TLC. Light is spilling onto the courtyard; he cannot pretend not to be here. *Fuck it.*

Not to worry; tell 'em to come back tomorrow. Briefly Roy remembers a couple of early-evening to late-night visits, back in the old days, when he had Bible Street Cars in North London, actually on Bible Street. Never a better thing had he done than leaving that borough. On two separate occasions, two men wearing heavy winter scarves around their faces had come calling. Roy had lost a fortune: in readies. Untraceable. Inside job. The second one was what had convinced Roy to get out of the Big Smoke. One of the reasons he had moved out here, to Bedfordshire, to the comparative sticks, was for peace and for a better standard of life. The only thing he's brought with him is the company's name; and these days his place of work is a business unit that opens onto a potholed yard behind a cut-price carpet warehouse, whose products Roy has long since suspected comes from other than viable, tax-paying sources. What's more, Roy's place of work is not visible from Stanbridge Road. The footfalls haven't stopped at Carpet Banquet, so unless this is one extremely lost hitchhiker, the objective destination is Roy's domain.

Comforted by the thought of the 200 millimetre heavy duty spanner in the top drawer of his desk, Roy remains where he's stood for the last few seconds, waiting. Things get busy, top drawer gets opened. Simple as. He's smoking his cigarette so close to the filter that it tastes like venom. But he wants to be holding the butt, and not a new one – a show of inner cool – for when his guest comes into view.

She does so now. Crossing over from gravel and crushed stone – crushed by wear and tear rather than by design – she enters onto the garage's bumpy but one-piece concrete flooring. Gratefully Roy eyes her up and down; her eyes blink into the illumination, with Roy knowing that it's a lot brighter in here than it can seem from the outside, in the gloaming or in the evening's dark. She is younger than he – a rough guess places her in her late thirties, early forties – with shoulder-length auburn and blonde hair, done in streaks, and a round face displaying colour from either the chill of the evening air or a problem with drink, or both. She is wearing a long dark blue coat, and Roy's internal gauge judges: Reliable. Dropping the butt into a pewter mug brimming with other smoked casualties, Roy takes a few steps in her direction, his worried simper settling into a grin.

'I'm afraid we're shut for the evening,' he says.

'God, I'm sorry I'm so late,' the woman answers. She shows him the palms of her red-mittened hands, pleading helpless resignation. 'It's a longer walk from the bus stop than I thought. Just come to collect.'

'I was just locking up for the night.' Roy is perfectly certain that his visitor has not visited here before. He adds, 'I'm sorry, do I...?'

'Oh.' The woman moves in closer. Roy can see traces of perspiration on the line where her hair meets her brow. 'I'm collecting a Fiat Punto for Mrs Anderson. She's my aunt.'

'Do you have the registration number?'

The woman fiddles and faffs in her coat pocket, at the same time taking the single second necessary for her eyes to locate the right car. 'It's that one behind the Corsa,' she tells Roy, nodding her head in the direction of a Punto. 'Hang on.' Wearing the mittens she can't find what she's looking for in her pockets. She removes them and opens her mouth wide in order to hold them between her teeth. The piece of paper she removes from her left pocket is the back of an envelope. 'Here. RO58 DXF.'

Roy nods his head in the same direction. 'That's your aunt's all right. But I did tell Mrs Anderson it won't be ready till *tomorrow*.'

'She said that. Thought I'd chance it. If it's ready, she said, I can borrow it tonight – I'm meeting some friends in Milton Keynes. If it's not, I'm back on the bus.'

Roy laughs quickly. 'There hasn't been a storm, has there? Phone's still working?'

'Yeah well… bit of exercise. So it's not ready?'

Roy examines a jailer's hoop of keys, all sizes. 'As luck would have it, I've had a smashing old day today. Yes it is.' He finds the key. 'Come with me.' And he sets off towards the back of the garage, into the cave of cars, past balancers, scissor lifts, air tools, welding clamps, sanding blocks, slide hammers… Followed by Mrs Anderson's niece, he stops at the far end of the garage: another desk. A metal cabinet, to the eye as secure as a bank safe, is drilled to the brick wall. The key in Roy's hand unlocks it, to reveal a backboard of more keys, on hooks. In a matter of seconds Roy has demolished the code, recalling the first part of the Punto's registration: RO58. You add the first two numbers together: the Punto's ignition key is on hook thirteen. The key to the Corsa – blocking the Punto's exit – is on hook thirty-one.

'Just move out of your way,' Roy explains unnecessarily.

'Shall I pay up now?' he is asked as he walks back past his caller.

'It's all paid for, darling. Your auntie leaves a float with me.'

'Oh right, I didn't know that. Can I ask why?' Once again she follows Roy.

'Why what? Why she leaves me a deposit?' Roy unlocks

the Corsa.

'Yeah.' The visitor moves between the two cars in order to get to the Punto's driver's side, squeezed close to the garage's outer wall. As she contemplates the space available between the door and the wall she watches Roy angle down into the Corsa's passenger seat and fidget his way across the handbrake and the gearstick.

'She's done it this way for years, apparently,' Roy calls from inside the car '—when the bloke before me was around. When I moved in last year I couldn't see any reason to stop the practice!'

He starts the engine as the woman tries her best to get into her own car in the orthodox manner. No use. She enters via the passenger side and starts the Punto.

2.

Head like a box of dead sparrows.

Crapulent and disordered is how Roy feels now. He turns off Stanbridge Road and performs the in-car boogie required – torso lurching, shoulders arching, head swinging like a pendulum – as part of any vehicle's passport over the various depressions to the garage. The only music is the sound of the van's engine to the thump of the shocks, but Roy's dance is no less vigorous for that. As he's reminded himself on a few thousand occasions, he *must* get someone to tarmac the driveway.

Ian waits on a BMX bicycle: a FreeAgent Trail Duster, as Ian has taught the team. The *Presely* of BMX. The *De Niro* of BMX. It was with no small collection of tears in his eyes that Ian had told Roy: 'Boss? It's the fucky *noley growl* of BMX, mate.'

Ian. Junior Mechanic Ian. E for short.

Roy parks up beside him. 'Before you say it, *don't* say it,' he warns.

Ex-offender (possession of Class B, with intent) and all-round quick learner in the mysterious ways of mechanics, Ian takes one look at Roy's face and says, '*Kerplunk.*'

'I said don't say it, E. Get the kettle on.' Roy unlocks the large doors.

'Celebration or commiseration?' Ian asks, wheeling his beloved bike into the workplace. 'Is that why you're a few minutes late?'

'Neither. Just a quiet pint. And I'm not late: you're early. It's twenty to.'

Finishing chaining up the bike, Ian consults the clock on the wall above the tyre pump. By displaying 7:44 it confirms Roy's story.

'*Bollocks* to it,' Ian says. 'I could've had longer in bed!'

Roy climbs into his overalls. 'Get a brew going – two sugars – and we'll make a start on the graveyard. The Mitsubishi first.'

Half the morning passes on a tide of Radio 1 cranked up loud, strong sweet tea, tools clanking against parts, and the soothing sneezes of the compression apparatus spending air. Roy and his apprentice make good time. The money will come in on the backs of elephants, that'll be the only way to carry it, the sole beast of burden strong enough to bear the glorious load. Through his dawdling but diminishing hangover, Roy provides signs and sentences of admiration for Ian – for Ian who is doing so well on the straight and narrow, his dealing days long behind him. It's not until eleven that the telephone rings, the noise vibrating the two extra bells installed for amplification, one high up on both of the side walls.

'Get the blower, would you, E?' He wants Ian to take the call for two reasons: the first is that he is wrist deep in the diagnosis of a five year-old Citroen, the crown of his head gently shaving rust from the underside of the vehicle's erect bonnet as he peers within. But the second is to test if Ian has it in himself to take messages and make bookings.

Seems not. The boy calls his name out; waving come-hither in the exaggerated fashion of a constipated window-licker at his first sight of snow.

'What is it?'

'She wants to speak to you, Roy!'

'Kinnelle.' Roy straightens up quickly and nearly trepans his bonce on the bonnet. Roy marches over to the front desk. *Who is it?* he mouths.

'Mrs Anderson,' Ian answers.

'Hello, Mrs A. Fine morning bar the rain.'

'Indeed, Royston. Royston, please, your young man employed there has confused my good self.' Her voice is plummy, marginally agitated. 'I was merely calling to ask if I might call a taxi to take me from Stoke Hammond to your depot…'

She pronounces the last word with stress heavy on the second syllable, as in Daniel *Defoe*. This, however, isn't what makes Roy screw up the wrinkles on his face into deeper grooves.

'Mrs A,' he says into the mouthpiece, aiming for a certain qualified poshness of his own, 'I gave the key to your niece last night. She drove it to meet friends in MK.'

'Assuredly not, Royworth. I sent no niece to conduct my affairs, nor would I.'

'A surprise, perhaps?' Roy chances.

'Because you see, Royness, I *have* no niece…'

'She had your licence plate number on a bit of paper. She knew your name. She said she was doing for a favour or summing.'

'Who did? Did what?'

'Your *niece*. Pick up the car…'

'I've told you, Royreth, I don't have—'

'I *know*. I know, Mrs A,' Roy remarks, feeling thoroughly

nauseous.

'Royly. Do you mean to say that my Punto is no longer present?'

'*Exactly*, Mrs A.'

'Then I suggest one of us calls the police, shouldn't you say?'

'Yes. Good idea, Mrs A.'

'Good idea,' Mrs Anderson repeats, while Roy turns three-quarters to take a gander at what Ian's up to – to see if the lad's buckling down to his work or trying to overhear the conversation. The boy's working. Besides, from where Ian's stationed, you would need the hearing of a whale or a guinea pig to make out anything over the din of Radio 1. Mrs Anderson is saying something else, and ironically it is Roy who cannot hear; he wonders if Ian might have it in him to have set this up. He'd know the make, the registration...

'Sorry, Mrs A, I didn't catch that.'

'I was just saying, Roymond, that this is positively *exciting*.'

III.

1.

These are my sad waters.

The bathroom sink is approximately half full of water, sludge-grey with suds and shavings. Where 'approximately' is as close to the truth as he can manage, due to the unconventional shape of the basin itself – that elongation to the right hand side that his parents, with laughter, had discussed at length and had described as their defeat at the hands of modernism. And although the boy remains bemused, he knows that the joke is not important. The leaf-shaped bowl is what's important. All he has done, thus far, barely forty-five minutes after its expensive installation, is stare at it, direct his visual venom in its specific direction, micturate against its newborn olive shine, having saved up his visits to the lavatory for four hours, and laboriously depilated his shins in its neatly contained pond.

As he looses the reservoir, the wet plug in his fist, he watches the scum as it jumps, laps and licks. There is a knock at the door, although he never uses the locks, but his attention is on the whirl-pool. Another knock, three pounds against the door panels. He answers 'Yes' but what he wanted to say is 'What is it?' The drain gurgles and clears its hair-tickled throat.

'Can I come in?' he is asked.

'I'm not wearing any clothes.' In fact, he is wearing minus clothes, a layer *below* the skin. He has cut himself with his father's razor, an accent of an incision to his left shin has produced three leaking tears of red. Nor can he recall if the wound was intentional or accidental. Once he starts bathing in the sad waters, he finds it difficult to remember much.

These are my sad waters.

'Your dinner's ready,' his sister calls. Then she opens the door and looks him up and down. Her eyes instantly weary.

'Oh *James,*' she says. 'What have you done *now?*'

2.

Not being able to help it, he counts the sliced carrots on his plate (sixteen), and peas, levelled flat and not in a pile, to the side of the pork chop (thirty-six); and then he adds the two numbers together. Sixteen plus thirty-six equals fifty-two. This is the age of his father; more importantly, fifty-two is a good number. On this secured basis, James is happy to eat. Silently he does so; he cuts up his food, aware that at any second he will be asked about his day. After a bare minimum of chewing he swallows his first mouthful. When possible he swallows without chewing at all. He has an answer prepared, but the daily inquiry is becoming a stretch. The food is heavy in his gullet. Rapturously the boy burps and asks to excuse himself.

'Granted.'

This voice belongs to his stepfather and not his father.

'Did you have a good day?'

'Yes thank you.' James has finished his peas and will now begin work on his carrots. 'I talked to a policeman.'

There are four of them around the table in the kitchen: Mother, stepfather Lenny and sister Louise. They all stop moving their cutlery – their 'eating irons', James remembers suddenly from an earlier meal – at what he has said. The second of silence feels like chaos. Then it is Lenny who asks, 'A policeman, James? Where?'

James always tells the truth. 'On the Downs. Police Constable Simon Kolko. He told me to call him Simon.'

'He wanted an ice cream, you mean?'

James doesn't like his peas but he wants to eat his carrots. He dislikes questions much more than he dislikes peas, so he definitely dislikes questions more than he dislikes carrots: because carrots have vitamins and help your eyesight, or so he's been told. He doesn't understand the benefits of peas because no one's explained them to him and he has never asked for clarification. 'Not an ice cream, a lolly.'

'Oh.' Stepfather Lenny appears relieved. 'But that's *all* he wanted?'

'No.' James looks at his carrots as if he's being denied them. 'He wanted to know if I'd seen anything yesterday.' James tries to visualize his carrots into a process of disintegration. Although he's not hungry he wants to continue eating, since eating is good for you. A refusal to eat is why James gets poorly from time to time; besides this reason, he wants to eat because it will mean he cannot speak. You can't eat and speak at the same time because it's rude. You have to push the mulched food to the side of your mouth and look stupid.

'Seen anything yesterday?' repeats James's mother. 'What sort of anything?'

'I don't know. He wouldn't tell me. He asked me if I'd seen anything.'

'We heard that,' says Lenny. 'But what was the conversation about?'

'He asked me if I'd seen anything. Yesterday.'

'Don't exasperate him, Len.'

'I'm being calm, Sal, aren't I?' Now turning again to his stepson: 'James. Please repeat what the nice policeman said. As much as you can remember.'

This, thinks James, is more like it – easier – though he's somewhat surprised to note that for once a demonstration of his condition of hyperthymesia is being actively encouraged. At first he treats the invitation with suspicion. Then he confesses.

After he's spoken, when Lenny says 'I'll call Leo', James starts eating his pork chop. He always leaves his protein until last, not because he prefers it to vegetables, but because it is tough to eat meat, regardless of the quality of its preparation. When he's into his meat he knows that pain will come, and then it will go, and when it does the meal will be finished; at that point he can go up to his room and not talk to anyone anymore.

3.

P.C. Kolko was too overweight to be a policeman. James watched him lock the door of his unmarked car; the backlights blinked a confirmation.

Mid-morning, and trade was slow. James had been alone for the better part of ten minutes, looking out over at the counter at the few people who had decided to brave the slapping, scolding winds on the Downs' crest today. A man in a chocolate-coloured suit was shouting into a mobile, inside his Saab; to James the halved argument, from this distance across the car park, made the man within sound like a wasp trapped under an inverted pint glass. Beyond where the car park's stones ended and the grass began, a young dad was failing to show his infant son how to fly a kite. The wind was too strong. Even James could have told them that. An older lady was chaperoning a Red Setter's exploration and befoulment of the general area, armed with a pink pooper-scooper and a turbid smirk.

The policeman, not wearing a hat, walked over from the car to the stand. He had big Pingu feet and either a bad leg or some other impediment that forced him to jut out his left hip with every left stride. At the counter he said, 'All alone, son?'

'Yes.'

'It's not half term, is it, son?'

'No.'

'Then why aren't you in school?'

'I was suspended.'

'For doing what?'

'Fighting.'

'And who were you fighting?'

'Some boys called me names.'

'Ah is that it?' The policeman tried to win trust by smiling, but James trusted smiles even less than angry faces and bruised knuckles.

'And what *is* your name, son? Not your bad name. Your real name.'

James told him, then asked if he would like to buy an ice cream.

'Go on, then: a lime lolly, please.'

Busy pair of hands is a safe pair of hands, thought James, sinking his enthusiasm into the task of retrieving from the chest freezer the correct iced sweet, then pressing the appropriate button on the cash till, saying the number that he read on the display, and holding out his hand for the money.

'Thank you.'

He deposited the coins in the tray, counting them out to check the amount given, placing each coin in the right compartment.

The policeman tore open the lolly.

'I'm Simon Kolko. I'm a P.C. A Police Constable. But you can call me Simon.'

Kolko waited until James comprehended that it was his turn to speak.

'Thank you.'

'…Who's looking after this stand with you?'

Kolko scouted the terrain. His right hand was used to shield his vision from non-existent glare. His gaze swept wind through the grass.

James answered the question. 'Leo.' Then there was another hiatus.

Kolko stopped taking in the sharp decline of the hill, down to the brambles and far, far below, the farmers' dormant fields; he became disinterested in the walkers' paths, the few people present, or even the way (James thought) the sky itself resembled another pasture. Point blank into James's befuddlement the officer inquired: 'Not gonna be difficult, are you?'

'No.'

'So who's Leo?'

'Lenny's partner,' said James, who because he was an apt learner, and because unexpurgated details seemed to be favoured currency, added, 'Lenny's my stepdad. Wednesdays are Lenny's day off because he likes to go betting. Leo does today.'

'Then where *is* he?' Kolko bit the end off the lolly; it was too cold for his teeth, James could tell by the man's acute wince.

'Does that hurt? I'm only allowed ice cream on special occasions.'

'Why's that then? And yes, James, it does hurt. I need to see a dentist.'

'There are chemicals in them my brain doesn't like.'

'Is that so?'

'Yes. Leo's gone into Dunstable in his Mini. We're short on ice cream cones because he forgot to order them so he's gone to town to buy some from the supermarket, out of his own money, but I'm not supposed to tell my stepdad because he might be angry.'

Once more the police officer waited a second. Then, with an expression that bragged of his being fleet of wit and gumption, Kolko nodded his head briskly, decision made.

'Do you sell a lot of ice cream in this weather, James?'

'No. But at lunchtime it's busier. We sell Coca Cola and Diet Coke, and Fanta Orange, and Dr Pepper, and Sprite—'

'I understand. Do you know when Leo might be back from leaving you on your own?'

'No. Shouldn't be long. He's been gone a while. We also do hot dogs.'

'Great. Now James, do you mind if I ask you a question?

'No, I don't mind,' although he did – he had had enough already.

'Were you here yesterday?'

'Yes. I'm here most days from nine to twelve when I'm not allowed in school.'

'Right. And did you see anything? Anything unusual,' Kolko clarified.

It took James no more than a second to play back yesterday morning, but he held on to the silence like a shield. He wondered why the policeman had posed this question but he didn't want to appear rude by asking. Instead he dished out the turkey: 'There was a man on a mountain bike. He had black sunglasses that went round his head, although it wasn't sunny. There was that woman over there, with her dog. She comes every day. She picks the dog poo up with a special bag and puts it in one of the bins marked Canine Waste. There was a man and a woman holding hands and walking down the hill. There was a man who arrived and went jogging. There were two other walkers, but not togeth-er. There was a fat man who came on a motorbike and smoked a cigar and his music was loud. He liked heavy metal.'

Kolko nodded. 'Could you put the rest of this in your bin, please, James?' he asked. 'It's a bit too cold for my teeth. I should have ordered one your hot dogs.'

'We do burgers too, and slices of pizza for vegetarians.

Cheese and tomato.'

'That's good, James. And the cars these people came here in – did they all come at once?' He acknowledged James's shaking head. 'Throughout the morning then. Yes. And would you know any of the cars again, do you think, if you saw it? Anything whizzy?'

'I don't know if a car's whizzy or not.'

'Okay. But do you think you can remember any of the cars you saw?'

'Yes.'

'That's good, James; *very* good. Are you a car fan?'

'No. I just remember things well. The first one to arrive after I started was a silver Mondeo, registration number YR07 HHT. The second was an Orion, registration number…'

Minutes later Kolko handed James a business card.

4.

Dear Dad (James types),

I hope it's been nice weather in Heaven today. The man on the weather with the big head and the teeth that are too small says we might have snow at the end of the month. I don't like snow anymore because I can't play snowballs with you. I'm too old to build snowmen but I'd like to play snowballs. Mum doesn't know how to throw properly and Lenny throws them too hard. You always knew how to throw snowballs just right.

Mum asked me today what I wanted for my thirteenth birthday. She said I'd been a good boy because I'd cooperated with a policeman the other day and she wanted to get me an extra-extra-special present. I made her cry and I'm very sorry; I said I wanted you back. An hour after that Lenny knocked and came into my room, saying that he loved me and you weren't coming back. I didn't like him for that but I know it's true.

Today in Chemistry we did an experiment to make hydrogen. We had to hold the end of a lighted splinter to the end of a test tube and the hydrogen made the fire go pop. It was fun. I wish I could go back to school every day but Mr Tanner has told Mum and Lenny that it might be too early. He calls it a 'phased return' – after that trouble I had. It used to be interesting going to the kiosk every day but now it's got boring, and I miss my friends at school.

Not as much as I miss you.

I hope you will be my birthday present.

I have to go. Louise wants to use the bathroom to have a soak at her leisure so she's asked us all if we want to use the room first. I said yes. I have to brush my teeth. She's waiting for me – but I'm getting much faster at typing because she's always waiting for me.

Love

James xxx

P.S. Does Louise ever write to you, Dad? She told me a few months ago that she found it hard to remember the sound of your voice. I called her a whore and I got in more trouble.

P.P.S. Lenny says he will take me to the canal when it gets warmer, to go fishing. I remember when you took me fishing, Dad, and I nearly fell in and you saved me. I wish I could have saved you and I hope you're nice and dry now and not wet.

P.P.P.S. Lenny is angry with Leo because Leo left me on my own at the stand. Lenny shouted at him on the phone and told him he was as thick as I was. He said I didn't have 'the right brain' to be left alone in charge of 'a few hundred quid's worth' of ice cream and fizzy pop. The right brain, the part where we process our perception of shapes/motions, where we develop intuition, the time concepts of the present and the future, and where we store our hoards of intonation and accentuation, pragmatism, prosody, and the ability to contextualize. But that's not what Lenny meant. I waited for a good moment and then said to Lenny, 'Thanks for your vote of confidence.' He didn't know what I was talking about. He just shrugged.

IV.

1.

As she approaches, from a distance, she sees two nurses, one black and one white, both young, both tired – a fatigue she can feel in emanating waves, as opposed to deducing it from any telltale signs such as eye-orbit bruised baggage – and they are maundering on about recipes and what they intend to rustle up in their respective kitchens, as soon as they've killed the shift and gone home. The black nurse has some chicken salad left over from the weekend; the white nurse will defrost a marine pie. They laugh. Curtains of thick smoke ripple as the one moving gets closer to the women, and Dorothy wonders: *Don't they see me?*

A return to full wakefulness is rewarded with smiles from the two nurses. 'Here she is,' says the black nurse. 'You were quite deep,' the white nurse informs her. 'You can't have slept for a while before this. How are you feeling?'

Dorothy takes a second to answer, the words breaking from her mouth like kindling popping in a flame. Her mouth is dry. As she answers 'It hurts,' she is confident of her facial appearance: skin matte, any previous shine deadened by the operation from which she's emerged, apparently unscathed, if the nurses' chit-terchat has anything to say for itself; flesh yellow as a streetlamp's beam through light mist; two sugarcube-sized encumbrances of milk-coloured, crusted-up spittle in the corners of her mouth.

'Well you will. Do you know where you are?'

'Have you got your wits about you?'

'You were sleeping like a cherub!'

'...Do you think I could have a glass of water?' Dorothy asks the nurses, closing her eyes, pinching her lips together and

drawing them backward into her mouth to key up the saliva production line.

'She's thirsty.'

'I'll get her a drink, shall I?'

'That's kind of you.'

'No problem at all!' one or the other of the nurses twin-
klingly announces; but when Dorothy hears no evidence of anyone having moved, she raises her lids, squints briefly for focus,
and as though inferring that some sort of permission for the project management of this task is required, she adds with a blunt
rattle: 'Well, *go on* then?' Suspended from her palate, hiding above
her tongue, her uvula sings with sudden sharp pain, and the dry
white clags attached to her lips taste of pencils.

Silence. The dividend of Dorothy's directive is not, as she
expected, a swift departure by the nurses – in the direction of
a cupboard of National Health beakers, thence to a tap – in
order to execute the order, but rather a balky and stoic standing still. The nurses' faces are armed with square white teeth,
expensive-looking. Now dispelling the notion that Dorothy has
been embroidered into the fabric of any semblance of reality
(she must be dreaming, or at least hallucinating – shackled still to
the effects of the anaesthetic), these same rich teeth centrepiece
smiles that shift swiftly from pedantically mucilaginous to vaguely
threatening.

'She's a cross-patch, bless her,' says the black nurse, holding
firm to a resolution to do nothing whatever but durably grin,
giggle and engage in baby talk.

'Bless her. Bless her,' twice repeats the white nurse. Movement is no more forthcoming from this quarter. Dorothy watches
as the two women in their uniforms swap identical patronizing
glances. The ugly smiles linger like slush. 'How are you feeling?'

'I've told you: I'm hurting,' Dorothy replies, deciding on

a less supine posture. Surprisingly, the nurses neither say nor do anything to prevent Dorothy's sitting up in bed.

There is no noise from beyond the thin plastic curtains that border the observation cubicle. Has the rest of the hospital gone to sleep? Perhaps I *am* dreaming, thinks Dorothy.

'Snoozy bubbeyes,' says the white nurse. 'You need your rest.'

'Mrs Anthony want snoozy bubbeyes!' the black nurse backs her up.

Dorothy waits. Actively listening for any sound now – any sound at all will do – she divides her concentration, as beleaguered as it is by some remaining fronds of anaesthesia, between the two nurses. She waits some more. And she wants to know the nurses' names (she doesn't recognize either of them): not only for the purposes of the email she'll soon compose, the one complaining about their unanimous perfidy against the principles of contemporary healthcare, but because she wishes to appeal to the adult side of their hybridised nature, if such a sensibility exists. She is frightened; fear is gathering within her, competing with a quantity of discomfort that is shocking in its length and breadth.

'One. Mrs Anthony is a Miss. And she does *not* want snoozy bubbeyes. I've just been asleep. Nor am I a crosspatch or an infant without her front teeth in place. Two. What I *am* is extremely thirsty, and if my request for a glass of water… is *unreasonable* for some reason, I'd appreciate it if you'd tell me what that reason might be.'

Although the brief speech is not half bad, particularly given the grogginess affecting her judgement, the speaker is disheartened by the lack of reaction from her angels. The unrustable smiles are fixed in place; Dorothy makes a speedy estimation of the number of lashes on the black nurse's left eyelid; the number of crenellations on the white nurse's lower lip.

'Fetch me a doctor, please,' Dorothy tells them, swinging her legs to the left. She struggles for the name. 'Dr Daniels.'

Anything earlier than a recollection of the double-barrelled shotgun of her surgeon's nostrils and nose – the former of a prodigious circumference – as he leaned over her vision, inverted as he stood behind her head, and accompanied her in a sing-song of ten down to one as the gas took hold, is carrion memory. Dorothy's ears itch as her brain flaps and picks at what's on offer at the roadside back through time. There isn't much. A sense of injustice, shared with what she'd felt on the morning of her most recent visit to London, is stinging – it's as raw as an anal polyp. And she should know: she's had those as well.

Woozy but spurred on by bullied frustration, Dorothy stands up. She swims through eyesight as mushy as grease on a windowpane. Blinking helps. As she steadies herself for a few steps – no, for an *escape* – Dorothy blinks hallucinations from her vision. Sickness calls into her throat. Torso pain intensifies. She feels hemmed in by the curtains around the bed space; despite her protests, she is indeed tired. Refusing to take notice of the nurses' frozen expressions – not to mention their new wordlessness – exacerbates a wriggling appearance of mild claustrophobia. An uncertain step towards a curtain… and still no reaction from the nurses – or none that Dorothy can readily absorb. Dread is real. Dread knows Dorothy's address… She detests the smooth silence. Scattered thoughts from her past play while pecking at them again: London comes back strong, she remembers her occupation. Free yourself from this madness, she thinks, and there's material for the next one. Scribble it down in the *vade mecum*…

At the foot of the bed in which she's come back to life, Dorothy yanks the curtain to her right. The resulting attack is immediate.

2.

It was with little more than mild displeasure that Dorothy received the unfortunate news, but it was with taut disapproval that she acknowledged the speaker's bluff burst of laughter directly after. While accepting that the laughter was of the *nervous* variety, and while thankful that the burst was short-lived, she was unhappy to discover she had nothing in reserve for the eventuality.

'Couldn't someone have called me this morning?' Dorothy asked. 'We could have re-scheduled.'

'I tried. You'd already left. I really am most awfully...' Her voice stalled.

Dorothy shrugged. 'Worse things happen,' she said. At least she had managed a good run on the book she was reading (for research) on the train on the way into the capital – this itself the second victory in a row, after that of securing and maintaining for most of the journey a double seat all to herself. The blow to her plans – that Julia, with whom Dorothy had an eleven o'clock appointment, had phoned in sick – was one she could surmount. To this end, Dorothy was casually shuffling the options of an unexpected opportunity to visit the Tate Gallery or the Science Museum, or both, when the other speaker added:

'This doesn't necessarily mean the meeting can't go ahead, though, does it?'

Her name was Helen. Along with a creepy, weak handshake she had offered Dorothy this much – and not much else.

'Won't you take a seat?' Helen smiled; she appeared to be relieved by Dorothy's absence of temper or animation.

Dorothy licked her lips. She smothered a yawn and thanked her interlocutor.

In keeping with the look of the office, the chair into which she sank was expensive but comfortable. After she had accepted

Helen's offer of a cup of coffee, Dorothy gave her eyesight a ticket for a tour of the room. Sleek and modernistic; there was a lot of black wood and polished glass. The desk that should be Julia's, but today was Helen's, as a result of the former's (and senior's) influenzic *abstentia*, was as large and dark as a mausoleum.

Carrying corpulent mugs leaking tissues of steam, Helen returned to Dorothy's presence.

'Here we are,' she sang.

The perfume she wore smelt warm – 'Thanks' – and clean and PR-endorsed. As Dorothy brought her mug up to sip, she was happy to concede that she quite enjoyed disliking this girl's company.

'When did the office get refurbished?'

Helen had sat in what had always been Julia's space. 'Just after I was employed,' she answered. 'About a year.'

Wishing she hadn't brought the subject up, Dorothy took onto her tongue too much of the scalding black coffee. She hoped her eyes weren't watering as she rinsed her tastebuds with saliva.

'You've done a nice job,' she added. 'Or the decorators did.'

'Yes. It was looking a bit…'

Helen leaned forward into the desk – a slight but significant movement. Was an air of mystery, of a confidence about to be shared – was an air of subtle inveiglement, wondered Dorothy, the young woman's desired effect?

'A bit fuddy-duddy, don't you think?'

'I rather liked it. But then again, I'm forty years older than you.'

Helen laughed. It was the second time she had done so, and Dorothy admired it even less than she had on its debut eruption.

'I really doubt that! I've read your bio a hundred times, Dorothy. And not just for the job! I got into you at university. You were born–'

'Don't say it!' pleaded Dorothy, the note of horror in her voice in no way feigned. 'Not sure the heart could take it. But thank you for the compliment, Helen. It's always nice to find a reader I'm not too fuddy-duddy for.'

'You're welcome. But I didn't say *you* were fuddy-duddy.'

'I'm teasing you, dear.'

'Oh.' Helen brightened. 'Well, to business then, shall we? By the way…' Again, she smiled. '…it's thirty years.'

'What is?'

'The difference: thirty years. I'm twenty-eight. Just in case you're interested, because sometimes people are, but time goes on and they think it's too late to ask, so they contrive little detective puzzles to work things out.'

'Helen.' Dorothy placed her drink on the desk. 'If I want to ask someone's age, on the offchance it's important to me, I'll do so. Then the onus is on that person – to tell me or not tell me. But what intrigues me more, right now, is your mention of business – almost as though, and correct me if I'm wrong, please do, as though you expect me to discuss my novel in progress with anyone other than my agent of the past twelve years. Disabuse me of this idea if I've grabbed the dogshit-festooned end of the stick.'

Dorothy peered into Helen's eager eyes, zestfully yearning for an impossible future when her own would appear as satisfactorily inky. She waited. *I see*, was what Dorothy expected; *I see*, or *I'm sorry*, or some species of rebuttal along the lines of the fact that despite her relatively tender years, Helen was capable of handling any one of the agency's clients. Perhaps there would even be tears – an outburst through which Helen might make it clear she was more than an Anthony-reader, more than a fan, she was a fully paid-up literary professional.

'You're really quite sick, aren't you?' asked Helen.

'…Beg pardon?'

'You're sick,' Helen told her, an unforced, not-for-show lightness splashing in the waves of the accusation. 'You're more poorly than Julia led me to think.'

'I'm not *ill.*'

'Is it malignant? No, don't answer that. Here.' Lips flexed in such a way as to concave her cheeks, Helen pushed across the desk a large white envelope.

The guess that Dorothy had made ran as follows: once the pecking order had been established, Dorothy would make a medium-to-big deal of acquiescing to Helen's suggestion to talk turkey. Nothing specific: just how far into the writing she'd got; an approximate delivery date for the manuscript; if matters paddled well, some light discussion on the topic of advances expectations – all of this, naturally, over a lunch to which, following two decades of convention since she'd first published, she would be treated.

'What's this?'

'From Julia. Some ideas on what you've submitted so far.'

Having unfolded the envelope's cuff (it wasn't sealed), Dorothy noted that what lurked inside was at least ten sheets long.

'Read it on the train home,' Helen announced, standing up and brushing both invisible motes of dust from her sleeve and the talks themselves from her diary. 'I concur with her thoughts, for what it's worth. It's not your best work, not so far. But we can live in dreams, I suppose.'

Was that it? Dorothy struggled erect, the sciatic nerve in her right leg pulsing painfully and without warning. The fact that rankled was her *fear* of how powerfully the diagnosis from this chit had punched her sternum. Since three years earlier, Dorothy had had good reason to read up on myocardial infarction, and now she felt unfamiliar twinges in her breastbone. Her heart raced. Was she being *fired?*

'I'll be speaking to Julia about this,' Dorothy warned – or tried to warn.

Helen nodded. 'She'll probably be back tomorrow. A twenty-four hour thing. I left her with two jugs of water and a thermos of flu powders. I'll pass on your concern while I'm microwaving her chicken soup tonight. Goodbye, Dorothy.'

3.

The noise is immediate: a panorama of sound. Voices, mainly. Through the shock that Dorothy experiences, she feels assaulted by the din. It's the wall of intermingled, raging sounds that makes it tough for Dorothy to shift position. A nurse speeds past, brushing Dorothy lightly; the noises that weren't there a second ago are beginning to make sense of themselves. Babel tamed.

Dorothy is looking at a hospital ward – the ward is looking right back at Dorothy. Visiting time. She is not aware of the hour – not even of the time of day, morning, noon or night. All of the other eleven beds on the ward are occupied; Dorothy is the only patient standing. A sweep of the head, a rough count behind her eyes, and Dorothy knows seven of her roomies have visitors.

With no shift in her stance, Dorothy looks over her left shoulder, a second after a feeling of self-consciousness at being in her nightdress sweeps over her. Curtains shut, she'd heard nothing but jibber-jabber from the nurses; curtains open, and the scene is ward-normal. She intends to demand an explanation from those in uniform who have upset her.

The nurses are not by her bed.

4.

The tanned light smelt distantly of the river, and Dorothy, querulous and shaken, needing somewhere to sit after the altercation in Julia's office, made her way towards the water, where she intended to read the report. The journey was simple: no amount of memory loss would have been able to erase the recollection of the path to the river bank, where she and her agent had dined on so many occasions. As Hannah is drawn to the air (or so she claims), so Dorothy is drawn to water, the rougher the better. She settled in behind a group of Oriental children, taking something – she was not sure what exactly; solace? comfort? – from their contented chirping and easy-to-match stride.

From a vendor she purchased overpriced strawberry ice-cream, and settled down with her matchbox-sized tub and a spoon so small it made her think of a thumbnail attached to a twiglet. The bench Dorothy sat on was cold stone; any rays of sun as had made it through the lacy clouds had done nothing to warm up the alfresco furniture; but, vestigially baffled, affronted and rattled as she remained, Dorothy regarded the chill to her glutes and her inner thighs with affection. For the moment she ignored the envelope. Let the sight of the Thames – sour-mooded and sombre as it was late mornings – soothe her first; water healed. The physician was Father Thames.

Chilled snack completed, Dorothy spooled the tape of the conversation with Helen one more time, intending it to be the final play. *Perspectivize*, as she'd heard Annette say at their last group lunch – a neologism that Dorothy had relished countering. But here it worked, with the tourists passing by, reforming into new patterns like swallows in urgent flight, and with students opening their books and listening to lectures on personal stereos – the business of the bank this day, as different from how it would be tomorrow as it was from how it had been yesterday – *perspectivize* was garnished with a peculiar apt spiciness. All this nonsense would take just a phone call to Julia.

She would ring after lunch. This gave Dorothy ample time

and chance to gather her disappointment and scraped-raw pride into something more coherent and vicious. Not that she'd be anything, of course, but icily professional. She and Julia went back a long way; Julia and Helen did not. She and Julia had made money for one another. Dorothy sighed; her fingertips caressing the envelope's sticky slit. She thought again of the new-look office. With undeniable sadness Dorothy admitted that a lot of time had lapsed since her most, but not very, recent trip on business down here to the Smoke. She sighed again. From the water a metre or so from where she sat, a decrepit-looking gang of gulls shrilly swooped to ambush an abandoned crisp, dropped by a child wearing oversized shades as she or he toddled past, dragging a parent or a guardian along by outstretched security reins. For a third and final time Dorothy sighed. The gulls' assault and the toddler made Dorothy glummer.

Read the report.

Her stomach told her it was too early to eat. Dorothy decided nonetheless on a table somewhere quiet, where she would feast first on words, be they roses, or be they thorns, over a remorseful and pensive gin-and-It. Depending on the severity of the critique, she would then order a second drink, and either a salad or something less punitive, nutritionally speaking. Taking intuition and her nasal senses as some sort of food guide, Dorothy selected her establishment and was mimed in the direction of one of any number of identical, unoccupied plastic chair-and-table combos in the jolly-looking eaterie. Before the waitress could get far, Dorothy surrendered it a bad day for her blood pressure, and asked for chilled gin. The waitress seemed to skid slowly away on lazy strides; she peppersprayed something in Italian – the drink order, perhaps – at a male, acquiescent voice, somewhere stage right – and Dorothy unsheathed the pages of her dubious fate.

'Bloody hell,' she thought aloud a few seconds later.

V.

1.

Buy locusts online, the advertisement reads.

Breeder direct! Tip-top quality. Postage free within the British Isles. Dealers welcome!

'Sabrina, come and have a look at this.'

'Look at what?'

'Come and look and you'll find out!' I tell her, nodding at the screen but not knowing if she's watching the back of my head from where she stands in the kitchen, waiting for the kettle to boil, a bowl of clicking cereal raised up to her mouth.

'Is it something yucky?'

'Very.'

I hear her crossing closer to where I'm sitting at my desk. *Our* desk; excuse me. Since the appointment to her new job we've been using the computer on a time-share scheme that doesn't always work out for the best. We need another machine; but where would we station it? There is scarcely room in this flat for us to extend our limbs.

'Yuck. Why would anyone buy *locusts*?' she asks.

She is dressed in a dark grey tracksuit – she's been to the gym – and now she stands beside me, to my right, her left hand over my shoulders.

'Pet owners? I don't know.'

'What eats locusts?'

'Snakes?'

'What are you looking at?'

'Just email. I'm tempted to click the banner to see how much they fetch.'

'Go on then.'

'Because if you click, they can catch your email address. Send you *more* crap.'

Sabrina laughs through her nose. 'Birds of prey. Gazelles.'

'That kind of thing, yeah.'

'Have you eaten anything?'

'I left you some pizza. Sorry. Should have remembered that before you had cereal.'

'I'll take it to work for lunch.' She pauses. 'Are you going in tomorrow?'

'I'll see how I feel in the morning. It's really sore right now.'

'Have you had some paracetamol and codeine?'

'Yeah. I'm chewing 'em down like Jelly Babies.'

'You're not supposed to *chew* them! — I'm taking a shower.'

I don't bother asking why she hasn't showered at the leisure centre, after using the gym, because I've asked too many times in the past and Sabrina becomes aerated if she has to repeat things more than twice. If she *has* to, that is: she has no problem retelling the same story (albeit with minor alterations of local detail and subsequent embellishments), forgetfully confident that this is the first time she's mentioned the matter.

At about the same time as the shower starts churning, the lesbians in the flat across the hall begin their bi-nightly argument. Shrill and Dopey we call 'em, and they're off again. I decide I'm not in the market for live locusts, nor do I have anything in my inbox but my usual daily link to a psychologist's blog that I don't know how to block, and come-ons for penis dismorphication and Botox jabs for crow's feet. This particular night's audio segment of the Lesbian Trials I don't much want to catch either; even if I did want to hear more — more allegations, more stringent denial, more insults — I would struggle to make out much through the thin walls this evening. Sometimes — as it is with Stephen's communications – the words are sharp and hard to miss; other nights, like tonight, Shrill and Dopey seem to be bellowing into pillowcases, across half a hectare of woodland. I turn off the PC. Stretch my poor back. Settle down on the couch with the unread local paper, five copies of which have been shoved, as they are every Tuesday, Thursday, and Saturday through the letterbox on the communal front door, to serve the five flats in this block: *The Leighton Buzzard Times*.

The headline is the politest weeny scream you've ever heard. Never let it be said that *The Leighton Buzzard Times* succumbs to wilful sensationalism, not even when the story manifestly deserves such treatment. This is the paper (and this is the town) in which a piece about a lost kitten can make it as close to the front page as page three. This is where future generations, or conquistadors from planets far beyond our extant technology's eyesight, will come to see the *definition* of small town existence in the British Isles. Where a mole 'devastating' the pristine shag of the golf course can exacerbate public outrage; where an affair between a boss and a secretary, in a bra factory, down the road from where I live, can cause a fire (a mistakenly dropped, post-coital cigarette), and gallop its way into print.

MAN FOUND DEAD, PERHAPS MURDERED, ON DUNSTABLE DOWNS, is the cautious headline. 'A man has been found dead, perhaps murdered, on Dunstable Downs. The discovery was made on Tuesday evening, by a man out walking his Red Setter dog…'

Love that *Red Setter* touch. Don't love the story. Through my living room wall, which butts against Shrill and Dopey's, I swear I hear the word *peanuts*. Over and over again: *peanuts, peanuts*. What on earth can they be rowing about *now*? I want to wonder – but the question in my head won't remain; it's salted down by strong sea spray – the waves in my head carrying pictures of Stephen in their surf – and all manner of logical thinking is eroded. I stand up again; I don't know whether to stand, sit – to cry out, shout up the dead, to wait for Sabrina to complete her process of bodily refreshment...

Refreshment! In the fridge – a whole eight strides from where I'm standing is a bottle of Finnish *sahti*, brewed with juniper berries, a treat for the tongue. I open the bottle. Half of it's gone before I've stopped thinking that the reported crime was Stephen's doing.

Then the phone rings, and I'm sure it's Stephen calling.

2.

Some killers can change their pasts in the manner that children are able, repeating an inexactitude with such regularity that they manage to convince their own memories that it happened this way and not the other: not the way that the police and the prosecution propounded; not the way that the tabloids and broadsheets had it in cold print. The spit-and-polished histories will now take root in a murderer's mind.

I know this from my extensive research on the subject.

Other killers, on the other hand, cannot do this at all. This breed is logorrhoeaic and sternly aortic with the truth. They can't help themselves; day in, day out, they talk about what they've done the entire time. Stephen counts himself among this clan. Or rather, he would if he had the first impression that they even existed.

3.

'Who was it?' Sabrina asks.

By now I'm in the other room, in the bedroom, reading Kingsley Amis, but I'm not feeling it tonight. His jokes aren't working. I feel like I've just discovered that something we believed in at the time, though we had no reason to believe it, has been disproved.

'Who was what?'

'On the phone. Rang while I was in the shower.' Confirming that there is no chance that this one-bedroomed flat will last forever. It's small enough when we're at ceasefire, but when I don't want her around, logging the times of phone calls, I count the new cracks in the plastered walls and feel absorbed by the hefty *anti-plenitude* of the place.

'Wrong number.'

'Who'd they want?'

'Billy Bollocks. I have no idea. Are you expecting a call?'

'Arrangements for Saturday.' Sabrina is drying her hair.

'Who's going?'

'That's what the arrangements are all about. Silly.'

The bedroom's not cold, but Sabrina takes her shower at a temperature that might give a sand beetle something to think about; the deluge she favours stripping ink stains from shirts. The temperature she suffers (without suffering) makes her shower more effective for laundry than the washing machine. As a result of her voluntary scalding, her skin, brow to ankles, is an apoplectic red. Punctuation marks of steam rise from her shoulders, her breasts; she is before me naked and gorgeous.

'Bloody hell, it's freezing in here,' she says.

'It's not. The heating's on.'

'Male or female. On the phone,' she asks abruptly, turning away from me to the mirror. Like a guy does she yanks the towel to and fro across the plane of her shoulders.

It was Stephen calling me; I know it was. I hadn't dared to pick up the receiver. I hadn't wanted to hear his voice; but now, something else is troubling. In comparison, this new worry is the equivalent, perhaps, of the page three lost kitten, the vandalous mole, the front page fiery frolic midst the knickers in the lingerie manufactory... I choose my words carefully.

'I think I'd know your friends' voices by now, Sab,' I lie to her. 'It was a man.'

Sabrina is drying her upper body. 'And he said what exactly?'

'He said: sorry, I've must've got the wrong number. Then he put the phone down. Why the interest?' I can't stop myself from asking. Just then the phone rings again.

'I'll get it.' Not a stitch to wear, Lady Godiva makes a play for the other room. I warn her, after her back, that I haven't yet closed the curtains, and if she turns on the light she'll be a feast of nudity for the neighbours in the houses behind to gorge upon. Before picking up the phone she quickly tells me not to be so melodramatic; but she doesn't turn on the light in there. My curiosity is piqued. As they say. It's with a note of disappointment that I eavesdrop on Sabrina saying, 'Oh, hi Hannah! How've you been?'

I wonder if Hannah knows that Sabrina takes phone calls while naked.

'I know,' Sabrina is saying, 'Isn't it awful? Annette told me at the gym. Is she coming, by the way? It'll be good to see her again. What about Dorothy and Sam?'

That's all the poor bastard's earned, is it? – that one rhetorical, 'Isn't it awful?' – and even then I'm only *assuming* that the subject is the body on the Downs. But that's right: get your arrangements for *lunch* sorted first. You can always discuss the corpse at the table.

I'm getting bitter. Sometimes there's a person inside me I dislike.

'Go on – who? You are *kidding... When?* Do the others know?' A longer pause. 'Well *you've* got plenty to talk about on Saturday.

Where are we going, by the way?' Pause. 'What do you mean? O*kay*. I'll look forward to that. I think… Me? Oh nothing much…'

4.

Of course I'm *grateful* for their monthly meet-ups. Where on earth would I be without them?

The five women congregate – Sabrina, Hannah, Sam, Annette and Dorothy – on the first Saturday of every month. Usually it's lunch; not always. The idea is for this quincunx to take it in turns to arrange the treat. One time when it was Sabrina's turn, she organized a hot air balloon ride for them, complete with a picnic hamper of sandwiches, pork pies and champagne. I won't pretend I wasn't jealous. *Why don't you want to go ballooning with me?* I remember asking Sabrina – and not once either. She couldn't really answer; there *wasn't* an answer. Hannah, apparently, loved it the most.

This time round – September – it's Sam's turn. I am as much in the dark as to where they'll be going as Sabrina is. Knowing Sam and her endless funds, it won't come cheap; but that's Sabrina's lookout. Her purse has nothing to do with me.

But her mind does. I believe that it's a right we have – to splash in the mud and the clay of another's consciousness – once we have invited that other into a home. Physical spaces are the same as mental spaces. I want to know all about her and her friends.

Sabrina is aware of this. Indeed, she treats the obligation with ascetic zeal, not fully comprehending sometimes that I do not need the creek, I need the nuggets of gold within it. My reliable narrator arrives home and tells me *everything*. I am able to sift for gold; smelt and agglutinate the nuggets into good, twisted brooches, into sour-looking rings from which I build my stories.

So of course I'm grateful for their monthly meet-ups.

This doesn't mean I have to look forward to them.

5.

'It's Sam's shout this month.'

'Yeah, you told me. – Do you know what's strange?'

'Apart from your hair? You really need a haircut, Tom.'

'I'm growing it long. What's strange is – the news isn't on the news.'

'The *news* isn't on the news?'

'The news about that guy on the Downs. Wouldn't you have thought it would be on the television news? It made it into our local rag…'

'Maybe it was.'

'We watch it every night!'

'Not last night, you didn't,' Sabrina reminds me. 'You fell asleep early and dribbled. You were having bad dreams before I'd even brushed my teeth.'

We are lying in the darkness. We are too tired to read. But we cannot sleep either; there is knowledge that neither of us understands, knowledge between us.

I've been expecting Stephen to get in touch. He is silent.

'She's taking us to a wacky new restaurant,' Sabrina tells me. She has told me this as well. She is talking into the darkness, not even necessarily to me; just talking for the sake of talking. Taming what they are that live in the night. I am frightened.

He wants me to go there: to the Downs. He has something to show me, to tell me: something to make me learn. This is why he is incommunicado. It's a test.

'I'll go there,' I mutter; the words leak out like broken wind.

'To the restaurant?'

'No. To the—'

'To the Downs?' she snaps. 'That's ghoulish. Why would

you want to do that?'

Why would I want to do that?

'Christ, Tom, you're sweating. Do you feel all right?'

'I feel ill. I'm not going to work tomorrow. I can't face it.'

She waits for a second. Our minds read one another. 'See how you feel in the morning,' Sabrina suggests.

'I can't face it,' I tell her again.

'I know. But *we* can't face not having your salary paid.'

'I'm still on half pay,' I remind her. 'Till the end of the month.'

'When the mortgage'll be due, Tom.'

'We'll manage.'

'I know we will.'

Rather testily I add: 'I am *looking* for another job, you know?'

'Yes I know. But you'll still need a reference. You can't just not go.'

This is going to curdle – this conversation – I can sense it. But I give back to the accusation all the same. 'I'm *not* just not going. I'm ill. And I've got a bad back.'

'Come off it, Tom.' Sabrina moves away from me and my perspiration; she is finding the right ground from which to send her missiles. It is night and we cannot sleep, therefore it's time for a fight.

'Dorothy had stones crushed in her *kidney* and she was working the next day.'

'Bully for Dorothy.' My sentence sounds petulant and thin.

'She's even coming on Saturday! That'll be nice. No one expected her to, so soon.'

'Bully for Dorothy. Maybe she's a tougher person than I am.'

'I'm sure it's painful,' Sabrina concedes. 'But it's a pulled muscle. You won't go to chiro because it's too expensive, and you forget to take your codeine. You're not helping.'

'I'm resting. I'm writing.'

'...What about?' Sabrina wants to know.

'You, as a matter of fact.'

'How interesting! Am I a princess in it?'

'No.'

6.

Sabrina shares my space in this hutch, and therefore she is partly mysterious to me. It can't help but be any other way. She is here – constantly reminding me that there is always more work on my part, more work to be done – because I don't know everything. I know about her cheerful but impoverished North London upbringing; I know about her education, and the lecturer she wanted to marry while she was at university. But I don't know *everything*.

Annette I don't know at all. I've never met her. But based on what Sabrina tells me, and on such little as I glean from my infrequent bumps into the other members of the quincunx, I see Annette as disappointed with her home life; boxing below her weight in a job at the leisure centre, enjoying it but too frightened to move on for more. As if I'm present personally, I can watch her planning her next affair – the one that she hopes will drive Richard away, but away on terms so good, so cordial, that they will maintain the spiritual upkeep and maintenance of the children. I watch her at work. Look! – she's teaching the butterfly stroke.

A mixture of sure-footedness and wannabe ethereality, Hannah lives and works at home, driving pieces of non-fiction on to her hard drive with the spirited precision of a chauffeur of long standing. She lives on air. Where does her money come from? How much can one university or another pay? Her ar-

ticles appear in medical journals and are used as think pieces
for undergraduates on Ethics courses, or studying for National
Vocational Qualifications in Care. She is writing about perioperative fasting. Two weeks ago she was researching the topic of visual short term memory. If I remember correctly. And next week
she'll be researching and typing up, I don't know, bladder cancer
treatments or hospital canteens' food safety.

Hannah is the one who appears to belly-dance through
life: she makes the difficult look easy; the muscular look sexy; the
grinding look fluid. Hannah is the only one of the five I've slept
with – it happened four times; five if you count one occasion of
impotence – and as a consequence I see her as little as possible.
Sabrina doesn't know about Hannah and me.

She knows about Sam and me, however, she knows that we
cannot stand one another. It's a brittle kind of love between us.
An American girl at university once told me, 'You can love someone without even liking them.' It sounds obvious now, now that
I'm comfortably into my thirties (without being comfortable); but
as an undergrad this struck me with a force like the ripping of
the sound barrier. Profound, I'd have said. Whereas it's elemental
these days that I hate Sam. That she hates me. What might be
trickier to discern is the love that floats between us, airy, ungrab-
bable, shifting. She doesn't come to the flat much anymore, but
she used to, a lot, and Sam would fry spaghetti or roast some
soup – or set to on some other ragtag recipe from the culinary
vanguard, insisting that it was *supposed* to smoke like that. An argument, once, between me and Sam, about the *right type* of spatu-
la to use to flip a fillet of cod – not the type that melted – was the
occasion that marked Sam's final visit to my place.

Sam Twyfield is forty-three years old, but you wouldn't
think it to look at her: you'd guess a decade older. A diet of ap-
ples, raisins, brazil nuts and cheap brandy – the last a known, un-

spoken secret – has meant that she's kept in shape in accordance with her eighteen year-old self's idealized size ten, but the face is a repository of unfulfilled ambition and unspent emotional tariffs. Sadly (for those around her) the choice of gluey makeup that she uses to disguise her inner grief doesn't help. She works, at a senior level, for a business in the airline industry. Though I'm not exactly sure what she does, I know that she's worked there for many years, chasing its concern around London as it moved from office to office, borough to borough, postcode to postcode. She was sixteen when she took her first tender footsteps on its reception room carpet; she was on work experience, arranged by her school, and this is where she first met Dorothy…

Who is a writer. As we all know. As anyone who breathes in the same waiting room as her, who shares the same plane, who dines in the same restaurant, will know. *She is a writer: got it?* Dorothy Anthony is a writer of three published novels (under her own name). A fourth is a work in progress – after a long gap. But she is not going guns on this project. I feel I know plenty about Dorothy; I like her. With her deep, endangered scowl, not perdurable in the least, always losing its steam, and dwindling to a twinkly expression of contented surprise, she gives the impression of liking me back. This might change. What I haven't mentioned yet, and what I probably won't ever mention, is this: her books *stink*.

They are the five. And this month it's Sam's shout.

VI.

1.

'I've had 'em all,' the old boy announces, adjusting the position of the blanket on his knees, his slippered big toes meeting so that his feet are in the shape of a chevron. He smacks his lips; motes of congealed spittle litter the underside of his white moustache. With a gesture that smacks of nervousness he adjusts his tie.

'Anything you could mention, girl.'

'I know, Dad. But the doctor says you mustn't…'

Annette is cut off in the middle of a protestation that she wishes she hadn't even begun. It's not worth the effort: the man will get his way.

'Breathlessness I've had; asthma, bronchitis, emphysema… heart failure!… and now me only daughter – me only daughter – denies me one of me last pleasures in life.'

The old man tips his chin, complicated as it is with dugs of bandy extra flesh on an otherwise taut and shapely face, towards the source of his most-recently cited former health complaint. He shakes his head; with a rasp that sounds like sadness, the chin scrapes across a plaid shirt a decade past its best.

'Me own daughter. I can't fathom it. Me own *daughter.*'

'All right, Dad.'

Annette uses her fists to lift her weight up from the armchair, deep in the broken coils and springs of which she's been pinned. Her back creaks with the effort of moving; she has noticed that it takes shorter and shorter periods of sitting still before a sudden movement causes discomfort these days.

'How about I make you a cup of tea?' The question is of-

fered in a tone of voice that smacks of a blatant attempt at jolli-
fication.

The old man raises his head and snorts. 'How about you make
me a cup of tea *and fetch me a bloody cigarette like I asked you?*'

Moving away from the man's toxic radius, Annette experiences both a feeling of weltschmerz – an easily earned but no
doubt difficult to spend depression, caused this time by the fact
that she has let him win again, even if she had no choice – and
a feeling of loss as she stands in the space-age kitchen; the kitch-
en that she can't come to terms with, its appearance so new, vibrant and zingy – so different, in other words, from the one he'd
shared with his third wife, Annette's mother, until the woman's
final days. The gutting of the room and the total refurbishment
had made Annette feel betrayed. It still does, she reckons as she
fills the kettle.

Dad keeps his cigarettes in a saucepan (also brand new,
bursting with light) inside one of the two cupboards situated under the sink. He hides them because he is certain that Elcin, the
Turkish cleaner who comes in twice a week, is determined to steal
them. As the kettle – made of rhodium or lutetium, no doubt, or
something equally costly – begins to moan and seethe, Annette
ransacks the cupboard, in search of fags. She finds them quickly.
The kettle is giving off a rapt, perky whistle when Annette has the
idea to smoke one herself.

She hasn't smoked since Mum. There are many things she
hasn't done since Mum, but smoking was the hardest promise to
make, let alone keep. But she made it. And so far she has kept it
(well, apart from the occasional odd lapse or two; but who's perfect?). Having fallen foul of the growth that would kill her, Mum
had lost much of her powers of cohesive thought; by the end she
had all but done away with conscious speech altogether, much
to her three daughters' grief and sporadic exasperation; but one

thing she mentioned, not calmly but forcefully, was a stark command that Annette would give up smoking. Eventually Annette had complied with the wish.

'Oh. And see your old man don't smoke neither,' Mum had added.

One out of two isn't bad, Annette has told herself. But statistically speaking, one out of two is bad. One out of two is lousy odds.

'What bloody kept you, girl?' the old man demands as soon as Annette has returned to the lounge. 'Give 'em here. Me lungs are singing.'

'You're welcome, Dad,' Annette tells him, voice pulsing with sarcasm, handing over the carton. The effort is wasted, he seems not to hear; murmurs of appreciation, uncomfortably close to a lover's dirty coos, dribble out of his mouth. Annette shakes the association from her head; she prefers to think of her father, now, as something of a barmy, wild-haired scientist, leading up to a shattering discovery.

Although the box has already been opened, the old man makes a grand show of tearing the top clean off it. He drops the litter on the small round-surfaced table, next to where Annette has placed his drink. Hands shaking slightly, he lights up and exhales before taking a long drag. After a second or two of dreamy rumination he decides: 'That's the ticket, girl.'

Annette sits down in her usual chair. 'The ticket to the cemetery.'

Her father laughs. 'There's nothing this fag can do I can't beat, love. I've already 'ad 'em all…'

'So you say…'

'I'm 'undred and four and they still can't knock me down.' He inhales again, holding in the smoke while he considers the cigarette in his hand; he stares at it as though he's never seen one before. Annette thinks it's the look of lovers at first sight.

'You're a hundred and two, Dad,' she corrects him. 'Nearly.'

He turns his attention on his daughter. Anticipating another fusillade of spittle from his lips, Annette sits back. Sure enough, white-flecked liquid accompanies her old man's retort.

'Well that's all right!' he shouts. 'Now me own daughter don't believe me! That's priceless that is. The bloody Queen believes me but me own daughter can't find it in her. That's charming that is.' As part of a highly affected sulk he's decided on he now smokes quietly.

'I give up,' Annette whispers. She wishes she had made a brew for herself when she had a chance. Without something to do with her hands she feels fidgety and nervous. She's always hated coming here.

The room is the same as before Mum. Nothing's changed. The lounge is the only room into which Elcin is not permitted; consequently it is dirty, already, the worst of the grime camouflaged in a dark maroon carpet and on nicotine-sallowed walls of patterned brown paper, and on the ceiling. One set of Mum's many sets of spectacles (the owl specs, she would call them), used for knitting and macramé, are present on top of the television that is never turned on. In photographs depicting much earlier bygone years, Mum is standing in front of an elephant, Mum is setting out a generous picnic, Mum is playing a piano while she's perched, still an infant, on her own mother's knees. It is hard for Annette to view these unchanging memories, but she cannot think of a good way to bring up the subject and she cannot face the thought, paradoxically, of her mother not being present.

'You go ahead 'n give up: that's right,' her father adds in a hard-done-by voice. He's not looking at her now, he is looking at the sideboard; he is looking at the cake stand, which is gathering dust. 'You give up on your old man when you can't get your own way. The bloody Queen send me a telegram on me 'undredth and that's not good enough for bloody clever-clogs here!'

'All right, Dad. You're a hundred and ninety-two. That better?'

'I'm a hundred and four,' he states slowly but with menace. 'If a hundred and four is good enough for the Realm, it's good enough for you, girl.'

'Fine.' Annette has another matter to consider. 'What time is it, Dad?'

The air between the two of them is alive with roiling gouts of expelled smoke; the quality of light is even worse than it is normally, which is a good thing, Annette is thinking. It feels like cover. Nonetheless, her father's gaze pierces with efficacy through the waves and he asks in a manner that strips the sentence of all inquiry how on earth he should know and if she hasn't in fact got her fancy watch on her wrist.

'So I have. It's just before four,' says Annette. 'I'll have to go soon.'

'Yeah, you do that, love,' her father answers, calmer now. 'I'll be all right.'

Dad doesn't do time. He didn't much, even while Mum. Less now. He doesn't own a watch and there is no clock in the lounge, which is where he keeps himself most of the day.

'Up with the bloody sparrows,' he used to say; 'down with the bloody dark.'

It's a system that has lasted with him his entire adult life: sixty years or more, give or take a disputed year or two. For the thousandth time, probably, Annette wonders what he does all day here. He doesn't watch the box; he doesn't play Sudoku or (in his word) 'waste' his time faffing around with crossword puzzles because 'the buggers are too easy'. And surely there's only so much drifting in the past that you want to do, with the passport in your head taking you places that only you and a select few others perhaps can go?

Alibi secured, Annette pulls the sleeve of her blouse down over her watch. It shows a quarter to two. Dad thinks it's four. She has two clear hours. She's on shift at five sharp.

'Did you enjoy that, Dad?'

Her father is extinguishing the cigarette; he is using the exaggerated movements of one plumping up a pillow.

'Not sure.' He laughs again. 'Acquired taste, girl. Need another to make sure. Another one won't hurt me at my age!'

'I have to go to work.'

'You don't know what it's like!' Shakily he eases the next smoke into his mouth, into the left corner. 'Tension 'eadaches I've had; lower back pain; electrical injuries…'

Annette objects to her father's use of but one of a handful of possible incipits − likeminded introductions to chants that seem Medieval (or older).

'I gave you the bloody fags, didn't I?' she demands. 'So you can spare me the list of what you've lived through…'

'Oh! Oh this is beautiful. Now she tells me she wants to hear about the ones I didn't live through. Is that right? You wanna know what nearly floored your old man!'

'Don't' be ridiculous. I've got to go…' Annette sighs.

'That's right. Don't listen to your old man's woes.' He is shaking his head, mock sadly − or at least in a way that implies mockery. 'Don't listen to me temporary blindness…'

'You've never been blind!'

'I said temporary blindness. During withdrawal. In Istanbul.'

'Bollocks, Dad.'

'Now she calls me a liar again! Smashing that is.' He is still shaking his head. 'She don't wanna know. Chest infections;

Crohn's disease; epilepsy; brain damage; cerebral palsy; deep vein thrombosis…'

Annette stands up. Today she doesn't want to produce her mental clipboard in order to tick off how many of her father's former ailments are the truth, how many fantasy; she's been given a clear two hours to use as she will. 'I'm off now, Dad.'

He hasn't paused on his way through the list. 'Stroke. Osteoarthritis. Broken bones. Thyroid gland. Migraine. Osteoporosis…'

'Dad.'

'Rheumatoid arthritis. Diabetes. Muscular Dystrophy. Von Hippel Lindau Disease.'

'*Dad.*'

'Obstetric cholestasis; cartilage balls-up; developmental coordination disorder; motor neurone disease; premature birth…'

'Right, that's enough, Dad,' Annette decides. Bending at the waist to kiss his forehead, she notices a soup stain on his tie and is flushed with relief at the thought of his remembering to eat; she smells the comfort he experiences in tobacco and melancholy.

'Huntington's disease; occupational dystonia; SAD; amblyopia…'

'Dad, are you listening?' Annette raises her voice. To her surprise she secures his attention. 'How long have I been here today, Dad?' she asks.

'Oh I don't know. *Too* bloody long.'

'That's right.' She is by the door. She opens it.

'Annette?' He won't face her when he says it but he will say it; he always does. 'Will you come and see me again soon?'

'Yes, Dad, of course I will.'

'Good girl. Do you need any money?'

2.

Kieran isn't answering his phone, which is a good thing, but Richard is, which is even better. With the latter Annette spends an important two minutes, bolting down the fact that he will be at work until six at the earliest, helping his typist (who can't type) to type up some of his handwritten departmental appraisals (which she can't decipher). *Sterling* news.

The third call she makes is to Alex. Annette does not so much as proffer a greeting. All she says into her mobile is: 'The house is free.'

It is less than an hour later when, plumped up and aerated by recent orgasm, Annette is shocked at the sound of the door-bell. Sensations other than panic immediately dwindle: ice cubes in fire. Panic is all. Swearing proficiently, Annette sits up on the bed, stands up quickly, and reaches for the clothes she's discarded with shovelling motions.

Recumbent on the dishevelled sheets, Alex is slower to move. Of all times (Annette will later consider) it is now when he drops his earthy geniality and decides to wax logical. 'It's proba-bly just a salesman,' he attempts to convince Annette.

'*Get dressed.*'

'Jesus. Chill pill time, babe.'

'Get dressed *now*... the fuck is my *bra*?' she mutters.

'Go commando. Okay okay...' With which Alex slides up to full, and considerable, height. 'I'd best be on my way anyway. Look. You've already established it's not Richard...'

'I haven't *established* anything.'

The door bell rings again. It can't really be a harsher, shrill-er sound than before, but it seems that way, the sound waves perverted and polluted by her panic. Say it's the kids. What if Emil or Jacob have been sick at school. She'd be called, wouldn't she? They wouldn't let them come home alone. Fucking *blouse*...

Sleeves tangled. Come *on*. Who else can it be? This time of the day. Maybe they've been driven home. But that's not allowed, is it? Health and Safety or some such nincompoop regulation…

'Wait in the bathroom,' Annette tells Alex. 'If anything happens…'

'Anything *happens*?'

'*If anything happens*,' she repeats, 'you're just who you are, okay. You've come round here…' Inspiration blossoms. Hardly astonishingly, given that this French farce is taking place in her marital bedroom, Annette's thoughts turn at a sharp angle to her husband. '…You've come here for us to discuss our staff appraisals next month. We're discussing strengths and weaknesses, okay?' She is dressed. The door bell rings again.

Alex is grinning. 'Oh I know *your* strengths, babe,' he says.

'Not now for Christ's sake! I said *okay*?'

'Yeah okay, okay. I'll hide in the toilet.'

Descending the stairs, ruffled, indubitably, but hoping to hold everything together, Annette's conscious thought is of Alex *literally* hiding in the toilet. He is pushing up the seat to have a peek out, like a child in a game of hide and seek.

'Yes?' She has pulled open the front door.

'Mrs Harrison?'

'Yes?' Her voice remains questioning, but it's a thinner, reedier sound.

The man on her doorstep is as tall as Alex but narrower in the shoulder; he has a handsome face, rigid with a duty to execute; a sense of… disquiet, is it? Thin lips, short hair.

'May I come in, Mrs Harrison? My name's Kolko.' He also wears a uniform. 'Police Constable Simon Kolko,' he adds, taking her open but silent mouth as an invitation.

Once he's over the threshold, Annette speaks briefly to his back. 'What's this about, please?' she asks, her options tumbling too fast around the spinning wheel…until one chuckles to a halt in the gulch marked with a zero. 'Christ. Is my dad all right?' In her mind's eye she sees him – Dad – still in his chair, rambling on about his martyrdom at the hands of diabetic retinopathy or eczema.

'I'm not here about your father, Mrs Harrison. Through here?'

'Yes.' Downstairs there are only two choices: the kitchen or the front room. The policeman has chosen the latter. Annette waits until he's conducted his three-second surveillance of the room. 'Is it the kids?'

'No, madam. Would you prefer I stand or sit?'

Odd question. 'As you like, officer,' Annette almost confesses – it feels like a confession at any rate. What she says chimes in with the feeling she gets, at least once a year, around Christmas-time but sometimes at Easter as well, when she hears religious music – boomed out carols, a snatch of *Songs of Praise* before the remote is used to change the channel – and she experiences the guilt of knowing she's missed thirty years' worth of Mass. An omission like that might take more than a few Hail Marys. And then, of course, there is all of the other stuff. Confession? She'd need to bring a packed lunch and a sleeping bag into the chapel with her…

'Please. What's this about, Mr Koko.'

'*Kol*ko.'

'Sorry. Kolko. What's this about?' she inquires again. A creak from a floorboard directly above her head is sufficient to advise her that Alex has ignored her request to stay in the bath-room. She can imagine him now, one ear down to the carpet, try-ing to catch what's being said. Annette is angry with him for this.

The sound does not pass unnoticed.

'Is there anyone else in the house with you, Mrs Harrison?'

Kolko asks.

'Yes. My colleague. He's using the facilities.'

'I see. Would you like to sit down, Mrs Harrison?'

'No I'm fine. What's this all about?' she asks for what she hopes will be the final time.

'I'm afraid it's about a death on Dunstable Downs,' the constable tells her, 'that we're treating as suspicious.'

'Oh...' Shallowly, quickly, she breathes into the silence. 'Do you mean murder?'

'Off the record we're treating the matter as murder, yes, madam.'

'Right... You'll have to excuse me, officer, but I don't see...'

'We have reason to believe that you might have been on the Downs yourself on the day the body was discovered. Tuesday.'

The panic that Annette has understood to be under control comes back to the surface of her emotions. In moments of high anxiety she blushes; she is certain she's blushing now. Thoughts of Tuesday recur, and feel like a self-betrayal, like adultery. She was there on the day in question – not for long, but she was there – and now she will need to explain.

She can't. Not yet; not straight away. She deliberates for a second or two. She wants to know: 'And what makes you think I was there?'

'You're not being accused of anything, Mrs Harrison. We're merely hoping to eliminate you from our investigation. Do you say you weren't there?'

Annette turns to the curtains. 'I was *there* but... but how did you *know* I was there?'

'We have a witness, madam.'

A *witness?* Who can that be? No one knows her in Dunstable – not that she's aware of anyway. And if that someone knows *her* – enough to be able to recognize her – then that same someone will know that she wasn't alone on the Downs. She was with Kieran.

The volume is lowered. 'This is extremely awkward right now, officer,' Annette states. A roll upwards of her eyeballs is how she intends to display exactly what she means: she doesn't want her colleague to hear any of this. Does the unspoken message get through? 'Is it possible we could do this another time? As I say, I have company.'

'A work colleague.'

'Yes.' Annette is armed with a good smile; it appears honest enough. 'And I wouldn't want it to get around at work that I was walking on the Downs on Tuesday.'

'And why's that?'

'I was supposed to be ill. I called in sick for the morning.'

'I see. But really you went for a walk.'

'Yes.'

'All the way over to Dunstable.'

'Yes. I fancied a drive as well.'

Constable Kolko waits. Annette half expects him to pull out a notepad and start to take down dictation. Then he asks it, as she has known he will: 'Were you alone?'

Instead of speaking she shakes her head. 'I was with a friend.'

It's impossible for Alex to have heard this, or indeed much else of what has been said up to now; but working on the premise of luck and chance obeying a collective law of diminishing returns, and also on the premise that Kolko is not about to leave swiftly, Annette makes the childishly dramatic gesture of placing a fingertip to her lips, a hint for requested muteness, and then takes the necessary steps back into the hallway. She calls Alex's name.

His departure from the house is brisk. Annette will have to discover at a later juncture how much the man has heard, if anything at all. Alex says hello and goodbye to the member of the constabulary, then offers a simple farewell to Annette, along with a face made and a supposedly forgetful addendum that he'll *catch up* with her on their break, after they've started their shift at five.

He didn't flush the loo for effect, Annette remembers. *Was that deliberate?*

'I was just about to brew up,' she announces. 'Would you like a cup of tea?'

'No thank you. Where do you work, Mrs Harrison?' Kolko calls.

Annette is in the kitchen. 'Tiddenfoot. I'm a swimming instructor and gym trainer.' She fills the kettle, both relieved at having Alex gone, but anxious at how much she must reveal.

Come to think of it, what's her job got to do with anything?

She returns to the front room. 'Here it is,' she tells the policeman, meeting his eyes. 'If I tell you something personal, are you, are you like a doctor, you don't need to say anything if it's got nothing to do with anything you're looking into. You can keep a secret, I mean.'

'No.'

It occurs to Annette, now at this very moment, that Kolko has not moved his body one iota since the moment he took up residence in the centre of her front room. His answer has weakened her somewhat. She fits her breathing into the dramaticized beating of her heart. With as much attention as she has recently taken in the contents of her father's lounge, she twists her head as though regarding her own for the first time. Instantaneously it seems smaller.

'We meet there sometimes,' she declares. 'My friend and I. My husband doesn't know. – That's the kettle. – I'd appreciate it if he didn't *have* to know. Really I would.'

Kolko is nodding his head. 'He has a name, this friend,

madam?'

'He doesn't need to be brought into this,' Annette tells the officer.

'I think we'll be the judge of that, Mrs Harrison. His name please.'

'Kieran. Kieran Milne.'

'Is he a work colleague too?' Kolko asks.

'No. And by the way, you still haven't told me how you knew I was there.'

'I haven't, have I?' the man replies. 'And can you confirm what you were doing between ten and eleven on Tuesday morning, madam?'

Annette sighs. 'I'll paint you a picture, shall I? We meet there because it's safe for us. Or I thought it was. He's got a girlfriend and I've got a husband. Does that answer your questions? We're not doing anybody any harm…'

The constable smiles. 'I wonder if your work colleague would agree with that.'

'*Excuse* me?' Annette splutters.

'I'll show myself out, madam.'

3.

Ousting her fear in favour of a more philosophical discomfort, Annette drives over to the leisure centre, tossing possibilities around in her head. It's while she's walking away from the car, in the decreasing natural light, and is almost up to the centre's presence-sensitive sliding doors, that Annette surmises that perhaps it's the car itself that holds the clue to how Kolko tracked her.

She turns on her trainered heels. Thinking *Is this really dumb or what?*, she gives the motor a tough-broad glance and for reasons of comfort adjusts the position of her sports bag's strap on her right shoulder, where a session of sunbed overtanning had left the flesh tender. Poor car. Poor victimized lovely car. This is dumb, she thinks. For the car in its borrowed bay is not conspicuous, either for reasons of loud colour, rare external specifications, or even size, being an ordinary four-door saloon, perfect for economic mileage and chugging reliability, with ample space for the kids and their schoolbags and art folders.

There were only five cars in the car park, she thinks, referring to the car park on the Downs. Would that be so difficult for someone to remember? With a gentle shrug Annette takes a moment to savour the appeasement that the deduction brings. There'll be Alex to fix next, she knows, but at least she is confident that she and Kieran were not spotted. Thinking this with glee, she bids good evening to Debs behind the counter.

'What have you got on tonight?' Debs asks.

On a funny afternoon in a very funny day, this strikes Annette now as more than something of a funny question. And not funny ha-ha. She comprehends a level of fatigue that she's been holding up by a brace against a gale. Shouldn't Debs, who usually knows such things, know this?

'College kids at five,' Annette answers. 'General swim six to sev—'

'No; I mean, what have you *got on*. What are you wearing? You can't work—'

'Shite. I can't believe I've done that,' Annette says with honesty, assessing her so-called workclothes for the evening. She is wearing the very same blouse and slacks that Alex helped her out of; her one concession to her place of employment this evening is a pair of trainers. Her *son's* trainers, which she now accepts with a jolt. The afternoon has cracked her. 'My mind's all over the bloody place,' she tells Debs. 'I'll have to borrow.'

'Maybe you packed some stuff in the bag,' Debs offers.

'Do you know something?' Annette beams. 'I can't remember *what* I put in there.'

4.

When the telephone rings at ten, Annette knows that the caller is Sam. She even greets the mouthpiece with 'Hi Sam!' and a smile that she hopes carries down the line. Not that she particularly wants to talk to Sam; it's more the case that if it's true what the quincunx says – Sam always knows when to call – then Annette, despite what she believes, must need to *be called*. Come to think of it, considers Annette, a brief natter after the day she's had might be nice. She must rein in her news, however; the next meet-up is only a few days away, and Annette does not wish to come to the table empty-handed, having spent her gossip already.

'It's me. Say *I don't buy things over the telephone* and hang up if he's there.'

The voice arrives as a shock; Annette jumps. Not a whole second passes before she has carried out, from her seat on the side of the bed, a search of the house. Part location-radar, part intuition, this ability to search has been a boon on many an occasion. What makes Annette so unarguably certain that Emily is in bed, beneath the covers, talking to someone on her mobile; that James is fast asleep, exhausted by a day at school followed by rugby practice and an hour's homework on the subject of long division, having discussed with Richard the latest signing to Tottenham Hotspur of a Brazilian left-winging *wunderkind*. The fires of his stressful workday doused, by now, by red wine, Richard himself is in his chair downstairs, watching the news.

'You can't call me here,' says Annette.

'I just have. You called me earlier.'

'No I didn't, Kieran,' she answers in a whisper. Despite the invisible laser beams at her disposal, the ones that can pinpoint any of the house's occupants by a sound, a smell, a lick of displaced air, Annette is not so cocky that she can conceive of not keeping an eye on the (open) door. One footfall, male or female, and Annette will hang up.

'Around three o'clock... I didn't have it with me.'

'I know, I forgot. You were at work.'

'We can't take 'em into the prison,' he explains for the umpteenth time to Annette, his tone rather drone-like, rather battered, slick with drink.

'Look. I had a visitor today: a copper. Are you listening?'

'Yeah. I've missed you, Annette,' he continues without a pause. 'Thought you'd forgotten about me. Where've you been?'

'Nowhere. Please listen, okay? On Tuesday—'

'That was great, that Tuesday.'

'Kieran, *listen*. Someone *saw us*.' She looks up at the light spilling dimmed through the lampshade. A tranquilized moth is going slowly about its bodily mortification against the buttery bulb. Its singed wings mutter quiet chants. 'Do you know who it might have been?'

'What are you saying?' His voice is sharper now; there's more clarity to the words.

'I haven't time. Just think about it. Call me from the prison tomorrow.'

'Someone *saw* us? Like, *saw* us?'

'I don't know exactly. I'll explain tomorrow...'

But Kieran isn't listening after all. 'I could lose my job. Public indecency.'

Indignant at Kieran's selfishness, Annette adds, 'Well, it was your idea, Kieran! Not that I needed much persuasion, mind... Gotta go!

The call's sudden end is due to the fact that her other phone – the mobile – is now singing '99 Problems' to the room, like a fat boy showing off at a wedding. The screen reads 'Private Number

Calling' but it can't be Kieran. It might be Alex, the conversation at the side of the pool, when they got a second to talk, had been terse, fragmented. He wanted more.

'Hello?' With no little show of relief she adds, 'Oh hi, Sam!'

'Hi. Just checking you're still okay for Saturday.'

'I'm looking forward to it.' This is true. 'Where are we going?'

'Hannah and I have found a great new restaurant in Milton Keynes. Called Profit.'

'Sounds expensive.'

'It is. But you'll see why it appealed to my sense of humour when we get there. Dorothy's going with Hannah in Hannah's car so I'll pick you up after I've collected Sabrina. About twelve-thirty?'

'Twelve-thirty's fine,' says Annette. 'Richard's got the boys.'

VII.

1.

The young man who opens the door to the sound of a heavy knock is flagrantly drunk. It's a quarter to eight.

'Pizza delivery!' the woman with the auburn and blonde streaked hair announces. She is wearing a long dark coat and holding a cardboard box the size and shape that would have once accommodated five or six vinyl LPs.

The young man is not impressed. 'We didn't order no pizza,' he tells her.

The non-uniformed pizza delivery girl frowns softly. 'Harvard?'

'I'm Ian Harvard. But I didn't order a pizza.'

'*Who is it?*' A voice from a room, above the din of *EastEnders*.

'Maybe your wife did? Your girlfriend?' the visitor holding the box asks.

'I live with me mum. Mum! Did you order us a pizza?' he calls over his shoulder; he is leaning against the wall. From the flat comes the smell of cooked food: they've already eaten.

'*What's that?*' comes the voice from within.

'There's a girl here selling pizza—'

'Not selling! It's all been bought and paid for!'

'We don't want none!'

'Hang up,' Ian starts to see light. '*Who* paid?'

The woman on the landing shrugs. 'I've no idea; I'm just delivering for some extra cash for my Sage Accounting course. At the college? Four-oh-five Ninth Street: Harvard.'

Ian squints at the box. 'Well that's us all right. All paid for?'

'Yep.' The woman fidgets from foot to foot. 'Look. Sorry to

be rude, but do you want it or not? My class starts in ten minutes. I've gotta get going.'

Ian holds out a hand that's scrubbed clean of the day's work. 'All paid for?' he asks again, as if in fear of a sudden trap that will leave him bankrupt.

'I'm just delivering.' She shrugs again. 'Enjoy it!'

'Well thank you very much, love!'

2.

'Royvinder, it's Amelior Anderson,' says Mrs Anderson into the phone. 'Have you a *momento* to spare-ee-poos? It's about my errant *Punto*, I rather fear.'

Roy is close to his working day tether; he's been about to shut up shop for the last forty-five minutes. Every time he's tried to leave, the phone has bleated. More work, more business, and that's good, but why not call during working *hours*? The Leper, with its localized saturation of charmlessness and smoke-free boredom, is calling him, finger curled. Tonight he'll be more abstemious in his quaffing, he's decided; but this doesn't mean he's in any mood to linger here among the cars, like broken turtles, when there's good money jangling in his jeans pockets to be pissed away. The last thing he needs right now is the amiable but loopy Mrs A, and her abstruse shenanigans.

'Good evening, Mrs A,' he says politely all the same.

'The police aren't telling me a dicky-bird, Roynox. Have you heard *owt*?'

'Not a sausage, Mrs A. I was thinking afterwards – well, I thought at the time, actually, when they were giving me the Gestapo, the woman said she's your niece she wore mittens.'

Mrs Anderson fails to respond to this ineffectual bombshell for the time it takes for the clock on the wall to click to 6:24. 'Is this fact earthshattering?' she finals asks.

'Well, it's prints, see, Mrs A. Fingerprints: there won't be none. She had mittens.'

'Oh, how positively Shirley Holmes, Royconut!'

'Yeah exactly,' Roy answers uncertainly. 'So I don't hold out much hope, Mrs A. That they'll get the girl done it. That's not to say we won't find your *car*, mind.'

Barely able to expel a glut of orgasmic enthusiasm from her voice, Mrs Anderson continues: 'But you *will* keep me up to speed with developments, won't you?'

'Of course I will, Mrs A.'

'How *copacetic* of you, Royker!'

Spiritually torpid, world weary, and buffeted (he thinks) by a malady of spirit that borders on the Biblical, Roy downs tools for the day and sets off out to get drunk. Not as drunk as last night, though. Not unless Tom's there again.

Not unless *I'm* there again, in other words.

Roy and Tom, in The Leper. Roy dons his overcoat now, not sure if he wants me to be there tonight or not. Once together, once chatting, they drink too much; their conversations are like thorny vines, twisting around one another; no other conversation can make it through without getting prickled. Last night in the pub, Roy had stared long and hard at two women at the next table but one from his own, the table in-between having been unoccupied. Roy and Tom had listened, having very little say in the matter, to the older, skinnier and much louder of the two women as she bragged her way through a recital of the day's events in the City.

'She's so rich,' Roy had posed to Tom, 'what the fuck's she doing living in the Buzzard? Fucking *move* to the City.' The men had laughed. The woman – early forties – had droned on. Like choir practice, with unenthusiastic choristers either refusing or unable to vary their delivery by any more than a *clef* either side of Middle C, her scalar transposition was only in evidence as the conclusion of a dreary thirst for approval, when her voice would rise minutely to ask: *you know?* Eventually Roy grew sick of the woman's public preening. To the *other* woman he said: 'This is your friend, right?' The quieter of the two had nodded her head. 'You deserve something better than the *shit* you've been listening to for the last hour.' And to the louder woman he's said, 'Change the subject. No one *believes* you.'

After that he got drunker. But he isn't going to do that to-night.

Maybe a *couple* – it's the weekend, after all – but not tonight.

The phone rings again. Give me *all* the Lord's strength, thinks Roy, picking it up and saying to himself that this *must* be the last one. He answers to the name Roy-Polloi. And at what Mrs Anderson has to say Roy is thrilled. The car has been found, in one piece, undamaged – not even vandalised – in a bay outside the ice hockey stadium in Milton Keynes. The key was left in the exhaust. 'I get my car back tomorrow! How *spiffing*!'

This calls for a pint.

3.

I am already in The Leper when Roy arrives. We haven't agreed to meet; this is lunatic attraction; this is some form of symbiosis. I knew he'd come. I've even paid Dave the barman for Roy's first drink; it's a shameful affair to know someone so well while you imagine you hardly know that person at all; but I feel closer to Roy some days than I do to Sabrina.

This is sadly not as difficult as it should be.

Dave is a relief barman – he's behind the pumps and off the subs' bench – called in by the management to cover Angie's period of convalescence. I asked Dave what was wrong with An-gie and he used the word *stress*. Stress? A *barmaid*?

I'd confidently expected Roy to share my scepticism, and for us to indulge in some good old-fashioned sarcasm for a while; but no, this wasn't to be. It *is* surprisingly stressful working in a pub, Roy opined; I'd be amazed. Well yes I would, actually.

My reservations notwithstanding, it is Dave who hands Roy his brimming glass; it is Dave who extorts Roy's promise that he'll remain on his best behaviour for the rest of the night. For it turns out that the very same choir-practice sciolist droner from last night had made a complaint to the management. About Roy and his (hindsightedly) brutal fact finding mission. Dave is embryo-forties; sturdy as a shit-house door; resolutely not to be fucked with.

'First time I've nearly been banned from a pub in twenty years,' Roy tells me.

'And *this* pub,' I reply. 'You'd think they'd be happy to have us. They're happy to entertain *rodents* and *you* get shit? Sorry, mate. I've got a curse of the indignants.'

'Don't bother, Tom. We *are* rodents. You and I: cheese-eaters in the *old* sense.'

I find I can live with being a cheese-eater. We get settled into our drinks.

That night, I share with Roy part of my story about Caitlin.

4.

Clear-headed and vibrant, Roy opens Bible Street Cars at an unprecedentedly early twenty to eight. It's been a while since he's pressed the button for recorded messages before eight.

'Roy, it's Ian. Mate – I can't come to work today. Sorry. I've been up the half the night being sick. Me and Mum. We got this *food poisoning* last night, off a pizza. I thought at first, like, it was just 'cause I had a couple beers, but Mum was rank on it as well. This cow? – well, she comes to the flat and she's like, someone's bought you a pizza. Want it or not? And we've already eaten fish fingers but I's still hungry so we said yeah. She musta put fucking *arsenic* in it or summing. We're *dying* over here…'

'Jesus,' Roy says aloud. It's original at least, he gives the boy credit for that.

'It was only after – like, four o'clock this morning – I remembered what you said about that bird who came and took the old girl's Punto off you. You said about her hair. Auburn and blonde strips. Could be coincidence, course. But the pizza bird had that hair too…'

I'm being set up here, Roy thinks urgently. He surprises himself with a chuckle. It's nice to be wanted by *someone*, I suppose. Whoever the crazy bitch might be.

Empties, 1: 'No torso to speak of'

1.

Some people make a fist against the world; some curl themselves into a ball. Stephen was one of the latter, and at last, I suppose, I can show him off. I'm ready; in my mind he has attained a critical mass. So I can talk about the uncle whose only words of rebellion, as far as I knew, were made with a carving knife, into the wood of a low, old-fashioned coffee table. OH GOD, he had gouged, WHY WON'T YOU FEED ME? His only *words* of rebellion, mind.

I barely remember him.

2.

Years later, he came back into my life with the force of a shredded covenant's repercussions. It was summer. Unmistakably summer, with the sun bleeding light on the family back garden. My father had always favoured a hands-off approach to horticulture, and the verdant grass was ankle-deep; the bushes as wild as dreadlocks; wasps danced from bloom to vibrant bloom... I was home, on holiday from a teaching contract in the Czech Republic. The book I was reading had grown hot to the touch, but the plot was diluted with character inconsistencies and a poor copy-edit; it was deadmeat-cold, and I fancied a drink.

In I went, through the door to the lean-to, which acts as a larder and as storage space for my mother's off-cuts and fabric remnants, even now. I entered the kitchen.

Mum was there, at the cooker – at the machine she loathed. Something was wrong. At first I assumed, with a gallop of panic, that she had burned her right forefinger on the ring. It was certainly her right forefinger that she was displaying as she raised her arm. But no; she was pointing. Not at me; at the door to the room that we always called The Room: the long lounge-cum-dining quarters, which also served as my father's office, when he wasn't upstairs, using the broad double bed as his desk. Her face was white.

'You just went in there,' Mum stated, her voice a quivering parody of its usual self.

'No, Mum, I was in the garden, reading.'

'You just went in there,' she repeated.

'Mum, what's wrong?'

'You-you…'

'Christ,' I said. We were alone in the house, Mum and I; or at least we should have been. But it had entered my head that we had, as unlikely as it seemed, an intruder: a particularly brave, ambitious and foolish one. From the top ledge of the cooker I snatched a saucepan, to be used as a shield or a weapon.

'*Someone* just went in there,' Mum elaborated, as I followed the bastard through, the panhandle held in the fist that wasn't tightly clenched.

There was no one in the room. My sudden movements stirred the budgerigars from their preening, and the four birds exploded from the top of the cage, to land on the curtain pelmet at the far end. I ignored them. There was nowhere for a person to hide. I stalked the length of the room and threw open the other door, into the hallway. Mum met me there; some of the colour had come back to her face. We were standing at the foot of the stairs.

'No one,' I said. 'Empty.'

'I thought it was you,' Mum said. 'The door opened but I didn't look up. I saw his leg out of the corner of my eye.'

'It must have been a breeze,' I answered, knowing full well

that I couldn't explain the leg, but frightened to climb the stairs. 'Shall I call the police?' I was aware that the question marked a significant contradiction to my previous sentence.

'No.'

We waited.

'I must have imagined it,' Mum said finally.

Two hours later we learned that Stephen had been found dead at his London home.

3.

Summers later, I am sitting on the balcony of my flat. Comparisons exist between the two scenes. Again, it is hot; again, I am reading. This time the drink has been achieved; resolutely alcoholic, pumpkin-coloured in a tulip-shaped glass, it throbs in my left hand as I turn the hardback's pages with my right. I am naked to the waist, my bare feet up on another chair.

The buzzer sounds. I get up; in the hall I press the intercom access button.

'Hello?'

I am expecting, perhaps, a postal delivery, a parcel too large for the communal letter slot. Instead:

'Are you the gentleman in the first floor flat?' a woman's voice asks.

'Yes.'

'There's a letter for you downstairs.'

Quite why anyone should object to my topless sunbathing is beyond my ken, but my first thought is that the letter contains an ambiguous complaint. I am correct, at least, on one point: the brief missive is indeed unsigned. But the message is anything but condemnatory.

Working as I do with words, with language, I have long since known how to acknowledge a confident hand from its opposite number. My own handwriting is a maniacal scribble, but it knows its function – its versatility. The writing on the turquoise envelope – 'the gentleman in the first floor flat' – is infantile, incapable and innocent.

I tear it open.

I've never done this sort of thing before. I've been alone for a long time now. If you're interested in having a glass of wine, call me. The square sheet of aqua-coloured paper is thick and expensive-looking; a phone number (obligingly including the local code) has been centred upon it.

Such an invitation makes the blood run faster; it makes me nervous, and I am intrigued to know who has set pen to paper in this way. For clues I return to the balcony, still carrying the note and its envelope.

Making the leap that the delivery is a direct result of my parading half-nude, I can count my options easily. Another few seconds pass before I decide to call. I finish my drink before I do so.

'Hello?' A woman's voice; but that's as far as I can go. No, not true. A *nervous* woman's voice. The voice is squeaky, high-pitched...

'Hello. Did you just leave a letter in my box?' I ask.

'Yes.'

There is silence; indecision. Divining that I might have the upper hand, I continue: 'Who *are* you?' It comes out more aggressively than I intended.

The woman is drunk. Her laughter tells me this. 'Well that depends, wouldn't you say?'

I'm trying to guess who I'm talking to. There's a very slim, very tall woman who lives in the flats somewhere; she parks outside. She drives a very old Fiat.

'Well, you must be able to see me when I'm on the balcony, otherwise I doubt you'd have written the letter. Can you see me now?' I am standing in front of the living room window.

'Yes. You're naked to the waist.'

'That means you're in one of the houses that overlook the car park, or you're in one of the flats to the side.'

'I don't live in a flat,' she slurs quietly.

'You don't drive a D Reg Fiat then?'

'No. I drive a Corsa.'

This doesn't help me one bit; not only am I useless with cars, but she probably parks on the far side of her building and not in the car park for the flats.

'You're not who I thought you were.' A pencil rolls off my desk; the sound it makes on the carpet is negligible, but it's enough to bring me to my senses. 'I have to say, I'm already with someone. Sorry.'

'You have a lady friend?'

Is this to assess the nature of my sexuality or to keep me on the line longer? 'Yes.'

'Don't apologize. If I'd known I wouldn't have written. She doesn't come around very often, does she?'

'Have you been spying on me?'

'Spying's an ugly word. Let's say...' Again she laughs. '...I've been registering my interest from afar.'

Registering it with whom? 'Listen. I've got to know who you are.'

'Not going to tell you *now*, am I?' She sounds more amused than ever.

'Please do. It was a lovely thing you did; I'm very flattered.'

'I'm embarrassed.'

'Don't be. It's not every day I get an invitation like that. Or of any sort. I just think, if you're off work today as well, you might work in education like me. Am I right?'

'Yes. I'm a classroom assistant.'

'Right. I teach English to foreign students.'

What am I doing? Dictating my autobiography? 'I have to go,' I tell her. Inspiration strikes. Taking a step backwards, I reduce the possibility of being seen from the houses to the left. 'Can you still see me?' I ask.

'You're waving.'

'You live in the house opposite, don't you? Two boys, about eight?'

'One's eight, one's seven; but yes.'

'Are you and your husband separated? I've never seen him.'

The sense of humour has not been knocked out of her. It's like when you played hide and seek; the thrill is in being caught, not just in the hiding. She answers my question with a tone of mild hauteur. 'Not that it's any of your business,' she says, 'but yes, we're separated. Divorced, actually. He left me.'

'Sorry to hear that,' I offer.

There is silence. No, not silence: easy breathing. It's time to hang up. The problem is, I don't know how to. 'I apologize,' I say grandly, 'for not being able to get involved. But thanks again for the offer. If I wasn't involved with someone... Goodbye.'

'Bye.'

'Wait,' I say. 'My name's Tom. What's yours?'

She waits a few seconds before responding. 'Caitlin.'

4.

I answered the door on the second ring of the bell. Mum had gone to the shops and Dad was drunk in the living room chair, watching a repeat of 'Allo 'Allo. It was someone who didn't want to go away, and when I opened the door I think I knew – immediately – why not. My first thought was not that I was confronting authority (problematic to me at the best of times), but that I was confronting an awareness of death. But what was it? The policeman's pallor, or the helmet worn – ready for the invitation over the threshold – in the right armpit? The arrow of sweat that traced his receding hairline? Or this?

'Is Mrs Lockington at home?'

My mother is incapable of doing wrong. The policeman wasn't here to question her; he was here to answer her, inform her. The only immoral thing she had ever done was failing to put stamps on pre-printed catalogue company envelopes. Her assertion? That the cheques 'always get there in the end'.

My mother was out – round the shops, as I say. This in itself, on a day that was already unusual, was further proof that stars had crossed, high above. Mum never left the house after 4 p.m. That was when she retreated into the third shed, to begin her day's stint at the sewing machine. Shopping was mid-morning work – mad stocking-up, the trough freezer jam-packed against the eventuality of Armageddon.

Like a vampire, a policeman on non-aggressive business needs a green light before entering a property. This was given by Dad, who had by now joined me at the front door. Given the hour of the day (anything after noon), he was drunk, but he was not irascible, though he hates authority too. He said 'Come in' with a weariness that spoke of futility. I closed the door.

Either deciding I was old enough to hear this, or sadistically impatient to deliver the inevitable into ears he had assumed would be unexpectant, the officer announced, before the two older adults had made it into the room: 'I'm afraid her brother has died.'

True, I was nearing the end of my twenties, but I was still climbing the stairs, seeking refuge from what would naturally be grownup concerns, when the words clasped something shut in my head. The world had changed.

5.

The second letter arrives about a week later.

I know you have a lady, and I wish you and her no harm at all. I just want to talk to you. I hope that's okay. I've never done anything like this before and I don't know if there are any rules to follow.

My husband found someone else and he left me and the boys. I wished him no harm either. It was something he had to do. Maybe I'm too passive. When he told me he'd met someone else, do you know what I did? I didn't throw pots and pans. I didn't even throw a tantrum. I put my arms around him and told him to look after the boys. He promised he would.

These two paragraphs have taken up the two sides of the first sheet of paper. There are another five sheets to contend with, and I read them all.

The phone number is not included this time. But it's on the first letter, weighed down under a clock that stopped working at exactly midnight. I can call her if I want to. She cannot call me. Even if she had dialled 1471, she would have found my number withheld.

Content not to be writing for a while, I have a drink and a cigarette.

Then I call her.

6.

'There's a guy called Norman Ricketts. Nice bloke. Usually, anyway. We used to call him Normal Norman. Well, Bob owes him money: twenty-six grand.'

This is my Dad. We are in his wild back garden, discussing the murder that has rocked the world of numismatism. Normal Norman is now awaiting trial, at her Majesty's pleasure. He has killed his boyfriend.

'It makes you wonder,' Dad says. 'What does it? Why *now*?'

'Well, discovering his bloke in bed with someone else probably contributed,' I offer, sipping my beer.

'I don't mean that. Expect anyone to get *angry*. Even Norman. But by all accounts – he went into the bedroom with a hammer *in his hand*. He didn't get home, find 'em at it, and *then* go mental. It was like a… like a supernatural thing. Arrived *home* with the hammer; just bought the bloody thing at the DIY shop. Norman? Doing carpentry? Forget about it.'

A pause. We both watch as a wasp faffs around in some flowers. We are both scared of wasps, as all sensible people are.

'And then he biffed him?' I ask.

Dad nods. 'And then he biffed him. But how did he *know*?'

'It'll all come out in the trial.'

'I doubt it. I doubt even Norman himself can answer the question.'

A supernatural thing, I repeat to myself.

7.

'I'm afraid her brother has died.'

It was only hours later I learned that the copper had, in his own sweet-suave way, attempted the diplomatic approach. While I was burying myself in music in my bedroom, the full details, in the room below, of Stephen's demise were coming to air. Nor were they pretty. Stephen hadn't simply died – as his mother had, suddenly, on a Wembley street, two decades earlier. No. He had been *found* dead – the door had been kicked down – and the retreat from life had not been recent at all.

There had been a stench…

8.

I say my name and wait for her to say anything at all. She

doesn't.

'I read your letter.'

'Do you know anything about regret?' she asks me. 'What's your biggest regret?'

I take the question seriously. 'Probably giving up playing the piano.'

'Hardly life-altering, is it?' she says.

Only mildly affronted by the put-down, I shrug as though she can see me (can she?) and tell her: 'I have no way of knowing.'

'Oh, you have,' she says. 'You'd have known if you were anything special. You wouldn't have been able to give it up: you'd have been compulsive about it.'

She won't be able to see me frown, so I make sure my words contain plenty of it to compensate. 'How can you assume so much?'

'How old were you?'

'When I quit? About eight. Same age as your lads.'

'Too young,' she states confidently.

'Are you a musician?' I ask her.

'No. But I love music.'

I already know this from the letter: it's one of the things, she had claimed, that keeps her going. The boys, and the music she plays when they are at school or with their father.

'Are you telling me you regret sending me the letter?'

'A bit. I don't want to cause any trouble. The offer of a drink still stands.'

'Thanks. But I can't. You know why. So what's *your* regret?'

She takes a long swallow of something – possibly only air, but I suspect I can detect the waves of drink from where I'm sitting at my computer. 'Let's just say I wasn't always a classroom assistant…'

'Yeah?'

'I had something in my hand,' she tells me. 'I can't tell you what it was, but I could have done some damage with it. I repeat: maybe I'm too passive.'

'I don't know what you're talking about.'

'No, of course you don't. Are you coming over?'

'No. No, Caitlin, I'm sorry…'

9.

'Oh no,' my father said, but the voice was strange – paltry, insufficient. It was the voice he used, and in fact the very words, on discovering that an admired TV programme in the schedules had been replaced by the snooker over-running, or by a miracle score in the cricket, in the darts: 'Oh no.' Usually he would continue by pitilessly lambasting the channel in question, by insisting the controllers have their testicles amputated, and by arguing that he was going to refuse to pay the licence fee next year. He always paid.

'Oh no…' This time he had nothing and no one to argue with. He could hardly take a swing at the policeman, could he? More likely, he offered him a glass of vermouth.

10.

'Dad?' – years later. I was eager – eager for the contamination of a long-suppressed secret. 'I need to know. I've waited all my adult life. I've got to know what you were keeping from me.'

Of course he said nothing. Of course not.

11.

'Why won't you feed me?'

He had lived on takeaway food – probably one meal a day. The house was a fire hazard of discarded wrappers, grease-spotted, from the local fish and chip shop. Although, on his discovery, the aroma of Stephen's decomposition was paramount, had he managed to live longer the air would scarcely have been inviting-ly fragrant. Along with the smells of deep-fried food, there were two decades' worth of dirt, dust and neglect to contend with. From the moment of his mother's death in '77, the house was uncared-for, unloved. The kitchen alone was a masterpiece of decrepitude. So much so that a different question looms: 'How could you eat here?'

Armed with a cloth and a lemony solvent, most people choose to wipe their dead selves away. Dust is us. We are dust. We leave our skincells on every ledge, in every seam; and our houses could end up, in a miracle of cloning, resembling us. But we scrub the threat to nothing.

Stephen didn't. He was growing more than mould. Alche-my was in progress. Definitely anti the mores of modern society, he was engendering a house-sized baby; he was building a new life in the only way – minus love, minus friendship – that he knew how. A progeny of slime and decay, of filth and rot, it would be something out of a horror novel. As indeed was its creator.

But I can't help thinking that the process would work, too, in reverse; that Stephen had begun to take on the house's charac-teristics, and not just in terms of his undeniable bulk.

It is fitting, I suppose, that his death went so far along its line as to begin to reduce him to liquid. By sinking into the car-pet, slowly, Stephen was giving himself back to the only home he had ever known; to the place that had always sheltered him. Where else could he have gone?

Symbiosis: it was the connection, the gesture of sharing, for which – if he had retained even the merest scrap of humanity – he had always longed.

His final companions were maggots.

I don't know why I feel I owe Stephen much, but I believe

he lived a life of almost criminal loneliness. The rest of mankind should be hauled up before the beak for what it perpetrated – for what our silence slowly did to him. I am disgusted; I feel guilty. I have to learn what happened. I have to know why this man, adrift in a world of drink and a lack of interests – who presumably bucked like an unbroken colt through the storms of his depressions, and who saw every interest he owned punished by something – was moved to madness, to suicide... I have a *right* to know.

12.

'"No torso to speak of," he said.'

This again was my father: this was his précis of the conversation with the news-bringing copper, whose name was Kolko. The killer line.

No torso to speak of.

13.

This morning *I* found maggots. On lifting a black bin bag, which in hindsight had been standing stationary in the kitchen for some weeks (through warm weather), I located a dozen of the tiny, wriggling bastards. My first thought was not of Stephen, or the discovery of his body. That was a later thought. My first thought was of disgust, and of being propelled into the act of annihilation. Performing a kitchen-wide dos-a-do, I heard the pitiful crunches of life that come from the death of something else.

Stephen. All the evidence suggests that he spent two decades of his life as a maggot, repulsive to others, and struggling through a meaningless existence. Which trampled upon him in the end. Even his house only loved him because he was a surrogate for his mother – and a bullwhipped dog still needs an owner, however harsh. Even the house, come curtain-time, was glad to see Stephen go...

Sabrina has a colleague at work whose boyfriend keeps the maggots he uses for fishing in a box in the fridge. The very idea is nauseating; complete in its unction of erupting great torrents of nausea. 'Can't you tell her to tell him to keep them in the garage? That'll be cold enough. Not even Stephen kept maggots in the fridge.'

'They haven't got a garage,' says Sabrina.

'On the front step then.'

'It takes all sorts,' she tells me, and after the anodyne imbecility of the get-out disappears, I realize absolutely that she's right. 'Besides, *you* don't have to live there.'

14.

Assumptions must be made, because they are all I have.

I *assume* that Stephen was unbefriendable. What alternative can be inferred from the fact that his death went unnoticed for so long? Passing through life, we inevitably attract friends – or people who become friends – but this didn't happen to Stephen. Despite his bulk he was made of air; like a ghost. Maybe it was he who longed for death, to give him a suitable status. Maybe, still, he floats along the walls of his former house. Unnoticed, unseen. Fundamentally nothing changed.

For he snagged on no one's attention, no one's care. Or perhaps he was made of grease. People tried to befriend him, but he shook them off like pellets of water from an umbrella. Women tried to get into his bedroom to no affect.

15.

When I was a boy, to have a maggot was quite the wrong thing; it was a disaster. To be accused of the same was tantamount to full-scale adolescent insurrection: it was fighting talk. 'You've got a maggot' meant that you had a tiny penis. And we couldn't go around accepting slurs like that, now could we?

How did Stephen feel? On his discovery he had considerably more than one maggot – oh, approximately a million more, all feasting away. Maggots in his maggot. Maggots everywhere. This was how they found him.

16.

What does it take – what have you endured? – before you fetch a carving knife and start to slice messages into the furniture? Finally, I find myself attempting to picture the shapes of a broken mind: Stephen's mind. At the time I didn't want to think about it at all.

'Oh God, why won't you feed me?' he had written. Well, what's the answer? God, we're waiting for your official statement.

17.

There should be people to question any absence. My mother calls me every Sunday, and if I'm not available she'll call on the Monday, or I will return the message (assuming that I've remembered to turn on my machine). She is aware of the patterns we form, the ones we tend to call our 'lifestyles'. And the corruption of them scares her. On only a few occasions has she left it a fortnight before hearing my voice, and vice versa. Should a second Sunday roll pass, she and my father would leave attentive behind and splash into anxious. They would move alphabetically through the adjectives, inexorably towards the Z, where all the terrible describers must live. They would visit, and pretend not to notice my ashtray.

I try to imagine an average day in Stephen's house. Apart from pornography (softcore), there were no books, so I can deduce that he didn't read. Perhaps he couldn't. Then again, he could have taken himself to the library every day; but that seems unlikely. So what did he do? He never even took out the empties.

18.

What's he up to? I was dreaming one morning.

Sabrina left. I could feel her parting kiss to either testicle, and I was ready to wave her goodbye from the bedroom, which faces the road. But too many seconds swept by. Sabrina didn't appear through the front door. Instead I heard the jittery rattle of her key in the lock's eye, and I wondered what she had forgotten. I cast my gaze about.

She delivered the envelope as if she was serving a subpoena.

The tell-tale turquoise stationery; the childish building blocks of letters on the front: 'Tom at Number 8.' It was a letter from Caitlin – from my stalker.

'Hey. I did nothing to encourage this, okay?'

'Why is she still writing to you?'

'She's lonely. She's empty.' I was tearing open the envelope. 'You read it first.'

To my annoyance and relief she reached for the letter. We were in my lounge now; it was dark outside and the lights were on, and I had yet to draw the curtains. My stalker, seated by the upper right of her windows, could easily have regarded the scene. She could have sold tickets. Abruptly Sabrina screwed up the letter.

'I suppose you want to know what it says,' she demanded.

'Not if you don't want to tell me.'

'This is your business more than mine.'

'I don't agree.'

Sabrina stuffed the crumpled-up letter into the wastebasket beneath my cup-cluttered sink. 'I'm off,' she announced.

'I'm sorry. Don't leave me.'

'I'm going to work.'

I retrieved the letter from the trash. *Dear Tom*, it began.

I don't know why I'm surprised when he starts to call.

Fear in Four Waters, 1: The Canal

I.

1.

'The lunge is an action,' Hannah says, 'that requires explosive leg strength; and doing it over and over again in a training session, or even more so, in a competition, requires a high degree of aerobic conditioning.' Empty-handed for the moment, but dressed in her full fencing get-up, she demonstrates a particularly aggressive lunge. She has a class of six students.

It's Saturday morning, and Hannah has slept well but not eaten. She never takes breakfast before giving a class; the exercise makes her stomach pinch. Between stints of monitoring her students' progress as they pair up and parry and lunge, she talks with carefree-sounding wisdom on the subjects of resistance training and plyometric training; on the benefits of jumpstretch bands, powerlifting, and the anaerobic threshold; but her heart is in her belly, and she's looking forward to meeting the girls again, for lunch.

When the session ends after its allotted sixty minutes, the students move away from where they've been working at the centre of the gym floor. She's reflecting on the session as she starts to roll up the first of the heavy mats. She's also thinking about Toby's phone call. She expects to bring the subject up at Profit. For this reason – in case she bottles out of her full confession – she has already passed on to Sabrina, on the phone, that he's phoned. There is no doubt in Hannah's mind that Sabrina will reach for the subject, even if she herself is flagging in her search for the right introduction. Toby's back. Out of nowhere; vocal notes of begging and self-chastisement;

the desperation for a reconciliation. Toby's back.

'Do you need a hand?' a voice calls. The gym is large and cavernous; sounds distort. Hannah looks around.

Dorothy is standing by one of the two doors that lead into the area. She is standing next to a battered metal cupboard that contains basketballs. She's dressed for a day out.

Waving a greeting, Hannah calls: 'Don't come in with your shoes on! Need trainers!'

Dorothy waves back, a gesticulation of acquiescence. She stands still, watching Hannah as the mats are rolled and secured in tight tubes by strings attached. As usual after she's rolled the mats, Hannah recalls a crowded carpet shop in Cairo. Carrying one of the mats under her arm, she walks over to her friend, a smile on her face.

'Have I missed something?' Hannah asks. 'Wasn't I supposed to pick you up?'

'Thought I'd save you the detour,' Dorothy answers. 'Plus, I needed the exercise.'

'Join the class! I could do with the numbers. I've just been telling them about aerobic conditioning.' Hannah stands the rolled mat on its end, next to the basketball cupboard.

'I caught the last fifteen minutes. Very *testoriffic*. I sent you a text.'

'It's in my bag; sorry, sweetie, I didn't get it. Never mind.' Talking loudly but not over her shoulder, Hannah walks back to the other mats, lying there like large sleeping insects. 'I'll just finish tidying up; shower off, get changed out of these Sweaty Betties, and I'm all yours. We're meeting the girls near John Lewis. I need to get petrol on the way.'

'I hope it's okay me being early,' Dorothy calls. 'I was hoping to have a quick word with you, anyway, Han. When you're ready. Thought we could talk in the car.'

'Fine. Not about fencing, I take it.' She hefts up the second mat.

'No. Well, maybe. Something about you.'

'Sounds delicious. Just so happens I've got something about me to tell you all too. Give me ten, okay? There's a coffee machine, back out where you came in; get yourself a brew while I'm freshening up. I won't vouch for it being brilliant but it's okay.'

In the car on the way to Milton Keynes, Hannah asks Dorothy what's on her mind. Dorothy starts talking about the manuscripts she's filed away unfinished since the disastrous meeting with her agent's junior assistant (and girlfriend) – the meet with Helen.

'But I think I've got something,' she goes on, pumped up. 'Something rich. See, I've set myself a challenge with this new book. To exclude anything I've used in any other book. So: no references to restaurants or racetracks. No references to sex – especially sex – to childhood—'

'No love?' Hannah indicates right. They are stuck behind a long line at the roundabout that will take them past the turn off for Water Eaton.

'None whatsoever. These are neutral characters. Or neutered, I should say. No love.'

'What's all this *traffic?*' Hannah asks absently. 'Why queue for *that* place?'

'Oh. It's some urban development project, the launch is today. I just remembered,' says Dorothy. 'It was in the paper. Someone important's cutting a ribbon.'

'We should have gone up the A5.'

'We're still early.'

'My stomach doesn't say so. *Come on!*'

'Anyway. As I was saying. You know my literary history, Han; I don't need to tell you. I need a hit. I'm getting on a bit too much now *not* to have a hit. I'll probably give some sort of bowdlerized version of my last meeting at the agent's office over lunch, but you know the full s.p. It was carnal. *They don't like my new book.*'

'I know. So you've done what with it. – Hurrah,' Hannah tacks on, her voice ironically far from genuine enthusiasm. The traffic is beginning to move again. They've been stationary for less than two minutes.

'Binned it.'

'You're joking.'

'I say *binned*. It's resting. I've got this other one – the one I'm trying to tell you about,' says Dorothy. 'Because I don't *want* to write for twenty-four year old or thirty year old women anymore. I'm not one. I'm nastily closer to sixty than fifty.'

They roll by the roundabout's circumference, the indicator ticking softly. Unused to hitting this particular roundabout at such a low speed, to Hannah it feels like the end of a fairground ride, when the motor is easing the whirling teacup to a halt. 'You want to write about fifty year old women,' she guesses.

'No. I want to write about you,' Dorothy replies.

'Me? I'm not fodder for a *novel*,' Hannah protests.

'Let *me* worry about that.'

'Seriously. I'm not.'

Leaving the lasso of the roundabout, the car picks up speed again. Hannah engages third gear, but she hasn't depressed the clutch pedal sufficiently, and a ragged tearing of machinery ensues. Hardly noticing the noise, Dorothy plays jigsaw with the available information. 'Are you saying no to Dolly?' she asks, preparing a grin.

'I'm saying no. Sorry. I don't *want* to be in a book.'

Dorothy hasn't anticipated this; she imagined that Hannah would feel flattered. 'I'll change your *name*,' she says. 'It won't be *you* exactly.'

'And call her what? *Anna?* Honour? It doesn't matter, Doll. I'm liking the fact you think I might be suitable source material, but really – no. No, thank you.'

Dorothy keeps a rein on her exasperation, but only just. 'Whyever not, Han?'

'Because it's hard enough living it.' This being the run-up to Milton Keynes, there is of course another roundabout; again they've stopped, this time indicating left. 'I don't want to read about it as well.'

'But there's the beauty, though. You don't have to. Read about it, I mean.'

'I suppose not. It could be the first book of yours I've ignored. – Hallelujah.' Hannah stamps on the clutch and dinks the shift into first. They lurch forward, narrowly avoiding the social embarrassment of a stalled engine.

Beaming, Dorothy asks: 'Is that a change of heart?'

'No. It's a change of mind. Go on then, I'll be your affair. On one condition: I don't want to know anything about it. Deal or no deal?'

'Deal. But that's a funny sort of affair. I could've just *done* it, you know.'

Hannah laughs. 'No you couldn't,' she replies.

'Why not?'

'Because you needed this win.'

2.

'Excuse me. Would you mind signing this for me?'

All such requests must surely be unexpected. The woman addressed, certainly, hasn't had such a request directed at her for some years. 'Why? Who do you think I am?'

'You're Dorothy Anthony! Or am I wrong?' A definite declension in mood here.

'No no, you're not wrong,' Dorothy answers gratefully. 'I'm just a little surprised. Bit rusty. I've been out of circulation a little while. I don't think there's been a photograph of me published since *Living Among Thieves*. And my hair was a lot longer and darker then!'

'I haven't seen that. But your picture's on the web a bit.'

'Ah.' Dorothy feels triumphant by being let down. It finishes a perfect week of the same. It's Saturday morning, and she's been dreading the weekend's mop and bucket – the one that will wipe clean the grimy floor of the past five days. She intends to remain disappointed; and this young lady – her dark hair as short as that of a Chinese monk – has provided the perfect antibodies against inner optimism. The literary world really *is* bad.

'I've only read *Nutcracker Island*,' the young lady adds quickly. But it is not the book itself that she holds towards Dorothy in application for a penned scrawl. The young lady is holding a till receipt, as long and playful in the wind as a gentleman's necktie. 'I got it in paperback. My name's Di.'

'Di.' If she says she bought it for a quid in a remainders shop, my week's complete, thinks Dorothy, taking charge of the till receipt in her left hand while seeking out a pen in her handbag with her right. Buying time she adds: 'You must be a perceptive young woman.' No photo of her was printed on the cover of *Nutcracker Island*, it wasn't done, back then. As a consequence of this sleuthing, Dorothy is delighted to demote this reader yet further down the food chain – but to what? Celebrity hunter? Dorothy is far from *celebrity*.

The expression of confused curiosity is a peach; it cannot be more exaggerated if it's to be found in a cartoon. 'How's that?' the girl asks Dorothy. Is this my readership? the author thinks: not happy, not sad; just needful of the knowledge. Dressed the same as when I first published? Same black, head to toe; the same short hair. 'Proto-feminist chic,' was how one reviewer had favourably summed up *Nutcracker Island*, thirty-so years back, when reading patterns were different – less frenzied and less geared to rev between gluttony, laziness and envy – and when the sophomoric concept of royalties had yet to be pooh-poohed as a phenomenon less likely than Halley's Comet.

'Even the pictures of me on the internet must be long out of date.' Dorothy uses the palm of her left hand as a clipboard. She scribbles her autograph. 'You must be quite perceptive, I meant, to have recognized me from those old Polaroids.'

'You've aged a bit,' Di concurs philosophically. 'Thank you.' She accepts the till receipt; the fountain pen's ink is spreading on the cheap paper. 'But it doesn't really matter what they say about you on the web, I think you're great!'

What they *say* about me? Dorothy thinks. She resolves to do something she hasn't done for as long as she's been able to stand not to do it: run her name through a search engine. It's been a good six weeks since she's done that.

'You think the novel is great, you mean,' Dorothy corrects her with a smile.

'And I *knew* how you'd look now anyway,' the reader announces with great gusto.

'How?'

'From the book!' the young woman tells her.

Where *are* you, Hannah? Where have you got to? Because they arrived early, Hannah 'popped' to the Post Office on the other side of the shopping centre. She'd tried to park there but it had been more likely to rain rats than find a space. So Hannah had parked the car and Dorothy had said she'd wait inside with Radio 4 on. She'd got bored. But worse than the boredom was the pain from the operation; Dorothy had climbed out of the vehicle, feeling feeble. She cannot go from the car – not even now, with her ardent fan giving her brain damage – because Hannah has kept hold of the key.

'From the book,' Dorothy repeats, making sure of what *type* this girl must be. 'From the words themselves, you mean?' *Please rescue me, Hannah!*

'Of course! They told me what you'd look like these days. Not that I'm crazy.'

'I didn't say you were, dear.'

'Or particularly intuitive,' Di goes on.

'Well as I say, I think you are,' says Dorothy.

'No, I doubt it. Thanks again for the signature. The autograph,' Di corrects herself immediately. 'Sorry I didn't have *Nutcracker Island* with me. Maybe another time, eh?'

'Maybe… What's wrong?'

The young woman is reading what's been written. 'You've spelt my name wrong.'

'Di? How many ways are there of spelling Di?'

'Sorry. It's your handwriting.'

'Oh. You can't read it. It says—'

'I can read it,' Di interrupts her. 'It's just – I was lying about the spelling. First thing that came into my head. Sorry. I was ambushed by your handwriting. Doesn't look like yours.'

'Like my what? My *handwriting*?'

'Yeah.' Di sighs zestlessly. 'I expected something… nobler, I suppose.'

'Well pardon me. I've had the same script since I was at university.'

Glancing away, Di frowns at some of the other cars parked. 'Now I've done it. Shot my mouth off.' She is talking to herself. Brightening – the colour control turned up in one strong yank – she's back with her literary idol. 'I didn't mean to cause offence!'

'You haven't, dear. Just a bit of confusion.'

Dolly calling Hannah. Come in, Hannah. Can you read me? Froot Loop Alert. Backup required…

'I always say stupid things. It's only – I've built up such a *picture* of you over the years – I've read everything you've ever written – and I thought I'd know your handwriting!'

Christ, thinks Dorothy at the woman's self-contradiction. Slapping on a smile as thick as warzone camouflage paint, the writer adopts a soothing tone. 'I'm sorry to disappoint.'

Di is cross with herself. Her attention claimed by her own frown, or so it seems, she has dropped the signed till receipt, and she shakes her head. 'I sound like a maniac, don't I? Would you mind if we started again? I'll do it right this time.'

'Started what again?'

The question foxes Di. 'It was a gift, it was,' she states.

'What was?' asks Dorothy.

'My copy of *Nutcracker Island*. I didn't buy it. Sorry about that. My boyfriend bought it for me. Well, my ex-boyfriend. He bought it for revenge because I dumped him.'

This line of attack, reasons Dorothy, is nothing if not novel. In the past – more specifically the *distant* past, when the book first came out – she received letters saying that *Nutcracker Island* was: good, great, inspirational (others, of course, thought at best it was total cobblers); it's been judged (by readers) as being as relevant as Erica Jong's early output, and as good a book to masturbate to as any. (Dorothy remains unclear how she feels about this particular plaudit.) Declarations of support, from a feminist *cause* that Dorothy did not realize she was tuned to arrived in flights. But no one up to now has ever mentioned the book as being a tool for *vengeance*. She can't let this pass.

'I dumped him because he gave my rabbit a cigarette.'

'I see. But…'

'He bought me your book and said how much it meant to him and would to me too.'

'That's nice.'

'But he were lying. He thought it were shit. But *I didn't*. So his plan flopped.'

'It did indeed.' Is that Hannah? If so, she's still a long way off; but close enough, surely, that Dorothy can begin the wrapping-up of this twittery. 'I really am delighted you like *Nutcracker Island*,' she says, relying on bankable facts as she's assessed them. 'Now if you don't mind, my friend's on her way back so I have to be—'

'I've annoyed you, haven't I? *Shit.*' Di bangs her own head with both palms. 'I'm *always* fucking doing that. What is *wrong* with me? Why won't I *learn*?'

'It's okay, it's okay, Di…' Thank the Lord - it *is* Hannah, returning to the camp fire, little knowing that the beasts she went to hunt have developed a taste for flame.

As abruptly as she began it, Di desists with the self-flagellation. 'I get so cross with myself,' she explains, her volume lowered to not much more than a whisper. 'Do you know what I do sometimes? When I'm cooking. I test the temperature of the soup or the bolognaise sauce, I test it with my fingers. Others slice. My thing's heat. When I was in prison one time—'

'I really have to go. – Hi Hannah!' Exaggeratedly.

The young woman hasn't really heard. 'I was in for arson that time—'

'Sorry.' Firmly now. 'I've got to go.'

Hannah is approaching the car: a few metres away. Dorothy leaves her station by the passenger side door and hobbles with pain over to her friend. 'Lock the door and let's go,' she hisses under her breath to Hannah's confused expression. 'She's a headcase.'

'Can I walk with you?' Di wants to know.

'Where?'

Di shrugs her shoulders. 'Wherever you're going?' she answers cheerfully.

'But where are *you* going?' Dorothy persists.

'Wherever you are!'

'Leave me alone, please. We have an appointment.'

'Together?'

Dorothy mumbles something about her nutcase radar needing new batteries.

3.

'Shame none of us do,' says Sam. 'Smoke anymore.'

'I never did,' Sabrina answers.

'They're talking about introducing random drugs tests at work,' Annette contributes. 'Can you believe that? A poxy little sports club in a provincial bloody town. *Drugs tests!*'

'What, for smoking?' Sam asks.

'For anything!'

'Can you do that?' says Sabrina.

'Smoking's not illegal,' Sam offers, the voice of contradictory reason.

'It might as well be, where I work. Disciplinary action if you're caught anywhere on the grounds with a cigarette,' Sabrina answers. 'But that's not what I meant. I *meant*, is it *possible* to detect nicotine? Can they do that *physically*?'

'I have no idea,' Annette replies. 'But it's got the staff up in arms. Apart from Hannah, of course – the part-time staff. *They* don't care; they're only there an hour or so a week.'

'But you don't smoke,' says Sam. 'What's the big deal?'

'Infringement of rights.'

'Well, exercise your rights to the full here, ladies. They *encourage* smoking up here.'

Sabrina surveys the terrain. 'No one else is,' she notes.

The three woman have arrived at Profit early. They've been seated upstairs, in the section that last time was referred to as

More Smoking. Sam thinks this is amusing, still does. Having no choice but to agree with Sabrina – there really is no one lighting up – she begins to wonder, and not for the first time, if she and Hannah had heard their waiter correctly.

They sip bottled water and nibble bread sticks.

'Here they come,' says Annette.

4.

'I love these menus. Who do you think in the kitchen's got a small penis?' Annette wonders. 'Because if you tell me that menus *this* large aren't some sort of compensation tactic I'll have you sectioned. Or have the five of us shrunk? – What on earth is Vapour Death Mango?'

'Bizarre…' mutters Sabrina. 'Raccoon chop suey… It's a joke, right?'

'We left here undecided,' Hannah answers. 'The bill isn't.'

Sam's laugh is mellifluous. 'Hark at her, still on about the bill that *I* paid. How many more times? You get what you pay for, and you pay for what you get. You had a *lovely* meal!'

Stung and chastened somewhat, Hannah pouts. 'I'm not disputing the quality.'

'Well then. Enjoy it; let someone else's wallet take the strain.'

'You're *not* paying for all this,' Annette protests. She is comfortable in the knowledge that the bundle of fifties her father palmed off on her are nestled neatly in her purse.

'Yes she is,' says Dorothy. 'I'm poor as a puddle of piss at the mo.'

Sam is shaking her head. 'The convention in this country, ladies, is to eat first and argue about the bill second. Is anyone ready to order?'

A table of dipped heads and murmurs to the negative

greets her question. It's Dorothy who says, not looking up, 'It all seems too good – in the wacky sense of good – to choose just one. We could go for the set meal for four, if anyone's up for that. You always get more than you can eat anyway.'

'That's not a bad idea,' Hannah agrees. 'Talking of wacky, Doll: tell 'em about your satisfied customer downstairs. Total bread, wasn't she?'

Far enough removed from the former incident, protected from the memory by her friends, Dorothy is able to chuckle about it now. '*Total* bread. Mad as a masturbating monkey.'

Annette is interested in the car park encounter. 'Why, what did she do?'

Dorothy nods. 'She was sniffing around for an autograph, which was fair enough; but then she just got weirder. Clingy.'

'Check your hubcaps when we go down, Han,' says Sam.

Hannah rolls her eyes, the indication being that she's thought this herself. 'Don't say that. Not even in jest,' she says. 'That's all I need, now I'm finally getting straight with my finances: new hubcaps.'

Annette shrugs. 'It's busy down there. She won't try owt.'

'We should order,' says Sam. 'Or at least look at our menus again.'

'Talking of wacky, though,' Dorothy defies her. 'I've got to tell you about something that happened to me in the hospital. It was really strange. Two in one week.'

'I'm very much drawn to the Punctuated Clams for starters.' Prettily Hannah squeezes her eyebrows together. 'I'm not sure this is the same menu. Do you remember clams, Sam?'

'I don't. *Or* the Radar Mushrooms.'

'Let's get a big mixed meal,' Sabrina echoes Dorothy's suggestion, 'and *forage*.'

The five women reach this consensus. Dorothy starts to explain what happened in the hospital, only postponing the recital when a waiter takes the order. Annette says, 'Can I ask? Why do you have all your tables set for seven people. We were talking about it.' The waiter takes an instant to form a suitable response. 'Seven lucky,' he answers, otherwise defeated by the language barrier.

'I *told* you it was lucky!' Hannah bleats, a finger pointing at Sam. 'You said it was China!' She realizes that her fervour is out of proportion to the victory won.

So does Sam. 'All right, all right. Calm down…'

Wincing for words he doesn't know, the waiter adds: 'Seven lucky *some* people Japanese. Ahhh. Buddhist, yeah? Seven time he live. You understand?' The waiter launches into a perfectly absurd mime: a dagger to the chest, death throes, sleeping… then wide awake with a *zing*, his face itself, in this last section, the very personification of an exclamation mark. 'And seven day after baby born – big party, yeah? And seven day after man die? Big sad.' The waiter rubs his knuckles into his eye sockets.

'*That* doesn't sound too lucky,' Sam mutters.

'Lucky lucky lucky…' the waiter sings, bowing shallowly and taking his leave. Amid the qualified hum of the restaurant's busy lunchtime trade, the women talk with a relaxed patience, discussing Dorothy's kidney stones, Hannah's report on fasting, and venturing (early) into a straw poll on the subject of what they'd like to do for next month's gathering, when it will be Sabrina's turn to organize. Annette brings up the hot air balloon, they'd all liked that, hadn't they? Perhaps they could go on an adventure like that again. Hannah mentions the dream she's been having, the one about the bi-plane. Sam, surprising everyone, suggests deep sea fishing, despite the fact that on the day trip to Dun Laoghaire last summer she had been sick on the ship's deck. The idea of fishing catches. And then they move on to the flower arranging class that Hannah attends weekly with Dorothy; to Sabrina's fight for promotion at work; to Annette's halfhearted will to leave the leisure centre and do something different with her life. The air is healthy; the mood good.

But the air and the mood are about to nosedive.

The topic of conversation has turned to pet peeves and bugbears.

'Do you know what *I* hate?' Dorothy says, treading on swiftly before she can be buttonholed with retorts such as: *Narrow it down, Dolly;* or, *You'll have to be more specific.* 'It's when I'm reading a book – a book from a major publisher, this is – and it's got typo errors in it. Even a missing full stop. A lower case letter when it should be upper case. The word *lightening*—' She enunciates the word clearly. '—when the author meant *lightning*. That kind of thing.'

'I never notice stuff like that,' says Annette.

'That's because you're illiterate. It drives me *spare*. Doesn't anyone *read* the bloody thing?' Dorothy notices Annette's wounded expression. Before anything more can be said she adds, 'And no, Annette, of course I didn't mean that.' Which somehow makes matters worse.

'Apparently not,' Sam answers Dorothy's question. 'Here's the waiter.'

As they all do, Hannah looks up expectantly. 'Ah. Carrying no food,' she says.

'This might be a sign.' Trust Sabrina to hold on for the positives.

'Yeah,' Sam tells the table. 'A bad one. – *Konichiwa.*'

The waiter drawing near is the same young man – snakelike in the hip, a laundry line quality, snapping in a zephyr – who attended to Hannah and Sam ten days ago. A little more enthusiastic on the hair gel, perhaps, but the same boy. A new argot, however, is brandished:

'Seat be seated comfortably?' he asks, '—my brave darlings?'

Sam gives the response: 'Yes, we're fine, thank you. Nice to see you again.'

The waiter smiles. 'Your beauties are the famous ones. I be back in a minute.'

Politure and puzzlement demand that the waiter is at least as far away as another occupied table – before the laughter begins.

'Did he really call me a brave darling?' Annette whispers. 'I want to marry him.'

'You're already married,' says Hannah. 'He's mine.'

'I'm just happy to have a beauty that's a *famous* one,' Sabrina offers. 'You're the only one,' turning to Dorothy, 'who's been in magazines and that.'

'Not recently I haven't. And even then I wasn't *famous*.'

'Oh, we shouldn't take the piss,' Sam contests. 'But it's hard not to, isn't it?'

'Hang on,' says Hannah. 'Here he comes again.'

'Bearing gifts,' Sam comments, referring to the tray that the man carries. As the tray is laid down on the table (Hannah moves the centrepiece out of the way), Sam says 'Goody' and the other friends make sheepish noises of homogenized approval.

'Before the main meal,' the waiter announces. On the tray stand five bowls of what looks like steaming, industrial-strength slurry. Matter lurks in the grainy fluid. '*Nanakusa-gayu*,' the waiter explains. 'Seven herb rice porridge innit! Make from *aki no nanakusa* – the seven herbs of autumn. For September full moon..'

Hannah is the first to pick up her ceramic spoon. 'It smells delicious,' she whitelies.

The waiter nods his head. 'Some people decorate with them,' he goes on, 'but some people eat them. Light and healthy. Enjoy! Main meal coming…' With which he again departs.

'Decorate with them, eh?' says Sam. 'I see their point.'

'It's not bad,' Annette counters.

'I like it,' Sabrina says.

'Remind me to invite him round to drink my fish pond. That's for decoration as well.' But Sam's sarcasm is light. Like they all appear to be, she is also having a good time among friends. 'I don't like porridge at the best of times. The texture.'

Dorothy adds, apropos of nothing at all, 'This reminds me of a restaurant I went to once called The River – when I was teaching in Eastern Europe. The same sort of quirkiness.'

Only Hannah knows the story of The River. Dorothy does not expand on the tale.

They are eating, therefore, when the man approaches their table. Eating when they look up from their food or away from each other, to greet him with questioning eyes.

Eating when he addresses first Sam and then Hannah.

His eyes are words; piercing through the women's grouped silence, his gaze is a sentence, strong on disgust and opprobrium. His skin is the colour, and baked hard by evident years of sun abuse, seems to have the consistency too of a turtle's shell. There is something disconcerting about the invisible sails of aftershave that ripple around his body – the body itself dressed in baggy clothes of prime colours. The aftershave is an attempt to mask something less pleasant: something rotten in odour.

It takes Sam a few seconds longer to recognize the man than it does Hannah.

'I said I would find you one day,' he tells Hannah, his English mannered, clippily confident in delivery, and marked with the leanings of a strong Egyptian accent.

'The bus,' Hannah tells herself, not meaning for the words to emerge aloud.

'And now I've found you, I face a problem,' the man before

them states.

Hannah grasps her self-confidence and gives the damn creature a shake to wake it up. 'It was a long time ago, mate,' she tells him, alarmed in an instant by the acceptance of how close he must have been all along, how close, not physically, but to her consciousness.

'More than fifteen,' Sam agrees, her voice shaky. 'Let bygones be bygones...'

'Who *is* this?' Dorothy asks, laying down her spoon.

'What problem?' says Annette, directly to their intruder. 'The only problem *I* see is, you're spoiling our lunch. So you can leave or you can be thrown out by security.'

The intruder – the *thief*, Hannah remembers; the thief with the masculine version of my own name – does not argue with Annette's bravado. Nor does he so much as listen. Those eyes – unblinking – veer between Hannah and Sam.

'I do not work in the public eye anymore,' he tells them both. 'Only in private.'

5.

'Bastard.'

'I can't believe it...'

'Oh my God...'

The five women are now outside. The meal has ended...To Sam, Dorothy and Annette (in the order they've spoken), Hannah provides one declarative catch-all balm.

'It's okay,' she says, 'I'm insured.'

They are standing nearby her car. Moving closer to the vehicle, as though unable to credit her own eyes, Sam's footfalls crunch on a liberal sprinkling of broken glass. Stunned at what she sees, she repeats the word *bastard* over and again.

'I'm insured,' says Hannah. But her legs are carrying water, eight gallons each, thawing from the form of ice into this current instability. She needs to sit down. Be strong, she tells herself. It's only a car.

'*Bastard*...'

After Hana's departure from the table, the story of the attempted robbery on the coach, back in Egypt, came out once more for an airing. Sabrina had heard it before, and could recall the pertinent details, but she sat quietly through the recital.

Dorothy's body aches. She wants to sit down as well.

Annette has produced her mobile phone. 'I'll call the police.'

'Witnesses, maybe?' says Sabrina, shock having eaten into the sentence.

'*Bastard.*'

Dorothy articulates the fear that's been niggling since the five of them finished eating, paid up faster than they normally would, descended the stairs, and left Profit in search of fresh air. 'Maybe it wasn't the thief,' she says.

In her head, Hannah tots up the cost of the damage. If it's do-able, private, she is thinking, won't affect the insurance premiums. Take it to Bible Street Cars, up Stanbridge Road. Windscreen? What's a windscreen priced at? And what about the driver's side window? – this has also been staved in. What about the key-scratch, from front wheel arch, all the way back along the bodywork, almost to the boot?

'The *bastard*,' Sam continues. 'How *dare* he fuck with your car!'

'It might have been the nutter who wanted an autograph.' Dorothy meets Hannah's eyes. 'I'm really sorry, Han, if it was. She was frontlobe city, after all...'

Hannah nods her head.

'I'm insured,' she repeats, sitting down on the pavement, the glass beneath her.

II.

1.

Much of what I've told you is apt to arrive via the medium of Sabrina…Sabrina, the fifth of the five friends, the newest recruit, the centre dot on the side of the die marked five. Sabrina, the fifth quarter of the whole; the Final Act. Sabrina, my partner of seven years – Sabrina Lake…

Unreliable as she might be in some respects (time-keeping springs to mind), she can certainly be trusted to be a good narrator. When Sabrina gets off the phone to one of her friends – or when she meets them for their monthly get-together – it is all she can do not to talk about what she's heard. What has scandalized the remnants of her Methodist Welsh upbringing; what has bored her half-blind and briefly mental. What she's loved. While once I would accept so much and no more, like a saturated sponge, now I make room for what she wants to say. Not simply for what I believed at first was a civil reason. No. I now lap up what Sabrina has to say about her friends for more personal, more psychologically nourishing, and for far more critical reasons. If nothing else whatever is gained, I get an opportunity to keep grounded – maintain some stability over this whole Stephen thing.

Don't get me wrong: I know there's no such thing as a perfect medium for communication; but Sabrina, I believe, is better than most. Her surname being nothing but coincidental – fortuitous in that it gave me the idea of signals through water – Sabrina at least *sounds* as though she's got more than the gist. She doesn't falter in the telling; she doesn't stumble. By and large she converses in paragraphs. But I repeat: *there is no such thing as a perfect medium*. Sabrina is not the boat, bringing news from ship to shore, through waters calm or restive. Lake is an ocean, Sabrina is the sea; the stories arrive, sometimes through squalls, through tempests, and are dumped on the sand, or pulverized against the shins of tall rock formations. However damaged, though, the flotsam and jetsam might be, it's beautiful to me.

Sabrina is not my only source. Loquacious though she might be, Sabrina is not my only source when it comes to material. There is Stephen (of course), however quiet he has been of late; there are emails from the rest of the girls, from time to time, which I can use to piece the story together. And, of course, a matter of moments from where I spend most days – out this room's door, down the stairs, out the front door to the flats, along the road to the front door at number 11 – is Dorothy. And she works at home. She is often in. For this meagre reason alone, she is excellent company.

2.

At a loss for anything better to do, Dorothy is indulging herself with what has become one of her favourite pastimes: she's writing about herself. Dorothy is writing the inside jacket author's bio – for the book that so far is not only *fore*-published, it is also *fore*-written, *fore*-plotted, and has only the presence of Hannah, hulking in its corners.

About the Author, she types. *Dorothy Anthony is the author of three published novels and six unpublished ones. At the age of twenty-four she defied advice and recommendation (her father, since gathered to God, was exhaustively vocal on the subject) by resigning from her position of Claims Administrator for the Civil Service on the day that her first,* Nutcracker Island, *was published. She worked her notice with the firm while waiting, with precocious naiveté, for the sales of her debut to go through the roof in the first month. They failed to do so, but Anthony left anyway, relying on the undeniable and well thought-out advertising campaign that consisted of author interviews in absolutely any publication that showed a scintilla of vague interest, Underground boardings, bus blurbs, and even spots on Radio 4, to carry their weight and get the ball rolling. To Anthony's eternal relief, the ad campaign netted the right amount of interest; and because she was in her twenties, and pretty, the book sold. She was able to buy a home, a place to work, and two grey cats – also, since gathered to God.*

Falsely assuming that she'd live in clover for the rest of her life, Anthony wrote The Orange Sibling. *It was accepted in the same week that Billie Jones, her editor at Mayne Publishing, took her own life with a cocktail of whisky and blues. And a car drive. In the turmoil and disarray that followed,* The Orange Sibling *had to wait like a footballer on the subs' bench. Even Anthony, slow-witted at times, knew something was wrong when her twenty-sixth birthday passed, and there were still only rumours of the novel's eventual publication. Mayne Publishing closed its doors, financially moribund. The quest, for Anthony, was about to begin from the start. Adventure ho! She taught in Eastern Europe for a while – taught English to spoilt children – and once had an adventure on a hill that sported a human face. That was odd, now that she remembers it. From a certain angle, in a certain light, the flora and fauna, the abandoned buildings, deteriorated stone borders and even the presence of a cave, had resembled a human face: there on the side of the hill. She hasn't thought about this for years, and there's only one person – her friend, Hannah Paddington – that knows about the face on the hill. Anyway…*

Spurred by the good sales of Nutcracker Island, *a smaller publisher, Riff Raff Books, commissioned Anthony to specialise in some of the racier material in the novel and write three 65K-worders of erotica. At first the author resisted the challenge: she had money coming in from the debut. But it was her father who convinced her (without knowing in any detail what the projects entailed) that any work offered was good work. Under the* nom de plume *P.P. Prober, she wrote two volumes of soft porn, and then a comedy science fiction smut-rag entitled* Space Babe from Uranus; *she changed her name to B.J. Liking for an unexpected fourth offer of employment – more erotica – and wrote, took the money for, but failed to publish* Hard Money, *which died like a denoted organ inside the publishing house when it developed, like Mayne Publishing, terminal cancer of the finances.*

No one wanted to publish The Orange Sibling. *It was better than* Nutcracker Island, *in the author's opinion, but no one wanted to publish it. Dorothy Anthony began work on* The Tight Blue Side *while temping in the airline industry publishing offices in which she met and befriended a very young Sam Twyfield, who was there on work experience from school. Anthony was thirty and Sam was sweet sixteen.* The Tight Blue Tide *was accepted by Maynard Publishing. Released when the author was thirty-one, a full seven years after her debut, it sold respectably, and based on its title, led to many a denial that it had anything to do with anal sex with dead people. That, she would joke in interviews, was for number three.*

Pseudonymia became a place for Anthony to live. Throughout her thirties, as well as taking on as much journalism as she could stomach – book reviews, poorly paid until a fellow reviewer took her to task for her naiveté in actually reading more of the book in question than the first fifty pages, a bit in the middle, and the last fifty pages, and author interviews with Dorothy on the working side of the Dictaphone – she wrote Hell of a West, *a western under the name of Clarence Flint, and Sick Doctors, an ejaculation of erotica-lite, under the name of Steph Walbank. Both found a small press audience, but the checks got lost in the mail. Waving her flag, she tried to publish* Eyesite *and* Window Pain *as herself. She might as well have tried resuscitating Mahatma Gandhi with a tyre pump. So she contributed short stories for slave wages to mimeographed small press fanzines that specialized in horror. 'The Magic Clitoris' was one story she managed to find a home for, as Dorothy Anthony. It was printed in an anthology of original science fiction erotica tales, and was nominated for the British Fantasy Society award for best short of the year. She published another five stories on its coat-tails, that same year, pounding them out fast and low to any bidder at all.*

Dorothy is amazed – it's been a long time since she's typed seven paragraphs without a break. Not one sip of coffee has she sneaked; not one ticklish craving for a cigarette has passed by her sinuses. Taking her resilience as a good omen, she repairs to the kitchen for a vodka. Just a small one; ample ice and o.j. Her story is a story in itself. She should write it up properly and send it to one of the rare internet magazines that actually pays. Or even one that doesn't, just to get her name out there again. It's been that long.

Wait a minute, she thinks, settling back down on her work chair. This is my obituary! The conclusion provokes an unexpected warming of her skin. She is happy in obscurity. Why shouldn't she stay here? Yes. It all comes flashing back now: because she needs *money*.

Beyond the wall that her desk faces comes the noise of a vehicle's throaty engine. Instinctively Dorothy leaps up from her chair, which sighs hydraulically at the sudden absence of weight. Her motion excites a flurry of pains and niggles through her system. She winces, clutches her back as best she can with an *Ow!* and straightens her back, her shoulderblades thrust back to an almighty cracking sound. *Ow!* she says again. She shouldn't move in bursts like this. If the doctors and nurses had their way, Dorothy wouldn't move *at all*. But move she does. She moves into the kitchen, with its window looking out onto the car park behind the flats. She likes to know the comings and goings of the flats' other occupants; it's something of an unpaid job for Dorothy. Occupation: writer and *nose*. Her flat is on the ground floor. Through the window she sees, immediately, her own allocated car space, protected as ever by a hardened plastic cone, orange and white, stolen by her very own hands from a mile's worth of roadworks, three years earlier. She doesn't drive, she doesn't own a car. But this doesn't mean that she will allow anyone *else* to park in her bay, and many are the infuriated notes that she's written and left on the windscreens of the cars of transgressors who have failed to intuit this simple axiom. No one is parking in her space. It is Ruth from the flat above, reversing into her own space, fresh home from work, the car too big for her, in Dorothy's opinion. A gas-hog.

From this uninspiring vista there is not much more for Dorothy to see. Uncurling herself from the driver's well, Ruth in her civvies waves Dorothy hello. Dorothy reciprocates the greeting, keen to keep on the good side of the neighbours. It doesn't matter that in truth she thinks Ruth is too ham-footed and heavy around her flat, occasionally bumping the light shade on Dorothy's lounge ceiling into a shiver. And there are times when Ruth's early morning micturation can be heard in Dorothy's bedroom, that seems to go on for *hours*. Ruth steps out of view. Dorothy knows the cars in the other bays too. From where she stands (sipping her screwdriver), she cannot see if the car shared by Sabrina and Tom is parked – their flat and bay are in the next block – but she always likes to know when they are home.

When the telephone rings, Dorothy thinks that it might be Sabrina calling.

'Hi, Julia. Funnily enough, I was just thinking about you.' This is not exactly untrue; it depends on the elasticity of that word *just*. Certainly it's true that since the meeting with Helen, Julia has been much on Dorothy's mind. She has left the other woman messages. This is the first that's been returned.

'How are you feeling now?'

'Rotten. Like an *entrail*. Have you had it yet?'

'No.' Dorothy runs through a checklist of ailments, remembering them (now that they've gone) like one-night stands. This year at any rate she has yet to sleep with Flu.

'I hope you don't. Helen said you were ill when you met up.'

Keep it calm, keep it friendly, thinks Dorothy, unable to

prevent her jaw jutting out in indignation.

'So she said. That was one of many things that rankled me about that day.'

What's been implied is ignored.

'But *are* you sick? I'm concerned.' Julia's voice stretches in preparation for a sneeze. It doesn't come. Dorothy can hear her sniff like a blocked plughole. 'Helen's good at that.'

'Good at what? Jesus, are you all right, Jules? Do you want to talk later?'

Julia sniffs again. 'It's suffer here or suffer at home,' she says. 'Might as well get some work done. She's good at knowing when people are ill.'

Resenting this, Dorothy slides her jaw out again. 'Well, I have just had a stone the size of Bruges pulverized inside a kidney, if that's what she's getting at.'

'I don't think she is. Get a check-up, Doll. Seriously.'

Dorothy is shaking her head. 'But you didn't call me to discuss my health, presumably.' She sips and waits – she is intent on Julia making the first conciliatory move.

'No,' Julia admits. 'Hang on,' she manages to add before a sneeze rattles at the other end.

Dorothy laughs. 'I almost got sucked in there.'

Julia groans. 'What have I done to deserve this?'

'There's a *swarm* of answers to that,' Dorothy is on the brink of replying, before realizing how selfish and self-serving it will sound. By failing to utter a word, however, she instead helps to build a nest of silence for the two of them to sit in. The situation hinges on the stark understanding that their friendship is not what it was. Dorothy continues the bio in her head. *When Julia took Anthony on as a client, she rescued her from potential further years of public inactivity, by negotiating the near-unthinkable and selling her novels all over again to Gangullus.* Julia asks:

'Shall we start again? How are you?'

Start again...These words wear sombre clothes nowadays; these words are the stick that silly, naughty children poke through the bars of the wolf enclosure. Don't tease me, thinks Dorothy. If I have to leave my pack to come over and see what's on that stick and it's nothing but birdshit I won't be pleased and you won't be spared. I have my pride, Julia, as weathered as it's become.

'To be honest? Let's see. Less than inspired, I think I can go as far as that. That report you wrote, Julia – the report on my one hundred and something new pages of fiction – the report you wrote on something longer and better than I've written in years...'

Julia interrupts. 'Longer yes,' she says. 'Better no.'

Rub it in, why don't you? 'It was less than fulsome in its praise, don't you think?'

'I agree. But you know I'm on your side, Dolly. I wrote as the heart told me, as I always do.'

Dorothy closes her eyes; behind her lids, zigzags wriggle and expand from lines into purple baubles. She relaxes the contraction of her orbits.

'"Spurious characterization, weak dialogue..." I can quote you from memory,' she says. 'More *cutting* than it needed.'

'My heart told me you're trying too hard.'

'How can you try *too hard* to write a novel? That's ridiculous. Like saying I'm trying too hard at breathing. It's what it *is*.'

'It's unpublishable. Forgive me, Dolly, but I always make it a point, as you know, to tell my authors what they need to *know*, rather than what they want to hear.' Julia sneezes again – a minor aftershock following its predecessor's detonation. 'So if that makes my comments sound *blunt*—'

'Blunt is one way of putting it.' Dorothy is not going to let the point go.

'—then I'm not even sure I should apologize for it. You presented the first hundred pages. Fine. I was *excited*, Dolly. But they read like an outline, with added speech marks.'

'Thanks. Fine. That's how I *wanted* it to read,' Dorothy answers, aware of the corrosive chill in that past tense of the verb to want. Is it *really* dead? she wonders quietly. Then, taking indignation as some sort of compass, she treads off on the path less chosen. She asks the same question aloud. And then she bites her lip.

She listens to Julia's sigh. 'It was never alive. Sorry, Dorothy.'

'That's all right.' Dorothy's voice is quiet – quiet to the point that she is asked to repeat what she's just said.

'Honestly. Do *you* think it's your best work?' Julia wants to know.

'Yes it is. I was trying for something different.'

'What, exactly? The characters don't have emotions. They converse in insults…'

'That's who they *are!*'

'Well I don't like them. Helen didn't like them either. And nor will the public.'

Dorothy sips her drink; the decision to say what she hoped the beverage would suppress is now no decision at all. It's what she's been building up to – and Dorothy hates herself for it. Indeed, she can forecast the emotional weather that will strike at Julia as soon as the words are freed. It is going to sound like tattle-taleing, but Dorothy lets rip anyway.

'Speaking of Helen,' she says coldly. 'She was terribly rude to me, Jules.'

Julia is also drinking something. Pink gin and arsenic, Dorothy hopes – sunning herself in the warm beams engendered by the hypothesis of Julia's violent suicide.

'I heard it was the other way round.' This is all that Julia has to say for herself.

Bristling at the absence of contrition, Dorothy asks, 'And who do you want to believe?'

'I left the playground a long time ago. He said this; she did that. It's irrelevant to me, Dolly. The important thing is, I'm entitled to expect from you your very best – especially after a gap this long. The readership, if you still have one, will expect something smart too.'

'Jules? I love your bedside manner.' Dorothy is tempted to extinguish the call.

'I'm against the clock, and I'm not feeling well. So forgive me if I'm curt. But to the bones now: what else have you got up your sleeve?' Julia almost demands. The succession of sentences has brewed up another storm of sneezes; the tempest blows.

Because of this squall, Dorothy has time to think. *Badly treated by her agent,* she writes into the rolling clouds of a volley of wet coughs, *Anthony nonetheless accepted advice, knowing that there would come a time when she could fire the bitch. All she had to do was get another book published. Have it sell in apocalyptically vast sums...*

'I've got a new story to tell you,' says Dorothy. 'I think.'

'Then tell me.'

'I'll write an outline. I'll do it properly. Synopsis and sample chapters.'

'Don't be silly, Dorothy; I'm not asking for any of that. Just tell me your idea.'

'I'll email you tomorrow.' Ending the conversation feels good; the feeling even lasts for another ten minutes or so, before a brush with insecurity knocks her astray. It's going to happen, isn't it? she thinks. For the occasion she turns off her PC, there'll be no more work today. The phone receiver has retained some of her angry temperature. Dorothy sighs. She prods the numbers at great speed, as though typing in a password. To dial this number she can bypass a flicking through of the address book, hardbacked, ancient, on her desk; given the frequency with which she's needed to dial it, it's almost perplexing that she does not recite the number in her sleep.

'Surgery! Can I help you?'

But it *is* a password, thinks Dorothy as she confirms her surname, date of birth, address. Now the entire network of her own health is open wide for her perusal. She hates phoning the doctor. But the appointment is made for the following Tuesday.

In the kitchen Dorothy refills her glass. She is shaky; by accident she knocks the glass to the floor. It shatters with a noise like a popping cap under the hammer of a child's toy gun. The noise scythes through Dorothy, leaving nothing but yawning silence as its harvest.

Dorothy takes her coat from the combination upright lamp and coatstand, outside the bathroom. She will clear up the broken glass later. Thinking about the damage done to Hannah's car, she puts on the coat and heads off on foot for the supermarket. Jamal's Minimart is closer but she has no change in her purse and at this time of the day it is Jamal's teenage daughter who serves, and she usually messes up the credit card transaction. The supermarket is only a few minutes away.

3.

The buzzer has made its frantic appeal. No one's home, thinks Dorothy, standing in front of the door to the block next to her own. Remaining in a state of agitated motion, Dorothy presses on the pad for flat 8 once again. Despite the noise of car engines behind her back, she clearly hears the buzzer sound within the building – dogged, peevish, and brat-like. *Come to me,* the noise commands; *and by the way, come now.*

Dorothy needs to speak to someone but that someone won't be Sabrina or Tom – not right now. Willing herself to calm down at what's just occurred, she attempts to dawdle through happier memories, but their chatter is atomized by the events in the supermarket. Her mind is on its own fun-slide, slippery and steep. It takes her back to the shop. *Calm down! A mere coincidence…* She keeps her eyes trained on the sky; her eyes water with a dull throb of pain. And as though a force celestial has read her mind, the curtains for her own performance – the curtains of cloud – part and a cabaret show of rain has its opening night. The shower is sudden, the light runny.

The box on the wall says hello. When she pulls on the handle the door swings wide; she steps in. The occupants of the downstairs flat are cooking curry; the aroma is pleasant but twisted with the scent of pine floor detergent, evidence of the cleaner having visited. Dorothy climbs. Tom is waiting inside number 8, holding open the door. There are gaps in what he says – gaps filled by Dorothy's own words, the essence of which she loses. What he says, in order, is: 'No, she's not home yet… Are you all right?… Of course… Take a seat… Would you like something? I've got some Czech beer… Saw *who* again?'

4.

'The nurses. Except they weren't nurses. I swear – I'm going mad, Tom.' She is speaking fast.

'Relax. Relax,' Tom repeats, his face showing signs of hard work as he grasps for the right expression under the circumstances. His sympathy muscle has been long underused.

A cow's tongue has manifested in Dorothy's mouth; it is larger than her own and it has trouble forming the words, chewing and lapping through them as if through cud.

'I *can't* relax, Tom,' she is able to say. 'It was just so weird…' Though she's declined her neighbour's offer of Eastern European lager, she nurses a mug of hot Marmite solution, from which she now sips, hoping to unglue her palate. 'They were checkout girls.'

Dorothy tells Tom about the hospital. As she does so, smouldering patches of discomfort on her body flare up again and re-ignite. Her torso hurts; her legs hurt; her ankles feel as though they've twisted. Between sips of hot Marmite she emphasizes the part played by the nurses – the white nurse and the black nurse – as they had babytalked her and invited her into the land of little naps. 'All they kept saying was, I was cross and I needed to sleep. Now they work in Morrisons!'

'Maybe you *do* need to sleep, Dolly. You've had an operation.'

'Oh *please…*'

'Seriously. Think of this,' Tom suggests, draining a good proportion of what remains in his mud-coloured bottle. 'You saw them in the supermarket, ages ago. Forgot about 'em. Then you have the operation and you're woozy and sleepy…'

'Don't *you* start.'

'…and you bring them into the hallucination you have when you're waking up. It's not impossible, Dorothy; the brain does funny things. Maybe you dreamt the nurses.'

Dorothy nods her head throughout this hypothesis. 'I can almost believe that bit,' she remarks. 'But why would they speak to me like that in the supermarket?'

'Like what?'

'Like I'm a child! Isn't it time for a sleep? Only a few months till Christmas – aren't I looking forward to it? Have I written a list for Santa. Have I been a *good* girl… Fucking creepy it was. Me, standing there with my basket, trying to pay for a few odds and sods. The black nurse serving me but shouting over her shoulder at the white nurse at the next checkout…'

'Except, as you say, they're not nurses,' Tom interjects. A

frown grasps at his forehead and pulls the skin forward. 'Come to think of it,' he adds, 'why couldn't they be? We're always hearing about their low pay. Maybe they're doing a bit of till-work on the sly.'

'*Both* of them? How would they know I was in hospital? Say I *did* dream the nurses. How did the girls in the shop know about my stones?'

'Is it impossible you've mentioned it?'

'I would have thought so, Tom. Oh, here's my debit card – and by the way, did I tell you I'm about to have my kidney key-holed? *I don't even know them, Tom.*'

The sympathy muscle is going into spasm on Tom's face. Dorothy knows the feeling, or sort of: her own sciatic nerve trouble has aggravated a new pain (welcome back!) that she thought had been left in the dust: a flexing in her right buttock. Her back aches too.

I do need a sleep, thinks Dorothy. I don't need to be here. She is sure that the smile she now produces looks wrong: like her face has taken the brunt of a great force. 'Too much poison in my head, perhaps,' she offers. It's a quirky comment, more in keeping with utterances from Hannah's mouth than from her own. As if to quell any further contributions of its ilk, Dorothy raises her mug to her lips and drains it of yeast extract and hot water. But she cannot resist a further recap of what went on when Tom asks:

'Was that all that was said?'

Dorothy shakes her head. 'No. They said something odd. They said they knew what my *snorename* was.'

'Your *what* was?' asks Tom.

'Snorename. It's the name you have in your dreams; it's your dream identity. So when your dream overlaps with someone else's you can be somebody completely new. You can be your snorename.'

'Do I look confused? I've never heard of anything like that.'

Dorothy places her mug on the table. 'No, you wouldn't have; that's the scary part,' she tells him. 'I haven't written it yet. It's in my notebook. It's an idea for a children's story. What I want to know is how they've read my notebook.'

'Who else have you told about the story?'

'That's what I'm trying to remember.'

'Okay. Which one said it? Maybe that'll help.'

'I don't follow.'

'Which of the checkout ladies – the black one or the white one – which one said she knows what your snorename is?' Tom asks slowly.

The question makes Dorothy feel worse still. 'They said it in unison,' she realizes.

III.

1.

Dear Dad,

On average, the adult male body is made up of 60% water. The adult female body is made up of a bit less, around 55%. They have more fat (although you wouldn't think so to look at Mum next to stepfather Lenny) and fatty tissue has less water than lean tissue.

The Earth is 75% water.

Add together the 75 with the mean of [male+female] and then present as an overall percentage and we can see that 66.25% of everything is water.

(Well, not EVERYTHING, I suppose. I haven't included the water content of animals. That might skew the readings. In the same way that different animals need different amounts of sleep per day – a python needs 18 hours but a giraffe needs only 2 – the water content of the animal kingdom might be too difficult to include.)

66.25% of everything on Earth is water. Yet a million Earths could fit inside our sun, which is considered a weeny-to-average size star. The Earth to the sun is of no more significance than one tiny drop of water among the billions of them in my body.

I am a son and I am a sun!

Water connects everything. It cannot be destroyed. It changes its consistency, to vapour or to solid, but you haven't killed it – you have only given it a new disguise. The rain falls and meets the rivers, meets the seas. Water is sprayed from the surface of the canal, or of a lake, and feeds the plants and enters the soil. Water leaves the swimming pool on our bodies and through the drains. Drop by drop it escapes. Water wants to be with other water.

This is why all water is sad waters. The waters want to join with other waters and become one water. The water inside me is seeking the water inside you.

The water inside my glass is sad water. I drink it to send it home. Drop by drop I am finding you, Dad. Drop by drop I'm still your sun. All my love,

James xxx

P.S. The percentages above are only accurate to two decimal points. Scientists argue over some data and I've taken mean readings where appropriate.

P.P.S. I dreamed I was water last night – walking water. And I was walking on water. I was walking along the canal. The ducks and the moorhen were looking at me strangely. I walked for miles, going north – past The Globe, past Milton Keynes, towards Northampton. And I told my dream to stepfather Lenny this morning when he was burning eggs. He said, 'But you ARE water,' and I thought for a moment he understood. But he was just joking, because he turned away from the frying pan and said, 'You're wet enough anyway.' I tried to laugh to show I have a sense of humour, but I was only being a parrot, copying Mum.

2.

There are three emails in James's inbox.

The first is from a boy at school – Wolfe by name, prick by nature – who is fast earning himself a seal of approval as an upcoming contender for the status of Playground Bully. The email James has received is an invitation to fight – politely and succinctly worded, in James's opinion. Bullying has changed its spots in recent years. James clicks on Reply and prepares to type. It is not the thought of the fight that concerns James; more the accusation that Wolfe offers in the line: 'You might have fooled most people with the nutter routine. Not me.'

Certainly this bothers James, and he is far from certain as to how to respond to it. He had expected that his string of fights up to now would be enough to *deter* any more boys from picking on him for his health conditions. Quite the opposite is the case. He is lining them up – taking bookings. He knows that if he continues he'll be excluded from school.

The time and place are now in the diary. James enters the details on his mobile phone calendar while the subject is hot in his mind. As for those small matters to be decided: the final statement, the P.S., offered partly as a way to put ants in Wolfe's pants, but partly out of genuine curiosity. *Shall we do hand to hand or do you have a preference for a weapon?* he has asked. He looks forward to Wolfe's response to *that*.

The second email is from Emil. 'Email from Emil,' James repeats to himself, a good few dozen times, impressed by the sound. Emil is happy that James has been allowed to return to school. Emil is experimenting with some new words, it appears; these new words are dropped into the muscular paragraphs of his message. Despite the inconvenience of being required to go back to full-time education following his suspension, James cannot deny that it is nice to have a friend, even if it's Email Emil, who's a bit of a twat.

Smiling properly, James clicks on Send and then Next Message.

The third email is from James's father. James closes his eyes, smells a funny smell, and unwittingly falls asleep for a few minutes. When he wakes up again he is breathing hard, and the message is still there on the screen. Dad is dead. Dad wants to talk.

Hi James! the message begins.

For the sake of a few seconds of privacy – just in case anyone comes knocking – James puts his schoolbag, packed with sports kit (football tomorrow), in front of the door. If Stepfather Lenny, or Mum or his sister, come to the door he'll have a second more to shut down. If push comes to shove he can always say he was looking at women with no clothes on. James doesn't like to lie but there are always exceptions.

Hi James! the message begins.

The voice has not changed one iota.

3.

At first sight, Sal's thought is not of a broken nose (for the boy has used the canal on his way home, to rinse the blood from his face, and the bruises will take another few hours to become prominent), nor even of the inevitability of a change of school. What comes to Sal's mind is a query regarding James's mood and temperament – his way of thinking, his funny few days – but as she finds him at the table, she plucks from her lexicon of maternal instinct catchphrases an altogether separate signifier of alarm.

'You've been fighting again, haven't you, James?' she claims.

James doesn't know how to lie. Ashamed, he lowers his chin then bends his upper body; his nose is no further from the table's placemats than the span of a baby's hand.

'Dear James,' Sal breathes. She closes the dishwasher door. She was emptying the machine when James spirited himself into the room. 'What happened? And don't say a big boy upset you…'

'That's what happened. I didn't *want* to,' James mumbles into the mat.

'Sit up when I'm talking to you, James,' his mother orders, waiting until he has done as required. She sits down beside her son and strokes some hair from his forehead. 'Where does it hurt most?'

James considers carefully. 'The face,' he decides. 'But he didn't hit me much.'

'Did you hit *him* much?'

'No. I pushed him in the canal.'

Quietly: 'Jesus, James,' says Sal. 'What happened? Did he jump you? Attack you?'

'No. it was all arranged.'

Sal sits up straight. '*Arranged?*' she repeats, quite unable to bar a scintilla of disgust from the word. 'How do you mean?'

'He invited me,' James answers. 'It was supposed be for Thursday but today he asked if we could re-schedule because he has an optician appointment. I said yes okay.'

'James. When will this sink in for you? You *cannot* go throwing your fists around every time someone bothers you!'

'But he *doesn't* bother me. I've hardly ever spoken to him before.'

'Then why did he want to fight you?'

'Because I'm different.'

'James. I don't know whether to laugh or cry,' Sal admits, the tears in her eyes giving the lie to her contention. She knows perfectly well. 'And what your father's going to make of this I *don't* know.'

'He's not my father,' James answers – quietly again.

'Don't start that, James. You're in enough trouble as it is... Does your nose hurt?' She cocks her head to the left, frowning deeper.

'Yes.'

'It looks wonky. I think you've broken it.'

'*I* didn't break it.'

'*Don't split hairs!*' his mother shrieks, breaking suddenly. She stands up so quickly that she knocks her chair over on its back. It lands on the lino with a brief, sarcastic round of applause. Immediately James closes his ears, the shutters for this act of self-deafening his own bruise-knuckled hands. Closing his eyes, he starts to hum his tuneless panic song; Sal hasn't heard this monotone version for some months and she panics too. She doesn't wait for it to build to a crescendo. She apologizes, with a flurry of activity. With a swoop (her back clicks) she retrieves the chair and sets it back in its former position. 'Quiet, James, quiet,' she whispers, taking her seat and claiming her son's hands in her own dampened grip. 'Quiet now. Calm. Calm, James…'

Mentally James flicks the OFF switch, and it takes him mere seconds to regain his composure. Aside from the reddened eyes – which might easily be the result of the skirmish as well as anything else – there is no sign that James has been ill-at-ease or put out in any way. Once more he is motionless, and quiet. Staring straight ahead, he ignores his mother, who makes little effort to cauterize her emotions. As she watches James, tears fall freely down her cheeks, and a chilling thought enters her head. She does not know how to touch her son, she realizes, immediately letting go of James's hands. She gulps, and once again she stands up. Not a word is said from either of them. And for a few seconds they cannot look at one another either.

The kitchen freezes.

4.

Dear Dad,

Don't be too cross but today I got into trouble again. I had a fight.

Once you've stopped turning in your grave I hope you'll be proud of me because I was defending your honour, in a way, and I gave him a good spank. I left him in the canal, and I hope he drowned. I don't really. But I hated what he said about you, and besides if I hadn't he would have called me coward names and you told me once that it's better to be an unsuccessful brave man than a wholly successful chickenshit, didn't you?

Sorry if you're angry, and I'm sorry for Mum and stepfather Lenny if I get removed from school, not much sooner than I got back in, but what else should I do?

Please write again soon. I loved getting your first email and I've written

to you back I think three times but I'm faster than you. Are you busy?
Your loving,

James

P.S. I'll find out what kind of trouble when I go to school tomorrow.

5.

As soon as James has finished with this problematic correspondence, he checks his inbox. There are three new emails. The first one is from Emil:

Reee-spect! Jangling James rocks! That was a WICKED fight, James! I thought you were going to KILL him. But you're gonna face the fucking firing squad tomorrow man! McAdam is gonna EXPEL your bollocks! You are OUT of school unless you've got some well fucking lucky stars!

See you tomorrow. If McAdam expels you tell her you'll kick her in the tits and film it on your phone for a networking site. Then tell me what her fucking face looked like!

As I say – reee-spect!

6.

The second is from Wolfe:

James
You won that one. I won't say fair and square because you could have drowned me.

Consider yourself dead, you weirdy cunt. No one does that to me. When you least expect it.

Violently yours…

7.

But it is the third email that concerns James the most. It reads:

Dear James

Please forgive any mistakes in what I have to say but I'm an ice cream man, not a journalist, and this is a new country for me, this typing lark. I'll make sure to correct as I go along – your mum's shown me how to delete and do caps – but if there's anything obviously wrong I leave in, just call me a sausage. OK?

This email was your mother's idea, to write instead of talking to you, because it don't look like my words are getting through. (That looks wrong already.) Or I'm using the wrong language or something. So if you'll forgive my errors and my repetition repetition (that's a joke), here goes.

When your mum and I decided to move in together we didn't take the leap lightly. It took a long time to decide, and as long again to get everything done once we made the decision.

Your mum was paranoid. That won't surprise you much, I suppose. But she had your best interests at heart, James – yours and your sister but mainly yours. I said from day that if I ever thought for a second I was contributing to you not feeling very well, or feeling worse, I would leave. Pack my bag, put on my suit, and leave. But I was gutless. That's all it boils down to in the end, isn't it? I didn't have the courage of my convictions..

Do you want me to leave?

All I can ask is you take a few minutes before you give me and your mother an answer. Think about what it might do to her, James, because you can call me what you want and you can think about me how you will, but you can't deny I make her life a little bit happier. And you won't see the back of me entirely – that's not up for discussion – but if you really think that this whole situation can't improve and it would be best to put on that whistle, I'll do it. Only give the matter your full attention, please, would you? For your mum's sake if not for mine.

That's what I have to say for now. I'll look forward to your response, either in writing or in person. I couldn't be sorrier than I am about what happened to your old man, James — I loved him like a brother, you know I did — but no amount of hurting, not for you or for your mum, will bring him back. I'm not trying to be him or take his place in your affections. I just want us all to get on and live together and face the harsh parts of this world as a single unit, untouchable and strong.

Best wishes

Lenny

8.

The house is quiet; not silent (it's never silent), but undoubtedly possessed of an out-of-place hush, a forefinger to the lips, that makes James suspect that the house itself, as well as its occupants, awaits his typed response to stepfather Lenny's posed query. It will not have to wait long.

REPLY, he selects. *Yes,* he types nimbly (no time like the present), *I would like you to pack as soon as you can.*

James selects SEND.

9.

James is reminded of the first time he rode the London Underground, pale faced with fear, heavy-bellied with his birthday treat mid-afternoon scampi lunch, his sweating left hand vice-gripping his father's concrete right. He was terrified, the crowds were made up of boisterous football supporters in identical shirts and raucous, discordant song, en route to the stands at Wembley, beer cans in hand and pumped full of good spirits, chanting *Away-away-away-ooo.* James squeezed his father's hand tighter and tighter, to the point where the man jokingly complained, a wince that James took briefly as cowardice and treach-ery combined. But he vowed to be stronger, for Dad. It wasn't easy. The atmosphere slurped at James's face like a dachshund's tongue; the damp heat split open only at the screeching approach of the first train. The football crowd surged towards the open doors; for an instant James lost hold of his father's fingers and palm, an amputation that shoved panic against his chest and wrenched open his mouth. They boarded. James's arms flapped; he didn't know what to do, even though his father was in view, and even though he'd heard a pep talk on the subject of what to expect. The gaining of his eighth year had taught him nothing except the need to be close, no, to be in physical contact with the man. As the tube doors slid shut it felt like a frightening and dis-graceful lesson. However, managing to keep from crying, James nested on the lap of his protector, proud that he hadn't let him down.

A current of slow menace is as trenchant now as it was in the intestines of Tottenham Court Road tube, all those years ago. Given a choice between the quondam cacophony and the mur-muring of the house this evening, with even the volume of his sister's SquareDub downloads subdued, either through reverence or nosiness and the urge to eavesdrop, James believes he would prefer the din. Perhaps that decision is made with the confidence of an experience got through. This evening's environment is new news, but James can still sense the train, its throat cut open, on its now-whispered approach.

His bedroom door opens. Stepfather Lenny is in the door-way, his face a mask of amphibian calm. 'You obstinate *little shit*,' he says slowly, quietly; James waits for more but none arrives. The man leaves his sight – if not his life.

IV.

1.

Though she has no way of knowing it, today is to be a day of two jolting recognitions.

At six-fifteen in the morning Annette walks along the canal path, on her way to the Tiddenfoot Leisure Centre. This week she's doing a split shift, the early bird, from six-thirty to noon; and then a late, five p.m. till the centre's closing time at nine. She is not looking forward to her day's toils, particularly; but she's in a so-so mood, ambling along past the water, obsidian as it is, the surface fluttered only by the distant play of ducks; past one brightly-coloured longboat after another – Daisy Chain, The Kite – and even past a solitary angler, awake but stone-frozen in the early morning nip. The angler's rod does not twitch.

Annette has almost reached the ramp that will take her up away from the water, back to the busy road that travels over the bridge, when she sees the boy. The boy is sitting on a bench co-loured brown in the early light, but one which Annette knows in good sunlight to be green. The boy is tearing slices of bread into squares. He seems content with this task. The bread squares he places onto one of three piles, on the bench beside him. The piles are approximate pyramids.

I know him from somewhere, Annette thinks, unconscious-ly shortening the length of her stride so as not to pass by him too soon. Where from? The dark, shapeless caul of hair; the face that needs no razor, pinched a little *rouge* by the temperature (or by former exertion); the well-made but unsmiling face, the loss in thought… Where have I seen him before?

The Downs! *That's* where she's seen this boy before: behind the counter – the refreshments stand. On one occasion Kieran had bought her a choc-ice. He had laughed on their way back up the slopes, back to the car park, saying that it had thrilled him, the resulting coolness of her tongue on his shaft. The boy tearing bread had given Kieran his change.

Annette regards this coincidence as sufficient to slow her stride down to close to a halt. She excuse-mes for his attention, which he gives with a worried and put-out frown. 'Are you the guy works on the Downs in Dunstable?' she asks.

The boy nods his head.

'It's been a bit hectic there, I bet.'

Now he shrugs. 'We don't sell much in September,' he answers.

'I didn't mean sales. I meant what happened to that poor man.'

'Oh. I didn't see anything. The police came and some journalists and some reporters with cameras. They put yellow ribbon...' He consults the half-slice of cheap white bread in his right hand, perhaps finding the face of God in it, a source of lexical inspiration.

'Not ribbon,' he corrects himself. 'Tape. They put yellow tape around the area where the body was found by that man's dog. The tape's still there, on one of the slopes.'

Strange boy. 'Are there a lot of people trying to get through the tape?'

'I don't know. I can't see it from the kiosk.' The boy's eyes remain fixed on the bread.

'Then how do you know the tape's still there?'

'My stepfather Lenny told me. He went to have a look.'

'Oh I see. Do you mind if I ask? What are you doing with that bread?'

'Tearing it into pieces.'

'I know. But why are you doing that? What do the different piles mean?'

The boy looks up. 'This pile's for the ducks, this pile's for the swans, and this pile's for the mallards. The moorhen don't get any bread because I don't like them.'

Annette offers him a smile. 'Why don't you like moorhen?'

'Their necks and tails twitch too much. They look like they're nervous.'

'Maybe they're hungry and nervous.'

The boy returns the smile. 'It's a jungle out there,' he replies.

Annette laughs. 'Indeed it is. I hope you don't mind me striking up this conversation,' she adds, 'but I was curious. Why are you here so early?'

'I like it here. These are my sad waters,' the boy replies.

Annette shifts the weight of her sports bag. 'That's very poetic,' she compliments the boy, feeling glad that she chose not to drive to work this morning as she often would.

The boy shrugs. 'I come here often,' he volunteers – his first contribution, thinks Annette, that is spontaneously given, not the consequence of a direct question posed. 'One day I'm going to swim it from end to end: the canal.'

'That's a long old swim,' says Annette.

The boy shrugs again. 'I could do it. I'm comfortable in the sad waters.'

Annette forms the opinion that the boy (she should ask his name) has just said something he didn't mean to say. 'Why are the waters sad?' she asks.

'They can't meet. They're alone.' He turns his head in the direction of the slope that leads back up to civilization. From the road comes the brush-on-porch swishing noise of traffic passing on the damp bitumen.

'Sometimes they're referred to as skitty coots, because of their nervousness.'

'...Who are?' asks Annette, suddenly lost.

'Moorhen.'

'Oh I see. Well I'd better be getting to work, I suppose. Bring home the bacon.' She is self-conscious at this moment; odd that she feels she should justify her onward journey.

The boy smiles. 'You work in a butcher's,' he says. 'Can *pigs* swim?'

'I don't know. They're usually very fat.'

'So are whales.'

Annette puts on a smile of her own. 'Fair point.' Close by a waterbird honks; Annette is in no mood to guess which species has made the noise, but all the same she glances around, uneasy though she doesn't know why. She experiences a familiar jar of jealousy – like a pulse – as she takes in the properties that back on to the water on the other side. Long, pretty gardens; more than she will ever be able to afford. Wooden tables, perfect for an early evening sit-down in the summer.

'Did the policeman come to ask you questions?' the boy asks.

Annette snaps back to him. 'What policeman? Questions about what?'

'Simon Kolko. About the dead man.'

'I'm not sure I follow you. Why would the police...?'

'He wanted me to tell him the number plates. Of all the cars.'

'That was you?' Annette's chest feels fluttery; in a different setting, with a different person, with a different amount of clothes on, the feeling would akin to erotic nervousness: when Kieran had gone through his phase of blindfolding her, for example. 'You remember my registration?'

The boy recites it.

Big deal, thinks Annette. He knows I was there; so what? He's a kid. It's none of his business; I've talked to that wanker Kolko. End of story.

By the time Annette has reached the leisure centre, however, her legs are watery, her pulse is too fast. Debs has also pulled an early; Annette greets the other woman over the reception desk, but perfunctorily only – there's no warmth or meaning in the address, and Annette doesn't wish to stop for a chat. Work to do. She only stops in her tracks because Debs says:

'Wait up!' The other woman is holding an envelope. 'This came for you. Hand delivered. Tucked under the door.'

Annette accepts the envelope, fails the test of identifying who the correspondent might be from the block capitals on the front, and tears it roughly so that the slit along the upper edge fans out and eviscerates the entire white rectangle, nearly ripping what's inside. Which is one single sheet of paper, removed without much care or finesse from a phone message pad.

'Secret admirer?' Debs is nosey enough to venture.

Annette laughs. 'Bit early for a Valentine! It's from my friend Hannah.' Pre-empting any further interrogation, she adds: 'God knows why she delivered it here rather than home.'

'Or calling you.'

Annette shrugs. 'Yeah. Or calling me.' Chills playing havoc with her spine and bladder, she moves to the female staff changing room, having memorized the contents of the missive with one glance. There is not much to remember. *I saw you on the Downs,* the letter reads. *He's not your husband...* No; there is not much to remember; but there is, on the other hand, a minefield to safeguard – there are bombs to defuse. There's a haunted house to explore, complete and bustling as it is with things that go bump in the mind.

And there is Alex to confront.

2.

'Raspberry Time! Come on, babe, we're on!'

'Don't *say* that. I hate it.'

'We're on?' asks Alex, wide eyed with faked innocence.

'You know what I mean. They're not raspberries,' Annette protests.

'Some of them are.'

'It's an offensive term. Please don't say it around me, all right? That's all I'm asking.'

Alex laughs. 'Oh loosen up, Annette-babe, I'm only joking.'

'No you're not. You say it every week.'

'And you usually laugh. What's wrong with you?'

'There's nothing *wrong* with me. I've got something to tell you, that's all.'

'It'll have to wait. Here comes summer.'

It's eleven o'clock, one more hour to go for Annette. It's the hour in which three lanes of the pool are cordoned off, reserved for swimmers from the Brian Westbrook School, a school for adolescents with physical and mental disabilities. They have arrived poolside, seven of them with three carers; in this particular group the swimmers are either very thin or very fat. At the sight of the stilled water one or two them start to scream. Annette is not certain if the noise is due to excitement or fear. It is always a pleasant (if noisy) hour, when Annette does this shift; there are certainly worse ways to finish a morning's work.

But today is to be a day of two jolting recognitions. Up to now Annette has only received her first. As she watches the far side of the pool, where a few other swimmers who are not part of the Westbrook party are free to exercise to their hearts' content, she notices someone who makes her need to breathe deeply the heavy, hot air.

This second recognition, if anything, is more shocking, the

shock of the familiar. Without a word to Alex she speed-walks around the edge of the shallow end to meet him.

'What on earth are you doing here?' Annette demands of the near naked man standing before her. They are both by the shallow end. Splashes and shouts come from the cordoned-off lanes. So far the man she's talking to has only dipped a hairy big toe in to test the temperature of the water. It must be suitable, he has his grip on the metal step-rail that is there to ease the less sure of foot into the pool. He immediately abandons the descent. He greets the abrasive nature of Annette's words with a baggy grin.

'What? You have a ban on old fogeys, do you?' Her father is obliged to up his volume; even with few people present in the water, there is a lot of amplified, echoed sound.

'I said nothing of the sort. I asked you what you thought you were doing here.' The air seems even warmer than it did a few seconds ago; opposite her father, his seal belly flesh white and drooping, like overlong stockings on thin legs, Annette feels somewhat overdressed in her track suit and trainers. She doesn't like the trade-off between worry and anger.

'I've come here for some vaccination jabs, haven't I? What do you *think* I'm doing here? I've come here for a swim.' As if to prove his conviction, he flaps his arms twice.

'You *can't* swim!' Annette reminds him, her voice an exasperated octave higher than she would like. *Where on earth has he bought those trunks? They are new.*

'Can you think of a better place to learn?' Again, the old man exercises his skinny arms, attempting flight; the flesh ripples from oxter to elbow, there are brown spots present.

'Okay, Dad: let me try again.' Calmly. 'Why, today, have you decided to take up swimming? At your age,' she adds, regretting the last part immediately.

'So you *do* operate a no-codger clause,' he barks at her in triumph. 'Thought as much. No coffin-dodgers, please! Their skin falls off and blocks up the plug 'ole!'

'Dad, please…' Annette glances around, spying for eavesdroppers. The raspberry ripples, as Alex would have it, are all but one now in the water. They don't care about her.

'Listen 'ere, girl.' Her father lowers his voice. 'I'm spending me money and me free time the way I want to, getting some exercise. Finally. Sick of sitting in that bloody chair. And besides, I just seen the film of your mother. Put me to shame, it did.'

Annette knows exactly the film Dad means. Twenty-four years earlier Mum had run the London Marathon, on a cool but bright spring morning on a Sunday in April. In the hope of Mum's efforts being shown on the television, Dad had recorded the BBC's four-hour coverage on two VHS cassettes. Towards the very end, near the finish of the second tape, Mum had briefly bounced into view; she'd grinned at the camera as she plodded past, looking puce in the features, wayward-haired, but her eyes had brimmed with mischief and joy. Annette knows that this tape only comes out on rare occasions. Dad doesn't like the TV much.

'Mum was sixty-seven years old!' says Annette.

'And I'm 'undred and four. I know,' the man states. 'Still put me to shame. A *marathon*. At her age! The least I can do in me twilights is doggy paddle from the shallow end to the deep end and back. Not too much to ask, is it?'

'We don't have a beginners' class until later.' Annette is defeated by his enthusiasm and pent up ire. Is there also, she wonders, an element of self-loathing in his demeanour.

'I'll wait in the vapour room then, shall I?'

'The steam room.'

'That's what I said. Or do you want me to have a swim unmolested?'

'I can't watch you. We've got a class for the disabled.'

'I got eyes, ain't I? I can see that. Go and do your job!'

'All right, Dad. Shout if you need me.' Annette sounds resigned.

'That's right. I'll shout as me lungs fill up with chlorine.'

Annette sighs. 'Oh don't be so bloody melodramatic,' she tells him.

'For the amount of money I give you, I'll be as bloody melodramatic as I fancy. *And* you'll say thank you for the privilege. Don't forget who's who, girl.'

3.

A stoic defiance of trauma-level boredom nearly always sees Annette through the less enticing tasks of the working day; but today is different. Everything she tackles scatters her concentration wider; she is upset, restless. Who could have written the letter? And why write it? Blackmail? She hasn't got anything to pay. (She'll have to ask Dad for another handout.) She wonders if the letter is connected to the boy by the canal. By the time the Brian Westbrook School students have left, she feels sleep deprived. She showers for a long time, wondering whether to avoid the canal path on the walk home for fear of locating the boy again. She considers feigning illness in order to escape from the next shift, this evening. She could do with an early night.

She won't get one.

V.

1.

What with the collection of blandishments she has nursed since Toby's manumission – kind words and compliments that she has recontextualized, smiled over and frowned at, and in some cases even needed to *forgive*, so graphically over-the-top were they – that Hannah is enervated and listless. He used to think the world of her, quote very much unquote. Hannah has become weakened by the reappearance of his flattery and of his hope. She is nervous too. Hannah waits for Toby to return, convincing herself that what they did by separating had been for the good. It hadn't been working. In the end, they had leeched the good colours from each other's petals. Simultaneously she both wants and doesn't want to see Toby again.

Too *many* kind words and compliments, thinks Hannah; too *many* were spilled – in either direction. Better surely to have ended with insults and blame – there's no coming back from that, if you do it comprehensively enough. It is a restless calm. Hannah has the strange impression that Toby will have changed appearance. Having rid himself of nice words, he will have turned repulsive, flabbier, into stone. Hannah finds herself leafing through a lexicon in her head, in the belief that there must be a word in the English language that means *the anticipation of nostalgia*. She is waiting for a chance to feel good about the old days, the time before Toby escaped. What is more, she concedes, she is looking for a word that means *the anticipation of the recognition of regret.*

2.

'I have something important to tell you,' he had said.

'So tell me,' she answered.

'I can't, not over the phone. I need to see you… Are you with anyone?'

The question had irritated Hannah. Had he meant in general or right at that moment? It wasn't as if the answer would be different, depending on the context implied.

'The coast is clear,' she told him with a faint background sneer of sarcasm – it was more that he needed to ask, that's what grated. The thought that what he had to say was so important that it couldn't be uttered if there was someone else present – romantically or otherwise – in Hannah's life.

'God, Toby…' She moderated what she'd been about to say. 'You're not ill, are you?'

'Well now that you mention it…' Sunny noises down the phone line, though it was night; it sounded like a beach. Where was he calling from?

Deftly, with brutal acuity, Hannah read into the silence. Heat flamed up from behind the breastbone, round the slalom of her ears, to lodge with a skin-reddening conflagration inside her head and on her temples. In a red-hot flash she saw the future, the trip to the doctor; his delicate, prissy reference to her 'natal cleft'; the prescription for the tri-syllabled cream; the wait by the supermarket pharmacy's cash tills.

'If you've given me an STD I'll teach you something about being ill,' she almost warned, but biting her bottom lip dammed the flow. 'What kind of ill is it?' she asked. If he'd passed on anything like that, she would have known about it by now, she reasoned.

'When can I see you?' he asked.

3.

Then again, perhaps he's thrived without Hannah. Minus

her influence, perhaps he's developed into something of a *flâneur,* dressed gaily, loudly criticizing the architecture of the flamboyant far-flung cities he walks among. Hannah attempts to stifle a laugh; the sound comes out as a honk. Why not transport the man back to the mid-nineteenth century? Have him strolling boulevards, walking a turtle on a leash. Get real. He's probably got a chill; got a bit of muddy gut-rot and feels leprous. Or lonely. Or horny. Thinking he can woo his way back into her thighs. Hannah huffs. She is suddenly cross about Toby's obscurantism on the phone. Why didn't he *tell* her? Damn him. Esurient Toby; attention seeking Toby, always demanding the last word. Why not *explain?* And why is he seven minutes late? Toby's never *late.* Her emotions hogtied together, she's breathing hard.

Her idea had been to have the computer on when he arrived. It would show him, she thought, that her work would not go unfinished because of *him.* The screen would be a prop; maybe even speed up the proceedings – make him feel that he was interrupting something important. For a different reason entirely from this one, Hannah addresses her screen while she waits for the doorbell to ring – the doorbell that she has already checked to see is working. She is composing a letter on spec. Having heard that some of the presenters of film review programmes on the more obscure cable channels are loath to go as far as to watch movies and write their own scripts to read to camera, Hannah is offering her services along these lines. See a latest release (keep the ticket stubs for her expenses) and then write four hundred words for some affected playboy to blather down the lens. How hard can it be? And it will certainly make a difference from writing about constipation or platelets. As soon as she's got her opening gambit watertight, she will mailshot every film review show on TV and radio. Furthermore, the very act of sitting down to write has been known to settle her nerves.

The doorbell rings. For a few seconds after the sound there is a continuing tintinnabulation in Hannah's head; the nerves around her brain clang. Hannah prinks herself in the hallway mirror. She answers the door.

Disappointment is the overarching sentiment. By appearance Toby is neither a well-heeled dandy, nor has life chewed on him and left him trampish. He is dressed in black jeans, with a mackerel-coloured shirt neatly pressed but untucked, struggling against the warm globe of his gibbous belly; the blue sports coat he wears over the ensemble looks baggy and expensive. His face has lost a little weight. To camouflage the effects of hair loss he's had a scalp shave; he looks tidy, prepared – he looks like he's out on a date.

'Come on in, Tobes.'

Why is Hannah careful to ensure the door is closed before she kisses him? Their lips taste the air around each other's earlobes – right lobe, left. A notion strikes Hannah that she wishes they'd agreed to meet somewhere neutral. Neighbours gossip; and there's a spiteful little quidnunc at number forty-seven – Mrs Bly – who is keen to share what she's seen to all who'll listen, night or day. But what has Hannah to hide? So what? Her ex has paid a visit.

'How are you keeping?' she asks Toby. Not waiting for an answer – in fact, turning away and walking towards the kitchen – she adds: 'Would you like a cup of tea?'

Hannah can hear his response before he makes it, but she hears it from another time and place. Back in the day, Toby had had a habit of infanticizing. Hannah hears him answering: *I'd like a cup of you.* But he doesn't really say it. He says something stranger.

'I was thinking, on the way over,' he tells her shoulderblades. 'One of the things I always liked about our time together was, we could talk at the same speed.'

Sure, thinks Hannah; but would you like a *cup of tea?*

'So many couples, you know − one of them talks faster. Not louder necessarily, just faster. And the one who talks slower doesn't say all he has to say.'

'Or she.' Hannah flicks the switch on the kettle. The water won't take long to boil; it's been in a state of deep heat for the last hour, the same water boiled over and over and not used. The cups, too, are ready; half an inch of milk at the bottom of each, stained muddy by the teabags that have been waiting for their scalding plunge. But was this a good idea, after all, such preparation? Now Hannah has nothing to do with her hands while Toby speaks.

Nodding his head, Toby agrees. 'Or she. But that wasn't the way with us, was it, Han? You interrupt a fair bit but at least we talk at the same speed.'

Fabulous. He's only been inside the house thirty seconds and already he's dissecting their relationship, and not for the first time either. Hannah doubts he'll remember all of the post-break-up phone calls (she hopes he won't anyway, for *his* sake), but no doubt, she reasons, he will have come out of the negotiations wearing a new rosette in the name of the peace he's brokered. Damn him. How *reasonable* he could be. How *sage.*

Try telling me we spoke at the same speed, Hannah thinks, when you bullied me half the night to give it another go. *Give me another chance, Han.* She is bitter; she is glad now that the water has only needed seconds to get back up to steaming temperature, it means she can turn her back on him legitimately, which she does. The bitterness she feels never fails to surprise her.

'I forgot,' Toby adds. 'I brought wine.'

Where? In the car?

Toby opens his sports coat as if he's flashing. How capacious it appears, now that he pulls from a pocket within it, on his left, a bottle of…

'Château la Providence,' Toby explains. '2000. Thirty-seven eighty a pop.'

Hannah frowns at the vulgarity. 'For a bottle of *wine?*'

Toby smiles. 'I don't know if you sound disgusted or impressed.'

'A little of both. Did you win the Lottery?' The question comes out quickly, and sounds rehearsed. 'Is *that* why you wanted to see me? You're landed gentry all of a sudden?'

'No,' he replies in two syllables, stretching the word to make it sound condescending.

'Then how can you justify spending forty quid on a bottle of plonk?'

'It's not *plonk*, Han. This is one of the finest wines known to humanity, to quote Withnail. And no, I didn't come here to talk about money. Or wine. But you might want one.'

Hannah is holding a cup of tea in each hand. 'I could have saved myself a teabag,' she tells him, her mouth lurching into some semblance of a smile that no other part of her body, nor her observer, believes in. 'I didn't know we were celebrating.'

Toby says nothing. Not needing to ask where to go, he opens the correct drawer to find the corkscrew. There is no more conversation as he takes a turtle's age to get the bottle uncorked. 'We'll let it breathe,' he decides. 'Shall I take that?'

Momentarily of recreant heart, Hannah says, 'Yes please.' Not because she's fulfilling her duty as a hostess; more because the cups, held together, are too heavy. She wants to sit down. But there is no shortage of anger inside her either; in fact, she is brimming – she's replete with the stuff.

Hannah takes a sip of her tea and speaks her mind. 'Tell me what's up, Tobe.'

'I've met someone,' he answers immediately.

The faces of her friends form a lightning-swift pageant in Hannah's mind, the justification for this cavalcade now doubled by the strident but cuddly tones of the telephone. She is stunned for a second.

'I have to get that,' she says.

Her closest friends know that Tobe has been expected; therefore they know not to call.

'Miss Paddington is that?' the voice enquires. Hannah listens; behind the question is pop music – a heavy beat – a radio is playing.

'Yes?'

'This is Bible Street Cars, Miss Paddington. About your Nova?'

Relief is warm and sweet. 'Is it ready?' Hannah asks.

'Well it *was*,' comes the reply; and Hannah hears the collapse of confidence in her caller's words.

'How do you mean?' she wants to know, picturing the wide face of the man to whom she delivered her battlescarred vehicle, having driven it there illegally (no doubt) with no windscreen in place to protect her face and rightly-pouting lips from winter insects.

The man's name is Roy. Hannah is alive to this fact because she has used his garage regularly – MOT examinations, a distributor replacement – and he is local and a close shave cheaper if you pay in cash and waive your right to a labour receipt.

'No easy ways to say this, Miss P,' Roy states – and Hannah images him, for some reason, cleaning an eardrum with the end of a screwdriver. Though she likes the way he says things like 'Miss P' and is quaintly bold enough still to say 'darling' and 'm'love' instead of 'madam', she cannot resist a ripple of frustration – a continuation of the perturbation she has experienced with Toby. After all, the two men – with their shared reluctance to talk turkey – are not dissimilar.

'To say what?'

'To *say*…' Roy sighs warmly over the noises from the radio. 'Your car's been nicked.'

Hannah waits before responding. 'As in stolen?' she says.

'Yeah. Not notched with a knife, not nicked in that sense. Though it was that as well, as you know. Nicked as in robbed. *Teefed.* I gets in this morning, I think – funny – Where's Miss P's Nova? Maybe she's collected it a'ready–'

'I haven't.'

'–but *that* don't make no sense cuz it was here last night!' Roy breathes all over her attention once again. 'I really don't know what to say, Miss P. There's no sign of forced entry, nothing missing…'

'Apart from my car.'

'I meant money. And I'm not being funny, Miss P, but it's a bit of a weird one. You seen the premises. Not exactly a fucking aircraft hangar – pardon and my French and wash me mouth out with salt.'

'It's okay. What are you getting at?' Hannah asks. She senses Toby's presence – behind her, and close. To snatch up the receiver Hannah strode into the lounge, though the extension in the kitchen where they were arguing would have been simpler to reach. She'd wanted the distance. By approaching, now, Toby has encroached; Hannah attempts to stare him down.

Toby has brought her a glass of wine. Wordlessly he extends it to her grip, which is unnecessarily pinchy, an expression of concerned hauteur on his features.

'I'm *saying*… it wasn't random, Miss P. It was specific.'

'Robbed to order?' Hannah tries to clarify, blocking thoughts of Hana her pursuer from her mental centre stage with slabs of speckled darkness. She doesn't wish to believe that the theft can be his doing.

'In a manner of speaking, Miss P,' Roy answers. 'Thing being – no offence – but there's a Merc here, right now, much older than your Nova: easier to nick and then easier to sell on.'

'If selling's the idea,' Hannah says.

'If selling's the idea,' Roy agrees. 'But the size of my place, love,' he continues, some of that formerly collapsed confidence rebuilding – his voice and its breath tasting fresher to Hannah, who takes a good drink of Toby's expensive present. 'The thief had to *move* the Merc get to yours. Still not sure how he managed that, nor's my apprentice. They were after your motor, Miss Paddington, no doubt about that. You made an enemy recently?'

'One or two.' Hannah drains her glass; she passes it back to Toby, nodding her head to indicate that a refill is required.

Toby makes his disapproval of the phone call perfectly clear; his frown is as deep as dirt in a farmer's thumbnail. But he claims the glass; he even withdraws as far as the door, his shoulders slumped, his back the shape of a violin bow. He knows his news has not hit the destined mark – the call is more important to Hannah than he is.

'Have you rung the police?' Hannah asks, halting Toby on the room's threshold. 'Wait a second,' she adds. 'You said *this morning.* Why's it taken you so long to ring me?'

'Been a funny old day,' Roy comments. 'You free to come over for a chat about it?'

'Sure. I'll hop in my car, shall I?'

'Oh yeah. Sorry.'

'Anyway, I'm busy,' says Hannah. 'Tell me what happened.'

'I was waiting for me apprentice to come back from the dentist. I's hoping he'd taken it for a test drive or whatever. Or delivered it to you.'

This is a source of cautious optimism. 'Well he *might* have, I suppose,' Hannah offers. 'Just let me have a look…'

'No he ain't, love. I asked.'

'So what did the police say?'

'Ah. That's kind of where I'm going with this,' Roy answers. Hannah notices Toby bowing his head.

4.

Before she started work on her perioperative fasting guideline – before she'd even had thoughts for its abstract – Hannah had been offered a different piece of research altogether.

The commissioner of the piece was Jilly Kerrimuir.

Jill was late forties, tall, cheek-boned, handsome; Hannah hated the woman but could not detract from her achievements. On documentation and conference badge alike, Jill eschewed the *Ms* for a well-earned *Dr*. She had studied in an area of psychoanalysis, adding papers to the professorial worship of the analyst John Steiner, and represented – to Hannah – all that was yet to be achieved in her *own* life.

'It's about the effects of sleep deprivation,' said Jill. The location of their meeting was the country and western CDs section of an Oxford Street music store. Jill was flicking through the New Imports section, seeking out God knows what.

'Yes! Here it is!' Jill offered in great excitement. Plucking this crock of gold from the other CDs, she brandished it like a badge – like a policewoman entering a crime scene. 'The Pallbearers: *Concrete and Buckshot.*' Her forehead crinkled. 'Thirty quid, mind.'

'Cheaper to download it,' Hannah answered. 'Jill, why are we here please?' There was no attempt to banish irritation from her voice. The tone seemed to dislodge her interlocutor's sense of self-absorption.

'To talk turkey of course! I need a researcher! I thought of you...'

'Well that bit's good...'

'Hang on. Just let me get this before my conscience cancels out impulse.'

With which Jill made off to settle up for her purchase. Hannah knew that she could make it to the front door and into the street before Jill returned. That would be all it took, an efficacious escape. Why not? They hadn't even talked project, let alone payment. If she ran for it now, there would be no need to think about this again. A few phone calls not to return, perhaps, but no need to speak to this insufferable slooze again.

She didn't run. Like an obedient beast of burden – like a camel – she waited where she'd been posted; she waited her turn to be laden up and mounted.

In due time, Jill explained her ideas.

5.

'Is that all?' Hannah asks, but a chill is upon her.

Toby pulls off the impressive trick of appearing both flummoxed and insulted, both at the same time. 'What do you mean, is that all?' he demands.

'I thought you had something to tell me.'

'I am telling you!'

'Something to tell me, as opposed to something to tell anyone. Or someone. You really pick your moments, you know that, Toby?' She shakes her head. 'For fuck's sake – why the cloak and dagger? Couldn't you just said that on the phone? I've been worried.'

'Well that's charming! Buy her a bottle of wine...'

'I don't want an expensive bottle of wine, Toby. Why are you really here? Is that it?' she repeats. 'You're getting married. Congratulations.'

Sheepishly Toby responds: 'I didn't say married.'

'You've got a girlfriend. I'm happy for you.'

'You don't sound very happy for me.'

'You sound like a teenager. I'll make sure the people I work with know, first thing in the morning. Is that good enough? And before you ask – no. No I'm not jealous.'

'You don't sound jealous either.' Toby won't meet her gaze.

'Meaning I sound jealous, presumably,' Hannah deciphers. She asks her fridge, 'Am I jealous of Toby and his girlfriend?' The smile this causes is unpleasant. 'Bad news, Toby, the fridge thinks I'm not jealous. Why would you think I'm jealous?'

'I didn't say jealous in the first place. You did. Anyway, I didn't finish. You know her.'

The silence that follows is sharp. Again, the faces of her closest friends flutter behind her eyes, but she scatters this deck to the rear of her own consciousness. For hasn't she felt this on its approach? Why else the flashback that caused such perturbation?

'It's Jill Kerrimuir, isn't it?' Hannah asks.

Toby's blinks say it all. 'How on earth did you know that?'

Hannah smiles. 'I have my sources,' she answers.

6.

She dreams of water.

She walks along a shore, not of sand but of skin, an eternity of grafts.

The dark is not her own; this is not Hannah's bedroom, in the small hours or at any other time. Nor is it the darkness of blindness.

The back that the man has turned to her is damp with night-sweat. Taking her time, Hannah slides her first two fingers along a spine that's far too long to be Toby's.

'Where's the light?' she asks, and by way of response she

hears his movement in the covers; then a click. The bedside lamp on the man's side smears buttery illumination through the smaller-than-expected room, giving Hannah the opportunity both to be gratified by the touch-sensitive instinct that has told her the sleeping man was taller than Toby, and shocked by her own nudity in his presence, although it's not for the first time.

Exposed to his navel, the man in the bed is Tom. His eyes blink quickly; his sight drinks in her skin, almost brown in the bad light. Feeling absurd and exposed, Hannah raises her right arm to cover her breasts; her left hand figleafs her pubic triangle – while Tom plucks his spectacles from the bedside table and puts them on.

'What am I doing here?' Hannah asks him. 'What am I doing in your bedroom?' she continues with more confidence, having made this logical connection.

'I could ask you the same thing,' Tom replies.

VI.

Dorothy knows to dress down for her visit to the doctor. The waiting room is of a temperature that could boil cabbage. Accordingly she dons a dark but lightweight blouse, heavy bra, and summer slacks of a pantomime brashness.

Dr Savro is in his early forties – a good age for a man of medicine, in Dorothy's opinion – and wears a brown turban of a material that looks like leather; an inverted bucket of whips or tamed vipers atop a wide head, a smooth brow, an odd pair of semi-circular spectacles, designed with the crescent higher than the vertical frame, and a plump black beard (surely dyed) that fails to disguise a hearty and well-meaning smile. He also wears a nest of necklaces, silver and as leather as his headgear, quite visible through the wide-open V of the paisley shirt and a copse of otherwise undisguised chest hair... While she suffers in the sweltering, coughing, baby-tears-infected waiting room, Dorothy pictures the man who will ask her questions and then invite his own fingers onto the incision scar she's been left with. And she cannot help herself, she cannot help liking her general practitioner. While the scared sensation refuses to vacate her body, Dorothy feels comfort in the thought of a compromise – that if she *must* be quality assured by someone in a surgery that smells of Witch Hazel, it had better be by someone she trusts. None of which, however, obscures the panicky flutter that Dorothy experiences as a grain of perspiration rolls from her brow down the left inside slope of her nose.

'Miss Anthony,' the box tannoy declares. Dorothy, in a fiction, might have made herself genuflect in praise and grateful madness. Instead, she climbs to her feet. A good solid pain, fist-sized and sharp, punches her in the sternum, and then, its gangwork completed, splits up into two roving factions, sending lines of discomfort through her upper body and down through the existing trapped nerve in her buttock, heading further south to freeze her legs momentarily until a cramp unlocks. Dorothy heads for the second door on the left. She could find it in the dark, so often has she been here in the past few years.

'Come on in, Miss Anthony,' says Dr Savro. His shovel-blade hand jabs a curt invitation towards a grey plastic chair where Dorothy parks her bottom. She answers his eyebrows' question (she knows the code; she knows the drill, her doctor's shorthand); she says, 'I've been fine, thank you, doctor. And you?'

'Truly?' Pumping notes into the computer keyboard as though it's a church organ, Dr Savro sounds surprised. 'No little pains? No distress?'

'Well yes,' admits Dorothy, 'a few small pains, I suppose. Nothing unexpected, though.'

The good doctor's smile is irrepressible; he has found an amusing tone in his patient's assurance. 'Now.' He has finished typing; he twists on an expensive seat, which sighs, almost a grateful noise. 'Pains where, Miss Anthony?'

Dorothy meets his inquisitive glare; the spectacle lenses catch light thrown in through the window, rendering the doctor apparently snowblind. The illusion vanishes, but Dorothy feels trapped in those semi-circles. *Pains where*? is what he asked; Dorothy does not know how to narrow it down. This feels like the worst kind of interview; whatever she replies will need to be qualified by a statement – that she always hurt anyway, even prior to the operation.

Words fail her; and all of a sudden she feels betrayed by herself. A chalky taste floods her mouth; something breaks behind her eyes, and the delible mask of confidence is wiped away.

With a bow of her head, feeling fractious and small, feeling weak as a wind-battered bird, she starts to cry and answers Dr Savro.

'*Everywhere,*' she says.

The doctor produces a tissue from the top drawer of his desk. It is a magic tissue, Dorothy decides; the thought simultaneously calms her while making her squawk through a volley of lubricious tears.

'Aches and pains are perfectly natural, Miss Anthony,' the doctor tries to soothe her.

'At my time of life.'

'No. After surgery.'

'But it doesn't even hurt *where* I had the operation,' Dorothy protests, her composure settling (the magic tissue doing its work, casting its papery spell). 'Not all the time anyway.'

'Again, perfectly normal, Miss Anthony,' Savro replies. He leans forwards; the chair moans softly. 'The body is a *funny* organism like that. Did you never get one of those headaches that feels like patches of pain on different spots of your brain?'

'Welcome to my world.'

'Same difference, Miss Anthony. It is your body protecting itself from further trauma.'

'Spreading the love all around,' Dorothy interrupts.

'If you like, yes. You must remember that for all the good we hope to achieve with our scalpels and our expertise, Miss Anthony, the art of surgery is still a most *nasty* act of violence.'

'Act?'

'Oh yes,' Dr Savro answers, nodding his head. His second head – the turban – also nods. Dorothy quickly hopes that it won't fall off.

'All the same I'd like to give you a once-over on the bed if you'd be so helpful. If you could strip off down to your brassiere and under-garments, please.'

You smooth talker you.

'There's something else,' Dorothy adds quickly – not fearful of the examination; concerned that if she says nothing now she might never.

'What's that?'

She cannot look at him, notwithstanding the beauty of his peculiar glasses. It is embarrassing to say it; but say it she must. 'I've had hallucinations.'

'Of anything in particular?' Savro enquires.

'Yes. Two young women. A black girl and a white girl,' Dorothy answers. The fear tastes stale in her throat; her sinuses ring uncomfortably, as if in anticipation of the chlorine-invasion they'll greet when she goes swimming after this session. *But I haven't brought my swimming cozzie,* she realizes suddenly; *what's wrong with me?* Dorothy clears her nose and then, the magic tissue's tasks achieved, she drops the wet paper into the bin by her feet. 'I keep seeing them, Doctor; and I don't know if it's some, some weird reaction, or if I'm going loco, or what it is.' She explains the events of what she has started to refer to as her hauntings: the hospital; the shop; the coochy-coo baby natter.

Throughout, the doctor keeps his eyes fixed on his patient. Looking for he alone knows what. Horns? Horns and a tail? Fur sprouting suddenly on Dorothy's cheeks? She keeps talking. Savro's stare is as patient as that of a plant preying on insects. As soon as he understands she's finished, he crosses his large hands on his lap. Instantly Dorothy becomes besotted with his wedding ring – the white stone as large as a sugar lump.

'Can I tell you a story about a patient of mine, Miss Anthony?' he wants to know. 'I shouldn't, hypocritically speaking, but if I mention no names it can't harm.'

'Go ahead, if you think it would help.'

'He's a diabetic. He forgets to eat and he's a diabetic, a

potentially lethal combination. He keeps glucose sweets in the car, just in case, but on two occasions – on at *least* two occasions, I suspect there've been more – he has had insulin problems that have made him black out. Through not eating. The first time he remembers trying to answer a ringing phone by opening the microwave door and talking to a bowl of steaming pasta sauce.'

The doctor leaves a pause you could drive a tank through – if Dorothy could drive. She cannot resist a smile that mirrors his own. 'Is this meant to make me feel better?' she wants to know. 'I don't see…'

'The second time, he thought his mobile phone was his door key. And as we know, phones can do a lot of things these days, Miss Anthony, but unlock a house they cannot.'

'He was going mad.'

'He was indeed; but that's not the point I'm striving for.'

Dorothy frowns. 'Forgive me, Doctor, but I can't tell what that point might be. I'm really sorry… I'm not usually so slow on the uptake. You're telling me what? His diabetes was strangling his mind?'

'In a manner of speaking.'

The doctor's grin is beginning to annoy her now. 'What's that got to do with me?' she asks bluntly.

'Deficiency, Miss Anthony; deficiency of something we depend on can cause the sort of illusions you speak of.'

This sentence at least is a ray of hope. Blazing through Savro's obfuscation, Dorothy ventures: 'You're saying I'm deficient in something.'

'I'm saying that this is a possibility,' the doctor agrees. 'Have you recently given up something you used to take a lot of?'

'No. I don't think so.'

'Savro nods. 'How much on average do you drink a week?'

'I haven't got the DTs, Doctor!'

'Please allow me to be the judge of that. Approximately how much?' he asks again.

'A few drinks, here and there. I've never counted.' The implied accusation has set her on edge. More on edge. She knows what is coming next.

'They didn't ask you before you had surgery?'

'Yes. I said five, completely arbitrarily.'

'Five what?'

'Oh five kegs of rum. For God's sake, Doctor, is this really necessary? I said five glasses of white wine, often spritzers. But I made it up.'

'So what *is* your poison, Miss Anthony?'

Odd choice of expression; then again, this was an odd choice of morning – if *choice* came anywhere near it or into it. Dorothy sighs. 'Either vodka or white wine, depending.'

'On what?'

'The situation! The week!' What else does he want to hear? *It depends on my menstrual cycle, Doctor. It depends on a complicated system of stellar alignment…*

'And have you gone on the wagon recently by any chance?'

Dorothy's response is intended a joke (the atmosphere has become too rich); unfortunately Dr Savro fails to smile on this occasion. More importantly, so does she herself. 'Quite the opposite,' she not quite snaps.

'You've been drinking more?'

'Maybe a bit. I've been stressed – work stuff. And some other things.' She wants him to ask, to confess all about the visit to the restaurant Profit, about the crazed fan. Also about the events in the lives of her friends, which make them by proxy events in her own life; the cloying undertow of menace she has felt beneath the surface of everyday existence in the last few weeks. Her sudden palpitations; her sweating marathons; her loss, or at least decrease, of appetite. But all she can tell him is: 'The black woman and the white woman, you know? They've made me discombobulated.'

This time Savro grins – the adjective appeals to him. 'And do you find you drink more when you see the women?' he asks.

'I suppose I do. Does this make me a nutjob, Doctor?'

'No. I don't think so, no. In fact, I think it might be the other way around: you're seeing things that aren't there when you're tipsy.'

'I doubt that. With respect,' Dorothy answers. 'I wasn't tipsy when I saw the nurses.'

'But you *were* coming out of anaesthetic. The mind can do peculiar things at such moments.'

Reluctant to sit still for another of the doctor's baffling anecdotes, Dorothy curses the lapse in wisdom that brought up the subject in the first place. I don't need a GP, she thinks, I need a psychiatrist. 'Shall I show you my war wounds?' she asks, standing up and pulling her blouse from under her trouser band.

The happy-relieved expression that Savro proffers convinces his patient that the man is immediately in more comfortable territory at this invitation – stitch-watching; incision-cleaning; post-operative care – this is more familiar ground.

When the examination ends, Dorothy dresses, thinking as she always thinks, when down to her underwear in the presence of medicine made flesh: *It would be a lot fairer if he disrobed too.* Not for the first time, the notion twinkles like a story idea – one she will never write, though has started it several times. On each occasion she has penned this GP down to a pair of lubbery breasts, or a nipple-ring; to a swastika tattoo, or the tell-tale scar trace of an intravenous injection, suggesting drug use – and then the story has faltered with stalled confidence; and the tale has died.

In the corridor the heat has worsened: a barnyard suffocation temperature. Dorothy heads back towards the reception desk, there to book her next post-operative check-up. A young mother is explaining her son's sneezes to a bewildered woman of tender years herself, who is clearly not in need of the medical theory; a sneeze is a sneeze, and one after another shakes the poor boy's body as Dorothy waits her turn.

Outside, the traffic's irritability tweaks nerves. It's too noisy and far too smelly. Leighton Road bustles and heaves with lorries en route to one of the industrial parks; a detour must be in place, Dorothy concludes. Wanting away from these belching twelve-wheelers, she walks fleet-foot back to the High Street, aiming (in her head) for a cup of tea, after a quick perusal of the bookshelves in the Cancer Research and Homeless Trust charity shops. A bus driver crosses the path in front of Dorothy, heading for his waiting vehicle – the 70 bus to the airport – and it is as Dorothy follows the line of his stride that the fear that has been dissolving in her after the doctor's visit solidifies again.

The bus windows draw her attention. The vehicle is parked at the end of the street; a congregation of passengers waits to board, but some of them have been left on board from the journey so far. Abruptly Dorothy feels sick. The black and white women – the two from the hospital, the same two from the supermarket – are on the bus, the white woman in the seat in front of the black woman. Their heads are turned to Dorothy; their faces are mouthing words.

The driver unlocks the door, which stammers open with a faulty connection somewhere. He steps up; Dorothy watches him through the waiting line of would-be passengers; he takes his place in the cabin behind the wheel and begins taking money and dispensing tickets.

Still the two women watch her, mouthing their secrets; Dorothy clenches her fists, moulding purple crescents in the skin with her nails. With subconscious boldness – nothing conscious or fully-grown – she has exercised one of the few rarefied privileges of her age: she has trampled her way almost to the font of the throng that had not quite formed itself shoal-like into a queue. Dorothy is third on board the bus: third only in deference to two separate, shopping trolley-wielding women in blue rinse, who are each a decade further down life's line than she is herself. She steps on. She coolly ignores the driver's hitherto unnoticed blonde but threadbare moustache as she sidesteps the man and his gigantic steering wheel with a deftness that belies the aches in her legs.

'Why the hell are you two following me?' she calls with leavened venom down the aisle. She moves towards her pursuers, the driver's protest as harsh in her ears as are her own demand.

'You need to buy a ticket!' the driver complains.

Dorothy cocks him a deaf 'un. 'I asked you a question!' she tells her audience – including a handful of other bewildered travellers. 'What do you want?'

'Darlin! Ticket!'

Dorothy has strode up to the white woman. Her lips have not ceased moving, though no sound emerges. This is brutal ventriloquism – and it scares Dorothy badly.

'*Say something!*' she all but screams. The black woman's lips also move; the revenants in Dorothy's life are speaking in silent tongues.

'You'll have to get off,' the driver says behind Dorothy's back – directly behind – the man has jettisoned himself from his cabin. He promises that he will eject her with his palsied bare hands if required. Dorothy shudders. All the same, against logic (against hope), she attempts to appeal to the man's basic human understanding and goodwill.

'These two woman are following me,' she say through taut

lips, casting her words over her shoulder like a scarf.

The bus driver's voice behind her begs to differ. 'These la-dies've been with me since Milton Keynes, love,' he counters. 'If anything, *you're* following *them*.'

Dorothy half-turns on her heels; what she's heard has struck a nerve. The injustice stings like chilli. '*Me?* I've done nothing.'

'Please. You can buy a ticket or you can leave. Unless you got a pass.'

The allegation is almost more than Dorothy can bear. She is *ringing* with rage. 'A pass?' she repeats, now turning fully in the aisle to clock her accuser. 'I'm not a *pensioner*,' she almost spits. 'I'm nowhere *near* sixty!'

'Then buy a ticket,' the driver reiterates. It is his turn – his limited speech executed – to turn his back on Dorothy. He returns to his cabin. 'Anywhere but Dunstable town centre; we can't stop there today. Roadworks.'

Dorothy does not hear the announcement of restrictions to the journey, although she will hear it later on through the medium of memory. Sounding high and aloof she says, 'Fine.' Dorothy follows her victor, fumbling her heavy purse from her handbag. 'A return to the end of the line, please,' she requests with an artificial sweetness.

'Luton Airport?' The driver slams shut his cabin door. He avoids this wayward passenger's angry and zany gaze.

'Yes. Or L.A. Airport if you'd prefer. Luton Airport, please. How much will that be?'

'Six-twenty.'

Into the black metal tray Dorothy slides the deposit of a cashpoint-fresh ten-spot; it quivers, as though fearful itself of the upcoming journey. The man in charge pauses.

'Got nothing smaller?' the driver asks, his voice just shy of unalloyed disappointment.

'Only my sense of pride. Or my IQ. Are you telling me you can't change a ten-pound note either?'

'What do you mean *either*?'

'You've got a driving licence presumably.'

'All right, love,' the driver says with palpable weariness. 'Could I call upon you, perhaps, to provide the twenty pee piece?'

'Just give me change from seven pounds,' Dorothy replies. 'I'll write off the eighty pee. It's all yours.'

The ticket jerks out of the machine's lips. Having snatched this paper tongue from its mouth, Dorothy makes her way back into the bus. The pursuers regard her. She takes the seat two behind the black ghost and seconds later the bus shuffles off.

In the early stages of the journey Dorothy finds a name for it: *anti-amnesia.* The flashbulb-popping effect of enforced memory-retrieval. Scenes brawl in her head and they have scarcely left Leighton for Stanbridge. Time was, she would make this trip fairly regularly. On her left, the offices of the Cooperative Funeral Company – one of the town's frontispiece showrooms for death dues and death duties. Inside this establishment, beyond the squirrel-grey glass, a good trade is underway. In fact, it is heaving in there. Death is a lonely business, Bradbury wrote, Dorothy thinks, referring to a novel she has owned for two decades but has never opened. Bradbury never died in Leighton Buzzard, she continues, her chest surging briefly in preparation for a cynical burst of laughter that doesn't pop.

Dorothy jumps as the bus crunches gears on its entrance into the Billington Park estate. There is tension in her back – a joint clicks – as the vehicle stops to drop off and pick up. Unnecessary tension as it transpires, the two pursuers in her life have not moved a muscle between them; nor have they shared a single word – not even an insult tossed in Dorothy's direction. Nothing. *Are they even on this bus with me at all?* she asks. *Didn't the busdriver say he could see them?* Perhaps this is a shared hallucination, but if so, who owns it? At any rate, it is too late to disembark: it is too far to walk back to town.

The bus turns right on to the A5, having waited at the intersection for nearly two minutes for a suitable break in the traffic. The gears sound as though the labour is all but beyond them. Dorothy deep-breathes; she knows how those gears feel. Her heart is still going a mile a minute, but she is feeling slightly better. She has told herself to concentrate on the scenery; there is nothing she can do until the two women – preferably together – climb off the bus. (And then? she asks herself.) A sign on the left advertises Christmas trees for sale. On the right, a motorbike rattles past with an engine that sounds like a sewing machine motor; on board the bike are a man and a woman not wearing brain buckets. The woman riding pillion is carrying a small dog dressed in what looks like a pair of oven gloves. The dog's tongue lolls, tasting the freshness of buggy airkill. Has the whole world gone stark raving loony today? Dorothy wonders as the bus draws to a whining halt. The traffic ahead is backed up on the approach to the large roundabout.

I should tell someone about this, Dorothy realizes. How often, in fiction as well as in life (though not in *her* fiction) could something disharmonious have been avoided by the simple act of making a phone call? But what will she say? *Hannah?* In Dorothy's mind the recipient of the call is automatically Hannah. *I'm on a bus, following those two headcases I told you about. Yeah, I'll call you later. Ciao! Ciao!* Surely laughable. All the same, the phone is in her fingers, fished from her cavernous bag in a motion of subconscious expediency.

They have passed the left turn to Houghton Regis, the fire station on the right; having entered Dunstable. Slowly, the bus moves, as if by electric shock, as if on the receiving end of a cattle prod's services. By experience, Dorothy knows that there is no such thing as a slack time for traffic in Dunstable. She makes the phone call.

'Hannah, it's Dolly,' she says quietly, her lips barely moving – her lips also a scant three millimetres from the mouthpiece. 'Can you hear me okay? An engine. On a bus towards Luton.'

Little more than this cursory synopsis leaves Dorothy's mouth; the recital concludes as the bus grinds up to the crossroads in the centre of town. No sooner has Hannah said that she'll call a taxi and meet Dorothy at the airport than the latter adds 'Oh God.' Hannah asks what the problem is, but with the line remaining open she is about to hear a running commentary all of her own.

'I think they're getting off,' Dorothy all but kisses into the mobile's mouthpiece. For indeed, at the stop outside The Quadrant shopping precinct, both the black and the white woman stand up, having waited for a number of other passengers to step off.

The black woman carries a handbag not much larger than a surgical sticking plaster. From it she retrieves – a gun. 'Oh God,' says Dorothy once more; other passengers utter their own injections, some much stronger on the ear than *Oh God*. The white woman's handbag is larger, but it concealed an identical bounty – a pistol; dead-fish grey, a weapon made for the smaller hand, for the more petite assailant or self-defender. Together the two women shout, 'We are taking control of this bus! This is a hijack!' The synchronicity of their statements is not performance-perfect, but the message is understood. The white woman has stepped to the front of the bus, by the giant-insect-eye windscreen. She drops the gun's muzzle onto the driver's temple, and with a smile on her face she orders him to…

'Drive straight on.'

Her partner-in-crime is in charge of crowd control – such crowd as remains. 'Nobody move a muscle,' she calls. The black woman points the weapon from one passenger to the next; Dorothy, nearest the back of the bus, is last for the treatment.

Oddly, Dorothy stays calm, or calm*ish*. She hasn't been truly calm for months; maybe years. The two woman toting pistols have had no obvious effect on her equilibrium. If anything, it is a result (she thinks) that finally they are doing *something* – although she wouldn't have guessed a hijack for all the tea in China.

Where will they go? Definitely not left, towards Luton and towards the airport. The bus has crunched over the crossroads, the white hijacker's pistol remaining on the side of the driver's head. What's this way? asks Dorothy, silently. St Albans, Harpenden…

Remember this moment. You'll need to talk about this later. Their clothes. Their eye-colour. The actions of the other passengers, but…

Actions? There are none. Dorothy notes the air of passivity – of complicity – on board the bus. No one moves. No one utters so much as a single word – as the bus feeds through Dunstable and past the turn-offs for the village of Markyate, where Dorothy once attended a wedding reception in the rain, fog glued to her freshly-purchased, expensive mauve hat like the bride's veil to her own. These memories tick along with the cluttered ratchings of the bus's engine and gears. Memories of how the bride had appeared, overweight for her dress, crammed in and stuffed like a doner kebab.

Markyate is left unconsidered, no more than green signposts in the vehicle's exhaust. That village is not their destination.

So where is it then? One man – right at the front, the journey's lone male representative – dares to pose the very same question. Standing up abruptly he demands in a clear voice for all to hear: 'Where are we going?' He is Dorothy's age, or a year or two older – he has crossed that bridge, now closer to sixty than fifty. He wears a brown checked jacket and baggy black jekylls; he has a birth mark like a plum on his left temple.

'Sit down!' the white woman tells him, pointing the gun at his head; but this bejacketed proponent of order has demands of his own.

'Where do you think you're taking us?' he asks.

The clothing he has donned for his visit to Dunstable, Luton or beyond is swiftly stained – painted into permanent disrepair. A bullet atomizes his incisors and molars; to a loud and violent report it leaves the gun, gets cold in the micro-second it takes to cross a metre and a half of bus-air, and enters the plaintiff's head to the squashed obscured noise of a pumpkin being dropped onto concrete. As the shot whips the man's body into a brief tarantella, Dorothy notes the stroke-victim's smile that the bullet renders, the left side of the man's mouth lifts up in response to high-frequency mirth; the right side stays planted in stoic neutrality. When the bullet leaves this man's hippocampus and skull, it is as if a child has thrown a balloon of red paint against the bus's window. The man leaps backwards to save an invisible shot at goal, his back connecting briefly with the glass and the blood that he has deposited thereon; then he slides back down into his seat, slumping forward, the blood on the window smeared and ruined.

He doesn't twitch; there are no death throes, no moans – certainly no further complaint on behalf of the man's fellow passengers. Silence has seized them all once more; the few squeaks and the solitary squeal having been hushed. It is all that Dorothy can do not to count her heartbeats; her eyes are fixed, not on the dead man who leans forward on his seat, like kids do when they're impatient to be somewhere, the arch of their back trying to speed the bus along, but on the window and its psychedelic mural of blood and shattered glass. From where she sits she can not quite see – but she knows it's there – a small white hole formed by the bullet's egress. She can imagine the edges of this break in the pane, the glass compacted around the absence like scar tissue smothering a wound. She can also hear a low but persistent whistle, a draught from outside, leaking in like air over ill-fitting dentures.

Window pain, thinks Dorothy at the back of the bus, spelling the homophone in the same part of her head that the man has had so comprehensively destroyed. The pain we see though open windows in someone's head. She closes her eyes; suddenly she feels lethargic and lazy, she wants to sleep. It's the wrong time to sleep; the wrong time and the wrong place. She opens her eyes after only a few seconds, half surprised that the world is as she left it. The smell of the gunshot has mixed with that of an opened human body; this miasma floats backwards, pungent, on the draught now spewing from the bullet hole. The fresco on the glass changes subtly as some of the blood crawls. Is that what she can hear? – the pitter-patter of blood-drops, like tears falling onto the love letter received by a Forces sweetheart? *Drip!* A pleasant sound, surely; dew tumbling from leaves at dawn, pearls of new-day life. But this is death. Dorothy can hear him not breathing. She can see him not moving. She can feel him not living.

The bus takes a left off the A5. The white woman has returned her attention to the driver; the black woman's role seems all but redundant, crowd control has never been simpler. With a grin on her face she even goes so far as to lower her weapon. As the bus rolls up the coiled ramp on to the M1 motorway, the black woman holds on to the back of the dead man's seat, for balance; the ramp is as tight as a spring.

They are heading north.

Hearing Aid

I.

1.

Roy is well used to the principles of victimization, having played both principle leads of the drama – the aggressor and the pusillanimous aggressee – at various junctures down the decades, circumstances demanding. He understands the power trip of bullying; but he is far from ignorant of the almost guilty pleasure of being a victim who must kick his way out of the ashes of the fires that have died around him, fighting back to reclaim a fresh equilibrium. He even respects the fact that someone, at the simplest level, might have it in for him, and nothing more; that someone wants him to pay for a former (and forgotten) misdemeanour. What Roy cannot stand is his own failure to comprehend.

Roy has had enough drink and enough of this nonsense. First the woman taking Mrs Anderson's motor, using guile and deception (he cannot deny it, he was fooled and bamboozled); but now Miss Paddington's, the thief having employed trickier strategies still – the strategy of breaking and entering. And yet... what had the investigating officer told him? No more than he had gleaned by himself, but it had seemed useful to hear the theory corroborated: that there were no signs of a break-in. Roy pours himself two knuckles' worth of beer from a can he abandoned the previous evening. The beverage is flat, warm from its twenty-four hour sunbathe on the kitchen work surface; and it tastes of the cigarette butt Roy extinguished in the can at the time of its devaluation. All the same, Roy consumes the vile concoction, hissing the ashes through his teeth like a connoisseur of choice brandies. Once more he rolls his imagination past what he knows of the car thefts...

The first thing being, of course, that Mrs A's Punto was returned to her, in A1 nick to boot. Nursing the ardent contemplation that a similar fate lay in store for Hannah Paddington's Nova will not make it so; but it does convince Roy that the same woman is responsible for both pranks.

She's out to get me, thinks Roy, finishing a slug of tepid lager. He relishes its acidophilus bitterness; it matches his mood, and it makes Roy thirsty for a proper drink. An impertinent red, perhaps, he considers, crossing to the rack in the cupboard under the stairs, and reaching back momentarily in his memory for the poorer times – jars of hot dogs, joblots of schnapps, the peachy sugary nastiness of which had been known to catapult him into migraine country for weeks on end. Until the next batch came along. As he selects his red, Roy remembers how he'd thought it nice to be wanted, back when he'd only mislaid one insane old biddy's motor and an attempt had been made on his workhorse's life through the idiot stealth psychology of simple greed. Pizza is good, free pizza equals better pizza. He chooses a rioja of indubitable charm, spiciness and above all, potency.

Who can it be? *I'm a good man now* sounds like a sophomoric protestation, but the fact remains that it's true. There were poorer times, rougher times; of course there had been. In whose life wasn't this so? But things get resolved. *I'm an honest geezer these days*, Roy confesses to an imaginary man of the cloth. He decants the bottle's contents into what used to be a goldfish bowl, back when he thought he enjoyed the company of pets. It does not take long for the alcohol to make its mark on his mood, by darkening it, but widening it also, opening Roy's intelligence to less stylised philosophical wanderings. In the sanctitude of his house's near-silence, Roy settles down to chew on his possibilities. In the lotus position he suffocates two sofa cushions with the deltas of his backside, as he sips red wine from a fishbowl and trots out gas via the successive lifting of either knee, thinking once again:

Three times is deeply personal.

He even vows to commit the gravid sentence to paper.

2.

Barring the necessity for bodily functions and the timeworn search for spectacles (always a joy in the morning after a night's drinking, as if my inebriated, waterlogged brain decides to play a little game, by burying this particular trove of treasure somewhere unlikely in the flat), my first positive action this Monday a.m. is to exercise. All things considered, this goes well. I conduct two sets of twenty push-ups; I wince a painful journey through the hostile weather of fifty stomach-crunches. But as there has been a paucity of similar activity during my convalescence from work, I am delighted with my efforts. Hannah herself would be proud of my cardioenthusiasm. No one else would. (Or I don't think anyone else would, but who knows? Maybe Stephen would. Maybe even Sabrina.) Then, these jerks achieved, my heartbeat slapping along and my belly efficiently squashed flatter, I embark on my second positive action of the day. A proper shower. Granted, this doesn't sound like much of a feat, but you'd be surprised. It tires you, staying off work; the ordinary tasks of a billion citizens every day is the sick, brokebacked bastard's twenty-four Everest, always there to climb in your heavy boots. I even shave. Using Sabrina's tweezers, or rather a pair she discarded that I rescued from her tampon bin, I pluck at the whiskery copse that straddles the bridge of my nose, connecting my eyebrows, which in turn receive due attention as I have spotted a couple of doomed white hairs.

While it is true that my back burns on with a pain sempiternal, the freshness of my discomfort sluiced and reawoken by my recent physical training, and while the case might be that I dread the arrival of a rep from the College's Human Resources department, who seems to have declared war on my absence from work, there are reasons the equal of my current jovial spirits.

The first is Roy. Impeccable material from the mechanic last night, the confession booth being The Leper (but does that make me a priest? – surely not), where he spilled beans of an unexpected genus. Such as what? Such as this: Roy's done time.

Roy's been inside; Roy's done bird; Roy's done a stretch. Over the carefully-timed provision of a brandy mack, on my part, Roy repaid my wintertime generosity with an expression of solemn, somewhat theatrical appreciation, a slow wrapping of his bear fingers around the rust-coloured beverage, as though the glass itself could ooze welcome warmth, and a slow, repetitive but ultimately fascinating rendition of a story about a man whose real name is Steve Birch.

And there's something else.

3.

'Three times is personal,' Roy told me.

'I agree; but what does it mean?'

'Dunno. Wish I could ask the bint.'

I didn't need Roy to specify who he meant. I tried to see it from his point of view, as indeed I do with Hannah and Dorothy, with Samantha and Annette – even Sabrina (though this is harder). What must it feel like to be invaded so... *tangentially*?

When you try to gauge the weather but the rain is too fine to see through your morning-dark window. You dress inappropriately; and you find that you're soaked to the marrow before you reach the postbox on the corner.

Roy is in a position like this, not certain he's being attacked (but fairly confident of the same), and certainly not sure if it's one person or more who's at fault; or why. He is soaked to the *atoms* in the invisible fine rain; he says it doesn't hurt but it annoys like chickenpox.

Experience had taught me to estimate justly the beauty, not so much of coincidences *per se*, but of the patterns that both precede these confounding ironies and then succeed them. And there are patterns at play, here in Leighton Buzzard in the here and now; patterns at work as well. It is not solely the case that the pairing of Hannah and Samantha, and singly Dorothy, have been visited by people with cargoes of bad news – the pair by someone from their joined past, and Dolly by two women from only the Fates know where; it is the short timeframe inside which these hauntings have occurred that seems significant.

Meanwhile (and is this also part of the pattern?) the person from *my* past – my mum's brother Stephen – is *loudly* absent, his silence as booming as fireworks, creating in my mind, paradoxically, an almost physical presence for which I am appetent. All of which leads me to query: where, if anywhere, do Annette and Sabrina fit in? Vulgar proximity to the principal leads, or is it something more pertinent?

Now take Roy. With a background like his, there might be any number of tasty eejits with scores to settle, finding their way back onto his run to scratch their feet and roost… We stepped outside to finish our pints on the patio, taking one of the many untended tables, the rain having kept most of the drinkers inside. Roy and I sat down on wet white furniture, under a table umbrella with the span of a pterodactyl's wings; by starlight and the amber glow of a patio heater I witnessed Roy's nostril hair writhe as he finished mumbling and shouting everything he deemed relevant. Then he asked if I fancied an Indian.

'It's late, Roy. I better be getting back. Sabrina's waiting up.'

'But you eaten yet?' he pushed.

'No,' I admitted; 'I don't have much of an appetite, tell you the truth.'

'Then why you getting so fat?'

'Because every time I fuck your sister she gives me a biscuit...It's too *late* for an Indian, mate.'

Roy laughed, as I knew he would. 'Never too late for an Indian, Tom. Never. Besides, you gotta eat; keep your strength up, to give that lovely missus of yours a good seeing-to.'

'Or your sister,' I reply.

'Or my sister.' Roy tipped his pot into the back of his throat and drained his lager. In a satisfied fashion he gasped; smacked his lips, and with a theatrical flourish he wiped his lips clean of foam with the back of his hand. 'Drink up, Tom!'

I drank. Roy stood up and eructated, before apologising in a debonair fashion. 'And you know something, Tom?' he said. 'You're a lucky man, you know that?'

I finished drinking. 'Why's that, mate?'

'My sister never gives *me* a fucking biscuit when I've done her.'

Wind pawing at our ears, Roy and I exited The Leper's car park; the gravel sounded grouchy beneath our heels, as we disported ourselves at ridiculing one another into giggles before we'd ordered our first popadom.

While it's true that Sabrina wasn't happy at my late arrival home, I closed and locked the door on a night of revelations, including a coincidence – a part of the pattern – that I chided myself for not acknowledging earlier.

The name of this jigsaw piece is Simon Kolko.

'Tell me more about that Caitlin next time,' is the final thing Roy says to me tonight.

4.

Sabrina's first question, disregarding the obligatory but meaningless one about the nature and quality of my day (meaningless because I always answer *Fine. You?*) is this:

'Why don't we take a holiday? It'll do you good,' she adds. 'Do *us* good.' She deposits the laptop case on the coffee table.

'We can't afford it.'

Sabrina shrugs, there in the archway into the kitchen, adopting the teapot impersonation – one hand on hip, the spout-like other arm reaching almost absentmindedly for a clean cup on the draining board rack. 'Stick it on the credit card, can't we? That's what they're for. Where would you like to go?' She finds her cup and starts to work on her first brew of the evening.

'New Zealand.'

'I'll only get a week off work,' she answers. 'New Zealand's too far.'

'I was joking. Where do *you* want to go?'

'What's so funny?'

'I didn't want one, thanks.'

'One what?' Sabrina looks confused.

'Brew,' I reply.

'I was going to offer! Jesus, Tom! Memory serves, it's me's been out all day working. It wouldn't hurt you, actually, to have a cup of tea on the menu for *me* when I get in. Anyway, I was going to offer.'

'Thank you. In that case, I was going to say I'd love one. Where have you got a fondness for? Holidaywise.'

'Maybe the Lakes?'

'The Lake District? Sounds nice.'

'Or the beach?'

I shake my head – not that Sabrina's shoulders can see me doing so. 'Too cold for the beach. Wrong time of year.' What is

Sabrina angling for?

'You may be right. The Lakes then.' Perfect play, Sab. 'I was looking on the internet today. It's out of season so some of the hotels are quite cheap.'

She's already booked, I realize. I wonder where we're going. Also wonder if she'd prefer to go without me.

5.

It's a small world, I want to say, but it comes out, mangled, as in: 'What a fucking coincidence!' 'Innit?' Roy ploughs into a dhansak of ambiguous meat origins. Crispy popodoms crackle in his wake through chutney, chilli and for-the-girls yoghurt. Roy is happy.

'You *knew* him?'

'Knew-ish,' is all that Roy will divulge. He has taken a polite sip of his lager; now he swills it around his cheeks in a mouthwashing action, like someone in the seat at the dentist. I nearly expect him to spit it out, all over the table; but Roy is on a warning from Dave the barman, remember; one false move and he's barred. And as Roy has mentioned many times, it would be an insult to be barred from a rectum like The Leper. Sometimes a name really *does* say it all. This particular public house is one book you *can* judge by its cover.

'Do they have dentists in the nick?' I ask, apropos of Roy's care with his beverage.

'Yeah of course. I quite fancied my dentist as it goes. I used to make up problems.'

'So you'd get sent to see her?'

'Exactly. Make up some molar malfunction. Gets you out of the cell.'

'And this was Lewes Prison?'

'Lewes Prison. Category B. Eighteen months of me life I

won't get back again.' Roy surrenders to the memory with a huge shrug; the telling of the tale has disturbed him. Forget the smile on his face, he doesn't like talking about this one bit.

'I can hardly believe it,' I tell Roy, watching him wipe a foamy moustache off the iron filings of his real one. 'I can hardly believe this coincidence.'

'That's if it *was* the same Stephen Meredith,' he is quick to qualify.

'It's gotta be: the way you describe him.'

'Fat. Far-away look in his eye.'

'Yeah…' Well it *could* be a different Stephen Meredith, but I'm inclined to buy the first shirt on the rail that fits. This is Uncle Stephen; my waters tell me so (whatever that means).

Stephen and Roy were neighbours on C-Wing. Stephen helped Roy with his reading; Roy helped Stephen not get beaten up. It was a marriage made in Devon.

'And he was in for robbery?' I ask again.

'Yeah. Was living a hand-to-mouth existence, the way he told it.'

'That sounds like him.' I am tempted to tell Roy again the story of Stephen's last years, the squalor in Wembley; the dirt; the undeniable mental illness.

The scratches in the table, like the jottings of an insomniac scholar; the sweat-riddled boffin, with his big brain and no paper for his theorems.

Why won't you feed me? he had written. It's a fair enough question, I still think.

What little I remember of Stephen is given new life; the memories dance and flicker, like flames; and then there's Kolko – the constable linking us all together. I try to bring Kolko back; I try to pump life into his veins, to make him a more solid person. It doesn't work.

Roy told me that Kolko was the investigating officer when Hannah's car was stolen. Kolko was the man who informed us (me, Mum and Dad) that Stephen had been found dead. Kolko this and Kolko that; but *years* separate these (and other) events. Is it the same guy?

I am starting to doubt some of my ideas.

6.

I tried to explain it to Sabrina.

'It's all right for you,' she argued sleepily, 'you don't have to get up in the morning. It's nearly one a.m. I need to sleep.'

'This is important.'

'So's my job.' But my reckless demeaning of her work role, as she would see it, had hit the mark nonetheless. Sabrina roused herself from the restive place she'd found, and turned on her side to face me as I undressed. '*My* job's keeping us off the streets, remember, Tom? Off government handouts? Remember *work*? It might seem an antiquated system to you but it'll be here for a bit longer – the idea is, you do something for somebody and they give you money for it. Then you use that money to pay bills. Remember bills?'

'I'm sick,' I answered simply.

'I know; but don't put down the one thing that's keeping the wolves from the door, Tom! That's ridiculous. Kojak can wait. My beauty sleep can't.'

'Kolko.'

'Kolko can wait even longer. Goodnight.'

She wriggled back to the position in which I'd found her, her back to me. Naked, I slipped under the duvet. I resisted the urge to cuddle in closer; I hadn't brushed my teeth and I didn't think, with her current temperament, Sabrina would take kindly to my perfume of alehouse and rogan josh. I killed the light. The room swam with purple loon triangles and navy-coloured insignia – sure signs of lower foothill inebriation.

I was tired but excited. It's not as though I live in a one-horse town, with one community-appointed sheriff and his faithful deputy; close to seventy thousand people live in this locale, so what are the chances that one man – a constable at that, the first foot on the law ladder – should police the whole area? Long odds, anyone would agree (even Sabrina). But what was I to read into it? The facts remained: Kolko *did* bring the detail of Stephen's discovery to our front door; Kolko *did* attend the break-in at Bible Street Cars.

7.

'So she stalked you?' Roy asked.

'Yeah. It was fun at first,' I told him. The subject of the conversation is Caitlin. 'Then it got a bit sad; I felt guilty for making her spend so much energy on me when I had no intention of letting it go anywhere. She kept sending me these *letters*. Long letters.'

'Did you threaten her? The police or whatever.'

'No; not exactly. I was drunk one night and I told her that it had to stop. I was supposed to be going out for a Chinese with Sabrina. Luckily I had enough time to leave the flat, and she was in, obviously. I rang the doorbell about five times, I think – that's the way I remember it anyway.'

'Don't tell me: little fluffy pink negligee.'

'No, nothing like that. She was wearing jeans; blue top, I think. I told her that I didn't want any more of this shit, okay? I was waving her letter – I hadn't even read it. She'd delivered it, like, two minutes before or something like that.'

'And did it work? Did she stop harassing you?'

'It got worse. She was like a *wolf*, mate.'

'I think I can see where this is going..'

'The first time, I could barely get it up. We did it in her kitchen. The only time I've ever shagged a bird leaning over the oven, pots and pans still on the stovetop. Jesus.'

'What?'

'My actions. I'm amazed I kept it quiet from Sabrina, that's all.'

'How do you know you did?'

'Because she would've given my bollocks to the charity shop, that's how I know!'

'She might be saving it up, Tom; payback at a later stage.'

I laughed. 'Is that meant to be reassuring? You're in a jolly old mood, Roy!'

'I don't get it, mate, from her pee-oh-vee. What was in it for her?'

'Contact? Comfort? You tell me, mate…'

Roy guffawed. 'What makes *me* some kind of expert, Tom?'

'You're divorced. You musta learned *something*.'

'You saucy cunt.' Then he sang that line from that old song by Space: 'The *fe*male of the species is more deadly than-the-*male*.' No doubt to the amusement of our compatriot diners, I joined in with this chorus. I can't remember the verses. For reasons unexplained, Roy then thought it appropriate to persevere with this ad hoc and *acapella* karaoke, gracing the room with a Cockneyfied, vowel-mangled version of 'Rhine drops keep falling on me, Ed' – before adopting a preposterous accent, part Lancashire and part Never Never Land, in which he informed all and sundry that once he'd been *afraird*, fockin petri*farred*. It was difficult to see Roy in any other light than that of soft disgust, it must be said.

By not checking his behaviour, however, what was *I*?

There and later on, I tried to rumour up Caitlin. Of course

I failed.

'Wait till I tell you all about her modelling,' I said to Roy.

'Airfix or fashion?' the bear-man joked.

'Neither. Or rather, it started with fashion, I suppose…'

'Oh? Bit of glamour, as they say?'

'Yes. Though it doesn't sound like there was much glamorous in it. Taking your top off in a grotty flat in Luton or wherever. That was just to start with.'

Roy raised his eyebrows. 'Porno?' he asked.

'Kind of.'

'And you turned her *down* to start with?'

'It was years earlier. It left her bruised, believe me.'

'What, mentally?'

'Yeah. Scarred like an old warhorse.'

'Well, then that was why she fancied you, Tom, obviously. There can't be any other explanation.' Roy laughed. 'Whatever happened to her?'

'She moved away. I thought I said that.'

'Afterwards.'

'I've no idea. I wonder that a lot from time to time.'

'Perhaps she's the mad bird stalking *me*,' Roy said.

'I wouldn't put it past her. What's happening to you sounds like Caitlin down to a T.'

'That's worrying. But why me? What have *I* done to her?'

'I don't know. Let's go home, mate; let's go to bed.'

Roy laughed again. 'Only if you promise we sleep head to toe.'

8.

To my surprise the buzzer buzzes. I answer the call box swiftly.

'Delivery for Lockington,' the voice mangled by distortion.

I get to the door and accept delivery and sign. The box is one that might contain four or five hardbacks, but this one is much lighter in mass. What I've got is not books. Sitting at my coffee table, I use my housekey to slice open the packaging to discover what I *have* got.

What I have got is a box. Specifically, I have got a shoebox... and it seems to be alive – small air holes punctured in the top.

I am worried as I slice open the smaller box's packaging, tightly wound in layers of heavy duty sticky tape. Before a few seconds have passed I'm grunting like a sweaty ape.

I manage to open the box. The final tassels of masking tape scratch free to the tune of low-key ripping noise, courtesy of the housekey. A vomiting occurs – from the box. Filling the room immediately, like a storm – thousands, four thousand, five thousand insects.

Locusts.

Someone has sent me a box full of locusts.

I don't know it for a fact – I *can't* know it for a fact – but I suspect it was Kolko.

I spend the following hour, or nearly, not reading (how could I read?) but planning the order in which I would read the next ten books that will gain entrance to my repertoire. All the while, locusts flicker and flatter by; the stench of them is appropriately appalling – the sort of stink that could knock a lazy buzzard off a shit-house roof – but I do my best to ignore the locusts' noise and hygiene issues. Instead, in this storm of wildlife, I arrange books. My rules of engagement are as follows: it had to go hardback then paperback, and so on, alternating; I was not allowed two consecutive books by the same author; if possible each new choice must be in a different genre from the one that precedes it. An hour of my life, with locusts landing on my head, on the ornaments, on the framed photographs on the window sill; on the painting prints on the wall; on my seldom used acoustic guitar. I throw open the windows – the curtains belly out into the sky – and then the back doors that give on to the porch where I once sat sunbathing, admired by Caitlin in the house opposite. Some of the locusts make a bid for freedom; the air thins but still seethes.

Leaving the doors unguarded, I repair to The Leper for lager. I have seven or eight locusts on my clothes; luckily there is no one in there that I know better than to share a nod of the head with (but Angie the barmaid, back for a trial run at work after her period of being signed off by the quack – Angie give me an odd look as she tickles my palm with hot change).

When I return to the flat – two hours later – most of the locusts have flown away. I hoover up dead bodies and bits of wings. It's enough to make a grown man queasy.

Has Caitlin sent me the locusts?

Has *Stephen?* (As unlikely as this seems…)

Why won't you feed me? was what he wrote – or rather, scratched deep into the wood.

Why won't you talk to me, Stephen? is the question I would ask him back.

I'm getting annoyed.

The franked postage strip says **MILTON KEYNES**. This could mean anything, I suppose. That's a wide, wide area to narrow down to a single sender.

Locusts from Milton Keynes. It's almost a song.

The package has arrived normal post. There is nothing to trace.

II.

1.

Suppositions and nuggets of myth-quality anger have clustered in Sal's head. No amount of paracetamol will shift this compound from her consciousness, a compound that feels physical, with mass and volume; almost with an identity of its own. It presses on her skull walls, like Smithy their cat used to do, a year ago, in the sturdy gated box used for visits to the vet – before James attempted to kill Smithy with a flamethrower made from a deodorant canister and a cigarette lighter stolen from Len. She needs air. Fresh air and some light, troublefree callisthenics; a brisk walk. This is what doctor after doctor has prescribed for James, is it not? An amble by the canal; a bit of sun on her flesh – it radiates the skin; helps you glow; detoxifies bad mood and feeling.

Sal is almost, but not quite, looking forward to meeting Annette again. They have agreed to meet outside Tesco, in order to execute their weekly shops in each other's company; their purchases deposited in the boots of their cars, to take a half-hour breather beside the water. They have matters to discuss, Annette had warned Sal on the phone.

What else can Sal assume but that these 'matters' revolve around James? (Everything else does.) Barring the fact that their sons attend the same school – the same class in some subjects – what else do the two women have in common? Sal knows next to nothing about Annette. She knows the basics, those that (again) revolve around James – that Annette is the mother of two boys, one of whom – Emil – is friendly with James; the other boy's name has been misfiled and Sal cannot remember it, or indeed if this other son is younger or older than Emil. Annette has a husband called Richard (*longsuffering* she'd called him, which had seemed odd), a taciturn boffin type; she has met them both at a parents' evening at school, an occasion on which she was told yet again that her son has a talent for waywardness and disruption – while Emil, no doubt (she considers with bitterness), will have been a candidate for Student of the Year. Other than that? Sal has shared words with Annette when collecting her boy from Emil's house after a tea-and-homework party; but that's about it. When Annette called her number it was Sal's first instinct to apologize for James's behaviour at their house the other night, even though she is not aware of any wrongdoing on James's part. That's the way Sal's life is: *apologetic.*

The day is fresh and clean; whipped dry by a brush-like wind, the mid-morning is inviting, welcoming; it feels good for Sal to get out of the house and into the Carrier. The roads are as clear as they ever get in this town. The lights are with her all the way. Sal parks the Carrier at Tesco, the choice of spaces a joy to behold. She has parked near the walkway that leads through to the canal path, near the vast receptacles for glass and newspaper recycling, where the supermarket's lower-tier employees craft smokes and drink fizz on their breaks from the deli, the warehouse, the tills.

Annette is waiting by the front doors. It is a moment of awkwardness. To kiss hello? To shake hands? Parental protocol has abandoned Sal; she can't remember what's best to do in the circumstances. With James's conditions and behaviour having passported them from shire to shire around the Home Counties, it is Sal herself who has often felt like the new girl at a new school, yearning to fit in. Luckily it is Annette who leads by example, leads with her nose. She angles her features towards the right side of Sal's face, depositing a brief dry kiss on Sal's earlobe, her lips as cool as a chilled bottle of wine.

'Thanks for coming.'

'Not at all.' With an exaggerated flourish Sal produces her prop – a shopping list written on the back of a flyer for a new pizza delivery service. 'I've got a few things to get.' Suddenly Sal experiences an absurd sense of shame for her own *handwriting*. She bets that Annette's script is tighter than her own infantile building blocks; and more controlled. It has only been two years since she weaned herself off the tendency to crown lower case *i*s with circles instead of dots. Her *d*s float high up off the guiding line, as though attempting to ascend the vowels that precede or succeed them. In latter days, if she handwrites anything at all (which is rare), she usually works staunch capitals.

They enter the supermarket. Guiding a trolley apiece, they embark upon this odd pre-lunch date, though they don't know it, each as wary and nervous as the other. It's Annette who appears more relaxed; she has dressed in sportswear, prepared for her shift at the centre in four hours' time. Like most of the shop's users, they are each accustomed to shopping alone; visiting unfamiliar aisles and counters is against the grain. Also they shop at different velocities; Annette is now required to slow down; Sal is obliged to choose with more deliberate insistence.

'I suppose you've heard,' says Sal. 'James has been suspended from school.' She clips the sentence short of the word *again*. 'For fighting.'

'Yes; Emil told me,' Annette answers, X-raying a bunch of emerald bananas for imperfections within the skins. 'How are you feeling?'

'To be honest, it's like a pair of slippers. Do you like them that green?' asks Sal, referring to the chosen fruit.

'Richard does. Nothing too ripe or ready for my beloved.' Tang of disappointment there; disapproval even. 'Steaks like roadkill. Fish with a trace of a pulse – that's Richard. And he likes his fruit underdeveloped. Hard as a bullet if possible. Do you need anything here?'

'No. We don't do a lot of fresh fruit. Or veg. I tend to cook around what James likes… Did he eat okay with you the other night?'

'He was fine, Sal. What boy doesn't like burgers and beans? I keep it simple when the boys have their friends over, don't you?'

They have pushed their trolleys into the bread aisle. Sal tells Annette: 'It doesn't happen very often – friends over. Not even Louise. She's ashamed of James, but she won't admit it. She doesn't know how to act around him; it's getting worse as she gets older, to tell you the truth. Louise prefers to go out. She's okay with a curfew.'

'I was going to ask you about that,' Annette replies, plucking loaves of raisin bread from the shelf, with the pinchy greed of an OAP under the weight of two decades of Communist rule. 'It was early one morning, couple of weeks ago, I was on my way to work – early pool shift – and I saw James by the canal. Just sitting there. I'll show you the spot when we've paid, if you like. Though I didn't know it was James, I hadn't met him then.'

Sal is already tired of talking about James. 'Should I be saying sorry at this point?' she asks. She selects a loaf of raisin bread, the same brand as the several that Annette has squirreled into her own trolley. She knows that James does not like anything with raisins.

'Whatever for?'

'I don't know. Was he rude to you?'

'Not at all. Can I be honest? I thought he was a little *intense*.'

'That's one way of putting it. *Creepy* is another way one sensitive soul informed me.'

'Another parent you mean?'

'No, a teacher. A *head*teacher, actually, in Berkshire. A good few years ago now.'

They walk on. 'People can be cruel,' says Annette, 'when they don't understand.'

It takes Sal no more than a second to convince herself that Annette has not meant to sound offensive. The patronizing declension – this is only in Sal's mind. Annette did not intend the sort of rudeness that she believes her James delivers frequently; Sal is tuned to a frequency that others cannot notice.

'And do you?'

'Do I what? Understand? I'm trying.'

'Why?'

'Why am I trying?'

'Yes. Why are you trying to understand my son?'

At the end of the aisle are batteries, inner soles, chewing gum, bulbs. Sal pauses, wondering which of these she needs least; she fingers the dangling gibbets containing batteries. 'I'm trying to remember toothbrushes,' she says as an announcement overhead obliterates all in its sonic range. A caretaker is required in aisle twelve. Annette waits until her hearing has returned to normal when she cracks the saliva bubble in her throat and ventures:

'I hope I haven't upset you in some way.'

'No you haven't. You were asking about James and the canal.'

'I *have* upset you. I'm sorry, Sal, I didn't mean to.'

'I know. A bit raw and sensitive at the moment. I didn't know he goes to the canal, Annette. He sneaks out, I don't know where he goes. Well I do now. He comes back in time for school. Ironically enough. What was he doing, by the way?'

'Just sitting there. Thinking, I suppose.' Annette pauses. 'Speaking of which…'

Sal raises her eyebrows: yes?

'Do we need anything in this lane?'

'No, not really. Microwave chips and ready bakes I can do without. Do you know, I've just noticed something.'

'What's that?' says Annette.

'*You* throw everything into the trolley. *I* separate things out so they don't touch. Like with James's food… I forgot to mention that about him, didn't I?'

'Emil told me. I made sure nothing touched. He ate it all up, don't worry. He was charming to me.'

'Well that's a relief. Do you need anything else? I'm finished.'

'Just some bacon, some yoghurts, then we're done,' Annette answers. 'Then it's time we rewarded ourselves with a glass of something at The Globe.'

'I'll meet you at the checkout, shall I?' Sal asks. 'I promise I won't run away,' she adds, and immediately hates herself for the dumb remark. While joining the queue at one of the few open tills, she chooses chocolate and wonders what Annette had had in mind by *matters to discuss*. She's none the wiser. She pays. Outside in the car park, she waits by the cash machines, clouds twisting overhead in a wind decompressing from moody to murderous, and she tries to remember where she locked up the vehicle. That's right, by the canal. As she pushes the trolley closer, ducks beckon her with quacks that sound drunken – ugly giggling from beyond protective hedges. Sal positions her plastic bags in the Carrier's boot.

I told her by the tills. Wank! Sal forgets to lock the boot and runs back to the front of the shop; she hopes that Annette will not think her common or ill-bred – will not conclude that Sal's run away like a pussy.

Annette is waiting by the Thomas the Tank Engine kids' ride. 'Thought I'd scared you off.' The dished-out grin suggests that the light-hearted tone is forced.

'I'm out of puff,' says Sal. 'I forgot we said tills; sorry. Listen... I've got... Jesus. Am I ever out of shape! Fuck *me*.'

'Looks like rain,' says Annette.

'Annette.' Sal recovers her breath. 'I have to ask – and I don't mean to be rude.'

'That's *my* job.'

'...What exactly did you have in mind? Please. The suspense is killing me.'

Annette leans heavily on the trolley's handlebars. 'Did James say the name *Kolko* to you?' she asks quietly. 'Simon Kolko?'

2.

The staining aroma of chlorine; the bliss of a pool undefiled by the day's swimmers.

'Need a word,' is all that Alex said, late last week. 'Your husband's on to us.'

'I really doubt that.'

'Don't pisstake me, Annette. I got a *call* all right?'

'Calm down. Call about what?'

'It was bacon, babe. Plod on the loose.'

'Speak English for Christ's sake.'

'I got a call from a cunt called Kolko. Do you know who I'm talking about? Yes? He said you'd made a complaint against me. Against *me*!'

'I'm confused, Alex. What exactly did he say?'

'That you'd accused me of raping you, in a nutshell.'

'Oh my God. And what did *you* say?'

'I said – what do you think I said? – I said it wasn't true. I said, we'd had sex a few times, and very nice it was too, but it wasn't... And then he interrupted me. He said: thanks, that's all I need to know. I wasn't thinking straight. So I said to him: what do you mean *thanks*? He said, that's all I need to know: you had sex a few times.'

'Why's he doing this?'

'Then he said: *You're a dead man.*'

'...I feel sick.'

'I feel angry. I'd *drop* the wanker, he was here right now. Drop him where he stood.'

'Yeah, that'd help. I'll call him.'

'Yeah, *that'd* help!'

'Well what do you suggest I do?'

'Have a word with your husband. Tell him to call off the hunt. You and me's over, right? That's what you said. You didn't want to do it anymore. I can live with that, but *this*...'

'I very much doubt this is Richard's doing, Alex. Very much.'

Annette wanted to jump in and splash, but she had a shift to start.

Tonight she'd call Kolko.

3.

The Globe is no more than an eight-minute drive from the supermarket. Annette chauffeurs Sal in her Renault. Rain invisible to the eye, crinkling the road ahead like warm cellophane, collects on the windscreen; the wipers squeak and yaw, seesawing through this nugatory moisture. Otherwise, they motor in silence. For want of something more constructive to say, Sal remarks on the peculiar weather they're having. Annette agrees with a toss of her head, a grunt, a slide down through the gears to first; they wait to turn right, and the car park's gravel clicks and shifts beneath the Renault's tyres.

There is a bridge for the two women to cross on foot. Annette remembers a time when she'd driven over it, right up to the public house, it had been a nightmare to get back out again. So these days, if she visits The Globe at all, she approaches on the soles of her feet. The last time had been with Kieran.

'Inside or out?' she asks her new companion.

'Let's sit out. The tables have got umbrellas if the rain gets serious.'

Lunchtime trade had not claimed all of the waterfront tables. 'If you roost there,' says Annette, 'I'll get them in. What are you having?'

'White wine spritzer,' Sal answers, sitting down.

'Girl after my own heart. Won't be a minute.' Inside the building, the atmosphere is crepuscular and warm. *Hairdryer* warm, as though someone has left all the ovens on full blast for eighteen hours. Annette cocks a twenty-spot for attention and orders three drinks – two identical and a separate double brandy, the last of which she downs in three swallows while the Polish girl tickles the till's gullet for suitable change.

'Who *is* this Kolko?' Sal asks Annette. 'No thanks.'

Annette has offered her a cigarette. She withdraws it with a natty flourish, scooping it into her own mouth in a diffident gesture. 'He's an irritant, it seems to me.'

'But what's he got to do with James?'

'That's the point. I want to understand the connection.'

'Shall I tell you what I know?'

'Please.'

'It was after the murder on Dunstable Downs. Kolko was the one who interviewed – as they say – interrogated James.'

Annette buzzes with drunk and undrunk, yet-to-drink alcohol; she lifts her glass, and it is miraculous – painted clear and cold by the dishwashing machine.

'He hasn't been the same since. Whatever *that* means.'

At first Annette interprets Sal's manner of staring off into the middle distance as rudeness, or of social inadequacy. Perhaps the woman is bored. Seconds later, and Annette starts doubting that she is giving the right impression herself; perhaps she is not holding it together as well as she believes. When she follows Sal's sight-line, however, she discovers that it's the ducks on the canal that have her attention. A mother duck leads her sixfold brood through the terracotta-coloured water, leads them with all the graceful indifference of a porter leading guests to a hotel room. To Annette's mind, Sal is poised on the ledge of tears; she tries to see it from the duck's point of view, simply going about its nature-given way of being a good mum. Perhaps the mother duck reminds Sal of her own failures in that department.

Annette thinks of different matters. Having made the connection with a high-class hotel room, she follows the porter there again, this time in mind only, though the scene she remembers was very much about the body. It was Annette's first adultery against Richard. It happened ten years ago, while Annette had pretended to visit a reunion of college pals, held implausibly far north in the British Isles. Richard had bought it. He had bought a lot since – a lot of deception, a warehouse full of lies – but maybe the letter was Richard's saying *No*. No more, Annette... She can even remember the room number: 47. The part about the congress occurring in Doncaster had been true; that was the only part about it that was. It is easy for Annette to recall Ben's aftershave, his initials on the room service dockets. Only a night. But sometimes a night can change everything, and it was true that Annette had never felt quite the same after that, so soon into her marriage to Richard; so bewilderingly *soon*.

It was Annette's first act of unfaithfulness against Richard. But it was not the worst thing she'd ever done.

Sal says, 'I'm sorry, am I boring you?'

'Not at all. I found myself thinking about my dad. Sorry. He just slipped into my head, the way things do.' Annette's eyes and mouth display humour, the latter also a clutch of gold fillings. 'He's always moaning about his health. To anyone who'll listen, really.' To assist her in the project of impersonating her father, Annette squashes her chin against the top of her chest. 'Psoriasis? Lift me scalp off like a blimmin' syrup of fig.' She laughs.

'Are you okay, Annette?' Sal asks. 'Maybe *I* should drive us back when we're ready.'

'He thinks I don't love him, just because he's a bit of an albatross some times. But I *do* love him. Even if he gets on my nerves.'

'I thought you wanted to talk about Kolko.'

Annette looks again at the ducks as she finishes her drink. It is not the subject of parental failure that they stir in Annette; they remind her of relief. Once, lost in woods, she and a man with her had followed a duck, in much the same way that the young on the water were led by Mother. It astonishes her how much she doesn't want to think about Kolko.

Is Kolko the devil she's been waiting for? She has wondered when one would be sent, for she has done so many bad things. Her mind flits back as far as school – hauled before the Head-teacher because of a poetry composition in which she'd rhymed *demon* with *semen*.

'Kolko has threatened me and threatened a friend of mine,' says Annette. Such is the fluency with which she casts off a bowd-lerised version of events that it might have been that the teller has practised for the recital. Nothing is further from the truth.

On finishing what she wants to say she lights a cigarette, remembering…

4.

It was her turn to buy lunch for the girls' get-together. She had gone to see Patrick – to borrow spending money. This happened nine months ago, give or take. As usual, he had wanted to impress her with moving stories about his triumph over illness and imposition.

'*Psoriasis*?' he grinned. 'Did you say *psoriasis*?'

'No,' Annette answered. Things were rawer back then.

'Don't talk to me about psoriasis, girl!'

'All right I won't.'

'Back in '62, got it so bad on me bonce that the scalp was coming away. Like a crust on a mug of 'ot chocolate it was. Frightful sight. Thought me brains would leak out. I could peel me own scalp off like a syrup of bleedin' figs. Like a *wig*.'

Annette clicked together the blades of the scissors that Mum had used to cut bacon for her hotpots. 'Thanks Dad, that's a nice image,' Annette told him. She clicked the scissors again: *snipsnip*. 'Right.' She stood behind him, in the kitchen; he was seated on a red stool, with one tea towel tucked into the front of his shirt and another in the collar round the back. The one against his chest, a relic from the commemorations of the marriage of Charles and Diana, resembled the cravat of a staunchly monarchistic sentimental homosexual; the one against his back had been drained, almost etiolated, by a decade of service washes, and it resembled the hard-luck hairdo of a formerly chart successful poodle rocker from the Eighties.

'Mohican again, is it?' asked Annette.

The old ones were the best. Despite the tension in the air, Patrick smiled and told her he wanted a bouffant.

'And then tidy the moustache and hack off me toenails, eh girl?'

Setting to with her trim of her father's white curls, Annette succumbed to the ineluctable pleasure of a revulsion shiver. The prospect of cutting Dad's nails was what ushered it into her skin.

'Did I ever *tell* you about me nails?'

'Yes, Dad.'

'*Nails? They was 'ardly worth the name!* I had *depressions* on me nails – they looked like bloody dice they did. Crumbling like chalk. Falling away from the nail bed. Gimme boils or impetigo any day of the week.'

And that was when it happened.

It is sometimes during the dreaming hours that the memory returns; when Annette recalls the emotion that ambushed her that day, standing behind her old man and his war wounds, with his immuno-deficiencies and his vulgar suppurations.

'I thought: *I could do it*,' she told her friends. 'Over in seconds.'

'Well apart from the prison bit,' Sam replied, the voice of reason for the nonce. 'There's *that* bit that isn't over in seconds. *That* bit might last a lifetime.'

'Knowing *your* dad, Annette,' says Sabrina, 'he's probably got anti-scissor-metal serum in his blood. The blades would ping across the room and embed themselves in a cupboard. How long did the feeling last?'

'A couple of minutes. I cut his hair – this is disgraceful – but I couldn't help wondering what it would feel like to cut his earlobes. He was annoying me *that much*.'

'Forgive yourself,' Hannah told her. 'You didn't, that's the important thing.'

'But I wanted to.'

'But you *didn't*. No harm done,' Hannah stressed in a QED tone of voice.

'It's the thought that was harmful. That little bit of dirt on the neck fat…'

'You're scaring me,' said Sam. 'I think I prefer it when you talk about sex.'

So, instead of talking about the truth, Annette told an old

one about the time that she and a boyfriend got lost in the woods, and were led out of there by a waddling duck.

'It's strange I can't remember his name, but he took me for a walk in the woods, near where he lives. Or lived at the time. Picture it: perfect cold January morning. Lots of love in the air after the Christmas break. It was delightful. And I'm assuming, all the while, that he might actually know where he was going. We were dressed up in our winter coats and he'd told me to bring a pair of boots to walk in, so we were dolled up perfectly. And he starts to take a series of turns off the beaten tracks, and it still doesn't occur to me that he might have got us lost; I was just happy to be there, do you know what I mean? It was the sort of place where people you've never met before say good morning to you.'

'I think I wrote this one once,' Dorothy said — the first words she had spoken since becoming utterly engrossed in her beef and ale pie. 'You're going to tell us he was a serial murderer. Luring you to his den in the forest, where the bones of his previous victims mould.'

'No, I bet he just wanted her to blow him under a tree,' said Sam. 'That's it, isn't it?'

'*Way* weirder, girls. See, it had started to dawn on me that he actually had no idea which direction to go in. And you know what I'm like with directions — I get lost in Tesco's car park — but even *I* knew we'd been past, you know, that particular *tree* in the last half hour.'

'So how long had you been walking?' asked Sabrina.

'About an hour, I suppose. Forty-five minutes happy and the rest in a deepening sense of panic. It *did* cross my mind he was trying to get us lost — or make me think we were lost — the old car's-run-out-of-petrol routine, you know, we-might-be-here-some-time. And that bit I didn't even mind, although I thought — bit *unnecessary*. It wasn't like I was keeping him waiting to get me into bed or anything. If he wanted sex outside he only had to *ask*. The simple fact of it was, to be frank, he was a bit of a *cock*. He was trying to be romantic, I'm sure, but it blew up in his face. He just didn't have a clue where we were.'

Sam asked, 'So what happened? This has turned into a no-sex story.'

'It *stays* a no-sex story. We kept walking, is what happened. And walking; and walking. My *legs* were aching; my *thighs* were aching; I desperately needed the loo. We'd *long* since stopped talking; but he hadn't admitted anything about his powers of navigation or anything. It was like two zombies lumbering around. With not a path to be seen. So I'm telling myself: just keep calm and try to walk in a straight line; you've got to make it to some sort of civilization eventually. Then I'll use the mobile and call a cab to take us back to the car.'

'Why didn't you call a cab there and then?' Hannah wanted to know.

'What? Pick us up from the middle of the forest, you mean? Use your head, Hannah! It was like something you expect to see David Attenborough chatting to chimps in. It was *Gorillas in the Mist*, babe. Then we came to a fence.'

'Ah,' Dorothy said, 'I was waiting for the fence. There's always a good fence.'

'Fences are good,' Annette agreed with a nod of the head that freed two identical barbs of lacquered hair from the Alice band that she wore at the time. 'But it was barbed wire.'

It was Sam who spoke next. 'Let me just clarify one thing, if I may?' she said. 'You do emerge from this tale unscathed, I take it.'

'Physically.'

'Ooh, intrigue,' said Dorothy.

'Drama!' Sabrina concurred.

'Because anything's possible in your stories, Annette,' Sam continued. 'I'm thinking of that guy who liked you to stick a silk hanky up his posterior and yank it out at his *moment*. To free the bowels, I think was the way you put it. This wasn't the same bloke, was it?'

'No. Funny thing is, I can remember *him* quite clearly.'

Hannah laughed. 'Pretty hard to forget, I would imagine.'

'But I can't remember the one who took me into the woods.'

Annette resumed her tale, partly embarrassed that there was so much told and so little left to tell. They followed the barbed wire fence, she and her suitor – not without a fight on the man's part, who insisted on knowing the reason for this when his plan was to carry on in a different direction. *Because who do you think put up a fence? The squirrels? A fence is a manmade device, to keep something out or to keep something in. It'll lead to a farmhouse or a woodland property or something.*

Where the farm dogs can yap at us! he protested.

I don't care if it's a nuclear reactor and we end up glowing and cough-ing out our own tonsils. I don't want to be in these trees anymore, do you understand? Go your own way for all I care...

The duck that led them to safety crossed their path a few hundred metres on.

5.

And I've faced everything I've feared, Annette reminds her-self, by talking to Hannah at work.

'I've faced it all.'

'I know you have, Net.'

'Though... you know, the bad reckless ways might be with me, sometimes – things I don't like to talk about much, things I do wrong – but I face my fears, Han. I faced that wood. I have faced my father, but that's a continuing struggle. I have faced my mother's death and kept him as happy as I can. I face Richard; I face his boredom – the boredom that he causes and the boredom that he must endure.'

'Richard's been good to you, Annette. Do you need a tissue?'

'Yes, please.'

'There are so many things I'd like to tell you, Hannah. I go wrong sometimes.'

'We all do.'

'Badly wrong, Hannah. I need to tell you something.'

'I've got five minutes of break left. Will that be enough?'

'What are you on?'

'Gym supervision.'

'I'm coming to see you. I'll just dry my hair,' Annette replied, 'but honestly no, I don't think I'll actually need the full five minutes of your time, Hannah. I've been unfaithful to Richard. I need to tell you about what happened on Dunstable Downs.'

III.

1.

Hope left them nearly half an hour ago − tossed from one of the windows along with the last of the mobile phones. Now the passengers have nothing; or *claim* to have nothing. Dorothy's mobile was the last to go. The black hijacker offered a lambent smile as she tipped the contents of Dorothy's bag all over the adjacent seat. 'What's your name?' Dorothy asked − however futile and desperate it seemed, to know a name was to own a part of that person.

They are on the M1 motorway, destination *somewhere north*. The lane signs plot their route, stitching the towns together on a map sewn in Dorothy's mind. With scant geographical nous to call her own, she builds these conurbations on her dreamscape, based on the miles-to-go provided on the signs: cockaigne hamlets of a score of houses apiece, smoke swaying above chimneys shaped like urns on thatched roofs.

I was asleep, Dorothy concludes, opening her eyes to the same bus and − she could swear − exactly the same stretch of three-lane ahead, although she is still at the back of the bus and this is impossible to discern. How on earth she's managed to nap in the circumstances is equally as confounding. The screams the dream gave her resolve into pitiful squeaks from the wipers on the vast screen. The rain is abusive.

Where are we going? seems the most poignant and pathetic question imaginable. Dorothy feels robbed of vocabulary; robbed of years; perhaps robbed of sanity.

If I'm mad and this doesn't exist, Dorothy thinks, I can't be shot − because there's no gun. There are no women − grinning their way through a hijack with the cooperative passengers. And… *if there is no gun, I cannot be shot.*

Dorothy rises to her feet; her sore leg clicks at the thigh; pain feeds through, back-of-shin to perineum, a wavering bolt.

'Sit down!' the black woman demands.

Simultaneously, both the black woman and Dorothy take a step towards one another, in the aisle.

'I can't be shot,' Dorothy states.

The black woman replies: 'Wanna bet? Siddown you silly bitch.' She points the weapon at Dorothy's chin. Her language – salty. No mouth-mimes; no choir-of-two recitals with her partner in crime.

'That gun's not real.'

'Wanna *bet*? Last chance: you sit down or you lose something fundamental to your equilibrium. On the count of three. One.'

'That dialogue's not real either.'

'Two.'

'Did *I* write that?'

'Three.'

'I don't *think* I did.'

Noise. Window pain. Heat.

2.

Hannah precedes her direct request with all manner of deflections: *I wouldn't ask if it wasn't an emergency.. If we can put that madness behind you – behind us I mean – I could really do with…*

'What is it you need, Hannah?' I ask her point blank.

'Your car, Tom.'

'I don't have it. Sabrina has it – she's at work.'

'You see, mine's been stolen.' Hannah is not listening to me; her panic is too loud.

'Yes I heard. Sorry about that,' I offer.

'You heard? Who from?' I have thrown a different noise into the howl.

'Roy. The mechanic.'

'Oh I see. Of course Roy. Maybe I could borrow a car from *Roy.*'

'Maybe. What's this all about, Hannah? Why do you need a car so urgently?'

'You'll laugh. Or maybe you won't. But you'll just have to trust me on this. I think Dorothy's been kidnapped. I can tell you on the way,' Hannah replies.

'The way where?'

'I *don't know*. I haven't got time for this, Tom. Can you get a car off Roy or can't you?' – with an exasperated tone that suggests she has asked me this several times when in fact she has not.

'I'm not his keeper, Han.'

'Fuck it, he owes me. He's the one who lost my car in the first place. I'll get a taxi there.' Her tone softens. 'Shall I detour and pick you up on the way over?'

Is that a plea I hear before me? 'Of course I want to come,' I tell her, but she's already gone; the line hums at me, censoriously and with admonition.

3.

'Did she win the bet?'

'Did she wet the bed?'

'Did snickums get a scratch then?'

'Did sniffles bump her nosey?'

Baby voices, but from adults; baby questions.

'Scrach her chinny-chin-chin.'

'Bump her Rudolph the Red.'

Dorothy asks: 'Why are you speaking like that?' Her voice

is slumber-drunk; sloppy-edged. She will need to work harder.

Rime dissolves; light sprinkles through a seal-grey gloom – golden speckles, hundreds and thousands on a cake, they taste sweet, pinpricks of illumination that Dorothy would like to gobble down, until she's sick.

'Why are you *speaking* to me like that?' she demands, forcing up her eyelids with dreadful effort. This open-sesame allows in more than light; in comes pain. *Window pain.* A recollection – a flare at the gun's muzzle – and then something burning on her left shoulder. While raising her right hand to touch the wound, she is alarmed to find that hand already in place. Her senses didn't tell her that she was attempting to staunch the flow. *I've been shot.* This must be shock. There is blood all over the hand, as close to the skin as a leather glove; as best she can, Dorothy watches it.

The passengers on the bus, and the hijackers, are looking at Dorothy; they have twisted and turned on their seats, as if shooshing a sweet-unwrapping, muttering noisy twat in a cinema theatre. Silently bemoaning the absence of sympathy flowing in her direction, Dorothy spends two seconds doing her best to stare them all out, these ugly creatures.

Didn't she point the gun at my face? wondered Dorothy. What made her change her mind and aim for her left shoulder, especially after the man who protested too much was hacked down in his prime?

They want me.

Somehow and for some reason not yet clothed in anything that Dorothy can see – *they want me. They want me north…*

The bus is moving, not quickly, in the left lane of three, and by now they might have reached the Midlands. But how? Where's the police siren whine? Where are the rescue copters, chugging overhead with the persistence of horseflies? Where's the media? It's hardly likely, after all, is it, that a stolen bus on the

M1 has gone unnoticed.

SWAY 2M, a sign reads; it snags on Dorothy's attention once she's swerved her eyesight away from the passengers and the pirates. Where is Sway? Dorothy has never heard of it.

'I feel dizzy,' she thinks aloud. With greater volume she adds: 'I need a hospital. This needs looking at.'

Apparently this is amusing to the black woman, who smiles a gale through the vehicle. 'Is ickums wet?' the woman enquires.

'Well of course I'm not wet,' Dorothy spits back. 'Unless you count the blood from my shoulder. Why are you talking in that manner?'

'Piggle cross,' the black woman calls to her partner, who dutifully sees the funny side.

For once they've got it spot-on. 'Yes Piggles is cross. And Piggles is about to get a whole lot crosser. I need to get this wound seen to.' Dorothy flexes her left fist – the gunshot seems not to have damaged any nerves – she can move her fingers at least, though it hurts to do so.

'Shut up for God's sake!'

This comes, not from either of the hijackers, but from a woman in her late forties who has twirled in her place in order to issue the directive. Her face is spherical and also made of spheres, a fleshy chin, tennis ball cheeks. And hers is a face that transacts in hard currency: Dorothy can imagine the woman's round face cracking up on hearing the one about the owl and the jockstrap. But now the currency is different – blissful anger – and the denominations shuffled out are high.

'You'll get us all killed!' the woman concludes.

Dorothy is chastened – partly by her fellow's words; as much or more by the singular lack of empathy that she's been awarded. *I took a bullet for you guys*, she can hear herself saying; but no one likes a show-off. Deciding to keep quiet, Dorothy listens to her castanet thoughts; her eyes grow blurry eating the road.

Evidently Sway represents more than a name on a motorway sign; it would appear to be their destination. Or if not the latter, it is somewhere on the way to their finish line. The bus has slid onto the off-ramp; they leave the M1. Up ahead is a large steep roundabout. As they start to encircle it, Dorothy foists focus on her eyes; she counts the exits. Not many to count. The bus leaves the roundabout at the second, and Dorothy pictures the same cartoon compass she has held in her head since she was a schoolgirl. On it the arrow points to nine.

They are heading west.

4.

On my insistence the taxi sets us down on the lips of the stone driveway, the one that leads down to Bible Street Cars and a few other small enterprise businesses. While Hannah begins to make her way on foot, I watch the driver three-point-turn his way back onto the Stanbridge Road; then I follow. Stones clatter underfoot. Spine tingles with unfamiliar exertion; the pain there changes shape.

'Wait up!'

'Come *on*, Tom,' Hannah calls over her shoulder, refusing to alter her pace.

It's like running on sand when you're a kid, my ankles twist with every stride; the grip is not familiar – and I've donned the wrong shoes. The soles are not adhesive – especially not for the damp pebble runway on which I am to gain ground – and before I've moved five metres my face is pocked with sprigs of sweat. 'For God's sake, wait up!' I say again, lunging harder; toothy pain gnawing a line down my backbone, into my kidneys.

All of this on top of the fact that I'm still reeling from a conversation in the cab. 'I don't know quite how to say this,

Tom,' Hannah had said, taking care not to look at me. 'I should probably just shut up but I wanted to talk about it.'

'Okay,' was all I could commit to.

'Well…' It is no more than ten minutes in the car from mine to Bible Street Cars. We had already covered most of the distance. Whatever it was would have to be dealt with quickly. 'I had the strangest, *strangest* dream – about you. It's been sort of… simmering with me ever since. Sounds stupid mentioning it now.'

'What was it? Is it.'

'You and me.'

I took a deep breath. 'I had it too. I had the same dream.'

'I'm being serious,' Hannah told me, making eye contact.

'So am I. You and me, in bed. Total darkness. Not your bed. Not my bed.'

'The *same* dream?'

'That's what I'm saying.'

'*Not* your bed?'

'No, not exactly.'

'…What can it mean?'

'I have no idea; but I don't like it'

'No. No, I don't like it either.'

Roy is waiting outside the garage. Although I called ahead to warn him of our arrival, I got Ian on the line and I wasn't sure that Roy would get the message. Poker faced, Roy stands in his once-blue overalls, smeared a darker rainbow of oilstains old and new; somewhat bizarrely, he is not only holding an umbrella (the rain is all but non-existent), but twirling it above his head, like a propeller.

'Yo Tom. Miss P,' Roy nods. 'What's the hoo-ha?'

Hannah takes the reins of this bucking bronco. 'I need to borrow a car. I think that's the least you can do seeing's my own car's been stolen from here.'

I could weep. We even dummy-runned this in the taxi; we rehearsed this very transaction. What did I say? Don't go on the offensive, I said. Not with Roy, I said. With some men, okay – with others you just *don't*.

Visibly bristled, as they say, by this slur on his security precautions, Roy sucks tuneless air in a whistle through his teeth. I know he doesn't wear dentures (as well as you can ever *know* such a thing) but right at this moment I form the opinion that he has indeed popped in some falsies. His temperament shifts battlefield grey; he sucks on his own jaw. The phrase *bear with a sore head* trifles with my mind.

'Please,' I add lamely.

Although Roy must surmise I will tell him everything in good time, there remain a few ins and outs to peruse. 'Where's the fire?' I am aware that the noise of labour within the garage has ceased. As if to gauge the efficacy of his own message-taking, Ian steps outside, rubbing a spanner down with a cloth in a motion most masturbatory; he forms the second line of defence, broadening his stance half a metre behind his manager's back, slightly to his right. He even folds his arms.

'All right, Ian mate?' I say.

'All right, Tom,' he returns. 'What's the name of the game? What's the scores on the doors? What's–'

'Shut it, E, eh?' Roy clips off the young man's clichés. 'I asked where's the fire' – thereby adding a cliché of his own. Confusion has made him confrontational. Before Hannah can bollix another word, I leap in. 'Our friend's been kidnapped, we think.'

Roy's eye sockets pulse. 'Fuck me. Sorry, Miss P. Why didn't you say?'

5.

Dorothy remembers the hill – the hill with the face.

That was how it appeared, from a certain angle – in a certain East European light. This was years ago, when Dorothy was still in her twenties, fearing the tiptoeing approach of the big three-oh. She was working on a book, earning her living by teaching English and Social Skills to spoilt brats with braces on their teeth.

The hill had had a face: the eyes made of caves, sporting tree growth for lashes and terse hedges for brows. A copse crowns the hill, giving the impression of a rakish hair-don't – a little boy's style, straight from the pillow, before being slicked back for the school run. A long demolished stone building – abandoned by time and wind-tide – resembles a broken nose; there are lines of other stones to form a mouth and a set of whisky teeth, the crenellations in the lips marked by fauna.

Dorothy used to walk on the face, especially between arguments with Ian or Bruno. It was a place of beatitude and swarming calm. She would don her heavy boots and climb; she would plot and kiss nature with an open mouth. Walk along the hill's moustache; read Pynchon or Ferlinghetti in a sleeping bag, on the cheekbones of a passive god. It was her way of escaping from the camp; the drills; her way of getting out alive from the clamour.

Why does this thought burgle her mind right now? She doesn't know. Nor is she entirely sure that what she is remembering is true. There was a hill, that much is certain; but something about the picture she's created – the pastoral sweetness, perhaps – plucks at her consciousness, trying to make sure she stays awake long enough to get it right.

The hill, yes; and yes, there was a definitive argument – with Ian. Not with Bruno. Something happened and she went to the hill, but it was far away from where the argument took place. The hill was not close to the camp where she taught the brats.

What happened? Dorothy stretches her brow to make room for more memories.

Blood loss? *Am I suffering from blood loss?* It seems so. Blood loss is the root cause for these hallucinations, these memories… Surely it is.

She had only told Hannah about the hill, and what had Hannah replied? Something about hills pointing to God, had it been? Something like that. How you sometimes imagined you could feel the presence of God – or at least of some minor deity or sprite of the verdant slopes. No; what Hannah had actually said was this: *You were walking on the Face of God Himself.*

An odd remark, even for Hannah; eccentric and baffling.

If that was God, I pity His poor missus. He was an ugly bugger, really.

Hannah laughed. *Maybe God's good in bed, to compensate. He'd have to be, wouldn't he? Being God and all.*

The two women had chuckled… but Dorothy had felt hollowed-out by the confession. You're supposed to feel relieved of a certain weight, by the act and trauma – the excision – of a confession. Dorothy, on the other hand, had felt the real world and its real rivers, torrenting in to fill the evacuated space.

She remembers clearly: *the hill was where they found me – after Gabe left. They found me in one of the hill's blind eyes.*

An eye is where you're supposed to locate peace – the eye of the hurricane – but it doesn't always work out like that, does it?

This is your blood talking, Dorothy thinks; your bitter blood – the blood that's leaving you for another woman. As though prompted, nerves send signals towards this epiphany – the wound on her shoulder *twists* (she would swear it) – twists and shouts; and Dorothy wonders again if she is dying.

She could have slaughtered you.

Who could have? Who's she – the cat's mother? *She's got a name, Dorothy –*

Yes, Mum…

So who's 'she' when she's at home.

Yes, Mum.

Louder!

YES, MUM!

Who's 'she'? She's the girl on the face of the hill. She's the girl in the eye in the face of the hill… and I don't know why, she swallowed a fly, perhaps she'll die.

Perhaps *you'll* die.

She didn't want me to die.

Who's *she* – the cat's mother?

No. She's the girl on the hill.

There were two of them, Dorothy. It wasn't one girl on the hill; there were two of them, and they weren't girls either. Young women; one with pale white skin, one with black.

Huts made of stone, Dorothy remembers.

They didn't want me to die. They wanted to die.

With which she collapses into unconsciousness.

6.

Hannah has insisted on driving, which is fine by me: my back hurts and concentration is onerous. As we make our way to the motorway entrance near Flitwick, she punishes that gearbox and revs the accelerator as though testing the weight of her right leg. We don't speak – which is easier (I assume) for both of us; definitely it is for me.

'Do you believe in ghosts, Han?' I ask.

'What?'

Indeed, what I have said is hard to hear: the senescent

jalopy that Roy has lent us makes unexpected and ridiculous sounds. The engine clatters, the belts whistle. The huckleberry Citroen is well over a decade old – it belongs in the last decade, in the previous millennium – and is in and of itself as good a reason as any not to converse. It sounds like The Harry Partch Ensemble, on a particularly grumpy day; it gives new meaning to the phrase 'courtesy car'.

Not because I want to talk – it seems a shame to spoil things in that respect – but because I know solutions do not arrive without effort, I repeat the question.

'No,' Hannah tells me finally. She has slid onto the M1; we are heading north, chasing, in pursuit, and she has taken her time to respond. She raises a limp left hand to gesture thanks to the driver of the workvan behind us, who has yielded and let us in. The driver's headlight beams play twice on our windscreen as he acknowledges Hannah's appreciation.

We listen to unspoken words, Hannah and I. The radio goes untested; wordlessness is good, at least up to a point. And besides, we have the Citroen's industrial shockwaves and din to keep us occupied; not to mention the fear that now we are on the motorway, our velocity increasing, the car might simply conk out or explode.

Where are we going? it occurs to me to ask. Still I say nothing. Am I *frightened* of Hannah, suddenly? Because of what? Because of a dream we shared? Ridiculous! *Mum* shared a dream with her brother, did she not? Mum shared a dream with Stephen at the moment of his dying, way back in that summer, when I was home from teaching abroad; when I came in from the garden and she saw his ghost precede me into the lounge.

This is how I like to think of it. At the moment that Stephen's melted corpse was discovered, he sent his sister a dream – and she shared it. She turned it into a wish-belief, she wanted the house's intruder to be a burglar, not her brother. It was too much information; but does that mean that Mum was *frightened* of Stephen?

Does this mean I'm frightened of Hannah?

I am wary of her confidence.

'How do you know where to go?'

'I called Travel Line while I was waiting for the cab. It was just a hunch – Dolly said something about the bus going to Luton and the route's got a diversion on it, some roadworks on Dunstable Road and Luton Road. The whole place is bumper-to-bumper going through the housing estates. So they're diverting some of the routes onto the motorway for a junction, up to junction 11 and 12.'

'So why are you feeling so anxious about Dorothy?' I ask, and it takes Hannah the duration of a slow-down and a gear-change to respond. Traffic bunches like furious insects on the trail. 'Why's she going to Luton anyway? No one in their right mind goes to Luton.'

'Well exactly. She's not well, Tom. Something's wrong with her.'

'Something's wrong with all of us, though.'

'Again, exactly. And I don't like being wrong in the head, Tom. I'll fight it.'

'It's not your head. There's something in the air.'

Surprisingly cross (surprising to me at least), Hannah barks: 'Don't be so airy-fairy, for Christ's sake! Grow a pair of balls, Tom, and *face this* with me!'

IV.

1.

James spells the name in his head.

Kay. Oh. Ell. Kay. Oh. Kolko. Simon Kolko, who said that James should get in touch if any more information came to light. None has; but James feels he should make contact anyway. Now where is Kolko's business card? James digs for it; but all he's known since Dad's single email has been fruitless searches. Although James has replied to Dad thirteen times (unlucky for some) there has been no more word. James has sent report queries to his own Internet provider's Helpdesk – and to Dad's. There is nothing to be done, technologically speaking. The relevant systems are fine; they are friendly with one another. IT is not the problem; *Dad* is the problem.

How can he not want to talk to me?

Several times since Dad's email, as cherished as a polished precious stone, James has replayed his interlocution with Constable Kolko. While it might be true that Dad's *remember-me?* has nothing in common with the murder on Dunstable Downs, Kolko had cut the closest thing to a comforting figure of authority that the boy has known for some time.

Using the Internet, James finds the phone number for Dunstable Police Station. It turns out to be a number for Bedfordshire Police as a whole. The prefix code James recognizes: it's been used on business correspondence to stepfather Lenny, an invoice for the supply of chocolate sprinkles, a factory in Bedford. So Bedford is where James is phoning. A voice asks him what she can do for him.

'I'd like to speak to Constable Kolko if I may,' James answers in his poshest voice. 'Constable Simon Kolko.'

'Him again! Someone's winding you up, sir. Or winding *me* up. There's no one of that name working here.'

James wrinkles his nose. Dad used to call it his 'slapped rabbit' face. 'I think he works in Dunstable.'

'No he doesn't; they've never heard of him over there either. I know because you're the second person to ask for him in the last two hours. I have to say, though, it's usually a better joke.'

'Joke?'

'The name itself. No one gets it. It's not funny.'

'It's not meant to be funny; it's not a joke…'

'Well maybe I can help you instead,' the officer interrupts.

'No, it has to be Kolko,' says James – but is this true? *Why* does it have to be?

'Are you reporting a crime, sir?'

'No. Yes. I'm not certain.'

'Can I have your name please?'

'James. Technical fraud. IT fraud.'

'Pardon?'

'Yes. Yes I'm reporting a crime. Someone's hacking into my email account. That's a crime, isn't it?'

'Indeed it is. James what?'

He has told a lie or he hasn't; he is not sure. He is confused. He only understands one thing, that he has not thought this through properly. The noise of water surges in James's head.

'James what?' he hears… but his name is not Watt. The noise increases.

Kolko lied. He is not a policeman; perhaps his name is not really Kolko. Sudden inspiration makes James reveal more of Kolko's work identity. 'He was investigating the murder on Dunstable Downs,' James blurts.

'Who was? *What* murder?'

'Kolko. He asked me questions because stepfather Lenny has an ice-cream stand there and I work there sometimes when I'm not allowed to go to school but I didn't see anything…'

'Woah there; slow down,' the voice says, but the voice is drowned in the water; the noise is even louder.

James lifts his own voice into a fair to middling falsetto; he is impersonating his sister Louise. 'Oh James! What have you done *this* time?' He replaces the receiver on its stand; it makes a sound like *bee-boo*. Still, the noise of water. James crosses the landing and runs into the bathroom. Although he cannot remember turning on the taps he knows he must have; it has slipped his mind for a moment, that is all. It's nothing serious. The bath has not over-flowed; James has caught it in time.

James kneels down for a celebratory stint of masturbation.

2.

James is unable to locate Kolko's business card, nor can he recall what it said – he can't have read what was printed on the stiffened paper. This seems peculiar. Unless…

Unless stepfather Lenny has destroyed the card. This is a strong possibility that James has weighed up. (Where's there's misery, there's Lenny, after all; this has been James's opinion.) Like a furtive PI, since Lenny's offer to leave the house, James has been watching him. Listening to him too. The long and the short of it being – stepfather Lenny is *still here* to listen *to*. Despite his offer, where are the goodbye, valedictory speeches? Where's the suitcase; where's the train ticket? Where's the housekey, slapped down on the glass-topped table in the hall (or maybe even placed there calmly, defeat-fatigue on his face)? Where are the farewell kisses from Lenny to Mum and Louise?

Instead, James is teased by housewide auditory clues, which the boy plots into a daily (and boring) narrative of Lenny's existence. From the banal – the return home from work, the confident click of the front door; his voice calling out an apostrophe with unnecessary volume, given the house's dimensions – to the scatological. James hears Lenny in the bathroom, about his business; he wonders if it's all men, or just ghastly stepdads, who micturate in two or more goes at a time – a proficient blast followed by one or two desultory aftershocks (and fervent windypops). This is something that James will look into. He has already made a note on his hard drive.

Stepfather Lenny has been giving James, not so much a wide berth as a wary acknowledgement of an equal foe previously considered unworthy of much attention. The atmosphere inside the house is of a high note, played long and loud; the four of them won't be able to stand it much longer.

After James spiders out of the bedroom window and negotiates the exterior plumbing, his climbing frame takes him to the left of the house as you look at it, where he sees a light from his mother's bedroom. Just as the light comes on, thumping a yellow cone into the pre-dawn darkness, James finds his footing on the crenellated rooftop of the two-car garage.

He has performed this feat of escapology a score of times. Why today, then – why this morning – is he so nervous? He jumps from the roof. Breath constricted and roasting in his chest, he hits the grass and flips forward, controlling his motion and velocity with a forward roll leading into a fully erect dismount. He exhales. There in the corner of the garden he raises both arms, just for balance, not for show. Then he turns to peer up at the lighted window; lighted although the time has barely scratched past five.

James is not surprised to see stepfather Lenny in the window watching his exit – critiquing it, probably; reviewing it in his own mind for future ammo. What surprises James is seeing his mother by Lenny's side. Lenny places his left arm over his wife's shoulders.

At this hour of the morning, despite the wintry bite in the air, the streets bring to James's mind the thought of molten metal, miles and miles of metal, crossed and latticed but not fixed in shape yet before they cool. Only from overhead will the system resemble a cobweb. Moving among these grids, a solitary fly, James predicts the kind of conversation he'll have when next he and Mum discuss anything at all. The noun *disappointment*, no doubt, will feature heavily.

For strength and for company James calls upon the power of the water he approaches – the water of the canal. Almost immediately (to the boy's delight) the image of metal falters, withers, dies; the replacement indication is that of more water. The streets themselves are canals; James swims on the surface of the murky brew like a duck. That milk float up ahead is an overturned insect. The milkman's name is Clive and he and James know each other solely on an early-morning basis; there is no need for more than a chirpy hello-and-how-are-you? Clive hefting an empty red crate and placing it on top of a pile of similar empties, the better to get at a full crate underneath, is the last thing James notices fully before he strides onto the canal path, when rain starts leaking – sulky rain.

The bully known as Wolfe is waiting at the rendezvous, as they've arranged by email. The rendezvous is the small lock, the one overlooked by an abandoned warehouse that used to sell pine and birch bookcases and TV stands at knock-down prices. 'Good morning, James,' Bullyboy Wolfe says politely. James thinks for a second that Wolfe will even offer to shake his hand, but of course such politure is not what they're here for. Like a pantomime villain Wolfe teases the fly legs of what constitutes his threadbare moustache. Lopsided smirk on his wide face he says: 'You didn't think I'd come.'

'I didn't think you'd come alone,' James answers truthfully.

'I meant at this ridiculous hour. You're a few minutes late, by the way.'

'No I'm not. Was it difficult getting out?'

Wolfe sniffs the air. 'I don't answer to anybody. What made you think I wouldn't come alone?' the bigger boy asks, casting a split second glance at the gate that leads away from the canal path, the lock and this clearing – the auditorium for the boys' forthcoming bout. It is somewhere down that path, shielded from sight by trees, James realizes, that Wolfe's cronies lie in wait for a signal – a whistle? a yelp? – before coming running

James if fluttery with nerves. He wonders how many apostles Wolfe has been able to coerce into this grey-light pummelling. 'A bully always likes an audience,' James replies; 'it's his way of justifying his actions – by the approval of those too ignorant to enjoy their own moments of achievement.'

The explanation halts Wolfe. Psychology and logic haven't featured in his plans for this morning.

'Besides,' James continues, 'I thought you'd be too chickenshit to meet me alone.'

Wolfe's eyes widen. His lashes, James notices (squinting his own eyes into em-dash slits), are long, almost wiry, less girlish than piggish. '*Chickenshit?*' he splutters.

'Yes. That's why you brought your bumboys with you.' This retort, and the one that preceded it, were learnt in the bedroom last night, after his daily wank; now recited from memory, like the gushings of a street poet busking for his bus fare or skag fund. 'Come out, come out, wherever you are!' James sings – a pathetic town crier.

'There's no one there,' Wolfe tells him.

'I can smell them. Don't lie to me.'

'You're weird.'

'Thank you, wolf-pup. That's what your sister told me when she didn't have her mouth full. But all the same, was there anything else you wanted from this?' James asks, watching either the wolf-pup insult or the less direct one about his sister burn two shooting stars of embarrassment onto his aggressor's cheeks.

'To teach you some manners.'

'I did nothing to you, Romulus. All I wanted was to make new friends and finger your sister. Tell me why you wanted to spoil my school career like I spoiled your sister.'

Taking a step towards James, Wolfe says, 'I couldn't give a fuck about your school career. I just don't *like you*. And I don't *have a sister.*'

'Yes you do. Your mum gave her away to the gypsies.'

'I'm gonna batter you, boy. Are you ready. It's *your* turn in the freezing water.' Wolfe closes the gap between them but he moves slowly, for reasons that James does not at first appreciate; moves as though he has hurt both legs from the knees down. It occurs to James now that his chickenshit arrow had hit the mark, not only because it showed Wolfe up for a moment (within ear-shot of the bandidos), but because it was actually true. Wolfe *is* frightened of me, James thinks, moving only slightly to swerve away from the bigger boy's first punch.

He almost avoids the blow. Knuckles clip the left side of James's head, by the hairline; it is a negligible strike at best, and one that causes James neither discomfort nor difficulty. Tensing his upper arms, James hurls his balled hand into Wolfe's stom-ach; unfortunately for him, this is lost in the padding of Wolfe's winter overcoat. The head will be the soft spot; the body, James knows, is a waste of time and effort, protected by Wolfe's teenage fashion choices – the coat that bunches its owner in, down to the waist. Quickly, James uses his right hand to swing a punch into Wolfe's temple.

Lack of formal technique ensures that the bout is messy; scrappy; the boys are like terriers competing for a greasy bone. It isn't long before blood is drawn. One of Wolfe's lucky uppercuts connects with his opponent's nose, already damaged since the previous fight. The pain is explosive. With a shriek, James backs away, blinded temporarily by red light jammed up against his field of vision. Wolfe works on animal instinct, seizing the opportunity. He runs towards James, his hands splayed for better distribution of pressure, as he intends to push James into the water.

Successful with a dandy skip half a metre to his right, James takes hold of Wolfe's body, pulling him closer as though heaving a bale of hay, and attempts to hurl the bulk on its way. The canal claps a round of watery applause, either stirred by the wind or by something equally unseen, equally powerful. But the water will have to wait to have its way. Wolfe recovers his balance. Surprisingly nimble for a boy of his size, he executes a nifty pirouette, his back now to the canal. As hard as he can he kicks James in the stomach.

James shrieks again; the noise muffled by his own expelled air. By doubling at the waist he grants Wolfe another easy target. Again, Wolfe uses the chance presented and he knees James in the face. It would all seem to be over, except…James does not know how to quit.

Retreating a few steps from Wolfe, James says, 'Are you ready to apologise?'

'I beg your pardon?' Wolfe answers, well-bred to the core. 'Apologise to *you*? I'm winning, y'prick!'

'No. To your family.'

'My *family*? What've they got to do with this?' Wolfe asks, as pleased as James is for the chance to catch his breath.

'You're an embarrassment to them,' James says. 'You'll be expelled like I've been in the past. It'll break their hearts. They'll be ashamed of you.'

'I don't care.'

'I think you do. I think you'll be ashamed of yourself too.'

Wolfe cocks his head. 'Why's that? Because I didn't need an *audience*? Because I didn't need my *bumboys* – to pulverize a weirdo like you?'

Both boys turn: Wolfe his whole body, to his left; James, just his head (his throbbing head), to the right. The impetus for these movements: the sound of footsteps. Someone is approaching on the path that leads into the trees and the fields beyond them.

'I knew it,' says James, now lifting his left foot to rest it on a bitt, which is there in sturdy black iron to help tie canal boats to the side. He turns back to mark Wolfe's expression, but is concerned that the other boy shows neither celebration nor relief. If anything, Wolfe looks as confused as James feels. Wolfe has told the truth all along, James comprehends, there are no back-up forces, there is no school-uniformed cavalry. There's just someone out for a wander…but who is it? Who would be here at this hour?

James coughs blood. Shifting his position, James quickly decides that the one approaching person must be a stranger. A dog-walker, for instance. But if this is the case, where is the sound of the dog's paws on the ground? Where is the sound of the dog's lead?

The new arrival emerges onto the canal path. There is no dog at his heel. There's a large man crammed into dated winter clothes. 'Boys, boys,' he says in lamentation.

'Who the fuck are you?' asks Wolfe.

James answers simply: 'Hello, Officer Kolko.'

3.

'Good morning to you both,' says Kolko. 'A fine morning

it is too to be settling differences.' His gaze strays skywards. Fine morning? The sky is as black as a scorched saucepan; the air is damp with rain that won't fall properly, but lingers like bad feelings.

'I tried to call you,' says James, 'at the police station.'

'I know. They told me.'

'Police?' says Wolfe, deflating inside his padded coat.

'They didn't know who you were.'

Kolko nods his head. 'They told me that as well. Someone new on switchboard, didn't know how to check properly,' he continues. 'What was it you wanted to talk about?'

'Not now. Why are you here, please?' James asks.

'What's going on?' Wolfe wants to know.

Kolko turns to the larger boy. 'I told you: a settling of differences; though I must admit I've been a bit disappointed so far with your half-hearted attitude. Both of you.'

'I don't understand,' Wolfe replies, sounding more the boy and less the man. 'Did you call the police?' he demands of James. '*You're* the chickenshit.'

'I didn't call anybody. I thought you brought your bumboys, I told you,' says James.

'Stop *calling* them that, would you?'

'Why should he?' Kolko asks. 'That's what they are, aren't they?' In an innocent voice that holds (the boys feel it) real malice; the disappointment he speaks of is genuine.

Wolfe goes for the easy option and tells Kolko to fuck off.

James has never seen Kolko angry; nor does he seem angry now, not exactly. What he sees is worse, he thinks; something deeper, richer, longer-lasting than anger. What James sees Kolko do now is *smile*. However, it is an imperfect smile; it seems (James searches briefly for the word) – it seems polluted.

'Fuck off?' Kolko repeats. 'Me? Were you addressing *me*,

you spotty little sop?'

'No,' Wolfe fibs, 'I was talking to Weird Boy.'

'Weird Boy, as you call him, has a name.'

'Yes, sir.'

'What is it, that name?'

'James.'

'James what?'

Wolfe's eyesight focuses on the canal; the water is filth-brown curls, combed and tweezed by breeze and (James concludes) by Kolko's very appearance.

'I don't know his surname, sir,' Wolfe admits.

Kolko nods his head. 'Yours is Wolfe, right?' Wolfe nods his head. 'Look at me, please, you masturbating little window-licker. Thank you. Yours is Wolfe, correct?'

'That's right. Wolfe.'

'Wolfe by name and wolf by nature, am I right?'

'I'm going home.'

'You're going nowhere, son, unless you want the full force of the law on your doorstep in fifteen minutes flat.' Still that smile, like curdling milk. The canal applauds. 'What do you want me to do?' Kolko continues rhetorically, sarcasm worming through his words. 'Do you want me to shout "Scrap! Scrap!"? *Finish each other off for Christ's sake!*'

Surely the fight is finished, however. The two boys regard one another with weary distaste, but this is not enough to re-ignite their leaking fuel; nothing is. Moisture in the air has dampened everything. Instead of raising their fists they raise their eyebrows; both see their own fear reflected on the features of the opponent.

'I can't begin to tell you what a grave disappointment you two are,' Kolko adds; and yes, the voice does indeed sound disappointed.

It is Wolfe who says, 'What do you expect *us* to do?' – turning the question on its originator. 'I taught James his lesson. I have to get home.'

'Why? Why do you? There's no one there gives a monkey's toss about you. And you know that. Why not finish the job you started?'

'He's had enough.'

'Have you?' Kolko swivels on his heels; he is full frontal towards James. 'Have you *really* had enough, James? I didn't have you pegged as a chickenshit quitter. What's your dad think of you? Mincing little pansy-boy quitter, aren't you, James?'

'Leave my dad out of this, please.'

'Aren't you, Jim-Jiminy? That's what he used to call you, didn't he, your old man?' Kolko continues. 'Jim-Jiminy, Jim-Jiminy, Jim-Jim Jaroo. Sitting on his knee, watching Disney.'

'How do you know…' James begins.

'I know a lot about Jim-Jiminy, James. You thought the cartoons were real, didn't you? You believed in the Disney deities. Saint Mickey of Mouse. Saint Pluto. And no one knew what was wrong with you then, did they? You thought you'd see a six-foot sailor duck every time your mum took you screaming to the shops. Tell the truth.'

'Why are you doing this?' James asks.

'James?' Wolfe makes a motion with his head, as though manoeuvring a football into a goal mouth. The signal, while scarcely surreptitious, is meant to say: *Let's run. Let's get out of here.* The problem is, James misses it.

Transfixed by what Kolko has said, James is rooted to the spot. He is as much a part of the earth as the iron bitt is. He starts to hum his panic blues song, which makes Kolko's grin widen. James knows where these feelings will take him: to the place where he makes a lot of noise and puts his hands over his ears to crush out every sound in his skull.

'You remember, don't you, James: there on your dad's lap, watching cartoons. Bugs Bunny made you want to try a whole raw carrot, but they tasted disgusting, didn't they? And all the while, you can *feel* him, can't you, Jim-Jiminy? Feel him underneath your lap while he sang your Jim-Jiminy song to you; while he moved you on his lap...'

'James, let's go,' Wolfe whispers, as though Kolko mightn't hear.

'Shall I sing it for you, James, like your dad used to, on his lap – moving you on *his* whole raw carrot? You found it uncomfortable, didn't you, James?'

'Shut up please, Mr Kolko.'

'No I won't James. I want you to remember, and I want you to act on this scrote's' – Kolko indicates Wolfe's presence with a languid flick of the wrist – 'insults to your dad.'

Wolfe protests. 'I didn't insult your dad, James. It's *you* I don't like.'

That itchy noise, building in the younger boy's cranium. James looks up, his eyes gluey with moisture and poor vision. Churning the waters of the sky, a flotilla of perfectly semi-circular clouds is in full flight, abetted by a wind; the sky is a host of tortoises, racing the one hundred metres, right to left. Purple patches in the sky are sharply focused.

'I insulted his sister,' James tells Kolko.

'He doesn't have a sister, Jim-Jiminy; it doesn't count. Think of that pressure where you sat... Can you feel it?'

'Too much noise,' James answers in a whisper.

'I'm going. I'm leaving you fuckheads,' Wolfe announces again.

'Now think of this worthless piece of shit,' Kolko carries on, '*sharing* what you had with your dad. Wolfe wants him too. Are you–'

James launches himself at his tormentor: not at Kolko; at Wolfe.

'—going to—'

With blistering speed he issues a volley of punches against Wolfe's torso, flanks and face. Hot breaths scream through his lungs and materialise before Wolfe's eyes.

'—let that happen?'

The fight is back on. If little form or technique had been exhibited in round one, round two is an even less structured affair; more brutal too. Stirred up by Kolko's taunts, James has taken one of his holidays from his own mind and acts independently of overt thought.

James headbutts Wolfe.

The strike is meticulous; it couldn't have been better planned. James's brow, for a split second, kisses the bridge of Wolfe's nose. The resulting crack is as loud as a duck's quack, and Wolfe howls with pain, while James shakes his head to make the stars fade and clear. Wolfe is weakened. Jumping up, James twists in the air – he presents his back – catching Wolfe's head in a lock with his two arms, pulling his down to a bent-double height. With Wolfe's head in his arms James now secures the hold, by gripping one wrist in the other, just until they are both comfortable. At which point James strengthens the stranglehold – his muscles like acorns but strong nonetheless – and releases his own left hand. This he uses for target practice on Wolfe's exposed face: punch after punch, like a workout, lifting weights. Wolfe wriggles in his grip, alternately clawing at James's securing arm and attempting to find something to punch.

Where is Kolko? The question only comes to James's consciousness once Wolfe has given up the punching game – to get himself out of the headlock requires a more tactical approach; and he can just about reach James's testicles… But where is

Kolko? There: behind them. James senses him present as readily as he feels Wolfe's vice-grip on his balls. Wolfe squeezes tighter. Kolko doesn't move. James continues pummelling.

Kolko says, 'Feel him touch you, James. Imagine it's not Wolfe with his hand on your erection. You *are* hard, aren't you, Jim-Jiminy? The violence has eroticised you. But it's not Wolfe touching you. You know who it is, James. Because you're starting to remember him. Who, James? Who am I talking about?'

James shrieks. The ferocity of his punches shifts to overdrive; this has become a barbaric assault, bordering on the murderous.

Too much *noise…*

'*Who*, James?'

The canal has never looked so inviting.

'I said *who*,' Kolko demands.

'Dad,' James answers, twisting Wolfe's battered body to the edge and thrusting him over the threshold – for the second time into the water.

4.

'Where the hell have you been?'

'Out,' James answers.

'I know you've been *out*, smart lad. Don't bunny *me*, son. Where've you been?'

'I'm not your son.'

'Lenny,' Sal attempts to soothe. 'Have you been to the canal, James?'

'Yes.'

'Sit down, James. Please.'

Here again is the kitchen table, the locus of a thousand and one rows.

James sits down, as requested. Full family meeting – even

Louise is in attendance, her school tie loose about her throat, like a necklace. Her eyes are downturned, table-facing; she does not want this argument, James infers, any more than he does himself.

'Give me strength,' Lenny whispers. James notices the hairs on the back of his stepfather's hands – still wet from the shower or from a post-micturation finger-rinse. The hairs are like trees, battered horizontal by a flood; the hands rest on the table, palm to palm, fingers extended. The gesture is reverential. 'We've been worried sick, James,' he continues, his voice swamped by a near-silent anger that rings like white noise. Change the frequency of your auditory channels and that sound would be deafening.

'No you weren't,' James answers. He studies his sister's bowed head – a lot of supplication in evidence this morning – and with his eyes traces the somewhat manly hairline, as if she will suffer from male pattern baldness.

'What do you mean we weren't? You go out at the crack of dawn–'

'Lenny,' says Sal again, keeping tight hold on the kite of her husband's temper – before a thermal can aerate it, send it soaring.

'No one's been sick,' James clarifies.

'And how would you know that, soft lad? *How would you know that?* You weren't here to *watch* us worrying…'

'Lenny, please,' Sal tries once more. 'Actually, James, your sister's been sick, haven't you, Lulu?'

'Mum…'

'But not with worry,' James argues. 'She's vomiting because she's pregnant – and you're both too thick to notice how often she goes to the toilet to bring her food up.' James starts laughing – laughing like a drain, as Dad would have said.

Other than these sounds, there is silence. Probably the silence does not endure for as many seconds as it feels; but a good few seconds pass, nevertheless. It is the accused who mashes this silence with a high-pitched defence. Standing up briskly, Louise points a finger at her brother and at his continued mirth.

'I am *not* fucking pregnant!' she squeals. 'Mum I'm not!' she implores her mother.

'Okay, Lulu,' Sal whispers.

Louise reassumes her assault on the only member of the room younger than herself, but it is not like bullying: it is anti-bullying. A midget's deathwish tirade against a Samurai.

'You mentally retarded little shit,' she screams. '*Stop laughing at me!*' James doesn't. Louise appeals again for maternal protection, but the snake is already in the stable; it's too late. 'Mum, I haven't even got a *boyfriend…*'

'I swear,' Lenny states, shaking his head. More calmly than his stepdaughter did, he rises to his feet. 'I *swear…*' he mutters again.

'Where are *you* going?' Sal demands – though she might as accurately be addressing Louise, now fleeing the room, pushed from the vacuum by the sound energy of James's laughter.

'Work.'

'Not till we're finished here you're not. James, stop laughing now, there's a good boy.'

To both parents' surprise James obeys. Instead of comedy it appears as though crooning is now on his mind. He starts to sing into the placemat before him – a photograph of the Rhine – a tune-free ditty of his own composing, dedicated to and inspired by his sister. 'Louise, Louise, she aims to please. She drains your rig on bended knees…'

'I swear…' says stepfather Lenny.

'*Knock it off, James!*' Sal shouts.

'Am I excused from the table?' James asks, suddenly calm – squall passed.

Wearily Sal answers, 'Yes, James.'

The boy stands, smiling a 'thank you' smile; without another word he heads into the hall, as his stepfather forms his hitherto slippery advocation.

'I swear sometimes there's a devil in that child,' he says.

'James? One more thing,' asks Sal.

James does not turn: he will take the question in the shoulderblades, like the arrows from a coward.

'Did you meet Simon Kolko at the canal?'

No one can see it, but James smiles wider. 'Yes I did,' he answers with his customary candour. 'I also met Dad's ghost.'

5.

Wolfe splashes in the water like an angry duck.

'Help me! I can't swim!' he gurgles.

'James? Are you going to help him?' asks Kolko, resting an arm on the boy's shoulders.

'No.'

'Good boy. Why not?'

'Because he managed last time.'

'That's my boy. Why else not?'

Considering the question, James toes stones into the water. 'Because he asked for it,' he answers. 'Because I don't care if he dies.'

'That's my boy. Let him drown?'

'Let him drown,' James decides, nodding his head. 'I should probably go home now.'

'Why?'

'I'm not at school; I'll be expected to sell ice-cream.'

'It's too cold for ice-cream. Hello, what's this? He wants the side, James. What do you have to say about that? What do you do?'

Control, thinks James. 'I kick him in the face,' he replies.

'Good boy. It's a nice morning, isn't it? With the sun coming up.'

'Very nice.'

'Kick him, Jim-Jiminy.'

It's the first time that the sobriquet has been used without the addressee feeling nettled. In fact, the opposite is true: James experiences satisfaction; a muckle of warmth. Comfort like codeine into his pain receptors: the bliss-out.

The kick shaves a dermis from Wolfe's brow. The larger boy struggles with gravity and aqua-positioning. His arms flap like unbalanced propellers.

'James, please!' he calls. 'I can't swim in these clothes!'

'But he's swimming *a bit*, isn't he, James? Else he'd have sunk by now. How deep is the canal at this point, do you think, James?'

The boy answers with zero effort. 'Four-point-six metres,' he says.

'Deep enough, yes?'

'Yes. Although it's possible to drown on a cup of tea, Mr Kolko. The amount of fluid isn't the only important factor.' He considers Kolko's previous statement in a double-take. 'Deep enough for what?' he asks.

'For an enemy to drown,' Kolko replies. 'You were on the right lines. He is your enemy, isn't he, James?'

'I'll get in trouble,' James says quietly; but he is not necessarily answering anything that's been said.

'You're already in trouble.'

'True,' James agrees.

'School doesn't want you.'

'True.'

'Your family – so-called – doesn't want you.'

'True.'

'Finish him off, James. We'll think of a story about where you've been this morning.'

6.

Hours and hours later, there is another attempt at a family meeting.

'Come away from the computer, James. We want to talk to you.'

Uninvited and unannounced, stepfather Lenny, Mum, and even Louise have entered the bedroom. Lenny takes a seat on the edge of the bed. 'Come over here, James,' he continues, patting the duvet, a scarecrow's crooked grin contorting his features.

'I'd rather stay here,' James answers, clicking the SHUT DOWN option on the screen. He faces his audience – his firing squad – fresh as they are from work and school respectively. James himself, on Kolko's implied suggestion, had refused point blank to join his stepfather at the ice-cream kiosk. It was indeed too cold for ice-cream; and James has decided that he will not be returning to work there, irrespective of the consequences.

'As you like it. We're all worried about you, James; that's why we thought we better have another house meeting.'

Standing by the door, Mum and Louise hold hands briefly; their fingers touch and tickle, then release – message of mutual support understood. Louise has had to be talked into attending these crisis talks, James is certain of it.

'I don't want to talk to you,' says James. 'You're not supposed to be here. We had a deal. You were supposed to leave.'

'Talk to *me* then, James,' says Mum. 'Talk to *someone*.'

'I don't want to talk to anyone. Not while this man is squatting in our house.'

'*This man* has a name, James.'

'Not to me anymore he doesn't,' the boy answers, body pounding with bravery. His palms itch; his scalp itches; he needs to use the facilities – but he won't be the first to move.

'What's that supposed to mean?' demands stepfather Lenny.

'Len, please – hold onto it. James – will you talk to me about what happened at the canal this morning? Please? What did you mean about Dad's ghost?'

James answers the first question truthfully but ignores the second one. 'No,' he says.

7.

'I'm gonna do that boy a permanent.'

'No you're not, Len; and that's no way to speak of our son, by the way.'

'*Your* son, Sal – he's made it infinitely clear he's not mine – as if that's supposed to make me, what? Jealous? Stroll on! Jealous of not parenting *that?*'

Sal replies slowly, '*That...* is my son, Len.'

'Well exactly. *Your* son. Thank you!'

'He needs a doctor. He's getting bad again.'

'He needs an exorcist! Is what he *needs!*'

'Don't push me, love. What did he mean by his dad's ghost? That's the bit I can't work out. Something *happened* there this morning...'

'His dad's ghost?' Lenny splutters. 'He's fantasizing and you're not helping by indulging him.'

Sal ignores the accusation. 'We have to speak to this Kolko.'

'Now it's *we* again, is it?'

'Yes it's *we*,' Sal answers; 'but there's no *again* about it. It was always *we*, Lenworth, as far as I was concerned.'

'You've all got a funny way of showing it, that's all I can say.'

'What's *that* supposed to mean?'

All of the above, and what succeeds it, James hears. He listens to the discussion by standing on his bed, at the pillow end, with a spy's device of his own contrivance to his left ear. Having found unsatisfactory the antediluvian method of holding the base of a glass against the wall (too many murmurs, too many unresolved bass-lines... too many ghosts in the wall, perhaps), James hit upon the notion, several months earlier, of *penetrating* the wall. This he achieved by stealing a dog lead from the chiffonier that they used to have in the lounge. The chiffonier's gone now, busted up one sunny Saturday afternoon, back in April, by Lenny and Leo – beer cans in one hand, mallets in the other – and its pieces have long since been obliterated to sticks at the Tidy Tip. The dog lead was never used because the dog was never purchased; never purchased because James had been more than customarily agitated and unstable in the spring just gone, and given the torture he had inflicted on Smithy the cat the previous year, the acquisition of a canine had been demoted to the bottom of the Good Ideas Table. The lead has a hefty buckle and the buckle has a fastening spike, as sturdy as a dart's tungsten tip. It is this buckle-fastener that James has used to drill into his bedroom wall, taking months on the operation. The hole is hidden by an embroidered pennant from a school trip to *la Mont St Michel*, when James was eight; the pennant is curling at the triangulated lower tip, shrinking upwards with age, ineffectively kept flattened by successive and ever-growing blobs of dried-out Blu-Tak to stick it to the wall. Whatever plaster dust was created by this primitive excavation, James ate. He licked the dust from the wall as the buckle-spike slowly drilled; or he snorted it up from his duvet.

The buckle-spike is as deep into the wall as it can go. On his feet on the bed, but slightly hunched about the shoulders, James wears the lead loose around his neck. His right ear (less bruised) is to the base of a pint glass, the rim of which is in contact with the buckle.

The argument in the next room escalates. James is happy about this development; he regards harsh words optimistically – each barb of blame a potential catalyst to expel stepfather Lenny from the house.

'...end of my tether, Sal. I've tried, you know I've tried – you've *watched* me trying – but nothing I do. You say be lenient, I'm lenient; you say be less servile, I'm less servile–'

'As if I've got all the answers!' Sal shouts. 'I'm learning as I go along, just like you, Lenworth. You think I can wave my wand?'

'Don't be ridiculous...'

'If I had a wand to wave, I'd wave the fucking thing. I wish I shared your Walt Disney view of life...'

Disney, thinks James – and the thoughts are like rollercoaster cars, bumping together in the queue before the ride begins. *Canal. Wolfe struggling in the cocoa-coloured water.* Are you going to help him? *Cocoa. Kolko.* That's my boy, *Kolko said.* They watched him backstroke to the far bank. His winter clothes dragged him down; but he kept bobbing up. Air beneath his padded jacket, perhaps? James didn't know. He and Kolko watched Wolfe grip handfuls of grass on the bank that was half a metre above his head.

You can see his dilemma, can't you, James? it's like the boy holding the balloon that lifts him off the ground. When should he let go? If he lets go straight away he is safe, it's only a few inches to terra firma, but the balloon's gone forever and he really does love that balloon, James; and he hopes his weight will bring it down – like the balloon will give up the fight before he does. But it won't, will it, James? So the boy is taken higher and higher, by the balloon he used to love but now hates.

It's a stupid story, James said. *It would never happen.*

The point of a story is not if it would happen or not, James. Kolko sounded patient but bitter. *The point of a story is what it tells us about ourselves. Why does the boy hate the balloon?* he repeated, as unwilling himself to let go of the metaphorical string.

Because it will kill him. Or take him somewhere he doesn't want to go. But it's impossible.

Why's that?

He wouldn't have a balloon big enough for his weight. And his arms would get tired... Mr Kolko?

Simon, please, James – call me Simon.

James nodded his head. *Simon, I think Wolfe is giving up.*

It looks that way, doesn't it? Kolko agreed. *Like the boy with the balloon: if he takes off his heavy clothes he'll have to let go of the side. Maybe sink, maybe swim; that's the gamble. But if he stays where he is, James?*

The boy smiled. *His arms will get tired!*

His arms will get tired. So what would you *do, James?*

Or he'll freeze!

Indeed. So what would you *do, Jim-Jiminy? You haven't really got many options at your disposal...*

I can swim, James countered.

I know that, James.

So the situation is different; I can't answer your question. He looked physically pained by the admission; he wanted to be a good boy and answer Kolko properly. *He's not making much noise now, is he, Simon?*

Getting tired, James, I would think.

'What the hell are you doing, James?'

The voice startles the boy from his two-second reverie. The canal slips away – sucked up by a vast invisible straw, this cocoa-Kolko milkshake of liquid and dead fauna – and James spins round on the uncertain, bouncy surface of his mattress. He almost topples; balance wavers. He sees that Louise has entered his room, without as much as the courtesy of a warning knock on the door.

'Get out, please,' he says with a calmness that confounds them both. His equilibrium regained, he turns to face his sister, his unenlargeable erection poking blame in her direction.

'Yuck,' says Louise, but she doesn't move. She adds up the equation's x-factors. What she sees is her brother, with something leather around his neck – something joined to the wall – while he stands bollock naked near his pillows. 'Trying to hang yourself?' Louise asks in a matter-of-fact tone. She even nods understandingly, as though auto-asphyxiation is the best that she can hope for from this scenario. Still she doesn't retreat, it is far from being the first time that she has witnessed her brother's stiffy. 'Or were you having a weirdo wank?'

'No.'

'…I want to know what you meant by me being sick because I'm pregnant.'

'I haven't got any clothes on.'

'*It doesn't matter.* What did you mean by that? That was hurtful, James.'

'Emil told me.'

'Who's Emil?'

'My friend.' James steps off the bed; the frozen sausage thaws at his midriff, making James thinks briefly of a deflated balloon.

We'll watch him for another couple of minutes, shall we, James?

Okay.

Then we better go. You'll need to get home, clean your face up a bit. Do you hurt?

Yes.

Whereabouts?

James floats around his room in search of his dressing-gown, fingers flickering from surface to surface like the legs of a crane-fly. The item of clothing is heaped beneath his computer desk.

'Some friend! Lies to you about your sister and you just swallow it!'

Tying the gown's cord about his waist, James replies, 'He used some of those same words about you.'

'Don't be gross.'

'What's going on out there?' shouts stepfather Lenny from the marital bedroom.

'James is being disgusting!'

'I'm not the one who goes into people's bedrooms uninvited,' James retorts.

'Go to bed, the pair of you!' Lenny continues.

'I'm having a bath,' James decides, purely to contradict the order.

'You had a bath at eight o'clock,' Louise reminds him.

'I won't be locking the door.'

V.

1.

Samantha wakes from a dream of waking; the sleep has seemed treacle-rich, but she is worn out, in need of a nap. Which would be fine if she happened to be in bed – her own or anyone else's – or on the sofa, on a beach, in a deckchair. But Sam is at work.

She shares an office with three other women and two men, all of whom report to her. All of whom have dabbled in conversations about her over the last few weeks; the general subject, in one guise or another, has been the deterioration of Sam's productivity and mental health. Depending on whom you ask, the medical verdict is that their manager has either lost it or is in the process of losing it.

'Sam? It's for you,' says Raymond, delighted by a way he has discovered of seesawing a telephone receiver between his thumb and first two fingers – like Groucho Marx balanced a cigar.

'For me?' asks Sam (she did not hear the phone ring); she senses the real world crowding in. She's been dreaming it away, but has she really been *asleep*? Sam crosses the office floor to Raymond's side. Accidentally she kicks his wastepaper bucket; it clangs against a metal desk leg with the sound of hammer on anvil.

'I wonder why it's come through to you,' says Sam, taking hold of the receiver. 'Did you get a name?'

'Hannah.'

'*Hannah?* Why on earth hasn't she called my direct line? Hello?'

Raymond will later tell Sam that the call *had* gone through to her own direct line; it had rung and rung, until under a heavy rain of glares from the other people in the office, Raymond had prodded the 'intercept call' key on his fingerpad.

'Hello?' Sam asks an empty line. 'Are you there, babe? Are you on the mobile?'

A silence. A *slithering* kind of silence, it seems to Sam.

'Hannah? Hannah, are you there?' says Sam. 'Is that you?'

'Yes. I am Hana,' says a man's deep foreign accent.

2.

Nightmares give way to more comical studies in absurdity. Sam wishes through jungle creepers made of memories and nonsense, indiscriminately and without pattern stitched together. As surely as she knows the weight in her bladder she knows that she has a call to make. A diary's responsibility, never absolved. Painted to within an inch of their lives, her cuticles tap for Hannah. Sam has never been one for SelectDial.

'Bang in the middle of something,' Hannah tells her, pleasantries observed.

'I'll be quick. I've got an inkling.'

Hannah sighs into her ear. 'I'm driving right now; I'm on the M1. I'm worried about Dolly. I'll pass you to Tom.'

'Tom, what's going on?' Sam asks when she hears my voice.

'Hannah thinks Dorothy's having an episode. I'm inclined to agree with her.'

A bitty recapitulation ensues.

'Will you keep me up to speed?' Sam asks in a voice that sounds strained and desperate.

'Yes, of course, one of us will. Were you calling for a chat, or…?'

'It can wait. But in a nutshell… I got a call from our Egyptian thief, here at work. He knows where I work, and now I feel sick.'

'Why, what did he say?'

'He needs me to remember something on our holiday. I told him I didn't want to speak to him now or at any other time, thank you very much, and I put the phone down. I'll try to give Dorothy a buzz…'

'By all means, but I've been doing that as well. It just rings and rings and rings…'

Empties, 2: 'Alone in the room of limbs'

1.

I do not believe it was suicide. I believe it was self-negation.

My contention is that Stephen did not try to kill himself; but he tried very hard not to live anymore. He expended a good deal of energy in the attempt – the effort not to live anymore. It was his hobby, his pastime – trying not to live was his one true love.

I am not sure, however, how much this explains.

2.

Ankles and hands, in a nest. In another are hip joints, pelvic bones, skulls.

I am in the room of limbs. It's the Luton and Dunstable Hospital, and I'm at work. I am nineteen years old; it's my summer job. The new term starts in five weeks.

There are rooms into which I may not venture. This is not one of them. The Room of Limbs is one in which I must cart my youthful domestic expertise and my rags smelling of disinfectant. I'm here to clean the artificial limbs.

I can build a human being, but there is no torso to speak of.

Years later, when finishing myself off on one occasion with Caitlin, I will remember this room at the moment of ejaculation. I don't know why. I will drive into Caitlin from behind, my pelvic bone cushioned on her rump, and this room of plastic bits and bobs will rise in my mind. I will collapse, duly spent, on to Caitlin's sofa and she will ferry over the half-full bottle of red, holding the glasses – one smudged with lipstick – by their bases, like castanets. She will pour the wine and tell me about her penniless days, when she wanted to be a model.

3.

She stood in front of the door and toyed with her hair. She prinked. Had the drive given her too much of a sheen to the forehead? Self-consciously she cleared her throat.

As if on cue, the door two along swung open brusquely with a squeak. The woman who stepped out was decked head to toe in the housecleaning regalia that the welcome mat she carried would have suggested was her current, and laborious, task. In other words, she was dressed in koala-bear slippers, track suit bottoms and a horseshoe-grey leotard top. Nipples like chapel hatpegs, thought Caitlin.

Moving to the rail, the woman shrieked: 'Tyrone!' Caitlin watched. 'Tyrone! Sebastian! If you don't get your fucking arses in here on the double there's no tea for you! And no fucky *nice-cream* neither!'

She turned to Caitlin. The latter proffered a faint but deliberate smile, heartwarming and sharing, or so Caitlin had groped for.

The woman regarded her from the midriff skywards. 'What you fucking looking at?' she wanted to know, when at last she wanted to know anything at all.

'Nothing. Kids, eh?'

'They're parasites,' was the unequivocal viewpoint dealt out. 'Not that mine are kids anyway. Fucking old enough to know better.'

Caitlin nodded. Evidently the other woman had lost interest in the conversation; she turned away, spat skilfully over the barrier and commenced to beating the daylights out of the mat with a heavily decorated fist. Dust and chips of unidentifiable matter sprung for cover, some of it in Caitlin's direction. Either I leave now or I resemble a mosaic, thought Caitlin.

Or I knock on the door. That's the third alternative.

'You here for the photos?' the woman asked, not tearing her attention from her mat-tenderising.

'Yes,' Caitlin said with some relief. It was good to know that the photographer within had something of a reputation as such. She was not queuing up to get murdered, at least. Furthermore, it arrived upon Caitlin (it made a chill scamper down her spine) that here, if worse came to worst, was a witness. 'Have there been many?'

'One or two. You hear things.'

'What kind of things?' Caitlin asked, taking a step away from the door and risking the mote-storm.

'Just stories,' came the enigmatic response. Then as Caitlin was about to add another question her informer said: 'He's into muck. Mucky pictures.'

'Not with me he's not,' Caitlin told her.

'So you say.' The woman smiled. 'So what's keeping you from knocking?'

Without another word Caitlin returned to the door and rapped upon it: three times.

It was answered as the woman took her refreshed welcome mat and her corncob nipples back into the warmth. The smile had decayed on her face but a vestigial sympathy lingered – like the scent of rain after a storm.

'Hello?' a man asked. He was short, thin on top, with peppery sideburns that writhed along a good percentage of his jawline. He was dressed in denim.

'I saw your ad?' said Caitlin. 'We spoke on the phone.'

'Caitlin?'

'Yes.'

'I'm Mark. Come in.'

That night she watched – listlessly, randomly – a documentary on soil exhaustion. She slotted and pricked in a new set of earrings (she felt naked without earrings) and she contemplated her overdraft, her lack of zeal, and her future. Sure, she had done the right thing. She had done the right thing, but would she do it again? She wasn't sure. In search of something sexy, she changed the channel. At last she settled on the news – a report on a minor earthquake in Bogotá provided her with a place to deposit her disgust. She opened a fresh packet of cigarettes.

The boys arrived home at eight-thirty.

4.

When I was between my first and second years of university, I took a summer job at the Luton and Dunstable Hospital, as a cleaner. For a student the money was good, and the work was local, easy and fair. Indoor work, anyway, and no heavy lifting. I was not expected – indeed it was forbidden – to enter the theatre. So what I had to do was mop the fast-lane corridors into that dooming room – the infrequent driblet of blood, the splash of vomit. Serve up tea and coffee to the patients. Tidy up in the room of limbs. This was the room where all the spare parts were kept, as I've said. More of a surreal experience than a frightening one, to enter the room of limbs was to encounter the plastic parts that might one day be locked onto a living section of flesh. Aged nineteen, that was a different concept to admire. Alone in the room of limbs, I entertained certain strange fantasies. I saw a wide stage – a Vegas stage, a Follies Bergere – and a chorus of can-canning, high-kicking pins. Just the legs. Naked. These dancers had no torsos at all. And the gap between the legs, where the slit should have been but where there was in fact only space, only air, was the crucible on which a hundred erotic daydreams would swing. I wanted to fuck that space; I wanted that absence of skin on my nose, lips and tongue.

I always enjoyed my placements in the room of limbs; but there was another room that I was not permitted to enter. To do so, I'd been warned, was a sackable offence. The Room with No Name... If an operation went wrong, there had to be a place where the body was stored until it could be carted away and investigated.

Malcolm – my supervisor – called this room the Banshee Hotel.

5.

Unlike in life, Stephen fails to rest; he squirms like a maggot in an ashtray of salt... and he is trying to tell me something. Dying to, died to.

Are...

But the broadcast point fizzes with the flashes of primitive star-shot cameras; stormy too. The transmission comes from a wind-tunnel in which a gross of parakeets have been enraptured to the torture-threats of whipcracks and loose fanbelts.

'What are you trying to say?' I ask. There is desperation in my voice. Before I wake I must decode the transference.

'Are? Are what?' I demand.

Are-kep... are-kep...

'Is it difficult to talk?' A redundant question; a time-chewer. I hate myself for posing it. In the dream, the camera eye opens and there I am, on my parents' bed, bedoodled with maggots. And maggots are much smaller than you imagine. There are more maggots on my skin than people living in the Czech Republic.

Are... he repeated.

Are-kep. He sounds stoned.

Are-kep dye-yer.

'You kept dying?' I am leaking away from sleep – or sleep is leaking away from me. 'You kept dying?'

When I wake, in my mind there is a picture – a solitary snap – of a feather in flame. It stops there. It is time for my first cigarette.

6.

It didn't matter what, in terms of speeches, I had prepared. A bottle of wine had prepared me more recently, and when you're an alcoholic, that's all that counts. The moment, the here and the now. I saw the letter, and I saw red. Unopened, it was transported around to its scribe. I knocked. Five knocks, if I recall, each as hard as its predecessor... it took a while for Caitlin, in the unlit house, to open the door into the unlit hallway.

I didn't wait for her to speak.

'I don't want any more of this fucking shit, do you understand me?' I dropped the envelope onto her welcome mat.

'Okay.'

Frightened; hoping. Above all, drunk.

I stalked off. I had a Chinese meal with Sabrina. Not once did I mention the denouement, because I couldn't believe that I had just participated in one. There had to be more. There was no more.

7.

Malcolm was my supervisor. A few years older than I was, Malcolm was a graduate of French, a competent jazz guitarist – and he cleaned toilets for the local hospital. He couldn't find a job. Every day he would arrive at work and don the smock. His face was like a pig-trough; a disaster of flesh.

When it was time to deliver drinks to the bedridden he

would say: 'Let 'em wait. Take a break. It's their fucking fault – for being ill.'

It is fair to say that he did not enjoy his work. This attitude may have had something to do with his inability to find alternative employment.

One day he said to me: 'Do you want to see the Banshee Hotel?'

'What's that?'

He explained.

'Are we allowed to?' I asked.

'Of course not. I wouldn't suggest it if it was legal. How many cups of cocoa do you think he'll need?' This tickled Malcolm; he started to chuckle – a rare enough occurrence. 'How many sugars does he take?'

I laughed, too, the absurdity of it.

'Who's "he"?' I wanted to know.

'They wheeled an old boy in there this morning. Gall bladder, I think. You know Rachel, the nurse with the tits?'

I nodded. With her small, pretty face, red hair, her loud Welsh accent, and her knockers like rucksacks in the rain, Rachel had proved difficult not to notice.

We set off for corridor H.

Looking from left to right – we were safe – Malcolm punched in a code. The number-pimples sounded sticky as they were pressed. He opened the door; an overwhelming aroma tided out – not of corruption, but of camomile tea. Bizarrely. I have since learned the scientific reason for the odour.

8.

At the time I struggled with a memory and not with an explanation – Sabrina, overclothed at her kitchen table, in the winter; her hands locked together around a cup – a cup of death.

To this day I cannot smell camomile tea without conjuring up thoughts of mortality.

'Go in.'

'You first,' I said to Malcolm.

'I have to keep watch.'

What was frightening me so? It wasn't like entering the cave of a shrieking predator. The body on the trolley at the far wall couldn't harm me.

Gingerly I crossed the threshold, uninvited, a gawker. The body – the old man – was covered by a white sheet; his toes stuck out the end.

I did not turn on the light. I crossed to the corpse, six strides, almost daintily – either scared to make a noise that would arouse suspicion, or scared to wake the fellow at rest.

The body beneath its sheet had a big belly; it had a great deal of torso to speak of. I tried to imagine the face. Calm and reposed, or set in a silent howl of understanding? – comprehension that the operation had been a failure.

'Take a look,' said Malcolm. 'Lift the sheet.' His voice seemed to come from a long distance away.

I faltered. Wasn't the sight of his toes, so white, quite enough?

9.

'Jesus!' whispered Malcolm. 'Someone's coming. Wait!'

The door slammed shut.

'No…'

There had been no time to voice any more of a protest, but the seconds that followed were full of words that I needed to utter. Unfortunately, my throat was clogged with the chickenfat of fear; I could scarcely breathe. I said, 'Malcolm…?'

The darkness was not quite total. 'Oh God,' I whispered,

standing still. Light was steady around the door jambs, but apart from that? *Nada*.

It was as though a tap dripped somewhere and I was the collecting bowl. Only, the liquid being dispersed was not water. Something colder, it froze on impact.

'Oh Christ, Malcolm...'

What was worse: being discovered by my superiors, or being left in a sealed room with a dead man?

I moved my arse not one iota. Heard nothing from beyond the door.

'Well, what did you expect to hear?' came a voice.

My heart had swollen. Like a clockwork figure on a music box, I turned. The air was different... fruitier.

The old boy was sitting up, with his legs over the side of the trolley. The only part of his body that the sheet now shrouded was the groin, and his breasts sagged down like failed Yorkshire puddings. My tongue was frozen raw.

'Well, what were you expecting?' he asked, raising his arms in the gloom; 'a Mariachi band or summing?'

My legs said *adios*. Down in a heap on my backside I fell. I grunted.

'Hello to you too,' said the corpse. 'Have you farted?'

'You're supposed to be dead!'

'I *am* dead. Don't mean that manners have to be left out to dry, does it?'

'No, but...'

'No indeed.'

'I want to scream,' I admitted.

'Go ahead, mate. See if I care... You don't smoke by any chance, do you?'

'No. Well yes, but I don't have any on me.'

'Well then. Your uses to me are limited, wouldn't you say?'

I tried to stand up.

'Jesus,' said the old man, observing my pratfalls. 'Bit of lunchtime drinking, was it?'

'Not at all. You're dead!' I said with my voice raised.

'And so are you if you don't keep it down,' said the corpse.

'I don't believe this…'

'Oh great: denial. Fucking evergreen, that. Well, son, how about this?' said the old man. 'Believe this' – as he reached through the hair-befuddled crease between his breasts. Surely – surely to God – it was a trick of the absence of light. It was conjury.

What the old man produced was black in the gloaming, but I suspected red in the freshness, the fullness… It throbbed like an erection. And the scent if offered… my Lord. Like a six-week-dead dog, in an avalanche of ordure, fish-heads and sprouts. It stank – as they say – to high heaven… and heaven's high.

'That's death,' the old man told me. 'Not me rotting. The actual noun.'

So *that* was death, I thought.

10.

What could he have meant? He kept dying.

That he suffered the successive failures of one in turmoil, and one in permanent decline? Or that he understood the un-washed deceased and their numbers – their cumulative weight? Or what?

He kept dying, that's what.

Stephen just kept dying.

11.

'What did you think you were doing?'

'I heard someone!' said Malcolm. 'But I got it wrong.'

'You fucking well did,' I said; but I had no idea of how to continue with the spunky denunciation. 'You're a liar.'

'Suit yourself, Tom. Christ, you're an ungrateful little cunt. I might've just saved your job, you know that? And what do I get? Next time I'll let you rot.'

12.

Saturday.

My bedroom is a medical camp of moist shirts and scrunched up undercrackers, all fresh from the washing machine. I lean gently on my iron, pressing down on its board – burning sense and order into my work trousers and pillowcases. I hate every moment. For company, and for encouragement, Mahler plays.

My mind has slipped free of its moorings, as it often does when I am faced with a dull, repetitive task. What brings me home sharply is pain. Carelessly, yet scarcely believably, I have ironed over my left little finger. '*Fuck.*'

The scene becomes neat custard pie, pure farce. As I slam down the iron, incorrectly, the better to nurse my wounded digit, I hear the sticky singe-noise as the heat marks a stain on my shirt-cuff. Tears in my eyes, I step backwards. My left leg is snagged in the bolus of the cord, and my motion pulls the iron away from my now-damaged shirt. The iron topples and plummets... or rather leaps, for its unlikely trajectory makes a beeline for my right foot.

Impact.

'*Fuck*,' I squeal, now hurting in two places. Maddened by pain and by visual information (the finger-burn is as red as blood), I hop and hobble to the bathroom. It hasn't ended. Half-way through dousing the finger in cold water, I smell what must be my bedroom carpet erupting into flame.

The burn mark on the floor is a copy of the ace of spades. After stowing the iron, safely this time on its quadrangled rump, I return to the bathroom to resume my first aid. When the water hits the scald there is a sense of relief that I can almost see. Black squares, circling slowly. Am I about to lose consciousness? I rest against the sink, as though heavily drunk. The black squares connect and spin around my face, like a mad angel's halo, worn unfashionably at the wrong angle.

Are-kep, I hear Stephen tell me – but to my shock I see my own lips moving in time with the words. My eyes are wolfily bloodshot.

I shake my head. I want Stephen out until the pain goes away.

'You kept dying!' I say. 'I hear you! But I don't understand!' *Are-kep...*

Again, there is the accompanying static, the whistles, the whines, in my head.

...dire-yee...

...dire...yee!

'Jesus, Stephen.' My face is still in the mirror, but the black circle is plumping itself up, obliterating what else can be seen in the glass. '...can't you just leave me alone...?'

Water gushes. Combined with the tinnitus in my skull, the noise is astonishing.

...dire-yee...tom...torm...dire...

And it comes to me suddenly, with a shock that soothes my finger but floods my heart with crazy chemicals.

Stephen didn't keep dying. No.

'A diary,' I mutter. 'A *diary*?'

...yessh...

'You kept a diary! My God...'

'...*aaahhh*...'

Pleasure or pain? For the moment I don't even care. 'Where?' I demand. 'Where is it? Where did you hide it?'

But the volume is slowly decreasing; the transmission is coming to an end. Feeling as though I know the answer anyway, I smile and allow Stephen to drift away...

Stephen, you kept a diary. You are trying to help me to reconstruct you; I comprehend. And you hid it in the house, I think.

I have to get inside 47 Rosebank Avenue. Dig up the floorboards if necessary...First I wrap my burnt finger in wet toilet tissue and lie down. I remain on my bed until the rhythmic throbbing in my hand sends me to sleep.

13.

My father knew rooms of limbs.

Dad was a fireman. There were two things he wouldn't talk about — the two worst things he'd ever seen. My mind boggles. For among the events he *would* tell me was this:

An old girl took a bath: sitting down, lumpily, and waiting for the tub to top up. But this old girl's old bones were ridden with the worm of arthritis; her days of moving quickly were well and truly over. Unfortunately, so were her boiler's days of working properly.

The bath filled quickly with water that you could have used to boil rice. At first the bather was merely uncomfortable. This changed. It was far too hot, but the old girl couldn't reach the taps. The scalding water continued to flow — to overflow. She shrieked, no doubt, for help; no assistance arrived.

Dad was routinely drunk when he told me about the old girl's discovery, so I can forgive his absence of discretion; but the account was *cold*. 'Imagine,' he said, 'a chicken that's been left in for too long… How the skin comes off the bone.' He paused. 'I tried to lift her from the bath. It was like those old comedies…'

'No, Dad…' I protested.

'…where the guy gets his suit pulled and the whole sleeve is pulled off. I had her *armskin* in my palm.'

'No, Dad.'

This is one of the ones he *would* tell me.

14.

47 Rosebank Avenue, Wembley.

A fortress; a citadel. Offering protection, though, from what?

My left little finger boasts a blister that resembles a condom's teat; the pain is bearable, low. Unimportant, anyway, with my new piece of knowledge. I am overtired but excited. Finally, I have a lead.

What I don't have, however, is a key. I have no way of getting in. When Stephen was discovered, the house was ransacked by the owners – an ambush of industrial cleaners and decorators. The building's guts were discarded onto a large yellow skip. There was nothing of worth: thousands of empties – blackcurrant cordial and whisky – and some low-grade grot (mainly breasts and bottoms; no intercourse; Stephen apparently did not go in for intercourse). How on earth am I supposed to find a diary?

Or, as I say, get in?

Suburbia is balmy this afternoon. Three children play kerbie, two on one side of the road, and the isolated player on my side; the ball they use is a basketball with worn markings and a slow puncture. I try to imagine how I might use these kids to get into the house; my imagination fails me and I sail away on an ocean of depression.

To hell with it, I'll just break a window.

Yeah, that's good – and collect a conviction for breaking and entering while I'm at it. But there must be something I can do – something legal.

Can my youth be of assistance? This is nearly a decade ago, after all, and I am not yet heavy with ill-used booze in my system; but what good will it do me to be possessed of an ability to shin a drainpipe? I am years away from working in a prison for Young Offenders; at least if I'd had this particular dubious privilege I could have asked one scrote or another for some tips on burgling.

The front door is sturdy. Smash a window, I'm still not *in*. Even now, in my younger, lither days, I can't possibly hope to sneak in through the gap that a broken window would grant access to.

Fear in Four Waters, 2: The River

I.

1.

It's one of the places where I went to teach. It should be some-thing I'm proud of, but how can you be proud of what you do not truly understand? To this day, I don't know why it happened, how it happened; and the sense of compounded injustice sometimes bores through my ear like the sizzle of a solitary car on hot tarmac. It stretches from that ear to the other, and then puzzles through my vitreous fluids and entices me to weep. And I'm not the weeping kind, ask anyone…

The question, I guess, to ask is what first?

What would you like to know now and what later?

It might or might not make a difference. You never know.

2.

But this isn't me, of course – this is Dorothy. The above is Dorothy, but you'd never know it (would you?) if I hadn't drawn your attention to the fact. This is *Dorothy* speaking – addressing her dwindling audience, like sending up a flare.

Through her pen, Dorothy finds her past. Or her past finds her. Through her pen, it's a continuation of her obituary that Dor-othy writes.

And through her conversations with me, of course.

A conversation is coming soon – a discussion contiguous with a panicked phone call that Dorothy makes to me, although she is home in her flat in the next block.

Dorothy, edging closer – as she herself edged closer to the stone hut on the hill with the face. I need to boot through those dangerous shards, as she herself strode through weeds and crabgrass and crocuses, on her way to the event that would first become a memory and then a repression. For more than twenty-five years she has fought with what now locates her: that lonely ascent through a mean and crepuscular late afternoon, with the environment matching her mood aptly.

3.

At the first school I attended, where I abandoned the violin, it was relatively simple to be the offspring of a famous musician. No one cared. At the second school, where I abandoned the piano and guitar, it was more difficult. Writing was not in my genetic blood, but it was in my spiritual blood; I knew that even then, despite the constant reminders about how lucky I was to have been born with a musical instrument in my grip.

Classmates would occasionally run errands for their parents – to ask me to get Mum's autograph. More often than not she refused the requests. She had, a reputation as a hard-hearted child-hater to preserve and nurture. At the third school, where I abandoned the flute, the competitive draw of chess, and thoughts of a name change by deed poll, I was known as Dolly or Dotty or Doo-Doo. Only my mother still called me Dorothy.

She despaired for what she referred to as my lack of ambition. You're in your mid-twenties! she would accuse. What do you want to do with your life? You can't assume it's going to happen with the writing, and you've already given up a good job.

A good job that I didn't want, in the Civil Service.

She had been the same way when I'd fought not to go to university.

Disillusioned with much, I embarked on a gap year in Eastern Europe – which is where I saw the hill with the face. The journey itself – the journey to get there – was onerous enough, and things did not get much easier.

At the camp in the Lubuski Region, on the border between Poland and Germany, I taught gatherings of early teenage Americans and Canadians how to play volleyball in the rain and scour woodland for edible wild mushrooms. The kids called me Doo-Doo. And although it was tough manoeuvring, for much of my time there, it was one of the happiest years of my life. I didn't want to go anywhere else.

I certainly embraced no desire to return home to England. I wrote short stories about wildlife – mice that engineered miniature vehicles, urbane, witty foxes, plants that argued among themselves when all the humans had put their heads down to sleep – and I foraged in my consciousness for the next thing to do.

I hadn't yet been to the hill with the face. The hill was but a story itself.

There, at camp, I met Ian, an habitual traveller of thirty-seven – a pretty dormouse face nested snugly in shoulder length brown and grey hair and a square beard that reached down to his nipples. He was kind and seemed wise. He had left north-western Australia thirteen years earlier, and did not intend to return. He'd quit an entire country in disgust. Well, in comparison I was no more than a novice at quitting things, but like attracts like and he was something of a guru, and before long we had applied to the camp manager for permission to move into one of the communal chalets.

I quickly got used to Ian's habits, as he did to mine. For him, the hour before an evening meal was sacred; I left him alone at these times, and he read or he practised the clarinet and the Tarot, or he stared into space and composed a few more sentences of what he claimed would one day be an internationally bestselling novel – a novel for which, I might add, he had yet to commit a single line to paper. I suppose I loved him. Eccentric he might have been, but not strange.

Strange came later. I had been at the camp eight months, having become used to the early mornings, and I was more physically fit than I had ever been. As enjoyable as the work was, however, I was conscious that eight months was two-thirds of a year and that Mum would expect me home by August. Time was running out. Without wishing it to be the case, I was being driven towards making a new decision. The question I had to face again was: what next? Move back to England – with Ian? without Ian? – and either start a course of education or a job. Nothing sounded attractive. My stories, I thought, were as dry as week-old droppings. The Orange Sibling *had still not been published, and I was worried about that too.*

Come back home with me, I said to Ian one night. You've been here two years; it's time for a new adventure. There's plenty of work for an Australian in England....

I don't want to work in a bar, he told me.

You don't have to. But you worked in a bar before, you said you liked it.

I do. I just don't like England.

We attempted a similar conversation on a dozen occasions, but it always fell flat; Ian would make excuses – he was tired, I was pressuring him – and eventually he'd turn away on to his side and pretend to sleep, leaving me restless with confusion and loss. Strange got stranger. I began to think Ian was using my mother's expectations as a way of breaking up with me. It made matters nice and neat. If I had to go home and if Ian wouldn't follow, well, that was the end of that, was it not? I accused him of this.

A month before my contract was due to run out, and I was being asked three times a day if I wanted to renew. My manager was pleased with my work, but couldn't I see his point of view? If I didn't want the job, he needed to know so that he could recruit. I gave in. I'm going home, Leo, I said. Moody and with my heart not in it, I played rounders – girls versus boys – after dinner, and when the light started fading I took a walk in the woods until an animal scared me, then I made it back to the chalet.

Ian wasn't there. He had gone into town with a couple of the other guys in the People Carrier; it was their night off, it was Pedro's birthday.

I brewed some tea, resigned to whatever. Sure I'd go home, but my heart manufactured a susurrus of dissent; I think I was seeking out anything but conformity. Angry with Ian and with his stupid pretence that all he owned in the world was what he could fit into his rucksack, I chose that very evening to look into said piece of luggage. I don't know what I thought I'd find – nothing in particular, memory tells me now, although I might have viewed matters differently back then – and the rummage made me feel better by not even one jot. There were only a few belongings – his passport, his box of earrings and necklaces, and his clarinet in its big orange sock.

The People Carrier arrived back at camp at a little after three. It had a noisy faulty exhaust, contributing no doubt to more than our collective's fair share of the planet's carbon footprint. I waited in bed. The revellers made their way to their chalets and dorms, trying hard not to make much sound in that exaggerated way that just makes people louder. Still, I waited in bed. It was like waiting for the rain to stop. I got up and pulled on Ian's dressing-gown – my own was in the bathroom and it was too cold to walk far – and I stood at the window for a watch. No Ian.

A guy named Mark stumbled towards me. I opened the door and asked Mark where Ian was. No idea, was the response. Well, did he come back with you or didn't he? Mark told me that he thought so. Where had they been? Some club in town. Which club? Mark didn't know the name of the establishment; then again, I doubted that he knew his own middle name at that point so I bid him a good night and with the door still open I pulled on jeans, two jumpers and my walking boots. If Ian had decided to go for nightcaps with the birthday boy, or for anyone else for that matter, I was about to advise him that this wasn't the best notion he'd had. He and I were on swimming pool duties before breakfast and we had to be up and in our costumes in three hours' time. He needed to rest.

After I'd knocked on his chalet door for half a minute, Pedro eventually came to the door. He shared with three other guys, two of whom had been on the charabanc and were already snoring confidently. Pedro appeared wasted. 'Despiértame a las ocho, mama,' *he said. Never mind eight o'clock, I spat back; what the hell have you done with Ian? I'll wake you when I bloody well want to. Pedro told me that Ian was fine; he'd climbed aboard the People Carrier along with everyone else.*

Pedro was making little sense so I went back to the chalet. My sleep was fitful, but I awoke on time and pulled on my bathing suit. Unluckily for me, the boss was not around – he was in the kitchen, preparing sausages and bacon for the kids' and staff's breakfasts – because if he had been at the pool he would not have allowed me to supervise the swimmers on my own. It went against Health and Safety strictures. The teenagers swam ably, and after twenty minutes Ian strolled over, fingering his now smooth chin. Amazement wrestled with anger.

You've shaved, I said, unnecessarily I'm sure. Ian nodded his head. Did it take you all bloody night to find the razors? I went on.

Sorry, he said. I got pit-stopped.

Pissed?

It was Pedro's birthday. We damaged some absinthe in an underground pub. I lost track of the time. Fell asleep in a bush.

You were on the People Carrier. Pedro told me.

Yeah… a bush by the basketball court, Ian added, and both the amazement and the anger drained away swiftly. Suspicion took their place. I asked: You couldn't make it another two hundred metres? To your bed?

All he would say was: Sorry.

Oh, sod off, you silly hippy, I said to him. I stepped towards the edge of the water and bombed in with all the grace of a hippopotamus – much to the squealed glee of a few of the thirteen year-old girls. For the next forty minutes we played water rugby and synchronized dancing while Ian nursed his hangover with a can of Diet Coke.

We ate our cooked breakfasts in silence.

The morning and into the early part of the afternoon was taken up by a visit to what had once been a working windmill but was now a tourist attraction to educate those who were interested in the subject of flour manufacture. I was with Becks – Rebecca – as Leaders of Group Green. We had seven girls and three boys to look after; following the guided tour (strung out to nearly an hour), she and I bought coffees in the cafeteria while the kids either played on the Jungle Gym, or (the two younger boys) foraged cutely for conkers in the small wood nearby, within easy visual range. She asked me what was wrong and I told her. She sipped her cappuccino and said could we move outside; she wanted to smoke. Although smoking was verboten in front of our wards, I followed her anyway. Half the kids had already asked her for cigarettes, at one time or another. We sat at a bench that was painted red.

Boys will be boys, said Becks, shrugging. Probably went to a strip club.

I don't mind that, I told her. It's the not coming home part. Where was he all night? If he thinks I believe he slept in a shrub he must think I was born yesterday. He'd be scratched up for one thing. I don't buy it…

Becks made a show of collecting in all of the children with her eyesight – of counting them, making sure they were all local. Clearly thinking about what to tell me next. I prompted her by inviting her to speak her mind.

She finished her brew. She said: Listen; can I tell you something? Promise you won't tell Ian because he'd have my guts for garters. I agreed to her terms. He's done it before, she continued, relieved.

Done what? Not come back to the camp?

Becks nodded again; she licked a Zapata of froth from her lips. Before you joined the camp. About a year ago. He nearly got fired. Do you want one?

She was offering me a cigarette, which I accepted, although I'd technically given up and had actually never taken up as far as my mother was concerned.

What happened? I asked, and then endured the kind of silence that is like three dots in fiction: something implied, something to be inferred. Oh I see, I said through a smile. You're surprised he hasn't told me already, is that it?

Not really, said Becks. I don't know the full story. Just, it was a bit more cautious then – the whole place. More rule-y. As in rules, you know? Strict curfew, that kind of thing. You break curfew, you better have a good reason. Ian didn't. Didn't have a good reason, I mean. It was chaos, Dolly. Police out, a hunt in the woods. Dogs. We all thought he'd been maimed or *something; left for dead in an alleyway.*

Don't tell me. Strip club.

Well, no; that's the thing. They did go to the strip club but Ian went somewhere else afterwards; they couldn't get him to get in the car.

Who are they? *Anyone I know.*

Becks shook her head. I think they've all moved on, she said. Maybe Anita was here then, I'm not sure. You know what this place is like. She laughed. Stay fifteen minutes and you get a gold watch.

It would make up for the salary!

Well, quite. Becks frowned. But the thing is, do you know what his story was? He forgot everything. Except for six bright red lights in the sky…

Hang on; is this a campfire story? I asked.

I swear that's what he said at the time. He saw six red lights and they were moving closer. That's all he remembered. Or said he remembered.

My boyfriend was abducted by aliens, I said to Becks. Where were the tabloids? Was he colonically probed?

Becks spat out smoke. He didn't say! Would that account for anything if he had been?

A number of his more unusual quirks, I answered. Seriously, what? He got drunk and got laid somewhere? That's what you're saying.

That was the common consensus, I must admit.

I didn't know him then. I can live with that.

But you know him now. Sorry. Shouldn't have said that.

I waved the apology from the air; she hadn't offended me by stating the obvious. I can't say it hasn't crossed my mind, I told Becks. Fuck it. He'll either tell me or he won't. The whole thing's probably irrelevant anyway. Couple months, I'm going back and he won't come with me for some reason.

Well he can't, can he? said Becks, standing up.

It was sheer coincidence – our moving together somehow lowering a defence mechanism in Becks' brain. She even did the cartoon thing of slapping the palm of her hand to her mouth.

What do you mean? He has a passport, I said.

Nothing. I shouldn't have said that. It slipped out.

Becks? What do you mean, he can't go to England? What…?

I can't say it, Dolly; please don't ask me. I've said too much.

Across the table from one another, I put my right hand on her left shoulder, intending to convey the message that it was okay for her to say anything, I wouldn't hold it against her. I added: Please.

Well, he's not allowed to, is he? Becks gave in. I beg you, this didn't come from me, okay? I'll have to deny it if it comes out…

Allowed to?

He's got a record. He's on a register.

There are some stories you want only to begin with Once upon a time. *You want ice-cream stories, pizza-stories: comfort food, in other words. When Ian began his own story, not with* Once upon a time, *but with* It was a long time ago, *accompanying the beginning of the confession with a hang-dog expression, so forlorn and full of woe that I wanted to bring the telling to a halt before it had hardly begun, I felt my pulse quicken and my back begin to sweat. We had not made it into bed. I hadn't wanted to undress in front of him.*

Tell me about it, Ian, I said, feeling sick – the sort of sickness that reaches up to your throat and wings out into your temples. Ian sat on the stool by the dressing table-cum-desk.

It was a long time ago, Jules. She swore she was seventeen.

Oh God… How old was she?

Fourteen. She was underage drinking with some mates from school. She asked me if I'd buy her a drink. I said yes.

How long ago? I asked.

I was thirty-four. Three years ago.

Jesus, Ian, I feel really queasy.

Sorry.

And stop saying sorry.

What else am I supposed to say? It meant nothing.

Oh, how beautiful. You old romantic you… I was thoroughly disgust-

ed and I made sure I let him know it. I'm going to the well, I said.

Should I come? he asked, causing me to turn at the door. I'd been about to leave the chalet without a coat or even shoes on. If you want to speak any more, I said coldly, about your past, you can follow. But I don't want it spoken about one more time in the place where I sleep, understand?

Partly through necessity and partly so that I didn't have to look at Ian, I tied my bootlaces. And two more things, I shouted at him. One: four years is not a long time ago. And two: it didn't mean nothing. It meant an offence register that you are now on for how much longer? Another year?

Another year, Ian agreed, his voice pitiful.

The well was covered with a circle of rusting portcullis. Arrested by the early evening chill, still coatless, I dropped two coins through the mesh and made a wish for this not to be happening. I had hoped for a bit of light pilfering – even, ideally, shop theft in the name of some cause or another. I had even been prepared to settle for an isolated incident of Grievous Bodily Harm – street fights can get out of control, even for a kind soul such as Ian.

Will you talk to me? he asked when he joined me.

Why not the truth, Ian? I asked him back.

You name it. Shame. Guilt.

And how do you feel now? Now that I've learned it from someone else.

He sighed. Ashamed. Guilty, he answered. I just don't want the hassle at Customs, Heathrow or Gatwick, all right? Chances are I'll walk in without any bother, but what if? What if your mother meets us?

She won't meet us. She'll send someone.

Or that then. How would you like to explain it away? Your boyfriend, who's already too old for you in her opinion – oh yeah! He also happens to have a criminal conviction against children.

So many queries helter-skeltered from my head to my gut. I couldn't help myself. The chicken casserole I had pecked at for my dinner came surging up. I wasn't sick but it was a very close thing.

Let's get you out of the cold, suggested Ian.

It's too late to be concerned for me now, mate, I told him. How the hell *did you get this job? Working with kids every day.*

I was totally up front. I went through the court case until they were bored, and then I went through it all over again. She could have passed for twenty-one, I'm not... what I'm guilty of more than anything is guilty of being stupid with my trust. Being lonely in a foreign country. I'm sorry.

Say sorry again and I'll scream, Ian. I didn't say this. I didn't say anything for a couple of seconds, maybe a minute.

Who told you, by the way? he wanted to know.

I promised I wouldn't say. I was hoping it'd be a dirty rumour.

Wish it was. What now?

What now what? I faced him eye to eye for the first time since leaving the chalet. My cheeks burned with the cold; I had wrapped my arms around my chest. I wanted to leave. Right then; next bus anywhere; next train; next airport; next flight. Who I wanted to see, oddly, was Mum. I'm going to bed, I said.

Undoubtedly sensing his status as persona non grata, *Ian asked me where he should sleep. I gave it to him straight.*

The bath or another bush, I said.

He chose the bath. For minutes while I lay under the duvet, Ian faffed around, gathering what he could in order to nest in the tub. He laid down a coat as a mattress; he piled the entire basket of dirty laundry on top of himself as a form of tattered blankets. He remained clothed. Working as he did in the dark, I almost felt – no, I did feel – sorry for him. Was I without sin or error?

Dreams drained through my thoughts as I tried to fall off. The worst one was the thought that Ian had spent last night with one of the kids in the camp. I couldn't shake it. I spent a dreadful night, made worse by the notion that I didn't want to pee if Ian was sleeping in the bath. Misplaced coyness for sure, he'd seen it all before, but it was how I felt.

The next morning, when I woke for duty, Ian was gone. No one had seen him leave. His bath was not made. His rucksack was missing. Predictably enough, rain fell as I toured from chalet to chalet, then on to where the tents were pitched; I was hoping for news, I found blank faces. I was asked if we'd argued. I said yes. But that wasn't it, I tried to say…

Leo was the name of the Camp Manager. It spoke of his reluctance to interact with either staff or campers, the fact that his office was on the very edge of the encampment; it took me fifteen minutes through the mud to reach his door. He offered me a mug of warm milk, with honey and lemon. I held the mug in both hands and the steam moistened the skin on my face.

Do you know where he's gone? I asked Leo.

Leo had taken to chewing chocolate cigars as a way to stop smoking. He said: Yes. But he doesn't want me to tell you.

That's not fair. Is he at least safe?

He's safe. He's on his way to Warsaw.

I see. Where's he flying to?

He's not. He's going to see his daughter. I shouldn't be saying this.

Then why are you?

Leo removed the chocolate cigar from his mouth. Because, he replied, I agree with you, it's not fair. I tried to talk him out of it.

The word daughter *was like a paper cut. Ian had not mentioned a daughter. It was like observing an ancient castle toppling down. How much had I really known about the man who had shared my bed? – the man who had shown me new recipes? – the man with whom I'd swapped earrings?*

Not much. Do you have an address? I asked Leo.

You can't chase him. He'll kill me for what I've said as it is.

I'm not going to chase him, I said. I'm going to write to him.

Really?

Yes, really. I don't want to see him again. I didn't know about the daughter. I don't know about a lot of things these days. How old?

The daughter? About three, I think.

I placed the mug on his desk. Emptied as it was of hot milk, it was still producing steam. Thank you for the drink. I have to go to watercolours.

Who are you on with?

Becks.

She can manage on her own for ten minutes. I want to be sure you're okay.

I could feel the low temperature outside as soon as I placed my hand on the door latch. It was freezing. How much else had Ian said to Leo?

Did he ever mention the spot of bother he had in England, four years ago? I asked.

After a pause Leo nodded his head. I knew about it, he admitted.

He hasn't gone to Warsaw at all, has he?

That's what he told me.

But he hasn't. Why would his daughter live in Poland?

Leo looked at me as if the question had been intended as a trick. Her mother's Polish, he replied. She was in England on an education exchange.

Oh, this gets better! This gets great! You'll be telling me Ian was her teacher next. Was he? How the hell did he get this job, Leo? I shouted.

That's none of your business, Leo answered quietly.

My face itched – as though I'd just sprouted a beard. That same sickly feeling lifted up and ring-a-ring-a-rosied round my organs. My God…

What?

He was here the night before last, wasn't he, Leo? I said slowly, moving back towards the desk – towards the steaming mug, towards the vapour. He told me he slept in a bush, but he couldn't have; he would have frozen to death. He was here, discussing his escape plans. Did he blackmail you, Leo?

There's no need for this. I know you're upset…

Did he blackmail you to get the job, Leo? What's he got on you?

You're not making any sense.

Yes I am. Your body language tells me everything. Ian taught me all about body language, funnily enough. The plot thins. The plot thins, Leo, and like attracts like. Don't you see? Did you have a spot of bother yourself?

Be careful, Dolly, said Leo. I resent the implication.

Resent what you want. There's something you're not telling me. Maybe you'd prefer to tell someone higher up in authority. What's your story?

I don't have a story, Leo protested.

The chalet was chilly, but I kept up my temperature by packing my

bags swiftly and efficiently. Brushing my teeth again, I regarded my compo-
sure from the outside – seeing how anyone else would view me. It was fine.
I would not get paid, but I was not going home to England. Nor remaining
in the Lubuski Region, making friendship bracelets for friendships I didn't
feel, or hiking hills avoiding goat crap. The last place I would visit would be
Warsaw.

So I thought, at least, at that moment.

Morning activities were well underway by the time I had checked if
I'd left anything behind, three times. It was as easy to slip out of the camp as
Ian himself had presumably found it. Like him, I was invisible; only I had
no confidante with whom to stack up a plausible story, true or not true. An
hour passed, and I was close to the border with Germany. I had never been
to Germany before. I took a bus. I didn't know where I was, but I knew...

4.

...I knew I couldn't stay on the bus.

It was full of the poor and the damned, or so it seemed.
One woman carried a catbox on her meaty lap, its inhabitant
spitting fur and curses like an old fishwife. A young man fingered
a Bible, like an actor learning his lines, lips flexing, brow like a
cauliflower.

My desire was to get off this ghost-train. Panic had mush-
roomed in my head. My spittle tasted of pencil lead.

Villages sucked us in. We veered unexpectedly up insane
inclines and through the skinny gaps afforded by ancient bridges,
walls made of lamb-coloured rock. All of us silently praying for
no oncoming vehicle; begging that nothing as big would be coming towards us from the opposite direction. We motored through
hamlets of nine or ten dwellings. I had no practical idea where
I was, and I didn't much care. Those straw-like lanes sucked us
up and in, a blockage in a vein, perhaps; something poisoning
– but if so, slowly poisoning the natives. Miles of greedy green

and scratchy brown to either side. The countryside breathing, as if after a good fuck. The bus belching its appreciation of a decent meal.

Bolení břicha, I told the driver. I had staggered to the front, via army games – athletic games – games of balance and skill – the result of the bus's crossbow twangs to the right. Nor was I the only one to invest the moment with its correspondent and respectful down-payment of fear. Other faces were etiolated, too. We were going too fast.

The driver stormed us through the villages like a plague.

I had gripped hard at a pole – me, a pole dancer for the first and only time of my life. The bus shook like a cocktail-maker; the air outside dimmed, holding pockets of clashing colours that I both liked and didn't like. It felt homely and alien at the same time.

Bolení břicha, I repeated to the bus driver – as if he happened to be a deaf in charge of a four-ton contraption carrying live quarry. I needed to disboard.

A sheep came to my rescue, thanks be praised. A stray sheep, either confused or attracted to the bright lights on the road, it had wriggled free of wire fencing and expectation. Out onto the road, the driver had no choice but to stop.

He sounded his horn – and so did I. I repeated *Bolení břicha* – meaning stomachache – on several fresh occasions, intending for the driver to pick up that I either needed to be sick or I was going to squat. And I didn't much care which. Because once I was out of the bus I was on my own, come what may. I had made that decision already.

Two women were at the front of the bus – one black and one white.

It was up to me to wrench open the door at the front of the bus, oddly enough to no verbal opposition or challenge that I can

recall. Stepping off the vehicle, my feet encountered the anticipated gravel dancefloor; my nose the competing odours of hills,
earth and sheep dung.

I saw the sheep in the road. Wool as dirty as dishcloths;
face benign and resigned – face pretty and blank. For the sheep
at least, this was the end of the road. Not for me. I didn't know
which direction it would take me in, but I knew the road had
some miles yet to lead. Disdainfully the sheep glanced up as I
disembarked.

The sheep blocked the road for me to get off. I still believe
that.

Partly.

5.

The aroma of a river. The sound of a river...

Taking instinct as my compass, I went off in search of this
majestic flood.

I didn't find it.

Tramp as I did over hills green as fresh seaweed, my motivation seemed to be to continue – to do nothing else but continue.

I had no idea if I was tramping on private land or open
pathway. It didn't matter – the frame of mind I was in.

The hill with the face and the river were bosom buddies.
Any casual eavesdropper on local folklore was aware of this
much. When I heard the noises of running water, and already
in the knowledge that I walked the general footprints of the hill's
million previous visitors, I became excited and felt noteworthy
and worthwhile – the first time in ages.

Of course I had not forgotten Ian.

But what could I *do* about the prick? He had run away. I
was not doing the same thing, or so I believed.

6.

I found it.

The hill with a face – beyond a field of woebegotten yellow shrubs. The place had no quality control attributed to it whatsoever. No care for its appearance.

The face was like that of a movie-star portrait.

Tender with battered nerves and humming with fear, I decided to climb it.

7.

Up its nibbled inner flanks I scrambled, searching for God – for God knows what. The sky a bruise of duller yellows, greens, an acne dot of black.

The nose was about halfway up the human face. At the top of the nose, where aerial spectacles might have perched, was where I stopped to survey the landscape.

The hill had been in a fight. The nose was broken.

I need to feel wanted by something.

What is the point of a hill with a face if no one is looking at it? If no one can melt at the smile. Was the hill on which I stood male or female? What sex was this creature with the battered nose? Was it attractive to other hills? Do hills wink at each other, flatter each other with come-hither grins?

I was conscious that what I was standing on was ancient.

8.

A stone hut perched like a pimple on the left eyebrow of the face.

It was at this moment that I missed Ian more than I ever had, but I can't explain why. Feelings mingled; emotions as rich as a sense of pathos, and hunger bit into my chest. I tried to remember the last time I'd eaten, but I failed – I couldn't remember.

You are dealing with the natural, I remember thinking. The force you feel is natural. And the eyebrow seemed to leak a lifeforce of its own. I took my good time regarding it, that's for certain; I was conscious that I had no idea what time of the day it was. The light said evening, but I could not be certain.

Even now, I'm not so sure it was even real time.

9.

Of everything that was there, it was the stone hut that I approached. It smelled of mildew and bad bananas; sheep shit and hill-breath. A flexing in my breast that might have been nervousness, or might have been indigestion grew within me. Thinking back, perhaps it was curiosity that killed my cat. I walked closer.

Having come so far in my telling, I cannot avoid talking about what happened in the stone hut, though instinct can be a harsh editor. I both want to and don't want to discuss it, but I can't swerve away from the tale, not now, not so late in. It doesn't matter how many times I told myself: *It happened, it did, and you were not to blame.*

I entered the stone hut.

I had anticipated desolation (if memory serves), but it wasn't what I found – or not exactly that alone at any rate. Two women sat in the filth, in the muck, and one of them – the black woman – cradled a baby whose skin was white and whose features were vaguely Eastern. I was utterly confused. For a long few seconds no one spoke. My lips were sore with pursing and flexing. My feet scraped on some trash on the stone floor.

The black woman and the white woman looked up at me.

We were miles from any form of civilisation, however rural or cut-off; the two women sat in squalor in their peasantish outfits, a baby to share between them. Wind curled and looped through the spaces in the walls that had once been windows, though probably never glassed. It was cold and damp, and it smelt of the moss that grew on the rocks scattered around – remnants either of stone decay or former furniture. The floor was littered with food wrappers – proof of a fairly recent visitor, I imagined, though the meal might well have been the women's own. Or the baby's for that matter. Not that eating had been the sole activity inside the hut: also present among the rubbish were beer cans (some burnt black by any one of the number of doused fires whose sticky soot smeared wall and ceiling alike); some condoms, like fat worms in mid-wriggle; and there were even a couple of hypodermic needles.

The women did not take their eyes off me. I asked them if they spoke English, which was foolish in retrospect, but I wasn't in full control of the situation. As a result of my question – nothing happened. Still, that greedy double gaze of theirs. Faces frozen in a macabre tableau. The white woman unfastened the first three buttons on her blouse. Beneath it she wore no bra and her breast appeared dusty and dirty.

Before my eyes, the black woman passed the baby (approximately nine months of age, I guessed) to the white woman. The baby, knowing the score, attached its lips to the exposed nipple. The black woman now smiled on at the exchange of power.

What could I do? As the baby suckled noisily, I longed for more sound – more than the baby's eager gurglings, more than the sigh of the wind speeding through the holes where the windows may once have rested. Anything would do. I repeated my question in English – *Do you speak English?* – then composed the equivalent sentences in German and Polish.

No reaction whatsoever came from the two women.

I couldn't wait any longer. I had lingered no more than a minute or two, but I was already itchy. I didn't belong here, but neither did they. Three quarters of the way up a spooky old hill, with a baby between them. It wasn't right. It wasn't natural.

10.

But that's not what happened.

Protest on protest, building a bonfire in Dorothy's mind. She can – she must – construct something that will ignite. Burn down those old stories; watch the blaze climb up a tinderbox the size of three coffins…Two adult-sized, one measured to fit a baby –

No. Dorothy slams down a creased fist. *None of that really happened.* That was part of *Nutcracker Island*, nothing more and nothing less. That was in the book.

Yet she *does* remember the hill with the face. She *does* remember running away from the camp – running away from an Ian who had already made good on a swift egress.

I fled Ian and found the two gypsy women. One of them stood up… Oh God. It really happened. It was nothing to do with fiction. I didn't write them into existence.

Rising to her feet, off her sofa, brings to Dorothy the memory of the black woman standing up. Though the light was poor in the stone hut, pinpricks of white found her eyes, giving the woman the appearance of wisdom. The white woman nursed the baby. Even down the passage of years – and even above the noise of the wind on the hill, a wind that sounds every bit as loud right now, in her home – Dorothy hears the baby's puckering on the breast; the pops and crackles of cartilege as the black woman stretches *with knees as bad as my own.* Dorothy winces in sympathy.

Convalescing is what she is supposed to be doing, but life's too short for inactivity, she argues. *It certainly was for that child.* As swiftly as her aching bones (and her brittle mind) will take her, Dorothy shuffles over to the tiny – almost token – section of her bookshelves dedicated to her own work. There are seven copies of *Nutcracker Island*. She hasn't touched the book for years. She pulls a copy free from between Kingsley Amis's *One Fat Englishman* and the next example of her own first novel. Then, on a sudden impulse, she removes the second of her *Nutcracker Island*s as well with the unreasonable notion that has struck her that the content of the two will differ. She feels peculiar. In her head she adds together her birthdate – 12 – and the month number – 11 – to make 21. Once she has sat down, this time at the dining table, she draws a deep breath and opens both copies of *Nutcracker Island* to page twenty-one.

To her relief the font is identical between the two. The words as well, as she is able to confirm once she has simul-read the first three paragraphs of each, which take up three-quarters of the page. *What did I expect?* Contentedly and with strenuous relief, she sighs.

Then the two women return to her head. The baby. The hut on the hill with the face in the wind – the Eastern European wind...

I wrote it all in this book, Dorothy argues with herself. It didn't really –

Read it then, her mother tells her. *You know you're wrong, but read that smutty garbage from cover to cover if you think i'm lying to you. As you always did, let's face it.*

Shut up, Mum.

I won't. You'd already written that filth before you went abroad, you silly bitch. Use your noggin. Use your noodle.

I said: shut up, Mum!

Don't speak to your mother like that! Just read it. See what you find and report back to me. Then the voice is gone.

Dorothy holds on to her head.

This is when she telephones me.

11.

As though in need of another run-up – like a high-jumper opting to lope past the pole set too high, rather than begin an unsuccessful backwards flop – Dorothy re-approaches the stone hut, as opposed to starting the memory film up with her body established inside. Will things be different? she wonders. This time she pays more attention to her surroundings, her thigh muscles gripping with her efforts on the incline, or is it not so much that she is more observant of the environment, and instead more that the memory has grown more detail to reveal? She notices the taut crocus buds, snapping open a crust that appears both stretched and impoverished by not enough rain. This iteration of the dream gradient displays a hundred details to Dorothy, details missed on the previous memory-trek, or maybe missing altogether, not painted in yet, and therefore unnoticeable. Or better yet... maybe ignored in the first place, more than a quarter of a century earlier. After all, she'd had greater worries on her mind at the time...

She pays due respect to the architects and constructors of the stone hut. It has stayed erect and mostly intact (*in my imagination,* Dorothy qualifies) for what? – a hundred years? Five hundred? Longer? Although there has been weather-wear and tempest-tear, some of the stones leaking crumbs, and although much of the east- and and south-facing walls (not the wall with the front doorway) have been bleached and etiolated by centuries of sun, it remains a surprisingly handsome structure.

Ugliness is within, *But it doesn't have to be. This is my memory and I can change it if I want to. I don't have to see the guns.*

Yes you do, Doo-Doo. Her mother's voice, even up here, most of the way up the hill. Worse than the intrusion into her thoughts is the understanding that Mum is correct, she has no choice. It's either now or it's later, but it's not a choice to say *don't do it at all.*

And don't fool yourself, Doo-Doo, that the women won't be in there.

'I know,' Dorothy whispers. 'You win. I'm going in. On one condition...'

There are no conditions.

'Please, Mum – just this once. On one condition.'

Oh all right. What condition?

'Stop calling me Doo-Doo. I never liked it.'

Thus resolved to enter the stone hut, Dorothy falls upon something so obvious that it almost roots her to the spot. True, she has to go in; but why should she have to go in alone?

This is when she telephones me.

12.

When the telephone rings I am reclining in an orthopedic chair that does nothing or little to soothe my bad back, and which makes drinking beer decidedly tricky. It's mid-afternoon; two-thirty or so. Like a hillside hermit I have become unused to the sound of the telephone (and the intercom buzzer) and it takes a few trills before I move. But move I do, hoping I won't sound too inebriated (I've only had four) – in case it's Human Resources at the College yet again, on my arse about a return to work and how-can-they-help? And fearing my eventual lawsuit for being made to lift heavy boxes in the first place.

Momentarily I think of myself, not as an employer conducting a job interview, but as a psychoanalyst as Dorothy moves past me – a light brush of perfume – and reclines in the chair I have just vacated. As though needful of slumber (join the club), she closes her eyes, face pickled wrinkly with nerves and anger. She makes no mention of the fact that I'm still in my dressing-gown and boxers, well past the day's midpoint. I wonder, in fact, if she's even seen me. Her breathing sounds like scratches; there's a key-like catch on the exhalation. Host with the most that I naturally long to be, I offer coffee. Dorothy shakes her head; shakes her torso, too. She asks for wine – or *anything stronger than caffeine*. The beer's out – I know that much – but to my surprise, on ransacking the cupboards, I discover a bottle of sherry, three-quarters full. Dorothy says quickly, 'That'll do' and continues to work on her breathing, which swoops like a stormy petrel.

'That'll do,' I echo, confirming the decision to myself. 'Sabrina'll never miss it.' I can't remember the last time Sabrina used sherry to cook with. *Erratum*: I cannot recall the last time Sabrina cooked, full stop.

Opening her eyes again, Dorothy awards me one long glance, equal measures compassion and contempt. Dorothy adds: 'If she does I'll replace it, okay?'

The first sip is harsh – probably more so for guest than for server. So *committed* is the coughing fit into which Dorothy is delivered that I wonder how she keeps the liquid down; how she refrains from vomiting. She has to lean forward to crush the coughs. The second, third and fourth sips she takes are progressively larger. Here's a woman who wants to get *drunk*. Fair enough, it's nice to have a partner other than Roy for a change, although what we've got in stock will not go far. Holding up the glass, Dorothy straightens her back and demands 'Another!' I vow to catch her up as I refill her vessel with the sweet brown bearpiss.

'Dorothy, what's wrong?'

'In a minute.'

Breathing shallowed, wet red lips smacked cleanly together, Dorothy looks my way for the second time. I have yet to sit down; I am standing under the archway into the kitchen. 'I want to tell you a story,' she says. 'Do you have time?'

'I'm all ears.'

13.

'So I entered the stone hut,' she resumes. It is water that she sips now, but the cooking sherry has played its part in opening her up. It has even provided her with a semi-pissed juiced-up lexicon. I haven't heard the word *tacked* in a thousand years.

'I tacked the incline and listened to the sermon on that particular mount, to full pulpit volume, I tell you. I was almost deafened by the wind, as I recall.'

She is miles away; years away, too. When her eyelids lower, there is movement within – a flexing and a settling – as her vision searches for something, blind, back then.

'What happened? She lifted her skirt…'

'Yes! A heavy skirt – heavy fabric. Patterns of flowers, kind of a gypsy skirt – or a farmer's daughter's skirt…I'm not sure exactly how to describe it.'

'Dorothy. The skirt is not entirely important,' I tell her.

She opens her eyes. 'But I disagree, Tom! By telling you about the skirt I'm rebuilding the scene; I'm knitting it all together with my twelve-inch needles.'

'Okay then. What colour was it?'

'Brown. Milky-tea brown. And dirty.'

'What else?'

'There were *conkers* on the ground. Inside the hut. Conkers.'

I wait. I probably shouldn't ask it but I do. 'And what's *that* got to do with anything?'

Dorothy perks up and widens her eyes. 'How long have I been like this?' she asks.

'Like what?'

'Brittle and confused. Tell me straight.'

'I wouldn't have said you were brittle and confused. What did she do?'

She nods her head, suddenly serious. She has a job to do.

'Lifted her skirt to her waist. Her groin was like Kew Gardens. Country girl self-respect, you know?'

I don't. 'I've never been to Kew Gardens. You mean unkempt?' I ask.

'Bushy.' The nod of the head, emphatic and large. 'But pretty. A mini work of art.'

'But why was she flashing you?'

'She wasn't; or at least, she wasn't flashing me her Minnie. She had a garter belt on her left upper thigh. God! I see it all so *clearly*. It holstered a pistol – a little pistol.'

'She pointed the *pistol* at you?'

Again, she nods. 'I thought I was a goner,' she tells me. 'But no, I wasn't to be the victim – how were they to have known I'd show up in my precarious emotional state?'

'How indeed.'

'She was waiting – not for me. Waiting for the white woman to stand up. Which she did, carrying the baby. She *handed me the child* and produced her own pistol.'

'Another garter belt job?'

'Yes. Her Minnie was shaved to the dermis; utterly bald. I followed them outside…'

14.

The wind hummed in the grass, playing notes against the aborted shrubs. Evening was low, in those few short minutes ink had run across the page of the sky; it was a beauty to behold. And the temperature had dropped to nothing, to minus numbers.

I listened to the river, thinking at first that it was the sound of the wind. I couldn't see it and I never did – the river. I couldn't see it but I could hear it.

The baby kicked in my arms. Stupid as it might sound, I was worried that I would disturb someone if he started crying.

That *I* would, since I am the one that had taken on the responsibility – a mother's responsibility. Stupid, as I say.

The two women had agreed to a twilight duel. That was
the reason for the pistols.

Not knowing what they were about to do, I followed them
out of the stone hut and onto the slope. Vegetation looks more
sinister in the gloaming. I was frightened and sparked awake, despite the fatigue in my marrow and behind my eyes from the
climb. Still I was tired all the time, even then. I think my problems with sleep began that year.

The baby wanted to climb up my body; The baby was
white, by the way; I don't think I mentioned that, and it didn't
seem so important – at that point – who the mother was.

Even at this point I didn't understand the rules of engagement. Nor even when they stood back to back, weapons raised,
and started the ten-step walk away from one another.

You've seen duels. I had, too. You seem to think you comprehend the imbecilic non-complexity of them from reading *The
Three Musketeers*, but believe me, you don't. When the black woman headed up the incline and the white woman moved down-
wards, I held a baby to my chest as if one of the combatants was
my husband or something in seventeenth-century France. Then
it dawned on me what was happening.

I shouted a protest, but one voice is not as loud as two pistol
reports.

The white woman went down immediately – first to her
knees and then face first into the sorry mud. The bullet had
punctured the very breast with which she'd given succour.

The black woman was hit on the right shoulder, the aim of
this shot less true.

The baby started grizzling.

I couldn't believe the *economy* of violence; and it was this thought that was to haunt me. My skull throbbed and rang with questions every bit as loud as the gun noises. Why a duel? What for? What was the disagreement? Why now, upon my approach? Was it so that someone could hold the child? If they had both died, what would have happened to the child if I hadn't ventured upon their suicide pact?

And, of course, 'What should I do now?'

I was struck by a *floating* sensation. Contrary and confusing thoughts pinged me – that it was the end of the summer; that the flowers around me were of the wrong month of the year; that the baby must be hungry again. I didn't know what to do. I felt… *October.* I actually felt like the month of October.

The baby started whooping. If my mood had been different, I might have joined in – he almost seemed happy, but this was no time for happiness. This was a time for panic.

The black woman began moaning.

I carried the baby to the wounded woman

The sound of the river might well have been inside my world – by which I mean my head. Wind and panic: the unlikely twins. She had laid down in the filth. Blood at twilight is a ghastly colour, and a ghastly aroma to boot – the perfume of the damned.

'Give him to me,' she said in English.

II.

1.

Three weeks have passed since the fight at the canal. It is Guy Fawkes' Night – November the fifth – and the sky is a kaleidoscope of hues, muddied by acres of smoke from fireworks that have expanded like accordions, and expended their brief existences at the zenith of the park in front of the train station, where a crowd of several hundred – man, woman, child and beast (a scattering of tethered, cowering dogs) – has congregated to pray and coo beneath the organized display and its violent beards of popping colours. Such warmth as the air contains is snuffed out by aerosol-strength drizzle. At every turn, flickering light battles in the darkness. The light (and heat) arrives from a bonfire at the centre of the park, on which donated items of decrepit furniture crackle in a yellow and strangely green blaze. Winking eyes of light sit at the end of wooden sticks, carried by children dressed up against the cold in so many layers that they are all but spherical. Sparklers on sticks are wielded like miniature weapons, hissing free eyelashes of golden flame, twisted like batons to form ephemeral coronas for the children to be entranced by. The park smells of a million matchsticks – and of burgers and hot dogs from the vans set up at the edge in the station car park.

Another volley of explosions takes to the air. James looks up. As the fireworks corrupt the night, his mother sings into his ear, 'That's a pretty one, isn't it, James?' He has had to promise to be good to earn this official outing. He nods his head. Since the fight and since his second meeting with Kolko, James has learned a lot about lying – its deployment certainly, but above all its efficacy, charm; its *aptness*. In fact, the fireworks are nothing special;

even James, with his limited experience of the subject, has witnessed much more grandiose exemplars. A rocket combusts on its trajectory moonward-ho; it forms the backbone of the letter *D*, joining up with a luminous pink crescent. The capital letter D fades; temporarily excited, James is anxious to read more of the new sky script. Among the chattering Morse Code conflagration of the same barrage, he picks out a lower case *i*, complete with a dot that expands and then chases its own green tail until the atmosphere exhausts it.

A *D* and an *i*. Convinced that there is a message in the fireworks, James maintains an upward gaze, his neck stiff, his eyes flooded not with sadness but with nervous anticipation. He is aware that his mother is watching him.

She's the only one who is. There have had to be compromises for this excursion – chief among them the non-negotiable guarantee from Len that he will not venture within twenty metres of anywhere James happens to be standing. As Len (along with Leo) has secured a Food Distribution licence for the evening, and currently tends a hot dog van that Leo has shares in, in the car park, this condition is not especially onerous – for anybody. But it's still *there*, this agreement: the bad blood between man and boy simmers. *What if we hadn't got the van?* Len had asked. *What if I actually wanted to see the display with my wife and my stepdaughter? Are you telling me I would have had to stay away from you all?* Sal had answered: *No. It means we wouldn't go at all.* Len had shaken his head and looked to Louise for support. *You're empowering that boy for an illness,* he'd said. Louise had shrugged her shoulders, saying *I don't care, I'm going with Chloe and Rachel.* Sal had wiped away a tear and summed it all up with: *I don't know what else to do. I can't do it all by myself.*

So…Louise is off with Chloe but not Rachel (who has a cold and has remained at home) – last seen chatting with some boys from school near the bonfire. Leaving Sal to mind James, who, in the glistening airborne curlicues of blood-red and sodium-flare, has deciphered his third letter since learning to read: a grooving *e*.

D-i-e, he has read in the sky. The thought (the command? the imperative?) makes him smile. Taking her son's expression as a good sign, Sal smiles too, and squeezes his hand. James is too old to have his hand held – both of them know this – but sometimes it soothes him, although there is no obvious pattern to when this pacification technique will work and when it will repulse. James squeezes back, fingers to fingers. They wear no gloves. James refuses to wear gloves, the material makes his skin itch. His own hand is warmer than his mother's. *D-i-e*, he reads again, although the impressions are long gone from the sky. Other fireworks whistle up. James attempts to decode the resulting chandeliers, rosy blooms and astral scrotums. At first there is nothing to see. Perhaps if they were closer to the bonfire, he conjectures – however, there is nothing logical in the supposition. Wordlessly, led by her dragged arm, Sal follows her son in the blaze's direction.

It takes another five minutes for James to note more letters. Locking what he's deciphered into his brain, he maintains surveillance for more of this strange dictation. There is none. The six letters in total are the sum of his memorandum: *D-i-e-l-e-n*. More than enough to make him smile (which Sal accepts with gratitude). That he needs no reminder is irrelevant – he's been working on plans to this effect since the canalside with Kolko – but it's nice to feel wanted; feel *needed*, even.

Ever since that morning, James has worked on the purchasing of a gun. If instinct hadn't told him what to do, and if Kolko's pep talk had been insufficient (it hadn't), this message in the sky, from his father, James decides, is enough to quench any smouldering doubts. A gun it is. On the acquisition front, he will have to try harder; but at least he knows what he has to do – James is sure about that now.

2.

Meanwhile, a large boy whimpers...

A defeated boy; a broken boy. The change in this boy (all agree) has been remarkable. In the space of three weeks. Not only has he been knocked from his camel, he's been pulverized into the sand, to grub about with the other mites and ticks.

Not that Wolfe says much about the events at the canal, of course. He is not even swearing revenge. He has stopped talking.

Instead he whimpers. He has taken a total of nine out of the possible fifteen days of schooling as sick days. Some of these days are even authentic as he really is ill. The contaminated water has done what it needs to do, it has contaminated him. He almost drowned when he swallowed the filthy water by the lungful. It is fortunate that he didn't die

3.

Meanwhile, other boys cause parents problems...

Two mothers discuss their sons; one of these mothers has become feisty.

'*Ground rules?*' she demands. 'Did I hear you right?'

'You heard me right; but I'm not sure my *expression* was right. Shall I try again?'

The location is once more The Globe, by the canal. Since their friendship began – a matter of mere weeks earlier – The Globe has become something of a regular haunt. Annette is fond of the superior grade of Polish and Czech incivility with which she is served; it means that she can order what she wants with no fear of having to remain pleasant. It's Annette who spends the most money because she gets herself a double every time she walks back into the building on the pretence of visiting the toilet. The system works. It works for Sal too, she is happy to go out *anywhere* for an hour or so. It has become the norm on these brief visits for Sal to drive; she is not exactly sure why this feels more comfortable for her – as yet she does not suspect Annette's drinking. There are no obvious signs to suspect. If pressed for an answer she would probably say *I just prefer driving. I'm a nervous passenger.*

'Yes please,' Annette replies. 'Try again, please.'

They sit outside. The Globe has installed outdoor heaters, near which the women perch, so that Annette can smoke the cigarettes that she can't smoke near her closer friends (or her husband) who believe she stopped over a year ago. With Sal, however, the slate is clean, and Annette can be whoever she wants to be – for now. So they sit near the heaters, in the crisp winter chill, fully coated and bescarved, enjoying a natter. Annette lights up. She takes a sip of red wine. Sal is content with a coffee.

Sal waits; she waits as though the correct construction is a carriage to jump onto, on a train idling by. 'I'm suggesting this for the sake of our new friendship, Annette.' Again, she waits. 'That we put aside whatever – we talk with honesty. Yes? We speak our minds? It just *happens* our sons are friends, right?'

Uncertainly, Annette replies: 'I suppose so…But I told you, Sal – James was charming to me. He's only *ever* been charming to me.'

'The other way around,' Sal tells her. 'I'm talking about Emil.' As swiftly as she's able to without appearing rude, she explains what James has accused Emil of, talking scrat about the teenage pregnancy of Louise. 'It really upset her,' Sal continues. The sentence hangs.

'Well I'm not used to this…'

'Annette, sorry. I almost didn't mention it, but I'm sure we can…'

'I'm not used to such *rubbish*.'

'Excuse me?' Sal sounds stunned.

'Are you serious about this?' Annette goes on. '*Emil? Emil* talked about your daughter sleeping around? Sal, even *I* knew that one. The controversial thing is why *you* don't.'

'She hasn't even got a boyfriend. She told me that.'

'And *my* son once told me that cheese is made of feathers,' Annette answers. 'They're *children*, Sal; part of their *job* is lying. So what? It's called an imagination.' She looks away for a second while she takes a few drags on her cigarette.

Not knowing what to look for, Sal studies her. She wraps her mittened hands around her cup. In the nippy air her coffee is already cooling. She drinks it quickly. Her heart goes hell-for-leather. 'Are you telling me you've heard *stories* about Louise?'

'Yes, Sal. All the parents have.' She turns back to face Sal.

'Because if you have…'

'I said yes, Sal. Yes I have heard rumours about your daughter that I've hoped can't be true. Sorry about that. Unless you want our friendship to swat away honesty.'

'That's exactly what I *don't* want. Maybe I wasn't clear.'

'You were clear enough.' Annette drains her glass of wine in one long swallow. 'You wanted to blame my son for your daughter's reputation. Right or wrong?'

'You sound angry…'

'Why would that be! Right or wrong?'

'I suppose right, but—'

'But nothing.' Annette rises to her feet and clutches her handbag. 'Don't lump my kids in with yours, Sal,' Annette says. 'Nothing could be further from the truth.'

'Where are you going?'

'Home. Where the heart is.'

'But I drove us here!'

'I'll walk the canal path. Then I'm going for a swim. Have a think about your words, Sal.' Only now, in this supposedly grand exit, does the slimmest trace of inebriation slide through Annette's words – not even prominent enough for Sal to notice, though others around might have picked up the clues.

Annette walks away.

4.

'Left anterior descending. Coronary artery; angina; hypertension.'

Patrick pauses while he searches in the medical dictionary that he retains inside his head. 'Ischemic heart disease,' he continues, 'elevated blood sugar. Poisoning of the gastric acids; rhinitis; nasal trauma; pharyngeal perforation; intracranial insertion wounding…'

'I know all this, Dad,' says Annette.

'Been sicker than any man's a *right* to be, girl.'

'I know that too, Dad.'

'Nasogastric tube misplacement. Periorbital bruising. Cerebral lacerations. Subdiagphragmatic trauma. Ionising radiation sickness. Erythema. Intussusception – a blockage in the intestine – and a problem with me gastro-oesophageal reflux.'

Annette knows that this is important – for him. For her it is essential. If the old man is not happy then there is little chance that he will offer her a financial handout, and she needs one. So she listens with weighted patience; she cannot think of anything else to do.

'Sepsis!'

'Yes, Dad, sepsis. Dad, do you want your cigarettes?'

'Well there's a first.'

Annette acknowledges the satire. Under her lowered lids her eyes roll in consternated aggravation; but even assisting him in his plans to smoke himself blue is preferable to listening to his war stories of diseases and ailments he's known and bettered. As Annette leaves the room in search of his smokes, she hears behind her:

'Dermatophytes. Eczema. Candidiasis. Squamous cell carcinoma. Erysipelas and cellulitis. Boils! Impetigo. Benign warts. Fungal infections…'

If only he put as much effort into getting over Mum…

The thought remains unfinished – a long note vibrating. Experiencing a peculiar combination of penitence and defiance, Annette returns to the lounge bearing gifts of nicotine. She even offers: 'Shall I light it up for you, Dad?'

'How much do you want?' Patrick replies, snatching at the box. Shakes take hold of his hands as he endures the pulmonary pulsing – the anticipation of gasped-in chemicals. It doesn't help that this is a fresh box of cigarettes; the smokes are as tightly packed in as rush-hour commuters on the Tube. Thumb and forefinger pinch together, nails golden, chipped and toughened to the consistency of ashtray glass.

'Can I help you, Dad?'

'No. I'm a free man,' says Patrick, apropos of nothing. 'I asked you how much do you want. You haven't come here for me elf.'

In the past there might have been disagreement – a protest, perhaps, from the daughter defamed. The protest might even have carried some weight, but things were different back then – back then before *Mum*. They both know it; there is no point denying it, denial takes time and they both have scarce reserves of time, or so they feel.

Annette clears her throat. 'Would two hundred be okay?'

she asks; her breath catching on the last word's consonant. She remains standing; she has yet to sit down since her arrival. Accompanied by a swift self-rebuking reflection of disgust, Annette acknowledges the reason why this is so – she has expected her father to direct her to where he has left her money. She hasn't shown one ounce of doubt that the cash register will cough up. She wanted to get down to business, and assumed that the money would be given. Promptly. Yet she hasn't even had the courtesy to look her old man in the eye. She is ashamed of herself. But it is surely too late to sit down and pretend now.

'Do I have a choice?' There is no mirth or indulgence in Patrick's question.

'*Yes.*' Indignant; snotty – as though wounded by this slander.

'You're me daughter! Of course I don't have a choice.' Patrick ignites the tip of his cigarette. The warm breath of pleasure. 'There's three 'undred under the cushion on the settee – the cushion with the book on it.'

To Annette's surprise the book is *The Tight Blue Tide* by Dorothy Anthony. She picks it up and flips back the cover. The fact that a biro'd inscription is scratched into the title page – *To Lesley, Happy 21st Birthday, Love Mum xxx* – suggests that Dad has bought it at a jumble sale or in a charity shop somewhere. Unless I gave it to him, Annette thinks.

'I could get that signed for you, Dad,' Annette offers.

'What's that?'

'The book – Dorothy Anthony. That's *our* Dorothy, my friend Dorothy. I could get the book autographed for you if you like.'

Patrick gives the impression of actually shrinking in his chair. 'And what, may I ask, leads you to think that might be a good idea?' he asks his daughter slowly.

'Well, Dad... it might be nice. Nice for her and nice for

you. Flattering for her.'

'What? Flattering for her to sign a book that someone's gave to a daughter, which has ended up in the cancer shop for a quid. Yes, I'm sure she'll be *thrilled*. Just take your money.'

While collecting the bundle of notes Annette adds, 'What's wrong with you today, Dad? Why are you so grumpy? There's more than three hundred here.'

'Keep the change; you sold yourself short.' Patrick makes the kind of noise sometimes presented in fiction as *harrumph*; an old man's style of representing the morally indigestible and the disgraceful. His hand twitches as he makes the act of stubbing out his cigarette into one of unnecessary violence, the ashtray wobbling under the pressure on its little table stand. 'You really do forget what you do and say to me, don't you, girl?'

Annette needs no second invitation to handbag the extra money. 'What do you mean?' she asks, genuinely confused.

'You've introduced us before, you know.'

'Really?' Now, with business conducted, she parks her bottom on the yielding sofa. *The Tight Blue Tide* remains in her grip. 'When was that?'

'The barbecue at Sam's place in the summer, for one,' Patrick answers, snickering like Iago in a bad production. 'Look at me, I'm 'undred and four and I got a better memory than this one.'

'Yeah Dad, you win. When else?'

'A few other times,' is all the old man will admit to. 'And I've seen her at the pool a time or two; not often, but we might have had a swim and a hot chocolate. So, Queen of Sheba, if I decide I want to offend your friend and mine by asking her to sign something that's been given away to charity by an ungrateful bitch of a daughter, I'll take it to Tiddenfoot with me on the offchance that I bump into the author. Fine by you?'

'Jesus, Dad, okay all right?' Annette surrenders with a display of both palms. 'Whatever's got you into this mood I don't like it. Is something wrong? Is it the money?'

Patrick maintains a sudden and vociferous silence. In lieu of a reply, he takes a second to crunch his dentures and to light a second cigarette, his mood less one of vituperative tristimania than one of scarred and battle-weary victory.

'Dad, please, what is it?' Annette asks, leaning forward now.

The eyes of father and daughter meet; the conjunction feels rare to them both, it has the spark of novelty.

'I got a phone call from one of your boyfriends,' Patrick answers, breaking the spell. 'I couldn't hear him right at first. Did I tell you about me earwax?'

'Fuck your earwax!'

'Charming, that.'

'What did you say about *boyfriends*? I don't have *boyfriends*.'

'Oh, please, who are you talking to? Postman Pat? He called me here – friendly voice.' Patrick inhales and exhales, whether meaning to or not, constructing the suspense. 'Which I didn't much like, I must be honest with you, girl. Do you know what the word *dormition* means? Pleasant as you like, "I'm Simon, one of your daughter's boyfriends, and I'm just ringing to wish you a pleasant dormition. I can't wait to see her again."'

Annette leans forward an inch or so more. 'Simon, you say?'

'I had to look it up. First time I've opened a dictionary in ten years, I reckon. Dormition. It was his voice – so chappy and chatty. Nice as pie, he was.'

'Simon? His name was Simon?' asks Annette.

'Yes. Do you remember that one?' Patrick says with great sarcasm.

Annette dodges the question and asks one of her own.

'What does the word mean? I almost don't want to ask,' she replies.

'A peaceful, quiet death,' Patrick answers. 'He was wishing me a peaceful, quiet death. That's *got* to be odd, annit? I'm not *that* far out of touch, girl, that something like that's normal for you youngsters.' He sips on his cigarette. 'Though at my age, I don't know if he was paying me a compliment or a wish to 'ave me away in me box. Maybe he thought he was being nice; it was the *intrusion* I didn't like.'

'He's no boyfriend of mine, Dad. He's a dangerous man. His surname is Kolko.'

'That's right, Simon Cocoa. Funny enough, I was having an 'ot chocolate when he called…' Patrick's eyes glint with the memory and the jokey coincidence.

Using the only method to get her dad's full attention that she knows, Annette stands up, leans towards him and plucks the cigarette from his mouth.

'Kol-ko. Kay-oh-elle-kay-oh. If he calls again, you're to telephone the police.'

'Give me back my cigarette. You're not too old to get a spank!'

'Yes I am, Dad. You call the police. I'm serious.'

'So am I. Give it back and get out of my house, you dirty cow.'

III.

1.

Who am I today?

On opening her eyes the first thing she does is check her hands for clues as to her age. They are not a young woman's hands; nor are they withered like fruit on the vine, however; they err on the boney side, but the palms and fingertips are smooth.

A writer's hands. Unaccustomed to heavy lifting or manual labour.

My name is Dorothy Anthony.

She opens her eyes for real, the examination she has just conducted was in her dreaming mind only.

She also dreamt of her friends and of some other jigsaw pieces from other corners of her life. Along with Hannah and Sam, Tom and Sabrina, Annette and her father Patrick, also present were Julia, her literary agent, Di, her rabid reader, and the beetling waiters from Profit. Furthermore, the Egyptian guy Hana had made an appearance. And they had, all of them — Dorothy included — frisked and frolicked in the shallows of an unnamed river. The sun, a white iron bolt; shone with splashes of naked skin. The river picked up speed, charged by the leaking sexual energy of the performers. More people — two of them Dorothy's nursery tormentors — had waded into the river with them. The sun bleached the *al fresco* squirmings, water washing light through everybody's skin, as Hannah floated on a beam of illumination, over to Hana, and like a ballerina she pirouetted, riding the light, bending at the waist and presenting the man with her rump. Even before his erection (the length and girth of which were surely exaggerated by the dream) moved into Hannah's body, a combination of delta tide and sunlight began to flay it raw.

The water dissolved the bodies, as though they were made of sugar. Tom appeared at Dorothy's waist, on bended knee; as he pressed his mouth to her sex to kiss her wetter, the water corroding the tongue from his face. It detached and moved inside her, crawling and slurping, moving on the track of her pubic bone. Before long, all had lost their identity – they were then all the same, shrunk by time and the tide into intersecting, merging pools of the wider, whitening, cresting river. Would they ever be the same again? *And who will I be when the river washes us out to sea? Who will I be today? Who am I today?*

Her bedside visitor confirms her ontological status – or tries to at any rate. 'How are you feeling, Dorothy?' asks Dr Savro, her turbaned GP. 'You've had quite a ride.'

'Where am I?'

The answer is obvious. 'You're in the hospital. How are you feeling?'

'Like I've been shot. A hospital in the Midlands, you mean?'

'No, the L and D.' Pausing briefly, he considers the wisdom of clarification. 'The Luton and Dunstable Hospital,' he says.

'I know what L and D means, thank you. How did I get here?'

'In an ambulance.' Savro sounds faintly puzzled, as if he can't quite believe the reality of her situation either. Or perhaps it's his patient's line of questioning that has caused him the confusion.

Struggling to sit up, Dorothy asks, 'What happened after I was shot?'

'Shot? I don't under-'

'Yes, shot, Doctor. Please don't make me repeat it. I'm asking you politely, what happened to me after I was shot? By the nurse.'

'You need to rest,' Savro replies. 'Why don't you go back to sleep?'

'Don't *you* start. I don't need to sleep,' Dorothy answers. 'The only thing I need is an answer when I ask you something directly. It's a matter of simple manners. In exactly the same way as *you* would expect an answer in your room at the surgery.' She chews on her words; they make contact but some only fizz and splutter, like fireworks. 'When you ask about alcohol consumption, for example.'

The Good Doctor smiles; and does so broadly (and apparently genuinely) that for the first time Dorothy notices a gold cap nested on one of his eye-teeth. 'I'm afraid, Miss Anthony, you've muddled me up with somebody else.'

'You're Dr Savro,' Dorothy insists briskly. 'There's nothing wrong with my memory, Doctor. You're my GP in the town of Leighton Buzzard, not more than fifteen miles from this very bed.'

'I'm Doctor Khan, Miss Anthony.' The smile dries up. 'Which I should have said right at the start; my apologies for *that* slip of manners. I'm afraid I don't know the practitioner you're referring to.'

Dorothy waits while her ears continue ringing; till the dizziness slips from her skull like evaporating mist.

'Miss Anthony? Are you all right?'

'Quite *un*-all right in fact, thank you very much,' she replies.

2.

'I love the limousine, you shouldn't have gone to so much trouble.'

'Yes, sorry about the car,' Hannah replies.

'Only joking. Which scrap metal merchant did you steal it from?'

'Yes-yes, Dolly, very good. You could walk home if you like,' Hannah tells the outpatient with a good-humoured-matron attitude. We will have our little jokes, will we not, Miss Anthony? Hannah lowers the sun visor on the driver's side and risks a joke. 'Or I could drop you at the bus stop if it's easier,' she says.

Fortunately Dorothy has not had her sense of humour excised during her two days under hospital observation. She cracks a smile, which leads into a fully-fledged laugh as Hannah feeds fifty-pence pieces into the metre to get out of the patients' car park.

'Seriously, where did you find it?' Dorothy asks.

Hannah explains the loan she has taken from Roy the mechanic – and the reasons for it. 'I spoke to him last night and he reckons it's the same thief who stole that old lady's car from him. The fit bird, as he puts it.'

'Maybe it was Hana,' says Dorothy.

'In drag.'

'It works for some!'

Both women laugh and chew on the same joke.

'That's enough about this accident-waiting-to-happen,' says Hannah. 'What about you? What happened to you, Dolly? I was so worried.'

The right turn out of the car park is impossible because of the roadworks on Luton Road; they will have to go left, and crawl with the other vehicles towards Lewsey Park and the swimming pool on the green.

'I'm assuming your silence has nothing to do with the splendour of seeing Lewsey Park again. Come on, Dolly, you must have assumed I'd ask you – you've been under medical watch for two days. What on earth is going on?'

'Swimming is one of the things I've been prescribed. Some healthy exercise, anyway.'

'Well that's fine, come to Tiddenfoot more often. That's not important right now.'

'I know. I'm working up to it. Remember once, Hannah, I told you a story. About when I was in my twenties and I swore you to secrecy. The one about the hill with the face.'

'Yes I remember. I never told a soul.'

'Didn't think for a moment you did. This'll sound crazy…'

'I've got one for you as well, a story, when we're ready. We all have.'

'Okay then. I think I went back there. It was almost physical,' Dorothy explains. 'No, it was physical. It's hard to get right, this. Let me try again. You know the two women who have been showing up everywhere I go? It was them in the stone hut on the hill – the same women. I saw them die, but here they are, nearly thirty years later. Try that on for crazy. I thought – I made a story in my head – I was on the bus, I thought they were taking me back.'

'The bus detoured to avoid Dunstable,' says Hannah.

'I know. I know that now. But when I was on it, we went north, north – much faster, I know now, faster than we could have done really. I was wondering where the police were. Of course the bus was doing nothing wrong; they tell me it was just a change of route for a week or so. It was in my head… but it also wasn't. It was real. The women were real. They want something.'

'Something from you? I agree. Just like that Hana wanker wants something from me and Sam. The question is what?'

'I can only think of one thing,' Dorothy replies. 'I think they want the baby back.'

IV.

A winking red light, the size of a grain of rice, informs Sam that her computer has successfully shut itself down for its daily nap. She rises and unhooks her second most expensive coat from the stand, where it nests with a crowd of cheaper outer garments.

Not that she wants to go home in the middle of the day, of course. Doing so feels like a failure, for which she is ashamed. All she can be sure of is this: there is something not quite right with her brain. Yesterday, after work, Sam had sat in a waiting room until her name was announced – but not by her own GP. Apparently Dr Jones was ill. Dr Savro was shouldering some of the Doctor's workload. He had seemed more concerned about paralyzed muscles in Sam's face (non-existent) than about memory loss, gaps in the patient's reality, or the fact that she kept *crying* all the time.

'Any history of stroke in your family?' he had asked.

No.

Savro had wanted to sign her off sick. 'Two weeks' rest should be the ticket,' he said. Sam replied that two weeks' rest wouldn't suit her – but on the contrary, here she is, walking past Reception and the security guard who speaks no English. Saying 'Goodbye!'

Jittery and with heart a-flutter, Sam crosses from the building – down the wide concrete steps, past the wheelchairs and deliveries ramps, past the cars whose spaces are reserved – to her vehicle.

The sun is out but it's been raining; a drain at the end of a row of cars gurgles ably, trying to suck moisture from a toupee thatch of vegetation. Sam blinks and frowns – not at all certain why the sight of the drain, or the sound of its drowning complaints, unsettle her so. Why is she nervous?

The car starts first time. It thrives on low-volume German efficiency. Sam waits a few seconds, then she taps the accelerator, just to hear the hearty roar of the engine. She depresses the clutch and engages first gear; she slides the safety belt around her body and clunk-clicks into the slot. More than ever she wishes to be away from this place

No other traffic moves in the car park, and within the minute she has moved onto the sliproad that will take her away from the business park.

She has several choices of route home – but does she really want to go home? Instinctively eschewing the option, straight ahead as she approaches the roundabout, that leads to the motorway, Sam indicates left. She'll take the road pointing towards Harpenden, then hang a right turn and drive through the villages – the scenic route. Maybe stop in the village for a white wine spritzer.

Half a mile down the hill towards Harpenden, she waits her turn. Vehicles approach from the opposite direction, travelling up the hill – even a tractor, chugging away. Will it make it up the incline? Sam imagines the driver panting, as if he is doing a Fred Flintstone and propelling the vehicle by leg power alone. The tractor passes and Sam, still indicating to turn right, attempts to catch a glimpse of the perspiring driver. She fails to do so. But as there are a few cars caught behind the tractor, and as Sam still can't turn, she follows the tractor in her rearview mirror.

Or this, at least, is her aim –

…but the rearview mirror is blocked. Sam gasps. A man's face fills the reflective glass. Sam can't breathe. Tea-coloured skin; eyes so dark they appear abyss-like. And of course she recognises him immediately.

Sam screams.

Hana has sat up on her back seat. Expression-free, he fills up all her available space.

Sam's heart starts to pound.

Hana says nothing.

Get out of the car, she tells herself; but a *roasting* sensation arrests her behind the safety belt. An unwilling participant in a process of being heated alive, Sam attempts to break the steering wheel with hand-strength alone. Her vision shuffles; it blurs; and she is back on a coach – back in the heat of a Cairo trip, years earlier.

He had a gun then, Sam remembers. What is to stop him owning one now?

The road is clear to proceed, and someone in a car behind her loses patience and sounds the horn.

'Drive, please,' says a voice lover-close to her ear: Sam can feel the breath tease those tiny earlobe-hairs, invisible to the naked eye. Her gut flexes; her body ripples through a spasm. The heat in her belly intensifies; she realizes that the mundane has morphed into the incandescent. A simple drive home is now at best – what? Revenge? Robbery, second act? Murder?

'If you'd be so kind,' the voice presses (the car-horn toots again) – and Sam blinks away the past – she even mutters 'Sorry' – and gives the car clutch and first. It pulls away grudgingly; Sam remembers the handbrake; it pounces into the turn, puppy off leash. Together, car, car-owner, and car-unwelcome-passenger, ease up to the speedcam-regulated 30. The village opens its arms in underhanging cloaks of unused fields, stained pomegranate-and-grey; Sam can smell inexpensive aftershave, applied with eye-stinging liberality, the sign either of unfamiliarity with the product or an attempt to please...

Maybe this won't be bad after all, Sam thinks, having no other way to rationalise the cologne's overuse. Cologne – and what else?

Food. More specifically, spice on his breath. He's already eaten.

I'm not being taken to dinner then, continues Sam's interior monologue; and the thought makes her laugh – just the once – it is so absurd.

'And indicate left, if you please,' says Hana.

Sam regards him again in the mirror – his blade-ish nose, his skin, the grey flakes in his hair, pushing the black coils into retreat from the temples – and says in something like wonderment, 'The *pub*?'

'Indicate, please.'

With a two-fingered slap Sam depresses the indicator stick and tells Hana: 'This was where I was going anyway. How could you have possibly known that?' – as they stone-crunch the car park behind The Sun. Gravel spits up against the hubcaps as they draw to a halt; it sounds like fat boiling. 'I asked you a question. How did you know where I was going?' But now she won't meet his eyes in the mirror; she stares ahead – at a wooden shed affair that houses either some pump or boiler, or the bins. Her eyes trace a patch on one of the vertical beams, where the paint is threadbare. She imagines that she can see the knots and patterns.

'Vacate the car, please.'

Making assumptions that feel sensibly cautious, Sam twists the key to silence the engine although she has not been told to do so. He's not having her car without a fight – or at least an explanation. The safety belt slides back to its carapace; on this occasion the buckle does not catch on the buttoned separation of her blouse, as often happens. Sam clenches the key bunch in her right hand: she knows that something solid inside a fist can increase the weight and force of a punch to a face. Cheating boxers used to secrete horseshoes inside their gloves. Sam opens the door, crushing her keys as though testing her own strength.

She climbs out, testing the taste of a sprint; but since she's in her work shoes, medium- if not high-heeled, she wouldn't make it far, she is sure of that. It is even with reasonable patience that she waits for her kidnapper to push forward the driver's seat and climb out. He resembles a chick struggling from an egg.

'All creatures want to fly towards the sun,' he puffs through this minor exertion. An enigmatic statement until Sam realizes that he's answering – or at least *might* be answering – her question of a few minutes earlier. *How had he known she would come here?*

Sam looks up at the white-painted side of the pub: in large green letters, THE SUN. *All creatures want to fly towards the sun*, her kidnapper had said. Surely he hadn't capitalized the final two words.

'That's the kind of thing Hannah would say,' Sam informs the man straightening up before her – taller than she remembers, even from recent acquaintance in the Profit restaurant.

'I *am* Hana,' is the response.

A brisk tally and visual frisk. The man is dressed in light-weight laceless shoes; his teak-coloured Chinos are crisply lined but dirty with food or newsprint. An emerald shirt flaps loose on his wiry frame. He looks tired.

'You know what I mean.'

He does not appear to be carrying a weapon.

'What you mean is not important. What *I* mean is import-ant.'

Sam sniffs. 'You think the world of yourself, don't you, mate?'

'Is important to *you*.'

This stops the train from leaving the station: in the face of male would-be supremacy Sam is apt to turn spiky quite quickly.

'Well what happens now?' she asks, subdued, a little daunted. She treats the keyring to a comforting good-luck squeeze.

Hana nods at the building. 'We all fly towards The Sun. Would you like a drink?'

'Are you serious?'

'It looks like rain again, as you are known to say in this country.'

Sam is flabbergasted. 'You kidnapped me to take me on a *date*?' she splutters.

'Kidnap is such an ugly word, Mrs Twyfield.'

'…How did you get in my car?'

Hana shrugs. 'You left the doors unlocked. The back isn't as roomy as it looks. How do your children fit in?'

'Leave my children out of this,' Sam snaps, but she feels the need for either further explanation – or for an additional patina of self-protection. She adds: 'They're away at boarding school.'

'I see. Shall we?'

Although Sam twists her heels in the gravel, she refuses to move from her spot. 'I wouldn't leave an eighteen thousand pound car unlocked, mate.'

'But you did.'

What better *ipso facto* can there be? In her current state of mind – well, it's hardly impossible. An instant of forgetfulness… the thief climbs in…

That's a point. Thief.

'If I give you what you want will you just leave me and my family alone?' she asks.

'I have no interest in your family, Sam.'

'Me then.' She notes his movement to her abbreviated first name. 'How much? How much to fuck off out of my life? I'll write you a cheque.' She prefers the *Sam* to *Mrs Twyfield*. She has always detested her married surname.

'I'm financially secure,' Hana tells her, somewhat smugly.

'You don't look it,' Sam retorts, bitchy and unnecessary.

'I have a pillow and a roof.'

'Then how do you think you're going to take me for a drink?'

'I didn't say I was paying.'

'Charming. I've been out with men like you.'

'No you haven't. Shall we go in? I'm quite sure that was just a spot of rain that I felt.'

As they stroll, as though comfortable, towards The Sun's front door, facing the road, Hana adds, 'Besides, there isn't a commodity you can offer me, Sam. It's what I have to give you that's important. This I've finally understood.'

'Which is what?'

'Your life story.'

V.

1.

Dorothy is unwell. A decision is made that a meeting should go ahead without her: a decision-making process led by Sam, 'fresh' from her insightful time with Hana the thief. 'We have lots to discuss,' is Sam's sober summation, on the phone to each of the friends.

The venue chosen is Profit, back in Milton Keynes. Even though it's not her turn, Sam is keen to point out that this month the meeting will be her treat. She wants to spend; it will make her feel better.

'Should we feel guilty, do you reckon?' Sabrina asks, 'not inviting Dorothy, I mean. It doesn't feel quite the same without Dorothy.'

'No, I agree: there are no insane fiction fans waiting outside to fuck up my car,' says Hannah, who misses Dorothy and whose wit is sometimes lost inside its overcoat of sarcasm. Picking up the vast menu that she's been handed by a waiter who called her 'my darling' (a flattering comment, she had thought, until he went on to call everyone 'my darling' while handing out the menus), she regrets the remark.

'I *did* invite her. She's being taken care of,' Sam replies. 'We have things to go into. I feel pale. Do I look pale?'

'I know…' Sabrina says. 'No you don't look pale,' she adds, not taking the bait – the bait that Sam has something that she urgently wants to blab about.

'Being taken care of by who?' Annette asks.

'Your dad, for one,' is the answer.

'He can't hardly take care of himself.'

'That's as it may be. He's got the job. Desperate times and all that.'

'Is anyone ready to order?' asks Hannah.

'What's the rush?' Sam wants to know.

'You know this place, they charge by the minute.'

2.

Hannah chooses wings. It seems symbolic of something; then she realizes that it's chicken wings and chickens cannot fly. Restaurants don't serve eagle – not even restaurants as wacky as Profit.

Sam plumps for the lamb pie. 'That sounds lovely. Nice as pie,' she tries to quip, her heart not really being in it. Her heart has not been in much since Thursday… when Hana the Egyptian thief carjacked her – and then broke her heart.

Annette chooses a Swiss Burger and Sabrina a salad, in deference to her weight and where she longs to keep it. And although diets is a somnolent subject, I admire her dedication to this particular cause. Not that she needs to diet, of course, but that's a different matter.

'What would Dorothy order?' Hannah wonders.

'A steak!' Annette emphasises. 'Medium rare. Lots of onions.'

'I think you're right,' says Sabrina.

'Here's to Doo-Doo!' Sam adds, raising her glass of exorbitant white. The massive menus have new steak selections. 'Would that be the Nervousness Steak or the Steak Libel?'

'Dorothy should write a piece about this place,' says Hannah.

'Maybe she is already.' Sam shrugs.

It's in the air and it's in the noise, the knowledge that they must discuss Dolly. It won't discuss itself; they must make it happen. No one is exactly sure how.

Having taken a long, refreshing glance at the ceiling, Hannah cleans and moistens her fingers on a wipette. Her friends wait. Trays in hand, the waiters wait. The *restaurant* waits, or so it seems (even the businessmen have quit their blather). It is Hannah who must step up. When I question Sabrina later – or interrogate her more like – it appears that Hannah moves slowly and carefully through the jungle of salient points. The resume is ninety per cent reportage; ten per cent emotional embellishment. But that's okay; that's a pretty good ratio, in the right direction. The quartet is suitably poleaxed.

'I can hardly imagine,' is how one of Hannah's emotional, discursive ingredients begins, 'how she must have felt carrying that child for mile after mile. Neither of them knowing where they were – not a clue.'

'How far did she carry him?' asks Annette, wiggling her smudged digits in the fingerbowl. She reaches for her napkin – the heavy material, a broken wing, of a white the inversion of blindness. She wipes her hands dry as Hannah answers:

'A couple of miles, she reckons. And in the dark. Until a truck picked her up on the country road.'

'Took her to town?' asks Sam.

Hannah nods her head. 'But the baby was really sick by then. It came on quickly – coughing like a hound was the way Dolly put it. She's not sure if he even survived... That's why she's seeing these women all over the place, I reckon. Not that I'm an analyst.'

'You surprise us, babe,' says Sam.

'But don't you think it's possible? Guilt? Repression? Come back to haunt her... There's no point *pecking* at me, Sam.'

'I'm not!'

'Because I'm not saying I have all the solutions – I'm only

trying.' She utters this retort in a tone of Sisyphean weariness. While we must imagine Sisyphus happy, pushing his rock, we are encouraged to imagine Hannah sad, gnawing on a chicken wing, her eyes drifting towards the ceiling fan, which gyrates slowly, stirring the expensive food aromas for the rest of Profit's diners to share.

The women are upstairs in the restaurant. Two tables away, a quartet congregation of suits, stretched either across chair-backs or their owners' fat shoulders; the conversation is business then football then Amsterdam – and its best-value brothels, pound for pound. From the vocal silence at the women's table, Hannah, Sam, Annette and of course Sabrina (from whom I gather so much of this stuff) are delivered into the men's patter and chatter, their swagger and swirl. As we all do, the women compare the quality of conversation – and find it lacking. Sabrina tells me it both enraged and engaged her, to listen to the businessmen's hollow blatherscythe, so much so that she vowed to up her game. In the history of their monthly meetings there has rarely been a silence – seldom a time when words stand still, stand on guard – and now, in this month of November, a silence cannot be permitted to survive.

Sabrina says, 'Shall we start again? Does anyone agree we need a total recap. Need to share our own individual stories. Not that I *have* one yet, unless you count the bugs someone sent Tom.'

The other three give her a strained look. Non-communication looms again – so soon after the previous outbreak – like a recurring disease.

Hannah saves them from the silence pandemic – and Sabrina from further scrutiny and embarrassment. 'Well, don't feel bad...' Hannah gestures to Sam with her bald, finger-length bone with its new spit-shined commas of sucked gristle. '...Sam and I don't have one each. We're doing sharesies.'

Sam dips her head towards the table; her hair shags her eyes. 'Actually, I've got a solo one for you as well.' She looks up again. 'I met him on Thursday.'

'Who, the thief?' asks Annette.

'No, the President. Of course the thief. His name is Hana.'

'We know that,' says Sabrina. 'What do you mean you *met* him?'

'Yeah, what do you mean by that?' Hannah adds, unable to dissolve her anger in the question. Into a small pot of garlic dip Hannah absentmindedly dunks the chicken bone that she's been wielding for a few seconds, temporarily forgetful of the fact that she has already sheared the cooked white flesh from it. Her eyes tighten with hatred. It is not fair that she's not the first to know such a thing.

'Sorry, Han,' says Sam, reading her mood and mind both. 'I've been grappling with this for two days. Thursday night I was too shocked and then too drunk to call. Last night I didn't want to disturb you on a Friday night, in case you were busy.'

'Yeah, with all that salsa dancing I do,' Hannah spits. Parenthetically realising her error with the chicken wing, she retires the dead soldier to the parade ground of its already fallen comrades. 'I was at my computer last night. Working. Final draft of fasting. Sent it to the commissioner at eleven-oh-six. I had a ball.'

'Don't be cross, babe.'

'*Cross?*'

Annette interrupts. 'What happened, Sam? With the thief.'

'He was waiting for me in my car, I must have left the doors open. Unlocked, I mean, not actually open. I've no choice but to believe that, have I? He lay in the back and waited for me. I think…'

'You didn't *see* him?' asks Sabrina, who has not finished her plate but has finished eating.

Sam shrugs. 'I was on autopilot, I was going home early ill. I just didn't – didn't *see* him there.'

'He was prepared to wait for you,' Annette adds, 'until the end of the working day.'

The reality of this gusts across the table; it's a wonder the saucers and fingerbowls do not dance in this river. And there's a new aroma, too. Of overwhelming cologne, worn by a different waiter from the one who took their order and delivered their dishes, who has approached with an illusive smile on his lips. He has daubed so much cologne on his body that you might think he exemplified the walking dead, smelling oversweet to fool the nose as to the decay beneath his cummerbund. The waiter asks, 'Is everything all right with your meals, my delicious beauties?'

A chorus of affirmatives and compliments. Only after he's retreated does Hannah grumble, 'Probably itemise asking us that on the bill.'

Sam is snappy. 'Don't worry about the bloody bill, I said it's my treat so don't spoil it… The man smells like Hana did.'

Hannah opens her mouth to speak, instantly believing the slight is against her; but they all understand the connection. Hannah plucks up her last remaining wing and dips it – the pepper sauce this time – in a desultory fashion .For the moment she is too tired for words.

'Said he'd give me my life story,' Sam says, 'and he did. Just not the one I remember.'

3.

'We remember it differently,' says Sam. 'The incident on the tour bus. That was the bit that was hardest to come to terms with.. Which one of us punched him, Han?'

'I did. You know I did.'

'I *thought* you did. Now I'm not so certain.'

'Because he told you that *you* did? What difference does it make?'

'We remember it differently, that's what I'm saying.'

'And I repeat, what frigging difference does it make?'

'Why would he travel all these miles unless he had a point to make?' Sam asks.

Hannah is defensive. 'I don't *doubt* he has a point to make, but unless you're going to come to it quickly I can't say I'm really too fussed about it. We remember it differently. Okay, fair do's; I can live with that. But I know it was me. And not because I want to be the heroine of the story or anything like that, but because that's the way it happened.'

'We remember it differently,' says Sam, looking down.

'Stop *saying* that! It doesn't make an iota of difference.'

'I think it does. What was he trying to do?'

'Steal our handbags and purses. Does he disagree with that bit, too?'

Sam nods her head. 'And so do I.'

This admission leaves Hannah flustered for a moment. 'This is rich. Go on, then. What other reason? Why was he there? To *give* us money.'

'He wouldn't take your money, remember?'

'I insulted his honour and pride, or some shit. I embarrassed him. And he was wise to want to cut his losses. You haven't answered my question.'

'He says he was there to protect us,' Sam replies. 'He's come a long way to tell us that, Hannah. Why would he bother?'

'I give up on this round of charades. You tell me. Why would he bother?'

'Because he thinks his god has given him a job to do,' says Sam.

'And let me get this straight. This *job* happens to be to protect us. Protect just you and me, or does he have loftier ambitions?'

'Like what?'

Annette steps in. 'Ladies – please – let's keep this civil. We're having a nice meal.'

'No we're not, Annette,' Hannah adds.

'Well you ate it!'

'I'm not talking about the food! I'm talking about the way we're still parrying away from this idiot all these years later; and for what reason? Protect us from *what*?'

'From death, is how he put it.'

'And you can't see the contradiction, Sam? He had a Beretta.'

'…What's that?' Sam asks her.

'Are you serious? It's a gun, Sam. The gun he held is called a Beretta.'

'There wasn't a *gun*.'

Silence squares up to these words – a few seconds of silence.

'Sam, the man had a gun,' Hannah explains with what sounds like strained patience. 'That was how he convinced people to let go of their purses and wallets.'

'If he did that at all. Which is the bit I'm not sure about, babe.'

'I am honestly getting worried now, Sam; please tell me you're mucking about. He was a thief – he probably still is – and he got on our bus and told us to give him money. We thought at the time that it was for a drug habit, but that might've been just our bluster. But you can't have forgotten the *gun*. Seriously, Sam.'

'The whole thing's foggy, babe. Hana told me things about my *life* – not just that day in Cairo. How would he know those things? Why would he ask about my children?'

'Because he's a creepy weirdo?' Annette answers.

'Well he might be. But he kept saying he was put on the earth to protect us, that's all I'm saying. Protect *us* – you and me, Han.'

4.

True to form, it is late when Sabrina arrives home. Sabrina's returning home late is at least *one* thing I can count on her for.

Being angry is another.

'What the hell is up with this carpet, Tom?' she demands by way of an introduction.

'What about it?'

'The *food* on it, what about it. Would it hurt you to push the bloody Hoover around?'

'Actually it might. I'm signed off sick with a bad back in case it's escaped your notice.'

'It doesn't hurt your back to vacuum clean.'

'Have *you* tried it? Try it, be my guest. The fucking thing's in the cupboard.'

'Don't swear at me.'

'What happened?'

Sabrina flumps in the blue rocking chair; it dandles her on its upholstered knee. Layers of stress fatigue lift from her face like makeup sponged off.

'What happened with what?'

'With your day,' I answer. 'Would you like a glass of wine?'

'Oh, you saved me some. Yes, please.'

'Of course I saved you some. Red or white?'

She answers white. Her breathing is slightly laboured – either because of anger or frustration or me, I can't tell. She says nothing else until I wait on her with a brimming chilled glass. She sips with birdy pecks.

'And I've done chicken,' I tell her.

'Is it my birthday? I ate at lunch, remember.'

'That was lunch. It's nearly nine. Where've you been, by the way?'

'Out. Chicken and what?'

'Rice or potatoes. You choose.'

'You haven't *started*? I know you like skinny birds, Tom, but this is ridiculous.' She gets up from the chair and paces, not looking at me.

Trying to push the notion from my head I say, 'I repeat: what happened? To put you in this foul mood, I mean.'

'I am not in a foul mood,' she answers with slowness, weight on each syllable.

The air in the flat swarms thickly with plump accusation. And the idea swells inside my head, that I do not know who this woman is any more.

Wordlessly (still not a glance in my direction), Sabrina carries her glass into the bathroom, pausing only in the hall to open the boiler cupboard door and to flick the switch to boost the hot water. So that's that then, is it? She'll retire into the bathroom, she will linger in the suds. So I *do* know her, after all. She is about to bathe (and that's the last I'll see of her tonight, most likely). Through slightly damp vision I watch the space where she has been.

Is it my birthday? she asked me. It stings at my conscience that for the moment I cannot recall that date. The memory is frisky and energetic of what we actually *did* on her last birthday – the blissfully spasmodic toil of buggery on the rocking chair, its shoulders clapping against the cream-painted wall while the Chinese takeaway congealed in a series of aluminium craters on the table. But if you were to put a pistol to my neck veins and demand of me to name the *date*, I could not have done better than to pluck something from the oxygen...

Sabrina is singing while the water belts out a Lou Reed

Metal Machine Music shield of noise. If I can decode her words correctly, she is warbling the words 'Jesus, you hurt me…' Is this the name of the song? I don't know.

The telephone ringing gives me a reason for action. No, I don't want to answer it, but the fact that it wants me to provides me with something to do.

I confirm my name when it is spoken to me as a question.

'This is Mandy from the College? From Personnel?'

Mandy, I want to say, you sound like a guy. 'Mandy, do you know what the time is? It's after nine,' I answer on her behalf.

'I'm working late. But I've been trying to reach you for a number of days now.'

'I've been right here, Mandy,' I answer.

'Have you had anyone else mention troubles getting through to you?'

'I can't say I have, Mandy. But then, no one really calls me much these days.'

'I see. Well, anyway, I was calling for an update. How's your back?'

'My back is not mending.' *And I am not coming back to work*, I fall short of adding. *So don't bother shooting me with any psychobabble.* 'You received my sick note, I hope. I'm still signed off. Everything's all right, isn't it?'

'Yes, we received it. You sound a little angry, Tom.'

'I'm not angry, Mandy.'

'Tell me about your day,' she says.

'Excuse me?'

'Your day. Tell me about your day.'

'I want to tell you,' I answer, 'that my day is not really any of Personnel's business, is it? I've paid taxes all my adult life and now I'm off work with a bad back and anxiety.'

'I'm only making conversation,' Mandy chuckles. It makes

me think of something heavy landing – landing in a lake – causing massive ripples and altering everything. The voice has just got deeper in tone.

Still I don't get it – call me slow on the uptake. It's not Mandy, I know that much – or my unconscious knows that much at any rate – and it's not the College either. Who is it?

'I don't have time for chit-chat. I was just about to go to bed...'

'You daft bugger,' a man's voice laughs into my ear.

'Roy?'

'You daft *bugger*... Try again!'

The voice listens to my silence – and reads it. I cannot speak, but I do not drop the receiver; my grip is frightened tighter still, if anything.

'Yeah it's me,' says the voice of Uncle Stephen. 'How've you been? You daft *bugger.*'

Part Two: The Lunge

An effective way to deal with predators is to taste terrible.
    Unknown

He that toucheth pitch shall be defiled therewith.
    Ecclesiasticus xiii. 1.

Forgiveness doesn't come with a debt.
    Mary Chapin Carpenter, 'I Take My Chances'

Window Pain

I.

1.

As November slides our travellers down, down towards the gaping hole that appears at the end of the year, *every* year, it is a winter both of discontent and of joyful recuperation.

Take Dorothy, for example. Well she might watch with suspicion as Christmas decorations and chocolate selection boxes sprout in the shops like garlands of fungus, but at least she makes a go of her own healing. Happy she might not be, but she takes to her new regime of swimming and walks along the canal. She needs to get healthy again – her mind as much as her body. Though she still cannot believe it didn't happen quite as she remembers it. That there *was* no gun wound. There *was* no Midlands trip…

It was all in her head – and with luck and a following wind, it will all blow over on to the page. She will write it down.

2.

'I've 'ad 'em *all*,' declares the old man Patrick. 'Hippocampus disorder, corrupting me memory function. *That* were nasty.' The old man buckles under the weight of unspent laughter. With a complicated sniff and a wipe of the brow he continues, saying: 'Monotonic decrease. Pre-eclampsia. Spondyloarthropathies. Acerbic aciobathy. Cerebral palsy. Dyspraxia. Protein deficiency, osteoporosis, and spasticity. *Throat* cancer. Iron absorption issues. Arthritis; cerebral palsy; prostheses twitch; kidney malfunction. Nerve injuries; polio; cornea transplant itchiness; dysarthria. Hip

replacements; Hurler Syndrome; borderline personality disorder...*That* were a bugger and no mistake. Acute stress disorder...'

We are at the swimming pool.

Dorothy is happy. She is happy to listen; happy with this
friendship. Although she has known Patrick for years, it has only
been over the last few weeks (she believes) that they've grown
closer. She likes his stories. She likes everyone's stories – true
enough – but she has always had a soft spot for the stories of our
elders and betters.

3.

'I found a copy of one of my books in a charity shop once.
The Tight Blue Tide.' Dorothy fondles peonies into an aesthetically
pleasing position, but not in her garden. Her garden is a tidy
rectangle of imbecilic green simplicity – and it perches on a windowsill in her flat. No; Dorothy is in a classroom, with Hannah;
they are being taught flower arrangement. They stand next to
one another, facing their own receptacles – Dorothy's being a tall
thin vase made of navy blue glass.

'And being the egotistical bitch I happen to be, I picked it
up – searching for clues. Guess what was inside. I remember it
word for word. *To Lesley, Happy 21ˢᵗ Birthday, Love Mum.* Then three
exes for kisses. I thought—'

'How ungrateful?'

'How *fucking* ungrateful! Woman gives her daughter a pres-
sie and now it's raising money for spina diffida. I was furious.'

'It's a good cause.' Hannah on the other hand is working
with a spherical orange vase. She has inserted a loose ball of
floral netting inside it and stretched it until it pushes against the
interior surfaces.

Dorothy hasn't looked up from her as-yet rudimentary display. 'You're missing the point...' she says, then twigs. 'Oh, go on

then, laugh. But I was *cross*, Han.'

'Dolly, *anything* could've happened to that daughter!'

'*Could* have.'

'What? You'd be in favour of full reading histories before a book was accepted for resale?' Hannah asks. Now that she has her netting in place she doesn't know what to do. She is loath to ask her tutor, Charlie, for assistance; she believes him to be a letch, and besides, his breath's been contaminated with onions.

'I would,' Dorothy answers.

The class is on the Bletchley campus of Milton Keynes College, twenty minutes from where they live; but to Hannah, at this moment, home seems like a plane ride away. The flowers for the students' usage are aromatic, fresh; their scents have mingled into a soup thrown together by a reckless chef, too carefree with conflicting spices. The room stinks of dying flora. Hannah takes stock of the shared apparatus on the table she shares. There is waterproof tape and waterproof clay; there is a pan melt glue pot, which she remembers is to prepare pan melt glue, and pan melt glue secures the ends of silk flowers in foam when making large arrangements. Fine; but this doesn't help her now. There are anchor pins, floral wires, floral foam and candle cups; and of course the wreaths of flowers themselves, four bunches per table, to mingle and arrange as the students see fit. This is the mock exam, and Hannah feels it in her irritated bowel, a curl of panic.

'Charlie's busy,' she answers. 'We're supposed to know all this by now.'

Dorothy snorts. 'Forgive us for having lives outside flower arranging.'

'But the exam's next week.'

'Were you thinking of putting it on your CV?'

'I already have,' Hannah says. 'Charlie?' she calls.

The teacher is at the back of the room, dealing with another student – the sole male learner enrolled. Charlie acknowledges the cry for assistance with a raised forefinger denoting *patience, my child*, and a supple writhing of his vile facial hair.

Dorothy answers absently. 'Shall we go to the pub after this?'

'*Natuerlich. Angeboren.*'

4.

The nearest public house to the Bletchley campus is The Enigma – named in deference to the ciphering machine used to decrypt top secret messages during the Second World War, and to Bletchley Park, the site where successful codebreaking took place. There is nothing enigmatic about the pub itself. It's a typical south-east England boozer, with a flowing trade in transit tonight; and it's the place where Charlie has decided to take his students for their pre-exam social drink, much to the horror of Hannah and Dorothy, who wanted to sip alone.

'You can *do* it next week,' his moustache has finished telling the seven members of the class who have turned up for a quick one. 'It's all about go-getting! About *faith*, team! Faith in yourself! Faith in your learning. But above all… faith in the *flower*.'

'It's a flower exam,' Hannah's saying to Dorothy. 'He made it sound like we were doing PhD orals in astrophysics.'

Dorothy takes taste of her vodka and lime. 'Do you know, I'm more nervous about next week than I was when I took my Finals!'

'Me too. It doesn't help having a bloody *spin doctor* for a teacher.' Hannah is halfway down her second Diet Coke (no ice) because she's chauffeuring them both.

'What did you put on your happy sheet?'

'The Course Evaluation? I gave him five out of five, all the way down. I'll go to Hell.'

'Why on earth did you do that?'

'In case he has any say in our final grades. I didn't want him angry.'

'Look at him over there. I think he's as nervous as we are.'

'Chatting to Malcolm, you'll notice. Has he stopped perving on women, do you think?' She wishes she'd accepted the offer of ice, her second Coke is breath-warm. 'What do you think they're talking about, engrossed like that?'

Dorothy's answer is immediate. 'Flowers.'

5.

'Endothelial dysfunction,' Patrick thinks aloud. 'It's a physiological dysfunction of normal biochemical processes, the ones done by the endothelium…'

Patrick opens his eyes and realizes that he is talking to himself.

Yesterday, at the pool at the Tiddenfoot Centre, it had been different. Patrick had felt as far from lonely as it was possible to feel, all because of his new friend Dorothy.

'You're a breath of fresh air, you are, Dolly,' Patrick had said – and now he reflects on these words – is it with embarrassment? 'No you are. It's been so lovely having you here around me, I can't thank you enough. It's been a long time since I could talk to someone about anal polyps without them squirming. I can't with Annette.'

'I should think not!'

'Talk to her about anything. She's only interested in me for me money.'

'I rather doubt that, Patrick. Annette loves you.'

'Loves me wallet more like. But you, girl. You! I dunno…'

'You can talk to me about whatever you want to, Patrick.'

'I know it. It's been an eye-opener, finding out there's still people like you in the world. It's been a while, Dolly.'

'What has?' Dorothy asked.

'Since I've had any *joy*,' Patrick resumes now, a note – is it guilt? – in his voice. 'Not since Annette's mother.' In the same way that Annette does, Patrick omits the last word of the sentence. (The word is *died*, Dorothy coaxes him silently.) Patrick chuckles.

'Most interesting for a while's been enjoying the company of a fly,' he says, 'that lands on me forearm. I try to pretend it's always the same one. I call her Patricia; no idea why.'

With a smile on her face Dorothy regards the man's forearms, exposed as they are by his habit of rolling up his pristine white shirtsleeves. She blinks at his tattoos. Time- and tan-blurred though the naval tattoos on his forearms have been rendered, the arms still appear strong. On a whim, an impulse, Dorothy leans closer and places her hands on them.

'You don't need Patricia the Fly,' she states confidently. Now. Are we going to chat or are we going to swim?'

'Can't we do both?'

'Not unless your aim is to drown.'

'It was once. But not now.' Annette's father copies Dorothy's dopey grin – just in time to see it fold into something tighter; a parcel of remorse.

'I'm sorry. Have I brought back something sad?' Dorothy asks.

'Only in order for me to kill it,' Patrick answers. 'Rather than let it kill me…' Indeed, he seems perfectly chipper at the association. 'I don't swim with them sharks anymore. Refuse.'

'Sharks?'

'Depression, Dolly. It's like a shark, don' you think? Or maybe you've been lucky.'

'No; I know depression. I just – I've never put the two

things together.'

'Believe me. Always hunting out emotional blood; sniffing around; never sleeping. Then, when you think you've stopped your panic-splashing enough for the bugger to go elsewhere, he's back for a clamp on your bollocks.'

Dorothy laughs. 'That's one way of looking at it,' she admits.

'Sorry. I forget we live in politically correct times. It can chew on your fanny just as well. I didn't mean to sound sexist, girl.'

'No offence taken,' Dorothy replies.

6.

After months of silence I have received not one but two communiqués from Stephen, the first on the last day of November. He missed my birthday but I forgive him.

'You daft bugger,' Stephen says to me. 'You're barking up the wrong tree.'

'You don't say. Why not be an angel and enlighten me,' I reply.

'Be an angel – that's good. That's *good*, Tom. 'You've never been known for your GSOH. Ask your mother.'

'...What happened to your speech impediment?' I ask. 'You're clear as a bell, mate.'

'You get the hang of it,' Stephen answers offhandedly, and he *sniffs* – right there into my ear – down the line. 'Now listen, Tom, I might not have long. It's tiring, for one thing. Now are you listening, you daft bugger? This is an important bit.'

'*Of course* I'm listening,' I answer tetchily.

'I don't see it all... but there's something about Roy and a set of keys, right?'

'He thinks someone must have got hold of his keys – they

got into his garage and stole a car. Well, borrowed a car, as it turns out, but at the time we didn't know–'

'Tom. It was something about a party. He lost his keys at a *party*, Tom… Ask him about the party…'

I decide to do so immediately. He has recorded a new message for his answering service – one in his poshest tones – and I say, 'It's Tom. Could you call me back, mate?'

The next morning Stephen calls again. This time he comes to me in the sort of dream that you refuse to believe is any such thing.

Sabrina has left for work. *Sabrina* does not take days off sick, irrespective of the fact that she needs them more (if I'm honest) than I do.

Sabrina climbs into clothes that marry her ambitions with the office in which she will no doubt achieve them. I am not always in favour of her work look. Today I am.

Today she could pass for a princess on hospital handshake duty.

She's gone by eight. I have a series of roll-ups and a glass of exotic red. Then a beer. By half past I am in receipt of a decent buzz and a whole carpet of events to unroll for the day, should I care to do so.

So my dead uncle Stephen – who might or might not have committed suicide (he won't tell) gets in touch at the tail-end of November, when I'm good and exhausted by the progress of the year. When I can't even judge if the cheese in my fridge is real, never mind anything else.

Half past nine. Sabrina is gone, in her Sunday best. She has a meeting today with clients. I don't know any more details than that. I swear – sometimes I don't feel I even know what my partner does for a living.

7.

'Where have you been?' I ask him out loud.

His answer gives me the giggles – I cannot help it.

Perusing is what he says.

8.

I want to know about the murder on Dunstable Downs.

Oooh and me both.

Cut the shit, Stephen. You did it, didn't you? And why's your impediment come back again, all off a sudden?

My impediment?

Your 'ooh' thing instead of 'who'?

He pauses. Whether it's for effect or for necessity I am not quite sure.

What murder?

The one you did, you cunt! I scream at him – though this is all inside my head.

Nort me… he replies.

I take the reins on my temper. *Fucking talk to me, cunt,* I insist.

9.

There wasn't a murder on Dunstable Downs, he tells me.

The transmission ends.

When Roy returns my call, he claims to know nothing about any party. 'My party days are over, Tom-mate,' he contends, even after I ask him if he's sure.

Then this transmission also ends, and I'm in need of another drink.

II.

1.

'I think…' Dorothy starts.

Sensing the twang and tautness of her caution, Patrick aims to soothe the environment. 'Speak your mind, girl,' he says.

'I think we've developed enough of an understanding – between us, I mean – to speak honestly. You've been able to tell me about the physical ailments you've endured…'

'With pleasure,' he adds with pride.

Again, Dorothy stalls, but this time not long enough to prompt further encouragement. 'What about mental ones?'

Patrick clutches the head of his walking stick in cupped hands: the protective fashion of a bluesman wielding his harp. He tests the familiar grip for size and says, 'Mental instability, eh girl? Yeah, I've got a story or two. Where shall we start?'

'With hallucinations,' Dorothy answers. 'So clear you think they're real.'

'But they *are* real.'

'You know what I mean. *Really* real,' says Dorothy.

Patrick is not trying to be difficult or pedantic, however. 'Know exactly what you mean, Dolly. Sort you finish and can't shrug off; they stay with you, like constipation.'

Dorothy smiles. 'Not exactly the comparison I would have made but I suppose so.'

'They've got a lot in common, believe it or not.'

Their conversation is interrupted. 'Are you lovebirds ready to go home?' asks Annette, approaching their table in the sports centre canteen. She wears a blue tracksuit; she has been supervising in the gym this afternoon – an extra shift on what should have been a day off. Kieran called in sick this morning with 'man flu', leaving the centre a member of staff short. 'Hannah's just drying her hair; she won't be a mo.'

'Ready when you are,' Annette's dad replies. 'Grateful for the taxi service as ever.'

Annette has sat down before she weighs up the silence. 'Sorry if I interrupted something,' she offers.

'Such as what?' Dorothy asks her.

'Well *I* don't know. What were you two yakking about?'

Dorothy is reluctant to be honest but Patrick answers immediately. 'Mental elf if you must know.' His accent is slightly coarser when he addresses his daughter, Dorothy has already noticed: the aitches more defiantly dropped; the glottal stops paraded with paramilitary precision. 'Remember when I went bonkers?'

The question rings in Dorothy's ears – it's like a challenge to Annette. 'Which time?' she asks.

'You guys ready?' is a different question posed at the same time. The voice, of course, belongs to Hannah; she has emerged into the pulsing light and the chlorine perfume familiar to swimming pool cafeterias. Hannah's locks are shiny and damp. She tousles them impatiently as she offers an explanation: 'The hairdryer's bust.'

The fields beyond the car park, which lead to the football pitch and tennis courts, eventually the canal, are as white as a page. In the bleak mid-distance, a figure de-sexed by the intervening metres and by what the wind's whipped up for an aerial dance, is the only black blot on the landscape. Annette sees him, too.

'What's he doing, do you reckon?' she mutters.

Patrick and Hannah have made good their catch-up. 'What

are we looking at?' Hannah asks.

Annette explains. 'That guy in the field, just standing there.'

'Walking his dog, probably,' says Patrick.

'What *dog*, Dad? Can *you* see a dog?'

'No – but then again, me ole peepers ain't what they used to be either. Cataracts I've had; conjunctivitis; detached retinas...'

'Shut up, Dad,' whispers Annette.

Hannah wants to be the voice of reason. 'He's probably got lost taking a detour from the canal,' she says. 'He'll catch his death. So will we if we don't move.'

'But that's my point,' Annette argues. 'Why doesn't *he* move?'

'Pharaoh's Corneal Disorder,' Patrick witters on, in the groove now – feeling the pulse of recital. 'Amazon eyelash poisoning.'

'Not *now*, Dad,' says Annette. 'If I didn't know better, I would swear that fella's watching us.'

'You're confident it's a he, are you?' Dorothy answers.

Annette nods her head. 'Yes. Yes I am.'

'Let him watch,' Hannah decides. 'He can watch me getting into my car. Watch me getting warm if he so chooses. To hell with the prick. I can't be out here with wet hair.' With which declaration she makes a move towards the hire vehicle from Bible Street Cars. 'Anyone need a lift home?' she calls over her shoulder.

Dorothy raises her voice. 'Hannah, you're missing Annette's point. *Turn around* when I'm talking to you. *Jesus.*'

Hannah does as she's told. Although she pirouettes with grace (her trainers squeak a fanshape into the lightly-settled snow), and although she wears a smile for camouflage or for padding, when she says 'Yes, *Miss*,' there is bitterness and hostility in her throat.

'And what might *Annette's* point be, Dolly?' Hannah demands.

Attempting to lighten a mood, Annette plays her ditzy card and says, 'Yeah, Dolly. What might my point be?'

'Don't shilly-shally, Annette.' This, surprisingly, is from Patrick. 'Let's not pretend we don't know who that is, watching us.' He points off into the alphabet of frost-laden gusts, there to interpret for anyone with the right reading glasses.

'Well, will someone tell *me*?' Hannah pleads.

'Who else would it be?' Dorothy starts.

'That's Kolko,' Annette realizes.

2.

Although the snow has not had much time to work with, the effort it has exerted so far makes for a slow progress for Annette and Hannah as they cross the field to where Kolko waits and watches. Very briskly it was decided that Dorothy should be parked in the hire car, with Patrick, the heater rattling.

Annette arrives at a state of comprehension first, but only by a second or two. By the time she and Hannah are close enough to recognize that the figure is too young to be a policeman, Hannah has worked it out too. 'That can't be Kolko,' the latter remarks. Annette pushes on with her thighs beginning to burn. She is physically fit but this is unfamiliar exertion; her breath is slightly laboured.

'Hello James,' she says to the boy. 'It's me – Annette. Emil's mum.'

James has not moved a hair's breadth. He has watched the two women draw closer, then near. 'Hello,' he says back.

'What are you doing out here in the cold, James?' Annette asks.

'Waiting.'

'Waiting for what? Or who?'

'My dad,' the boy answers simply. 'This is where I last saw him: somewhere over here, I'm not sure exactly. I was by the canal at the time, you see.'

'I see,' Annette tells him. 'But do you think it's a good idea to be out in this weather? Even if you *have* got a nice scarf on.'

James shrugs. The scarf writhes as the mouth beneath it smiles. 'This is my dad's scarf. I can smell him on it.'

Hannah needs to take control. Disappointment and concern are conjoined within her – disappointment that she hasn't yet encountered the elusive P.C. Kolko; concern that if they stand here much longer, Dolly and Patrick will have to send out the St Bernard with the barrel of rum round his neck.

'James? My name's Hannah. My car's parked back there and if we all squeeze in I can give you a lift home. Unless someone's coming to pick you up.'

The boy shakes his head.

'Right. Shall we go then?' says Hannah. She is the only one who moves.

'She tried to wash him out of the scarf,' James continues.

Annette seems content with the conversation. 'Who did? Sal? Your mum did?'

'Yes. Sal,' James repeats. 'I'd better call her Sal. She's not my mother anymore.'

'Why not, James? Have you had a nasty argument?'

James shrugs.

'Can we talk about this on the way home?' Hannah interrupts. 'Only, they've got the heater on and it might drain the battery on that old jalopy.'

'But water is sad because it's a circle,' James continues, no longer regarding his interlocutors; his gaze has strayed skyward. There is going to be a snowstorm.

Tough love is what's needed, Hannah realizes. 'I'm taking your dad and Dorothy home,' she begins, thinking that if Annette can walk to work, she can walk home as well.

The words have an unexpected effect. Abruptly, the boy returns his attention to Hannah and Annette. There is a look of unalloyed panic on his face. 'No! You can't take my father!' he pleads, he panics, he threatens – all in one.

Somewhat taken aback, Hannah holds up hands. 'I was talking to Annette,' she says to James, meeting his stare. 'Are you coming, guys?' Hannah asks.

'James? Would you like a lift home with us?' Annette wants to know.

'No thank you. Not going home.'

Hannah begins to trudge back the way they came. She notes the mismatching footprints, even her own two are mismatched – where she's pressed down with a little extra weight on her right leg, to compensate for the slippery surface; where her foot has twisted to use her ankle more in the negotiation. She listens out for the sound of footfall behind her, but instead hears:

'You can't stay here on your own, James. Why don't you ride with us?'

'I've nowhere to go,' the boy replies. 'I need to talk to Simon.'

Annette suggests: 'You can come back to mine. How about that? You and Emil are friends! I'll make hot chocolate and we can call your mum and let her know you're safe.'

'She won't answer. Only Louise escaped.'

'What does *that* mean?' asks Annette – and then the breath she inhales makes Hannah think that it must have hurt the woman's lungs.

Hannah turns.

'Jesus,' whispers Annette – and somehow Hannah hears

this too, her auditory senses suddenly as delicate as a tuning fork.

The boy James is holding a gun.

3.

'One occasion, it was in Burma, during the war,' Patrick says slowly, corralling his memories. 'It was a voodoo ceremony, and I witnessed it.'

'In *Burma?*'

'Yes. I'll spare you the details, girl, especially as I don't emerge from the tale in a good light. I shouldn't've been there in the first place.' Patrick waits. His fingers dance on the walking stick's head. The two adults have temporarily taken the front seats of the cut-and-shut lease car, and the walking stick's vulcanized rubber base is deep in a footwell clogged with banana skins, soda cans, and reams of notepaper covered with scribbles and doodles.

'Do you mean you deserted?' asks Dorothy, as she continues to prod and poke knobs on the dashmount – she is trying to get the heating back on. The inside of the car is as cold as a fridge.

'You could say I borrowed some time,' Patrick answers.

'Do you want to tell me about it? Seems we've got a bit of borrowed time ourselves.'

Patrick needs no second invitation. 'The smell of bleach is what I remember most. Place stank of it.'

'Bleach? Like, domestic bleach?'

'Like you'd swill down your khazi, girl, that's right.' He has closed his eyes; and for a moment his mouth is shut too. His breathing is via nostrils clogged as densely with hair as potted plant are with roots. 'They bleached the bones,' he continues after a few seconds. 'Boiled 'em up; bleached 'em in chemicals; then ground 'em into dust; for us all to snort up like cocaine. You ever done that, Dorothy?' asks Patrick.

She attempts to make light of the question and its implicit accusation. 'No, I've never sniffed mashed up bones,' she says. She gauges the temperature of Patrick's stare on her face – it is hotter than anything the car-heater could manage. 'Or do you mean coke?' she asks, cool as apple-pie.

'I meant bones. *Everyone's* done cocaine,' Patrick teaches her, a note of disparagement about his lesson.

'Actually, I only did it once or twice. It's not as widespread as you might imagine.'

'Everyone *rich* has done it. If you moved in my circles you did it…'

Dorothy frowns. 'There you go then,' she replies, 'I've never been that kind of rich.'

'Nor has Annette and *she's* done it – loads of times. She used to do it with her mother, bless her socks.'

'You're kidding! Mother and daughter…'

'Oh yes. Every other weekend, rain or shine. Thought I didn't notice – and the truth is, with the missus, maybe I wouldn't've. But not Annette. There was no disguising much with my Annette, not when she was on the drink or drugs.'

'I had no idea.'

'You already do.'

Dorothy leans his way, and her hand joins his on top of the walking stick. She squeezes his hand gently. They kiss.

A gunshot.

'What the hell was that?' Patrick demands.

III.

1.

It cost him plenty, and the commodities were time, patience, courage – and money. *Stepfather Lenny's* money, to be precise.

Well, James reasoned, if all went to his sketchy plan, Lenny wouldn't be needing the money for much longer anyway.

2.

'I can forgive you for attempting to make Mum happy.'

'Oh you can, can you? Well that's good of you, James, I must say.'

'But I can't forgive you for failing in your duties to me.'

'What duties? *What* have I failed, you arrogant little prick? Be specific. I have tried my very best by you and your sister.'

'And I can't forgive you for going into my computer and pretending to be Dad.'

'This is stupid. Have you any idea what you're saying, James? *Me?*'

'Yes I do. Yes, you.'

'I can't even work a pissing computer properly! Think before you accuse…' Lenny stands up. 'I'm going for a shit, a shave and a shower. When I come back I'll expect you to be down from this manic phase and I'll expect an apology from you.'

'You didn't protect me. You didn't protect Louise.'

'You exasperate me, James. Be very clear – take your time if you need to, I want to get this. *What exactly* didn't I protect you from?'

'Dad.'

Lenny is baffled; he hadn't seen this coming. 'You're angry

with your dad now?'

'No. I'm angry with you. You were his best friend; you should have known.'

Lenny sits back down. When he speaks his voice is quieter. 'When you say *protect*, James – *protect* you and your sister.'

'You should have known.'

'Known what, James? Please. Did he hit you? Is that what you're saying?'

'No. It was primary and secondary category sexual abuse,' James recites – and his eyes are as dead as those of a fish on ice.

Lenny recoils from the news; his back straightens as if he's been called to attention. His scalp twitches. 'That's a terrible thing to say, James,' he says quietly.

'I know.'

'So you made it up?'

'No.'

Lenny's back relaxes as he exhales. Though he's felt in the past that the kitchen is too small for the four of them, he has rarely felt it too cramped for two; but he does now.

'I'll…' Lenny begins. He crosses the word out. 'We'll have to talk to your mother when she gets home. She's out doing the food shop.'

'I know. She's meeting Annette for a coffee afterwards.'

'That's right. Are you going to cry?'

'No. I want you to leave the house,' James tells him.

'And we know that can't happen. So we look for some sort of compromise, James. That's what people *do*.'

'I'm not people.'

'You can say that again. Listen…'

'*Why* can't you leave?' James asks

'Because I'm married to your mum,' is the slow and de- liberate response. 'And your threats don't *help*, James – your de-

mands, I should say. What you think might hurt me hurts *her*...'
He stands up again. 'I'm going for a three-S, okay? A shit, a
shower and a shave,' he doesn't need to explain.

James watches his stepfather leave the room.

The opportunity slot will be narrow. James will have only
a few minutes if he wishes to catch stepfather Len in the shower.

In the other room the toilet flushes. Water scythes through
the house's pipes, hissing. James's heartbeat gallops; he pulls out
the lowest drawer, where the knitted vests he refuses to wear still
remain. James detests the vests but he acknowledges that they've
done a good job on this occasion; they've hidden the gun. Not
so comprehensively that a careless rummage wouldn't have dug
up this heavy treasure, but well enough to fool the naked eye in
passing.

James lifts the gun to the bedroom lightshade, for what must
be the eightieth time; once again he is surprised by its weight.

He was surprised by its weight from the first. After he'd
taken possession of it – a claiming that had forced James into
rare and frightening territory – a dawn journey from Leighton
Buzzard to London, and not even *North* London; the quest had
seen the boy armed only with cash and a travelcard, and he had
fought his fear of the Underground system, twisting south on
trainlines whose names made no sense.

James steps onto the landing, crosses it in his usual three
strides, and tells himself that these exact three strides are taking
him that bit closer along the path to being a man...

The man he met that morning, after the journey and the
Tube, in the rain, in a flower-gardened corner of Streatham
Common, on a park bench, was older than James had expected;
but surely that was okay, because James would have been *younger*
than the other man had expected. At any rate their age difference
went unremarked. The seller asked to see the colour of James's

money. James had seen it in films, he knew you brought money in a plain brown envelope, so that's what he had done, too. He handed it to the vendor, who said:

'There's no one around, you know – not in this weather. Not at this time of day…'

James didn't know how to reply. The thought that things might go differently somehow if someone was out walking the dog (say) had not occurred to him. For the journey down was the bit he'd really feared, not this meeting. At a loss as to what to say, James looked at a raindrop on the end of the man's nose and wondered how long it would take to detach itself. Getting wet was not a problem for James, but he was starting to get hungry; he had brought no extra money for a breakfast.

'What I mean is,' the salesman continued, 'I could check it right here.'

'Okay,' James replied, uncertain.

'But I won't. You know why?'

'No.'

'Because I believe in your cause, son. I believe in it. You need it to fight, right?'

James hadn't anticipated needing to lie; he wasn't prepared. He did his best, saying, 'Something like that.' It felt good to be someone else for a few minutes, and a few more seconds went by before James was satisfied that the man was not only envious, he was frightened. *Frightened of me.*

'I gotcha. All things spread out from the Smoke, don't they? So now it's getting crisp in the Home Counties.' He laughed and gulped at the same time; the result sounded like eggs cracked into a bowl, but amplified.

James did not understand. Luckily for him there was no gap left open in the conversation for him to respond.

'You bangers: I *get* you, son. It's your gang versus the other gang. Turf, innit? Holding ground. The necessary.'

James's stomach clenched with hunger. 'Can I have the gun now, please?' he asked. Rain on flowerbeds was agitating a series of itches in his sinuses. A parabola of bile was catapulted up inside his body; all of a sudden he felt nauseous. *Food.*

'Sure, son.' The salesman reached into a jacket that reminded James of the one that Wolfe wore, by the canal – the jacket that the other boy had almost drowned in. What emerged was a plastic carrier bag. 'See, I was a gangbanger once meself.' He handed the bag to James. 'Can't say I don't miss it as it goes. Banged in Bricky. You know Bricky?'

'No.'

'That's Brixton to you out-of-towners. You country boys, eh, son? Eh?'

'Brixton.'

The man laughed again, watching his punter check the contents. 'It's all there, son. Don't peek at your presents before Christmas, eh?'

'Why is it in an envelope?' James asked.

'Why, did you bring a holster?'

'No.'

'Then that's why it's in an envelope. Where I'd advise you to keep it until D-Day, son. The cunt's loaded. Safety catch on… You want to see it, don't you?'

'Yes,' James admitted.

'Good. You can't be too careful, can you?'

'No.'

'Well be quick then, and then I'm on me way. Have fun. Don't do nothin' I wouldn't do.'

He thinks this is funny, James understood. 'Would you kill a man for breaking a promise?' he said.

'Those days are gone, son.'

'When you were my age. Would you have?'

'You can't be older than fifteen. Things are different now,' replied the seller.

'You're avoiding the question.'

'Maybe I am. I don't know, is the honest answer. It would depend on the promise, wouldn't you say?' The man stood up.

'No I wouldn't.'

No it doesn't, James thinks, taking aim at the bathroom door handle. He holds the gun in both hands, supporting its weight; he is aware that weapons kick – he has done his research. Squeeze. Noise. The door swings back and open, the handle and the lock on the other side in smithereens. James's pulse has quickened; his ears ring with the sound he has created; sweat oozes.

Stepfather Lenny is whimpering as James enters the room. The air is muggy with steam and the combined aromas of body gel and excreta. The shower door is open. Framed by this door, solid in its rain, Lenny stands shaking with fear. He has taken a good protective grip on his genitals – not that decency or modesty is the extent of his worries. His face is a picture of fear-stoked rage. His body doesn't know which way to take him. Scant seconds have passed but for both of the males in the bear-cave the time has stretched, and neither of them knows fully what to do next.

'James, put the gun down, there's a good boy.'

'I didn't think it would smell like this,' James replies, then smiles. 'The gun smells because he's eaten his dinner. The gun's *parping*, Lenny! The gun's blowing off!'

'What *dinner?*'

'The door! The gun says thank you and yum yum. But the gun's still hungry, Lenny.'

'Fuck are you on about, James? Are you *on* something? – 'cuz if you're on drugs, boy, you're in a lot of trouble…'

'I'm already in a lot of trouble.'

'Where did you get that gun, James?'

'London. Because I lied.'

'What?'

'Good boys don't tell lies, do they, Lenny? That's what you always say.'

'Put the gun down, James. Let's talk about this.'

'I lied to you. When I said I could forgive you. Because I can't. Not for anything.'

For the second time James squeezes the trigger. As loud as the report had been on the landing, the sound seems even more remarkable in the bathroom's confines. Shower-mist is briefly stained red: Lenny's chest has exploded. The red fog is calmly beautiful – serene – which is more than can be said for the victim. Brute strength and ignorance keeps him upright for a moment – then, not even the shower stall's back wall can do a decent job of maintaining his posture – stepfather Lenny crumples; he slides down inside his vertical, frosted-glass coffin, what once had been inside him pulsing out into the funeral's hot precipitation. He comes to physical rest on his backside, one leg creased beneath him in a yoga-like position, the other leg stretched out in front as if he'd tried to kick the toilet bowl. Words from another language crowd his lips.

James closes his eyes and interrogates the ache in his right shoulder, caused by firing the two shots. Seconds later, when he opens his eyes again, water from the shower nozzle is suspended in the cubicle; it won't fall. Even water from a showerhead refuses to touch stepfather Lenny. Instead it spells a word. The word is *GOOD*. The word is written in water and backlit by blood on the ceramic tiles on the shower's back wall. James blinks again – if only to make time re-start.

'James?' Lenny croaks.

Holding the gun at his side, James takes two steps forwards on the damp carpet. Inquisitively, he tilts his head to the left – almost as if the word alone, his name, is an unfamiliar sound. He resembles a newborn puppy, investigating life in the garden for the first time.

Lenny slides a few centimetres down the tiles. Both of his hands press down on the wound above his right nipple. This means that there is no opportunity for false modesty – his genital area is on full display, like something freshly butchered. Indeed, there is kill-blood on his glans.

'Can you hear me, James?' Len croaks.

'Yes.'

Len's eyes are closed. Inside James's chest, his heart bumps and grinds as if eager for escape.

'Can you hear me, you little shit?'

'Yes,' James answers.

'About your dad…' Len coughs. No blood is jettisoned by the cough, but a good deal of spittle is. 'I *knew*, James. Do you hear me? I *knew* about his tastes. I knew about you.'

A clock ticks in the boy's head. The ticking is loud – so loud it is difficult to hear Lenny through the rising rage. 'You *knew?*'

'I helped him. I held you down,' says Lenny. What flits across his mouth is an attempt at a smile.

James lifts up the gun.

'But… James, you still there?'

'Yes. I'm close.'

'It's getting dark.'

'It's about to get darker.'

Len coughs again, and this time blood sprays from his lips. 'Don't be stupid, son–'

'I'm not your son.'

'Just ring for an ambulance. It hurts like buggery.' Again,

that smile, or maybe-smile.

'Did you hurt Louise as well?' James asks, his voice wavering. He has pointed the gun at Lenny's head.

'No. Your dad didn't like girls,' is the answer given. 'I don't know why.'

Horror rips through James with the force of fire down a line of spilled petrol. What he sees in his mind's eye is the ice-cream kiosk on Dunstable Downs. All year round, but especially in the summer, children line up for cones or 99s from mid-morning until the sky blushes. That's a lot of exposure to children…

'Are you still there, James?' Len asks, sounding desperate.

Perhaps in times when you're facing an eternity of loneliness, James considers parenthetically, even the voice of your assassin is a welcome diversion. 'Yes.'

Len smiles; a more successful endeavour on this occasion. It's a smile that says: *I reject your disgust of me.* 'Your mother's going to *kill* you, James.'

'Yes.'

'You'll go to prison. If you don't get me an ambulance, you'll go to prison and that is where the big boys will have you. It'll all start over. They'll love you…'

'Why don't I remember it?'

'What?'

'I don't remember it happening,' James elaborates – it might as well be to himself.

'James?'

'Yes, I'm here.'

'Your mother's pregnant, you evil little spastic. Get me a fucking ambulance. *Now.*' His face wrinkles like cracks in dried mud.

'No.'

'The baby will need a father.'

James's finger tenses on the trigger. 'But you're *not* a father, Lenny. You're impotent. Dad told me. You fire blanks.'

Len's eyes open – which is what James had intended. The eyes are swimming – could it be in *tears?*

'Please don't, James. I was lying to you… all lies… James…'

'Goodbye, Lenny.'

Noise.

Lenny's face erupts like an overripe pumpkin dropped onto pavement.

From downstairs comes the thud of the front door closing. Someone has arrived home. Sal's voice calls 'Hulloo-oo' in her customary *I'm-here* falsetto, prompting James to leave the bathroom, the shower head still spurting behind his back. With the gun ever more comfortable in his right hand, he moves towards the stairs.

3.

James is halfway down the stairs and his mother is removing her gloves, plucking at her fingers one by one as though peeling a satsuma. She no more than glances up at her son; she is preoccupied. 'Where's your father?' is a sentence that confirms this preoccupation.

'My father is dead,' James answers truthfully.

'Sorry. Where's your stepfather?'

'In the shower,' James answers truthfully again.

Sal's nostrils fidget. 'What's that smell?'

'He had an accident.'

Sal pays more attention. She has pocketed her gloves and is in the process of shrugging off a heavy-looking dark blue coat. 'What do you mean, an accident? What's so funny?'

'I'm not laughing.'

'You're grinning from ear to ear.' Sal crucifies the coat's

rain-sodden deadweight on a sturdy wooden hanger. She claps the package – hanger and coat – onto a wooden peg on the wall-mounted coatrack. She calls out: 'Len! I'm home! Could you help me with the shopping out of the car?'

'He won't obey you,' says James, remaining as he was, halfway down the flight of stairs, leaning over the banister that shields most of his body from view.

'You're worrying me now, James… Why have you left the shower running?'

'Have I? How do you know it was me?'

Sal gives herself a second to catch up; her breathing is a little troubled. 'What do you mean, an accident?' she repeats, her first foot on the first stair, where traffic and travel have worn down the carpet on the hip. '*Len!*' she calls again.

'He won't obey you,' James also repeats; the declaration unlocks something rigid and lumpy; wet laughter breaks through this dam and he drools on his chin.

'Get out of my way, James.'

'You can't come up here.'

'I'm not messing now. Get out of my *way*…'

'We've been planning a surprise. Like the one Len gave me. Like the ones Dad used to give me.'

Sal has reached the fifth stair; James is two stairs higher, towering over his mother for once. On the woman's face, confusion clashes with worry.

'Is that *blood* on your clothes? My God, James, what the hell's–'

'It's a *smelly* surprise. But *all* surprises are a bit smelly, aren't they, Mum?'

Sal's brow freezes. Although there are urgent questions bubbling on her lips, she has decided that as her son is in no mood to respond in a mature fashion, then she is in no mood to pose them. She climbs towards James, who doesn't move.

'You're already in trouble, young man,' she begins to warn him, but does not get a chance to compose her threat. Contact morphs briskly into conflict; mother and son lock into shambolic pantomime of unarmed combat. Neither has the requisite skills, but both seem suddenly refreshed by a new source of energy. The wrestle for a few seconds.

It is only when Sal loses her footing and her balance that she has no choice but to give up the struggle. Though she collapses down the flight she remains upright, grasping hold of the banister and sliding down to a few stairs lower. Beaten by an opponent with bloodspots on his jeans; with madness in his eyes; and with an undeniable, if temporary, height advantage.

Mother and son breathe raggedly. Sal orders the boy to: 'Tell me what happened. You said there was an accident. Is Lenny hurt, James?'

'Len is dead. Good riddance to bad rubbish.' After making a clicking noise with his tongue, as though geeing on horses, he adds, 'I shot him.'

'That's not funny, James.' But doubt clouds Sal's features: a sudden storm of ambivalence. She eyeballs her son, toe to head: there are spots of what seem to be blood on his clothes... Len not answering... the shower running... the *smell*...

'I think you knew too,' says James.

Close to tears now, Sal demands, 'Knew what?'

'About Dad. What he did to me.'

Sal shakes her head. 'And what did he *do* to you, James?'

'Touched me. Where he shouldn't.'

'Are you... are you *insane*, James?'

Though posed rhetorically, and in anger to boot, this question is one that James is content to answer. He has been answering it, on and off, for a long time. 'I live on the autistic spectrum, with a narcissistic complex and a variety of borderline patholog-ical symptoms. My moods are largely controlled by medication. Which I have stopped taking, by the way, Mum.'

Sal is horrified. 'Why?'

'It makes me weak.'

Maintaining a keen eyeball bead on the boy's midriff, Sal backs a careful retreat down the remaining risers. In seconds she is back in the hallway, by the door through which she entered the property, near the coatrack from which she now plucks her damp garment. The scene is being played in reverse: a dream. Backwards she will walk to the car. In reverse she will drive to the supermarket. *None of this happened.*

'Your father loved you, James. I can't believe you would think bad things about him like this.' She fastens her coat.

James has not shifted position on the stairs. 'Kolko told me,' the boy answers simply. 'Then Len confessed it as well.'

'*Len* did? You lie.'

'I don't lie,' James protests – but the defence tickles trouble-somely: the declaration that he is a boy who doesn't lie is not true anymore, and they both know it.

'Then you're confused; you're mistaken,' Sal allows. 'Your stepfather would never agree to such a wicked thing. Agree with, I mean. Kolko has twisted Len's thoughts,' says Sal. 'It's the only thing it can be.'

James sits. With his head cocked slightly he asks, 'And why would he do that?'

'Well *I* don't know! I've never met the bastard, but when I do–'

'You won't.'

'…Why not?'

'Because *he* chooses.'

'So maybe he'll *choose* to meet me, we can have a nice little *chat.*' The last word pongs with sour sarcasm. 'Right now I'm calling the police, James, something funny's going on here. Maybe your precious Private Kolko will attend the scene.'

'He's a constable.'

'*I don't give a fuck what he is!*' Sal screams.

'Don't do that.'

'Why not? You're hiding something upstairs, you've got blood on your kecks. Give me one good reason why I *shouldn't* call the police.'

'You forgot the bit about Len being dead. But don't call yet. I'll show you the gun.'

Sal's fingers tremble like leaves fallen onto the surface of the canal. There's a crack in her voice. She says, 'Yes. Let's do that. Show me the gun, James.'

The boy's smile is charming, despite the chaos that surrounds it. He does not need to venture far; all he does is lean back, flat against the stairs, and with his legs bent he propels himself a few steps higher. The weapon is on the landing carpet, just around the corner out of sight.

'Ta-*daa*,' James announces, producing its heaviness with the exuberant flourish of an amateur but diligent magician. In doing so he sits up straight again.

'Oh by Christ,' mutters Sal. Like slow, heavy birds, her hands flutter up to her. 'Is that real, James?'

The boy nods his head. 'I bought it off the Internet.'

'...*Why?*'

'To kill Len. Because he lied to me.' The boy's brow wrinkles; he has ceased laughing. Aware as he is of the word *hypocrisy*, he cannot find it in his lexicon at this moment. He is not sure why what he's said sounds wrong.

Sal whispers, 'Oh my God... Oh my God, James, what have you *done?*'

'Killed stepfather Lenny.'

'Do you mean *really*?'

'Yes.'

'Oh my God… Will you give it to me now?'

'No.'

'Why not?'

'I'm not finished with it.'

Sal nods her head. She is right by the door; there's a chance… The words sink through to her comprehension like a pebble through quicksand. 'Do you plan to kill me?'

'I don't know.'

'What will decide you?'

James stands up on the flight of stairs. He points the gun at his mother, both hands taking its weight at its owner's arms-length.

'Your side of the story,' the boy replies.

IV.

1.

My back shows no obvious sign of improvement, irrespective of the light callisthenics or the long hot baths that its impatience has earned. Having stretched my bones, I lie in the soap-milky water, deep to the chin, and listen to a recording of Beckett's *Malone Dies*.

Where is Sabrina? Those hours that she doesn't spend with me – where does she spend them? Her place of work? Sure – when she slammed the front door this morning I knew that her place of work was where she was heading. But what happens *after*? Does she *really* spend so long at the gym? So long at Pilates? So long at her once-a-month book club? I have mentioned before that she might be cheating on me, but with whom? Her wardrobes and drawers give no clues.

I need to get out of here, surely I do. The good stuff happens elsewhere. *My* life is in my head, after all: information gratefully received helps to build the big picture. Then there is Uncle Stephen – Stephen and his holiday so extended that it makes me wonder if he was ever present, even in my head, in the first place.

I know he was. If I find myself doubting Stephen, where does that leave me? He *phoned* me, for Christ's sake. It doesn't matter that he's dead – he *phoned* me.

Perhaps I need another night out with Roy. Like me, he's just another bear in his cave. I try to imagine where he lives, based on snippets and gobbets; I have a far clearer image of the cell in which he did time, way back when. However, Roy – this is simply bald instinct talking, nothing more – Roy is important to all of this. I don't know how and I don't know why; but he clutches in his paw at least one piece of the jigsaw puzzle.

Every one of our ragtaggle group has been visited by the past or by something that can't be explained, the two matters not being mutually exclusive.

Dorothy has her psychotic nurses. Hannah and Sam, their Egyptian gunman. Roy, his thief (and pizza-poisoner). And Annette, a strange boy and a stranger police officer and who knows what else?

Leaving *me*, I suppose.

Oh yes, and leaving Sabrina; Sabrina, who I find I know less and less as time goes on. Sabrina is becoming estranged from me; Sabrina is leaving me. One day I'll be arriving and she'll be going, and that will mark the end of *that*.

Tonight she is late home again.

I wonder, when she arrives, if Stephen will call me on the phone, like that other time. Sabrina and I will argue, Sabrina will retreat to the bathroom as I have deliberately cooked no dinner for her, to exacerbate the problem, and then he'll ring. And he'll stay on the line longer than it takes to call me a silly bugger as well, I hope.

A short phone call it had been – if it had really been a call through the telephone in the first place. Maybe it's expensive to ring from the afterlife. He could have reversed the charges; I would have picked up the tab. *Your charges are in the form of a piece of your soul*, some celestial operator might have said. He ended the natter pretty *tout-suite*, as soon as I mentioned that Sabrina was in the tub.

That didn't go down too well with Sabrina either, of course. Sod's Law, but where I'd expected her to spend half the rest of the night in the water, she had only gone in for a quick dip. She had seen me drop the receiver onto the cradle immediately after I'd told the caller that she was soaking herself.

2.

I can remember – easily – when this town attracted no pollution.

This is what I'm thinking as I wait for Sabrina's arrival, as I stare out of the bedroom window, past the road that leads up to the factories, the industrial estate, the Working Men's Club, my back-stretching clinic, my dentist's surgery; past the shoelace of tributary canal, fizzing softly with its flotsam and jetsam of abandoned supermarket trolleys and fish-and-chip papers; past the rugby club and its alien glow of floodlights, beneath which boys of approximately James's age shout and rumble; to the church spire in the distance, poking holes in the bellies of fast-moving chestnut clouds.

The sky is filthy. The snowfall, as violent and robust as it has been today, has done nothing to ease the sky's load, it would seem. Pollution has come to this town, just as confidently (but as deftly) as our individual visitors have slipped back into our lives. But where is mine? Is mine Sabrina? Is Sabrina *my turn*? To use words that Hannah Paddington would appreciate, we have parried for a long time: long before we understood the nature of the lunge. But where is the lunge against *me*?

Scrabbling free of the visual quicksand of the chestnut-coloured sky, I am midpoint to the telephone in the other room. I am about to telephone Roy, to ask if he'd care to join me for a cheeky couple and a chat in The Leper – when the intercom sounds by my left ear. A harsh buzz, as unexpected and raw as the noise of a wasp. For a second or two I wait. No one calls here – certainly not at this time in the evening. Only parcel-delivery staff and Human Resources representatives, come to check on the unlikely possibility of a return to work, deliberately press the intercom button for Number 8.

'Hello?'

'Tom, it's Hannah. Can you let us up?' The sweeping, the *collecting* sound of a large vehicle passing, no doubt *en route* to the estate. 'It's really important.'

3.

At some point during the afternoon – I don't know when – it is clear that I have experimented with some of Sabrina's clothing. I don't know why. Nor do I have any recollection of doing so. Evidently, however, I have worn a bra over my Fred Flintstone t-shirt for the last little while.

Hannah stares at me. What was I *thinking*? Not only, during the afternoon, have I donned one of Sabrina's brassieres; I am now acutely conscious of a tightening to my skin – on the face. I have daubed my features with her makeup as well.

The boy ascending the stairs behind Dorothy – he notices the makeup and says nothing. This must be James, I understand, but what an introduction! He has come here – been dragged here for all I know – to meet this halfhearted transvestite before him.

James sniffs the air and tilts his head back, still climbing; he resembles one on the last leg of a journey up Mount Kilimanjaro. Weary before his years. Blood on his clothes.

I eyeball his features and something kicks and jolts, belly deep. A thud of recognition.

Uncle Stephen is in the boy's features. The boy reminds me of Stephen.

I can't speak. Hannah slides past me, into the flat with a soft promise – 'I'll explain' – tracing the salty, spicy air that has left the oven of the flat below and risen. The whole block smells of cooking when the people downstairs brew their curries and their casseroles; their culinary fireworks have made me envious on more than a couple of thousand occasions – a world I cannot reach – but they do not make me envious now. The boy's face is a picture, *my* picture, of how Stephen appeared; but it the appearance of the final guest that unlocks my tongue. She weaves upwards; I recognise her; she recognises me; and together, duetting, we both say:

'*You…*'

4.

In they file, into my cave – five of the Seven Dwarves. Making me the sixth. (Am I Sleepy or Grumpy?)

Who is the seventh? Sabrina or Roy?

Heads are turned, as if in respect, away from me and my attempts at reconstruction. If the man chooses to wear ladies' underwear, let him be, seems to be the message. Ditto cosmetics.

5.

'*You*,' I repeat.

'Yes, me. *Annette.*'

'You're not Annette, you're Caitlin. You used to live over there.' I wave in the general direction of the balcony doors. 'You were my stalker.'

'Tom, have you been drinking?' asks Hannah.

'Yes. What the hell is going on? I feel invaded.' I look to Dorothy – my ally, I might surmise (incorrectly as it transpires); Dorothy, my sister-in-arms, we're joined at the mental hip by our flakiness, our weak spots.

She turns away from me. It is always Hannah who aims to get to the bottom of things.

'You say hello to Annette, Tom, every month when we have our lunches,' she tells me in a soft voice. 'Why don't you take off that bra? Make yourself comfortable in your own home.'

'I bet you say that to all the boys,' I answer, but I do as she has said anyway. My comment has stirred up an indistinct ripple of non-committal laughter. I toss the bra into the kitchen sink, where it lands on top of the attention-seeking crusty washing up.

Internally I'm protesting: *But I've never met Annette – not when she was Annette, anyway…* 'I've never attended one of your lunches, Han.'

'Yes you have, Tom. You always come as Sabrina and we're never supposed to mention it. But it's too late now not to have full disclosure, wouldn't you say, especially after what we're going to tell you.' Hannah sits down at my desk.

'This is nuts. I go as *Sabrina*, you're saying? Do I need my ears syringed?'

'You need *something* syringed,' says Dorothy – a comment that doesn't actually make much sense in hindsight but which strikes me with a fist of lead at this moment. I sit down on my blue rocking chair.

'Has this town gone loco?' I plead.

The boy parks himself, perched on the coffee table. Instincts with the force of airplanes make me want to shout at him to get off the table, this isn't the monkey house at the Whipsnade Zoo. But my youngest visitor, with perfect posture, hand in hand, gaze fixed at the Bs and Cs book shelf, is more pageboy than primate; his manners seem impeccable. I hold back the remark. Standing up instead I announce: 'I'm going to call Sabrina.'

'We have things to talk about, Tom,' argues Hannah. 'I didn't expect *this* to be one of them, I must say.'

'Did you really not know?' Annette wonders.

I snap at her. 'Not know your real name is Caitlin? Not know you attacked your own children with an axe? Yes I did happen to know that one as a matter of fact…' Turning to Hannah: '…and *this* would be my disputed girlfriend's existence, would it? Forgive my manners, Hannah. Which one of us did you actually sleep with?'

Dorothy splutters, '*What?*'

'Not now, Tom, for Christ's sake. He's talking about dreams.'

'He is not talking about dreams. I'm talking about you lot losing your neurons, is what I'm talking about.' I run through the names in my mobile as I go through my protestations. SAB WORK. Thumb on the CALL button. 'CALLING 123456789,' I read quickly on the display. I hold the phone to my ear.

'We're sorry, we have been unable to connect your call. Please check the number or try again later. We're sorry, we have been—'

'Wankers,' I mutter to myself.

'Dead line?' suggests Hannah.

'Must have changed.' Defiantly (but feeling weak).

'It was never there, Tom.' Sympathetically.

I float, I hover… For just a second or two, I swear, my feet leave the carpet and its crumbs; I look down on a beige sea, an abandoned archipelago of fallen biscuits. 'What's happening to me?' I ask, soaring higher. I bump my head on the lampshade and waft back down.

Skin tightens across my chest; feathers prickle my throat; my temperature rises – in my mind's eye I see the gauge, the needle flickering around the red maximum.

'Do you need to lie down, Tom?' Hannah asks, making me believe that just at this moment she is the only person left on the planet who can speak.

True terror has a taste as distinctive as rare steak. Every steadfast thought – every notion you have previously assumed set solid – is now en route to somewhere else: to somewhere and something that will change it. Every thought is intercepted by armed freedom fighter personnel, and either allowed on its way or incinerated there and then.

'I don't know what to say,' I finally admit.

'Then allow me,' Hannah adds softly. 'I think we all need to tell our stories right now.'

Dorothy speaks. 'Have we all forgotten something?' She nods towards the boy – and by extension towards the claims that he's made.

'How fast can we talk?' says Annette. 'We might have time before. You know.'

'Before what?' I ask her, unable to ban the note of nastiness from what I'm saying.

'Before we have to call the police, Tom. What do you think? Before D-Day?'

'Hey Annette, that's not bad,' says Sam. 'Let's keep it all nice and sarcastic.'

'I learned from the master.'

'Well fuck you, Annette. Jesus, she's getting on my–'

'*Everyone* shut up,' says Hannah. 'Let's just do it properly, or as properly as we can.'

Maybe *Hannah* sent me those insects, but why would she?

Maybe it was Annette. Or Caitlin. Delete as applicable.

Maybe it was me. No, it wasn't me – I'm sure of that.

It isn't long before the subject of Kolko is raised.

'How would you go about finding who he is?' Hannah asks.

'You're asking us? You're the bloody researcher,' says Sam, sore from being thought ill of. She is trying to rebuild some standing.

The accusatory implications of the sentence come as something of a shock to Hannah. 'Yes I am, aren't I?' she replies quietly. Transfixed by her wine glass, she holds it up in front of her eyes, like a compact mirror

'I'm going to find the fucker,' Hannah answers.

'Do *you* know where Mr Kolko lives?' Annette asks the boy.

James shakes his head. I say to him, 'Why don't you tell us what happened?'

6.

'She asked me if she could sit down and I said of course she could, it's her house, so she sat beside me. She was shaking. She kept looking at the gun on the table. I wanted to tell her to stop looking at it because it was making me nervous. I don't think she had ever seen a gun before, but most people haven't, I suppose. Have any of you?

'She asked me where I'd got it and I told her what I told stepfather Lenny: I bought if off a man selling it on the Internet. I suppose I'll go to prison, won't I? Is it true they try to rape you in prison? That's what Lenny told me but he was a liar, so I don't know if he was telling the truth or not.'

Nobody wants to give voice to an answer. Only the silence of held breaths greets the boy's words; but James doesn't seem to mind. Though there is no obvious abreaction – no discharge of emotion in the boy – he seems content enough, ploughing his gaze into one of my rugs – the bluer and the filthier of the two.

The silence seems to sting, the longer it reaches; it's like a case of sunburn. When you don't appreciate the sun's heat because of the wind factor or because you're pissed, and it's only later that you feel the tenderness on your shoulderblades, on your shins... *Someone breathe,* I plead; *say something, say anything at all.* No one speaks.

So it's up to me, then. And while I don't know where the question comes from, I'm glad it comes from somewhere, it means that I can exhale.

'What are you going to do with the gun?' I ask James.

As the boy answers 'I don't know really,' the others regard

me with facial expressions that also approach a certain tanning factor. I can feel the heat chapping my lips. What I've learned from recent conversations – especially those concerning Kolko – is to shake the rat once you've got it in your jaws.

'You don't *know*? Then you really *are* in trouble, son. You haven't even thought it through properly, have you?'

James lifts his chin; there is water in his eyes. 'Please don't call me son. I'm not your son,' he tells me – a voluptuous dignity about the words.

I don't give a fuck about his dignity. 'No, you're nobody's son, are you, James?' I tell him. 'Because you killed your parents.'

'I killed my mother. Stepfather Lenny was just a cancer.'

'Tom, I'm not sure…' says Hannah, who no doubt (here I fantasise, of course) would care to remind me, given the chance, that the weapon remains in the boy's possession, and that if all is true, he's not exactly a piss-poor shot. But I do not give her this chance. The hand I raise to beg for silence does not give her this chance either. Making a mental note to apologise to Hannah at a later time, I peck on at James.

'What happened to your father? Did you manage to leave him out of this?

'He died. Myocardial infarction.'

'Come again?'

'He had a heart attack, Tom,' says Hannah, visibly peeved at my interruption – perhaps also peeved by my manner and de-meanour, uncommonly aggressive, which she fails to fathom but which stinks like a goat's anal gustings.

Not that I'm entirely certain of what I'm doing anyway.

'He had a problem with his heart,' James confirms. The thousand-yard stare remains fixed on me, but I know he doesn't see me: he is looking at his old man. He is looking *through* me, into a past I can't know unless he wants to tell me all about it. If it's the truth that there is an engastrimythic quality to my own words, as though they're being spoken by someone else – again, *through* me* – then it's every bit as true to say the same thing about the boy.

James talks as if he's reading a script. Once the juice flows there's no stopping the lad; he speaks in paragraphs. What we hear next is a loving testament to his father, and a total recall summation of the man's life and death. Fascinating though it might be, I find my attention drawn to Annette; it is impossible to segregate my thoughts and portions of attention. She is Caitlin, not Annette, and she used to live in the house opposite my flat, across the car park. She was my stalker. I had sex with her on several occasions, just as I had told Roy in The Leper; I *can't* have made that up. And yet…

And yet no fucker believes me. By insisting on the existence of Sabrina I have devalued my own trustworthy stock.

Sabrina is at work, I tell myself. She is only *not here* because she is *at work*, and she can't be in two places at once. I did not make her up; this must be more of Kolko's doing, I am convinced.

But what does Sabrina do for a living? Right now, I don't know; I *can't remember*. But I'm sure I knew once. I'm sure she told me. If only I could remember.

Caitlin lived in the house opposite – with her boys. With the boys she killed with an axe. So why isn't she in prison? Double homicide: life sentence, you would think. Early release maybe, or even a minor tariff in the first place, the grounds of diminished responsibility having been taken into account. Rehoused; then given a new identity. (But in the same geographical vicinity?) Annette, eh? Almost too funny if it's true: a play on words. A net. One in which she is caught forever. She will have to report to the Probation Office in Milton Keynes every fortnight… *But she's got a job, Tom*; she works in a leisure centre, which includes working with children They do checks on you before they give you that kind of employment. *Criminal* checks. How on earth could she have faked the CRB clearance?

'You haven't answered my question, James,' I interrupt. 'I asked you what you were going to do with the gun and you said you don't know, but I hope I made it perfectly clear that that answer's unacceptable. You've started something so now you have to finish it.'

'For God's sake, Tom,' Annette snaps, 'just leave it with the gun, all right? He was just getting to the murder on Dunstable Downs.' She appears distressed, and so she should. I am about to discover why; we all are.

'I know that!' I lie, quite concerned with myself that I have allowed my attention to stroll askew.

Listen to the boy, says Sabrina. *For once, don't stick your oar in. Just listen.*

So I do.

7.

James adjusts his position all over the coffee table. I should be forced to pay the little bastard for polishing duties. And then he says to us all, 'I shot her in the throat.' This shuts up my thoughts for a sec.

'She tried to get away and I couldn't allow that to happen. So I shot her. There was blood in the sink, on the tiles. There was blood on the dishwasher – I didn't expect that. There was blood everywhere. It was like a murder scene.'

'...Is that meant to be a *joke*?' I ask him.

'I can't tell jokes, I've tried.'

'You bet your arse you can't.' I address the auditorium. 'Can anyone remind me why the fuck we're not calling the filth over this? Let's get this little maggot banged up.' Now, to James.

'And yes, they do rape boys in prison, you dirty pish. I *work* in one. I know.'

'You don't work anywhere, Tom,' says Hannah.

'I'm on sick leave, if I need to remind you. I have a bad back.'

'Did *Sabrina* advise you to say that?' asks Annette.

'And *you* can fuck right off. In fact, what are you doing in my home? I don't have to accommodate a murderer!'

'You already are, without me!' she answers.

She is right, of course, but I don't want to hear it. I would like to kick her out. Then again, I would also like to set her on fire and toast franks on the flames rising from her cunt; but we can't always get what we want, can we?

I need help here. I am lost.

Fortunately, Annette seems willing to pick up the dropped baton. She asks, as calmly as she might, 'And what happened after you shot her?'

James has expected this. 'I took off. I ran. With the gun in my coat.'

'Where it still is, I assume.'

'Tom, for fuck's sake...'

'Hey, excuse me if I take a general interest in who sits on my fucking furniture. Come to that, what the fuck are you doing sitting on my table. You born in a barn or summing?'

'Now's not the time, Tom,' says Hannah.

James stands up. I wave him down again. As soon as he parks his buttocks, he lapses into a rendition of his life to date. Including the stuff that I've slipped into this account, in the early chapters. You can say what you want about James, but the cunt's a reliable narrator. Sooner or later – I feel it's later – he comes to the stuff about the canal.

8.

Much later I dream of a giant army – an army of giants, swinging giant arms. Arms that are out of proportion to their owners' bodies, and stretching longer with every oscillation. And they are chanting something that I can't hear, although I hover above their shaven heads. What exactly do people mean when they write 'he woke with a start'? Well, to hell with it, I'm with you guys. That's exactly how I woke, whatever it means.

I wake with a start and Stephen is breathing down my brain. *You took your time,* he says into my head.

'You can talk.'

Nice dream?

'No, not particularly. Why did you hang up the phone?'

I was tired.

'Then why did you contact me in the first place?'

You wanted me to!

'You could have chosen a time more convenient for you.'

Now he's being picky as well! Jesus! Do a man a favour...

Does he giggle at this point? And does he giggle, more specifically, on the word *man*? 'What favour, Stephen?' I ask him, cross now.

Hey, here's an idea, Tom – why don't you grow up for a second and fucking listen? You have to find Kolko.

'God, that name again,' I answer. 'Who the hell *is* he for Christ's sake?'

He's my son, Stephen answers. *Now listen. The business on Dunstable Downs...*

'Tom?' It is Sabrina's voice, behind me. When I said 'I woke with a start', I made it sound like I was sleeping, either in bed or on my rocking chair. But neither of these is the case: I am in the kitchen, somnambulently in search of a glass of *milk* of all things. When my partner speaks my name, she catches me in the guilty act of pouring from the six-pint drum.

Turning quickly, I slake the work surface with a whip of white liquid.

'Who are you talking to, Tom?'

'No one!'

'I heard you. Who is she, Tom?'

'I'm not talking to anyone!' I get it together and turn my back on Sabrina. 'Besides,' I follow up with quickly, 'you don't even exist. You're not real.'

'…Are you okay? Are you sleepwalking?'

'Through life it seems.'

'Come back to bed. I thought you were on the mobile. To her again.'

'There isn't a *her*. Is there a *him?*'

'It's too late for all this?'

'In our relationship? Or tonight?'

'Tonight. Tonight, Tom. I'm not at all certain about the relationship. Are you?' she almost pleads – or that's how I hear it anyway.

'What time is it?'

'Late. I think you're sleepwalking a bit, drunk a bit too.'

'You may be right. But you didn't hear what I heard today.'

'Then tell me.'

'Is there a *him*, Sabrina.' I still can't face her. 'Is there a him?'

She waits a while; it feels like an autumn. Everything is dying in what we had; all the leaves are brown and the skies are grey. 'Yes, there's a him, Tom,' she answers me with a weary groan.

'I see. May I ask his name?'

'What good would that do? His name is Tony.'

I cannot help but flinch and snigger at the same time. 'Well, at least it's not a name that I'm likely to forget. You had to choose someone with the same name as my dad.'

'Tom, I'm *talking* about your dad.'

I face her as fast as I can, once more sending milk splashing across the kitchen – this time the floor. But it's not Sabrina I face.

My mother stands in the kitchen with me, naked and with a finger in her left ear.

'Jesus, *Mum*...'

I am also naked. I hide my shame with the bottle of milk – it's cold.

'He was telling me about the murder on the Downs,' I tell her, gabbling – just something to say for the sake of saying something.

'Who was?'

And when I blink I open my eyes to torrential blackness. My limbs stiffen, my extremities thrash. Someone breathing close to my face. Lying down. Both lying down. Too much darkness, no air to pass through it...

'Sabrina?'

'It's me, Tom. Hannah. I stayed with you. Go back to sleep.'

'What are you doing in my bed again?'

'You're in *my* bed. You had a turn after the hospital.'

'...What hospital?'

'The L and D.'

'No – no, why were we at the hospital?'

'You insisted.'

In the bedclothes, in there with me, is something sharp. *Hannah's nails?* crosses my mind – and it's a sleepy slow crossing. Is she in here with me? Sticky pictures of the Luton and Dunstable Hospital: the room of limbs: they squelch past my consciousness, these pictures, but each one is adhesive, reluctant to leave my sight; each one is peeled away like dead skin that is somehow moist. The room of limbs, back when I had the summer job cleaning – what was that guy's name again? With a smile on his face he lifts a prosthetic hip to his mouth and says *hockey mask.*

'Put it down,' I tell him. 'We shouldn't muck about in here, we'll get sacked.'

'Who cares? Shitty job.' He laughs at me; it sounds like a dentist's drill. Turning away dismissively, he underarms the hip into a stiff plastic basket, waist-high, where it rattles before settling. He says something about it being time to stir the pot.

'What?'

'I didn't say anything,' Hannah's voice tells me.

'Turn the light on, Hannah. Please.'

'I can't, there's been a power cut, Tom. How are you feeling?'

The prognosis isn't good, I must admit. 'Scared.'

When she lays her hand on my brow there is a sizzling sensation which licks my face and travels into my neck. It is neither pleasant nor unpleasant. It occurs to me that maybe I've suffered a stroke. From beyond a pane of glass that I can only imagine, a car moves briskly, creating a sizzling sound of its own, as though the road is saturated.

'You're burning up. Drink some water, James.'

'My name's Tom,' I tell her fiercely. 'Why can't I see?'

'There's been a power cut, Tom. We'll be all right in a minute, don't worry.'

'I'm in your bed, Hannah. I can't move. I can't see.'

'There's been a power cut, Tom.'

'Stop *telling* me that, I heard you the first time…'

'There's been a power cut, Tom.'

'Why were we at the hospital?'

'There's been a power cut, Tom.'

Making more effort now, I try to move, but pressure stretches athwart my torso, like two criss-crossing straps, one shoulder connected to its opposite hip. My backside grinds into a sturdy mattress. I must have had a heart attack.

'Why was I at the hospital?' I shout at Hannah.

'It's where the sick people go.'

'Who was sick? The boy James?'

'No, you, Tom.'

'I'm not sick.

'You're injured; it's the same thing. But they managed to save it.'

I think of eyes for some reason – my own eyes. 'Save what?' I croak.

'Your cock, Tom. I'm sorry, it was all my fault. But you would keep demanding I suck harder, so I did. As hard as I could. I sucked and I sucked and I sucked it right off. But I had to take it out of my mouth to call the ambulance. In the next room.'

'…Hannah?'

'Yes, Tom?'

'You're a liar. This isn't real, I'm dreaming all this.'

'Then who exactly is the liar?' Hannah asks, flapping her arms and twisting in flight toward a window that I can suddenly see, dim though it might be, and off with great velocity, horizon-bound.

Yet still I cannot wake; all I do is move from one dreamscape to the next, each one insisting on its dreampound of dreamflesh. The night I sift through is inelegant, ugly; there is nothing refreshing about nibbling at its vast universal limbs, like a speck-sized mosquito.

9.

'You can be a bit of a burden, I hate to say it, Tom.'

'Is that right, Stephen. Have you any idea of your own presence?'

'No, not really.'

'Well allow me to educate you. You are the one who's dead. *Now* who's the troublemaker, eh?'

'But you're the one who sought me out.'

'I did nothing of the sort! I hardly knew you!'

'Not consciously.'

'And what's *that* supposed to mean? Not consciously, my arse!'

When did this conversation happen?

I remember – as the song says – I remember as though it was yesterday, but that doesn't mean it was yesterday. It doesn't mean anything at all, because memories are not bricks, they are clouds; they reform. They don't stay in place.

The thing your mind returns to – the happy thing, the sad thing – isn't true.

10.

Dorothy informs me that it was Sigmund Freud who taught that dreams are our way of not going mad. No doubt he put it more elegantly than that, but that's it in essence.

Didn't he have anything better to do than state the bleeding obvious?

But what if the dreams themselves, while trying to stop you going mad, make you mad? What if the dreams themselves are the problem?

How has the world lost the will to live so suddenly? Where have all these *phantoms* come from? Were they *always* here?

No incident occurred on Dunstable Downs. Does that mean I *dreamt* it? I couldn't have because it was not only me that the script affected.

No incident could have occurred to the back of my flat either, across the car park, in Caitlin's old place. This is trickier to fathom. Because it happened. It was a scandal. It made the news.

Hannah doubts that Toby ever went to the house.
Who do you believe?

11.

I believe the boy. I believe James.

Still sitting on my coffee table he said in that low, robotic voice of his, 'I beat the bully in a fight. I wouldn't let him out of the water. I'm just not sure why now. It was as if I was being directed; I was being told what to do. Kolko was egging me on.

'Then he showed me my father is happy. He made the boats dance.'

Here James stopped. Talk about an after-dinner speaker – talk about a *pro*. It was Annette who broke the silence. Her voice as soft as toilet paper she asked, 'What do you mean, James?'

James nodded his head – in silent acknowledgement of the fact that he had known that this would be explored; that he hadn't given enough information. And for this kid, that is what it's all about now, giving information.

'I couldn't believe what I was seeing, but Mr Kolko was conducting the boats, making them come closer. He was waving his arms, like an orchestra conductor.'

I knew it was probably a dumb question, but someone had to say it. 'Are you sure it couldn't have been a coincidence? That they started up at the same time? Maybe they all wanted to move on at the same time,' I said.

'Oh, they didn't start their engines, if that's what you mean,' James replied.

'Yes, that's what I mean. What are you saying? The boats moved *on their own*?'

He nodded his head. 'They moved faster than they should have as well.'

'Weren't there people on board them?'

'I don't know. I didn't see any people but there might have been.'

Hannah asked, 'What happened next?'

'They started to fly.'

'The boats?' Hannah clarified.

Again, the lad nodded his head. 'I was scared but it was beautiful at the same time,' he said, and only shrugged at my interjection of 'I bet it was!'

'When you say the boats flew...' Annette starts.

'They left the water. It was like a dream but it was really happening.'

'And where was the bully boy at this point?' she continued.

'Are you thinking of asking him for a corroborative statement?'

'There's no need to be nasty to Annette, Tom,' said Hannah.

'I wasn't being nasty! It's a fair question, isn't it? If the other boy was there as well...'

'I couldn't hear much,' James carried on. We might as well have said nothing at all. 'There was water crashing all over the place, but I could hardly hear it. Especially when the canal boats were in the air... They were dancing!'

'And then what happened?' Hannah wanted to know.

'The boats made a smile for me! And it was my dad's smile. And Mr Kolko explained that he was happy with me because I was doing what Mr Kolko wanted. That I had to carry on doing what Mr Kolko wanted. Because then he would still be happy with me. And then he told me to *remember* my dad, but that was the bit that didn't make any sense – because I can't do anything *but* remember my dad.'

'A smile, you say. How many boats are we talking about?'

James counted the boats in his memory, looking up at the ceiling, where a trio of tiny flies moved among the lanes in the paintwork. To assist him in the project of recalling a precise number, James moved his fingers. 'There were three boats to make the smile,' he answered; 'then there was one for the nose, hanging completely upside-down; and one each for the eyes. It was my father's face.'

A dreaded silence. It beats and beats. The only sound is that of the files in their aerial combat, or courtship.

As if she had read my mind Hannah asked James, 'What else did Mr Kolko say?'

'How long were they up there?' Annette asked at the same time.

James took the second question first. 'Just a few seconds. He wanted me to make my life perfect, and if I did he could make my dad come back to me.'

'And that's the word he used? Perfect?' Hannah said.

The boy nodded. He told us, in a staccato that chilled more and more as it went on, about the night he'd seen the fireworks instructing him to kill his stepfather. He told us about the trip to London to buy the weapon – he had mentioned this already, but now he went into it in more detail. He told us about what he'd heard of the broken fate of the boy called Wolfe. He told us what I have provided to date.

It was like an inventory.

'And he wants me to wait for further direction,' the boy concluded a long time later.

'I bet he does,' I said to no one in particular, and I said it with bitterness in my mouth.

When he finished, the silence wasn't pure. By this time in the day, vehicles had started to arrive in the car park behind the flats, people home from their day's work. Doors slamming; a rumble of a bag on wheels across the bricks. Was that a bird I heard singing or a squirrel chirping? Keys skittered into the locks on my block. And I was grateful for all of this noise; appreciative of every car horn tooting from Billington Road, of every juggernaut grumbling past the front of the building…

'May I use your bathroom?' James asked.

'As long as you don't try to kill yourself,' I *didn't* say – but it was a close one. It was a swift and brutal exercise in self-censorship. 'Sure, go ahead.'

Great minds thinking alike and all that, Annette said, 'Why not leave the gun here, though, eh James? I'm going to give your mother a call while you're in there.'

'My mother is dead. I shot her in the throat.'

'Okay.' Annette's voice (or was it Caitlin's voice?) was stern and crisp. 'But you might have been mistaken, James.' And what was it that bothered me so about the voice she used to talk to him? With a nod of my head, I had it. Her voice was too level for someone who didn't lie regularly. Or for someone who had never contemplated cutting up her own sons with an axe during a bout of depression. 'I would like you to leave the gun here anyway, is that okay?'

'Okay,' the boy agreed. The gun was in a pocket inside his coat; I didn't know that coats came with pockets as big as that. The gun was gigantic.

He placed it on the coffee table, where he'd sat.

'First on the left,' I told him, though surely the directions were unnecessary; it's not as though I live in The Ritz. In something tasting like horror we watched him leave the room; go into the khazi.

'I wish I had some dope,' Annette muttered.

'We're not allowed to smoke anything any more. Including weed,' said Hannah.

'I'm not going to. I just said I wish. There are times and places for special circumstances, surely. If *this* doesn't qualify as one, I don't know what will.'

'Shall I pose the obvious question?' I asked. 'What do we do now?'

Dorothy had been quiet for a long time; Patrick too. Now, as though a multi-tasking ventriloquist had his arms up their individual spines, they gabbled as one.

'It's the police,' said she, 'it's got to be.'

'The boy's not as cracked as you might imagine,' said he.

I looked at the old fella. 'What was that you said, Patrick?'

'He's had his mind played with, no question of that, but he's not a loony tune. That would be my own interpretation. I've seen things myself, boy – things I couldn't explain.'

It had been a long time since anyone had called me *boy*. I found I quite liked it.

'I had some psychosis once. I've 'ad it all, son. Neurosis, psychosis, palpitations…'

'Dad. This isn't the time for your deathbed confessions, all right?' Annette – moody.

'No it never is with you, is it, girl?'

'He'll hear us,' Hannah said.

'I don't care if he does! This is my home!'

'We have to tell the police,' said Dorothy.

'I know. I agree,' Hannah answered. 'There's just something…'

'Don't get wet, Han,' I said to her. 'Dolly's right.'

'I *know* she's right. What do you mean, wet? This is out of control, Tom.'

'Exactly,' said Dorothy. 'We'll give it to the professionals to deal with.'

'But what makes us think they'll do any better?' I argued, stupidly. 'I know I'm fighting against myself by saying this, but seriously. This won't be in their rule book, you know.'

'Yes it will. Violent crimes happen every day.'

'Not around here they don't!'

'The police,' said Dorothy firmly.

Then we heard something unexpected. From the bathroom came the sound of running water, and we looked at one another with befuddlement.

'Is he running a bath?' Hannah asked.

'It sounds like it,' I answered, standing up. 'I don't want his parents' blood in my tub!'

In the hall I banged on the bathroom door.

'Open up, James! Open the door right now!'

No reply. I tried the handle and of course the boy had locked it from within.

'Jesus, this gets worse,' I muttered. Dorothy had joined me. She called James's name through the wood. I jumped up and tried to get a look through the window on top of the door. I couldn't see much. 'You'll have to break it down,' Dorothy said to me.

'This is all I need. *Come out of there, James!*'

Still no reply. With my right shoulder I nudged the door, knowing in advance that any such exertion would cause shock-waves of pain to whip through my bad back.

Back in the lounge, Hannah was standing at my desk, the phone in her hand. I heard her ask for the police. She had dialled 999 for Emergency Services.

Sweat on my face, like a rash. Sweat all over my body. The panic fit on me, as heavy as lead. When I ran my fingers through my hair, either my fingers or my hair was limply damp with per-spiration. 'Grovebury Road,' Hannah said. 'Number eight. Up-stairs flat. There's a boy committing suicide in my friend's bath-room.'

Committing suicide? Had I really considered that? I suppose I must have because her words failed to shock me. I hit the door with my right shoulder once more; the pain shot through my lower back like volts.

'What've you got in there?' Patrick asked. 'For him to do himself a mischief, I mean.'

'Don't give him *ideas*, Dad!'

What *did* I have in there? In the moment I couldn't recall. There were probably razor blades; but then again, maybe the lad had seen enough blood for one day and would go the drinking-lubricants route. There was enough shampoo to drown a buffalo; I was sure about this because I hadn't been using it lately. I hadn't been washing any more than was strictly speaking necessary.

'Have you got a screwdriver?' Dorothy asked.

'A *screwdriver?*'

'Yes, a screwdriver, Tom. Do you own one?'

'There's one of top of the fridge, in a blue box. Why do you want one?'

'Jesus. I thought I might make a nice wine rack. What do you *think* I want one for?'

She disappeared back into the lounge.

'I don't know; that's why I'm asking!' I was a little bit stung by her reproof.

'To take the bloody door handle off, of course!'

The idea seemed sensible. 'There's a hammer there as well.' To the door I shouted, 'Turn the water off, James, it's not yours and you don't pay for it. And if you've got blood on my carpets I am *not* going to be happy, do you understand me?'

James said nothing at all. Perhaps he was already dead. Perhaps he was slumped against the door itself and that was why I couldn't barge my way in. All that came was the sound of water crashing into my bathtub. It falls quickly and only takes a few minutes to fill to the brim; we didn't have long to play with.

From outside, from somewhere in town, came the sound of sirens.

I couldn't say for sure that the Emergency Services would be too late – I had no way of knowing that – but I had an inkling; that's all it was. Save your petrol, boys and girls; there's no rush – the kid's brown bread. The nutter's completed his own personal trilogy.

Let him rest now.

V.

1.

Tousle-haired, wiry, wired with a cocktail hangover, from reluctant sleep and breakfast nerves, junior mechanic Ian arrives at Bible Street Cars on his skateboard as the lines on his digital watch make the subtle transformation from 7:38 to 7:39. He spits into a darkened acre of gravel; contemplates his walk to the garage's wide doors. As much of the morning as can be seen in the bad winter light is fair; the fresh air to Ian's shaved chin is a valuable tonic. He stamps down on the back end of the board; the front end leaps up into Ian's right-handed confident grip. His trainers slide and crackle on tiny stones; Ian hears this crunchy rhythm even through the barrage of jungle that he sometimes thinks is too *thick* to climb through his iPod's earbuds.

'Well fuck me,' Ian whispers to the wind as he gets closer. At the sight he hastens his pace, lengthens his stride. He knows that Roy is already at work – the office light is on, as well as the harsh floodlight set in the wall above the garage doors, which drenches the forecourt in a sickly beige illumination. Stepping into the office, Ian is in epiphanic spirits, hoping that he can tell Roy the news – he hopes that his employer was too strung-out or hungover to have noticed what is parked outside. 'You'll never guess…' Ian begins, but stops dead. It is not Roy in the office.

'Morning, Ian.'

'Morning. Where's Roy?' Ian asks, instinctively adjusting his grip on the skateboard, making it a weapon if necessary.

'He's at stool. My name's Kolko.' The other man takes a step and holds out his hand.

To take it for a handshake Ian must relinquish his grip on

his means of transport and his potential ally in a fight. Ian places the skateboard on top of the waist-high fridge, next to a red tray burdened with an industrial-sized jar of supermarket-brand coffee the size of a bongo, some ill-washed utensils and a sugar bowl whose contents are polluted with syrupy stripes of coffee granule contamination.

'He's what?' Ian asks, shaking the visitor's hand.

'He's having a dump, Ian,' Kolko replies. 'I was trying to be polite.'

'No need, around here. Roy swears like a fishwife. Are you bringing one in or collecting?'

The smile on Kolko's face seems as fixed as a clown's paint. 'Funnily enough, Ian, a bit of both. I've already done the collecting and now I've brought it in.'

From Ian's left side, beyond the wall, the toilet flushes. Water moves in complicated surges in the pipes; the sugar spoons rattle on the fridge in metallic applause. The penny drops.

'Oh, it was *you*,' says Ian, 'brought Miss Paddington's motor back. It was you, right?'

'Yes.'

'Did you nick it in the first place?' Ian jokes, leaving no time for a response. 'I'll brew up. Coffee or tea? The coffee's shit but the tea's not much better – keep meaning to bring in some quality.' Ian has turned away from Kolko; he has picked up the kettle. It is already heavy, and hot from a recent boil. 'I was hoping to surprise Roy with the news. Like the Car Fairy paid us a visit.'

Wiping his hands, the manager appears from stage left; so, in his wake, does a shitbat of density and squalor. 'Are my ears burning?'

'My fucking *nose* is burning,' Ian replies. 'Close the door fuck sake!'

'Is that any way to speak in front of an officer of the law?

Have a seat, officer. Where's me manners?' Roy closes the door to the khazi.

'Coffee or tea?' Ian repeats.

'Nothing for me, thanks,' says Kolko.

'Black with six, cheers, E. Got a few cobwebs to blow away, you know how it is. Now, the car. Where was it?'

'Milton Keynes. Near the Council offices.'

'That's where *I* live,' says Ian, pouring water.

'Yes you do, don't you?'

Ian turns. '*I* didn't nick it.'

'Bit of joyriding, was it? We call it twocking, Ian, you probably know that. Taken Without Owner's Consent.'

'Wait a minute, officer,' Roy interrupts.

Kolko turns slightly to face him. 'Or maybe it was you, setting him up.'

'Woah there. It weren't neither of us!'

'Do you know what the penalty is for wasting police time? Or for making a fraudulent insurance claim?'

'I've no idea, but—'

'You've no idea? Why not? Done a stretch, haven't you? You must have *some* idea.'

Roy dips his chin. 'Not in front of the lad, please.'

'Have you done porridge?' Ian asks.

'Long time ago.'

'Old habits, eh, Roy?'

Roy's voice is firm. 'I have an honest, respectable business here, and this is harassment, Kolko, though God knows what you intend to get out of it. But I'm aware of me rights. And I'll be reporting you for these accusations.'

'Will you now? Well fire away, with your grubby fat fingers – who'll listen to *you*?'

'There's no need for this. You've found the car, I can return it to Miss Paddington…'

'You'd like to fuck her, wouldn't you, Roy? Be honest; no one would blame you. She's a good-looking sort.'

'What's that got to do with anything?'

'She'll be nice and grateful, Roy, even to a fat oaf like yourself. Putty in your greasy paws. Probably let you earn your brown wings with her.'

'Why don't you leave?' asks Ian.

Kolko smiles again. 'I think I will. I never could stand for too long a place smelling so *strongly* of failure and manure. Change your diet, Roy. You'll be dead in five years.'

Kolko is out of the office. Ian watches him with the attention of a trainee sheepdog, following. At the wide garage doors the policeman turns. He says, 'I'll be watching this place.'

'We've done absolutely nothing wrong, mate; my conscience is as pure as the driven. Someone's got it in for Roy, that's all it is… What was he inside for?' Ian adds in a whisper.

'Running guns to Africa.'

Roy appears to them. He sees Ian's eyes widen – in wonder? in fear?

'What's he say?'

The question is directed at Ian but Kolko takes it.

'Says he thinks someone's got your number, trying to whittle you down. Is that what you think too? Because of two *robberies*?' Kolko asks nastily.

'And the pizza thing,' Ian adds.

'…What pizza thing?'

'The poisoned pizza, delivered to my door at home. Sick as a rat I was.'

'Did she now?' Kolko murmurs.

Roy steps closer, sniffing blood, albeit from a tiny cut. 'What makes you say *she*?' he asks. 'No one mentioned *she* about the pizza.'

Kolko's face is a picture, Roy reports. 'Face like a rent boy's ringpiece,' are his exact words – when I next meet him in the public house.

2.

'She had to have a key for the front door to let herself in. She had to know the code to turn off the alarm. *Then* she had to know where the safe box is, where I keep the car keys. *Then* she had to know which car keys to take, drive the fucking car onto the yard... *Excusez-moi,*' Roy belches, 'then do the whole operation in fucking reverse to lock up again.' He simmers with disbelief.

'It's a wonder she didn't park it back inside the garage, instead of leaving it on the forecourt. Daredevil behaviour like that,' I say to the big man, 'and for what?'

'To show she can. No other reason. I know a bit about showoff crime,' he adds darkly. Curls of beer foam chug down his throat like soapsuds down a drain. 'You want another?'

'Pope Catholic?'

While I'm waiting for Roy, I scan the crowd with the lazy-lidded gaze of the quasi-blottoed. A young man walks past in a T-shirt bearing the London Underground logo. The words on it read MIND THE TWAT.

'Here comes summer,' Roy announces as he places down the pints. For a minute or so nothing else is said. While I noodle on what Roy has told me, a mobile rings. Both Roy and I go for our own, gunslinger-swift. It's his, but he's adjusted the ring tone since last we supped. It's the same as mine now.

'Yellow... And a good evening to you as well, Mrs A. You well?'

Evidently the answer to this question of welfare is complex; Roy is gone for some time, attention-wise, the scalene triangles and frowning musculature of his face setting *denser*, more defined, as he listens.

On completing the call, Roy sits back slightly, forgetting that he's on a stool, not a chair with a back, nearly falls, breaks wind (the sound of an inquisitive puppy), then snatches back his balance, accidentally punching the side of the table, spurring into circular motion both the base of the table itself and the glasses thereon, which spin like coins, before he smiles at the demonstration of kinetic energy as it whirs and clinks to a halt, plumply sighing with satisfaction and assessing the situation with a greedy-eyed critique of 'No harm done.'

'No harm done,' I agree.

'You'll never guess who that was, Tom.'

'That was Mrs A.'

'That was Mrs A, well eavesdropped. But talking of coincidence, which we weren't, you'll never guess who Mrs A happens to *be*.'

'Who is she?'

'Mrs A is Amelior Anderson – owner of the *first* car that cunt took off me. Funny timing, that – us just talking about it…'

'Is it? Never mind,' I add quickly.

'Why, don't you think it's a coincidence? We could've been discussing carburettors.'

'I take your point. It's just, I'm not sure I believe in them anymore. Coincidences, not carburettors. What did she say?'

'I'd like to hear your views on coincidences another time,' Roy replies, and from the piglet iron gleam in his piglet-squint eyes it takes no miracle of investigation to infer that he is far from unhappy to be abandoning the topic. Roy wishes to discuss Amelior Anderson as much as I do.

'She said…'

3.

'I don't get out as much as I used to, Roydoodoo. I'm sure you can only imagine that, still at your age, but the years they go by fleet of foot, Roypopo, believe me they very much do indeed.'

'Is there something wrong with the Punto again, Mrs A?'

'No. Come down off there, Nob! Down! Good boy! Come to Mummypoos, good boy. No indeed, Roytylicious, the car is ticketybooboos. Now don't scratch, Nob, there's a lovely tomtom. I've got a fat Nob in my lap, Royker, pardon my attention span. You know what it's like, but I wouldn't be alone, I don't think anyone should be alone. Are you alone, Roymood?'

'Yes I am, Mrs A. About the Punto.'

'Well don't be. Get yourself a Nob or Nob substitute for your lap. Rear from young is ideal, not always possible I grant you. The Punto! Yes! Well as I say, I rarely drive – the pet shop for a particular canned pilchard that Nob prefers. Insists on, don't you, Nobbywoowoo? Yes you do, *yes* you do, but I thought I should rather *clean* it a tad don't you know. The *inside* as it were. And *what* do you think, Roymaster, what do you *think* I should discover on the floor beneath. Beneath the driver's old *seat* do you follow. It gave you a scare, didn't it Nobcheese? Yes it did!'

'What was it, Mrs A?'

'What was what, Roystander?'

'You *found*, Mrs A.'

'Why, it was a wig, Royllover. Rather a woman's *wig*. And while I must concede I am no more than an armchair Miss Marple, it must be said, neither was she. Miss Marple I mean. And I think I'm old enough and ugly enough to put two and two together, Roypaste. It's the *thief's* wig.'

'What colour is it?'

'Auburn. Blonde streaks.'

'It could well be, Mrs A. it might well be at that.'

4.

'Let's say it is, Roy. Or Roy-no-more, I should say. Roy-no-suffix…'

'Yeah yeah.'

'Let's say it is. Where does it leave us?' I ask. 'Instead of looking for a woman with *that* coloured hair, and *that* style, which was vague enough by the way, you're now looking for a woman with *any* coloured hair, or no hair at all, in any style.'

'Or no style at all,' Roy interrupts me. 'I know, I've thought of that. But you can only fuck with the cock you've been given, Tom. You want another, or is it home to toast and marmalade?' He has drained his pint.

'Yeah another.' It is actually my turn to buy but Roy seems not to have noticed, and you don't look a gifthorse in the mouth. 'What's *that* supposed to mean, the cock you've been given? You looked like you'd won the Lottery!'

'Yeah? And *you* look like you've just come inside her and reached round to find she's got bollocks.' Unsteadily Roy rises to his feet. 'It's a *wig*, Tom. She'll have left, fucking, *follicles* in it. You never heard of the DNA process? It's revolutionized–' He belches roundly. 'Pardon *me*. Revolutionized police work.'

'Sure, mate. I've got my own testing kit at home; it's linked up to the fucking, the FBI database of all known offenders. What you been sniffing?'

'I'm not suggesting *we* do it, Tom, you silly toss. Put your tongue away and give your brain a chance. I'm talking about the filth. They have access to technology like that.'

'The police?' I ask, my chin tilted upwards through necessity, not through choice. Towering high above my seated position, Roy hasn't moved; or rather, he hasn't shifted his feet. There is nothing about Roy you'd call *still*; paralysis is not one of Roy's worries. Muscle tics, head shakes, hip realignment for the purposes of balance; all of the above are in ready evidence. We have drunk a lot already. 'Why would they bother testing a wig?'

'It was a crime wunnit? They do still check up on such matters, correct me if I'm wrong. I pay my taxes. Sometimes when they're due, not even late. Besides, what have we got to lose? I'm going round there; collect it – the wig.'

'Not now you're not,' I tell him.

'No, not now – after the next round.'

He has taken my protestation as a criticism I'm making that it's his turn up the bar – which it isn't anyway – and that he's shirking his duty. 'Not then either!' I go on quickly. 'It's nearly eleven o'clock, Roy; she's an old lady.'

'Yes genius, and *she* just phoned *me*. They don't need to sleep much, old ladies. Like *Thatcher*. Four nights an hour apparently. Be back-a minute.'

I am not against Roy's proposal in principle. It is more the case that across the moat of beer I've drunk there is no sturdy bridge of rationality. Or to put it another way (I feel I should), I don't know what to *do* with the wig. Later on (a matter of minutes) Roy will reveal to me his plan of handing the wig to Kolko – as if *that* might help. Roy thinks he needs to vindicate himself (and Ian) in front of the man.

Not for one moment do I imagine that Kolko will give a fuck about a robber's hairpiece. Wouldn't surprise me to learn, in fact, that Kolko planted it in Amelior's car. For Kolko wants trouble. Kolko *loves* trouble. *Agent provacateur* does not come close; does not do it justice. Kolko is more than a shit-stirrer *par excellence*. Fucker writes the manual – writes the *exam* – on shit-stirring.

Our pints concluded, and against my better judgement, Roy and I venture in the direction of Stoke Hammond, towards Mrs A's house. Having made calls to Leighton Taxis (one a piece, just in case of operator fibs), we learn that tonight a taxi-drought is in operation; there are none for hire, neither for love nor money.

'Come on, we'll walk,' Roy decides, 'pick one up in the market square.' But there are no cabs there either. Ever the optimist at such times, Roy says, 'Walk a bit further; bound to be one in Linslade.'

'And if there isn't?' I ask.

'And if there isn't, we can both do with the exercise,' he answers.

The walk will take two hours, and it has started raining.

On the way to Mrs A's, we talk about Stephen. I hereby confess, what with the rain, the surprising noise of the pub kickouts, a fight outside Kebab Ye (two fat girls in cowgirl *ensemble*, a minute earlier a hen party presumably, now a feisty Dodge City showdown of nail and slur), some of the conversation is sketchy, inkblotto, marred by inner and outer storm. What I *do* recall is Roy's reiteration that it was Stephen of all people who taught him to read – taught him to read while they rotted at Her Majesty's Pleasure… As the road mounts a slight rise to clear the canal by a Tesco supermarket (the very place where Annette first met the boy James), the rain strengthens – it falls harder. A barrel of thunder rolls, up and left a bit, towards Wing, towards Aylesbury, or so it seems; but nearly simultaneously, lightning tiptoes on the water, nimbly, as though wary of being extinguished.

'That was close,' Roy states the obvious. 'You ever been hit by lightning, Tom?'

'Funnily enough, no, mate; it's one of my life's ambitions. We should see it realized this very evening; or should we take shelter?'

'It's only *rain*, Tom. Yeah okay,' he reconsiders swiftly: another drum of thunder, beaten deep into the sky, prompts this change of mind.

Under the bridge, by the supermarket, near the bench on

which James sat to talk to an Annette on her stroll to work, is where we carry on with our discussion.

'I can scarcely believe it's true,' I tell Roy. 'Stephen didn't do *anything*. Except drink. Even his porn was low ambition. Low calibre.'

'But you didn't really *know* him, Tom. That takes confinement, midnight secrets.' The rain being no better but no worse, we decide to take off, away from the bridge's shelter, but along the canal and not the road. If nothing else, it's the scenic route (I don't get to the water too often these days), and although there is obviously no chance of hailing that long-sought-for taxi, and despite the lateness of the hour and the certainty in my mind that Amelior Anderson will not be up when we finally get there, I find that the walk is doing me good. In truth, my back has not felt so healthy for weeks. In addition, it serves my spirits well to be Roy's appointed tour guide this night.

'This is where Annette first met James – this very bench.'

'This is where James fought with Wolfe, the school bully. Then he had his vision about his dad, not sure exactly where but along here somewhere.'

The canal path walk to The Globe is easy enough ('This is where Annette meets James's mum, or used to at any rate'), the rain loosening pockets of mud but remaining more or less solid to the tread. It is beyond The Globe that conditions deteriorate. The path becomes runny as raw egg; my feet are freezing; I need a jimmy. What seems like a whole night later, the oasis of the Grand Union public house rears up, the security spotlights triggered on by our movement, the click of a camera activated, the rain appearing sugary in the custard illumination.

'Shame they're not open,' says Roy. 'I could murder another pint.'

We are dead on our feet by the time we reach Amelior Anderson's house. It's the furthest I've walked for years – possibly the furthest I've ever walked – and my muscles ache even where you would think no muscles have been used. My chest feels like I've been benching rounds of fifty for the last two hours.

'What now?' I ask Roy.

We are on the pavement outside the property. The only sounds are the result of rain; gargling in the throats of drains and gutters; tapping on car roofs, including the 'errant Punto', parked on the asphalt driveway; entertaining bits of ornamental rockery, and making flowers bow their penitent burdened heads. From across the field at the end of Mrs Anderson's road, from a stable building no larger than a gravy cube or a wrap of resin at this distance, floats the mingled aroma of grain, harness dressing, rubber boots, rope and hay; but even the horses within are silent and asleep.

'Seriously, Roy, we look like burglars. What're we going to do now we're here?'

'I don't know, I've sobered up a bit. Ring the bell?'

'Let's go home, mate; this is stupid.'

'Going home would be stupid,' Roy replies. 'We just got here! Least we can do is get a cup of tea! We're soaking wet for the old puffin!'

Looking straight into Roy's eyes, I tell him: 'Roy, listen. We should have turned back an hour ago; this is madness – we're gonna get ourselves arrested!'

'For doing what?'

'Loitering.'

'Without intent. Free country. We can stand here like twats if we so choose.'

'Well you said it.'

'No *law* against it.'

'We're gonna catch our deaths,' I add.

'No law against that either,' Roy snaps, and unfastens the sneck that holds the waist-high gate closed. He swings it open; steps onto the property. A short narrow path bisects the front lawn; Roy strolls along it, five strides and he's at the front door. Hanging baskets brimming with night-dampened colour, like monstrous earrings in the great lobes of the porch, they twist and swing gently in the wind the rain's brought.

As Roy pushes the divot to sound the bell, I hasten myself on to the path and fasten the gate behind me. The bell has five notes, on a rising scale. As though I might need to use him as a shield, I tuck in close behind Roy and peek out from his right side. I am made more nervous by movement to the edge of the garden. *The hell's that?* I'm about to say, when the creature's identity becomes clear and I am saved the bother of forming the simple words. It is a cat; Mrs Anderson's cat, I'm willing to bet – the famous or infamous Nob. The light green eyes of radiation, piercing; the tomcat simply sitting there, in a flower bed, in the torrential rain, watching his mistress's visitors with a gaze stern and true… The cat puzzles me. Aren't cats supposed to loathe water, run from rain? *This* cat doesn't and *this* cat isn't. Butch and brawny, independent it would seem of mind and body, this cat Nob merely blinks in a manner that appears disdainful – curtaining off for a fraction of a second that unbelievably green stare – and continues to watch me watching him.

'One more ring,' Roy assures me, 'and then we're off, we're giving up. I've got work in the morning, unlike some.'

'It *is* the morning. Check the moggy,' I add, pointing at Nob.

Roy clocks it. 'What about it?' he asks, leaning forward to press the divot again.

'Sitting in the garden, watching us. Cats hate the rain, don't they? They take shelter under cars or whatever. Or even under this porch.'

'Well, this cunt don't.'

'Exactly.'

Roy fails to read my mind. 'It wasn't under the porch, Tom. We didn't scare it off or nuffing,' he says.

'That's my point, Roy. *Something* did. Why else has it not gone home through the catflap?'

'How do you know there's a catflap?'

'There's always a fucking catflap!'

'Hang up, mate, I hear movement.'

So do I; but why does this lead to the expansion of dread in my midriff? Very suddenly I want to be sick, but it's not about lagers downed.

A horizontal yellow aurora, above the top of the curtain in front of the door. Mrs A has switched on the hall light. The curtain flips back – a whispery rattle of wooden hooks – and her blurred, showerglassed appearance through the door's dimpled windowpane.

'Who is it at this time of night?' a voice croaks, but croaks with appreciable volume. Mrs Anderson juts her chin and face towards the glass and the darkness beyond; towards her visitors.

'It's Roy, Mrs A: the mechanic. You called me about the wig?'

'…Who?'

I can't tell you how grateful I am – how relieved – to view, albeit as a smudge, this short old lady, made wider than my mind's-eye has expected, either by the incorrect lens prescription of the door's pane; by the voluminous nightdress that she seems to wear (which is fair enough, given the hour); by the rainfall hampering my own eyesight, with drips clinging to my eyebrows and my spectacles; or by any combination of the above. What has made me think that someone else would answer?

'Royvinder, Mrs Anderson. Roy-Roy. Roywalker. Roy-pol-loi.'

'...*Who?* It's very late, you know. I don't open the door to all and sundry at any hour, let alone in the middle–'

'It's Royston, Mrs A. You called me about a wig.'

'What wig?' she calls through the door. 'What the devil are you talking...'

'She's gone loopy,' Roy whispers.

'It wasn't her, mate,' I whisper but with greater ferocity. 'Let's get the fuck out of Dodge, Roy.'

'What?'

'I'll call the police!' cries Mrs Anderson.

'*It wasn't her, Roy!*' I crabwalk back in the direction of the gate. '*Come on, let's go! Now! Now, Roy!*' Energetically I wave him away from the door; my biceps stinging.

But Roy seems reluctant to shift one iota. (Silent up to now, Nob the cat hisses – or is it a feline sneeze? I do not want to be here to find out.) Roy has dug deep in the sand for his treasure, and he won't leave carrying anything less than a shell... He looks back into the glass – and from the gate, so do I, although for me half the pane is obscured by Roy's torso. It doesn't stop me seeing...

'Jesus,' Roy mutters, then louder he shouts: 'Mrs A! *Behind you!*'

In the two dimensions I can make out on the distorted screen – height and width – the man I myopically observe is larger than Mrs Anderson. He finds his place behind her shoulders, in much the same way as I did with Roy. The difference being, the man in the dark uniform has no intention of using Amelior as a shield.

Dry words crackle in my throat; I cannot speak, not even raise the kind of warning that Roy is sallying forth. At my back, in a house across the street, a light is turned on. I feel this rather than see this, I cannot turn either. I can't do anything but watch – and listen.

Listen to Roy as he thumps on the glass and the frame around it, bellowing *Mrs A! Mrs A, look out! Behind you!*

There is not much of the window left to see through now that Roy has adopted this new position, but there's enough. I see the man behind the old lady wrap his darkly-clothed left arm across her chest. My paralysis at an end, I step in closer. The man's right hand is holding a knife. He draws it across Mrs A's throat. And I see that worst horizon: a throbbing blood-red line.

Then the attacker allows his victim to fall to her knees.

She doesn't scream – perhaps she can't – and for a second it is only the cat who is willing to voice any condemnation: a vociferous hiss. Then the cat stretches; Nob takes a run-up, bounds up and over the front perimeter wall and hurtles into the street, where he leaves my consciousness.

Roy is frozen by the front door, all but catatonic through the shock of what we've witnessed. I see that lights have gone on in two more houses, one of them Mrs A's immediate next-door neighbour. It's impossible to ignore the fact that we will have been seen, committed to memory, maybe photographed; none of this, however, stops me wanting to run away. 'We have to go, Roy,' I manage, the words hardening and assuming new significance even as they leave my mouth.

It has to be Kolko within. Kolko is Amelior's killer – and now he approaches the door, filling the space, with a *smile* on his face through the glass.

'You fucking bastard,' Roy whispers.

'I'm leaving. I can't do this. We'll call the filth.'

'He *is* the filth.'

'He's got a knife, Roy! Unglue yourself!'

On the other side of the door, Kolko wipes his weapon clean on the curtain.

Roy backs away – stunned into sense. *'Call the police!'* he hollers at anyone who might be taking notes for near-future statements. He doesn't wait for me to open the gate, his size thirteen Doc Martens pound flat a flower, and hauling himself up, he performs a ragged version of the Fosbury Flop as he clambers over the same wall via which Nob the cat had made good a more elegant egress.

Leaving the gate swinging behind me, I tear into the street. Roy has gained a few metres on me; I follow his thick back as he sprints ahead, surprisingly *lithe*. The mobile is burning a hole in my jacket pocket; as I run I fish it out, wanting to call Sabrina but knowing it must be 999 first.

5.

Rain like a disease, like an affliction, as we make our way back to the canal path.

We don't speak much. What we've witnessed has eaten our words. I have phoned the police, much against Roy's strong opinion on the matter; breathing heavily I have explained the situation as best I can. The operator tells us to stay where we are but I tell her it's not safe to do so. I listen out for a siren; I hear nothing of the sort, but maybe this is not so strange: the roads are empty – there is no need for a copper to hit the blues. Behind our backs, somewhere minutely north, a car should roll into Amelior Anderson's road.

'Dump the phone now,' Roy tells me. 'In the water. No one'll ever find it.'

'What do you mean? It cost me eighty sheets!'

'Get rid of it, Tom, it's a dangerous thing to have knocking around.'

'For who? I've done nothing wrong, mate. I reported a crime!'

'I don't wanna be involved, mate, in case I ain't made that point perfectly fucking clear. Get shot of the cunt.'

Panting like panthers, we look at the canal as it shivers in the wind; at the moon through its cloudy wrappings, the colour of aged meat. Absurdly I fancy a swim. I take the mobile from inside my jacket, having to lower the zip to do so. This releases a pint of warm air, thick with rich body odour. 'Are you sure?' I ask Roy, and he nods his head with childish enthusiasm, naughtyish.

It sinks; the water gulps; we stand there, frozen in time until I say, 'We should go to the police station – recite it all again. Give our statements. Why are you shaking your head?'

'Because of what I just told you, muppet. I was never here tonight, Tom, neither was you. We were tucked up in our jim-my-jams, snoring like walruses, you got it?'

'They'll find out.'

'Find out what? There was no one to see us.' He starts to walk away from me.

'The neighbours saw us, Roy,' I reply to his shoulders, which shrug.

'As you say: we did nothing wrong.'

'You're not making any sense, mate.'

'I'm still pissed.'

'Well so am I, but even I can see–'

'Just leave it, Tom. Stop *nagging*, you're like me fuckin ex. Grow up for a minute. You got an alibi for tonight?'

I think of Sabrina but the picture fades as quickly as ripples on the surface of the water. 'No I haven't.'

'Then I'll be it. And you can be mine; and everything can be snugly. Blood brothers, Tom; soldiers in arms and all that ca-per. In the ditches filled with blood and piss.'

'Now you're a poet, right?'

'We got tanked up at The Leper, we went for chips…'

'Where?'

'Kebab Ye. No, we went for *kebabs,* that's better.'

'They'll *check*, mate.'

'Listen: we ain't done nothing *wrong.*' Roy raises his voice.

'Seriously, Roy, it's the police station and the truth. What are you running away from?'

He turns; never before (as far as I can recall) have I felt in his presence so much like a puppy in the wake of a Great Dane. 'A murder, Tom,' he answers me slowly, boldly, as if I might not be able to grasp the finer points of his terminology. 'We are running away from a murder, mate. Of an old girl I happened to like a fair bit, as it goes, but even if I didn't – a murder, Tom. And I'm trying to get my head together, okay? And to do that I really don't need you yapping in my ear and giving me a brain disorder, okay?' With which he starts walking again – striding away from me, towards town.

'Well *I'm* going to the filth,' I call after him, already regretting losing my phone.

'You do as you please, mate. It's between you and your conscience innit? It's a free fucking country the last time I looked.'

'I'm going back to the house.'

'Now you're using your noodle! That's what I'm talking about!'

'Amelior's house, I mean.'

This stops Roy again, in his tracks. Pirouetting with comfortable ease he tells me: 'You're *doing* no such thing, twat. You developed glaucoma or summing? You did happen to witness the fact that there's a man with a knife back there.'

'He won't be there now.'

'Then why go back? For what *purpose*?'

'I don't know. I can't just go home and have a nice snooze.'

'No; you can go home and give your other half one. Wake her up. And give her one, all right? Then when you've laid your cement you'll fall asleep.'

'Hey presto,' I say sarcastically.

'Hey presto indeed. What's the time, Mr Wolf?'

'Nearly two. Mate, I'm scared.'

'Me too. Let's walk faster.'

6.

The one thing in life I think I trust right now is Kolko.

Tonight I stared into the mirror and tried to picture Sabrina; I tried to wear Sabrina's skin over my own. To assist me in the project I had carried a paintbox of her cosmetics from the bathroom to the lounge. I had sat in my blue rocking chair. I had smeared my face with lipstick, powder and paint.

Could I see that girlfriend of mine through the makeup?

I thought I could. I could. And she was calling to me from somewhere. As I stared into the fingerprinted compact mirror, Sabrina called to me and begged my solemn forgiveness, which of course I will never give. I won't forgive you, Sabrina, any more than I'll forgive myself.

It came to me in a moment of frenzied, restless calm.

Kolko – the word – is the backwards of *o'clock*, albeit with a different spelling.

Simon O'Clock.

But I don't know what significance this has. Simon, by implication, is time backwards.

Kolko is worth trusting because I know that he represents something evil. It is undeniably worth knowing, in the same way that you don't play silly buggers in the pit of the rattlesnake. You don't mess with the sea.

These are bigger boys than you and they can make you cry.

7.

What with all the mental hullaballoo that my head encases, it is astonishing that I should fall asleep; but given the fact that I wake up, it stands to reason that I must have at least dozed. My room is the same; the taste and effects of alcohol, papery yet paste-like, in my mouth – these too are the same. Blood is neither on my hands nor on my walls.

Evidently, before retiring, I got as far as removing my jacket; nothing else; that's as far as my aspirations reached. As I roll off the bed, my erection jolts inside my trousers, equal measure morning glory and piss-sustained; I must micturate and masturbate, probably in that order: because *nothing has changed*. Even my clothes remain damp, either with rainfull or sweat. I can imagine Stephen saying: *You can smell murder, can't you? Funny aroma. Not like you'd expect.* And then I ask him: *What do you want?*

When the telephone rings I am halfway through the first of my planned twin-set of bathroom activities. It's a point of principle (and fear) that I never fail to answer a call, so I tense my bladder to increase the rate of flow, and snatch up the receiver with my palms greasy with perspiration and my old chap dangling out of my britches.

'It's me,' says Roy. 'Didn't wake you, did I?'

'No.' But Roy hardly ever calls me; it's a surprise to hear his voice – I had expected the call, for some reason, to be from the Personnel Department. 'What's up?'

'I thought I'd call about the weather. What do you think?'

'No picnics today. What's up, Roy?'

'I just spoke to Amelior Anderson. She's still alive. Well obviously she's still alive if I just spoke to her, but. But did that actually *happen* last night, Tom?'

'What did she say?' I do not wish to answer his question because I'm afraid of it; and because I don't know how to. What did she call you, first?'

'What did she *call* me?'

'Yes. What name did she use?'

'Errrm. Roysnap, I think. Why do you ask?'

'Because I don't think it was her – any more than I think it was her on the dog about the wig. I wanted Kolko to do something wrong: call you Roy straight up, for example. Then we'd know it was definitely not Mrs A. If that makes sense.'

'I think so; but you haven't heard what she said yet. I says to her: How you feeling? I couldn't think of anything better than that, I think I was in shock.'

'I'm not surprised. What did *she* say?'

'She said: fine as rain on roses, Roygasbord. Then she told me about a dream she had. "I had rather a naughty dream, Royjob. A burly policeman came to me in my sleep and he gave me *such* a fucking, Royband – fucked my cunt to *jam*. He fucked me to ribbons! I'll be pissing clementine chutney for a fortnight." This from a woman who never swears.'

'It's Kolko. He's dicking with us.'

'But why? I don't even know the cunt!'

'Neither do I, but he's aiming at us – you, me, Dorothy, Hannah, Sam…' *Annette*, I want to add, but cannot. 'He's got a bee in his bonnet about us, about me if I'm the common link, and who knows how many other people he's doing this to… Do you believe in ghosts?'

'He's not a *ghost*, mate.'

'I didn't say he was. But do you?'

'Your Uncle Stephen used to; used to tell me about his dreams.'

Because I don't want to hear this right now I interrupt.

'How did the call end?'

'That was it. I was so stunned I didn't even ask about the wig, about *anything*. She sounded great.'

'As fine as rain on roses. There never was a wig, Roy.'

'I'm starting to come to that same opinion. What are we doing wrong, Tom? This has got to be punishment for something, hasn't it? We've done *something*.'

'We haven't done anything. Things are speeding up.'

8.

Hannah hasn't been lucky.

'The police force have never heard of him – you knew that much – and neither has Directory Enquiries.'

'Ah bless. You mean he's not listed in the phonebook? Go figure.'

'Yeah, well at least I'm *doing* something, Tom. That's more than I can say for you.'

It's ridiculous how rapidly this sentence feels like a swipe at my undoubtedly doughty constitution. Voice pinched I add: 'I wish I had your perspicacity, Hannah!'

'No you don't.'

'I'm doings things too!'

'Skiving off work doesn't count. Why are you being difficult, Tom?'

'I didn't know I was. What else did you try? Don't tell me the Internet.'

'The Internet. Why is that a dumb idea?'

'What did you find?'

'An Australian golfer.'

'Maybe he's putting on an accent.'

Although she chuckles briefly Hannah says, 'You don't have to be so sarcastic, you know? I am trying *muchos* hard here.'

'I'm sorry again; I'm edgy. I have something to tell you about last night.'

Kept crisp and brisk, the recital takes less than ten minutes, even including Hannah's need-to-know interjections and all-but-comical endorsements of my common sense with reference to my insistence about going to the law.

'But I *didn't* go; I bottled it,' I tell her.

'No, *Roy* bottled it; *you* didn't. *You* didn't do anything wrong.'

'That's become a bit of a refrain for us.'

'So what do you think he's doing? Other than putting on a show for us, of course. Which means, by the way, he *can* do accents.'

'Maybe he *is* an Australian golfer after all. Roy's suggestion is he's punishing us.'

'For what?'

'What's the worst thing you've ever done?'

Hannah chuckles. 'I'm not going to tell you that! Can I buzz you back?'

Hannah calls back too soon for my liking. I have not even booted up the computer; I want some adult entertainment to take my mind off things. Preferably with a model or two who resembles Han.

'There was no murder last night, Tom, in case you're wondering. I just this minute spoke to Mrs Anderson. She told me about her geraniums and called me Hannah Rabbit for some reason.'

'Because she's insane, that's why.'

'Perhaps. But she's live and kicking.'

'How did you get her number?'

'I rang Roy for it.'

'Does he know you know?'

'Yes. I'm going to call him back in a tick; relieve his tension, just like I'm relieving yours, I suspect.'

'Resisting the obvious innuendo, Hannah, can I ask what happens next?'

'The search goes on.'

'How's he doing it? I'm tired of the why. Let's look at how for a change.'

Hannah smiles down the line. 'Let's look at how,' she agrees.

9.

What choice do I have but to accept it all? To accept that there never was a Sabrina. To accept that Kolko is playing tricks with our minds…

To accept that a boy killed himself in my bathroom.

VI.

1.

'How did your flower arranging go?'

'The exam was last night. Fine, I think. We get the results in a couple of weeks. But I did everything old Charlie taught us. He took the whole class for a drink afterwards at The Enigma.'

'What did Dolly think of the exam? She do okay?'

'As far as I know. I wasn't really paying attention to her. Or to my exam, to be honest. There was an element of auto-pilot,' Hannah admits.

'How do you mean?'

'You'll cringe. It was a weird dream.'

'Oh dear. Flying again?' Sam asks.

'No. Swimming, actually. Or at least that's how it started.' Hannah explains her dream of having swum in the memory sea, before recounting the experience of waking up in Tom's bed, the latter half of the recital not without a good deal of steel and reluctance.

Both women are tense and controlled. They have chosen to meet on the High Street in Leighton Buzzard, near the old fire station which is now a restaurant. It is Tuesday, market day, and the weather is favourable enough to walk along either side of the street, stall-shopping and talking among the crowds – this means that they do not need to look at one another too much.

'They look nice.' Hannah beelines towards a stall selling Greek and Mediterranean nibbles. She buys a punnet of black stoned olives and a tub of sundried tomatoes.

They walk away from the vendor and his aromatic produce.

'I got dressed. Tom's still in bed, watching me; smile on his face like the cat that got the cream… Speaking of which, do you need anything from Boots?'

'No, not really. So did you and he… or not?'

'I don't know! That's the killer. It *felt* like it, but… I can't remember a thing about it if it happened. Or how I got there, or anything between watching TV at my place and that dream about the sea. It's like I've woken up with someone else's memories, but just for that little while.'

'Sabrina's, presumably; but let's not get *too* metaphysical.'

'Why not?' Hannah leaves her question unanswered. 'All I can think of is how determined I was to get out of there. Soon as I had my kit on I left the flat… and it's all real, Sam. There was no waking up in a chill; nothing. My car was outside; my keys were in my handbag. I drove home. Two thirty-nine by the clock on the dash when I pulled onto the drive.'

'I'm a bit jealous,' Sam admits. 'What's he like? Physically speaking.'

'Sam, please! I'm spilling out a crisis and you want to talk cock size?'

'Could you say that a bit louder?'

'Sorry.'

'You have to remember, this confession might be as close to a sexual encounter as I get this year the way things are going. Don't get censorious on me *now*.'

'I'm not. He's average.'

'Good. Thirteen inches. No sense in getting squeamish about *that* part.'

'I'm squeamish about the whole thing! I'd especially be squeamish if he *was* thirteen inches, by the way.'

'Unlucky for some.'

'Exactly.'

'Lucky for others. Including Sabrina.'

'Look, are you going to take my mid-life crisis seriously or aren't you? So I know.'

'Is that what you're having?'

'I can't think of a better explanation, can you?'

'Well, if *you're* having one then I'm having one as well.'

'We're *all* having one!'

2.

Yes, we're all having one, including me, and I'm still in my thirties.

When I have time to think, I finalise some fairly outlandish speculations: that Kolko is storing up our memories – the logical synthesis for the fact that we're all dredging up pieces of our past; that Kolko is a foot soldier in God's Army (don't laugh) and God needs our memories because He's growing forgetful.

3.

Dorothy's crisis is different.

As far as Dorothy is concerned, too much has become inverted. When she is awake it feels like sleeping, and not even somnambulistic zombie-shuffles through a daily reality, but actually a shallow-breathing rest for her organs and limbs. While properly asleep is when she wakes up. When she's asleep, her dreams concatenate – the mundane with the bizarre, the humdrum with the erotic – and she executes her business with a smile in her chest.

Take this afternoon. Dozing while standing up (as it turned out), with her forehead against the cool fridge door, Dorothy dreamed of making a cup of tea. So far, so ordinary. Ah! but the kettle she filled with golden water from the penis-tap was not an ordinary kettle; far from it! Inside this womb of metal and reinforced plastic, little lives could grow. And here they came! Rising on the tide as the water continued to gush, tiny adults, waving not drowning; one of them was herself, the size of a thumb, but herself in her twenties; two others were the women on the hill.

Why couldn't you leave us? called the woman with dark skin. Dorothy had had to fight an urge to push her down deep into the kettle.

Is this a bad dream or a bad memory? wonders Dorothy, undressing for the second time today. The first time was in the changing rooms of the Tiddenfoot Centre: to go swimming. She had nearly drowned. Waking up in the deep end, Dorothy had forgotten what she needed to do. As helpless as a baby, she had felt her limbs soften; she'd descended a watery ladder, rung by rung to the pool's floor, on tiptoe. Her stomach still hurts, now that she undresses for bed at not even a shadow past seven p.m. It was Annette who had dragged her up; Annette who had gone through the lifesaving procedures – squeezing the body, forcing sausagey oxygen into her lungs – while Dorothy slept on.

What the hell is wrong with me?

In Doctor Savros's opinion, there is nothing wrong that a month of rest wouldn't cure; but two real obstacles stand in front of the physician's modest but lacklustre prescription. The first is that *no one* gets a full month's worth of rest these days – not even full-time students reading Peace Studies. The second obstacle is more cerebral.

'There is something inside my head,' Dorothy says aloud, her raised voice shocking her system into a period of wakefulness. Without knowing she has done so, she has walked into the kitchen. She has made her announcement to the kitchen window, looking out at the darkened car park; and this by itself would not be so alarming were it not for the fact that Dorothy is stark naked. And even *this* – her nudity in her own home – would not be so distressing but for the fact that her raised voice has caused two people to turn their heads in her direction.

At first she panics. One of her observers is a black woman, thirtyish, heavy of breast and rump: but it is not the black woman on the hill with the face. Her name is Rebecca, Dorothy remembers; she lives in the next block along, she drives a Datsun; on one occasion the postman mistakenly delivered a piece of mail to Dorothy that was addressed to Rebecca and Dorothy had taken it round to claim her reward of a thank you and a cup of tea and a biscuit. Simply a neighbour; probably returning home from work.

Dorothy's other observer is Tom Lockington. Me, in other words.

4.

I have gone round to the car park to take out the trash

Then, Dorothy's lifted voice, with or without which I would have peeked at Dorothy's kitchen window through force of habit; and there she is, framed by her window, a nude portrait.

She does nothing to hide her modesty. Does she *see me*?

'Dorothy hasn't been well,' I say to my neighbour. 'I think she's sleepwalking.'

'Well I don't know much about that,' says Rebecca, and gives me a see-you-later and precedes me back to the road and the doors to the flats. Rebecca climbs the steps to the first block we greet (Flats 16-20), but me, I stop outside Dolly's.

She must have watched me. The buzzer sounds and the door clunks unlocked.

Dorothy is hiding herself as best she can behind her front door; she has had no time to slip into something more uncomfortable.

'Are you sure?' is all I say.

Dorothy says nothing; in lieu of words themselves she steps away from her open door. I walk into her flat and she is in the hallway. Her shoulders slope; two sexy parallel cambers of flesh trace her backbone up and down. Her bottom is dimpled; there is a mole on her left cheek. On the spectrum between lust and disgust I do not know where I stand. I *want* to be aroused, and part of me is.

'Are you sure?' I repeat, closing the door behind me.

'You've seen it all before, Tom.' Dorothy has moved into her lounge. 'But *they* haven't. I better close the curtains before things go *awry*,' she adds with a definite sardonic tone. 'Would you like refreshments? I have some rough gin and some even rougher vod.'

'The rough vod, if you please. Why are you putting on the strip show, Dolly?'

'I'm having a senior moment. I thought it better than soiling my twin-set and pearls. Would you mind pouring? It's in the fridge or the freezer, I forget which.'

'Sure,' I reply, stepping into the kitchen. 'Why *rough* vod, by the way?'

'Because I'm poor. I have more in common with the tramps on the gyppo camps in Eaton Bray than I do with the literary intelligentsia.' She laughs. 'Where's my fucking advance for another book, Tom, that's what I'd like to know.'

'Found it. Would you like to put some clothes on, Dorothy?'

'No, not really, it's my home, as far as I know. This isn't the first time you've seen me naked, Tom.'

'Yes it is. Would you like me to shed my outer garments as well? In sympathy.'

'In sympathy? In sympathy no. For any other reason, let's discuss that.'

'What would you like with your vod?'

'Pure air and fresh oxygen. There might be a lime.' Dorothy laughs. 'Wave the little green bastard in the general direction of the glass rim.'

I laugh too. 'Any ice with that cocktail, madam?'

'You decide. You're the bartender. Do you really not remember? You took me to bed a few years ago.'

'Of course I remember,' I lie. 'Was I any good?'

'Ah, Tom, it's either feast or famine for a woman of my age. You were a *god*.'

'A god I can live with. Here.' I hand her a wine glass full to the brim: vodka, fresh air and ice – with a token slice of handbag-textured lime.

'*Muchos gracias*, Tom. I am losing my mind.'

'No you're not, we're in the grip of something – like a virus. Have you been writing?'

'Yes I have a bit. I don't know if it's worth what a squirrel passes through its alimentary canal, on the other hand. Sit down, won't you? I feel like a duchess.'

'A nude one. Do you need help?'

'My doctor thinks not. He says I need rest.'

'Then rest.'

'I'm trying to! Do you know how hard it is to rest when you don't feel rested?'

'Yeah I do, unfortunately. This *is* rough, you were right.'

'You're welcome. What else were you going to do tonight?'

'Oh I don't know. Wait for a call from the plod.'

'Why?'

'Are you sitting comfortably?'

'No.'

'Then I'll begin.' And I tell her about last night.

5.

I have managed to convince myself that a woman named Sabrina lives with me in my flat, but she doesn't; I live alone. I wear her clothes. I am in denial of this fact (says Dorothy), although I don't want to be. I want to believe everything, like when I was a child.

Not long after I tell Dorothy about last night I kiss her and she opens my shirt with shaking hands. She licks my chest and says 'Salty'. It is not mindblowing sex (what is?); but it is comfortable, comforting... friendly, even.

'Tell me I'm not imagining it all, though,' I ask her, staring straight up at the ceiling.

'You're not. Tell me I'm not either, Tom. I was on that bus, I swear it.'

'I believe you.'

'But there was no gunfight. No hijack to Cuba. Nothing.'

'I know, I believe you.'

'The others don't. They reckon I'm going nuts.'

'Maybe *they're* going nuts,' I try to please her.

She takes the suggestion seriously. 'Tom? Did you want to be a little girl when you were a little boy?'

'I wanted to be Hutch. As in *Starsky and*. When I was at St Christopher's – my first school – we had a class on Tuesdays I think it was, an Arts and Crafts class. We had to make – I don't know what you call it. You get a big piece of paper and folder lengthways, over and over, so it's like a fan.'

'Then you cut it,' Dorothy says, 'you cut shapes into it.'

'That's it. And the shapes are cut into all the folds. I cut mine in the shape of Hutch.'

'You fancied David Soul.'

'Maybe. But Mrs Gill said, "That's a nice picture of a man." I said, "It's not a man, it's Hutch." And she thought I meant a rabbit hutch, even though I'd been writing about the programme every Monday morning for weeks. We had to write about what we did at the weekend; I always wrote a review of

Starsky and Hutch – or *The Professionals.*'

'Now I'm with you there. I fancied Martin Shaw.'

'I fancied Lewis Collins. Just loved those flares.'

'So where did Sabrina come from?'

'I don't know. Why did you all indulge me?'

'What else were we supposed to do? You look good as a woman.'

'I look like Harvey Keitel in a dress.'

'No you don't, Tom. You fooled plenty of waiters.' She rolls over on to her side to look at me but my glance is still fixed heavenly north. 'We thought it was a game for you.'

'A *game*?'

'Maybe game's the wrong word. An adventure. Do you want some music?'

'Yeah, get out your clarinet. Acker Bilk me.'

She has an oldfashioned turntable in the bedroom. She has a clutch of albums stuffed ill-fittingly into a container designed for magazines; they slope out with the bottom angle protruding upwards.

'Do you have any punk?'

'I've got Chopin or Handel or...'

'You choose.'

I study her buttocks as she slips a record from a battered sleeve. And I do mean study: I even reach down beside the bed to pick up my spectacles to assist in my research. Those buttocks I have held, I have clasped.

'I didn't really upset you, did I?'

'No of course not, I was just messing.' She drops the needle into the groove with a *whoops* and a burp of irritation from the speakers. 'Too loud. What time is it?'

'It's not late.'

'I'll turn it down; we need to talk. Why Sabrina, by the

way? It's quite a posh name.'

'She's quite a posh bird.'

'What does she do?'

'She works in business.'

'Well that's helpful.' Dorothy lies down on the bed as a strain of violins swells. It sounds like flowers growing.

'Was there a Sabrina in your childhood?' she asks.

'I don't think so.'

'I'm trying to salvage something from the wreckage.'

I nod appreciatively. 'That's a good way of putting it.'

She is not sure if I am making fun of her. Evidently she decides to give me the benefit of the doubt.

'What are you girls saying about me and Annette?' I go on.

'We're not saying anything. *They* might be. I don't get that either.'

'Tell me about it.'

'Did you really not recognise each other before she came to yours? She's seen you *hundreds* of times, Tom. Well not hundreds, but lots. And you can't both be such good actors.'

'It wasn't an act. She was a woman named Caitlin and she lived on Billington Road, with the back of her house facing us, and she was a stalker, and she killed her boys with an axe.'

'Except she didn't. That's the part I think we can all rest easy about.'

'Have you ever seen her boys?'

'James has. He goes to school with Emil.'

'I'm not sure he's the best witness we could hope for.'

'I don't agree. He has total recall and trouble fibbing. He's a prosecutor's nightmare.'

I turn to face Dorothy. The light isn't winning against the force of darkness outside. Her face is grey; her face is a sculpture.

'...Are you still horny?' she asks.

'I am a bit, yeah.'

'Give me what you liked to give Sabrina,' she says, lying back and opening her arms. She closes her eyes and waits for me. I don't keep her long.

6.

While I won't claim much knowledge on the subject of Obsessive Compulsive Disorder, I do know that I share some of its defining characteristics in that I check I've unplugged plugs, locked windows and the balcony doors, and turned off the cooker and the iron before I leave the flat, even if I intend to return ten minutes later from the corner shop.

Leaving Dorothy's flat, by contrast, is a blissful experience. Dorothy has even handed me a ten-spot that she's located in her tights drawer, with which to pay for two bottles – one of each, red and white. I exit the building, walk past my own block (hereby proving myself unable to resist a glance up a storey towards my own window), cross the road, enter the shop, choose one of each, deposit my selfless tuppence change in a charity box collecting for lifeboat crews; then, all aglow with my success and with the pristine symmetry of the manoeuvre, I leave the shop, cross the road (the plastic bag clinking), walk past my block, take a *good* look up at my window, re-enter Dorothy's building, her flat and her bedroom, where I disrobe again, starting with my crinkled black socks.

'You're sweating a bit,' Dorothy informs me.

'There's someone in my flat. Red or white first?' I have deliberately chosen screwtops rather than corks. Our glasses are already beside the bed.

'*What?* Why did you get undressed?'

My laugh is somewhat bitter. 'Do you think I'm going *in* there? Behave yourself, Dolly. *Red or white?*' The two bottles are on the bedcovers.

'You have to call the police!' says Dorothy.

'He *is* the police!' I reply, opening the Merlot. 'Hold out your goblet.'

'No he isn't, Tom.'

'He's *our* police anyway,' I continue, tipping the beautiful scent of oxidised grape into my finger-smudged receptacle.

Of course there is another possibility, and Dorothy knows this too. 'It might *be* the police,' she says, 'considering everything.'

'Which makes me even less inclined to go home. Let's watch the news. Let's have a few drinks and do something else.'

'Like what?' Dorothy asks.

'You mentioned you've been writing. Tell me a story. But first let me fill your glass. Especially as you paid for it.'

It is plain that Dorothy is not certain, but she goes as far as holding out her glass while saying, 'I'm not sure about this, Tom. When!' she adds to indicate I should stop pouring.

'If it *is* the police, I don't want to talk to them, Dolly,' I say.

'That's not how it works, though, is it? *They* want to talk to you.'

'I'll be a fugitive from justice then.'

Away from the bed, in the other room a few seconds later, Dorothy calls, 'What makes you think there's someone in there anyway? What did you see?'

I raise my voice. 'Just a figure at the window! Could've been a trick of the light! Could've been *Sabrina*! Back for vengeance!'

'Don't joke about that, Tom,' Dorothy replies, returning to the bedroom carrying a sheaf of papers.

'That was quick,' I tell her.

'They were only on my desk, I printed it out earlier on.' Dorothy slips back under the covers. '"The Trespassing",' she reads, then pauses. Briskly she nods her head and continues.

'"You could take a shortcut up Carterweys – the road where the two girls lived – and at the top there's an alley that leads straight through onto Hadrian Park. Me and Franco used to go on our pushbikes, as my Dad called them, with the sun on our backs. We were eleven or twelve years old, with all the time in the world. We all remember it, don't we?" *You* remember it, don't you, Tom?' Dorothy asks me.

There's a beat of time while I decide at what point she stopped reading. The question is a real one. 'Like I was there,' I answer. 'I even knew a boy called Franco,' I tell her. Call me slow but I have yet to catch on. At this precise second, what Dolly has said seems of no greater gravity than idle coincidence. Maybe it's the wine that has strangled my powers of perception.

'Can you remember the rest of your story? Without reading it, I mean,' I ask.

'Can *you*?'

'Yes. It's going to be the same, isn't it?'

'Shall I read on?' Without waiting for an answer, and without a glance in my direction, she does so.

'"The park seemed vast when we were kids, and it was often empty, apart from seagulls, which never made any sense because we were miles from water. You occasionally saw someone walking a dog, some other kids. If you were really lucky you might see a couple of teenagers snogging and you could whiz by and hope for a glimpse of her bra or knickers."'

I laugh. Dorothy smiles. 'Does it have what they call the bitter ring of truth?'

'Indeed it does. You were never sure who was more nervous – us on our bikes or the couple getting off with each other. But you're going to tell me about the handicapped school, aren't you, Dolly?'

She nods. 'I think I am – after a bit of scene-setting. There was a set of swings.'

'A roundabout, a slide… a kind of dip in the ground you weren't supposed to go down. So of course we went down it. It led to a metal doorway – probably not as large as I remember it. I don't think we ever did find out what was behind it. Some said something about sewage, but I can't believe they'd have sewage maintenance under a kids' playground.'

Dorothy places her left hand on top of her manuscript, making a show of blocking her own view – like the playing card magician donning his blindfold.

'Why don't you read the rest of it?' she suggests.

Shrugging my shoulders I answer, 'Sure, hand it over.'

'No. Why don't you read it from memory?'

'Uh…well okay. Um. They were building something on the land to the right of the park as we looked at it. I'm not sure what the direction would be. They'd closed off some land. They were digging up the ground, laying foundations… What's the matter?'

'Have I gone white?' she asks.

'Well now that you mention it, you look like you've seen a ghost, ho ho.'

'I knew you were going to say that.'

'Did you feel the blood?'

'No, not that. The bit about the park – I knew you were going to say *that*. Where my thumb is.' And she passes the manuscript sheaf closer. Squinting without my specs, I read the words *bully smelly*.

'Hang on, I need my glasses.' I reach down to where I've left them on the carpet in a nest of socks. With my vision corrected the *bully* clenches clearly into the word *building*. The *smelly* becomes the word *something*. The sentence reads: *They were building something on the land to the right of the park as we looked at it*. 'Jesus. That's what I said, isn't it?'

'Word for word,' Dorothy answers, claiming back the paperwork.

VII.

1.

Roy enters The Leper and orders a pickled egg, a triple brandy and a pint.

I make the introductions.

'Dorothy – this is Roy. Roy? You remember Dorothy.'

'Howdodo.'

'Howdodo.'

'So we're just waiting for Ian,' I say to Roy.

'Knowing him, he'll be here on skateboard,' says Roy. 'He stayed at work. He's typing up the week's accounts.'

In due course, Ian adopts the novel approach of using his skateboard as a tray for the four drinks. They wobble slightly but nothing is spilled.

I introduce Dolly to Ian, and vice versa, calmly aware throughout that everybody knows we are here. Late afternoon I called Hannah, whom I caught at her desk, as ever. I explained where we were meeting, and why; I even invited her along. Of all of us, I think it's Hannah who has taken the boy's suicide bid the hardest. He *had* managed to drink down a new bottle of shower gel before the paramedics broke the door down.

Next I called Sam…

'Sam Twyfield!' Sam sang.

'It's Tom. Sam, have I ever called you on this number before?' I asked.

'Loads of times.'

'Me. Not Sabrina.'

'I'm trying to remember, babe. You didn't call just to ask me that, did you?'

2.

And I awake from a dream of violence.

In this dream I swim north in the canal; I swim right up to Amelior Anderson's front door. It is night. An anthropomorphized version of Nob the cat allows me access with a toss of his head and a clownish wiggle of his sword-sharp whiskers. In I walk. Amelior and Kolko are in her bedroom, naked. The latter boasts an erection unlikely in real life; as I wait he *smears* it over the old lady's dugs, depositing cubes of his own rotting flesh.

They are aware I'm there in the room.

Briskly, impatiently, the humanized Nob bounds on his two back legs to the side of the bed. Amelior Anderson plucks from his chops one of those sharp whiskers of his. She then uses it on Kolko, stab, stab, stab into his back and shoulders. They're as drunk as crabs. Their howls of enjoyment become a song in my ear, high-pitched.

'Who's there?' I ask in the darkness.

'Who do you think it is?' Sabrina's voice asks me.

'Are you in my bed?' I sound calmer than I feel, I reckon.

'I'm in *our* bed, Tom. You were dreaming. I was singing you "Go to Sleep" from *Snow White*. I think that's what it's called. It used to calm you down, when you were a boy.'

'I didn't know you when I was a boy.'

'Yes you did, Tom. We used to play together.'

'Are you real?'

Sabrina sighs. 'I died a long time ago, Tom. I was twelve,' she answers. 'I drowned in a swimming pool in Portugal. Family holiday. Not one of my smartest moves – I tried to swim two lengths of the pool underwater, I ended up down in the deep end, I didn't make it.'

'My God...'

'Well, quite. It's fair to say you didn't want to let me go. So in that sense I'm real.'

'But you're all in my mind?'

'You can touch me right now. Do you want to hold hands like when we were kids?'

'…I'm so ashamed, Sabrina, I just can't – I can't remember you.'

'Hold my hand, Tom. We don't need to speak for a while.'

Our fingers touch. She is here again.

Empties, 3: 'Eutexia and the middleman'

1.

Back then, Stephen came to me in my dreams. He became my affair – my illicit passion, part nervous energy, part thrill-seeking enticement, part fear – but he would be gone for long periods of time. I learned to build longing into these gaps in our schedule; they became as important as the situations of contact.

Needless to say, I kept all of this from Sabrina. Would Sabrina have believed me anyway? That's the question. Would she believe me now? That's another.

2.

Eventually I had a brain scan, but it took a long time to convince my GP that there was anything wrong with the toys and the abandoned furniture in my attic. *There's nothing wrong with you, Mr Lockington,* I heard – not once – it must have been a hundred times. *Then why am I hearing voices?* I would argue. *Because you drink too much,* was the general consensus – but it took a good few visits before any physician had the nerve to come right out and provide me with that diagnosis. By that point Stephen had moved in.

As Sam is to Hannah, I am to Stephen – I am his diary. The problem is, Stephen is not exactly a loquacious writer; or perhaps I am not much of an amanuensis.

When I first made Stephen's acquaintance, he was eloquent in a kind of through-a-tunnel, lockjawed kind of way. He talked to me regularly.

Maybe he's sick of me now. I've had my fair share of situations in which I'm dumped, but never by a dead man. When the dead get bored with the living you can be sure that there is trouble somewhere.

My brain scan showed nothing remarkable. My liver scan said: *Slow down, Charlie.*

I slowed down. I waited for Stephen.

Estragon has got nothing on me, the cunt.

3.

In my adult life I only visited the house in Wembley on three occasions.

The second was when I busted the window and climbed in.

The first was a moment of madness.

The woman who answered the door was unwilling to grant me access. Built as she was like a Rugby League fullback, I was inclined to agree with her assessment, but I'd come a long way. Not geographically a long way (not really), but dare I say it, spiritually a long way.

'I know this sounds a bit odd,' I started with. 'My uncle used to live here. I wondered if I could have a look around,' I eventually said a few seconds later.

'You expect me to let you in because your *uncle* used to live here.'

Had I known then what I know now from working with prisoners, would I have done anything different? True enough, I have eavesdropped on various brags and snippets of criminal autobiography – enough for me to have picked up a tip of two – but would any such knowledge have helped me break into Stephen's house?

I waited. Any criminal on the planet will tell you that the success of a job depends on careful timing, and that patience is a virtue. A predator will say the same.

47 Rosebank Avenue, Wembley, is suburbia – or was, at least; a long road of identical houses, with nowhere for a spy to

hide. It was far from easy.

Three streets away, well out of voyeuristic range, sat a pub – I forget the name. It was there I waited, nursing a drink, while I formulated a strategy more reliable than putting a brick through a back window.

The woman who lived in 47 would now be vigilant, but for how long? How much time would pass before the daily routine blotted out the memory of the visitor who had asked for access?

Having finished a third drink, I all but tiptoed back to Rose-bank Avenue. Malarial with alcohol and panic, I kept thinking of what Stephen had scratched into the surface of the coffee table: O GOD WHY WON'T YOU FEED ME? All I knew was that if a knife and an absence of food was what took him away, a knife and some sustenance might bring him back. As crazy as that sounds to me now.

It took a good long time to find the relevant shops. In one of those private ironmongers that have since been replaced by chainstores, I bought a Stanley knife and ripped open the pack-aging. Two streets away from that I bought a bundle of fish and chips – one of Stephen's favourite meals, judging by the number of discarded wrappers that had been found in the house. I rang the doorbell again. I wondered if I should have brought whisky and blackcurrant as well.

The large woman answered, this time wielding a baby against her right hip. I had surprised her; she hadn't expected to see me again. Quickly her surprise filtered away, however, and the front was erected. She said:

'You're still not coming in.'

'I've brought food.'

'I don't care if you've brought a large cheque, you're not coming in.'

'I've also got a knife,' I told the woman and I stepped over the threshold.

…The second time I broke in I just hoyed a brick through a window.

A fuck of a sight simpler.

4.

'Are you there?' he asks.

'I'm here. Where have you been?'

'Would you believe on holiday?'

'No.'

'Well it's true,' says Stephen. 'I find I can visit places that I used to only dream about; it was the best I could do.'

'How?'

'How do I travel? By dreaming my way there, mate. So this was what my imagination was there for all along… It's harder than you might imagine. They *watch* you, they do; but as long as I concentrate good and hard I can manage.'

These conversations really happened – I know they did – but I mix them up with other conversations, discussions that I was not privy to. They happened without me, but I remember them as if was at the head of the table. Things that Caitlin told me.

'Okay, darling, that's beautiful. Turn around. Turn around, girl.'

Caitlin felt a snowball melting in her gut as she inched a slow pirouette. It did not make her feel better to hear the photographer's instant appraisal.'

'Bewful, babe. Up on your – up on your tiptoes now: tighten the muscles. Cool…'

Or when the policeman talked about the stench in Stephen's house, before the door was broken down; or rather when the facts were indirected my way at a later stage, I thought of the dead in the Banshee Hotel at the Luton and Dunstable Hospital, where I had worked one summer. I remember the old boy and his last-chance-saloon stab at life.

'What did he die of?' I asked.

'Drink. Depression,' said my father.

Loneliness, I thought. Utter emptiness.

Or maybe I summoned these opinions later on. It's hard to tell now. But I knew what the policeman had located. I knew what they found when they kicked down his front door, heavy-booted and insistent.

Stephen was not simply dead. He was eutectic…

Put simply, he was making the gradual move from the flesh to a heavy liquid. A broth; a strengthening soup. Insects were eating his eyelids. He reeked.

But the pigs were eventually called because of a dripping tap. So mundane. And I can only conjecture that Stephen had got it into his head that it was time to do the washing-up. A wrecking yard of crockery was in place. Why else would he have jammed the plug, if he hadn't intended to fill the sink with water? However, he did not turn on the tide. If he had he would have been discovered – the authorities would have been notified – much sooner. It just dripped, like a boring man's heavy point of view.

Weeks passed.

Drip.

Months.

Drip.

Slowly the sink filled; it was coming, this square bowl, to the end of its utility. It was approaching the end of the line.

The water overflowed. It soaked the kitchen floor. In the next room along, Stephen was close to the coffee table; he collapsed like a tonne of potatoes. It was the last time that he would do so.

What is wrong with me? I have no motivation. Don't worry, I've noticed. I am not blind, am I? I'm just directionless.

This is me turning into my Uncle Stephen, drip by drip.

5.

He told me a story once.

Stephen, aged nineteen; a warm foreign beach, with the darkness and the campfire playing tricks with the eye. For all the world it looks as though the sea is as still as shellac and it's the land in lazy motion.

Stephen lies on the sand. He is not alone. Cartographically, our man traces the knouts and fissures, the ramps and curves, of a fully-clothed woman's ample body. Her name is Anke, and like its homophone she has weighted him to the spot. Stephen has made up his mind that he will not leave this spot until she has agreed at least to unbutton her blouse.

The signs are favourable. An hour earlier, the last of the other beach party guests took their leave; now the fire is down to glowing embers. Even Stephen's tent-mate – Brendan – has long since departed, alone, and much the worse for consuming single-handedly an entire gallon-keg of red wine. Off up the sandy slope he'd scurried, crab-like and complaining of a pain in his eyes…

Stephen kisses Anke again. Though both drunk, they make a connection that seems secure and honest. They explore. At the pit of Stephen's stomach there lurks an acidic rigidity, and one which he takes his time both registering and comprehending. At the moment that the light changes – the sky is ripped open by iridescence – he gets it. Hope for the shag (naturally), but also hope that he has found someone with whom he can share… and communicate.

'What is that?' she asks, lying back into the sand, with her hair now arranged into four short ropes on either side of her wide head. Her face is smiling; and Stephen recovers in an instant from the powerful sense of embarrassment that the question has engendered. Why, he thought she was talking about his erection: the one that he'd been spading into her navel for the previous fifteen minutes. But now he is not so sure. Her German accent says again: 'That! In English!'

Stephen looks; his head bows upwards. The night sky, as still as a pond, has been scarred by –

'A shooting star,' says Stephen.

Anke nods; it takes Stephen a full few seconds to realize that he has never seen one before either.

Someone or something has spooned sugar onto the scene. Not at all reluctantly, Stephen mirrors Anke's smile; they observe the remaining two seconds of the sky-zip. They are alone.

'So much nicer in English,' Anke says. 'Shooting star.'

This is it, thinks Stephen. She's getting sentimental and more promisingly his splayed fingers have divined a good deal of moisture at her crotch, even through the bottle-green denim that she is wearing.

'Will you come back to my tent?' Stephen asks.

Anke pauses before replying. 'What about your friend?' she wants to know.

'He drank a gallon of wine. He'll be asleep.' Stephen hopes Anke cannot hear the undertone of panicky hope in his voice. As it turns out, he's telling the truth.

Again, she pauses. Then she says, 'Okay. Let's go.'

Angel wings flutter in Stephen's chest. While climbing to his feet, the *clish-ma-claver* of the sea deposits a strong sensation of nausea in Stephen's brain. He helps her up; their hands are cold. She takes his arm.

They walk to the tent.

'I better just check he's asleep,' Stephen says to his new friend. Indeed he is, on the floor, in a puddle of red wine vomit, half in and half out of his clothes.

'Perhaps we'd better go to your tent,' Stephen suggests; but Anke doesn't want to – on account of *her* travelling companion and what *she* might say.

Stephen does not want her to leave. She is having second thoughts, and he cannot let her go; and he holds her arm too tightly until she tells him he is hurting her.

Stephen has a fine way with the ladies. You can't take that away from him.

6.

What was in Stephen's fridge?

Some rancid margarine, and some homemade (and dangerous-looking) self-generated yoghurt in a milk carton. A few small cartons of Um Bongo fruit drink (with straws); half a slab of chocolate. A jar of jam with a centimetre's diaphragm of protective green sponge above the red tide. Half an onion.

No maggots. No drugs.

What has put the drugs idea in my head?

7.

Years later, and a knock at my door. Not a buzz from the intercom system but a knock at the door to my flat. I haven't been aware of anyone returning home while I've been having a day off work – sometimes the lady at number 7 pops back for lunch – but maybe it happened while I was reading in the bath.

It is Officer Kolko. His hat is growing out of his armpit. 'Your neighbour let me in,' he explains. From upstairs I hear the door to number 10 slamming shut. Nobody in this block knows how to shut a door quietly.

'It's fine,' I tell the man. 'Do you want to come in?'

He crosses the threshold. I want to ask him to remove his shoes, the carpet still glistening from a rare bout of hoovering.

We enter the lounge. 'Do you know why I'm here?' he asks.

'No.'

'I'd like to ask you about a woman called Caitlin Bryant. Do you know the name, sir?' Kolko removes a small pad and a tiny ballpoint from an inside pocket.

'She used to be my neighbour,' I say. And now she is dead; of that I am certain. She has killed herself, and fingered me in her envoi. Why else have I been bothered at this hour, or any hour?

Officer Kolko writes something on the pad. It's much more than I have said. What is he doing? Drawing my starsign chart? He leaves a silence.

My heart yammers to fill that silence, but I have no more words to provide. What is more damning – to clam up or to elaborate? And why am I feeling so guilty?

'And was that the extent of your relationship, sir?' Kolko asks.

'Yes. Well, no. I mean, there was a sort of incident, or series of incidents. Which is why she probably mentioned me on her note. Otherwise you wouldn't be here, would you? Do you fancy a brandy?' I say to conclude my babble.

'No thank you. What note, sir?'

I blink. 'The one she left. Didn't she?'

Now Kolko blinks. We are like a diner and a waiter of different nationalities, frowningly attempting to find some common ground over a dish containing artichokes or asparagus.

'Left where?'

'Well I don't know. Behind.'

'Perhaps you'd better tell me about your incident,' said

Kolko. 'Or series of incidents.'

Was he mocking me? Rising up out of my chair I said, 'And perhaps you'd better tell me why you're here.'

To which he added something wholly unexpected, something childish: 'I asked first.'

'It's my house,' I countered.

'But I'm the one wearing the uniform. Sir.'

I paused. I moved into the kitchen. I wanted a beer but the cupboard was bare, so I poured myself a brandy. 'She was my stalker.' Drink secured, I sat down and added, 'She sent me letters. I've kept a few; you can read them. She was lonely and wanted some company.'

It felt strange to reduce those desperate months to a few quick sentences – and not even concentrated sentences either.

'I did nothing to encourage her, I promise you,' I concluded. 'She just got it into her head that I was someone to talk to, I guess. Failing that, someone to write to. I never wrote back.'

'I see. When was this?'

'Do you want to read about it?' I asked, absurdly.

'Read?' said Kolko as if the word was a new arrival to his lexicon.

'I'm writing about it. The manuscript in front of you. I could fish out the relevant pages…'

Some of the light had left Kolko's eyes.

8.

'But you talked to God, didn't you? Or tried to at least. "Oh God, why won't you feed me?" you wrote. And I quote.'

'I didn't write exactly,' Stephen contests. 'But I take your point… No. I didn't communicate with God, although I hoped to. You know who God is?' he asks. 'The next part of yourself. Your next port of call.'

'So what am I doing,' I enquire, 'by talking to you? Maybe I should salute.'

'Don't be sarky.' Stephen's voice, while remaining familiar, is high-octane, supererogatory. 'Smartaleckry doesn't suit you. You're getting the dirt here, mate. Be grateful.'

But I am grateful, I long to protest. I really am. And it occurs to me that access to Stephen's new realm – whether or not it's what he believes it is – has entirely been the result of nothing more than my interest and enthusiasm. How can it all be so easy?

'So tell me this,' I say, 'can you dream your way into anyone's existence?'

'Not existence exactly…'

'But anyone's?' I push.

'Theoretically.'

'Good. I've set you up with a date.'

9.

I dream my way into Stephen's death.

His organs fail before me. There is panic and plaque in his mouth; his breath reeks of whisky.

Somewhere towards the end he suffered an epileptic fit. He fell… People in my fiction are always bashing their heads when they fall, but Stephen didn't. With a shock that even stabbed through the onset of unconsciousness, he landed on his left hand and tore his little finger backward.

Brill. A fortnight of spasms and a seriously busted digit. Makes you have to wonder, should you be so unfortunate, as to endure these indignities, if someone somewhere is testing you – feeding off your pain.

He is mentally intact as the end approaches. Of this I am confident. He hasn't lost it… Stephen feels it when his heartrate trebles, his rectum prolapses, and his sweat starts to smell of goats and doves…

Stephen is still there, with his brain like a jewel. And all I can do is watch.

10.

But does anyone ever go away? Do they really go far?

It's a question I want to pose to Stephen, but I can't find him.

Sabrina, likewise, has floated away from me, for now. Warmth that shields my body convinces me she'll be back.

This morning I spoke to my mum. I asked her if she remembered a little girl called Sabrina. She doesn't, but I'm not taking this as much of a knock. Why should she? It was a long, long time ago.

But what does it say about me? She was there; she was not there for a lot longer; and then she was here with me for years. We *lived* together. It is simply the fact that we must re-examine the word *lived*. She was real to me.

She is real to me again; I don't care what anybody else says.

It doesn't matter that no one could see her.

She's as real as Stephen is.

Fear in Four Waters, 3: The Sea

I.

1.

It has cost me a fortune to get here. I am in Reykjavik. And Uncle Visa helped me out: I put the whole trip on plastic after Christmas had passed in a wounded flurry and I had stared into the vacant corridors of a new year with a sensation of horror.

I needed help sleeping. I needed help staying awake.

It was Hannah who demanded I take a holiday. There was no room for negotiation. She said I looked shocking and that I wasn't looking after my personal hygiene. She told me to book a flight somewhere sunny; I told her I hate the sun. She said she didn't care; I couldn't go on the way I was, which was true (and still is).

So I came here. Somewhere *sunny*? I am in Iceland in February, contemplating the sea from my hotel balcony. I have seen sunnier *teapot interiors*. But at least I am away from it all, unless I'm not – and I keep myself busy with touristy palaver. I don't have to *like* it.

2.

By now I have read all of the correspondence and notes.

Surprisingly it was Louise, James's sister, who supplied a good deal of the material above on her brother. It turns out that the little whackjob kept a fairly comprehensive diary, and when I say *surprisingly* I do so because I hadn't expected her to want anything to do with me and my questions. But a handwritten note was all it took. More or less as soon as James had been stretchered away from my flat to have his stomach pumped at the Luton and Dunstable Hospital, and of course to be referred to psychiatric assessment, in the spirit of striking while the iron is hot I hiero-glyphed some autobiographical and pleading nonsense on to the back of a credit card bill envelope and popped it into the post to the address supplied by Annette via Hannah. (I still can't speak to Annette, though I know I must at some point.) It's fair to say that such was my inebriated state during the composition of this note that not only can I not recall precisely what my drunken hand scribbled but that I'd also forgotten that I'd penned any such mis-sive. A few days passed before Louise replied..

She regretted snooping around her brother's computer's alleyways, but she'd done so for a long, long time. It had been 'nothing difficult' to guess his password. It was 'FATHER'. And subsequently, in the hope of helping him (she was insistent about this) she would log on as James whenever opportunity knocked. As a result, I have seen the lad's letters to his dad; his thoughts; his musings: Louise emailed them to me. She had everything backed up and safe. The police had taken James's computer. She sent them to me in case I could take off some of the pressure.

Good luck to you, Louise, wherever you may be.

3.

Directly preceding and then over the Yuletide period, there are no further complications and no further contact from Simon Kolko. (Perhaps he's killed himself.) Though I expect it every day it doesn't arrive, like bad mail you don't want to receive but need to read for one reason or another.

Several emergency meetings and symposiums are hastily arranged. They have the feel about them of post-disaster support groups. And we *do* need the support; the problem is we cannot find the disaster. Not the real one. Not the one that must have started everything off (assuming that pressure has a beginning). So instead of doing much constructive or creative, we disagree and argue and go over old stories, seeking out, ploughing for the truth. Are we drifting closer together or further apart? I couldn't tell you.

So we fling our lassos wider, trying to reel in ever-more-distant memories. We apply the dictum that detective fiction has informed us – that even the smallest detail might make a difference. Endlessly, during these meetings, hour after hour, I listen bored to shapeless narratives about dead pets and lost jobs; about disappointments and longings and sexual derring-do. Everything seems open to discussion, dissection. It's worse than I imagine counselling ever to be; this is a metaphorical open heart surgery. This is *abuse*. And it also means, naturally, that I must discuss Sabrina…

Of course we get plenty of opportunity to discuss matters – to hone our stories, as it were – with the law enforcement reps of this green and pleasant. We are all interviewed… Interviewed. What a lovely word for such a terrifying procedure. We all swear that we will bring Kolko's name up as much as we humanly can. Later we confess (among ourselves) that we do nothing of the sort. While not one of us refuses his existence, or tries to hide him, there is no sense of bringing him to the fore either.

I don't know why not.

Paradoxically, given my distaste for the woman, it is Annette who draws some muted praise from at least one officer, who concedes that while the first option of leaving James where he was on the snowy fields should have been the first and safest choice, at least he was with a somewhat familiar face when Annette took him into the party that removed him from the leisure centre, all five bodies crushed into the car that Hannah had borrowed from Roy. No; it *isn't* much to go on, this reluctant thumbs-up, but at least it means I am allowed to travel. To embark on my Hannah-recommended deportation order to Iceland.

No one will face charges of abduction. That's *something*, right?

4.

I am scheduled to go whale watching. Hours before my mid-morning departure, I stare at the sea, which is stained a plum colour by strange early light, and torpid, slow; it makes me feel restful, and I should bask in the sensation. Somewhere near the harbour, so distant that its motor sounds like paper being crushed, a motorbike putts and stalls. Above me, gulls and other seabirds hang sharp angles. In my mouth is the sweetish residue of the rollmop herrings I ate at breakfast. Reykjavik is still.

Sad waters? The boy James thought that water was sad. *These are my sad waters,* he wrote in an email to his father – and at the time he referred to a bowl of shaving suds. Imagine how he'd feel if he saw *this*! Not that he will now, of course.

I wonder what he dreams of, that boy; at his nighttime escritoire, what dreams does he scribble? The *oeuvre* that Louise provided reveals little material in this regard; but there's no reason why it should. Kolko told him that he'd see his father again; all he must do in return is kill his mother and that guy Lenny. Oh, and himself, of course; that goes without saying. So why did he hand over the gun? Can it be that James finally doubted Kolko? Already prone to guilt and depression, James had been securely hoodwinked up to that point; did something change in his mental make-up? Dreams fade, after all. He could have shot himself – it wouldn't have taken a second or two – but he tried the poison route instead.

My dream, last night, was of the prison where I allegedly teach English. Roy was in it, only briefly (the dream, not the prison). It was not in the Education block, it was on F Wing – the Wing for vulnerable prisoners… The fabric of the dream has the odour of damp tobacco. I am in a cell much larger than exists in real life; I am tied to a cot. At my left side, similarly restrained, is my Uncle Stephen; but whereas I thrash against my bonds, Stephen is calm, motionless; even though it's night I see that his face is serene. After another fruitless protest on my part, he tells me to *relax, we'll be out of here soon.*

Why are you here, Stephen? I ask him.

I killed a girl before I had my first kiss, he replies. *I drove drunk. I lost control. I knocked her off her bike. She died.*

Here in my dreams, I meant.

How do you know it's a dream? is his enigmatic reply.

I thrash against the belts that hold me once again, as if for good measure.

Relax, Tom! Just give it time!

I haven't got any time! But even as I utter the words I know that the escape committee has arrived. Battleship grey, they swarm in through the cell's walls, a writhing, pulsing multitude of *rats.* They cover us and gnaw at our bonds; we spring free. The rats carry us out of the prison – cross-legged we ride the magic carpet – and up the street, where the traffic is thin.

You're my protector, I say to Stephen.

I always was.

Protecting me from what?

From Death; he knows your name, Tom.

I board the whale-watching boat at the allotted hour; the name on its escutcheon is *Dottir.* Daughter (n): the female child of a larger parent vessel. Queuing for my waterproofs, I remember from the dream Stephen's line about death knowing my name; a sudden nervousness pinches at my chest.

After little preparation the boat climbs out of the port – and climbs is right. Even so close to the shore the waves are playful, energetic; the sea has become boiling milk, ready to blow – a far cry from an hour or so earlier. The *Dottir* seems to struggle against the waves for the first mile from land.

Up on deck I eat the cereal bar I've brought with me and drink the scalding coffee I've bought from the bar downstairs. The sky is spoiling for a fight; it looks threatening. As testament to the general gloom, if testament should be needed, the photographs that my fellow passengers take send out flares of flashes from their tiny silver cameras.

I should have brought my camera, I realize for the hundredth time. It doesn't matter. We bump and grind into the slate-coloured water; the waves inch higher and higher. The sky is permed with purple and dark brown clouds; a nasty periwig.

By the time the *Dottir* arrives near the site of some hot full-feeding action, having passed Puffin Island, I am slightly queasy with motion sickness, grateful I thought to bring the cereal bar with which to line my stomach. Grateful too that these heavy waterproof suits were provided: the waves are high and mighty; a patina of salt from the spray coating my lenses.

Our guide is a young woman who speaks in a cute squeaky voice through the P.A. system. 'Minke whale at two o'clock! Fifty metres!' she enthuses, and we all turn to our right and squint to see the whale's black back rise up and out of the water to feed on the fish that have attracted the chattering birds, themselves flocked as thick as TV static on the dark screen of the waves behind.

The nervous sensation that assailed me when I boarded now returns. I am certain it is more than *mal-de-mer*: It feels like when I saw Amelior Anderson (not) being killed; but I fail to place it now. Too many other tourists? The bad weather? Perhaps the weight of the waterproof suit, which has amassed incrementally, it appears. In spite of the swaying of our vehicle, it should feel good to be out in the open air – at one with nature – but something troubles me, tickles at my gut – it seizes my teeth and renders them oversensitive. The cereal bar rolls in my stomach...

Rain starts to fall. Exhausted by its two-second cameo, the whale has descended backstage for a rest. Gulls hover, swoop and peck, their cries like a sharp unpleasant taste.

Then a voice from behind me says, 'Fancy meeting *you* here, Tom.'

5.

Once I read a description of a man being doused in benzene – it made him freeze.

Being doused in chilly sea-spray, at this moment, does not make me freeze; it feels like my insides are *simmering*.

Churning too. The man who has said my name is dressed, as I am, in an orange rubber romper suit, with the hood up and over his forehead, his face only visible from the eyebrows down to a marble-sized chin. If it's sweat on his face I'd be surprised – the waves are kicking harder – but it's sweat on mine. It is hotter than ever inside my Day-Glo gimpware.

'Hello, Stephen,' I say to his smile.

Is it perspiration or saline that stings my eyes? Although my eyes hurt, it is not this smarting that dissolves Stephen's face almost as soon as I've recognised his features. It is not the misty smear on my glasses either. The obvious fact is that Stephen is both in and not-in his waterproof suit. I could lose him any second.

'How've you been?' Stephen asks, his small area of available skin thickening again into something more than a pink oval blur.

'You've grown a goatee.'

'So have you, Tom. Any grey bits in it yet?'

'Yeah, a few. I'm glad they're not so obvious that you have to ask.'

'I wouldn't take *too* much comfort from that, mate. You're a bit of a smudge on the windscreen if you wanna know the half of it.'

'Likewise. Your face faded out—' *A second ago*, I am about to add. Our whaleguide's excited bleat shatters the thought.

'*Minke twelve o'clock!*' she shouts through the P.A. so loudly that the acoustics warp and distort.

The dream envelope tears; these seconds of conversation with Stephen flap away, carried off by the wind. A quick glance to my left and right reassures me that if anyone actually heard my sentences with Stephen, they either didn't care or comprehend. Maybe the weather was on my side – the noise of the gathering storm, of the water, masking what we said – but I might not be so fortunate again. So unexpected had Stephen's appearance been that it had put me under some kind of spell.

Not again, I vow to myself… but where has Stephen gone? I remain near the prow, facing twelve o'clock. It feels like solid midnight straight ahead, the clouds congealing into uglier bruises. A chorus of gasps educates me to the fact that this leviathan-lite has been spotted again; but the ghost of my uncle, if 'ghost' is the right word, is my own quarry. My own gaze veers to *six* o'clock.

He is retreating towards the stern. Do others see him? In all other circumstances, the brightness of the suit would be difficult to miss (that's the point of it, after all, in the case of man overboard), but now there is no one to move out of the way as he approaches – everyone is up the front with me.

I ease through the throng; and they are happy to move aside – it releases a space for them to get closer to the prow for a better view.

Finding Stephen takes no time at all. He's a hard man to miss, whatever the weather. He has sat down on a white-painted box that houses lifejackets. Of all strange things, he is rolling a cigarette with his banana fingers.

'You shouldn't smoke, you know,' I inform him.

Stephen laughs. 'It's not going to hurt me *now*, is it, boy?' he asks.

'I don't mean that. I mean smoking laws have got stricter since you went away.'

'It's the open sea!' he protests, actually reasonably enough – I'm tempted to join him. 'What are they gonna do? *Kill* me? *Drown* me?' He laughs again.

I sit down beside him. I don't really know what to say. I was wet behind the ears when last I saw him in the flesh. I am wet behind the ears *now*, but for a host of different reasons.

'How's your mum?' he asks me after a few seconds, sparing me any further silence-fuelled embarrassment. Before I can answer he adds, 'It's a bit choppy out here today innit?'

'Yeah it is. She's okay. Do you ever say hello to her, Stephen?'

'Nah. Too much water under the bridge,' he says, immediately finding this response nothing less than hilarious.

'*Minke eleven o'clock!*' our guide yelps.

'I know it's none of my business, so tell me to sod off if I'm intruding–'

'Sod off, Tom.'

'–but what actually happened between the two of you? I *say* it's none of my business, but who knows these days?'

Stephen's gaze is to starboard; a momentary blend of fag-smoke, spray and possibly a dip in his own internal energies causes Stephen's features to morph and then vanish. Again I stare at the pinkish, detail-free void inside his hood.

'People drift apart,' he answers, a sad note in his words. 'But I didn't come to talk about your mum; I came to talk about Roy. By the way, I took a big risk to be here today.'

'Who do you report to?' I ask him, pleased that the image

comes back clearer – the image of his face – like a candle flame guttering in a draught; now it's returned.

'It's not as simple as that. Did you ask Roy about the party he went to?'

I have to cast my mind back; the context isn't clear. Then I remember: Stephen told me to ask Roy about a party, some time ago; before Christmas? It must have been. 'He didn't remember a party,' I say to Stephen.

'Well he does now. He'll call you soon about it. He'll be excited.'

'Call me *here*?'

'Maybe. I don't keep his diary, mate.'

'Okay… And is this thing about a party some kind of breakthrough?'

'Perhaps it is. It proves you-know-who has a limit to his powers of suggestion.'

'I don't follow.'

'He'll tell you, Tom.'

'*Minke feeding at eleven o'clock!*'

Frustrated, I answer, 'What *can* you tell me, Stephen? Because all this is seriously getting on my tits. You say you took a risk to be here, and I believe you, but what the hell's going on? I don't *understand* anything anymore.'

'You mean you used to?' he asks me with scepticism in his voice. 'Grow up, Tom, the world don't revolve around you any more than it does around me. We're cogs, mate. Cogs.'

'I never said it did revolve around me!'

'You used to think so, believe me.'

'When I was a boy?'

'Even later than that. The problem is, you don't remember nuffing.'

'Then tell me something! Tell me *anything*!'

'I'll tell you something. Minke whales are the sprats of the whale kingdom,' he says. 'You have to go out a lot further to see the big boys.'

I am all but ready to lamp the twat. God give me strength, I think, glancing up into the near-Biblical sky, the gulls swooping and barking... Then suddenly the boat's engine shouts in a different accent as the pilot changes gears, and we are on the move again, chasing whales. At first I think it is this – the alteration to the stroke of the engine – that causes the vibrations along the top half of my body. Then I comprehend that my phone is ringing.

Frisking myself to find the phone in my strata of clothing is not simple. The waterproofs are only the first layer; the phone is buried deep beneath clothes I have piled on – advice from the hotel reception girl on the subject of going out to sea. I am jittery at the thought of missing the call, however. Half a second (I reckon) before the voicemail function kicks in, I locate the instrument and the panel reveals all I need to know and what I have already prognosticated. It reads ROY MOB.

It does not occur to me to marvel at the fact that there's even a signal, however many miles out into the briny we are. The transmission is as clear as a churchbell at midnight.

'Royvinder,' I say into his hearty cough.

6.

The call does not take long, but it's long enough for Stephen to leave me again. I watch him go, but I do not miss him, and do you know why? Because I know if he's done it once he can do it again. He's learnt how to pay visits; I'm his new holiday destination. And that's a great feeling to have – to know he'll be back. Sometimes it's nice to feel wanted.

Royvinder, I say to his hearty cough, as I have mentioned.

'You asked me about a party, Tom,' he says, a firelight of

excitement in his voice. 'I couldn't remember it – I didn't even want to be there, I only stayed about an hour for a bitter shandy. See it was the word *party* that threw me, I reckon – it was one of me ex's evening bashes she sometimes invited me to when she's feeling sorry for me or wants to show off.'

The stern heaves and sashays. It makes me think that the *Dottir* herself is impatient for what Roy has to explain. Attempting to prompt him along I say, 'So what happened?'

'She'd appointed one of her bumboys to take everyone's *keys* as they arrived. Just in case anyone got wankered – you don't get your keys back. Though quite how that little *fry-up* was going to stop me having me own keys back remains to be seen, but there you go.'

Does Roy sense my confusion in the silence I give him? All he can hear, I am certain, is the *whump* of air pockets in his ear; the cymbalisation of the waves; perhaps our whaleguide. From this I infer that Roy thinks something is vital in what he has to say; otherwise, wouldn't he ask a question about what he can hear?

'Don't you see what this means?' he asks.

'I'm afraid I don't, mate.'

'I called the ex. She weren't too impressed with the accusation, but she belled the key guy and he told her there was a bird who took the biggest set of keys, which was mine, and then *brought them back* a few minutes later, saying she made a mistake – she didn't want to leave straight away after all. A few minutes is long enough to press a set of keys into individual blobs of clay to get the imprints. Do the maths, Tom.'

'And what did this bird look like?' I ask.

'Medium height, medium build–'

'Well that's helpful. That narrows it down.'

'With auburn hair with blonde streaks. Same as the woman

who nicked Amelior Anderson's Punto!' Roy can scarcely disguise his enthusiasm.

'It also sounds like Annette,' I realize aloud.

'*Feeding frenzy at three o'clock!*'

'Tom, where are you, by the way?' Roy wants to know.

'Watching whales.'

'You're in *Wales*?'

'Not *in* Wales. *Watching* whales. In Iceland. Northern Europe.'

'I know where fucking Iceland is, Tom. What you *doing* there?'

'On holiday innit,' I answer.

Roy is incredulous. '*Now*? With all of this going on? He doesn't wait for a response, which is just as well: I wouldn't really know what to tell him. 'Thought you had no dosh,' he retorts suspiciously.

'Credit card. Say it *is* Annette doing these things – the thefts, the attempted – I don't know – botulism pandemic. What does it actually prove? What's so good about any of this?'

'It shows Kolko is not the magician we're giving him credit for being. Sure, he can create *illusions* – we both know that – but even he needs a physical object, like a key, to get *in* places. Or his worker bee does anyway – Annette, if was her. Whoever it was.'

The notion disturbs me – and what also disturbs me is the fact that I have until this moment given little real credence to the possibility. 'You think they're doing it together? Kolko and Annette?'

'If it *is* Annette – yeah. Don't you? We need to wake up, mate. It's too much of a coincidence otherwise. How would he know so much about us all? He can't be *everywhere*, can he? He needs spies.'

'Annette. Maybe Stephen.' Though it seems ugly to speak

ill of the dead, I cannot deny this possibility either. Besides, it's getting a bit late to start having morals.

'You're fuzzy, mate. Say that again.'

I repeat the accusation against my deceased uncle; it seems uglier still.

Roy says, 'I doubt it, mate.'

'Just thinking aloud.'

'I could chat to this Annette bird,' Roy offers. 'You got her number?'

Thinking of Sabrina's address book, and the fact that I transferred Annette's number into my mobile, I answer, 'I'll text it to you. What are you gonna say?'

'I don't know yet. I wanna see her face to face.'

'She works at Tiddenfoot.'

'The leisure centre? Leave it to me.' Roy coughs; recovers. 'Listen, mate – this must be costing me a packet; I didn't realize you were in the fucky *Norf Pole*. You gonna send me a postcard?'

'Wait; before you go, Roy. You can use the Internet at the library, right?'

'I've got it at work. Ian uses it for BMX sites, and whatever else, when he thinks I don't notice. Why do you ask?'

'See if you can find out about Caitlin Bryant – you remember my stalker? Killed her sons with an axe?'

'Of course I remember. I remember you *telling* me about it at any rate. That don't mean it's necessarily so, Tom, as you're well aware.'

'Are you doubting me now? Because *I* am. Could you see what you can find out?'

'I'll get E onto it. Pronto.'

'Cheers, Big Ears. I'm back on Sunday.'

'Pint at The Leper?'

'Twist my arm.'

We end the call, and I stare out to sea: in the direction of six o'clock, at the opposite end of the *Dottir* from the rest of my excitable travellers.

Stephen is in the sea, vigorously splashing for some kind of paradoxical purchase in the water, no doubt the 'trick' he alluded to. For my eyes only, a great white whale that has no business here in these relative shallows, rears up out of the waves and crashes down, taking Stephen into its vast mouth.

'Man overboard,' I whisper, and I smile when I return to the prow of the boat.

II.

1.

Inconspicuous as a pimple on a genital helmet, the dark blue chuffwagon-shitmobile that Roy loaned to Hannah is stationary in the car park outside the Tiddenfoot Centre, which is enjoying a decent trade on this February evening. In the hull, Roy sits fuming indeterminately, his brain as busy as a wasp. He watches the building; the sky is mauve with a daylight that seems sluggish to leave – it should be darker. Feeling as though he completely fills the car, Roy is fidgety, anxious; a cramp twists behind his left knee. Is it time to get out of the vehicle and approach the building? He brims with self-loathing at his own inadequacy: disgusted that he has come here without so much as a firm plan to execute.

The car-thief had come into *his* place of work. Therefore he should go into *hers*.

Symmetry.

With a grunt and a burp Roy exits the vehicle, experiencing a twinge in his back. The only piece of preparation he has made is to pack a plastic carrier bag with sportswear. Or at least with a pair of Bermuda shorts, a pair of trainers, and a highly unflattering once-black vest that could be used at a pinch. Although he has no genuine intention to join the gym, or anything silly like that, he was aware that he might not be granted access to the building without some show of disguise. He takes the bag from the boot, locks up, and walks over to the sliding doors.

'Hello, darling. I was hoping to have a word with Annette.'

That *darling* does not go down well.

'I'm afraid she's about to start a class, sir.'

Roy nods his head. 'Yeah, that's what I mean. I've come to join her class.'

The young lady on front desk must have worked through experiences like this before; it is to her credit that she conceals her surprise.

'She starts at seven. The advanced class,' said as if to make Roy confirm that he has the correct time and day.

'That's right,' Roy bluffs it out. 'Where do I need to go?'

'Men's changing rooms are down there on the right. Then you'll see the sign to the gym. But no offence, sir, are you sure it's the *advanced* class you're after?'

'Yes,' Roy answers, only half feigning his offence (the other half is genuine enough offence). 'Is that a problem? Just because I've put on a few pounds…'

'She usually asks everyone to start with the beginner's class. And I don't think I've seen you here before, have I?'

'I did the beginner's class somewhere else. In Dunstable.'

'Oh I see. Well okay then, that'll be six pounds, please.'

What if it's not the same woman? he wonders. Six squid down the drain and the potential for a heart attack. Nice evening. I could be at home with a glass of red…

Upon entering the changing room, the first thing Roy observes is that of a naked man. The man is towelling himself down while gazing with adoration into floor-to-ceiling mirrors. As Roy hustles past, the man, still un-towelled, bids him a good evening and Roy feels obliged to return the same.

Six squid down, a heart attack, and a naked male floorshow.

It's the gift that keeps on giving.

As soon as he has changed, Roy glances at his watch – 6.55 – and follows the green signs to the gym. His heart scurries and scampers. He does not know what to expect.

Bracing himself for the inevitable sly glances of pitying

concern, Roy strolls into the clanking noise pollution of dance music, hydraulic exercise systems and weights being lowered, some more tactfully than others. A woman as young as the one who greeted Roy on front desk karate chops the supercooled air, indicating his direction of onward travel, and he enters a dance studio, where class is close to beginning. Dance is one thing that Roy has not considered; the full horror of what he's volunteered for – *paid* for – stalks his veins as surely as imperfections in a bloodstream.

Nine other people are present – and all of them are women, dressed either in leotards or sweatwear; most with their hair tied back. Their feminine eyes draw Roy hither. Right at this moment it would be harder to walk back out than to continue on in. A few of the women even smile in sympathetic greeting.

Including the trainer. Roy spots her easily enough – not so many months have passed since he first clapped his peepers on her, back at Bible Street Cars. Back at *work*. And now he's infiltrated *her* place of employment. Justice. 'How does it feel, darling?' he wants to ask, but doesn't – and doesn't for an interesting reason. Unless she happens to be an actress in her spare time… that smile seems straight-arrow enough… *like she don't fucking recognise me!*

'I paid the girl at Reception,' Roy offers by way of explanation. 'Don't be fooled by the blubber.' Rather hopelessly he adds, 'Unless you've no room, that is.'

The dance studio could safely garage a private jet while class was in session. 'We've got plenty of room. You're aware this is–'

'Advanced class. Yes,' Roy bites a little irritably. To his surprise his legs are leaden; somewhat twitchy with nerves. Bit like how stagefright must be, he compares, all the while keeping a bead on Annette's features. Drilling his eyes into hers – or hoping to.

'Well then, let's see how you get on, shall we?' says Annette. 'Tonight we're starting with some light skipping to get the heart and muscles warmed up.' To the rest of the group Annette says, 'Ladies! Ropes at the ready! Have you got a skipping rope, uh…'

Very distantly, somewhere in Roy's head, is a chime that informs him that he is being asked for his name; however, he is snagged on the word 'skipping'… *Skipping?*

'Roy,' he all but blurts. 'And no I haven't, I'm afraid. *Roy.*'

'Yes I heard you, Roy. I've got a spare in my bag. Ladies! Leisurely warm up, please, while I help Roy–' Annette is turning away.

'Roy the mechanic. Bible Street Cars.'

Annette frowns briefly.

'I think we've met before,' he tells her, his voice lowered.

Nothing: not the merest glint of recognition on the woman's face.

'I don't think so; I'm usually quite good with faces. But I really must start the class, Roy–' as she turns again.

Can it be that she really does not recall entering the garage that night? Not a flicker of anything approaching distress has crossed her features, after all, and she has clearly been cornered.

There is one final bullet in the barrel.

'You picked up your Aunt Amelior's Punto from me, didn't you? Wasn't that you?'

'No, it wasn't me; you've muddled me up, Roy.' Still there is no suggestion that she's fibbing. Nimbly she jogs to the edge of the studio, where she has left her workbag. Bending at the waist, she pulls from the bag a length of rope – and Roy's reality shivers.

He is conscious of the women in the class; of the whirr of their ropes; the slap of each rope's individual downward trajectory against the wooden floor; of footfalls landing, breathing increasing in speed and the ruggedness of its quality. He can almost hear the women's *sweat*... And yet he is scarcely present. It is not until Annette hands the rope to Roy that the latter can even recall what country he lives in.

'Time's a-wasting,' she says, the smile on her face re-established.

Cardiovascular innit, thinks Roy, quoting a prison officer from the time of his brief dalliance with the penal system. The memory strikes him with a fist of lead. The prison gym, Stephen holding the punchbag, Roy lashing out his frustrations on it, gloved up and panting; then the reverse situation. The punchbag, the dumbbells... the skipping rope – before that incident of attempted strangulation – nothing to do with Roy or Stephen – which had resulted in the confiscation of all the ropes.

Roy starts skipping. He pools all of his concentration; he focuses on the far wall. Deliberately he does not face the other members of his class, he does not want to be distracted by their bouncing breasts. Roy trips against the rope, bollocksing the rhythm. He doesn't hesitate, he starts again. *Skipping, skipping. Cardiovascular innit,* he repeats in his head, over and over. He trips. He starts again. He trips. He starts again. He trips. He starts again. As his temperature rises, the time between trips lengthens: he's getting better. 'Agile footwork, Roy,' Annette compliments, but Roy scarcely registers the voice, he is in the prison gym with Stephen. Sweat bubbles on his face and shoulders. He is in the prison gym, and Stephen is saying, 'I could knock that cunt out, no worries at all.'

'What cunt?' Roy asks.

'Screw Baldock. He's a waste.'

They skip – Roy and Stephen. Roy says, 'Why would you want to knock out Baldock?'

'I could.'

'I'm sure you *could*. Why would you *want* to?'

'He's a waste.'

'That's not a reason, mate.'

'To stay here longer,' Stephen admits.

'Stay *longer*?'

'Yeah. This is comfy, mate.'

'You're a mug. *You're* the fucking waste round here if you think that.'

'Come on, boys, put your back into it, eh? Let's get them man-boobs off you.'

'I'm not ready to go home,' Stephen answered.

Institutionalised; brainwashed. Roy had seen it before; but now he re-registers his surprise that it's Stephen saying these words.

'You've done this before, haven't you, Roy?' asks Annette.

Roy doesn't hear her. Despite the fact that she stands a metre from him, he doesn't hear her – not at first.

Music erupts from nowhere: a heavenly salutation of guitars. It pumps. It's Shania Twain – 'Man, I feel Like a Woman!' How apt. How *ironic*. The volume is atrocious.

He skips as though the floor is on fire.

What do you mean, ready? Roy asks the past, and Stephen answers the question.

Too much pain on the outside.

On the inside as well, Roy thinks, referring to his hammering heart. Perspiration streams into his eyes. He feels like a boxer, but he has lost his mantra – or it has lost him. His mind asks its owner questions.

Why doesn't she know me? How could she forget me? Was she drunk at the time? She hadn't *seemed* so, true enough; but Roy knows that he himself can hold it together until the fourth or fifth pint of wine. No one is ever the wiser.

Skipping faster to whip away such thoughts, Roy is distraught to hear Annette call an end to their warm-up session. He is just getting into it.

'Ropes on the floor, ladies and the gent.'

Roy moves to the back of the class. Watching arses will be okay – they must have come here prepared for the possibility. No one ever said it was ladies only.

The song has changed to 'Simply the Best'. Facing the congregation, Annette begins with star jumps. And lo, the gathering does follow, Roy included.

Annette changes the nature of the exercise. She marches on the spot.

The class obeys.

Eventually the hour ends. Roy has developed worrying twitches; his chest throbs with the exertion. Silently he sings the survival blues… but his work is not yet done.

Roy waits until two-thirds of the group has walked in the direction of the changing rooms (the remaining three women mop their brows) before he approaches Annette.

It is as though she expects him to do so. She has bounded to the side of the studio, to collect her workbag. Now she turns and says, 'You did good, Roy.'

'Thanks. And thanks for the loan of the rope.'

'You're welcome. Will we see next week?'

'You've seen me before, Annette.'

'So you say. I swear I don't remember it, but if you're sure, then okay.'

'I'm a friend of Tom's.'

'Tom who? Oh *Tom*. Why didn't you say?'

'I'm saying now.'

'I see. Well can I just make one thing a little bit clearer? I've got a husband and two kids, so if that's what's on your mind. I don't want to put words in your mouth, but if it *is*, I'm sorry and all that, but.'

'I ain't chatting you up, Annette,' Roy answers.

'Then what? We've met before – I take your word for it. I don't remember.'

'I think I believe you.'

'Well that's a relief.'

'Kolko's made you forget.'

'*Excuse* me?'

'You heard me. Let me tell you what I know.'

Annette looks worried. 'They kick us out in a few minutes. Then I'm going home to a nice bath and to my hus – My God. It was *you*.'

'Me what? What was me?'

'I'm leaving, Roy.'

'*What* was me?'

'The blackmail shit,' says Annette.

'That was Kolko. Before you did your deal with him.'

'What *deal*?'

'Let me tell you what Tom told me, shall we?'

'Oh I know the gist. My name was Caitlin. I *stalked* him, of all things. Then I killed my sons – the sons at home with their father right now, shall I remind you? – the sons I love dearly – with an *axe* fuck's sake.'

'You had an affair,' Roy replies levelly. 'You fucked him on Dunstable Downs. Not that it's any of my business.'

'You're damn right it's none of your business! This conversation is over.'

'Just hear me out.'

'I'm going home.'

'His name was Chris. Or it might've been Liam. You had affairs with both of them, and I can't remember which one works here with you, but one of them does.'

'Did. He's left. Congratulations, and so what?'

'You can listen to me or wait till I've taken that information to your manager.'

'And tell him what? I've done nothing wrong!'

'To your husband then.'

'You're as bad as Kolko.'

'Not even close. Are we talking?'

Resigned and beaten, Annette answers, 'Spurt your poison, you disgrace for a man.' 'Thank you. Your private life reminds me of my own ex-wife's,' Roy says, picking his words as he might better fruit from the vine. 'And as such, it disgusts me. But it's none of my concern – although you know her, I think.'

'I know a lot of people Get on with it.'

'Kolko came to you via James – the autistic boy. He memorized your licence plate. And at some point he won you over, Annette. He put fog in your head. So you can't remember things you done. Like stealing cars. Delivering poisoned pizzas.'

'Yeah that sounds just like me. I do those things for a hobby. Are you mentally ill, mate? Maybe I should be thinking about calling the Care in the Community people.'

'You may be right. But you don't recollect any of this because of Kolko. He put a spell on you.'

'Are you done? You need a shower. So do I.'

'Just think about it. He came to you with leverage – you were knobbing some bloke from work. And he said he wouldn't tell. If.'

'If what?'

'You followed his trail of tears. Like James. You find a weakness and dig in the blade.'

2.

I take a deep breath and call Annette's number.

As the ringtones collect, I wonder parenthetically if Annette and I ever had sex. *Caitlin* and I did; but Annette and I?

'Hello?'

'It's Tom.'

'I've been wondering when you'd get in touch. Well?'

'Roy called on you.'

'Yes, at work. Thanks for that. Your decision, I presume?'

'Nothing to do with me, I assure you. Now I want to tell you a few things you told me. Back then. About the modelling days.'

Annette pauses. 'You'll have to be quick, I've got the dinner on.'

'Are you alone?'

'Richard's in his study. The boys are upstairs. So for the moment – yes.'

'What are you having? For dinner.'

'Fish. Would you like to read anything into that?' Annette demands, her voice as brittle as spun glass.

'I'm having fish as well.'

'I'll notify the press. What do you want, Tom?'

'You used to be called Caitlin.'

'Not this again.'

'Caitlin Bryant. You lived on Billington Road.'

'And I was your stalker. Right; I remember the script. I wrote you letters, we had sex, and Sabrina made you end it. Except there never *was* a Sabrina. And then I killed my two sons with an axe. The ones doing their homework upstairs.'

I quickstep away from her sarcasm. 'But you don't remember it,' I tell her, deadpan.

'It didn't happen!'

'No. Someone is protecting you – same way Dolly only recently remembered the hill with the face. Same way Hannah and Sam misremembered the thief.'

'*Protecting* me? They've got a bloody funny way of showing it! And who might my guardian angel be, Tom? No, don't tell me: Simon Kolko.'

'No. It's your dad. It's Patrick.'

The surprise I hear down the line has an abrasive quality, and it tastes foul, like liver and pineapple. It does not take a second to recognize I've hurt her. Drawn blood.

I end the call.

3.

Dorothy asks a question.

'I was cleaning my ears with a cotton bud and it came to me. What happened to Patrick during the war? The voodoo thing he mentioned.'

I can scarcely believe what I'm hearing.

'Are you asking me? He's *your* boyfriend!'

'Oh, what have I done, Tom?'

I lean over and kiss her right nipple. 'Nothing to worry about,' I attempt to assure her.

'I shouldn't be talking about this. Not with you. Not with anybody.'

'Does he know about me yet?'

'Of course not! He'd kill you.'

'He's a hundred and four don't you know.'

'He'd still kill you.' Dorothy gets out of bed and leaves the bedroom. She calls back, 'I can't believe here I am in my fifties, one boyfriend who's a nutcase and another boyfriend who's a geriatric!'

Is it jealousy that I experience now? *Something* is infiltrating my system, and it sure smells like jealousy.

Dorothy returns. Her stomach is lined with shallow red marks from where she lay on a mountain of pillows while I fucked her from behind. Otherwise her skin is very white.

She hands me a glass. 'It's something new,' she says.

I take a sip. 'It's water.'

'Something new,' Dorothy repeats.

'I don't like it. Do you have any vodka?'

'In my bra drawer.'

Cracking open the bottle releases endorphins, which spin around my skull. I add a gill of the beverage to my glass.

'You?' I ask as an afterthought.

'Yeah, we've come this far, Tom. Why not?'

'Why not indeed. Will you tell me about Patrick and the voodoo?'

III.

1.

Entering Patrick's house makes me feel like an intruder, even though the old man himself ushers us into the hallway. It smells of jasmine. The wallpaper is dark, floral; a trio of porcelain ducks flies towards an old-fashioned mirror. It is ugly beyond words.

I experience an Alpha Male Moment; I am on another beast's territory, and I am uncomfortable. Can he guess what Dorothy and I have been up to, for instance? Animals smell fear, and sexual competition, too.

Outside the taxi pulls away from the kerb as we enter Patrick's parlour – his choice of word. Air as rich and stuffy as the inside of a pet shop – an aquarium atmosphere.

We sit down. No refreshments are offered; I'm not thirsty anyway. I am twitchy. There is no preamble either, Patrick is all over his story like someone eager to establish an alibi.

'Some of the stranger things you see during times of war are not on the battlefield. They are civilian matters – people trying to cope with fear.

'I couldn't cope. I ran away – it's nothing I'm proud of. Who would be? But when you've seen enough belly wounds, pestilence and diarrhea, the prospect of being chased by the Army authorities loses some of its sting.'

'Tell Tom about the voodoo ceremony,' says Dorothy.

'I was sick. I reckon I might've mentioned I've had just about every illness and health condition known to man,' Patrick answers.

'And some that aren't.' Dorothy smiles. 'Yes, it might have

crossed your lips.'

Patrick stares at the carpet; the pattern draws him in, efficiently as a rotating spiral. He is mesmerized by his floor furnishings.

'I heard there were tricks they can do, these shaman. Authentic like.'

'What was wrong with you?' I ask.

'I should say Delhi Belly, shouldn't I, son?' Patrick laughs. 'But it were worse than that. That were only *part* of it. I had problems with me breathing, me peeing, me pooing. Problems with my eyesight. So I went to one of these healers.'

'And he led you to the ceremony?'

'No, girl; he was 'andy as neither use nor ornament. It was one of his other patients. It was him who told me about…'

'Go on,' Dorothy and I say as one.

2.

He led me through a maze of alleyways. Looking back I reckon I should have been frightened – alleys that dark, and to be honest, they stank. I didn't know where I was; I was feverish. I remember thinking, *this is like strolling through a nightmare*, but still I weren't frightened. In my mind, I think I'd given up, girl. Life couldn't get any *lower*, after all. I wasn't even scared about being caught – to be frank, I was probably suicidal. So I followed him. I have no idea of how long we walked because I already give my guide my watch. Valuable though it was, I didn't feel I'd need it again. And I remember thinking as well, it don't matter if I get mugged, got nothing left to steal.

We entered a heavy, stone building smelling of spices and manure. And some things I didn't recognize at first, things that turned out to be cooked sperm, boiling blood – you name it. We went up to a third floor room, its ceiling so low that we had to bend over. And he asked me to disrobe and he gave me a drink. That was when it all began.

I don't think I'd eaten for three or four days straight. When that drink they gave me went down the hatch it set fire to all the timber in the hull. I went down like a felled oak. Naked, feverish – heart like a road-drill, son. Thought I was dying!

There were five other people in that room. Including the bloke who led me there, excluding me, so six in total. But no furniture, nothing except for the small fire they lit in the middle. Smoke was everywhere! Not *big* flames, but big enough to roast a chicken – and there was a whole chicken on the blaze. But not cooking, hadn't even been plucked. Hadn't even been beheaded. Just a whole chicken with 'alf its feathers burned away, the other half damaged with soot. But as I say, they weren't cooking it – not to eat at least. They were *singing* to it.

I don't know how long it went on. The smoke got thicker and the singing became louder. I couldn't move. It was like I'd been batted in the spine. But still... I was calmer than I been in weeks. In months! I could've suffocated from smoke inhalation; I didn't care.

The only part of me body I could move was me 'ead. I twisted it on me neck, to count the people in the room. At first I thought me eyes deceived me, counting up to the five. At first I didn't see them all, but there was another man in the corner of the room! In the shadows. Bollock naked – just like the rest of us round the fire. He was carrying a bowl of something white – a powder. I don't know where it came from; but for the first time since I ran away, right at that moment I felt afraid.

I saw a figure taking slow steps towards me. Through the smoke, not through the noise. There *was* no noise. Even the fire – I swear it – was soundless. You could've heard the roaches on the wall; maybe I did, at that. All I remember is this figure, as I say

– *shaped* like a man, naked, but that's as far as the similarity goes. Instead he wore his skeleton on the *outside*, for example; but it didn't cover skin. Didn't cover *flesh*. Behind the ribs and the femur and you name it was nothing but rubbish and filth. Screwed-up paper smeared with faecal matter. Busted bottles, glass, containers, wrappers.

The figure was the alleys and roads I had walked down to get there. I turned them into this man. Why? Because I wasn't allowed to see him properly. My unconscious was protecting me, son, from the real appearance – if there *was* a real appearance.

He asked me what I wanted, and I told him, and he told me what it would cost, and I agreed. Then he said: *Are you sure? This will affect you and the ones around you. For the rest of your life and their lives.*

I was lying still on the floor. I'd tried to get up but I was like a newborn baby; I didn't have the back muscles. Not an ounce of strength in my body.

He leaned over me, close. His face was inches from my own face, and when he spoke to me he dropped ash and cinders through the hole in his skull where his mouth should be. Behind the skull was just more of the compressed, compacted rubbish. There were insects crawling in his eye sockets; and the ash and cinders fell onto my lips, into my own mouth. Like a filthy kiss, our faces were that close.

I swallowed the ashes and nodded yes – I could just about move my head properly to nod it. I'm not sure if I spoke aloud; not sure he did either. His skull was only a skull; the bone didn't make any alteration, but maybe the refuse behind the bone did.

He asked me one last time if I understood the terms and conditions, as we might say now. *The fucker was nervous himself!* He was a bloody amateur! Then. Not now. But then he said: *So be it. I can make it so you live. I can get you home, and protect you from the charges of desertion. Protect you from anything. You can have yourself a long life,*

Patrick, but don't imagine it'll be a free ride.

I paraphrase slightly but that was the gist of it. He said: *To stave off a cold you must first contract a cold, for your body to build up the resistances it needs – the necessary antibodies, if you like. So, to stave off every disease known to the world you must contract every disease known to the world.* And weren't *that* the bleedin' truth! I've 'ad 'em all! And I've *recovered* from 'em all! I been in sick beds with war wounds – no pun intended – that would have floored a bloody commando, with doses of tablets that could knock out an elephant, and yet I've jumped up and danced the Can-Can.

He was good to his word in that respect. But time went on, and sometimes, boys and girls, the memory sours. I started to forget about the agreement. Believe me or don't believe me but it's the truth. I would catch a dose of some pox or another and I'd fight it off like a bit of flu. It was just something I had to do – it was part of the pattern of life. Of *my* life.

What did he want in return, you'll be asking yourselves? Well, I wasn't so far gone that I didn't ask the same thing, of course. And do you know what he told me?

Control. When I desire it. Of you and those around you. For this I will grant you your wish for good health and a long life. Again, for you and those around you.

So all of this is my fault, I reckon. I can't see any way out of that interpretation.

3.

Neither Dorothy nor I say a word for a full minute. Nor do we glance at one another, we only have eyes for Patrick, who appears oblivious to the scrutiny, and lights up a fourth cigarette.

When eventually I open my mouth it is to say, 'You made a deal with the Devil?'

Patrick shakes his head, exhaling smoke in an even fan as

he does so. 'He weren't the Devil, son. The Devil has impeccable manners. And better breath.' Patrick laughs.

I remain stoneyfaced, leaning forward, my hands clasped together in what might have seemed, under other circumstances, as a parody of prayer.

Dorothy exhales sharply, as though she too is smoking (which she is not). I will do the smoking for the two of us, I decide, and I roll up and lick the paper as Dorothy says:

'He's been protecting Annette as well then? For a lot of years?'

Patrick nods his head. 'A *lot* of years, yes girl.'

'So much so, she can't remember things she's done. Is that right, Patrick?'

'On the money.' His voice sounds fainter; he will not meet our eyes.

'But *you* do, don't you?' I ask.

'That's part of my punishment.' Water has filled his eyes, and it's not the cigarette smoke that has caused it. 'Part of the *deal*,' he concludes, acid dripping.

Without a single modification to my tone – no scintilla of sympathy is evident – I push on with my swiftly-baking thesis.

'She really *was* called Caitlin, wasn't she?' I demand, and Patrick nods again. 'She really did kill her sons, didn't she?' I demand, and Patrick shakes his head.

'She did it with an axe. I *remember* it, Patrick!' I am suddenly angry – as furious as I've ever been. I stand up and lean over this old man, not even feeling ashamed of myself.

Does he know I'm here? Nothing on his face – not even an expression of *disappointment* – leads me to believe so. He stares at the curtains.

'She tried to. Someone stopped her,' Patrick answers, his voice low.

'Who? *Who* stopped her, Patrick?'
The old man peers up at me.
'You did, Tom,' he tells me, 'You did.'.

IV.

1.

I have made it clear they can bring whatever they want to drink but that I'll touch not a drop.

We're at my place. The curtains are drawn shut; the lights are on. The heating, too.

We wait for Stephen.

So far we have seen fit not to mention to Annette that she has a secret history – secret even to herself – but Hannah and Roy have been brought up to speed on the point: by Dorothy. I wasn't sure which way to go with the information – to tell or not to tell – but Dolly exhibited no such reservations or internal turmoil. She blabbed while Roy uncorked the first bottle of red wine. In truth, this surprised me a little – her oiled tongue – but in retrospect I am not sure why it should have. After all, these are not normal times.

I intend to share Stephen with Dorothy and Hannah. (I have already shared him with Roy, of course.) We are all in this together, are we not? Neither Sam nor Annette have been invited along… Actually, that's not wholly true. Sam was half-invited, in the sense that I asked Hannah to ask her. It was Hannah who failed to pass on the message, not by accident but by choice. They remain in a position very far away from their previous friendship. It was Hana, the thief, who separated the women. Guardian angels have a lot to answer for

Where is Stephen?

2.

My expectation that Stephen, if he comes at all, will come

via the telephone, as he has in the past, demonstrates a lack of faith, I must say, in his burgeoning powers of resilience, strength and stamina. It would do me good to acknowledge his appearance on the *Dottir*.

This time Stephen walks right up to my front door and knocks on the wood.

When I hear the brief tattoo, my initial reaction is: *Police*. My second is to panic because of the first. The law is the last thing I need tonight.

'Do you want me to get that?' Hannah asks.

'No, I'm all right.'

Along with my three guests, I have been sitting cross-legged on the carpet. I doubt if any one of us is quite certain why; it was a silent decision, with our tesseract chatting warm breeze and with Roy doling out the maroon refreshments (I gave in eventually).

Stephen's presence is on my welcome mat, and it slaps me with a wet rag. Perhaps understandably, my greeting is ridiculous.

'How did you get in the building?' I demand.

'Are you serious? How do you think?'

'Well actually, you've never explained any of that.'

'You've never asked. Are you gonna invite me in or do you wanna reduce me to tears? You little *tit*.'

He is stronger than he was on the whale-watching boat; more together, more materially dense. More real.

Into the lounge Stephen swans.

'Ahoy there!' he calls to the others, his arms wide open for maximum theatrical effect.

3.

'I get the picture, Stephen; you're not allowed to talk about Kolko in the definite third person.'

'I'd rather you didn't say his name.'

'I could use his old one if you prefer. Or one of his old ones anyway. Annette's dad told me and Dorothy he used to be called–'

'*Don't say it!*' Stephen interrupts. 'I don't wanna chance it, Tom. Not worth the risk.'

'Not to you, maybe.'

'Not to any of us! You don't understand.'

'Which is why you're here, and where I started from. *You* might not be able to discuss the ins and outs, but *we* can, and we can ask you questions. In theory.'

Stephen nods his head. 'In theory, yes.'

'But we'll have to be quick, right?' I add, almost hopefully. The reality strikes me that in fact I don't want him to stay long, though I've waited a long time for his arrival. Odd.

'I've got time. If I sound a little cagey, assume someone's tapping the line, so to speak; but I'll be as open as I can, for as long as I can. Okay?'

I have had the opportunity to marshal my thoughts and opinions. While they might not add up to much, I am ready to launch the attack.

'The earliest we know about is when Patrick made some sort of compact with him during the Second World War, when he defected. He ran away and ended up sick, but he was promised a long life in return for control of those in contact with him, however indirectly. Which means us. And *would* mean you if you were still alive, I think. How he *asserts* this control is by changing our memories, which I think makes him stronger somehow. But what he didn't reckon on were other… other spirits… other angels if you like, taking umbrage at this – getting fucked off with the fact that the bits of our memories that *they're* in have been altered… How am I doing so far?'

Sitting with us on the dirty blue rug, also cross-legged, Stephen nods his head once, curtly and cautious.

'Good. That's a start then. Finally,' I breathe. I take a sip of wine; we have embarked upon the third of the three bottles. No one – not even Roy – is drinking quickly, but there is no joyful sense of savouring the bouquet either. Tonight the wine is a tool.

'The other…I'm going to have to keep saying angels, or ghosts, unless you tell me otherwise. I'm sure there's a better word.'

'Not that I know of,' Stephen replies. 'You don't think we all sit and around and chat, do you? There's no village gossip, Tom. You have to stop thinking in those terms.'

'Can you see one another?' Dorothy asks. 'Do you know who my visitors are?'

'No. To both.'

I do not wish to relinquish hold of the reins, not now that I believe I am getting somewhere, so I interrupt any further contributions.

'What is making Mr K stronger is making others weak,' I say. 'Is that right?'

Again, Stephen nods his head; only this time he appears confident enough to elaborate. 'It creates an imbalance,' he adds. 'We all feel it.'

'All?' says Hannah, wrapping her fists so tightly around her empty glass that I'm certain she's about to break it. 'All you dead, you mean?'

'By your definition of the term, yes,' answers Stephen, unpredictably eloquent.

While I pause a beat to reflect on any other definition of the term, an anxiety prickles me – an anxiety that once again I have had the reins snatched from my hands.

'Our visitors really have come to protect us, then?' I ask

Stephen.

Derisively he snorts; this infinitesimal slip of poise is enough to vanish his chin and nose for two seconds – a blatant reminder (to me if to no one else) of what and not whom we are addressing.

'Protect themselves, first and foremost, I would say. Call me cynical.'

'They're just doing their *jobs*, aren't they? Their duties, if that's better. Tell me I'm right, Stephen,' Hannah insists.

He nods his head, wincing slightly.

'They don't *want* to, they *have* to. To what? To maintain that balance you talked about? To maintain their identity?'

'There's no identity crises, but you're on the right lines. It's some people's role to watch others–' Stephen starts.

'From up there?' Hannah asks, wide-eyed; she fidgets in excitement, twisting her rump on the rug and fingering the rim of the wine glass that I really should get around to offering to refill. The two things that stop me are: one, the sense of urgency I mentioned – the sense that time may be finite, *seriously* finite; and two, the impression that she's had enough already. When it comes to alcohol, Hannah has always been a lightweight.

'Up where?' Stephen asks her. 'Do you mean *Heaven?*'

'Sure!' Hannah answers, undeterred.

'You got to be joking, darling! You believe in *Heaven?*' His smile is biting.

'Don't you?' Hannah asks him, her face collapsing slowly.

'No I don't. I should know. You think I sleep on a pillow of white clouds? Come *on!*'

'Knock it off, Stephen,' I tell him. 'We're all kind of new to this, in case it's slipped your attention. There's no need to be sarcastic. She doesn't know.'

'Neither do you!' she hisses at me.

'I didn't say I did! If it's not called Heaven, what's it called then?'

'It's not *called* anything. It just *is*. And it's either in a state of equilibrium or it's not.'

'And right now it's not,' says Roy – the first words he's uttered in a long time.

'That's right: right now it's not.'

'Why's it got to be so hard for us to ask questions? Why can't you just tell us what's going on here, from what you can see ... on the other side?' Hannah says as she reaches for the bottle on the coffee table, needing to lean her torso into the task.

Evidently sensing that not all is well with the rest of the group, Stephen takes the opportunity to say sorry. 'The truth is,' he says, 'a lot of things aren't clear, not even to me.'

'Well you've been dead long enough to have made some enquiries!' I tell him – a rebuttal that actually makes Stephen roll his eyeballs back into their sockets in exasperation. One of the eyeballs – the left one – does not return for the remainder of the conversation. Eyesight would not seem to be important to this ghost. And none of us is impolite enough to mention that all we can see in his left orbit is the snowblind whiteness of the worst cataract in Christendom.

Hannah pours herself and Roy a top-up; Dorothy and I decline an identical offer. Stephen is not asked, but shows no sign of disappointment. He wants to explain himself – or perhaps it's to *defend* himself that is his uppermost goal and aim.

'It's not about how long you've been dead,' he says. 'It might as well have happened last Thursday – time has no meaning here. There are no watches. There are no calendars. As far as I can tell, the Ice Age was last July. Do you see what I mean?'

Roy nods his head with the most vigour. Here, it appears, is a concept he can accept... Parenthetically I wonder how Roy is taking all of this. By far and away it is Roy who has been the quietest of the welcoming party quartet, but what does this mean? No doubt in due course (in The Leper) I'll find out; but meanwhile, I can't help it, I experience a sense of sympathy for Roy. Of all of us present, Roy knew the man the best – Stephen taught him to read – and now… and now he doesn't.

'Stop thinking, if you can, about sight and sound, taste or touch. They don't apply. You are mind. You're not even a brain. You are mind. Thought. With only connections to what you've left behind.'

The work of the explanation is plainly draining Stephen. His colour fades and deepens; he's a starved plant suddenly in need of rain. He has lost the cocksure air with which he arrived – it has abandoned him. He will leave us soon. I recognize his waving-not-drowning demeanour, maybe even more than he does himself.

'I can't say if my experience was the same as anyone else's. We don't discuss anything.'

'Tell me something,' I interrupt. I don't care about what looks I might receive. 'I was in your house twice. I searched for you and you didn't answer. But you knew I was there, didn't you?'

'Yes. The second time I was sure. The first time…I felt you, yes, but I wasn't sure what I was feeling.'

'No one had tried to find you before that.'

'As in life, so in death…'

'That's sad,' says Roy.

Stephen turns to face him. 'Is it? I'm not sure. When Tom made the effort, it was like being woken up; but I didn't *want* to be woken up. It reminded me of what I wasn't. Wasn't wanted, wasn't needed. The second time… by the second time I was hungry for it. For communication. I knew where you were.'

'I was in your lounge,' I say.

'I felt it.'

'I broke into that lady's house. For you.'

'I *know*.'

'And you still didn't answer me.'

'But I tried, even though I felt…that sense of imbalance I've mentioned. I was aware you'd thrown something into the still waters. You made a splash. But I didn't know how to make a splash as big as your splash, Tom; I didn't know how to attract *you*. That took more time.'

Here is another comparison for which Roy is grateful, something on which to hang his known facts. 'It's like a sea, then. Death is.'

'Like a dry sea,' Stephen compromises. As though intensely aware at this second of a deficiency with his eyesight, he uses his right pinkie to peck at the innermost canthus of his left eye. The eyeball rolls back into place.

Out of respect I turn away. Or possibly it's nothing to do with respect, maybe it's more that I can't bear to watch someone else leave me.

When I open my eyes, Stephen's gone. Roy holds out his hands, palms to the floor, shaking. Hannah's gaze is fixed away from us on the ceiling. Dorothy has wet herself, though she doesn't know it yet.

I reach for the bottle with a sigh.

4.

The sea rises up to crush me – to pulverize my bones into flotsam – wave upon inky-dark wave of it, until the pressure is unbearable and my eyelids leap open with tiny clicks. Still the darkness persists, shoving at me; I don't even know which way up I am. I'm in the grip of a dry panic. Opening your eyes should bring the light, but the waves of darkness, dry now, all the more terrifying for that fact, crash against me…

And someone is breathing. A slight hiccupping catch on the exhale.

'Who's there?' I try to demand – but the question is more of a whisper than a bellow.

No one answers.

The darkness rolls by in tubes.

Am I lying down or standing up? Or am I in the sea, waiting to be swallowed by a minke whale?

'Stephen? Is that you?'

No one answers.

'Dorothy?'

Surely to God it can't be *Roy*. Surely to God I can't have gone *blind*…

Piles of darkness now, squirming on me…

Must be Hannah, I decide. After all, it has happened before, has it not? Waking up in the same bed, blessed or cursed with no memory of what happened to get us there, or what might have passed while the darkness gathered against us. So I say her name too.

No one answers.

I flap my arms; stretch out my legs. Try to swim among the dry black waves; a breaststroke through the sea of my mind.

'Sabrina?' I plead, knowing that if indeed it's my ex she will not be best pleased to be my fourth guess.

'It's time to open your eyes, Tom.'

A voice I strain to recognise; soft but sure; almost a lullaby whose intention it is to invite the recipient to do precisely the opposite of the spoken words.

'Who are you?'

'It's time to open your eyes, Tom,' I am told again.

'I'm trying! Am I blind?'

'Not in the sense you mean. Try harder. You can do it.'

I feel my brow strain to furrow. There is something about the nigh-on paternal encouragement of the words – something warming and hopeful. Something that inspires my confidence, despite it all.

It's like being spoken to by my dad, and for an instant I almost say his name as well. What stops me doing so (stops me dead, you might say) is the simple fact that the voice is utterly wrong. It's not Dad. It's not Dad in my room, and it's not Dad in my head.

The truth is but a heartbeat's step behind.

'Let me see you Kolko,' I tell my visitor; however, immediately conscious of life's reality – that sometimes slow and steady wins the race – I stitch on a word of manners. 'Please.' My voice is steadier than I might have imagined it would be.

He cannot hurt me, this is why.

Kolko has not hurt anyone – not directly; that's not his style – so even though there's a first time for everything, I am not so panicked as I was when the darkness rolled onto me.

'Has the cat got your tongue?' I enquire of the gloom, which swirls about my vision – clearing, but clearing too slowly for my liking. 'Or should I call you Otrenxus?'

5.

'Where did you hear that name?' he asks me, his voice both truculent and sulky.

'You sent it in a Valentine's Day card.'

'Well, that's a turn-up for the books,' says Kolko. 'I suppose you think you're doing something smart.'

'I *suppose* precisely the opposite.'

Kolko waits for my clarification.

'I used to dream I could fly,' I tell him. 'A few metres off the ground – nothing more. Does that resonate with you?'

'I don't know what you mean.'

'All right, saying that I believe you, allow me to elaborate.'

'No. I'm the one that asked you a question. Where did you hear that name?' he asks again.

There is no point in lying.

'Patrick told me.'

Kolko strums his fingers. I wait for him to burst – to scream – to whatever.

'And who the hell is Patrick?' he asks me.

V.

1.

She is dressed in her Sunday best. The suit is worth more than she can afford, but then again she is not the one who bought it. Daddy bought it.

Patrick bought the suit for his one and only, as a mark of personal shame. It is worth the cost of a year's worth of electricity, and Annette looks good in it. She wears her father's money well.

Locks click competently in front of Annette; one at waist-height, one at shoulder-. Electronically hinged, the door swings in away from her, and the woman who has unlocked the door is revealed; a taut, broadly-built redhead, dressed smartly in a long grey woollen skirt, flat shoes and a thick pullover. She wears no jewellery but she does wear a smile.

'You must be Annette,' she says, holding out a plump hand.

'Dr Bragg?' asks Annette, shaking the other woman's hand.

'Please – call me Vanessa. We only use prefixes in front of a select group of patients. Would you like to come through?'

The corridor is long and wide; it smells stuffy – it smells like her sons' bedrooms. Artwork of a great range of quality has been framed and hung on both walls.

'These are the inmates' pictures?' Annette enquires.

'Yes. But we do prefer the term patients to inmates, regardless of the locks at the end of each corridor.'

'Sorry.'

'Not at all. It's an easy mistake to make if you're new to the field, which I take it you are from your letter. Is that correct?'

The floor is covered with a dark grey carpet of spiky shag;

there is no sound of footfalls.

'Yes it is. It's very quiet. I expected it to be more…'

'Gnashing and wailing?' Vanessa guesses. 'A common mistake, too. Here we are.'

A decal on the door reads INTERVIEW ROOM 2. The words have been formed from earnest calligraphy, with curlicues and elaborate purple-inked flourishes; instead of dots the two *i*s sprout flower petals from their heads; from inside the two circles of the second word beam happy faces.

The work of a privileged patient, Annette surmises.

Beneath this decal is a rough but functional grid that illustrates appointment times, the patient in question, and the expected visitor. When Annette sees her own name on the grid she experiences a chill.

'I know we went through this on the phone,' says Vanessa, 'but so we're clear, okay?'

'Okay.'

Vanessa has her key-card ready, in the palm of her right hand, but she does not slap it onto the sensor.

'With James, we are experimenting with a way to deal with his lack of anxiety tolerance. Do you know what I'm talking about?'

'Not really.'

'Anxiety tolerance is the extent to which anxiety *additional* to the patient's habitual stock leads to further pathological behaviour or symptom formation. Or regression to an earlier physical or mental state. With James, we use a tranquilizing medication. And he will have had his dose this morning, before breakfast. So as I said on the phone, you might not want to expect too much from him.'

'Anxiety?'

'You sound surprised.'

'I am. I can't remember ever meeting someone so calm and collected. That's one of the spooky things about him, I thought.'

Vanessa says nothing. Very gently she nods her head; she purses her lips and savours the bouquet of this announcement.

Annette finds the silence uncomfortable and asks, 'What?'

'Let me ask you a question. Would someone so calm and collected, as you put it, go to the lengths James went to, first to procure a weapon, then to kill his parents? Believe me. There are levels of anxiety here quite exceptional for a male of any age, but certainly for a boy of James's. Not that we think that's the end of it, of course. There's a lot more going on here than anxiety; but I mention it because of the symptoms you might witness. Ready?'

Annette tugs in a brisk shallow breath. 'As I'll ever be.'

'You remember the drill? You hand him nothing and you accept nothing from him. He shouldn't *have* anything, but just in case. James is not above the occasional Sneaky Pete trick, although he's shown no sign of further violence.'

'What sort of tricks?'

'Oh, all of our patients play up from time to time, don't be worried. We caught him secreting some of his medication under his foreskin.'

'Jesus.'

'Are you ready?'

Vanessa taps the key-card to the sensor. Locks snap back with a sharp sound.

'Just one thing,' Annette adds quickly. 'Does he know what he's done?'

'Oh yes. He's quite proud of it, in fact.'

Vanessa pulls open the heavy door.

2.

'Do the police know you're here?' James asks.

'Not from me. Should they?'

'I think they monitor my visits. They want to know who calls on me.'

'Well, perhaps Dr Bragg will inform them,' Annette answers. 'How have you been?'

James sits on the other side of a table-and-bench made of reinforced plastic, which is screwed to the floor. His hands are on the tabletop, fingers splayed. His nails have been bitten into ragged sawtooth shapes; the flesh beneath the cuticles is angry.

James does not wish to respond to Annette's question; perhaps he does not know how to. He wants to finish up on the existing topic.

'They want to know *why* people visit me as well. Were you searched?'

'Yes.'

'What do they do with your handbag?'

'Why do you ask?'

'You're the first woman to visit. It's the first time the question's seemed relevant.'

'After I was searched I had to lock it up,' says Annette.

'Where's the key?'

'In the front office, on a hook on a board on the wall. These questions–'

'Do you worry that right now someone might be going through your bag?'

'No. Do you know one of the major ways you've changed, James?'

'Yes I do. Would there be anything embarrassing in your handbag for anyone to find?'

'No; there's nothing embarrassing. One of the major ways you've changed is, you ask a lot of questions now. You never used to.'

James shrugs. 'I never thought I needed to.'

'Why not?'

James sniffs his disapproval. 'I used to think I either had the answers already, or the answers weren't worth having in the first place. I've grown up a lot. And not just in terms of puberty.'

'So you're not getting much intellectual input, you mean.' Annette is not sure how else to address this statement. 'How do you spend your days?'

'Interpretive dance. How do you think?'

'Don't be sarky with me, young man.'

For the first time since Annette's arrival, James smiles. 'I don't think I can get in any *more* trouble, do you?' he asks wryly.

'That's no excuse for mislaying your manners, James. Is it?'

The boy's smile thaws and melts away. 'No, it's not. I do apologise.'

'That's better.'

'But why *are* you here,' James continues. 'If you don't mind my asking.'

'I don't mind at all. I'm here because the puzzle remains unsolved.'

'Not for me.'

'But it does for me,' Annette pushes on. 'So I've come to ask you for more help.'

'I told you everything. In that man's flat. Tom's flat.'

'I know you did. But hear me out, James. Because I think you and I – we've got things in common. More than your mum. But to find out everything I'll need to ask *you* some questions. Will you permit me that?'

'*I* will. Though I can't speak for my jailers. I don't know what *they'll* allow.'

'They're not your jailers, James. You're not in prison, you're in a hospital.'

Shifting slightly on his side of the bench, James enquires, rhetorically, 'Are there locks on every door?'

'You're ill, James.'

'Not any more. I excised my cancer.'

'When you killed your stepfather?'

The boy nods.

'And your mother?'

'To a lesser extent; but yes.'

'Okay. You see, James, you see… I think I killed someone as well. People tell me I did, but I don't remember doing it, so is it possible I did?'

'I don't know. Who was it?'

'My two sons… This is difficult. Deep breath… Do they record these conversations, do you know?'

'I'm not sure.'

'What would be your guess?'

'My guess would be yes they record these conversations.'

'Mine too. So you see how much I'm trusting you here, James, with this confession.'

'Is it true?'

'A confession is always true. But you've met my sons, right? You have actually *met* them. *Played* with them. I didn't imagine it.'

'Of course not.'

'I'm confusing you. I'm confused myself. Here we go. I have been told – repeatedly – that I took an axe to my two boys when we were younger. Yet they're alive. And I am not in prison.'

'Unlike me.'

'Unlike you. The question being, how is this possible? How can I not remember something like that? And I thought of you. And I thought of Kolko. Which brings me to the next questions, namely – has he come to see you?'

'Kolko? No.'

'Are you sure?'

'Am I *sure*?'

'Because I think he can trick our memories – I have no idea how, that's the hard part – and I think he can make promises. Like the one he made for you, James – the one you haven't told us about.'

'I don't know what you're talking about,' the boy protests, squirming as if he needs to make wee-wee; a boy again, an infant.

'Yes you do, James,' Annette continues; 'or maybe you didn't remember any of it at the time. I can easily give you the benefit of the doubt on that one.'

'I don't want to talk anymore.'

'To me or to anyone?'

'To you.'

'Good; that means I was getting close. You see, James, a funny thing happened. Some friends of mine went to see my dad, and they asked him all sorts of questions, and he told them all sorts of answers. Except for a very important thing, and I suspect that's what's happened to you as well, James. Even if you don't remember it… Sit down, James.'

The boy has stood up; his fingers clench and curl at his sides. His hands are like desperate crabs.

'I said: *sit down*, James. Unless you want me to notify Dr Bragg. Is that what you want?' Annette's tone of voice might have been addressing a two year-old holding a teddy-bear to his chest – a child who will not stay in bed – but the rebuke hits home, and the projected sense of guilt finds its mark.

The boy reclaims his side of the bench. Once more he lays his hands on the surface of the table. He blinks his eyelids shut and holds them there for long seconds.

'Thank you.'

Annette takes a moment to inspect the damage to the

room's equilibrium. There is little to discern. The buccinator muscle in the boy's left cheek pulses tensely, but other than that all remains as it had been. For many more reasons than the obvious one, Annette thanks James again.

'I think he promised you something, James; something it's impossible to get without him. Just like he did with my dad. You see, James, my mother. My mother. My *mother*.'

'Died?'

'Unexpectedly. Old, but unexpectedly. But Kolko had already vowed to Dad he'd look after us – look after all of us, though I didn't know anything about it, and even if I *had* known anything about it, I'm pretty certain not a lot could have changed. But how can this be? you find yourself asking. If he's supposed to be so shit-hot at looking *after* us, what happened to my mum? Some protector! Do you see my point, James? I think you do. Because he promised you the same thing as he promised my dad recently. To prove he's still the boss.'

Annette pauses.

'James?'

'I heard you. I don't know what you want from me.'

Annette leans forward, her breasts on the table. 'Just tell me I'm right, that's all I want from you. For now. *Am I right?*'

'Yes, you're right.'

'He's going to bring them back, isn't he, James? Your father and my mother: that's what he said to you, as long as you did the things he asked you to do. And you did.'

'Yes, you're right,' says James, robotic now, and closing his eyes again.

'He told you he could bring him down, didn't he? Back from the dead.'

'Yes, you're right,' says James, sounding all but braindead now.

'Good. And we're going to *help* him. Aren't we, James?'

VI.

1.

In the mail are three letters for me: a credit card bill, which goes in the bin unopened, unread and unasked-for; an envelope with my address upon it handwritten, which stimulates my interest and although I don't recognise the calligraphy, I'm reminded of when I used to receive letters hand-delivered from Caitlin Bryant, when she lived behind me – oh yes: and before she went nuts and axed her sons into kindling... This letter I leave until last. The third piece of correspondence is from the Personnel Department at the College, and the contents strip me down to my ugly cold bones – I have run out of sick leave and I will not be paid anymore after the end of the month. I will be broke and I will lose my home and everything will crumble into dust and shite... I need to sit down. True enough, I've expected this for a while, but this doesn't make the surprise any less spiky.

The thought of pennilessness invades my head and I start to panic. No money coming in; no Sabrina to earn us more. I will have to go back to work, to trigger my salary to be reinstated. This notion does nothing for my burgeoning panic attack, unless you count making it worse. There is sweat all over my body; fear's upon me like a case of the lurgy

Mere metres from where I stand, in her own flat, Dorothy picks up the phone. 'I'm having a panic attack,' I tell her.

'Welcome to my world. I was just thinking about you, funnily enough. I was reading a book by a guy called Ernest Gellner and he says: "People find it impossible to remain passive in the face of acute and recurrent anxiety."'

'No shit. And you thought of me? How sweet.'

'I thought of all of us, I suppose. What are you doing today?'

'I can't afford to do dick.'

'Fancy lunch out? Or a drink? My treat.'

We make our plans and my heart settles down. The probability of a fair-to-middlingly easy-to-achieve fuck – either antipasta or post-prandial – is not an easy one to ignore.

Around mid-morning I open the third letter.

It's from James's sister, Louise. She has something to say about Annette's trip to the hospital where James is being held.

2.

'What do you miss most about Sabrina?' Dorothy asks me.

'Miss most? There isn't a most. It's her. It's her I miss. And it's funny you should mention her now: I was thinking about her earlier on.'

'I know. That's why I asked.'

'You *know*?'

'Tom, you're using a lot of emphasis in your questions these days. Has anyone else mentioned that?'

'No, I can't say they have, Dolly. What exactly do you mean by *you know*?'

'Don't tell me you're *surprised*.'

'Well pardon me if I am; I'd forgotten about your long-standing talent for hypnosis or whatever it is.'

'It's not hypnosis. You're getting angry. Would you like some dessert?'

'Will it stop me from getting angry?' I demand. Now what have I told myself before about making a scene in public? It's not big of me and it's not clever.

'No,' Dorothy answers – with reasonable balance, considering. 'Probably the last thing an excited child needs is more sugar.'

Why can't I resist pecking? Why not simply let it go?

'Then why offer me more sugar?' In truth I don't *know* why I'm so cross. We have just enjoyed a tasty pub lunch at a place in town called The Crown; neither of us had fancied The Leper. You can have too much of a not-very-good thing. And Dorothy has already repeated her offer of picking up the tab.

'You're an adult now, Tom.'

'An adult *now*? I'm thirty-three years old!'

'An adult since Sabrina left you. You were catapulted through the stages of bereavement in record time. You did well to come back to us.'

I sniff; it sounds disparaging. 'Where else was I going to go?'

Dorothy shrugs her shoulders. 'Where the other lost souls go? Who knows? Do you want a dessert I asked you.'

'No thank you. Another brandy, perhaps.'

'Another? You haven't had one yet. You've had beer.'

Dorothy sips her spritzer. Crenellations such as those on the rim of a coin appear at the corners of her mouth. I feel like I might ask *What's so funny?*

When she returns to the table she is carrying two glasses of brandy. Doubles, no less. While my curiosity is all for challenging the provenance of the cash required for this afternoon's feast, I fear that to do so will be to kill the Golden Goose. I accept my tumbler with gratitude.

'Anyway,' says Dorothy, sitting back down, 'you didn't answer my question. The one about how you miss Sabrina.'

'Yes I did. I told you it wasn't about bits of her.'

'I worded it badly. Shall I try again?'

Dorothy sips her brandy; considers her wording. 'What did you use to do the most that you miss?'

'Argue. Or rather, argue is what we did most; I don't miss it.'

'Are you sure?'

'Of course I'm sure!'

Dorothy smiles. '*I'm* not so sure. You're more argumentative since she left you.'

'No I'm not.'

'There you go.'

'And stop saying she *left* me! She was never there, Dolly!'

'Never *here*, you mean.'

'Now who's being argumentative?'

'It's an important distinction.'

'To you or to me?'

'To *her*, Tom. Important *to her*. No one else is important. You believed in her; that means she was here, just like Stephen is.'

'Just like you are.'

'No. *Not* like I am. But like the black girl and the white girl are *to me*. Real as thunder. Real as radio waves. Real as touch.'

I drain my brandy in one go and ask, 'So what are you saying?'

'Only you can bring her back, Tom,' Dorothy answers.

3.

Only you can bring her back, Tom.

This is how far we've come, nothing rattles us anymore; nothing seems out of the ordinary.

The meal to which I was treated was the consequence of some humourless hard-arsery from Dorothy in the direction of her 'so-called' agent, Julia.

'May I speak to Julia, please?' she asked in her friendliest tones, as though she hadn't already made a score of similar requests. When informed that Julia was saving refugees in Uganda, or splitting the atom, or turning water into wine, or whatever the excuse happened to be this time, Dorothy went on with: 'I see. Tell me, dear, did she ever mention the holiday that she and I took in 2000 to Phnom Penh? No, I thought not; I imagined she might not have. Suffice to say, she and I frequented a particular bar – a specialist bar, you might say – where we solicited the services of a beautiful twelve year-old boy prostitute. Tell Julia I still have the Polaroids of that afternoon and I'll expect her call within the hour to discuss a project I want to write for her. Good day to you, my dear.'

The call came. Of course Dorothy was obliged to deflect a full ten minutes of crystallized invective, which she did with aplomb and patience. Then she said, 'Are you finished with this talk of libel?'

'I think so, Dorothy. I think we're done with each other full stop.'

'Hear me out. I have something I've started writing.'

'Couldn't you have put it in a *letter*? Like everyone else?'

'I'm *not* everyone else, Julia. We go back a long way, you and I.'

'Not to Phnom Penh in 2000 we don't! Not to a boy-whore we don't!'

'It made you look, it made you stare; it made you lose your underwear.'

'I'm not entirely sure what to say to that.'

'Say you're ready to hear my synopsis.'

'Will it stop you goosing my assistant?' Julia demanded.

'I would imagine so, yes. No promises.'

4.

'*Our* story?' I ask.

Dorothy nods her head. 'Is there a better one you know of? A five hundred pound advance. From her. Not the publisher: from Julia's own bank account. It makes you feel wanted again. Even if it turns out to be a sympathy bung. Another brandy?'

We walk home shortly after.

To our *separate* homes.

VII.

1.

During the night, snow has dipped low to the ground but has since largely retreated; what results on the country road from Stanbridge to Bible Street Cars is a kind of meringue-tough silky-grey slush, through which Ian, Junior Mechanic Ian, attempts against the odds to skateboard, while wishing that he'd opted this morning for the BMX. It's heavy going. He disembarks, stamps the board's stunter end and the device leaps up into his grip like a trained poodle. He will walk the rest of the way – a matter of fifty metres – while cleaning his brow free of sweat with the frayed end of his aubergine scarf.

He is satisfied with this decision. What knocks Ian's stuffing out – what obliterates his sense of self-importance – is what he sees parked on the forecourt at Bible Street Cars.

It's an ice-cream van. Though presumably (logically) pink and white in paintjob, under the unsatisfactory forecourt light the pink appears oxblood; the white the unappetising colour of three-quarters cooked pig's liver. The frown does not leave Ian's face as he carries his skateboard closer to the vehicle; his frown deepens. Not only because of the ice-cream van's presence, which is odd enough. More disturbing is the van's consistency.

Kicking up filthy sludge, Ian halts a few metres from the vehicle. It seems to be shimmering. Pulsing. Every second or two Ian can see right through it; then it regains its solidity and substance.

At first Ian blames a hangover – a hangover he doesn't even own, the previous night having been dry – and he rubs at his face and eyes with the plump flesh of his free hand. Nothing changes (he knows that it was not going to); the ice-cream van dims, *thins*; Ian takes in the sight of Roy's courtesy jalopy, parked beyond it; at which point the van seems to flex its muscles, and here comes the metal again, away goes the vehicle's gaseous countenance. Ian wants to touch it.

He is spellbound. A curiosity, almost infantile in its intensity, shoves him forward. Not that recklessness has taken over completely, however: standing close by the van now, he uses the skateboard (and an outstretched arm) to test the water, as it were. The skateboard taps against the van's bonnet; the sounds is as it should be. But when he taps his testing stick once more, a few seconds later, there is no noise; the vehicle has thinned out again – been spirited away – and the skateboard moves slowly through the diaphanous image.

Remembering to breathe again, Ian is shocked awake from the vision and the experience. He turns on his heels and makes a beeline for Roy's front door.

The garage's floor is already wet, and in his inappropriate footwear Ian slips, and it takes a flap of his wings before he is able to right himself. Then he stops still.

Voices leak from the office, one of them Roy's. Ian strains to hear the other one, who he thinks must belong to Kolko. Who else? Who else would visit this early in the morning, the cunt? And although the presence of the ice-cream van remains unexplained, Ian strides towards the office, fuelled by a steam of indignation, and in full protective manner, his skateboard no longer a substance-tester but a cudgel.

Roy is sitting in his big chair, on the business side of the desk. A fat mug nests in his heavy grip. On the side of the mug is a joke, referring to the beverage within: IF I'M HOT, YOU CAN ALWAYS BLOW ME.

In one of the two customer seats is a figure that Ian fails to recognise.

It is not human either – or at least this is Ian's foremost initial opinion in his soup of thoughts and sensory attacks.

'Man' he might once have been, but 'man' he is no longer.

'Christ,' Ian whispers.

'In the sense of resurrection from the dead, you've got a point, Charlie,' the visitor agrees. So quickly does he then stand up and extend a hand to shake that Ian backs away and nudges his gluteus maximus into the squat little fridge. On top of the fridge, the tray bearing cups, a kettle, spoons and a bowl of manky sugar rattles hard – appropriately skeletal percussion.

'Sorry,' says the visitor.

'Jesus *Christ*,' Ian whispers, his eyes fixed on his interlocutor's ill-formed physiognomy.

'It's okay, E,' Roy offers from behind the desk, and judging by his relaxed appearance it *looks* okay – at least as far as Roy is concerned – but how can it be?

The man who has paid them a visit has no *face*.

2.

The visitor sinks back onto his chair.

Ian's head feels muzzy and cramped; the sweat that formed on his body on his trudge to work through slush now reappears. His throat feels busy with a lolling tongue, a sense of suffocation, and a rhythmic spasm of the muscles in his cheeks.

When Roy repeats 'It's okay, E,' Ian turns to his employer, unconsciously raising the skateboard to his chest like a shield.

'The fuck's going on here, Roy?' Ian demands.

The visitor adds, 'I was just going anyway…' as if to excuse himself from present company.

Although there has been no move to stand up again, Ian points a trembling finger and says, 'You stay right where you are, mate,'

The visitor nods in agreement, in deference – and a beak of skin on his forehead slips forward and laps over his eye sockets like a fringe.

Ian lifts the skateboard to his chin and breathes disbelieving expletives into the lacquered plastic. The tray on top of the fridge clanks and tinkles once more: Ian has backed up against it again.

'Sorry about that, too,' the visitor mumbles. 'Still getting used to this.'

'It's all right, mate,' Roy attempts to assure him. 'Happens to the best of us.'

Scarcely able to credit his own powers of hearing, Ian turns to his boss again and asks, 'Are you nuts, Roy? His fucking flesh's falling off!'

'I know,' say Roy and the visitor as one.

Ian's eyes drink in the sight of the man in the customer's chair.

He is dressed in white: not a suit but a tunic, apparel that identifies him (in Ian's mind) as the driver of the ice-cream van outside. His collar, cuffs and trouser hems are a navy blue; further decked out in a sailor's cap he might have passed for a career seaman on shore leave. But there is no hat on his head; there is not much skin either. The man is all but down to the bone, to the skull; in much the same way as the van outside had guttered and flickered, the man's head and face move in and out of a more and then less respectable appearance, though they never quite make it all the way to fully formed.

Ian knows that what he's about to ask is a stupid question, but he poses it all the same, for his sanity's sake.

'Have you been in an accident?'

The man laughs at this, while at the same time fixing his forehead back into its correct place. 'I've been to Hell and back,' he answers, which elicits from Roy a muted sniffle of comic approval.

Roy says, 'We mustn't tease him. Make yourself a brew, son.'

'No thanks,' says Ian.

'At least take a seat.'

'No thanks,' says Ian. Then it spurts out: 'I don't think I wanna work for you no more, Roy.'

The big man raises his eyebrows. 'Just when it's all getting interesting? Come on, E. We've both got a brew; make yourself one.'

'*No thanks*.'

'All right, I'll make one for you.'

'*No thanks*, Roy! Jesus! How can you act as if this is normal. And what's with the fucking ice-cream van outside?'

'What ice-cream van?' Roy asks.

'Oh, that's mine.'

'I guessed it was fucking *yours*, cunt! I mean why's it keep disappearing?'

Missing what Ian regards as the salient point entirely, Roy asks his guest, 'How come you drive an ice-cream van?'

The man in the white tunic shrugs. 'I used to sell ice-cream. I drove an ice-cream van when I was alive.'

'Oh I see…'

'When you were *alive*? Fuck it, Roy, I'm leaving, I've had enough of this.'

'Just hear him out, E. He don't mean noh'arm, do you, mate?'

A shake of the head. The visitor picks his coffee up off the desk.

'This is Mick,' Roy tells Ian. 'He's that lad James's dad – the boy I told you about?'

'The fruit loop?' Ian says without thinking.

'Hey come on,' his father protests. 'I *am* right here you know!'

'Sorry, I'm mashed. What's *up*?'

Roy nods his head. 'He's come here to say thank you to us, E. Because he used to be dead and now he ain't. So he's come to say thank you. To us, son.'

3.

Thin lips pinched against the end of a rolled cigarette, Roy draws breath, takes stock, and engages first gear. 'You sure you'll be okay for an hour, E?' he has enquired of Ian, and although the answer was a confident affirmative, Roy is far from cocky. He expects to return to Bible Street Cars to find it razed to the ground: a freak fire, a suicide bombing, a meteor storm. He eases into the flow on Stanbridge Road.

In The Leper's sports bar is where he meets me. Although I'm not taking part in or even viewing any sports, it is where I have built my psychic retreat of the day. It's but a shadow after noon, and I am already three drinks to the wind, or nearly (early opening on Tuesdays for some reason, for the market traders on the High Street? – I've never asked) and Roy greets me with a nervous bonhomie, for we both know we're not supposed to be here.

'Wet your whistle?'

'I'll have another.'

'Why are you not in the lounge?' he asks.

'Fancied a change. Why're you?'

'It's busy in there.'

'It's always busy in there.'

Roy nods his heavy head. 'Needed some P and Q, mate,' he answers. 'I was just on me way to see Mrs Anderson, in Stoke

Hammond.'

'Why?'

Roy sidesteps my question.

'Something told me to come in,' he says in a tone of frustrated wonder. 'Were you thinking about me, by any chance?'

'Roy, my darling, I'm always thinking about you.' My glass is empty, for one thing, and as you know, funds are low.

'Straight up, Tom. No laughs.'

'All right, Ange?' I say to the passing barmaid, who is carrying a tray of empties with such care that you'd swear she was about to remove an appendix. But *now* who is dodging the issue?

'All right, Tommy? Got an ear infection now, innaye? One thing after another at the moment. Never rains.' All the same, Angie exhibits her customary good girl cheer.

'Affecting your balance, is it?' I ask, not willing to allow this distraction to slip away.

'Feel like I'm a toddler again! All right, Roy-son? Ain't seen you in here in a while. You succeeding?'

'Breaking even, Ange. I was here last night. You served me.'

'I weren't working last night, mate. Monday night's me Pilates. You're losing your sense of time!' Angie laughs and retreats. The glasses rattle on her tray; it sounds like applause.

It is not unfair to say that Roy fails to take Angie's quip in the best of spirits. In fact, as he stands there swaying like a sailor on shore leave, his face purples and he froths with displeasure; he cracks his knuckles.

'I *was* here last night, Tom,' he argues.

'I didn't say you weren't, mate.'

'No, but *she* did. I've lost me thirst, Tom.'

'Pish and nonsense. Get the fucking ale in!'

'Yeah all right.'

While he's away (a surprisingly lengthy interlude, the bar

staff with their hands full serving next door) I consider a return visit to Mrs Anderson as well. The memory hasn't healed from last time yet (far from it).

'I'm coming with you,' I announce to Roy as soon as he returns.

He doesn't have to ask what I refer to. He nods his head as he places the pints down. He sits heavily; sighs. He frets with a beermat. He says nothing. He drinks with a bloodhound's thirst. He says nothing. He wipes his lips with his scarf. He belches. He waits. He belches. He waits. 'Pardon me,' he says finally.

4.

Amelior Anderson is not pleased to see us. She peers through the fairground-mirror glass of her front door, the tip of her nose touching the pane and cultivating a small rose of condensation.

'Who is it?'

Roy identifies us in his broadest, most lovable tones.

'Go away, please,' she replies.

'But it's me, Mrs A! It's Roychele! Roydottir! Royvinder!'

'Go away, please, or I'll call the police.'

Nob the cat watches us from the perimeter of the small garden, a lazy sentinel if ever there was one.

'I hate that fucking cat,' I whisper.

'Shut up, Tom. We've just got a few questions for you, Mrs A. You keeping well?'

'The Punto's fine, thank you, Roy. The Punto's blessed.'

Roy turns away from the glass. 'Did you hear that?' he asks me, and I nod my head. 'It's not her, is it? She *never* calls me Roy.'

'I don't think it is, no.'

'What's he *done* with her?'

I shake my head.

'Let's go. Cat's giving me the creeps. I'm developing an allergy.'

'Or we could kick the door in,' Roy adds. 'That's always an option.'

'I prefer the first choice.'

No sooner have we buckled up in Roy's jalopy than we hear the siren – a police car.

Roy's face is a picture: fear and amusement. 'That can't be for us, can it? It's too quick.'

'Unless he's been waiting.'

'Who?'

'You know who, mate. Drive!'

'But why, Tom?'

'*Fucking drive, Roy* I can feel him. Can't you?'

'No.' Roy starts the engine. He three-point-turns us back onto the feeder road.

An unmarked car approaches, but lights are flashing on its roof and there's no one else around; it must be for us. Sickness grows in my stomach like yeast. 'Oh my Christ…'

'That's him,' Roy confirms. 'That's the one came to Bible Street. What do we do?'

'We stop for a nice little chat. There's nothing else.'

'I could probably outrun him.'

'In this? Dream on!'

'Oi, that's out of order,' Roy tells me, his voice sounding genuinely hurt.

'We have questions to ask him,' I reply, trying to sugar the pill.

'Yeah. Let's ask him his fucking blood type, the cunt.' Roy kills the engine and unbuckles the belt.

Kolko gets out of his vehicle. He stops advancing at a distance of two metres from Roy's runaround. He squints at the number plate as though he's just learned to read and is attempting to make a word out of the letters and numbers.

'Do we get out, I wonder?'

'Wait for his instructions,' I reply.

'Why? Who put *him* in charge?'

'He's a copper!'

'No he's not, Tom. Sod the uniform. It's just *clothes*.'

Although Roy has a point, I remain cautious. I know what Kolko is capable of… or at any rate I know what he is rumoured to be capable of. Those two things are not the same.

Kolko stands by Roy's side window. In TV dramas he might knock on the glass with his truncheon but no, Kolko waits.

'Roll it down. Let's get it over with,' I suggest.

The window glides down with a faulty hum. The face that leans into the space is chubbier than I have expected; the skin around his chops glows either with a shaving rash or with dermatitis. There's a squint about his eyes that might convince you that their owner is considerably short-sighted.

'Can I help you, officer? Roy asks, if only to break the uncomfortable silence.

'Have you any idea how fast you were going, sir?' Kolko replies.

'We were hardly moving.'

'Exactly. Do you know it's an offence to drive too slowly on the Queen's highway?'

'Is it bollocks. What's this about?'

Good old Roy; *reliable* Roy. I suppose I should be grateful and relieved that he managed to hold it together for an entire sentence.

Kolko is unamused. 'I'll thank you not to swear at me, sir.'

'We just started! I weren't even in third gear!' Roy protests.

I say nothing.

'Could you step out of the car, please, sir?'

He's not a real policeman, I fight to assure myself, but he *looks* real enough, and he *feels* real enough – right down to the atomised crumbs of onion bhaji that float into the car on the magic carpet of his breath.

Roy is sweating. 'I don't suppose I have much choice in the matter, do I?' he asks, but I'm not sure to whom the question is directed.

As Roy opens the driver's door, Kolko takes a step back – and I land a gentle right palm on Roy's knee, lover-style, and lean into the metre-squared warzone between them and say, 'Would you mind if we saw your credentials, please, officer?'

The car's roof obscures my view of Kolko's face, but I hear him sniff. Again, he bends at the waist, but this time he addresses me.

'Are you trying to be clever, son?'

'No, officer. I would guess we're within our rights to validate your authority, are we not? Please tell me if I'm wrong.'

'What the fuck do you think this uniform is? Everyday wear?'

'You can hire them from Party Hearty on North Street. Do you *object* to showing us your credentials?'

'So. You want to see my badge, is that it?' Kolko demands.

I shake my head. 'I didn't mention a badge.'

'Tom?' Roy whispers.

'...We want you to show us something like you showed James.'

'Who the fuck's James?'

'The mentalist kid. By the canal, you showed him the canal boats dancing in the air.'

Kolko snorts. 'Do you see any *boats* here, son?' he asks.

'No. An equivalent.'

Kolko returns his attention to Roy. 'Get out the fucking car. I won't tell you again.'

'On what authority?' Roy wants to know.

'The authority of the breathalysing equipment in my vehicle. I suspect you've both been drinking, and you, fat boy, have just lost your licence for at least twelve months. *So get out the fucking car!*'

Roy gets out of the fucking car.

And then he punches Kolko – square in the face.

I clamber out of my side. To join in.

5.

'I thought you were dead,' I tell her.

I'm whatever you want me to be, Tom, she answers. *I'm the perfect dream.*

We're in Oxford or Cambridge; a university city at the very least. A nice day. Annette walks towards us but doesn't see us. She walks past.

Do you want me back, Tom?

'Of course I do. I need you,' I tell Sabrina, and with a blink it all vanishes, and I'm in bed.

I'm not alone. There is form beside me: mass. The quiver of female scent as she twitches in her sleep; her skin is mauve.

What happened last night? Did Dorothy and I slip back into our old ways? Did it happen again? I can't remember.

Perhaps it's Hannah.

I touch my Thomas for evidence of last night's lovemaking, but I detect not a sausage.

'It's me, Tom. You've won me back,' whispers Sabrina as she rolls over to face me wearing my own features.

I want to wake up again, but there's nowhere closer to reality. This is as eyes-wide-open as it gets.

'But you're not real.'

'Don't you listen to your dreams? I'm as real as you want me to be.' Sabrina smiles. 'But rest now, it's the middle of the night. You've got a busy day ahead of you.'

'Why, what am I doing?' I whisper back to her.

'You're checking death records. And then tonight we're going out to dinner.'

'I can't afford it.'

'You won't be paying.'

The Taste of Taste

I.

1.

'What are you doing here?'

'I've come to serenade you. I've come to buy you lunch. I want to clear the air between us, Han. So would you care to break bread with the wicked?'

Hannah sighs. 'I don't think you're wicked, Sam, but I'm working. You see this tracksuit I'm wearing?'

'I thought it might be designer,' Sam jokes. 'What time's your break?'

'Two-thirty. After I give my class. I can meet you here if you like, but there's no air to clear, Sam. I was pissed off with you; I'll get over it.'

'I'm about to piss you off some more,' Sam replies. 'But what nicer place to do it than a sports centre caff?'

Hannah laughs. 'Piss me off over a cream cheese bagel and a hot chocolate. I'm off to teach. Have you brought a book to read?'

'No, but I've got the laptop in the car; I'll do some work while I'm waiting. It'll do my profile good to log on at some point today.'

Hannah turns on her sneakered heels before righting herself and addressing Sam again. 'Is the reason I'm going to be pissed off with you something to do with the thief?'

Sam opens her arms wide. 'But of course!'

'He's been to see you again, hasn't he?'

'In a manner of speaking.'

'Don't be abstruse. Has he been to see you or not?'

Sam frowns. 'Not in the way that I'm here before you now, but I saw him with perfect vision. With emmetropia, you might say.'

'Where? In a dream?'

'Precisely. In a dream.'

2.

But it wasn't a dream. Not exactly.

Sam was on her way home from work. Since the day that Hana had camped on her car's back seat, she had exercised the utmost solicitude with respect to matters of her personal safety. These days, not only did she check inside the body of the car itself for unwelcome stowaways, she checked inside the boot.

It was as she approached The Sun – the pub where Hana had taken her to discuss her history – that it happened.

She went blind.

'What do you mean?' Hannah asks, picking at a crumb of raisin cake with the tines of a white plastic fork. She has had no choice but to abandon her dreams of a cream cheese bagel: there has been a run on them this lunchtime and the cafeteria has sold out. The hot chocolate is nice, mind.

'What do you think I mean? I couldn't see, you silly cow!'

'Keep your voice down, Sam. I work here, remember.'

'Then stop asking me dumb questions!'

'Forgive me, do. You went blind.'

'And I was still driving! Do you remember that time – it must've been fifteen years ago – you were taking me to the airport and there was ice on the roads. We'd had a cold snap.'

'I remember.' Hannah shudders, gripped by the memory and shaken by the scruff. 'We went off the road on the road to Eaton Bray.'

'It felt like that. Completely out of control. It didn't occur to me to just hit the brakes – don't ask me why...Do you trust me?'

'I beg your pardon?'

'That's what he said.'

'What who said? Hana?'

'No, the King of Siam. Of course Hana.'

'I thought you said you checked the car for stowaways.'

'I did! But then I heard his voice.'

3.

'Do you trust me?' the voice said.

'I can't see!' Sam shouted.

'Do you trust me?'

And she felt his hands on hers, on the wheel; he had a grip as warm and damp as a camel's tongue. It was oddly soothing, this grip.

'Yes, I trust you,' Sam answered, though a part of her brain that hugged hard to logic was demanding some responses of its own. Where *was* he, for example?

'Good. Now open your eyes.'

'They *are* open!'

'No.' Hana's fingers flexed on top of Sam's. Sam felt the pressure more on her left hand, he was urging her to steer in that direction. 'Not physically.'

'*Then what do you mean?*' Sam yelped.

'As I said: *open your eyes*.' His tone was as infuriatingly neutral as a bad weather forecaster's, promising a tsunami to accompany the morning honey oats.

'Why don't you fuck off out of my life?' Sam asked; and she made a deliberate attempt to counteract the pressure on her left hand. To hell with it: if this wraith wanted her to angle left, by God, she would angle right. Nobody rebels like a good ex-Catholic schoolgirl.

Then Hana answered her question. The words sucked the wind from her sails.

'Why don't you fuck off out of mine?' he asked, his voice still level.

Sam limped and jellied in the driver's seat. For the first time it dawned on her to stamp on the brake, which she did. Were it not for Hana's hands on her own – glove-like, insistent – she would also have snatched at the handbrake. When she tried to do so, his grip strengthened – it *solidified*.

'You told me you trusted me.'

'I say a lot of things.'

'Just open your eyes, Samantha.'

We're still moving.

She pictured the darkness as the inside of an eyelid. If the darkness was hers – if she possessed it – then she could lift it: like an eyelid. She could make the world blink. Maybe not too many times, but at least once.

Sam concentrated.

The darkness flipped open like a beak, like a bin-lid. And Sam saw...

4.

Stocky birds, climbing the sky; birds, from a distance, with the shape and grace of a paragraph of print. A strain to imagine how they remain airborne. Stubborn blots of text against the fresh-page sky.

Where am I?

There is no one to ask. Sam is alone, in the desert – pecked at by a dusty alkaline wind. She is certain that she has never been here before, and yet it appears glamorously familiar. *Sexily* familiar. Sam senses that she could give a guided tour of the place.

The wind takes her. It rolls her around her own bedwarfed hectare of sky; she has neither mass nor appearance, but she refuses to be frightened. This is fantasy, after all. Somewhere else – back in a world coloured by a different quality of light – she is driving home (or perhaps she has crashed; perhaps she is dead), and none of these somersaults are shared between the two existences.

Where am I?

And what is the smell that she regards as so adorable? As she sails the fragrant air, her rectix twitches and sturdies; it sends her forward in the right direction, swimming towards the exterior of someone's flat.

A dead man's flat, as it transpires. The tenant hangs out of the window, one end of the rope reef-knotted around his neck; the other tied around the wooden base of a single bed that his suicide has dragged across the room, so that it's wedged beneath the windowsill. Very gently he swings, whenever there is a breeze, which isn't often.

Neighbours two buildings away heard his neck snap.

'He was my brother,' Hana explains.

The voice summons Sam back to the interior of her vehicle. A moment passes before a strobe of nausea, remarkable its potency, slinks slowly away and leaves her alone.

'He couldn't bear the shame. When I was caught,' says Hana. 'I come from a law-abiding family.'

'You could've fooled me,' Sam replies.

And Hana answers, 'No. I don't think I ever could. Not you, Sam.'

5.

'Why did you say yes? When he asked if you trusted him: why did you say yes?'

The question arrives after nearly a minute of silence between Hannah and Sam. The only sounds come from behind the counter, where the salesgirl prepares fresh coffee; and from the swimming pool, acoustic traces, not of people, not of thrashing, but of the water itself. Both women can hear the water.

'I don't know.'

'Because he's brainwashed you, Sam – *that's* why. You'll be announcing your engagement next.'

'Be reasonable, Han. *I'd gone blind.* Temporarily as it turned out, but how was I to know that? And he asked me if I trusted him.'

'He coulda driven you into a tree! Or a crocodile of schoolchildren crossing the road!'

'But he didn't, did he?' Sam snaps.

'No he didn't. I find myself asking why not.'

'But that's not all you wonder, is it, babe? You're also wondering: why me? As in me, not you. Why's that common thief bothering with me and not you. Admit it, Hannah: you're a little bit jealous.'

Hannah drains her mug of hot chocolate. With a satisfying puckering sound she smacks her lips; she cleans her upper lip of sugary foam. She says, 'Yes. Just for the record, Sam – yes. I *am* jealous. But it's an emotion with a bittersweet flavour, because, on the other hand, I wouldn't want to be so gullible that the bastard would want to use me in the first place.' Hannah stands up. 'Thanks for lunch.'

'That's all you have to say?' Sam is aghast.

'I have to get back to work, Sam. I don't pretend to have any answers for you.' Hannah has swapped sounding angry for sounding tired.

'And what about forgiveness?' Sam asks. 'Do you have any of *that* for me?' 'How forgiven do you want to be?'

'One hundred per cent, naturally.'

'You got it, okay? You're one hundred per cent forgiven, Sam, though there's really nothing to forgive.'

'Then why are we still arguing?'

'*I'm* not arguing!'

'Uncomfortable, then: why are we still uncomfortable?'

'I'm not uncomfortable either! Maybe we can discuss this another time, Sam.'

'Maybe; but I guess we won't. Don't you? Be honest now.'

'I'm always honest with you. That's one of the things I still like about you, you make me want to be honest,' says Hannah.

Both women take a breath; individually they examine their bodily responses to the sting of the words.

Sam breaks the silence. 'Well, I can't fault you for holding back on me there, can I?'

'I'm sorry.'

'Don't sweat it. It gives me a clearer picture, so thank you for that.'

'You're welcome.'

Nodding her head, her fake smile as stiff as a girdle, Sam says, 'I'd better go.'

'I'll see you around, Sam; but just one thing. You've built this up into a big thing but I really don't see it that way. It doesn't bother me as much as it bothers you. Have fun with your thief! Take him to bed for all I care. Just don't tell me about it, okay – that's the only thing I ask of you. Maintain a respectful silence on the subject.'

Hannah turns away, too quickly to notice the tears in her friend's eyes.

In more ways than one, Sam watches her go. She mouths 'Goodbye.'

6.

Her shift completed, Hannah clambers into her car and closes her eyes – to examine the depth of pain and discomfort that she has sustained while lunging during the second of her fencing classes this afternoon. The problem is her left knee; she felt it click. It will need an icepack. Or she'll need to hobble for a fortnight. Perhaps she will need to anyway, icepack or not; but it's better to be safe, she concludes, than sorry. And she starts up the engine. The fan heater breathes into simultaneous life.

A moment passes, and Hannah listens to the percussive notes in her knee. The tattoo's regularity both appals and appeases her, as she sniffs in the fan's dusty air and her lunch turns forward rolls in her stomach. Her knee throbs: Boom Boom BAM. Boom Boom BAM: like the rhythm in Queen's 'We Will Rock You'… While shifting into first gear, Hannah contemplates the wisdom of driving home. She could call a taxi; collect the car tomorrow. But in the end, feeling antsy and disputatious, she comes to a compromise. She will drive, but not drive *home*.

Instead of indicating right at Wing Road, she turns left into a customarily petulant stampede of traffic here at the Linslade end of town. When she is able to duck under the railway bridge without being made to wait at the traffic lights, she takes it as a good sign that she is doing the right thing.

Her destination is Aylesbury – and specifically, Toby. Although Hannah has been under the impression that she has not thought about him for a long while – not, in fact, since shortly after their argument in her kitchen, when he had arrived at hers with the expensive plonk – it is made real to her, the fact that he has squatted in some cerebral bedsit near her synapses, for longer than she would confess to even to an abbess; that what she has to say to him has brewed for longer than a full moon roaming the sky.

She parks near the prison, parenthetically musing on Tom and on whether he would ever return to work in that termitary. In a small convenience shop near Toby's house Hannah buys a bottle of wine, scandalously overpriced for such a simple everyday vintage; but decorum insists that she mustn't arrive empty-handed, especially after he had brought that sixty-quid red.

You don't even know if he'll be in, she tells herself; *let alone if he'll want to sit and…* What is the phrase Sam had used? 'Break bread with the wicked.' That's it. She rings the bell.

Barely a second before Hannah hears the door being unbolted on the other side, she experiences a belated surge of nerves. It's not Toby answering, she is certain of this much, although there has been neither clue nor giveaway.

The two women face one another. Much, much later, Hannah will employ the odd comparison of terriers trained for combat, circling one another with their tails down and their teeth bared; one further extrapolation will be that Hannah wished, at this moment, that she had tried to chew off the woman's *testicles*.

Hannah smiles and says, 'Hi Jill.'

Jill remembers Hannah from the sleep deprivation experiment, years earlier: or at least her eyes suggest this is the case. Her tone is a lot more surprised, but the greeting sounds amiable enough.

'Is Toby expecting you? He didn't say…'

'No. I was just passing, I thought–'

'Of course. You had no way of knowing I'd be here.'

'It's not like that exactly. I need to talk to him for a few minutes, that's all. Is he in?'

'He's at work. But I hope you won't waste the wine. That *would* be a crying shame.'

'The wine's not for Toby. It's for my nephew.'

'What's the occasion?'

'His coming-out party. He's now officially gay through and through. What time's he expected back?'

'Back home? I'm surprised you don't remember, Hannah. Around seven.'

Hannah takes the punch with good grace. She feels she deserves it; that it's Jilly's unconditional right. For she has placed herself in Jill's shoes and let her vision loose on the vista. She is disturbed that that the shoes fit so well.

Of course she's cross. So would I be.

'Look, Hannah, if I'm quick, will you accept a home truth or two?'

'If you're quick?'

'Before the poison sets in,' says Jill. 'I tried to do the right thing by you, I've really tried, okay? I sent him to you to explain that he's with me, and face facts – he didn't need to do that. And I didn't need to ask him to.'

'That was you?'

'Bless your faith for thinking it might be Toby. Not a chance. The wine was my idea as well. Was it good?'

'It was lush. It was *you*?' Hannah repeats. Toby always brought wine, usually an expensive bottle, as well. Her fingers tense on the handles of the carrier bag from the convenience store. She is sure she is nailing imprints into the heels of her hand.

'Wasn't that fair of me?' Jill wants to know.

'You're a saint, Jill, there's no question of that.'

'But now you're here with wine. You'll forgive me, I'm sure, a certain irritation. What *else* was I supposed to have done to keep you away?'

Jill closes the door.

7.

Argument three in Hannah's day arrives at a quarter to

nine that night.

The phone rings. 'It's Toby.'

Hannah knows that this has been on the cards. Undulating under the effects of the overpriced vino, she has settled on her couch with a bag of frozen brussel sprouts on her left knee.

'You still have feelings for me, don't you, Han?' Toby asks.

Hannah waves air into her face. Her face is so hot she is worried about fainting.

'No.'

'Sure you don't; it's so obvious. Turning up with a bottle of wine.'

'I was passing.'

'With a bottle of wine.'

'Which I've drunk.

'I don't doubt it. But that's not the question, Hannah. Do you want me to come round?'

'To mine?'

'Yes. Are you alone?'

'I'm alone; but no, I don't want you to come around here, Toby. Fuck a *duck*, no I don't! I'm going to bed.'

'Jill's in the bath.'

'Well, she won't be there all night, will she.'

'I wasn't proposing an all-night visit.'

'Spoken like a true gigolo. Why don't you go and sleep it off, Tobe. You're gonna be embarrassed in the morning.'

'So are you.'

'Oh I think you're right. I don't know what got into me.'

'Jill said you had a question or two,' Toby answers.

'I did. I don't now. I have all the answers I need.'

Toby pauses. 'Are you sure?'

'I'm absolutely positive. I've learned a lot today.'

'I can be there in fifteen minutes.'

'You're not listening to me.'

'I'll bring chestnuts.'

'…You'll bring what?'

'Chestnuts! Left over from Christmas. I know how much you love your chestnuts, Han. They're in the fridge fright now. Just say the word.'

'The word is *no*. As I said, I'm going to hit the pillows.'

'Hit them with me. I miss you, Hannah.'

'No. The answer is no.'

Toby arrives half an hour later.

8.

'Are you going to let me in?' he asks.

'Against my better judgement I suppose I am.' Hannah steps aside. 'Rather inside than on my doorstep.'

Toby crosses the threshold. He removes a silly hat − a light blue gardener's hat, tinselly bright with raindrops in Hannah's hall-light − a hat that manages to age its wearer by two decades. Taking it off has the opposite effect, and despite herself Hannah is happy with what she sees. 'You look well.'

'Thanks. So do you. Happy New Year, by the way. A bit on the late side, but…'

Hannah closes the door. 'Where does Jill think you are?'

'The pub. The Weaver's.'

'She could check.'

'She won't. Am I taking my coat off or not?'

'You might as well, now you're here. Did you bring those chestnuts?'

'No. They were gone when I went back to the fridge.'

Hannah takes Toby's coat; she hangs it by the hood on the banister newel and pops the silly hat on top of it. 'She heard you talk about them, Tobe; she's thrown them away, or hidden them, or eaten them.'

'She was in the bath. She hates chestnuts.'

'She was in the bath listening to the phone call, is the point.' Hannah leads the way into the kitchen.

'She's not like that.'

'Not like me, you mean. Maybe not. Maybe I'm projecting all my worse traits onto the totally blank canvas of her Snow White innocence…Would you like a glass of wine?' She indicates the bottle on the draining board.

Toby remembers where the glasses are kept; there is not an instant's hesitation.

'Thanks.'

'Can I ask you something, Han? Are you actually spoiling for a fight with someone – with anyone – or does it have to be me?'

'It has to be you.' She pours the wine, a grin on her face.

'Well that's clear as anyone could want it. Now may I ask why? Thanks,' he adds as he takes careful hold of his tipple.

'Because these have been some of the strangest months of my life.'

'I see. And I'm responsible in what way precisely?'

Hannah lifts the wine glass to eye level, testing for impurities. 'I think I might be leaking some of the strangeness into the lives of those around me,' she says.

Toby does not take this in the spirit that Hannah intends: he concentrates on the wrong portion of the message. With a note of hope in his voice he says, 'So I'm still someone around you, then?'

'I suppose you must be. Or I wouldn't have wrestled with my conscience for the last month just to get to the point where I bottled up the courage to knock on your door.'

Toby nods his head. 'You knew she'd be there, didn't you?'

'How would I?'

'Her car's parked on the pavement outside.'

'I don't know what she *drives*.'

'Still. There *is* a car parked on the pavement outside my house.'

'I didn't notice. Truly. What I'm asking is, has anything untoward happened in your life over the last little while?'

'Like what?'

'Like anything. Don't ask me to feed you the answers, Tobe.'

'What answers? I don't know what you're talking about.'

'Anything!'

He thinks about it for a moment and sips. 'There's some graffiti that's a bit weird,' he answers. 'Do you mind if we sit down?'

'Not at all. Where?'

'At the station. On the steps leading down to platform two and three. On one of the steps it says: *I love you Hannah.* On another one it says: *I love you too, Toby-Wobe!*'

'Jesus.'

Toby takes his seat and says, 'Don't you think it's time to explain this?'

Hannah slumps into the chair beside him, her head bowed as if in penitence.

They talk and argue for an hour.

II.

1.

Stimulating an immediate reaction from her neighbour Rebekah (who has chanced to step outside into the rain at the same moment), Sabrina pauses on the top step down to the pavement and blinks into the streaky wet darkness, like someone who was being held prisoner an instant before.

So it is that it's the neighbour Rebekah who first witnesses Sabrina's reappearance, two doors down on Grovebury Road. The immediate response is a faceful of strained surprise, which Sabrina catches briefly during her moment of tasting freedom. She smiles and blinks... Sabrina blinks; Sabrina breathes. Sabrina turns away from Rebekah, as the latter skips the steps down to the pavement and turns left – presumably on her way to her car round the back of the building. Sabrina stays put; she adjusts her handbag's strap on her bare left shoulder and she relishes the nothingy flavour of the rain, absorbing the deep hiss of car wheels in puddles, and what she deciphers as the approving murmur of engines.

Not even darkness and not even rain can camouflage the full gaudy impact of her rebirth from Tom's fetid chrysalis.

Seconds later, her second named witness has emerged from yet a third front door – the door between Sabrina's and Rebekah's blocks of flats. It is Dorothy. Gingerly Dorothy descends to street level, dressed in going-out-black and restaurant cream. She takes one look at Sabrina and raises the hand not busy carrying a matching handbag to her mouth. As she approaches Sabrina she says, 'You are not...'

'Hi Dolly!'

'…going out like *that*. Surely to God!'

Sabrina joins her on the pavement.

'You'll freeze to death, Tom!'

'What?' The smile rots on Sabrina's face; when she frowns a few snowflake traces of makeup powder slip free of their position on her brow. 'Have you been smoking scouring powder again? Why'd you call me Tom?'

'Excuse me?'

'You said Tom.'

Dorothy shakes her head. She acknowledges her mistake and replies, 'I'm sorry, Sabrina. How *is* Tom?'

'He's okay. I'll tell you about him at dinner. We've got a lot to catch up on!'

'Well that's as may be, but to return to my original point… Sabrina… you cannot. Go out. Like that.'

'Why? What's wrong with me?'

'Where shall I start?'

Sabrina is dressed in a pelmet red leather miniskirt and just-been-raped black torn leggings. For maximum shock contrast she had donned a sleeveless sheer lilac blouse through which an unnecessarily heavy brassiere can easily be viewed (along with the wads of tissue with which it is packed). Her face is clownish with exaggerated makeup; her hair is teased into tufts and spikes.

'Never mind,' says Dorothy. 'No time to change now; Hannah'll be here in a minute.'

'Seriously. What's wrong with me? The restaurant's always as hot as a bath anyway.'

'It doesn't matter.'

But it *does* matter – it matters to Dorothy. She experiences a red hot wave of something like rage. It perplexes her; she doesn't understand its origin, and the fact distresses her that it has come out of nowhere.

Perhaps she is simply jittery about the planned meal, at Profit. Why this should be she has no idea. Compelled to write earlier this afternoon, she sat at her desk and scribbled notes about how the meal would go. (It was a horror story.) She has already chosen from the menu; she can taste the fizzing bite of her first gin and tonic.

'What are you noodling on?' Sabrina asks her.

'I was thinking of a story I wrote about fifteen years ago. It was about a dead dog. A little girl's pet.' Dorothy licks her lip and folds her arms against a bluster of wind that brings the sounds of cheering from the rugby club, a mile or so away, a freak of noise and a momentary absence of passing vehicles.

'Sounds chirpy.'

'It was surprisingly upbeat, given the subject matter,' Dorothy replies. 'The girl's dad hated the dog. Really *hated* it. Which made the little girl love it all the more, of course. Then one day a driver knocks it over and it dies in the road, licking the girl's hand. She saw it happen – so did the dad. And the driver sped away and the dad wraps the dog in his fishing jacket and carries it into the house. Really tenderly. And they bury the dog in their tiny back garden, and the girl understands that she loves her father as much as she loves the dog. Because he treats it respectfully and enshrouds it in his favourite jacket – the jacket is the clincher, because the girl knows how much he loves his fishing jacket, and now it's in the ground with her dog. It was called "Little Things." *The New Writer* published it.'

'I'd like to read it.'

'Sure. Aren't you wondering why I was thinking of that right now?'

'I was. You haven't seen a dead thing in the road, have you?'

'No, nothing like that. Here's Hannah.' Dorothy is relieved as their chariot approaches. It means they can stop talking for a while. They climb in.

Hannah is not slow to notice Sabrina's outrageous get-up. 'Is the circus in town again, girl?' she asks.

'What do you mean?' Sabrina answers.

'The makeup. Which you appear to have applied with a gardening trowel.'

'Oh fuck off. Just drive, will you?' Sabrina retorts from the back seat. Her eyes flash in the rearview mirror, and Hannah and Dolly exchange brief what-the-hell glances. Hannah slips the stick into first and they pull off.

Hannah laughs. 'While we're at it, Sabrina, you might want to think about keeping your knees together. I can tell your religion with your skirt that short.'

'I repeat: you can fuck right off, Hannah. Or would you like me to translate that into another language, you stuck-up cow?'

They drive on in complicated silence.

2.

Profit has changed, Sam is quick to mention. This gobbet of opinion is not delivered at the table; Sam meets them outside, on the walkway. Agitatedly she shifts her weight from foot to foot; she has about her the nervous energy of a doomy soothsayer.

'You mean it's got even weirder?' says Sabrina.

'Exactly the opposite! It's been *neutered*, girls. It's gone *bland*. It's so exciting!'

'Is Annette here?' Hannah asks.

'Not yet. The table's not ready, anyway; we've got a few minutes.'

'Since when has this place given a monkey's toss for appointment times?' Dorothy muses.

'Well exactly! It's completely different! I love it!' Sam answers.

'Be honest, you came out here for a cigarette, didn't you?' Sabrina asks her.

'I did. Have you been in a fight or something?' Sam asks Sabrina.

'What makes you say that?'

'That explosion of warpaint on your face is what makes me ask that. It's not like you, Sab. And when women start daubing on the blusher as if it'll be made illegal tomorrow, in my experience, she's covering up bruising or cuts.'

'In your experience,' says Sabrina.

Dorothy asks, 'Is she right?'

'Shall we go in? It's nippy out here,' Sabrina answers.

'Well it would be, with your anus hanging out.'

'*Have* you been in a fight?' Hannah wants to know.

'I'm cold. I want to go in.' Sabrina opens the door and holds it, like a doorman at an expensive hotel.

One by one they enter the building, in an air of expectation and vexation.

Dorothy passes her mouth close to Sabrina's left ear, close enough for a kiss. 'I have something to tell you,' she says. 'And so have you: something to tell me. Am I right?'

Sabrina nods her head.

3.

The menus have shrunk to the size of tabloid magazines; the paper has not been laminated. Ink smudges under their fingertips.

'Has this place gone downmarket,' asks Hannah, 'or is it me?'

There seems to be no more excited that Sam can become; her appreciation gauge is wobbling in the dangerously red. 'I know! It's fantastic!'

'Perhaps we can leave without selling the deeds to our houses,' Hannah continues sourly.

Sam is smarted by her friend's ongoing pessimism. 'Oh what do you care how much the food costs? I said it's my treat again, didn't I?'

'Again,' repeats Hannah, but no further examination follows.

'Well then,' Sam tells her and the others at the table. 'Let's just enjoy it all.'

Hannah looks ready to spit feathers. Sarcastically she says, 'Yes, let's just enjoy our mucous macaroons.'

'They're off. Will you tell us what fight you got into, Sab?'

'When Annette gets here. But it wasn't *my* fight exactly. It was Tom's.'

There is a stiffening at the table; a setting of awkwardness and mood. No one is sure how to respond. If *Tom* has had a fight, why has Sabrina earned the bruises? Or perhaps she is not admitting to that after all…

It is Dorothy who appears the most anxious of all, and in fact as Annette sweeps in on a tide of apologies for her lateness, it is only Dorothy who fails to acknowledge her with a hello. She can just about squeeze out a smile. And why is this? Because the Tom/Sabrina thing, it was never a joke, a fad; it was never a *choice*. And now that Dorothy has been sleeping with Tom, where does this leave her with Sabrina, now that the latter is back in town in her new tarty ensemble?

Is this what guilt feels like? wonders Dorothy, reading the menu with a faux-intensity that borders on the autistic. She thinks of James. She thinks of Tom in bed. She thinks of *James* in bed, but of course that never happened. *Did* it?

'Earth to Dorothy. Come in, Dorothy.'

Must confess, Dorothy is thinking when Hannah's words

zone her back to the table. She adds, 'Sorry. Miles away.'

When would be a good time? To explain to Sabrina that she has entered into a habit of anal sex (among other peccadilloes) with her live-in boyfriend. Or to put it another way, when would be the least-bad time to admit to such a no-go indiscretion? For there is never a *good* time, surely to God.

'I have some news from Tom,' Sabrina states; and then adds to the waiflike waiter, 'The chicken, please. Chicken and chips.'

'I miss the fried platypus, I must say,' she says to her friends once he has retreated.

4.

Sabrina delineates most (but not all) of the events with Kolko – Tom and Roy's events, near Amelior Anderson's house – and concludes with a surprising interpretation. 'It means it's nothing, don't you see? An impersonator. He's nothing *special*. He's *playing* at being a cop.'

Dorothy spears a scampi ball on the tines of her fork. 'It's not a solo game, though, is it?' she asks, chewing in a strange bovine manner indicative of toothache.

'What do you mean?'

'Whose puppet is he?'

Hannah nods her head, about to add something, when Sabrina says, 'Uncle Stephen's. Stephen's still alive. He never died. It wasn't him.'

5.

Earlier this afternoon I telephoned my mother. Her surprise at the call was enough to convince me that I don't call her much anymore.

'If it's okay, Mum,' I said, 'I would like to talk about Stephen. Your brother Stephen.'

'Again?' she answered, in pain, then levelled herself to add: 'It was so long ago, Tom. What does it matter now? Why go digging up graves?'

'He was never buried, Mum.'

'…Cremation plots, then. No need to be pedantic. Have you been drinking again?'

'Yes. He didn't die, Mum.'

'What are you saying? Don't be so bloody ridiculous.'

'He's still alive, Mum,' I told her, my tone nowhere near as sympathetic as I'd planned for it to be; but was sympathy the right thing anyway? I wasn't telling my mother that her brother had died (someone else had done that, more than a decade before), I was telling her the opposite. I was saying that every single thing that she had experienced since the sunny afternoon when she thought she saw Stephen's ghost stepping from the kitchen into the lounge; since that same afternoon when the policeman arrived at our door and told my dad in the hallway that Stephen had been found dead in Wembley, had been a lie.

Sympathy was what I'd planned – sympathy because I had now challenged her hold on the past, not for anything else – but my mother did not receive sympathy from me. I wasn't *capable* of sympathy, perhaps. I've had a good deal of my own past challenged, after all…

'And I think you've known for some time, haven't you, Mum?'

She was silent. The phone line buzzed in my ear. Had she fainted?

'Are you still there?'

'I'm here, Tom,' she answered wearily. 'I see his ghost sometimes…'

'He's not dead, Mum.'

'No. But I wish he was.'

6.

We were never close, Mum has said to me on (who knows?) a couple of thousand occasions over the years; but on each occasion she had lied. And a lie is like a tumour, building and becoming stronger at the same time debilitating its host. Because you *were* close, Mum, you and Stephen; you were magnetised together by the crime or indiscretion that he committed.

Or *you* committed.

'You've been keeping a secret for a long time, Mum,' I said softly, cradling a glass of lemonade in both hands. The lemonade fizzed and spat, making tiny rounds of applause at my deduction. I scarcely dared to raise the drink to my lips, for fear of swallowing all those atomic clapping hands.

'Because you *were* close, you and your brother. Something you shared between the two of you and no one else, bonding you together. What was it? And what went wrong to break it all up?'

Mum stared at me for a second or two, her face smoothed by the steam curling up from her brew. She will deny me one more time, I thought, and then it will be gone forever; or she will spill out everything, every sewery, shitty portion of her and Stephen's decaying past.

For isn't there a rule of thumb when it comes to confession? Isn't there a breaking point for either party? The confessor wants to confess, even if she doesn't know she wants to. Ironically, the questioner might not really want the answer.

'Tell me, Mum. Please.'

And Mum started crying. 'It was so long ago, Tom,' she blurted through her tears.

'*What* was? What did he do, Mum?'

But I already knew the answer. I just wanted the confession now.

'We were lovers,' she gulped.

7.

Naturally, Sabrina is the emissary of the news.

'She made it sound like the most natural thing in the world,' she says of my mother's admission. 'Just a brother and sister, sharing a bed.'

'Well, sharing a bed would be fine if that's as far as it went,' says Hannah.

'Yeah. And if they were still seven,' Annette adds.

A horrid tramp's beard of cloud is straggly on the moon's cheeks by the time they emerge from Profit, and the air is effervescent with static rain. Although Sam has paid, and the others have doled out change to make up an overgenerous tip, there is a sense that the night is not complete. No one wants to drive back home yet.

Dorothy's shoulder hurts. It aches where the bullet that didn't go through her went through her. Wincing as if at a tasteless joke, Dorothy raises her right hand to the spot and uses up a wish in hoping that none of the girls will notice.

None of the girls notice – but Sabrina notices. The two of them are a few steps behind Hannah, Sam and Annette, under the block-long shelter.

'Is something giving you gyp, Dolly?' Sabrina asks.

'Only my conscience.'

'Oh that. I had mine removed years ago. Worth less than the appendix. What's up? Seriously.'

'Seriously? I'm knocking on a bit more than you girls. I get pains from time to time.'

'Are you telling me the truth?'

'Partly. I have something else. Something about Tom I have to tell you.'

'You're lovers, aren't you? I had an inkling. I knew it was *someone*. I'd rather it was you than a total stranger.'

'Really? Why?'

Sabrina shrugs her shoulders. 'Because I want the best for him, of course,' she says. 'Now I'm getting *really* cold. Where are we going?'

'I'm following *them*,' Dorothy answers, and they fall silent for a moment… Sabrina is not Tom in drag; Dorothy must remember this (they all must); and although they share a set of vocal cords, they are two different people. Or at least two different characters.

'I don't believe this!'

The voice – startled and outraged – is Hannah's, and she makes a break from the leading trio, exploding into a sprint. Towards her car.

'The *bastards*…'

The windscreen resembles the layer of sugar on top of the chocolate cake that Dorothy has just eaten for dessert; the paving slab that has done this damage lying on top of the bonnet, like a huge carbuncle.

'They've done it again!'

Dorothy and the girls observe, stricken, while Hannah circles her vehicle, assessing the damage.

'Why *my* car? Why me!' she shouts, but all that anyone can do for a second is coo or murmur; Hannah completes another circuit, totting up an inventory of the situation. 'They've put a coin down the side; that's about five hundred quid right there. The back lights; a few hundred…'

Dorothy watches Hannah from her position under the shelter. Getting closer to the broken car is not going to help; nor is getting wet. This was for me, Dorothy decides. Standing close by is a big-bone girl wearing a plastic silver crown and carrying a sceptre. Her eyes, upper cheeks and lower forehead are black with a bank-robber's mask of caked makeup. Only Dorothy recognises her, at first. Furiously, striding closer to the girl, she hisses: '*You.*'

The girl does not flinch, it's as if she has this coming; in fact, she nods her head – not in greeting but in a tired form of supplication that sits at odds with her would-be regal appearance.

'I knew you'd be back,' is all she says. 'Someday.'

'Was this your doing?' Dorothy demands, gesturing towards Hannah's beaten vehicle.

Hannah herself takes notice at this point. She attempts a different tack from her friend's confrontational approach, by asking: 'Did you see who did this?'

The girl flits her eyeline between her two interrogators. Although she does not seem panicky, the ceremonial composure has already begun to look strained and fake.

'It was always going to happen.'

'What's that supposed to mean? Are you a witness or not?'

To everyone's immediate surprise and swift dismay the girl begins singing 'Are you a witness or not?' A great beaming smile on her face, she pirouettes on nimble toes (Doc-Martened toes) and changes her tune to the Human League's 'Don't You Want Me?', falsettoing capriccioso: 'I was working as a witness in a cocktail ba-har… when I met you…'

'She's a fruit loop,' Hannah whispers.

'No she's not,' Dorothy argues, watching every move the young woman makes – receiving the coronational penance of the girl's shaken sceptre with less good grace than fear.

'How do you know her anyway?' Hannah speaks as though the other woman cannot hear her.

Dorothy feels betrayed. 'Don't you remember her?' she demands. 'The *last* time you had your car attacked here, she was here then as well. My *fan*, if you recall.'

'I still am,' says the young woman, suddenly breaking off

from her near-operatic rendition.

Annette calls over: 'This is a police job, Hannah. Call them now. There'll be CCTV.'

Although Hannah nods her head, her words give her away as completely suspicious of the suggestion. With a customary bite of sarcasm she says, 'I'm sure I should, but we'd probably get Kolko coming over on his bicycle.'

'No you won't,' says Sabrina. 'Kolko is otherwise engaged,' she adds when the girls turn her way.

Undeserving of this compounded scrutiny (or so she believes), Sabrina performs an act of exaggerated deglutition and bows her head to her scarcely covered chest.

'I didn't quite finish what I was saying about Tom and Roy,' she confesses. 'And Kolko…'

'Well?' Sam shouts.

'They did more than just beat him up and leave him there.'

8.

They return to Profit and the restaurant feels like it's breathing. It wants to hear the latest gossip. 'What's your name by the way?' Dorothy asks.

'I wasn't named. I wasn't even born, not in the normal sense. I was found.'

'Where?'

'On a hill.'

Dorothy accepts the information by crossing her arms, she is not attempting to keep it barriered out; she clutches it to her bosom, this knowledge, this masterpiece. It warms her, somehow; it drives some of the chill from her ribs.

'A hill with a face?'

'That's the hill.'

'You're the little baby, aren't you. The one I saved.'

'The one you damned.'

'A bit harsh.'

'*You* try living it.'

'I thought you were a boy,' Dorothy mutters.

'And *that's* not very nice either,' the fan replies.

9.

I remember a sentence from *Nutcracker Island*: *The bomb knocked the hat off the building.*

I imagined, when I first read it, a building dressed as a businessman, a tidy, sleek black suit, impeccable in appearance. And then, in the story, a bomb detonates in the fifth floor mailroom, and I saw the building doff its bowler or its trilby to the midmorning sun, which was rolling over a pillow of mist on the bed of the backdrop lake. I forget the city in question.

A bomb has detonated in my own fifth floor mailroom. And with expert precision it has knocked my own hat to the sky.

My mother and her brother were lovers. My mother and my Uncle Stephen were *boyfriend and girlfriend*. Consensual, guilt-fuelled acts of physical and emotional intimacy, the stuff of nightmarish confessionals.

'I don't want you to judge him too harshly,' my mother says, lifting to her lips the cup of tea from which she never quite sips. 'It takes two to tango, Tom,'

'Did Dad know?'

Mum shakes her head – then she nods it, thinking twice of introducing further lies. 'He was…' she begins. 'Tom, I'm going to tell you something disturbing now.'

'Like you haven't already? What were you thinking? It's illegal!'

Mum frowns. 'Why, fancy!' she says. 'You know that didn't cross my mind.'

'…I have to get out of here.'

'It was you who wanted to know!'

'I thought you'd covered up for him or something. I didn't expect *this*!'

'Covered up?'

My hands have taken on a life of their own; they flail wildly, as I'm trying to bamboozle someone – hypnotizing my prey.

'I feel sick,' I tell Mum. 'Yes, *covered up*. Like he's robbed a shop or something and you found out about it; gave him an alibi.'

'Oh I did that as well.' Mum sniffs, places down her cup and reaches inside her left cardigan sleeve for a crumpled-up ball of toilet tissue. The laugh she produces sounds bitter; she dabs at the buxom pouches beneath her eyes. 'Did that sort of thing plenty of times, too!'

Squirming in my armchair (it has grown several sizes in the last few minutes, unless it's I who has shrunk), I make an effort to steer the topic to something comparatively sane.

'He was a criminal?'

'We both were, Tom,' Mum answers, unwilling to meet my eyes.

III.

1.

Hats off to the architects of torture chambers, interrogation suites and incarceration facilities the world over. It's not as easy as it looks, is it, designing and constructing a suitable place to remand your prisoner? It takes Roy and I several attempts to get it right.

At first, in the road outside Amelior Anderson's house in Stoke Hammond, I am not even certain what Roy intends to do, beyond giving Kolko a kicking.

'Don't let him move, Tom.'

Move? It's unlikely he'll be able to *breathe* unaided for the next fortnight.

Roy returns to his car and pops the boot. When I shake my head I produce a corona of sweat that fizzes in the air.

'You've got to be joking.'

But Roy has already bent at the waist, near Kolko's groaning head, and is in the process of hefting the other man's torso. He forces his wrists and forearms under Kolko's armpits and barks an order:

'Get his feet, Tom!'

'Roy, come *on*, man. We can't take a *prisoner*.'

'Why not? What's the fucker done to us all these months? *Get his feet.* He ain't gonna lift himself.'

Who knows how many witnesses there have to be, curtains palpitating, but I get the feet anyway, and we carry moaning Kolko to the boot of Roy's car, where our victim seems to experience a momentary recovery. While Roy forces the boot down, Kolko tries to push and kick his way out of his new coffin.

'Jesus.'

'Not as easy as it is in films,' Roy remarks ruminatively. 'You're driving his. Back to mine.' He stalks around to the driver's side. Inside the boot, Kolko thrashes and stretches; the noise alone is horrendous, let alone the thought of him suffocating in there.

'Ten minutes,' Roy tells me. 'Fifteen tops,' as if he's read my mind. 'He'll be okay.' He curls into the driver's seat, leaving me with not much of an alternative.

I jog to Kolko's vehicle. Though I'm willing for there to be no key in the ignition, my prayer is ignored: it's there. All I have to do is turn it.

Furthermore, attached to the ignition key is a ring, and attached to the ring are another four or five keys. I turn the former; the engine starts. We might have his house keys here, I think clearly; and all of a sudden I am certain of where Stephen is hiding.

2.

To the bass-line accompaniment of Kolko drumming inside the boot, we must build our cell to contain him.

'We'll have to be nifty, son,' says Roy, at least coming round to my way of thinking on this point if on no other. 'We don't want him to get too panicky he starts asphyxiating on us.'

'You don't say,' I reply. 'That don't sound like panic, Roy.' I nod towards the thuds and scratches. 'That sounds like major pissed-off anger.'

'Well that's all right then. Anger we can handle, eh? Cunt can get *angry* as he fucking likes. The keys are in the little box.' Roy points towards the back of the garage.

I am nonplussed. 'The keys to what?'

'To all the motors! Keep up, Tom!'

Shaking my head I add something about my psychic powers needing a new battery and being a bit below par this afternoon.

Roy sighs with what I take to be longsuffering tolerance.

'It's simple, mate. We take the cars I've got in the garage *out*. We put *my* car and the police car that ain't really a police car *in*. Right at the back. Then we move all the *other* cars back in – tight up to *his* car, where he'll be, by then. Up close tight enough so he can't even open the door to get out. Then we can leave him there to sweat.'

Roy fans out his hands – *ta daaa!* – with a great fat grin on his face.

There might be the teensy problem of how we're going to transfer Kolko from the boot of Roy's car to this or any other car, but what I actually say is:

'He can still climb out the window. Tight or not. He might be a fat bastard but…'

Roy interrupts me. He points at the forlorn jalopy, now parked on the yard in the rain, that Hannah once borrowed. 'Not in the courtesy car he can't. *Nothing* works on *that* cunt. Not even the windows. Let's move some cars!'

3.

Kolko trapped in Roy's courtesy car puts me in mind of one of those aged grey-blue lizards in its heated tank at the garden centre, where I used to take Mum for Sunday lunch to look at the prospective pets. To my restless consternation Kolko grins from ear to ear; he appears content. He even points an index finger in our direction and starts crooning.

Roy and I watch him from a car away, standing inside the garage while outside the rain adds its own ingredient to the boiling pot of storm, just beyond the wide-open doors.

It is dawn – pre-dawn morning – and we're up with the

crickets. Kolko has been in his cell all night.

'So now what?' I ask. 'We've got him snug as a bug, Roy, but now what?'

'The fuck's he singing?' Roy mutters, distracted.

'He's a jolly old soul, isn't he?'

'But what's he *singing?*'

Turning my head on a neck that stretches stiffly after a bad night of sketchy and insufficient sleep, I regard the side of Roy's unshaven face – the underscore of jowl-flab. 'You're missing the point, mate,' I tell his profile. 'He *didn't get out.*'

'Perhaps he didn't want to.'

'Bollocks. He's just a man, Roy, just like we thought. Well, this proves it. Didn't even have the strength to kick the windscreen out!'

Roy faces me now. 'I've been wondering about that meself. But I don't like that song, Tom. He's too happy.'

'Cabin fever?' I suggest.

'What's that?'

'Madness brought on by claustrophobia.'

'So soon?'

'A night in the dungeon can bring out strange reactions, mate.'

'Tell me about it.'

Inside the courtesy car, Kolko turns up the volume. His torso swells and quivers as he reaches for a higher register – going through his jailbird scales.

'He's singing in foreign,' says Roy.

I listen properly now, to please or assure Roy, my partner in crime. 'It's French.'

Nodding his head, Roy adds, 'Go on then, Pepe. What's it say?'

'Christ, Roy. It's been a while, mate.'

'Don't tell me your state education was wasted on you. Even *I* can get some of it!'

'Go on then, smartarse.'

'It sounds like *si j'etais vous…*'

'If I were you,' I translate.

'Cunt's getting on me nerves. Why don't we give him something to sing about?'

Because we've already provided him with a spanking, I want to say; and it didn't work, did it? We've broken nothing, not even Kolko's spirit; and if the entire *raison d'etre* of a solid beating is not to *break* something then I don't know what it is.

'Ian'll be here soon,' Roy announces.

'What'll you gonna tell him?'

'Sort of speaks for itself, I would say. Wouldn't you?'

'As to the whys and wherefores.'

'No idea. But E won't be disappointed, I doubt. He hates the bloke as much as I do.'

Kolko starts laughing. The courtesy car shakes.

Roy shivers. 'Do you fancy a brew in the office?' he asks.

I nod in the direction of the car. 'What about him?'

'He ain't going nowhere. He's been here all night, fuck's sake.'

'I didn't mean that. I meant, do you think we should give him something to eat and drink? As our prisoner, like.'

Roy joins Kolko in a round of laughter. 'Do you wanna quote me the Geneva Convention, Tom? Look at the size of the pig. A few meals he ain't gonna miss.'

'Some water, then. It might be stuffy in there. We don't want him keeling over.'

'There's no space for him to keel over!'

'You know what I mean, mate. When *you* were in the nick you would've started a riot if you didn't get your cup of tea or whatever.'

'It's hardly the same thing, Tom.' Roy shrugs the back of his shoulders to me, as he is heading towards the office. 'But okay; we'll give him a glass of our finest *eau* if it keeps you happy.'

4.

Nor should I skimp on the details of what occurred between our kidnapping of Kolko outside Mrs Anderson's place, and our entrapment of him in the car. For a start we made sure that Kolko carried no more keys; we relieved him of his mobile, his wallet; we stripped him of all but his uniform. Then we hemmed him in, as described above. Throughout the procedure, our convict was alert, deferential, and he was studious – strangely so – about not giving either of us a hard time in this regard. You might even say cooperative.

Was he playing along for reasons of his own? Had it nothing to do with concussion, after all?

5.

When the telephone rings, it disturbs me from one of those stupors, possibly self-inflicted but in this case not, at the end of which you have no idea how you've been spending your time.

'I'm sorry if it's late.'

'You can't help the time, Han. What you mean is, you're sorry you're *calling* so late. Is anything wrong?'

Hannah chortles into my ear – a masculine bark. 'Tom, our *lives* are wrong. Haven't you noticed? Are you alone?' she asks.

'Yes; Sabrina's not home yet. Actually, I thought she was with you.'

'I dropped her off with Dorothy about an hour ago. They're probably at her place. Why? Are you worried about her?'

'Well, naturally. Did you see what she was wearing?'

'She's a big girl, Tom.'

'Don't I know it.'

'So you don't know what we talked about yet, at Profit.'

'No. I didn't even know that's where you were going. Did you have a fun night?'

'Action packed, as they say. Dorothy met an old friend and I had my car mangled.' Hannah waits. 'Tom, have you ever heard my favourite joke?'

'I don't know; what is it?'

'It's about Hell. I'll give you the radio edit if you like. A guy ends up in Hell and the Devil says to him: You've got to choose one of these three doors. Whatever one you choose, that's what you're doing for eternity, son. Got it? Whatever's behind it, I mean. So he opens the first door and he sees a million people in fire and ash, their skin burning, and he thinks – fuck that. So he opens door number two, and as far as he can see, millions of people are frozen in ice. Fuck *that*, he thinks, and he opens the third door and there's a million people up to their knees in shit.'

'I remember it now,' I interrupt.

'So he thinks, hardly pleasant, but better than being boiled alive or having my cock frozen off. I'll take the shit option, he decides; and he goes through, and the foreman says, Okay, you've all had your tea-break. Back on your headstands.'

Hannah pauses.

'You didn't laugh.'

'It's the way you tell 'em. Sorry. It's an oldie. I grinned *wry-ly*, as they say.'

'But what does it mean, Tom?'

'The joke?'

'I used to think it meant – be careful of first impressions, because the guy ends up doing a headstand for eternity in a wasteland of doodoo. But *now* I think – now I think it's more like, we're in it as deep as that guy at the Gates of Hell.'

'With our heads in the *merde*.'

'No, Tom!' Hannah says excitedly. 'That's exactly what I'm getting at. I thought of it on my way home after I dropped off Dolly and Sabrina. It's only a joke, I know, but *in humorous veritas* and all that. We've been so long thinking we're the ones with our heads in the shit, we've forgotten there's a breaktime. You get a *rest* from the shitty headstands, Tom. The foreman tells you, every once in a millennium maybe, you can stand up for a while and take your face out the poo.'

'And that's where we are now?' I want to clarify.

'I think so.'

'Are we back to the angels theory then? Our visitors, if you want to call 'em that, are here to protect us. Are we back to that?'

'I don't think we ever left it. But no, if we're being protected from anything, then I think it's because it's in *their* interest to do so. It's got nothing to do with *us*. We're just words in a god's language, Tom. This is *bigger* than us.'

I wait. Then: 'I miss you, Hannah,' I blurt into the phone. Despite the fact that I'm terrified of how my confession will be received, it seems to surprise *me* more than it does my interlocutor.

'I miss you too,' Hannah replies quietly. 'You could always come over. I won't bite.'

'I should be here for when Sabrina gets home, but I'm tempted.'

'I wouldn't worry about Sabrina; I think she and Dolly have a lot to talk about. You won't believe some of the stuff we discussed at the restaurant.' She purrs into my ear: a sigh.

But I don't want to hear what was discussed at the restaurant; not at the moment. It's too late, I'm too tired, and I'm nowhere near drunk enough.

Perhaps this is Hannah's opinion, too. 'Listen. About us,' she says, 'you and me, okay? While we're kind of on the subject. Do you *really* remember sleeping with me?'

'Yes. Do you really not?'

'I don't; but I'm doubting myself more and more.'

'I know the feeling. It happened, Han.'

'I'm sure it did.'

'So why do we remember different things? Is that what you're asking?'

'That's what I'm *answering*, I think,' Hannah replies. 'We have to get our heads back into the manure, Tom.'

'Something bad?'

'*Oh* yes.'

'Okay. But it had something to do with the old friend you mentioned?'

'Very much so.' She goes on quickly: 'We're being shielded from something, I think. *For their benefit*, though. Look at Hana, for example. He's got me and Sam believing two different versions of the same event, but what if neither of them are true? It happened *in a different way altogether*, Tom! But it's in his interest to have us fighting over the memory because it means we'll never stumble on to the *real* memory!'

I liked it better when Hannah was almost but not quite inviting me into her bed again; this return to The Story is head-spinning, especially so late at night.

'Don't know what to say,' I admit.

'What's the one thing that could blot out memory, Tom? The one thing we all of us run like a bastard from, man or beast.'

The riddle is too easy, and I provide my solution with confidence.

'Death.'

'Yes! There is death in our backstory, Mr Lockington, and

we're all shit-scared to confront it. We're in *mourning* for some-thing.'

'The same thing?'

'Different people. But yes I believe so: the same thing. So I think it's time to do our headstands, mate; get our heads back to *terra merde*.'

At length, when Hannah allows me to speak, I say to her, 'Fine. I buy all that; seriously I do; but what are you suggesting we do?'

'We get away from it all,' she says.

'I tried that! I went as far north as you can go! All the way to bloody Iceland, for Christ's sake, and Stephen still followed me!'

'But *did* he, though? A couple of days ago, and you were saying he's not a ghost after all. He never died, that's what you said. In which case, how did he appear to you on that whaleboat? And I mean that question literally.'

'No idea. But *everyone's* seen him – right here! On my car-pet!'

'He knocked at the door. You let him in,' Hannah counters.

'You *know* there was more to it than that, Han.'

'Okay, agreed; but I didn't mean bugger off abroad anyway, when I said get away. I was talking about somewhere else.'

Hannah sketches out her plan, the recital of which involves an account of where she drove tonight after dropping off Sabrina and Dolly. 'Audacious' is not the word for this plan. 'Foolhardy', 'dangerous': *these* are the words for this plan.

'And one last thing,' she adds, 'about our nights of love, back then – if they were indeed entire nights... Was it good?'

'Yeah it was good.'

Hannah chuckles; it's a much more feminine sound this time, I'm relieved to hear. 'Then you can definitely come over now. Have you money for a cab?'

'Just about.'
'Then use it. Dial for one now.'

IV.

1.

'What is the name of this village?' she asked slowly.

'The name?' she asked again, close to tears, biting her bottom lip to spur on a lick of pain that would remind her to persevere.

She was in a gathering room of some kind; a committee hall, perhaps. Not a bar. No drinks or snacks were on sale.

At the building's front door she had been relieved of the baby she'd rescued on the hill with the face. She wondered where the child had been taken. Wondered also why she had been brought *here* (as opposed to a police station, for example): to this assembly point, with its hectare of unvarnished floorboards, its stacks of grey plastic chairs lining each wall, its vast central table – pride of place, dark mahogany …

If the desultory collection of weatherbeaten fenestrated shacks to which Dorothy had been driven could justifiably be called a village, then the people who had met here to greet her were obviously the villagers. They were dressed in an almost unanimous shovel grey, with the only tip of the hat to the exotic being threadbare patches of filthy brown leather, sewn over holes here and there.

Nor had this welcome committee's collective sense of personal hygiene been unfairly represented by the poverty of its dress uniform either. The people stank. Though it almost hurt Dorothy to admit it to herself, what she was experiencing was *a snooty reaction*. These people needed a *bath*. This was the long and the short of the matter; but still, their issues of cleanliness aside, Dorothy was pleased to be off the road – delighted to be away

from that fucking *hill*. She just wished she could feel a bit more
certain about things.

The campsite she had left seemed a universe away.

'Does anyone speak English?' Dorothy asked again, that
fruitless refrain of hers.

'*Eeengleesh*,' someone shouted – someone at the back of the
crowd around her – and a tipple of amused titters and a very
light round of applause ensued.

Someone else repeated, 'Eeengleesh.'

Dismayed and getting panicky, Dorothy asked similar questions, first in German and then in Italian. For some reason, with
every word she attempted, she seemed to be playing to the audience; they got the jokes. A reluctant comedienne, then, Dorothy had found her level, and she could now ride a lucky comic's
streak. The only problem being… she didn't feel like being funny.
Recollections of events on the hill swarmed around her; shock bit
into her nerves. She was tired. How would she make these hillbil-
ly corndogs understand that she had witnessed and interrupted a
crime? That the baby she had cradled in her arms on her stagger
down the side of the hill, for several miles along a track so strewn
and obstacled with rubble that it had no business being thought
of as a road – was a fortunate survivor of an intermitted duel, a
baby who had had time, luck and God on her tiny side?

The baby had also had Dorothy on her side; but Dorothy
wondered quite how aware of this obvious fact these yokels happened to be. Although it was fair to say that Dorothy was not in
the baby-saving business, she had expected something other than
this when that rattling grenade of an old truck had lumbered
up behind her, squeaking on its axel, every nut, bolt and panel
apparently loose if she were to judge by the vehicle's din. On the
other hand, it *was* a vehicle, surely it had been better to flag it
down, as she had, than to have continued on foot… *surely*. For the

baby's sake if nothing else…

In the truck – squeezed onto the front seat between the toothless driver whose pockmarked jowls wobbled with every pothole over which the vehicle clambered, and a younger man, red in the face but more on the nose, a man who might have been the driver's son, who wore his alcoholic's broken capillaries on his conk with a kind of idiot's pride – Dorothy had forcefed herself on the rescuers' combined body odour, with a variety of relieved ambition about her bones. It might have stunk to the heavens in that truck, but at least it was heading somewhere definite. And Dorothy had sucked comfort from it all. Even as the baby had started bawling, startled from a nap by a particularly deep dip into a ridge, Dorothy had felt that it was all okay; this nightmare would soon be over. The men's sweaty bodies proved they worked on the land, surely. And this would imply that somewhere not far ahead would be a farmhouse, a telephone…

Now she knew less than she had even then.

'Can I have some *water*, please?' Dorothy asked. She cupped her left fingers around an invisible mug or glass and mimed tipping a drink into the back of her throat.

The performance drew fresh humour from her audience – from the crowd in the hall, the crowd that was expanding. Had the whole village been notified by now, however large in population the whole village might turn out to be? Perhaps they would all cram into this Mission Hall – or whatever on earth it turned out to be.

Dorothy was not comfortable, not about anything. And it wasn't only shock setting in afresh because of what she had witnessed and walked away from on the hill. It was newer – a sensation of stultified panic … It wasn't only that Dorothy had been ushered into this building; nor simply the sheer numbers who were avidly taking peeks and gawps at this stranger in their midst.

While in the truck, catapulting along, she had viewed it as un-expected the fact that the men who might have been father and son had not responded to her questions posed in any language she could think of. However, they were men of the soil, Dorothy had opined. Why should they be multi-lingual? In the hall, now, this argument failed to wash; it failed to wash in the way that the people – mainly men – crowding her closer to the vast central table failed to wash.

Dorothy had traded discomfort for fear.

2.

Dorothy closes her eyes and gasps.

'I remember thinking about their teeth,' she says, lifting a hand to where the fantasy bullet struck her on the shoulder; the wound throbbing again. 'Their yellow teeth, outlined in black. Or missing altogether. And big noses with an armpit's worth of hair climbing out of each nostril. Their teeth. They were all *smiling*,' she says.

The young woman wearing the crown says, 'I remember. I remember their teeth, too.'

Dorothy searches the young woman's face. 'You were a baby.'

'I'm your memory. I have no choice.'

The women fall silent; just a few seconds. Their waiter hovers close-by, not desperate for them to re-order, only listening.

'Did they hurt you, Dolly?' Sabrina asks.

'Yes, they hurt her,' the young woman answers when Dorothy doesn't.

Dorothy has her face in her hands.

3.

Hannah makes a call to her vehicle breakdown hotline and

explains the problem. In order to qualify for faster service from the operator, she pretends to be a alone – the company has a policy about prioritising lone female breakdown callouts. She is told that an engineer will be there within the hour, and Hannah asks if she can be phoned when he's on his way as she is not inside her car; she is inside a restaurant, keeping warm.

The call comes quickly: Dorothy has scarcely begun unpicking her memory.

'I'll be back a.s.a.p,' says Hannah. 'You'll have to tell me what I miss.'

The breakdown van is painted a tainted yellow colour. Resembling a slimline, clean-shaven Roy, the mechanic hops down from his cab in a set of overalls as disarmingly lemon in hue as the hull of his vehicle. In his right hand he holds a regulation clipboard. 'What seems to be the trouble?' he asks.

Hannah is in no mood. 'The cigarette lighter's broken. What does it look like?'

'What does what look like?' Roy-Lite replies, his tone suggesting that he has taken his share of glib nonsense in his time and that he's not in the mood either.

Hannah pinches shut her eyes; silently counts to five. 'I was rather hoping,' she overdoes it, 'that you could see your way clear to replacing the broken glass in my windscreen. So that I can drive myself and my friends back home.'

Roy-Minor scowls. 'This came through as an LFN.'

'An elephant?'

'L.F.N,' the mechanic repeats slowly. 'Lone Female Night call.'

'Oh. Well I was. On my own, that is. I just met them by chance.'

The mechanic is a dog with a bone. 'You said *back* home. Drive them *back* home,' Roy-Imitate argues pedantically. 'Clearly inferring you drove 'em here in the first instance.'

'Implying. Not inferring. *Implying* I drove them here in the first instance. Well I didn't. I met them here and it was pure jam. Now. Do you intend to fix my windscreen or not, may I be so bold as to inquire.'

'No.'

'Excuse me?'

'No. No I won't. Because I can't see anything wrong with it.'

'You can't *see*–' begins Hannah, spinning around to face her car.

The windscreen is intact. To look at there is nothing wrong with the vehicle; and the vision makes Hannah gasp in rainy air.

Forgetting her instantaneous animosity towards Roy-the-Younger, Hannah turns back to his uncertain grin and implores him: 'It was broken! Not fifteen minutes ago! Fifteen *seconds* ago! When I arrived back here there was glass everywhere! There were *scratches*…' she blurts.

'Well there aren't now, madam,' the mechanic replies cool-ly. 'You know I'll have to put this on your file, don't you?'

'On my file?'

'With the company. Un-call,' he sounds like he's adding.

Hannah imagines Stephen and says, 'Uncle?'

'Un-call. Unnecessary callout,' he elaborates, sighing with an inadvertent whistle. 'Wasting your time and mine, madam.'

'The car was damaged!' Hannah protests.

'What, the leprechauns fix it, did they?' With which Fun-size-Roy reopens the driver's side door of the horrible margarine van. His complacency penetrates Hannah painfully.

'Why the fuck would I call you out if I didn't need you?' she demands.

The man shrugs. 'To meet a fella?'

'…Tell me you're joking.'

His Cheshire grin tells her otherwise.

Hannah turns her back on him and stares at her new and improved car. She doesn't want to enter it to check out the interior, which is what she had planned to do while the windscreen was being replaced. Behind her back the van moves away.

I'm not getting in, she decides. Turning on her heel, she heads back to Profit.

4.

'I don't know how many of them there were, holding me down on the table. I just know I couldn't move...' Dorothy sips the brandy that their waiter has brought her without being asked to do so. 'I kept shouting and thrashing but they were too strong. I remember thinking – this can't be happening. I know it sounds clichéd, but that's what I thought. It can't be me. They can't mean what I think they mean. Then the one at the head of the pack unbuttoned his fly. I'd never seen such a big penis. But the other villagers had. I wasn't the first this had happened to, I can safely assume.' Dorothy sips her brandy again.

Eyes turn to the girl, who taps on the table with her sceptre, conducting an orchestra in her head. Her face is as unreadable as hieroglyphics.

Standing closer to them than ever, the waiter wrings his hands.

'They tore my clothes open. And they did what they did. And they *laughed*.'

Dorothy finishes her brandy in one swallow and clutches her other hand to her chest to trace the burn down through her body. 'How do you know this?' she asks the girl she saved. 'None of this is new to you so I want to know how you know it.'

'I've told you – I'm your memory of the incident. I have no choice in the matter.'

Dorothy grips the skin at the point on her shoulder where the bullet did not go through. 'What happened to me here?' she demands. 'If you know all the answers, *what happened to me here?*'

Adjusting the crown on her head, the young woman answers, 'It was the boy.'

'...What boy?'

'It was the idiot boy,' the girl replies.

Such colour as has remained in Dorothy's face now drains away. 'Oh God...' she whispers (the waiter swoops in to replace her empty glass with a fresh one, brimming).

Sabrina asks her, 'What is it, Dolly? Do you remember?'

'There was a boy,' Dorothy answers. 'He had learning difficulties, shall we say. He tried to fuck my shoulder.'

Annette's eyebrows pinch together. 'What, with a knife?'

'No; with his penis. Believe it or not. They held me down and took turns between my legs – but this boy with gap-teeth had other ideas. He was on his knees on the table, trying to drill his stubby little erection into my *shoulder*. Eleven or twelve years old.'

She tips some of the new brandy into her throat; at the same time memories tip out before her eyes, through her ears, into her nose... She cannot stop thinking of teeth: bad teeth. Breath so rank it would knock a lazy buzzard off a shithouse roof. The *dampness* of their clothing; the movement of the erections inside her; the taste of ejaculate, cyanide-strong; the patchwork of stinking stains on her clothes when it had finished...

'How did I get out of there?' Dorothy asks the rescued girl. 'I need to know.'

The girl smiles, a trifle smugly. 'I'm your key.'

'Yes, I know. So unlock the rest of it for me, please.'

'I was your key then as well. I started crying; it seemed to burst the bubble. The mass hysteria was over. They climbed off you. They even looked ashamed of themselves...'

'So they should've been… And?'

'And they released you. They let you walk out the way you'd been driven in.'

'Because you started *crying*?' Dorothy sounds disbelieving. 'After *that*?'

The girl shrugs her shoulders. 'Don't ask a baby!'

'But you're not a baby now,' Sabrina tells her. 'So if you'd be so kind as to explain this to someone who *wasn't* there, what is going on?'

'Oh my Lord…' Dorothy adds. 'Outside the village I found a bar in the middle of nowhere. A shack, really. I went in. I *fell* in. And there were about fifteen people in there and they turned to me *and they all had my face.*'

'I don't know about that,' says the girl. 'I wasn't there for that.'

Not being able to hold back any longer, Dorothy starts crying. Sabrina is swift to console her, moving her chair closer in order to flop her bare arm across Dorothy's shoulder.

People turn in their seats, at their tables, to see the woman crying. The lingering waiter has business elsewhere, and looks pleased to have been called away to work.

5.

If illusions are to red herring us away from what's really real, thinks Hannah, what is happening right now? Why the illusion of the damage to my car?

The answer is chillingly simple, she believes.

To separate me from the rest of the girls.

She picks up her pace, walking as fast as she can back to Profit. Should she run? For sure she is fit enough – never fitter – but no. She thinks not; and she thinks not for paranoid reasons, running is the sort of thing that gets noticed on cameras. HahH

A fantasy of flying strokes past Hannah's mind. Inappropriate as it is, she shakes it away. No time; not now. Thus it is at the fairest clip of which Hannah is capable that she rounds a corner out of the precinct, on to the final straight back to the restaurant, when she all but collides with the stringy body under a horribly familiar face.

'It's your turn now, Hannah,' says Hana.

6.

The girl removes her crown. She shakes her head (her hair doesn't move much) and she leans forward, crossing her arms on the table. 'I can only say as much as I know,' she says.

After taking a spoonful of cappuccino froth from her mug and sipping it as it were medicine, the girl says, 'No one has names there. The village doesn't even have one. So you won't find it on a map; you won't find it if you search for it. *It finds you.* It calls out to the lost.'

'Well, I was certainly lost all right,' Dorothy agrees, dabbing at her eyes.

'Not just physically lost. The traumatized; the desperate. On a different day, with a spring in your step, with the sun overhead, you would have walked straight through it and never known it was there; you wouldn't have seen anything. It doesn't even have a country; it doesn't *belong* anywhere. But they found you. Your pain was delicious to them... I'm surprised they didn't eat you.'

Sam clears her throat. 'This time last year I would have tucked myself up in a sanatorium for so much as *thinking* of what I'm about to say, but here we go. Do you mean to tell us that those people were dead? It's a village of the dead? Even with the campsite Dorothy worked at less than a day's journey away?'

To each of these questions the girl has nodded her head.

'So why were the two women duelling on the hill?' asks Sabrina.

'I know, I think.' Dorothy clutches her glass as if someone has threatened to take it from her. 'They'd *escaped*, hadn't they?'

Another nod of the head.

Dorothy rolls on: 'They'd managed to get out... but they didn't know how to get any further than the hill with the face. The village was a *prison*.'

'I think so.'

'You *think* so? You lived there, didn't you?'

'After a fashion.'

'But you made it out as well – like the black woman and the white woman did?' Sam ventures. 'It's not impossible.'

Fingering the fake jewels on the crown in front of her, the girl shrugs her shoulders once more. 'I'll go back. I don't think I'll have much choice. I'll go back.'

Dorothy clears her throat. 'I remember something else. Not about then. About when I first met you. You asked me to sign your book. You said you were a fan.'

'I am. I love your work! It tells me so much about you.'

'And you gave me your name. I'm sure I signed it to Di.'

'To *die*?' Annette misinterprets.

The girl smiles. 'It seemed appropriate somehow. I had to give you *something*.'

'So I call you Di?' Dorothy asks.

The girl laughs. 'I'm *your* memory. Call me anything you bloody well choose!'

7.

Hannah and Hana, outside 'I Second That Emulsion!' – the DIY shop with the huge cardboard cut-out of Smokey Robinson in the window that Hannah has never understood. She has never got the connection between Motown and home accessories.

Her mind tries to tell her that Hana the thief can't be here. But he *is* here – something just shy of a smile on his thin lips.

'What do you want?' Hannah demands. 'Haven't you done enough damage?'

'Haven't you?' He makes a big show of displaying his empty hands.

'What have I ever done to you? Apart from smacking you one. When you were *trying to rob me* and the other passengers. What have I *done to you*?'

'You'll remember,' Hana tells her quietly.

'My friends are waiting for me.'

Hannah dances to the side, fully expecting Hana to block her way. He doesn't. He doesn't so much as flinch or cross his arms. Instead he watches her pass, the smile on his face becoming vulpine, mocking. It's either the smile or the thief's apparent lassitude that stops Hannah in her tracks, once she's got by. She turns one-eighty and is presented with the surreal vision of the thief with Smokey Robinson's head on top of his own – Smokey grinning from the shop window, with the cardboard speech bubble anchored to his face. It reads:

IF YOU FEEL LIKE GIVING ME
A LIFETIME OF REPULSION…
I SECOND THAT EMULSION!

Hannah hiccups, catching air; she blinks her eyes hard – and the words in the bubble shrink and twist; they rearrange themselves like Scrabble tiles.

I SECOND THAT EMULSION! is all it now says; but all the same, Hannah takes a step to the left so that Smokey's head is no longer on top of Hana's. The sight was disquieting. 'Did *you* do that?' she asks.

'If I did it was for your own good…'

'Says you. And if you didn't?'

'You need to see an optician.'

'Nice one. You know, I'm beginning to find you pathetic, Hana.'

'So am I. But do we have a choice in such things?'

'Got an answer for everything, haven't you?'

The thief considers the question. 'Most things,' he admits.

'Then answer me this. Was it you fucked my car up?'

'Why on earth would I do damage to your car?'

'So what did you mean by it being my turn? My turn for what?' Hannah makes a face. She raises a finger almost to his nose. 'I'm going to say this straight, just this time. I don't *care* what voodoo spell you think you've put on Sam – she's a big girl and she'll have to learn to take care of herself – but it won't work on me. *Capiche?* So leave me and my friends the hell alone. I've had enough of this magic bullshit.'

With a snarl on her face (her upper lip trembling slightly with the confrontation), Hannah looks away from her hunter. Her reasonable expectation is that her legs will take her in the direction she wants them to go, but they don't. For one or two panic-stricken seconds she is locked to the spot. Held down, but held down by *nothing*. Like someone who's been hypnotised into thinking that her feet weigh nine hundred tonnes each.

Hannah whimpers. Hana glides into her peripheral – the left side. His movement sends heat to this side of her face, as if he bears fire. As if he *is* fire. She tries to speak. She tries to move. Pain lights up in her throat and sinuses; it burns a path down to her groin. All that will leak from her vocal cords is a pitiful simper. She has felt fear before – but never this.

She turns her head as best she can. Inside the shop window

the effigy of Smokey is turning to mush; although the structure stays put, what was painted on the cardboard runs like wet paint down a fence. His features curdle first.

Hana has moved behind the motionless Hannah. She can feel his erection against her backside – and from her rear he rubs at her stomach, gently, caressingly. In horror she watches his left hand slip lower.

'*Leave me alone, I said*!' Hannah shouts.

The paralysis breaks. It is over as suddenly as it fell upon her. The leg muscles she tensed while in the spell's grip now spring her forward; it is all she can do to keep her balance, now that her movements are hers once more. Out of Hana's embrace, Hannah turns round to face him for the second time this evening.

'Is *that* your game? You came all this way for a *grope*?'

Hana the thief laughs. 'Not exactly.'

'Then *tell* me!' Her voice contains a note of pleading. She'll be saying *please* next! Minding her manners… *Run*, says the voice in Hannah's head. *This isn't right and this isn't seen by anyone else. Haven't you noticed there are no people around?*

Hannah runs all right: she runs directly at the thief. It is only a matter of three strides, but she knows what there is to know about the lunge, and into her flexed open fist she piles as much energy as these strides will generate. Knowing where to hit him for the best effect, Hannah aims her fingers at a point below his ribcase, aiming the open-hand *upwards*. Get the fingers under the bony ridge; knock the heart out of place if you're lucky…

Her punch connects; Hana sags immediately, the reserves of his air bursting forth on a tide of gaseous meat-and-vodka. For good effect Hannah raises her knee to juggle his balls. Although the knee misses, there is damage enough done for the attacker to feel fuelled.

Hana drops to his knees. She backs away from the man

who has become her prey.

'It can't be murder,' she tells him as he struggles for air. 'You're already dead.'

8.

Hannah drops Sabrina and Dorothy on Grovebury Road, outside the flats.

They wave bye-bye.

By driving away quickly Hannah spools up two whips of dirty water from a roadside puddle. They watch her red lights vanish; and both of her passengers wonder where their chauffeur needs to be in such a hurry, this late into the evening.

'Are you feeling awkward?' they both want to ask, but it's Dorothy who gets there first.

Sabrina smiles. 'I'm feeling *something*.'

'Cold, I might venture. Well I warned you.'

'Yes, Mum. A nightcap? A middy of ale for me lady?' asks Sabrina.

'Wine before beer – makes you feel queer. Beer before wine – makes you feel fine.'

Sabrina laughs. 'You were drinking gin and brandy. The rhyme doesn't work.'

'I was drinking wine *before* I was drinking gin and brandy. In there.' She nods towards her flat, the next door along. 'But there isn't a rhyme for that.'

'Any left?'

'I have, as a matter of fact.'

'Would you relish the company?'

'Oh come on in out of the cold, little sparrow,' Dorothy chuckles; she feels tipsy, and not only with alcohol. She is drunk on stories; pissed on the truth; cabbaged on memories.

In Dorothy's kitchen, the hostess drains what remains of a

bottle of deep red, divvying up these liquid spoils into two identical glasses, one of which she hands to Sabrina.

'Bottoms up.'

'Chin chin.'

Dorothy experiences the oddest sensation (she vows to recount it to Tom, not Sabrina, when the time's right) that she is not tasting the wine, the wine is tasting *her*. The wine is sipping at her lips, drawing her deeper; she imagines the wine-dark sea and she is on that sea, the waves becalmed, but they want to taste her body. She is not on a boat, or a raft: she *is* the boat; and the waves of blood-red want her down, down, the sea-bed for her pillow…

Dorothy opens her eyes. It's the telephone ringing.

'Leave it,' Dorothy says to Sabrina, noting that the other woman is halfway to the desk. 'The machine's on.'

'It might be important. It's late.'

'And it might not be. I'm too tired.'

'I'm not surprised. Do you know what just happened?'

Dorothy chews on her response. 'Not really,' she admits; 'it was like a nice dream – for once – a beautiful dream, in fact.' Amused, she sniffs. You didn't lace my glass with LSD when I wasn't looking, did you?'

The telephone stops ringing; the answer machine does not kick in.

Sabrina laughs. 'It was weird. You fell asleep standing up! I don't think I've ever seen anyone do that before. I've *heard* about it…'

'Not even Tom?'

'Especially not Tom. He never sleeps… Have you any more wine?'

'Yes, but I've had enough. You can finish this one if you like, I'm going to bed. I hope you don't mind.'

'Not as long as I can come with you.'

9.

In the intervening hour between delivering her passengers at the flats on Grovebury Road and calling Tom, Hannah busies herself plotting. She knows it's late; it has been a jampacked evening. She is even alive to the probability that she is about to make a ludicrous error.

She has parked outside Toby's house – more accurately, Toby and now Jill's – and she longs for inspiration to float some words into her mouth.

It's midnight now, or as near as damn it, and what if they're asleep? What if they're *having sex*? What if they're fucking like *baboons*? Something rolls in Hannah's stomach; a crushing sense of something that feels like jealousy holds her hands tight on the steering wheel. She can picture Toby naked, of course, but she cannot conjure up Jill in the same fashion, as nature intended. So it is that Hannah makes Jill perfect; as she loosens her digits from the wheel she dresses Jill in a nudity that would make goddesses weep with envy. What's more, the woman is a Mata Hari in the sack: she is a lover who will not be left, who will not be abandoned. He won't dump *her* – not when she's *this* good in every department!

They *deserve* to be interrupted, Hannah concludes.

Hannah walks to the front door and rings the bell. Upstairs, a light is turned on and its rays dip down the stairs and into the hall. She hears: 'Coming!' And although she knows this means *I am making my way to the door,* the word reminds her of the sex scene that she has just created – reminds her that she did not finish it. Who came first?

Toby is on the other side of the door now. 'Who the hell is it?' he calls.

'It's the Avon lady.'

'...*Hannah?*'

'Open the door, Tobe. It's as cold as Christmas out here.'

Obediently Toby opens the front door; he glances over his shoulder, up the stairs. As predicted, he wears a dressing-gown.

'Don't ask me if I know what time it is,' says Hannah. 'I know it's late.'

Toby is puzzled and petulant. The air laps at his exposed chest; he pulls his gown tighter. 'You're damn right it's late! What's got into you, Hannah?' he demands. 'You can't keep *coming* round here! You know why…'

'Yes I do know why. And this will almost certainly be the second and final time. Can I come in?'

'It's not a good idea, Han.'

'I didn't say it was. Can I?'

'*Toby? Who is it?*' Jill calls from somewhere upstairs; most likely from the boudoir, where she lounges post-orgasmically on a raft of satin pillows.

'Jesus. You've woken her up,' Toby hisses, panicky.

'Sorry. You'd better answer her.'

Toby calls, 'It's fine, babes. I'm up in a minute.'

'You never called *me* babes.'

'*Jesus*. Would you have wanted me to?'

'No. In fact, I think I would have stabbed you if you had.'

'*But who is it?*'

'It's no one!' Toby calls.

'Well thanks a bunch,' Hannah answers, feeling plump and cocky now; ready for anything; galvanized.

'Go home, Hannah. You pick your moments, I'll give you that,' he adds. 'It's too late now. Go home.' Whisper-whisper he continues, 'I'll try to call you tomorrow, okay?'

'No.'

'No what?'

'No, sir? No thank you! I'm not interested in speaking to

you tomorrow, or even right now, if I'm honest, Tobe.'

'The hell are you talking about?'

'It wasn't *you* I came here to see.'

10.

It is not the first time that Dorothy has undressed a woman, but it's the first time she has done so for nearly two decades, not counting that regretted fumble with Julia, her agent, way back when, when they'd stumbled into the mews office, in from the snow, and had been giddy on brandy and an autograph-session high. She unbuttons Sabrina's sheer lilac blouse, prepared for the tissue-stuffed bra clearly visible through the fabric (as it has been all evening). But Dorothy's memory has not finished... What had stopped them – she and Julia – on that wintry afternoon? Why *didn't* they, there in the office? Julia had kissed Dorothy's neck, as Dorothy now kisses Sabrina's. Julia had laid Dorothy on the desk (knocking a miniature Christmas tree and its tiny necklace of chocolate baubles to the floor), in the same way that Dorothy now lays Sabrina on the bed...

The light in the bedroom is curious; the bathroom light has been left on – with the extractor fan whirring and occasion-ally rattling faultily as a result – and this illumination crawls timidly into the bedroom, as does light from the lamps in the street (the curtains are open). Because of the bad light Dorothy is not alarmed at what she sees, she knows it is one of light's conjuring illusions. This is all that it *can* be, this appearance, in the quarter-light, of Sabrina on her bed, the blouse wide open like a swan's wings, and the brassiere that has been beneath it, now revealed, and to the naked eye – to Dorothy's eye – it is stuffed not with tissue paper, nor with socks, but with skin, curved skin, fatty skin – the skin of a woman's breasts. Confused but not concerned, Dorothy tipsily removes her black trousers by the side of the bed. A split second of weighted consideration later, and she pulls down her equally dark panties. Fully dressed, then, only from the waist up, Dorothy kneels onto the mattress and then straddles the pelmet miniskirt at Sabrina's waist. Then she arches her mouth to Sabrina's breasts, intending to locate Tom's flat chest, the hairs thereon…but this is not what happens. The body that Dorothy kisses is a woman's body, the breasts full if not large inside their support. Even now there is no sense of alarm; when Dorothy pulls on each cup to release the breast, she is more intrigued than anything else. Not once does Dorothy placate the strain of logicality within her system, or even attempt to; she is well aware that she's not dreaming, so what is the point of insisting that this must be a dream? This is *Sabrina*: Sabrina, not Tom. *We meet at last*: but that's not correct. Sabrina was always there, for lunch after lunch, activity after activity. They only *thought* it was Tom they were talking to.

Dorothy turns around on the bed, and presents her bottom to Sabrina's eyes, and a few seconds later, her sex to Sabrina's mouth. Inverted along one another's torsos, she licks and kisses at Sabrina's thighs, only momentarily frightened of what sex she will discover beneath the leather mini and the black tanga briefs; but then realizing that in fact it doesn't matter. As she feels Sabrina's tongue, and the slippery makeup on Sabrina's face, squirm around her upper thighs, and then the former push open the plump folds, to unroll inside her body, Dorothy fingers aside the elastic of Sabrina's underwear. Although it is too dark to see what awaits, the sharp taste is one clue, but the lips that respond to her tongue's probing are the definite proof.

V.

1.

'Melanoma. Multidrug-resistant tuberculosis. Intravesical therapy at transurethral resection of a new bladder tumour...'

'Yes, Dad.'

'High density lipoprotein cholesterol. Cardiovascular disease morbidity. Spastic duodenum. Dropsy. Diabetic retinopathy...'

'*Yes*, Dad; but I asked if you wanted–'

'Chlamydia trachomatis! Breast cancer lesions! Dropsy! Pulmonary modules. Rotator cuff disease...'

Annette sighs into her fingers; the fleshy cave of carbon monoxide that this action produces informs her that her breath reeks of alcohol. As is increasingly the case these days before a visit to see Patrick, she has paid a visit to The Globe. (She has fallen in love with the Polish barmaid's attitude problem.) She jogged there from home, along the canal path, and then she jogged back, albeit in a less determinedly straight line. She had four double vodkas in thirty minutes, and on arrival at her father's house she had been under the impression that she'd drunk enough to take his nonsensical exaggerations on the chin for today; now she knows that this estimation was miles off.

'Would you like, I said, a *cup of tea*?' Annette repeats.

But Patrick is lost again – adrift in his stories – and he sits as motionless as a mummy in his armchair. As ever, to Annette's nose, there is about the place the stench of the familiar. It has always been the same since Mum; but her mother is retreating – it seems that with each consequent visit Annette pays, her mother is less and less keen to keep her company.

Did he *really* say chlamydia? Annette wonders… and then he's off again, his pit stop completed. Splashing around in his memories.

'Vertebral artery stenosis. Hodgkin's lymphoma. Respiratory piecemeal silicitis…'

'Enough, Dad!' says Annette, screwing tight her eyes with such determination that the bags underlining them twitch with a second's discomfort.

'I've had 'em all!' Patrick roars.

'I *know*, Dad! You've *told* me! I just don't want to talk about your ailments anymore. I asked you if you fancied a *cup of tea*!'

The colour in Patrick's face has turned a worrying puce; there is no doubt of his anger from the way his head minutely shakes, although his expression is blank.

'A cup of tea, Dad,' Annette says softly; and equally as softly Patrick says as he turns away from her, 'What gives you the right?'

'The right to do what?'

'To come into our house *reeking of gin*, you selfish brat!' With the first strong motion he has made since his daughter arrived, Patrick thumps the arms of his chair, two coordinated gusts of dust and cigarette ash ascend and dissipate.

Annette is stunned. Leaving the room, on her way to the kettle, she attempts to recall the last time her old man spoke to her in this way. Unexpectedly, she recalls instead a picture of her mother, and as she fills the old-fashioned metal kettle to its brim, she reels from a bolt of mourning which clubs her – rabbit punch! – right across the rear of her skull.

The blow is all but enough to floor her; only by gripping onto the handle on the fridge-freezer door does she steady herself, but the appliance is rocked on its base. Indeed, the objects on top of the fridge-freezer rattle together – a first aid kit, a plastic drawer of objects like batteries, a tape measure, some rusty screws, some string – and a small purple bottle of cough mixture tumbles out into the air. Annette tries to catch it, but all she succeeds in doing is jabbing its progress from vertically *down* to horizontally *across*. The bottle hits the wall with what appears (to Annette) to be a negligible velocity; but it breaks anyway. Catastrophically. Gluey, stinking medicine rains all over the wallpaper; it starts to slide down, red, stickyslow, for all the world a dead ringer for blood.

Annette falls to her knees.

'What are you doing in there?' Patrick shouts. 'Breaking our owce now, is she?'

Striding away from the minor wreckage, back towards her father, Annette demands, 'Who are you *talking* to? This is getting on my nerves! "Our house." "Who's busting our house?" Who are you *talking* to, Dad?'

Patrick smiles. Unaided, he has raised himself to his feet; he seems proud of this achievement. 'There's someone I'd like you to meet again,' he announces.

2.

Movement in the hallway; Annette snaps her head towards the door.

Annette knows who is coming before this visitor is framed under the lintel: scent: it's something familiar but not quite identical to. It smells like. But it can't be.

'Hello, dear.'

'*Mum…*'

'Hello, dear.'

'Mum, I don't…' Annette shifts her gawking between her parents; her father sports the widest grin she's seen on him for an age.

'Well don't I at least get a hug?'

Annette has tears in her eyes as she springs over; emotion is trapped in her throat – she can't speak.

The embrace feels natural; it feels good; they hold it for long seconds.

'But I don't understand,' Annette is finally capable of saying. 'I thought.'

Mum is smiling: the same face, perhaps a few years younger. Hair a little thinner. Body a few pounds lighter. Not quite *right*; but very close.

Wiping tears from her cheeks, Annette asks, 'Have you been on a long journey?'

'I've only been to the shops, dear. But I forgot what I wanted, and I don't know where I've left my shopping bag. I wanted *carrots*, I know that.'

The shops were where she fell down. Poor Mum: stately, proper, and displaying her bloomers for any passerby, while a volcano erupted and roared on the left side of her brain.

'I can't think,' Annette admits.

'Then take a seat. Hello, dear,' the new arrival continues, acknowledging her husband for the first time. Creaking slightly at the hips, she bends down to kiss his spotted forehead. He has not said a dickybird. Annette's mouth gapes and puckers, like that of a landed fish.

'Would you like a cup of tea, dear?' the visitor asks Patrick, who nods his head. 'And what about you, Caitlin? Tea?'

Annette shakes her head. 'Pardon?'

'A cup of tea?'

'No. No, *what* did you call me?'

'Caitlin, of course. You'll always be Caitlin to me, dear. No matter what.'

3.

Annette hears Dorothy's voice in the hall, but for Dorothy there is no clue that Annette is in the house. When she claps eyes on Annette, having entered the front room, she is surprised and ruffled. 'I didn't know you were here. How are you keeping?' Dumb questions; inane questions. 'Hello,' she adds to the other woman in the room, the one she does not know, the one who smiles at her.

'Hello, dear.'

'Dorothy,' says Patrick, behind her, in the doorway. 'This is Justine. This is my wife.'

'Oh. I hope I'm not interrupting anything,' Dorothy offers, instinctively switching her eyes away from Justine to Annette – an evasive tactical saccade, the purity of which is spoiled only by a flush of mottled red skin that betrays her embarrassment on either earlobe.

'All my girls,' Patrick sighs contentedly; allowing gravity to claim him, he collapses backwards into his armchair. A whoosh of air from the upholstery, like a mimic of Patrick's sigh. 'Altogether.' And his fingers drift onto the packet of cigarettes on his side table; his face shows comfort, his lungs burn for their feathery toast.

Justine tells him, 'No, dear.'

The old man fingers the cigarette back into his near-depleted box. In this way Justine has managed to do what neither Annette nor Dorothy have succeeded in: getting Patrick to quit, albeit in the short-term. Justine has shown the room her strength.

Annette asks, 'Shall I make some more tea?'

'Would anyone be terribly offended if I asked if there's anything stronger on offer?' Dorothy replies. 'I've had a hell of a time recently, Patrick. Maybe Annette's said…'

'No, I haven't had time. I was going to, but this has sort of been front page news.' She nods towards her mother. 'My *Mum's* come home.' She starts crying again.

'There's champagne in the fridge, Doll,' says Patrick. 'Four glasses, eh?'

'Champagne? You knew this was coming, didn't you, Patrick?'

'Yes. I've waited for this reconciliation for a long time.'

4.

A beautiful journey. A mystical experience.

Justine mentions neither of these possibilities. In her telling she is ultramundane and unflappable. Because nothing happened – in her world – nothing happened but death and resurrection. No great distinction between this and choosing between two brands of bread, or at least, this is how she makes it sound. From Justine's adumbrated account of the afterlife, you would think that she has been to the hairdresser for a blue rinse or something.

This is Dorothy's interpretation of the account. She is partly envious of the fact that Justine has come back at all – and more than a little concerned at how the personal dynamics are going to change. Right off the bat, Dorothy might well deduce that her place in Patrick's heart was never fixed with nails, only with Blu-Tak. This seems clear; but the disappointment this results in takes Dorothy by surprise. It's not as if she's exactly been faithful to Patrick, after all; she wonders about the density and breadth of her stung pride as Justine potters on, licking her lips every other sentence. Being ousted by the older woman is one thing; being ousted by an older woman who's been *dead and back* is a curious one to unpick.

More specifically (and more painfully) Dorothy is envious of the journey that Justine has taken. She wishes she'd held that same ticket… but perhaps she did. Or rather, a similar ticket to a different destination. An *alternative* land of the dead; a rural patch; how many of these pockets of the dead could there be? One for everyone? A pasture, a house, a conurbation, tailor-made to dredge up and expose that individual's darkest terrors?

Well, Justine has not faced her darkest terrors. On the contrary, she has become more animated in her telling. 'I thought I was young again,' she says. 'I was the full match – not the match after it's struck.' Warily she looks around her audience. Dorothy nods her head, indicating that she understands. 'And I had all this *energy*!' Justine announces. 'Like having a transplant…' Now *Patrick* nods his head with understanding. 'It was like a new me!' And Justine tongues at a helping of dried spittle at the corner of her mouth.

Is that a reference to me? Dorothy asks herself. Is she having a go?

'Was there a gap between then and now?' asks Annette; and if no one else can predict the answer to this question, Dorothy can – or so she will later believe.

Justine answers: 'No, not really, dear.'

Is she bluffing? Dorothy thinks suddenly. What if she's making it all up! How would we disprove her story? But why would she?

'Can you tell us,' says Dorothy, 'what you saw and heard. And felt. I mean in detail.'

In the two seconds that follow the request, Dorothy senses a tightening in the room's air. Has she committed an indescribable *faux pas*?

'That's a lot of information, dear,' says Justine. 'Let me see, what can I tell you as you're so curious. Where do I *start*?'

'I'm sorry if I sound pushy,' Dorothy adds. 'It's just, I'm fascinated.'

'Of course you are… Dorothy. Who wouldn't be curious in your position?' Her smile (to Dorothy at least) appears guarded and fake.

What's that supposed to mean? *In your position.* What's *my* position? My position as Patrick's bed-pal? Well pardon me, sweetheart; we kind of thought, as you were busy being dead in the ground and all that…

No, don't play games, Dolly. She knows something. Even if it's not what you think it might be – she knows more than *you* do. She knows something *you* need to know. Even if she's lying.

'Aren't we supposed to see lights?' Justine asks. 'I thought we're supposed to see lights, but I didn't. There was a colour I haven't seen before. There were noises I've never *heard* before. There were smells…'

You've never smelt before, Dorothy thinks.

'That's right, dear,' Justine tells her abruptly, although Dorothy has said nothing aloud. The confirmation appears to perplex both women.

'Right about what?' Annette asks – Annette who hears only words spoken, Dorothy realizes with a start. Annette who has not just read her dead mother's mind…

'I've never smelt before, dear,' Justine resumes. 'So I don't know how to compare it to anything I left behind. It was the strangest dream.'

A sweat has broken on Dorothy's forehead; she pools all her effort of will into calming down her heart, repeating like a mantra: *it was just a fluke, it was just a fluke.*

The problem is, to Dorothy it didn't feel like a fluke; it felt like Justine heard Dorothy's words as she thought them. So not so much mind-*reading* as mind-listening.

'It was painless and still,' Annette says – Dorothy tunes back into the conversation – and she pauses to sip champagne from the flute she holds in her left hand. Her right hand is in Patrick's grip. Patrick remains in his favourite chair.

Fire rises in Dorothy's belly. She has to know one way or the other. She sits up straight, enunciating the following words clearly in her mind.

What's your favourite colour?

'...the nice sleep,' says Justine. '...so nice I didn't even know I wanted to be home. I'm so sorry...' She turns her torso slightly to her right, to address a point directly to her husband. '...I'm rather afraid I forgot you both. But it was nothing to do with anything–' She turns to Annette; Annette hangs on her mother's every word. 'Nothing to do with anything *here*. It's simply what dying *does* to you. It robs you of *memories*.' Justine scowls; she stands up. 'Oh I must pay a visit – all that tea, I expect!'

Halting at the door, Justine sends Dorothy a smile that swims through the air between them. '*Yellow*, dear,' is all she adds.

5.

Pleading a headache that is not entirely false, Dorothy leaves Patrick's house minutes later... leaves Patrick *and Justine's* house, to be accurate.

How are they going to explain it to the neighbours? This is the question that's got her going. She is one street from the main road before she doubles at the waist. A swamp of pre-digested biscuits and champagne clogs her gullet; the blockage burps; to the accompaniment of a loud retching sound she deposits this lunch on the pavement, then recoils from the spattering as if from another's excrement. She walks away briskly. If fortune's on her side, no one saw that.

Her withdrawal from Patrick's house has the mental texture of an escape. Not only is she lucky to have got out of there, she imagines, she is lucky to be alive.

This is how it feels to Dorothy.

When rain begins to tip down, Dorothy veers off her chosen path that will take her more directly to Grovebury Road, and she ducks to the right, crossing the library car park with her legs at full stride but her mood composed of an imperturbability. If anything, she is grateful for the downpour – for the distraction it brings. She decides to wait out the storm in the library's lobby.

Plenty of other people have had the same idea. The library doors slide open as Dorothy draws near, revealing a crowd of shelterers in various degrees of dampness, wetness and virtual saturation.

6.

When she tries to scream, a freak gust buckets rain into the back of her throat. As a result, instead of screaming she is close to gagging. No sound emerges; her mouth is frozen, her tongue a dead stump.

She tries to turn away from the villagers, the idea being to run – to sprint as fast as her heavy legs will allow – but this intention is summarily hampered too, by the rain. The rain becoming thick as a wall; with little momentum behind her flight, Dorothy leans into something not quite solid, but something gelatinous enough to kill any acceleration she might muster.

Panicking, shaky, Dorothy is as stuck in the deluge as an insect is in amber; and this trap lasts for a good few breathless seconds, with Dorothy scarcely able to remember her own name, let alone consider any alternative escape route...

Slowly she turns around to face the people in the library lobby. As sure as she is of the fact that this can't be happening, she is certain emphatically that it is.

She remembers their smiles. She remembers their bad teeth. She remembers how they held her down on the table in the hall, and the idiot boy – here he is now, being ushered by the others to the front of the congregation, his fingers already toying at his clothed groin – the idiot boy who tried to penetrate her shoulder with his erection. And Lord! how that shoulder throbs now! Wincing and in pain, Dorothy feels pressure to her back.

Dorothy is ushered from the lobby into the main library. She is prodded towards the stands displaying New Fiction. Crammed to a groaning point, these shelves hold nothing but copies of *Nutcracker Island*. There are more on the display shelves than actually sold.

Then Dorothy is hassled along to the staircase. She doesn't speak.

They don't stop at the first floor – music and non-fiction. The second floor – the theatre – is to be their destination. There is no higher storey to visit.

The white woman and the black woman support Dorothy through the ticket sale area (there's no one on duty) and into the auditorium proper.

Dorothy is sat on the front row.

The noise behind her – the sounds of people finding their seats – represents little more than a murmur. No one speaks – in any language.

The large screen flickers into life and the house lights dim.

7.

Dorothy is not surprised to see that she is the star of the show.

What *does* surprise her is that the film is so humdrum. Forced to predict the content of what's to follow, Dorothy has pictured a re-run of the rape scene in the European hills: her starring role. But no; at least, not yet, and plenty of time has passed. She hasn't dared look at her watch so she has no clue *how much* time, but it feels like in excess of thirty minutes. Of what?

Of randomly shuffled scenes from Dorothy's life. And that's all. Here she is in a childhood outfit of burgundy suede and Chantilly lace (collar, hem and wrists). She remembers that purple dress with a strange affection, though she'd hated it at the time. Or not the *dress* exactly; it was more that she'd hated the frequency of how often she had to wear it, every single time that she and her mother had visited Uncle Paddy and Auntie Em. (She hasn't thought of those two for decades.) And now, in the film, Dorothy the younger is complaining to her mother that she (Mother) is *pulling my ponytail too tight... OW!*

Stop bellyaching, Dorothy!

Yes, Mum.

And stand STILL while I –

In the auditorium, looking up at the big screen, Dorothy smiles in spite of everything. It's rare that she misses her mother, but she wouldn't be human without a pang or two of yearning from time to time. Now is one of those occasions. However, the emotion is short-lived. The scene changes.

There are lots of childhood and adolescence reminiscences, some flashing past so swiftly that they are little more than snapshots. The family dog, Bruno, who had died after being run over; ballet lessons; violin recitals – oh Lord, how the nerves had threatened to pulverize everything, every note that her mother had coerced her into learning, perfecting – how she'd strangled every pip of pleasure from the act of picking up an instrument.

I'm not going to be the best, Mum, the screen-Dorothy says.

Yes you ARE. I INSIST!

'Yes, Mum,' Dorothy mouths in the darkness. Becoming sad by what she's seeing, she tries to discern some form or sequence to the compilation; try as she might, though, nothing is obvious. What now? School, work, writing, research, well at least this has some sort of logical order, but then the pattern is obliterated, she is taken back to a stage – a physical stage – on which she is a lone child in a spotlight, attempting to give an audience a bowdlerized snippet from Tchaikovsky's *Serenade for Strings*.

In her purple suede dress. With the Chantilly lace cuffs... As the screen-Dorothy grimaces and searches for a note to rely on, the theatre-Dorothy shifts her seated position, suddenly uncomfortable, though she has no idea why.

Cut to the camp in the Lubuski Region, on the border between Poland and Germany, where she'd taught; her relationship with Ian; the day she'd bid farewell and hunted down a bus... *Oh no*. This memory is as close to the events on the hill with the face as she'd come so far. Dorothy is hot under the collar. When she reaches for her neck she can almost feel that Chantilly lace again.

Was I never happy? Dorothy wonders.

Something lurches in Dorothy's metabolism, a *mal-de-mer* sensation. A hard round rock is in her stomach; she feels sick.

She's in an orchestra, panicked into full-blown paralysis. She is lost in Elgar's *Falstaff*; it's too noisy and she can't remember where to put her fingers...fingers... On the screen the film obediently closes in on the little girl's hands, the lace at her wrists; and now, mid-performance, she drops the bow and the violin. She starts crying, standing there among her more talented peers.

She whispers 'Help me' and so does Dorothy in the theatre. The older Dorothy feels sicker than ever.

What *happened* to that suede dress? she asks her brain. Did I really grow out of it?

Here, on the screen, is the dress, and the fire that's about to consume it. The dress in the grip of Uncle Paddy, in the backyard. He hadn't known that Dorothy was watching from an upstairs window...the bathroom window, that was it.

Why did he burn my dress? Dorothy tries to remember. *I am standing with one foot on the edge of the bath, one foot in the sink, and I'm looking out of the window, watching Uncle Paddy throw my dress onto the small bonfire he's made near the patio. So what was I wearing? What did I wear to go home again?*

She looks out from the orchestra, past the stare of Mr Milgram, which manages to combine a withering quality with sympathetic tenderness and concern, and into the faces of the first three rows. In the third row, there is Mum, Uncle Paddy, Auntie Em; they all look worried. But it's too late, she has dropped her expensive instrument, she won't play again, neverever…and Paddy *grins*. He grins at her, filth made flesh – *what's he got to look so pleased with himself?* – and Dorothy watches his face age before her. He gets older, older, though even then he was no spring chicken. The sickness has reached Dorothy's throat; her body tells her – her *adult* body tells her – that she is close to making a connection.

Find it, Dolly.

'Can't you find it, Dolly Doo-Doo?' says Auntie Em, her voice loud above the Elgar. 'Perhaps you need snoozybubbeyes.'

No I don't need snoozybubbeyes.

Uncle Paddy's skin drops below the jawline; his hair greys and whitens, falls out; he grows a moustache, it whitens, too; his teeth shrink with wear, and yellow… and she recognizes him in the wink of an eye – *his* eye; winking at her, a *child*… and it was Paddy who *took off my suede dress. Always the same dress. His Favourite. And Auntie Em and Paddy – they. They. And Mum knew, she knew – she took me there in that dress, how many times, and I know this man.*

There is little in Dorothy's stomach to fetch up – to 'cat up', Auntie Em had called it – but her strangled sounds of regurgitation are nonetheless resonant. Leaning forward, Dorothy deposits a puddle of foul-smelling drool onto her shoes, as on the screen her early tormentor makes his final metamorphosis into the man whose bed Dorothy has shared. She can even hear his triumphant refrain: *I'm 'undred and four you know!*

Uncle Paddy is Patrick, Annette's father.

And he has had sex with Dorothy at both ends of her life

to date.

It takes Dorothy a minute to recover from the shock, for her heartbeat to slow down. By the time she opens her eyes, she is alone in the theatre, or as far as she is able to tell she is alone. The lights are off; so is the film. The screen is as grey as a seal, and Dorothy stands unsteadily. Taking a deep inhalation, she walks towards the door with the green light above it.

The foyer is loud with brightness. Dorothy steps out, yawning and feeling ill. Directly in front of her is the Ladies'. Maybe she should wash up; at the very least dry her eyes. As she steps towards the door, it opens; a middle-aged woman exits the toilet and says, 'Sorry, was it tickets?'

'…Pardon me?'

'Did you want to book tickets for a show?' the employee elucidates, returning to her desk and her computer and talking to Dorothy over her shoulder.

'No thanks. I uh. I just came in to get out of the rain,' Dorothy explains.

'Oh, has it been raining?'

'Yes, Just a little bit… Were there other people up here a minute ago?'

'No, it's been very quiet. Have you lost someone?' The saleswoman sits down.

Dorothy smiles crazily. 'In a manner of speaking,' she admits.

8.

She doesn't walk directly home; the thought of returning to her walls and to solitude is repugnant. Instead of turning left out of the library and embarking on the ten-minute stroll back to the flat, she turns right and heads onto the High Street, reading anger in the clouds. Though the intensity of the downpour has lessened, the intensity of her thoughts and memories has not. Her memories flow freely now, vivid and unstoppable. It's as if she has drilled into an oilwell, she thinks, what gushes up is as black as sin and its spray coats everything and everyone around. Very soon she is wet again, not just with rain but with the perspiration that these memories prick from her body. She feels oily, her clothes are heavy; but there is (she can't deny it) a sense of freedom to be had, if she wants to capture it. A sense of something lost, now refound; or rather, something she'd forgotten was lost, now newly rediscovered.

The market traders have had a miserable time. It's been too rainy for people to browse the stalls on either side of the road; equally, however, it's been too wet for the traders to dismantle, pack up their wares, and go home. A forlorn bunch they look, Dorothy thinks; on a whim she stops at a stall selling anoraks, and fishes in her purse for sufficient small change to purchase an umbrella. Although she knows it to be of inferior quality, it will last her at least a few storms, and it'll be good to be under its turquoise-coloured protection.

She has no idea where to go; for the moment she is content to explore her shock and simply amble in the downpour, the pavement hers and hers alone. No one else is foolish enough to be out walking, and it's their loss, Dorothy opines. Walking in the rain is good for the thought processes. She dictates some of these directly to the stenographer that all writers keep shackled up in their heads.

My uncle is Patrick (she writes). *Or Patrick is my uncle. But we only called him 'Uncle' – there is no bloodline – it was a way my mum had of making me trust him and Auntie Em… who wasn't a real auntie either. So who was she?*

I haven't thought about either of them for over twenty years, I don't think. Maybe longer! Repression's been good for my soul… or has it?

The air in front of Dorothy is murky with rain, but the air behind her, figuratively speaking, is pellucid, clear as day. She knows what Patrick did to her when she was a child, but the right question might be: *Does he?* Does *Patrick* remember?

At the end of the High Street, near where the buses stop and pick up, Dorothy buys a piece of fresh mackerel from the fish van. The vendor informs her that she's the first customer he's had in two hours; his thanks are fulsome.

Before long Dorothy is at the canal; she's decided to take the long walk home. She will turn left and follow the sludgy green water south, as far as the next bridge, which is the one that leads on to the other end of Grovebury Road from the end where her flat is. The walk'll do her good; and besides, she hasn't been here for an age.

Ducks are on this near side, their heads curled into their feathers for protection. Under her new umbrella Dorothy watches them, the mother ducks and their young, and wishes that *she* had feathers and that feathers were all you needed for protection.

Feathers wouldn't have protected ME! Not if my own mother knew what was happening.

There were other adults, as well. Patrick and 'Em', yes; but there were others there too, sometimes. Deliberately hurting a child. She can't remember their faces, but she can remember their fingers, their mouths: on her skin, or pushing solidified fire inside her body… Some watched. They didn't participate.

And I wasn't the only child there either. Sometimes there were other children.

Where did it happen?

'Are you all right, love?' a voice asks to Dorothy's left.

Dorothy is pulled from her trance. She slaps on her best smile and answers, 'I'm fine, thank you.'

The man is about her age, simply dressed, holding up a

black umbrella in one hand; in the other is his dog's lead. An aged spaniel at the other end of it is champing to get home.

'I see you crying, that's all. Are you lost?' the man continues.

'No, I've just had some bad news,' Dorothy answers, 'about my mother.'

The worst news, really. Thank God the woman's dead so that she doesn't have to discover her daughter's disgust and disappointment.

The Samaritan doesn't know what to do with this. 'If you're sure.'

'I'm fine. But thank you for your concern.'

The man chuckles. 'Nice weather for ducks, eh? Come on, Pixie, let's get you home.'

Dorothy takes a few strides after owner and pet; but something nags at the back of her mind. Something she's missing; something about this canal, perhaps, a matter concerning this very stretch of moss-hued water... What *is* it? About a mile behind her back was where James fought the bully-boy Wolfe, with Kolko's intervention; further back still, further north, was where Tom and Roy used the canal path as a route to reach Amelior Anderson's house in Stoke Hammond, on the night they saw Kolko 'murder' her. And of course, just further on from James's fight with Wolfe is The Globe, where Annette would meet James's mother, Sal.

It's the middle of these options – it's something about Tom and Roy's visit to Mrs A – that sticks in Dorothy's craw.

Stoke Hammond.

Dorothy repeats the words silently, yearning for clarity – for epiphany. Nothing happens. The words are familiar, of course – she has lived in this general area for most of her life – but no specific resonance is attached.

VI.

1.

'We were wondering if you intended to join us,' a voice says into Sam's ear.

Sam squeezes her eyes in the direction of the display panel on the telephone, as if attempting to juice the figures dry of more meaning.

5283, the panel reads: an internal line call. Someone from within the company; but Sam cannot place the voice.

'Join you?' she stalls.

'Yeah, very funny, Sam. Come on, they're waiting for you.'

A bluff is required.

'I got held up,' Sam answers. 'What room are we in?'

'Four-oh-one. Quick.'

'Where are you calling from?'

'Fourth floor kitchen. I'm making them *yet another* cup of tea. They're not best pleased, Sam. Your show had better be the bollocks. No pressure.'

Her caller's words – her *female* caller's words – scrape. Deducing from the caller's use of the word *show* that she, Sam, is expected to deliver some kind of presentation is enough to lift her temperature two or three degrees.

Quietly she gathers together the facts – as though assembling ingredients for a recipe. Most apparently she is currently late for a meeting of some description; she is expected to perform something for people who have not been named.

The lapse in memory is frightening – but probably no more so than any of the other dozen such lapses that occur on a daily basis these days. Not only can Sam not recall her journey to work this morning, she can't remember what she's done since she got here. What time is it, in fact? While rubbing her right wrist, where an expensive watch should lie but is not in place, Sam knocks the desk with her left knee. The resulting vibration is ample to shake the mouse on its pad on the surface; her computer screen blooms into colourful life as the screensaver dissolves. Words on white – a document of some description, one that Sam has no recollection of opening, let alone working on – is behind the glass for her to read; but instead of doing so, she eyeballs the digital clock in the lower right corner. 11:15. So the meeting started at eleven? No; it was *due* to start at eleven, Sam infers.

Try not to panic, she hears.

Easy for you to say! *You* don't have to wing a presentation in ten seconds' time.

You can do it. I believe in you. Like you believe in me.

And this is one voice that Sam *does* recognize: it has been with her – *within* her – for weeks now. Oddly soothing it's become, now that she's got used to it.

The thief's voice, of course; Hana's voice. With a curiously anaesthetic effect in its every word, even when it is heavy-breathing platitudes of offensive blandness.

Sam opens her online calendar at the appointment set for today at eleven. The entry is all in initials: 'TEMPO RECON? ST, JS, DM. ST TO PRESENT.'

Well, I am ST.

Sam is sure of this much at least. Sam Twyford. Samantha Twyford nee Hamilton. 'That's me!' she whispers harshly.

A voice to her right answers, 'Pardon?'

'Thinking aloud.' Sam knows this colleague, sat at his own desk, by appearance; that's as far as she can go. The colleague returns his attention to his own screen.

Sam cuts 'TEMPO RECON' from her diary and pastes it

into the search engine. A dozen or so pages crammed with sug-
gestions are returned to her to select from.

'Fuck,' Sam says.

'What's the matter?' the same colleague asks, standing up
for the ostensible purpose of cracking his knuckles.

Deciding on the spur of the moment on a policy of honesty, Sam says, 'I'm losing my fucking marbles – that's what's the
matter, babe.'

'It's been funny all morning,' the man tells her, now picking
up a ledger which he tucks into his left oxter.

The phone on the man's desk chirrups; the guy reaches for
it, while Sam is immobilized by what he's said – she stares at the
side of his head as if he's announced his undying love, bowed
down barebacked at her knees, waiting to be flogged.

It's been funny all morning –

('Jim Dwyer,' the man identifies himself into the telephone;
a part of Sam's memory receives the words with gratitude – a
thankfulness for their now-jogged familiarity.)

funny all morning…

Has Jim felt it too? The amnesia; the silent plague of weird-
ness; the *ennui*…

'Yeah, I'm heading offsite… Only Dunstable; gotta be
there for twelve… Got it in my arms right now, no worries. You
thought I'd forget to *bring* it?' Jim laughs. 'Well then! *Ciao*! Later,
potater.'

…funny all morning…

'What?' Jim asks, continuing with a spot of laughter, but it
sounds forced, strained. 'Why are you looking at me like that?'

'You said funny all morning,' Sam reminds hm. 'You too?
The whole memory thing?'

'Could be, I suppose.' Jim shrugs. He clicks on the end of a
ballpoint and tests its ink flow on some paper on his desk. 'They

never really tell you, do they?'

Sam smiles. 'No, they don't, Jim,' she continues with beaming, cordial, formidable *jouissance*. By chance, through utter blind fluke, she has discovered this man *who comprehends*; who knows what she goes through, day after day – the solitude of the irreparable amnesiac...

Oh, perhaps he's different, of course; he might not be, and his details might not be, *exactly* precisely the same (his reference, for example, to a 'they' has Sam baffled); but at least there is a similarity, however ambiguous – a conflation, a synchronicity; a chance.

'We're just a job, aren't we?' Jim shrugs again. He holds up the pen. 'Gotta scoot. Lunch meeting at The Old Palace Lodge.'

'Just a job?'

'Basically. Don't you think? To them we are. Don't think I've ever met one, have you?'

'I don't know. Do you know where they live?'

Jim laughs. 'Fifth floor. How long have you been here you don't even know where their office is? Sort of proves my point, really... Weren't you doing a presentation about now?'

Sam stands up. No traces of a smile remain etched into her features; on the contrary, she has a face like thunder and blue murder combined.

'Who the hell are you talking about, Jim?'

'The I.T. guys. Why, who are *you* talking about?'

'I don't – Memory thing, you said.' Sam sounds desperate, especially to her own ears.

'I said it *might* be the memory. They didn't explain it; they just fixed it when it was going too slow, earlier on.'

'Fixed what?' Sam demands, but the answer has sprung fully formed into her head, no sooner than the words pass her lips. 'The computer,' she adds.

'Yeah of course.' Jim looks nonplussed and uncomfortable.

'What did you think I meant? You said fuck, I thought you were having the same problems I had before.'

Demoralized, challenged and beaten, Sam nods her head. 'It's been funny all morning,' she repeats softly.

This man is no *ally*; he is nothing in her plight – neither salt nor sugar on her plate. A semantic misunderstanding: this is all it has been.

Jim exits the office, a wary expression on his face.

Sam says it once more: '*Fuck.*'

A telephone rings, and it takes Sam seconds to understand that it's her own. Calling her again. Checking up. *Where are you?* People waiting. Presentation.

Sam wipes her brow (inefficiently) on the back of an envelope. As swiftly as possible she dons her coat; she picks up her handbag; and she is all set to leave, to sneak out down the back stairs, avoiding the lift, when the condition of courtesy halts her. A word is needed; surely a word of explanation is the least that her workmates can expect. She tarries a few seconds, a metre from her desk, then she takes the two steps back to her chair. In big block caps on the same envelope she's just used she prints:

SICK. GOING HOME. SORRY.
S X

Which she leaves on her keyboard, paying notice to the fact that she does not identify with her own handwriting. It's not hers. It can't be, or she'd recognize it.

A few minutes later Sam tastes the late-morning drizzle in the charcoal-and-sepia air. The day is spoiling for a storm; something big is brewing up.

Sam is not surprised to find the man sitting in the passenger seat of her car, listening to Classic FM. After all, it's where she left the man to wait for her a few hours earlier.

'Where to?' she asks him, buckling her safety belt and frowning.

'Towards the rain,' Hana answers, and turns off the radio.

2.

'You know I'm married, don't you? I wouldn't like there to be any confusion on this point.'

He has taken off his shirt. To her surprise he wears a white vest underneath it, it flatters his physique; it shows off his slim muscles nicely, and the contrast of white on his dark skin is erotic – erotic to the extent that it increases her nerves; it doesn't calm her. The fact that she wants him so much is more than mildly alarming, her expression says so. Evidently there is a matter that Sam feels the urge to explore.

'I mean, not *actually* married. We're divorced; but I think of us as married, sometimes. It wasn't long, there's still contact. Vicious contact admittedly. On his part... Christ. I'm not doing very well here, am I?' She speaks quickly, as if she's been caught out; caught doing something she shouldn't be doing.

The thief smiles. Wordlessly he toys with the belt through the loops on her skirt; the belt falls open. Embracing her, Hana kisses Sam's left temple; then he draws his tongue along her hairline, left to right across her forehead.

'I know I come across as brash – and blasé. Overexperienced.' Sam arches her head back on her neck; she clings to his eyesight. 'But the fact of it is, babe – I've always been a bit nervous around men. I'm a little rusty, to tell you the truth.'

The thief is still smiling. By reaching behind Sam's back he has unhooked a button; now pulls down the skirt zip, slides his fingers into the limited space between the skirt's material and that of her black panties.

Not a word does he offer. Not a word has he offered since they arrived at The King's Reign Hotel. Nothing. Unblinking he watched as Sam tapped in her credit card PIN…

Sam laughs. 'You're the silent lover type, are you? I didn't think you'd be–' Twittishly, skittishly, she shakes her head like a colt and mutters, 'Shut up, Sam.' With a wiggle of her backside, she assists Hana in his project to push her skirt to the carpet.

'You are quite, quite beautiful,' Hana states. 'This show will be a wonder.'

'Thank you, Hana.' Sam twists her head to one side and stares straight into the lens. 'I really wasn't expecting the camera,' she adds. 'Maybe that's why I'm jumpy: I've never done it for the camera before.'

'There's a first time for everything, Sam.' Hana palms his hands into the rear of his lover's underwear.

'Then again,' Sam gabbles, 'this was always going to be one of the strangest seductions, wasn't it? Take that as a compliment.'

'I shall. I wanted to keep a record of our time together.'

'But only you will see it, right?'

'Of course, Sam. Who else?'

Sam declines to answer.

'This show will be a wonder,' Hana repeats, then his face breaks open – his grin is a wonder itself – and, removing his hands from Sam's panties, he pushes her shoulders; with a shriek she falls backwards onto the bed, and bounces on lousy springs. Hana removes his vest with one movement; he drops his slacks and steps to the edge of the bed, his erection beating time in his briefs.

'Give me that,' says Sam. She sits up and removes Hana's briefs; he kicks them aside. Sam nuzzles his depilated scrotum with her tongue. Hana combs his fingers through her hair, rear-ranging her do into punky spikes. Sam grips and pumps on his shaft, teasing him with sips to his glans. She keeps him waiting. Minutes later, when she absorbs half his length into her throat, he hums appreciatively; she spends a long time slobbering on what fills her mouth, making noises of her own, before lying back suddenly and flicking off her panties and tossing them in the direction of the tea-making facilities. Yawning open her legs, she smiles for the camera using both of her pairs of lips: a perfectly framed shot.

'Is it true,' says Sam, 'that Arab men don't lick pussy?'

Hana masturbates for a few strokes, an expression of puzzlement on his face. 'I'm afraid I don't understand the question,' he admits.

Sam fingers her lower grin and explains. 'Your face. Right here. I want to feel your tongue inside me.'

'Soon.' Hana lies down on top of Sam, kissing her neck and angling his erection into her heat. His movements are anxious and swift.

'Slow down, babe. No rush,' Sam tells him; but her words are no more than ice in fire. If anything, they spur Hana on to a yet swifter rhythm. Besides his velocity, his thrusts are powerful. 'Try not to come,' Sam whispers in his ear. 'Go slow for me, babe.'

Hana speeds up. It is to the accompaniment of this ragged pace that the thief now raises his hands to Sam's throat, this movement as fast as his lovemaking. Sam is too surprised to block him. His fingers pinch into her neck; his weight falls into his grip for extra purchase. Sam thrashes, an entirely new performance for the camera. She tries to scream; she tries to kick – but Hana's body is between her legs. With her head whipping wildly from side to side, she does not react visibly to the spittle that Hana projects onto her features. Instead she produces some of her own, a bubble of it that pops from her right nostril.

Most of this is captured by the camera in the corner of the

room. Some of it is obscured by the muscles on Hana's back, or by his head when he is forced to adjust his position to stay atop his victim. What it easily records is the diminution in physical energy expenditure, the weakening of Sam's tortured cries. Little by little she ceases her complaints; her exertions are drowned by the waves of Hana's counterviolence.

Her eyes are bloodshot red by the time that Hana rolls off her. He lies by her side, panting and sweaty. Almost tenderly he takes hold of Sam's left wrist and curls her fingers around his penis; tightens her grip. Then he fucks her dead hand until he boils over onto her expensive wristwatch.

He stands up and approaches the camera, its red light blinking.

VII.

1.

Dorothy waves from the postbox down the road; from such a distance I can just about make out that it's her. I stand in the rain, waiting. She takes a long time to swim nearer; the light is fading fast and she seems to lose clarity even as she approaches.

'What've you got there?' she says.

I hold up the bag. 'Need you ask?'

The bottles I've bought clink together as we climb the stairs to my flat.

In my kitchen, while Dorothy makes herself comfortable in my chair, I say, 'Where would you like to start? Red or white?'

'Anything wet,' is Dorothy's reply.

I stick the white in the freezer and pour out two glasses of red. 'Shall I put the heating on?'

'I'm fine.' Dorothy sucks down half the glass in a gulp, giving the lie, I believe, to her statement.

'We should probably get out of these wet things at least. Do you want a towel and my dressing-gown?'

'No, I'm fine, Tom. I need to tell you about my day, but let's have some peace – just for ten minutes, okay?'

'Yeah that's fine. What about *eine kleine nachtmusik*?'

Dorothy exhales harshly; the sound makes me think she's mad at me, but her torments are internal.

'You have no idea how close to an exposed wound that question is, Tom.'

She looks up; she sees my puzzled expression, and adds, 'Just a few minutes. Let me enjoy this scooter fuel they've suckered you into buying.'

'Fine. I'm putting some music on anyway.' I choose some early Springsteen, key it up; the wine is smelly with chemicals, unless it's my saturated clothes. It's like something that Sam would drink and then bunch her fingers together in appreciation.

I wait. Dorothy's agenda is off-kilter, and in the end it's only a five-minute gap that's required before she opens her account.

'I've met Patrick's dead wife, Justine. But she's not the one who used to abuse me.'

'I'm all ears,' I sigh into my glass.

2.

What with interruptions for tears and refills, it takes Dorothy the better part of an hour to recount her story. In the room the dusty dry smell from the heater combats the whiff of our damp clothes. I open the balcony doors.

'What are you doing?' Dorothy asks.

'We need some fresh air.'

It feels enlivening to stand on my balcony, unprotected from the rain for half a minute... In the house across the car park, where Caitlin used to live, I can see the family preparing for dinner. The couple's little boys carry cutlery from the kitchen to the table near their back window, then return for a pat on the head from their father. It seems happy and safe. Steam rises from pots that the lady of the house stirs. Quizzically she sips at the end of a wooden spoon, testing the sauce; then she offers the spoon, loaded end first, to her husband or partner, and he takes the gift into his mouth without handling the instrument and expresses his satisfaction with a nod and a pleased smile.

I step back into the flat. I am alarmed that Dorothy is not in the chair where I left her, and her glass is not on the coffee table or the bookshelf... It isn't panic that reaches for me – not panic exactly – but the immediate interpretation I have is that she wasn't here in the first place. I have been drinking alone, as usual; imagining a conversation with Dorothy.

Then my toilet flushes.

Dorothy comes back into my lounge wearing a shirt that I know I discarded on to the to-be-washed pile in my bathroom. Her bare legs make me wonder if she's kept her underwear on. She rubs at her hair with one of my towels.

'I was getting cold with the doors open,' she says. 'You don't mind, do you?'

'You could have had a clean one.'

'It smells of you. It's fine.' Dorothy sits back down in my favourite chair. 'Besides,' she adds, '*what* clean ones?'

'...Shouldn't we get Annette away from Patrick and her ghost-mum?'

'I'm sure we should, but she won't come. You should have seen the gleam in her eyes, Tom – it's all she ever wanted, to see her mum again.' She picks her glass up from the chair-tread on which it has been perched all along, and I fill the second's silence.

'Do you want a refill?'

'Do you think I might have a bath? I'm not keen on going home.'

The sound of water in the pipes; the satisfying first drops into my tub... Dorothy is able to move through my flat with the grace of a ghost.

'Do you think she's in danger?' she asks, directly behind my shoulder.

'No less than you were, surely.'

'But she's an adult now.'

I hand Dorothy her refilled glass and say, 'That tells me a lot, Dolly. You don't doubt for one second he did it to her too. Do you?'

She sips and shrugs. 'How can I? I mean, *something* turned

her from Caitlin to Annette. Even her mother called her Caitlin when I was there.'

Sitting down on my sofa, I put my feet on the coffee table. They're sore from all the walking I've done recently.

'Do you want to hear a *really* fanciful one?' I ask Dorothy.

'He killed Caitlin. Patrick, I mean. He killed his daughter and Annette is the – the reincarnation, or whatever we wanna call it. Fathers with psychopathic sexual leanings show a marked predilection for anal rape, as opposed to vaginal; and the murder of a child is sometimes a punishment – not for the victim, but for the father himself. He punishes himself by getting rid of the thing he uses for pleasure and for control. In this case, a daughter.'

'In *this* case, Tom – our friend Annette,' Dorothy corrects me.

'*Your* friend Annette,' I correct *her*.

She lets it go. 'Where did you learn that?' she asks.

'I work in a prison, remember. There are plenty of sex criminals in there.'

'Well… Okay. I can't believe I'm agreeing to it, but what choice do we have? He killed Caitlin. He arrived at some deal that brings her back as Annette, sins forgiven – or forgotten. Is that roughly what you're saying?'

'I suppose I am, yes. But she made it to adulthood as Caitlin, and she had two boys. She was broke and she did dodgy glamour modelling for on-your-toes cash. And I swear – in *my* memory she flipped her lid, killed her boys with an axe, and went to prison. I even visited her, once or twice. But am I painting her in a prison based on what I've seen *working* in a prison? Because Patrick said…'

'You stopped her killing the kids.'

'So why can't I remember *that*? Would be nice to remember the good bits every now and then, wouldn't it?'

Dorothy nods her head and gets up to turn off the bath-water. On her way back she stops on the threshold, a puzzled expression on her face. 'When did you last have steam in here?' she asks.

'I don't know. Yonks. I'm trying not to use hot water unless I need to.'

'Whyever not?'

'To save costs. The college is not paying me, remember.'

'Well, that would certainly explain the state of your wine-glasses – not that I'm complaining, before you snap.'

'What are you getting at?'

'If you write something in the steam on a mirror, the next time it steams up the writing's still there.'

'What's written on my mirror?'

'"My dad's coming home." Are you telling me you haven't cleaned this mirror since James tried to kill himself?'

'Sabrina cleans the mirrors. That's *her* job…Anyway, it might've been me wrote that.'

'And why would you have done that?' Dorothy asks.

'I miss mine as much as he misses his. I might've done it when I was cabbaged. So what about it? Kolko convinced him his dad would return – we already know that. Which, according to Roy, has happened. So maybe Kolko's not such a Judas after all. Am I missing your point?'

Dorothy frowns. 'I'm not actually sure yet.' She chews her lip. 'The police were here, weren't they? Scene of the crime and all that.'

'…So?'

'Well, didn't they do their checks on things like this?'

'How the hell should I know, Dolly? They did their stuff. They didn't exactly walk me through the proceedings.' Standing up again, I slip into the kitchen for yet another top-up, that one having gone down like shit off an oily seabird. 'I don't know what you're getting at.'

Dorothy, once more, moves in behind me. 'Tom, where is James being imprisoned?' she asks the top of my spine.

'In a *loco* hospital.'

'Yes, but where?'

I turn around. 'Are you thinking I've had a newsflash you missed? I've no idea.'

'Well, Annette knew!'

'No she didn't. She couldn't get to see him – they wouldn't let her in.'

'*So*, my little drunken genius,' Dorothy starts to slur, 'she *went* somewhere and she got kicked out. How do we know this? From a letter from James's sister, right?'

Now it's my turn to chew on my lip. I need another swallow of alkaline Chablis to lubricate the inference through from my brain to my lips. 'Are you suggesting it wasn't her who wrote to me? Then who was it?'

'What about James himself?'

Shaking my head, I am confident of this one. 'They'll be monitoring all outgoing post.'

'Outgoing from where? From the place that hasn't been mentioned? *Think* about it, Tom! What if he's free! What if he wants us to *believe* he's locked away! You've just told me the police came and went in about the time it takes a budgie to tweet.' Dorothy crosses her arms. 'So why *can't* he be free? He's signed some sort of deal with our favourite police impersonator, all he has to do is convince a few people that he attempted suicide. Get us out of his picture, and *vice versa*. The kid's free to be with his old man...'

'But he was here! He talked for ages! We called an ambulance!'

'Did we though? I'm not so sure.'

'Oh come *off* it, Dolly. We were *all* here when he locked himself in.'

'Yeah! Convenient!'

'For who?'

'Whoever wants us to think he didn't get away with it…You never met Sal, did you?'

'No, I didn't have the pleasure. What's that got to do with it?'

'So you don't *know* she's a person.'

'Annette told us all about the meetings…which I admit right now might not amount to much. I see your point.'

Dorothy has no intention of rubbing anything in. 'I wonder if he exists at all,' is what she adds.

'Why don't you take your bath?' I suggest with enough emphasis to indicate a direct order.

'What does he look like?' Dorothy asks.

As best I can I describe James, although I would rather stop talking altogether, to be frank. Put Springsteen back on. Go and get some more wine, funds permitting. While I roll a cigarette Dorothy tilts her head to one side and sighs.

'Yes, that's what I saw too. Would you like a nice bath with me? I'd like to wash away a few things.'

'Just a sec, I'm calming down now.' I smoke. 'If there's no James, what's the story? What are we talking about?'

'I'm not saying *no* James. I'm saying *different* James,' Dorothy answers. 'I don't know if I'm right any more than you do, but it's worth the consideration, surely. That he played us.'

'He was special needs,' I interrupt. 'He's not capable of playing his own wristwatch.'

'Or Kolko did. Or whoever's playing Kolko, given everything you've told me. I repeat: Would you like a nice bath with me?'

'Consider me already stripping.'

In the bathroom I can't help but notice the statement about 'my dad', and although it's not my writing, this means nothing. My own script on the whiteboard at work bears little resemblance to my customary hand.

Did I?

And then a more paranoid thought calls my name.

What if Dorothy's lying?

We almost displace the water. The bathtub groans (cheap plastic rubbish) and the meniscus at the tub's banks wriggles every time either of us moves. After a while I don't care about the splashes, it's only carpet. I wash her face and breasts with a sponge, while the taps gouge dents into the fat on my back. She washes my chest, saying, 'Yes, though. I think we should get Annette away from her rapist father.'

But I haven't finished thinking about James.

How do I get in touch with the boy?

3.

She knows it is only a nightmare, therefore it will end. But it feels as real as oxygen is real to her lungs, and even inside the dream's tapestry Dorothy looks for a way out, for somewhere she can breathe again.

Rather than a scene, or interconnected images, and rather than sounds, this nightmare is constructed of stench and atmosphere; miasmas cooked and coded together; colourless shapeless landscapes through which her mind wanders, following its own nose. The nightmare is suffocating; there is nothing to breathe but stale air drained of oxygen, and fetor. And inside the nightmare's folds her head throbs for release from this tight asphyxiation.

Wake up, Doo-Doo! Dorothy's mother barks.

And yet she does nothing about executing this order; she

continues to roll through the infinite stink, seeking something out – or allowing this identical entity to seek *her* out.

Come on now, Dorothy. Wakey wakey. We're going to Uncle Paddy and Auntie Em's today, remember? I've ironed your best dress. You need to get up and wash.

Now the fabric of Dorothy's nightmare tightens; this squeezing bursts something – a bubble of some filth – and for a second the odour is worse than before.

Dorothy rolls over, not conscious of whether she flies or swims.

Where is she?

Underwater, it would seem: as soon as she forms this very interpretation, she bobs to the surface, her brow then nostrils breaking open a caul of green slime and algae that hums to high heaven.

I can swim. Mr Nye said I was a confident swimmer... Despite the fact that this water feels different from the water in the swimming pool (and it certainly tastes and smells different), Dorothy kicks out and rotates her arms horizontally, treading her way to stay afloat.

It's the canal... *I'm in the canal!* And Dorothy remembers to panic – because that's what she did, back then, she panicked. She had fallen in the canal and she had flailed, until such time as she recalled the strokes and beats that would maintain her head above water. She had swivelled her hips, turning round on the proximate spot, and she had seen...

What?

We have to remember, adult-Dorothy informs child-Dorothy, though the medium of sleep. *Turn around again,* she says into her younger self's brain.

In the water, the girl turns to face the opposite bank and a low eggy sun in a cradle of cloud. On the bank, Uncle Paddy and

Auntie Em… and Dorothy's mother. Watching a child splashing about in filthy canal water.

They pushed me in… she recalls with a start so intense that it nearly rips the nightmare fabric asunder – it all but catapults Dorothy back to wherever she's fallen asleep.

My God…they tried to drown me!

With which recollection, Dorothy feels again the same pressure to the area just below the shoulder: the exact same spot where the bullet either did or did not enter her body; where an idiot boy resident of a village had tried to penetrate her with his stubby erection… or hadn't.

Where Patrick had shoved against her, sending her sprawling into the canal.

And then they watched her.

Dorothy pictures their faces as pale mauve ovals; their motion goes without comment. Seconds pass, and Dorothy is dragged to the side with a scarf that Auntie Em lends Paddy to toss out.

She is dragged from the odorous water. And she knows, as an adult, that she wasn't raped that night. Her survival stunned them all. In silence she was driven away from the canal, and for the first time Dorothy can all but picture parts of the route. One sign she sees is for STOKE HAMMOND. She pictures a house.

I went home wrapped in a towel, she remembers. Then he burned the dress in the garden. The wet dress. No wonder it wouldn't take fire.

4.

I sense her nearing the completion of her nightmare's span. In the darkness I ready a glass of water for her reappearance.

She opens her eyes. It's not quite a gasp she emits before she studies the surroundings – my bedroom – and judges them safe. She takes the glass in a trembling hand and thanks me for it.

When she tells me she needs to make a phone call, I don't question her, I don't point out the hour. Instead, I hold her hand and lead her to my desk. I sit close by.

Dorothy opts for speakerphone; and the short conversation, in its entirety, runs as follows:

'Patrick, it's Dorothy.'

'…Hello, girl. You all right?'

'No, not really. A question. Did you ever live in Stoke Hammond?'

A longer pause; before Patrick answers wryly, 'How would you know that?'

'That's a yes then, I take it.'

'It's late, Dorothy. I'm talking to my wife.'

'Your second wife. Or maybe your third, I don't know – you've lived a long time. You're a hundred and four don't you know.'

'Nearly a hundred and five,' Patrick adds proudly. 'August.'

Ignoring the boast, Dorothy ploughs on with her inquisition. 'But you split up from your first wife, didn't you? Or the wife *I* know about, anyway. Her name was Em. To me her name was Em. Short for Emma? Emmerline?'

'Amelior, actually,' the old man tells my room. I feel chills.

Patrick and Amelior Anderson?

I notice Dorothy gulp: the admission has come easier than either of us expected – and quite likely easier than Uncle Paddy himself has expected in the decades since he used to partake in the worst thing.

Dorothy's voice breaks when she offers her royal flush.

'Patrick? I know what you used to do.'

'I was a soldier. Then I ran.'

'You were a child-molester, Patrick,' Dorothy continues. 'I

was one of your victims.'

The silence hangs as heavy as a guillotine's blade. Any nanosecond now he will slap down the phone. There'll be silence.

Patrick surprises me.

'You were the *only* victim, Dorothy,' he answers, his voice full of a quantity so close to pride it's sickening. 'There was only you. You were *our favourite.*'

No denials are on the menu; there's nothing but bragging in Patrick's tones. Probably not feeling as sick as Dorothy feels, but feeling sick nonetheless, I watch her staring at the receiver – almost daring it to repeat what it's just emitted.

'I've waited a long time for you, Dorothy. I went *decades* without the pleasure of your company, so what do you have to say for yourself?'

My thumb is two centimetres from the phone's cradle; I can end this immediately. So why don't I? My reluctance has nothing to do with looks or face from Dorothy, for she is not looking at me at all. Eyes wild, red and crisply dry, Dorothy gazes out into the coffeestain-coloured night. I wish I'd closed the curtains.

'I'm sorry,' says Dorothy.

My thumb clamps down on the widget that kills the call. The result is a burr of absence – and Dorothy's hairtrigger anger.

'Why did you end it?' she demands.

'I'm *sorry*, you said. You're telling *that* cunt you're sorry? It offends my ears.'

On her retreat back to the bedroom, Dorothy scolds me. 'Well, it's not your history to judge, is it?' she asks, slamming the door behind her.

'No. But it is *my flat.*'

The door opens.

'You want me to go?'

'I want you to see sense!'

'God, I *had* him there, Tom. You fucked it up.'

'Fucked what up? You were kowtowing to a kiddie rapist.'

Placing her hands on her hips, Dorothy answers that she'd been ready to swim with sharks; she'd prepared herself to confront Patrick, not with vengeance and outrage, but with acceptance. It would have inched her closer.

I remain unconvinced. 'With what in mind? And why didn't you *say* any of this?'

'I only just thought of it!'

Stepping into the bathroom, Dorothy harvests her clothing from the side of the tub, from the sink and the shower fittings, where she left it to dry an hour earlier. She piles it all on the toilet seat and unbuttons the shirt of mine she's wearing.

'Are you leaving?' I ask.

'I'm ready to face my own home, yes Tom.'

'Don't go, Dolly; I'm sorry – I didn't know what you were doing.'

She dresses in jerky movements and says, 'You should've trusted me.'

'I can see that now.'

'I'll call him back,' she tells me – or tells herself, more likely. 'Maybe this is something I need to do on my own – whatever it is. Could you step out of my way, please.'

Against my better judgement I do so; all Dorothy has to do is reach for the door, but it appears as though some of her rage is dissipating. Uncertainty is making a comeback. I open my arms as wide as my hallway will allow. Gratefully she slips into my embrace; I feel her fingers tracing patterns on my spine.

'I don't know what part to believe,' she whispers.

Rubbing her back, I tell her, 'What if none of it is true?'

'You just heard him confess, Tom. You did hear that, didn't you?'

'You know I did… Why don't you get out of those wet clothes again?'

'They're nearly dry.'

'They're damp. I'll stick them in the machine.'

'No point. It's still raining outside.'

'Then why don't you stay here for the night?' I ask as we lie down on my bed.

'…Where's Sabrina, Tom?'

'She's not here.'

'I can see that. I asked you where.'

'She doesn't tell me. Maybe she's found someone else.'

Dorothy tenses beside me. Her left hand stretches in my right, as if to relieve itself of cramp. 'Tom, I have something to get off my chest,' she says. 'You might want me to leave now anyway. It's about Sabrina…I'm sorry, Tom, I slept with her.'

'I thought you were going to say that. It's okay. I'm already sharing you with an old man who's a sex offender.'

'Not anymore you're not!'

'And I can't keep tabs on Sabrina. I never could.'

Dorothy waits a beat before adding: 'Do you want to hear something really crazy? I think I know where she is. I think she's at my place.' Dorothy smiles. 'Waiting for me.'

I reclaim Dorothy's hand and say, 'Let her wait.'

It is too much for me to admit to my recent night with Hannah. Another thought has crowded in.

'She talked to you. In your mind,' I think aloud.

'No, nothing like that,' Dorothy answers. 'It was after the meal at Profit and all the adventures that evening brought. It was comfort…'

'Not Sabrina,' I interrupt. 'Forget about Sabrina for a second. You said Patrick's wife could hear your thoughts, right? Or something like that. So if there's a kind of… of channel open, what's to stop you going into *her* head?'

'Why would I want to?' Dorothy asks. 'To *spy*?'

'Well *I* would if I had the chance,' I tell her.

5.

Dorothy revolves around the room, dialling for a signal; she wants to listen to the two old people in the room talking to their daughter.

The three of them watch the swimming pool from the spectators' gallery, with Dorothy an invisible character sitting next to Justine and perhaps even sharing the older woman's eyesight... Not that there is much to see, for now at least. Annette takes her place atop the lifeguards' ladder-chair; she studies both the water and the few people who are still swimming, this close to what must be the pool's closing time.

Dorothy glances to her left. Patrick has freed his penis from his underwear, and there is no selfconsciousness on display about his masturbatory method. Although Dorothy wishes to look away, her gaze is fixed: perhaps at Justine's insistence. Only when her vantage point is unlocked from afar can Dorothy return her attention to the water, in which the same people who were present seconds earlier have now shed years each. Both Annette and the customers are represented as children, but they're easily recognisable to Dorothy.

What is better to observe? What Patrick is doing to his personal equipment, or the fantasy that causes him to do it?

Dorothy hovers and waits for something to happen, hanging on the dream's every unspoken word. The water in the pool darkens and starts to move. Move slowly at first; barely noticeably, and not in whirls and not caused by the swimmers' splashes either – as the swimmers dart from the deep end to shallow, shallow end to deep, butterflying, frontcrawling and backstroking their years away, dwindling backwards along time's path, growing younger for Patrick's pleasure with every arm crash into the water.

Annette watches the tide as well. By the side, the toes of her trainers poking over the edge into air, she views the pictures projected onto the surface of the water – but projected by whom? By Annette herself? By Patrick? By Justine? Then the current drives the image along and a new one takes its place. The images are fully the width of the pool in height, drifting past Annette's eyes (and Dorothy's consciousness) with sloth, but with the attention-stealing attribute of a circus parade.

The procession is Annette's history. What runs along this conveyor belt is clear to look at (to Dorothy's eyes) but confusing; Dorothy has no memory of Annette's childhood to use to fill in missing context; some of what she sees could be happiness masquerading as sadness, some *vice versa*.

Up in the gallery, Dorothy speaks to Justine. *He did it to her as well, didn't he?* she asks, for the first time regarding Patrick's second wife as some sort of ally, or at least an oracle. *It was me years earlier* – Justine nods her head – *but there were others. Including Annette, years later.* And Justine nods her head again, her eyes full of the reflection from the pool. *And then he made us forget.*

'Justine, tell me, please,' Dorothy says aloud into my bedroom. The beg is a sleep-muddied murmur, but for me the message is clarity itself. 'How did he make us forget?' she asks, nearly awake now.

I have taken the precaution of having the bedside light on, ready for when Dorothy paddles back to a conscious surface. But before she emerges fully she asks her dream interlocutor one final question.

'What did he do to *you*, Justine?'

Then Dorothy is back to the land of the living; her breath is a struggle, haggard and wheezy with what otherwise I might think of as hay fever tubes. Dorothy and I blink into each other's faces. I don't bother with the are-you-all-right bullshit. A lover knows without asking.

'We have to go to the leisure centre, Tom,' she tells me. 'What time is it?'

'Just about half nine. What did you dream?'

'I'll tell you on the way. We'll need a taxi,' she adds, standing up.

'I'll phone for one. But what's happening, Dolly?'

'I think that's where he's going to kill her.'

6.

In no uncertain terms the operator tells me that due to the weather earlier there is no chance of a cab within the hour. There's a backlog of delayed bookings, airport runs, train station pick-ups. She's full-on apologetic, but her hands are tied, priority will be given to journeys longer than the one I've mentioned.

We'll have to walk.

'Or call Hannah for a lift,' Dorothy adds.

'She's doing her sleep deprivation thing.'

'Roy, then.'

'He'll be pissed.'

'So are we!'

'No we're not – or not on his scale anyway. Besides, I don't want him there,' I admit.

'Why not? This is all for one and one for all, isn't it?'

My answer comes a beat too late; and with Dorothy already perched on the brink of an authentic temper tantrum, my reluctance is reason enough for her to snap.

'I want to know why you waited. Why don't you want Roy present?'

In case you're wrong is the answer, but I don't provide it. I scroll for Roy's mobile number and I give him a beep.

'It's Tom,' I tell his answerphone. 'If you get this, and if you can drive, can you meet us at the leisure centre, mate? Dorothy says it's urgent and I'm inclined to agree.'

We have wasted important seconds. I could have made this call while we walked. The centre is a twenty-five minute lung-buster from here. I collect my key from my desk and follow Dorothy down the stairs, out into the rain.

Empties, 4: 'Early blinking'

1.

Where do you buy an axe from anyway?

Caitlin killed the older boy first, and even in this decision we glimpse the propinquity of a guarded choice. Get the tougher one out of the way; you never know how much trouble he's going to give you…

The blade chopped into Toby's chest in the early hours of the morning. How on earth she recovered from that initial blow is still a mystery to me.

Swinging her weapon like a lumberjack, Caitlin cut off Toby's right arm, and then tried to wipe some of the blood from her face.

But what did it take? To get to this point, what had Caitlin endured? An hour too much of overloud pop music? A failure to tidy away some toys or magazines? A row?

When does madness solidify?

2.

Except… I *saved* her from doing these things, according to Patrick.

He told me – with Dorothy my witness – that I *stopped* Caitlin from taking an axe to her sons, in the house behind my flat. Before she was Annette. But if I did, I don't remember it. I don't remember doing anything of the kind. In fact, I have memories that substantiate the criminal intent and action of Caitlin Bryant.

How can this be?

3.

There were questions asked…

The interrogation room into which I'm led is the grey of overripe steak; it doesn't stink – I expected it to stink for some reason. It doesn't stink of cigarettes because you're not allowed to smoke. And it doesn't stink of b.o. because the investigating officers are all business.

'We need to get it down, sir – on paper: your relationship with Mrs Bryant.'

This is Officer Kolko. Already I feel like I will be sending him a post-card the next time I go away anywhere.

Kolko interviewed me after Caitlin killed her sons.

'Did you sleep with her?' Kolko asks.

Though I couldn't see what earthly difference this might make, I said, 'No.'

'May I ask why not?'

These were strange questions, I thought. And they come back to me now with force. I have found what I was not looking for.

It is my turn to find a memory, and I have found one.

For this I have to thank my visit to 47 Rosebank Avenue.

'Because I didn't fancy her,' I answer. The simple response seems best.

I do not know why I lied about this. Nor do I know for sure that it happened.

4.

There were even prison visits – me to her new dwelling.

'Am I allowed to offer her a cigarette?' I ask.

'If you show me the packet first,' the officer replies. 'You'll have to take the fags in a cellophane bag. In case you're smuggling in a razor blade or a lighter.'

'Well I've got a lighter,' I confess. 'Is that wrong?'

NO TOUCHING, reads a sign in the vestibule before the

visitors' room. In case I haven't understood this fully the guard in front of the door kindly elaborates.

'No holding hands, no kissing. No hugging. No removal of clothes. And no massage.'

'Got it,' I tell him.

'Are those cigarettes for her or you?'

'Both.'

'How many do you want to give her? I'll have to do it personally.'

'Can we say four now and then renegotiate if necessary?'

Except…

…except none of this actually happened, did it?

Fear in Four Waters, 4: The Deluge

I.

1.

Prefatory matters attended to (the final draft on perioperative fasting pinged over to the project's commissioner by email; the electric sockets freed of contact with plugs; some food approaching its sell-by date disposed of in the outside bin), Hannah hefts up her overnight bag onto her left shoulder. The bag is heavy. At the front door she turns and says goodbye out loud to her house.

Since taking part in Jill's experiment on sleep deprivation all those years ago, the laboratories have shifted location. Hannah drives north up the A5, past Milton Keynes (customarily as far north as she ever drives) and on towards Northampton. She'd wanted to go by train, but Jill had advised her that the labs were miles from the station and that it would cost a king's ransom in taxi fares at the other end; Hannah had concurred. Not once had Jill offered to drive Hannah to the labs: this isn't the kind of relationship the two women have.

At length Hannah pulls up at an orange-and-white striped barrier; a squat man in a khaki uniform emerges from his sentry box holding a clipboard. She gives him her name; he thanks her, returns to his box; the barrier lifts a half-circle with a complex wheeze of straining hydraulics. And Hannah is in; simpler than she'd imagined.

2.

Jill leads down a dimly-lit staircase.

'It's not at all like before, is it? The other place you had. This is like a farmhouse.'

'The bit you can see from the front is, definitely. That's the point. The last thing we need is the wrath of the anti-scientific ethics brigade, camping outside the grounds with their placards and Pot Noodles.'

'Did you get that with the old place?' Hannah asks.

'All the time. One of the labs was working with animals and some of the activists got wind of it. They used to ambush the egg deliveries – the eggs they'd be working on, I mean. As if stopping eggs getting to the lab would kill the research. Some of them even *threw* eggs – supermarket eggs this time. I still don't know if that action was intended ironically or those people were just *thick*. In any case, here we are.'

At the bottom of the staircase is a door with a number pad at Hannah's eye level. Hannah watches Jill tap in 6600711; she commits the combination to memory, more in a spirit of waste not want not than through any serious notion that the number will be vital. She turns the sixes into 'sexy' and the '007' is easy to remember as 'James Bond'. Legs eleven is what's called out in Bingo, so: Sexy Sexy James Bond Legs.

The lock pops open. Jill pushes on the door; it swings wide on electronic hinges.

'This is where you forget about comparisons with a farmhouse.'

Beyond the door is a vestibule, and on the wall directly facing any visitor is a large sign in caps:

STEP IN ONE AT A TIME.
STAND ON THE X.
PREPARE TO BE PHOTOGRAPHED.

'Daunting,' Hannah remarks.

'The first couple of times. We learnt our lesson at the old place. It looked too flash from the outside and it wasn't flash enough on the inside, security-wise. We've redressed the balance.' Jill steps in and waits on the X. A lightbulb pops as her picture is taken.

'And no trouble so far?'

'Not so far. Say cheese on your way through.' Jill steps into a doorway suddenly created in the wall: a door springs open, Jill moves through, the door slams shut again.

As soon as Hannah paces into position on the cross, the door behind her closes. An instant of suffocation; claustrophobia; the vestibule with the affects of a fat coffin. The photograph is taken, the camera whirrs. Hannah feels reprieved.

'Home sweet home,' says Jill. 'You won't be needing that,' she adds, holding out her left hand.

'Needing what?'

'The bag. You sleep in what you arrive in. Or rather, you don't.' Her mouth winces with self-satisfied humour. 'Old joke,' she confesses. What I mean is, there's no creature comforts. That's the point of it. What you decide to keep now is your own affair–'

'I decide to keep my bag.'

' – but it must be on your person. No accoutrements.'

'*Accoutrements*? An overnight bag?'

'Or you give up before you start.' Jill shrugs. 'Your call.'

Hannah thrusts out her right arm; on the end of it is the bag.

'Are you sure?'

She nods her head.

'You're not due on or anything?'

'No,' Hannah answers resentfully. She bites her lower lip.

'Good. So you're in this room for an undisclosed period

of time. I'll take your watch, thanks. And the idea is to record…
your ideas! Whatever they might be. The walls have sensors for
voice, heat and electroencephalographic output. Among other
imperial data.'

'Romantic.'

'You're a moth on a pin,' says Jill, 'for the next n hours.'

3.

The first hour is the easy part: it gets more difficult after
that.

For the first hour Hannah is alone with her thoughts, her
scattered urges. After this, her thoughts are alone with her. It is
eerie to be a plaything of a notion.

By this point she is sitting in the corner of the room. The
ceiling is high. Hannah spends her seconds in calculating the
height of the ceiling; she dabbles with thoughts of her own personal hygiene. What she said to Jill was correct: she is not due on
soon. But what if? The body is not a machine; and Hannah has
known periods both early and (more locally worrying) late. If it
comes on now, what then?

She will have to provide the products. Surely.

But what if Jill refuses to take her calls, so to speak?

Hannah stands up and jogs on the spot. She pictures her
class in the gym, and in the space of a drawn breath she is there
– the metallic acoustics, the scent of wooden floors and perspiration the perfume of gymnasia the world over. Kitted out in her
fencing gear, she lunges out. She can *feel* it; she holds her epee in
her right hand, Z-ing the air like Zorro. She lunges again. Blood
and oxygen race in her body. Lightfooted (and feeling *sexy* of all
things) Hannah dances her attack ballet; she conjures up a series
of opponents. Toby then Jill; Hana then Kolko. Even Stephen
makes a surprise guest appearance.

You're going mad, you know that, don't you? Sam asks.

Hannah dismisses her class and hits the showers.

In the sleep deprivation chamber she undresses as if for bedtime. Disrobing to her underwear, she wonders where her nightdress is. Has she left it in the utility room, hanging to dry? Funny, she can't remember doing the laundry. It's not even laundry day!

Was I asleep?

Hannah clenches her fingernails into the fleshy heels of her hands.

Enamel…

At school (for a while) she was Hannah Banana; then Hannah Bean. The Palindrome. Then her surname had been made use of, and Hannah became known as Paddington Bear or Marmalade Sandwich. Lady Marmalade. Sarnie. Arnie. Then there was that rough patch of monikers, with Arnie linking easily to Schwarzenegger, or The Austrian or Swiss Cheese. Then came The Bodybuilder (her fondness for the gym and aerobics, even in her teens, had helped this one through its rite of passage). And Hannah had played along; she had secretly enjoyed the attention. Best of all she had liked Hannah Enamel.

Taste of something rotten in Hannah's mouth. Haven't eaten anything. Burning sensation on my tongue. Gas. A leak. *Gas is leaking in!* Visible now. It's a gas, gas, gas… Puffs of purple-tinted vapour eke from the wallpaper, blurring Hannah's vision and igniting her lungs. Fight or flight? she wonders. A song shouts in her synapses. Nowhere to *run* to, bay-bee… nowhere to *hide*. No choice: so breathe, now exhale. She lifts her arm to cover her nose and mouth; her forearms smells of the gas.

What do you do now, Hannah Enamel?

Not sleep! Find the *place* where you don't sleep. Step over that border.

Vice grips on Hannah's temples, there's something in the gas – something toxic, corrosive. *I'm going blind. I can taste my own tongue…* A slab of raw meat in her mouth; a watering-can's volume of slimy chickenfat in her throat.

I'm being punished. I nearly slept and the wallpaper sensed it, and now I'm being punished. The room needs me up-and-at-em.

Hannah adopts a boxing posture and jabs her left fist at the wall. 'So why can't I remember Cairo?' Hannah demands suddenly. 'Why do Sam and I remember it differently?'

She is sure she knows the answer. Her chest rises and she ignores the coughs that the vapour induces.

If she and Sam disagree on what happened in Egypt, something worse did. Something the thief doesn't want them to recall. *So he's keeping us at each other's throats,* Hannah concludes, feeling more awake than she has for months.

4.

Why won't you feed me? Stephen had asked, but had this interrogative been only for God's attention? He'd lost his mind; he could have been trying for the attention of anyone.

'You were a prisoner, weren't you, Stephen?' says Hannah, deliberately raising her voice so that the microphones in the wall will pick her up. 'Not figuratively. *Literally,* you were a prisoner. Weren't you. So who was keeping you alive, Stephen? After your mother died. Who was it?'

If she has expected the walls to articulate some kind of response she has been mistaken; but this does not stifle her soliloquy.

'I've got your number, Stephen. Or I think I have. You were a sexual deviant. A pervert, in other words. You did it with your sister. And I think you did it with Tom as well. Tell me if I'm right.'

But the walls remain *schtum*.

Pangs of hunger cause a momentary panic; Hannah tries to imagine never eating again. She amuses herself briefly by guessing how many meals she's missed. With little variation in the quality of light it's impossible to tell how long she's been locked in.

'Talk to me, Stephen,' she whispers.

5.

Above a beige canvas of sand Hannah soars; from here the desert floor appears flat, though she knows it is not. She beats her wings; air resists her, resists her, yields; she feels it pump past her tail-feather; she climbs higher up into the sky, her vision sharp, her movements natural. It is cold and clean. She dives, as if for prey; but there is nothing to hunt. She glides, swerves; she beats her wings.

In the distance, ripples on the beige canvas. A Pyramid. Hannah soars; her heart soars, too. *The Pyramids was where it started.* Hannah widens her beak, testing her vocal cords. Diluted by chilled air, the squawk is brittle. She swoops in the direction of the Pyramid, which multiplies in her vision, like an amoeba – the Pyramid squeezes out of its own body a second perfect replica of itself, then a third. Even from this distance, the crowning points appear huge.

She beats her wings; she sails closer. The temperature warms as she takes a gentle gradient down out of the sky. It's the heat of the earth; the heat of the people crowding on it around the structures. Hundreds of people; possibly thousands. Hannah's keen eyesight picks them out and divides them by the colour of their skin.

The buses as well – she sees the buses, either vomiting out their human waste, or sucking great clods of it back in, back behind the windows.

Then Hannah sees what she's been looking for.

She sees herself. She sees Hannah and Sam, boarding the bus to leave the site.

With the loudest squawk she can summon, Hannah-as-Bird circles in the temperate eddies, a tight wheel of motion, the equivalent of treading water, the best she can do to hover more or less in one place.

The bus is her prey. She wants to eat the bus and all the human-sized bugs upon it. She squawks again and completes another soaring circle, waiting for the bus to move.

Very soon the bus coughs its engine lungs up; it shakes itself awake. When it drives away, past some resting camels and the owners who charge for rides, past a stable block, past drinks vendors, food vendors, postcard salesboys, Hannah traces its progress from on high. When it stops for other traffic, she squawks and circles; she flaps and changes direction, but never once loses sight of the vehicle.

It is on the bus that Hannah and Sam met Hana the thief. She will not let it go.

6.

'I won't let it go…' Hannah mumbles. Something about the words – their vibration against her skull, perhaps – rips her back into the present, where she finds herself leaning against the wallpaper, face first, her forehead making contact with the ghastly print.

'I wasn't asleep,' she wants to assure the wall. 'That wasn't dreaming exactly.'

She sits down, her back to the wall. Parenthetically she wonders why she is clothed only in her knickers and bra; she cannot remember disrobing. She hugs her breasts tight, tighter, tightest; she wants to experience something on her skin. In this way, the memory might vanish; it might be squashed flatter than a plateful of piss, as Tom would say.

'My God, *we killed him*,' Hannah says to the wallpaper.

7.

Hannah throws herself from wall to wall ('surprisingly padded,' she will judge, although the bruises on her upper body tell a different story). She shrieks for freedom; she wants out. Her cajoles and her threats get her nowhere, but failure is no impediment to further strain. If anything, she howls louder – the snatches are feral – but still no door swinging wide, certainly no rescuer. 'What do I say to get out?' she screams. If she was given a magic word she has long since binned it, buried it beneath panic and mind-rubble. She cries and yells; writhes and moans. Urine flows down her left thigh.

'Tom, I have something important to tell you,' Hannah says directly to the wall. 'I don't know how crazy or random this is going to sound, but I'm going to say it anyway.'

A stray thought passes through the concentrated mass of notions that she is struggling with how to articulate. The stray thought is that she wishes she had worn better underwear. Hannah knows that she is playing a part; she's not *acting* as such, but she is presenting a persona – or a series of characters. Might have been wise to have selected sexier knickers for her audition.

'You can be my diary. Sam used to be but we don't speak as much as we used to, so you've got the job, Tom, if you're good with that. And I'll try to keep this in some sort of order.

'I dreamed I was flying…'

She pauses; absentmindedly she fiddles with the bra strap that has slipped down her shoulder. She says, 'No; that's wrong to start with…'

Hannah stares at the wallpaper, urging the patterns to move.

'...Tom, he's dead because of me and Sam. We killed Hana – they tore him to pieces on the bus in Cairo: the other passengers. After I punched him... It was a lynchmob, Tom.

'I can see it now. Clearly. He was passed up and down the bus and *everyone took part*. Including us, Tom. They used him as a rope – a tug-o-war. I can hear his bones cracking. It was like... dismembering a chicken. With the bus still moving through the traffic. It was mass psychosis. Kicking. Stamping... Someone set fire to their travel documents and made him eat them.

'We killed him Tom. And that's why he's back for me and Sam. Why *all* of our visitors are back. It's not *us* who have forgotten, Tom. *It's them*. They need to be told what happened to them, to bring them to life. We've *been* their killers. Now we have to be their diaries.'

II.

1.

Through my work and my numerous conversations with Roy on the subject (when he's in the mood to stir this particular stew), I know enough about prisons and the mechanisms of the penal system to understand that much of Annette's account of her visit to see James on the psychiatric detention ward is hogwash. Not that I blame her for believing it, of course. *I* would trust it, too – the memory – if I wasn't aware of what a treacherous thing the memory can be.

Despite what Annette says (and thinks), she did *not* go to see James in his padded-cell quarantine.

And how do I know this?

Because he has told me so.

Or, to clarify: it is *Louise* who has told me so – in the letter I mentioned before. Not an email. A letter. An ink-on-white-paper, stamped-envelope *bona fide* letter.

2.

Dear Tom (it reads),

James is as expected – and so am I. Ghastly, in other words.

He's protected from a lot of what's going on, but he gets to hear leaks, and someone told him that people are trying to see him. Ghouls and journalists. Same thing.

But one woman was really throwing her weight around in Reception, apparently. Screaming moral outrage, this, my expected rights, that. Shaking the ceiling plaster with her voice, rumour has it.

The only reason I mention this is because of her name. She kept shouting I'M ANNETTE! I'M ANNETTE! And this was my mum's new friend's name, and I think your friend, too, and I thought it might be worth mentioning.

After a while, when they were escorting her off the premises, or booting her out (take your pick) she changed her chant, or added to it:

I'M ANNETTE, I NEED TO SEE HIM! I'M NOT CAITLIN! I'M ANNETTE!

Do you know a Caitlin?

Does this mean anything to you, Tom? I promised myself I'd tell you everything, so that's what I'm doing. It means SOMETHING, not necessarily to you, I know that.

I hope you're well.

Best wishes,

Louise

3.

Kolko has been in Roy's garage for four days now. He shows no sign of wanting to go home. Actually, most of the time he shows no sign of anything at all. At one point, regarding his open-eyed silent passivity I was put in mind of a family holiday when I was young, when the crab in the pool in the rocks had *looked* dead, so I'd poked it with my plastic spade to check... I can still see those vicious claws, snapping at me, click clack – trying to cut off my willy, or so I'd believed at the time for some reason.

But why is *Kolko* laying low? Neither Roy nor I are willing to believe that he's hotelling in the courtesy car for his health; so what's he up to?

Kolko sits on the back seat of the car. Not once has he tried to escape; nor does he protest, scream, cry, wail. He doesn't even thrash around for a smidgen of exercise (his legs must be aching like hell), and neither of his captors has seen him sleep. A silent hypnophobe, who offers us, if anything at all, the occasional wry smile, the less occasional burst of song (his singing rehearsals did

not last long, but when he *does* croon he still croons in French),
Kolko is a food-refusing famished mute who withdraws into a
psychic retreat for hours on end.

'It's not natural,' Roy tells me when I arrive at Bible Street
Cars on this, the fourth morning following his capture.

We're in the office, Roy and I; the door's closed and although we've come to the agreement that we don't need to watch
the prisoner, still it remains the case that our voices are lowered.
There's no point pushing our luck. We don't want him to hear us
discussing him, it might hurt the cunt's feelings.

While we're talking I mention the on-foot dash to the leisure centre that Dorothy and I had made the previous evening.

'Yeah, I got your message,' Roy tells me. 'What was it all
about?'

I delineate the nightmare that Dorothy had had, and her
fears for Annette's safety. There are no flies on Roy, and he picks
up on something.

'You mean she phoned you when she had a nightmare,' he
says.

'Well, not exactly. She was at mine. Where she *was* is not
the important part of this...'

'Are you two shagging, Tom?' Roy asks matter-of-factly.

There's no point trying to lie to Roy. 'It's between you and
me, okay? I thought you knew already.'

'Does that mean your missus is free?'

'No it doesn't.'

'Are you sure? It's been a while, Tom: be a mate. I'm swollen up like a sack of spuds!'

'Yeah I'm sure, mate. Anyway. We walked all the way there
and the place was locked up for the night, as I imagined it would
be. We walked around the grounds but we couldn't get close to
the pool building as it was chained off. So we walked back home

again before we raised suspicion. In the rain.'

Roy gulps his tea and flicks at his left nostril with a mahogany little finger.

4.

It's wrong to bait bears, it's wrong to make elephants dance; it should be wrong, by the same token, to elicit a performance from Kolko, but it feels fine. I figure he owes us one, and so does Roy.

He won't play, though. Kolko doesn't want to know us, it transpires, after all this time, during which it seemed that he did little else but clamour for our hot applause. But what if Kolko's inaction is a ruse? What if we are not holding him but he's holding us?

Or try this on – one of Roy's. Kolko's resting. Summoning up his energy for a Big One, whatever it could be.

By my age I'd like to trust the veracity of my own eyesight... but suppose he is not really there. The stratagem is to make us *believe* he's here, when in truth, assuming that my earlier faith in eidolism is now discredited, his physical body, if he honestly owns one, is elsewhere. What we see, in other words, is his projection.

5.

We would have to feed and water him. The question was: whose job would it be to do so?

Roy and I were airing the vicissitudes of this second dilemma on the second day that Kolko had graced us with his company – or the first full day, I suppose I should call it. That's by the bye. It was lunchtime. Sitting, the three of us – me, Roy and Ian – in Roy's office with pre-packed sandwiches from the supermarket, where Ian had ridden to and from on his BMX, it was Roy who had nodded to the extra sandwich on the desk.

'That one for Kolko?' Roy asked.

Pretty obvious that it was, but I guess we all needed to be on the same page.

Through a mouthful of luncheon, Ian answered, 'Yep.'

'How do you know the wanker likes cheese?'

'It's *cheese*! Everyone likes cheese, mate!' Ian swallowed. 'If he don't – fuck him!'

Junior Mechanic Ian has taken to Kolko as he might to a new pet, or more fittingly, to just another task he must overcome on his way to becoming a fully-fledged mechanic.

Having volunteered to be the delivery boy too, Ian scampers over the cars he needs to scamper over in order to reach Kolko's new home. He pops the boot and leaves food and water therein; it's never eaten. It's an old-fashioned car. You can get to the boot by adjusting the upholstery on the back seat – the cushions come down – and we've explained it to Kolko in shouted instructions, but he doesn't want to know. From this we have established that he's not hungry, or he is not taken with our food choices.

The idea I like least is that he doesn't *need* to eat.

6.

I'm reminded of something Hannah said: the bit about what we're seeing being for someone else's benefit. It makes sense, but I don't know what to do with it. Kolko wants us to see this – his portrait of an artist as an old lag – but what's he doing in the background, elsewhere? Today I find out, perhaps.

Today I'm returning to 47 Rosebank Avenue. My grandmother's house; Uncle Stephen's house; and I suspect, too, the bolthole where Simon Kolko has been laying his hat.

7.

In the same way that Hana the thief is clicking Hannah and Sam together like billiard balls, is my Sabrina playing new tricks on an old dog like me? Is she really dead? (Was she ever alive?) What if Sabrina is using me; making me believe her story, entirely for her own benefit?

No wonder I'm paranoid.

Am I mourning her? That's the question. If I'm not mourning Sabrina… who *am* I mourning? Stephen?

Mum informed me that Sabrina died, as a child, in a drowning tragedy while on a family holiday: and now I'm haunted by her.

But did she, though? *Did* she drown?

Mum has lied to me, and lied and lied. Why should I assume that she told me the truth about the swimming pool accident?

Because Sabrina corroborated the report.

Big deal.

Maybe they're in this together.

8.

From downstairs, the sound of post arriving into our rattling communal letterbox.

I dress quickly and go down to see if there's anything for me. There is – a small parcel, no larger than a pack of cards, tightly smothered in sellotape, with no stamp on the wrapping – it's been delivered by hand. It's the only thing in the letterbox, now, and the Royal Mail was not responsible.

I return to my kitchen. So carefully has the parcel been wrapped that I need to use scissors. It's a memory stick.

What do I feel as I plug it into the socket? This emotion is fairly low-grade fuel, the truth be known. After everything I've seen (and done) I'm hardly likely to catch the willies by turning on my computer.

The movie file has been named SAM. It's the only file on the stick. It occurs to me that I haven't sat here at my desk for a while, and I wonder how long it's been since I last turned on the machine.

Then Sam appears on my monitor, and suddenly there's nothing else to think about.

She appears nervous. This I can see without much help from the below-par lighting.

It's not the fact that I'm spying on a sex tape involving a friend that creates my ill-feeling: it's the fact that this is a record of Sam's last words.

Halfway through being sick, the phone rings. I make it to the desk on the fifth or sixth ring, but I don't want to be so close to where I watched Sam's final performance.

'Tom, it's Hannah. Are you all right?'

'No, not really.' I log off and pull the stick from the socket. As it's evidence... Jesus, *evidence*... I should keep it, shouldn't I? So why is it so tempting to lay the stick in an ashtray in a nest of torn newspaper and ignite the fucker?

'Why, what's up?' Hannah asks.

'I have absolutely no idea of where to begin,' I tell her.

'Well, snap. I've just got back from the sleep deprivation thing...'

'You're back already? I was just about to ask...'

'...which I need to talk to you about, but as I was leaving I got a text from Sam's ex-husband, worried he hasn't heard from Sam. You know the funny thing they've got? He sends her money and she replies with abuse?'

'Yeah, I know.'

'Well, he sent her a cheque a few days ago and she hasn't

once called him a piece of shit. He's getting concerned.'

'But why's he calling you?'

'I've just said – he can't get in touch with her. And neither can I. She's not answering and she's not at home. She's not at work either; I tried. I was wondering if she said anything.'

'Hannah…'

'Though God knows why he's got *my* mobile number, I see what you mean. I never really knew him when they were married, let alone now.'

'Hannah, listen. Please.'

But how do you say it? In spite of everything that's happened, how do you actually say it out loud? 'Can you meet me?' I ask.

'I'm on my way to work. I have a gym induction to do.'

'You'll have to cancel. Or get someone else to do it.' A thought occurs to me. 'I thought you'd booked annual leave anyway. You're not supposed to be working.'

'I did. I called my manager last night and said I'm home earlier than expected… Is this about what I've said about Sam?'

'Not on the phone.'

'Oh God. Just tell me she's okay, Tom.'

'Not on the phone, Han. Is your car working all right?'

'Yes, it's okay. Where are we going?'

'To Bible Street Cars. I'll see if Dorothy's free as well. We should all see this.'

'See Kolko, you mean?'

'Well, that as well. Another witness or two can't hurt.' I sigh loudly and it's like a burst of microphone feedback in my left ear. 'Maybe it'll prove that Roy and I aren't off our rockers.'

Hannah laughs. 'You're counting on *me* for that?' she asks with a kind of squeal in her voice. 'I'm not exactly a reliable narrator.'

'We should hear what happened to you as well,' I tell her. 'All of us. Even Annette, if you can get hold of her… Or is that a stupid idea?'

'I don't know, Tom. I don't know what you've got in mind.'

'…A catch-up. I want us all to hear what everyone else has been up to. But not here. And it's far too early for the pubs to open.'

'…Even Sam? Is Sam coming?'

After I've said it, I feel disgusting and cheap; but I swear I don't mean it as any kind of joke when I say, 'I'll bring Sam.'

Hannah is confused. She says, 'But aren't I bringing *you?* And Dorothy?'

'Yes, I'll…I'll get dressed right now and call Roy.'

9.

'Mum?' I say into the phone, hours later. 'Got to ask you something difficult. Sorry in advance.'

It's the first time we have spoken since she told me about her and her brother. Even now it's not me who has extended the olive branch (how can I?), *she* phoned *me*. She wants to know *how I am;* although I long to be sarcastic, I can't keep that up long with my mother.

'Do you remember the day we found out that your brother had died?' I ask her. 'This is a bit I don't get – one of many.'

Your brother. Not *Stephen,* and certainly not *Uncle Stephen.* His name – for me – has become a bridge too far, I think. I can't even *talk* to her about him.

'Ye-es,' Mum answers cautiously, like a question.

'Do you remember the name of the officer who came to tell us?' I ask.

'God no,' Mum answers, a springclean of relief in her voice. 'Why?'

'If I said it, would you… maybe? His name was Kolko. Simon Kolko.'

'Yes, possibly. Tom, I have better things to think about… Why do you ask?'

I've been expecting and dreading this. The sooner I address the problem, however, the sooner we can all move on to other matters.

'It was my test. For you, Mum. To see if you're lying to me.'

'Lying?'

'Yes, Mum, lying. To me. And you are.'

'…I don't like your voice, Tom.'

'I shouldn't think you do, Mum,' I reply. 'Do you know where I am?'

'You're at home. This is my call. I thought *one* of us had to.'

'I've had my calls transferred; I'm on my mobile right now. I'm in your living room – where the upright piano used to be.'

'Tom, what are you talking about?' Mum asks.

'Because you'd never forget a name like that – not the man who told you your brother has been found dead. It didn't even strike me as strange at first, how vague you were about Sabrina's drowning. She didn't drown, Mum – you lied to me about that as well.'

My mother's voice is soft but I hear her just fine. 'Where *are* you, Tom?'

'Your old house. In Wembley. Where it all happened, I think.'

At first she says nothing at all. Then she says, 'Where what happened?'

A wave of dizziness takes hold of my senses. I consider what happened to Dorothy, the film show that she was made to sit through in order for her to learn her past; and the reason I think of my friend is because something along similar lines is happening to me. All of a sudden I am outside my own body, and not only looking at myself from a different perspective, I am looking at myself in a different *time*.

'It all got out of hand, didn't it, Mum?' I go on quickly, while there is air in my lungs; I don't know how long this might continue. For one thing, she might slam down the receiver. 'It was you your brother was having relations with – I know that now – but it wasn't *only* you, was it, Mum? There was me, for a start. And I think there was a girl on his list called Sabrina.'

'Tom, you're not making any sense…'

'She and her friend – when we were kids – she followed me and my friend Franco into a school for the disabled that was being built. Stephen followed the girls following us. And Franco and the other girl – Sadie – got away. I don't know how. But Sabrina didn't, did she, Mum? And neither did I. Then don't let's get started on the prostitutes he must have…'

'…Is that what you remember, Tom?'

I am all but in tears by this point. 'I don't know if I remember it or I've created it. *Have* I created it all, Mum? *Tell* me.'

'No,' Mum sighs. 'No you haven't. Not exactly.'

She ends the call. I stare around the flat, searching for clues as to what to do next. My bluff about being in the lounge of her former home has worked to an extent; but now I have more information – the usual thing – I have no idea what to do with it.

Of course I *had been* to 47 Rosebank Avenue, on the same day that Hannah went into the sleep deprivation room. But I wasn't allowed in. The woman who answered the door remembered my face, I think, or perhaps had a strong sense of *wrong* when it came to visitors on her doorstep. She'd got a lot older; so had I.

There on her doorstep, I decided that neither of us needed the hassle. Life's too short, and besides – I mightn't get away with it a third time. I said 'Bye' and turned and left. For a ten-second conversation I would make a three-hour round trip. On the platform at Wembley Park, I trembled in the blustery rain, cursing the law that forbade me to smoke. I would take the Bakerloo up to Harrow, then change onto my line back to Leighton Buzzard.

I did not walk home straight away that day. The rain had stopped a bit – or as much as it ever seems to stop nowadays – so I strolled down to The Globe, on the canal. Despite the weather I sat outside, and I did my best to feel for them – to reach out for Sal and Annette in my mind – using their previous connections to this place.

This morning Hannah and I went over to Bible Street Cars to watch the film. They both wanted to see; this despite the fact that I'd warned them what the file on the memory stick contained.

We watched it in the office with the sound down. From outside we could hear pop music on Radio 1, with Ian working and singing along. The concatenation of image and sound was obscene. Before the film ended, with Hana approaching the camera, Hannah excused herself and slipped into the bathroom. I could hear her being sick.

'He'll be coming for me next,' was all that Hannah seemed to want to say for a while. Roy and I took this in. I had considered the possibility; I don't know if Roy had. 'I wish we'd made a better job of it when we killed him on that bus in Cairo. I'm going to leave now. Do you want a lift home, Tom? But I'm going right now.'

There was no discussion about 'sticking together' or anything like it. My impression is that not one of us wanted to be with either of the others.

'Just one thing before you go,' Roy said. 'The memory stick.'

The prospect of watching it burn was the only thing that could have delayed Hannah's flight from the garage and its yard this morning. As a matter of routine, Roy siphons petrol from the tanks of cars that have been in accidents and which the insurance companies will write off as unworthy of the investment needed for further repair. He keeps the siphoned petrol in a series of stoppered glass jugs that once held strong, expensive Somerset cider.

Roy unlocked a filing cabinet and removed one of these glass jugs. Wordlessly Hannah and I followed him outside (Ian watched us go with an expression, I think, of jealousy) and we set fire to the stick on a pyre made from a solitary truck tyre and a torn up copy of last week's *Exchange and Mart.*

Hannah dropped me home, but the phone call from my mum has disturbed me something peculiar. I didn't want to be here on my own. Nor did I want to slope over to The Leper in case Roy decided to shut up shop early and drop in for one (or ten), or in case Angie wanted to tell me something about her love life or her health scares.

Nor did I wish to speak to Dorothy.

Stepping out into the rain, I let my feet decide; and they take me to the left, up Grovebury Road. I walk as far as the path that leads to the canal, which I follow; then I stroll back along the canal as if I was heading for home, but I don't turn right at the supermarket, which is the way to walk back through town. I keep walking; and walking; and walking. The wind like ice at my temples; the pain refreshing.

I could walk as far as Northampton, I consider. To the Midlands!

The fact of the matter is, I'm tired after an hour, which is opportune since I have just begun my approach to The Globe at this time. I buy a drink and sit outside under a vast umbrella, smoking.

I phone Roy.

His voice is unexpectedly cheery; it's as if he's just heard a good joke and he's struggling to process it without any further laughter.

'What's tickled you, mate?' I ask him. Truth be known, I find his good humour creepy.

Roy is immediately on the defensive. 'Why, what's the matter with you, Tom? You sound like you lost a tenner and shat your knickers.'

What does he mean: *what's the matter?*

'I'm tired, mate. I had a late night.'

Does he imagine our phone line to be insecure?

'That all? Wait a sec, mate – *Ian! Turn the radio down, would you?*'

This is going nowhere. 'Are you free for a pint?' I ask him.

'Will be soon. Just got a service on a Mondeo to finish up. The Leper?'

'Why not? I can walk there, half hour, forty-five minutes... How's Kolko?'

'We need to chat...' Roy half-sighed, half-chuckled. '... He's gone, mate.'

In the last few *hours*? So loudly, and with such appreciable violence, do I say '*Fuck-a-duck*' that a couple of the ducks in the water turn my way, as if in alarm at the proposal.

'How did he get out?' I whisper into the mobile.

'He didn't,' Roy replies. 'Not escaped gone, Tom. *Gone* gone. The man's dead. Gone as in brown bread, mate. And I'm somewhat hysterical at this moment in time. I've been calling you for a while—'

'Not on the phone. The Leper!'

'...The Leper,' Roy agrees.

10.

It's a long time before I enter The Leper. It's been a marathon walk and my feet are hot. Throat's burning for beer; emotions as tangled as Christmas tree lights in their box… Kolko is dead. Not just gone gone, the cunt is dead gone. *Real* gone; a goner… and I simply don't know how to feel – not that one should be able to choose anyway.

Roy greets me as though I'm back from a ten-year Antipodean emigration; he even hugs me. Roy! Roy, whose concession to any pleasantries involving bodily contact is strictly limited to a before- and after-sale handshake.

Leaving Angie looking mildly put-out that we do not require her company (The Leper is half empty and she's bored), Roy and I move across to a table. He's already steaming. His rump knocks the table and the menus flap to the floor; Roy giggles. It's a relief when he finds his balance on a bench, his back to the wall. Still he does not stop chuckling. I collect the menus off the carpet and sit opposite him, near the open fire. Instinct informs me that I should be as drunk as he is, but I can't get there.

'So.' Roy takes a break from laughing. 'Have you had a good day then?' he asks.

No one's perfect; I can't help it either – the monumental absurdity of it all – something triggers the laughter in my own brain, and sucks it out through my face. It's as though we've just heard the best joke going. From over behind the bar, Angie wipes a glass and gazes at us imploringly, as eager for a taste of the witticism that's infected us as a dog is for a bite of meat at the family barbecue. But what would I say to her, even if I could say anything at all?

'I've had better,' I answer, 'I've had worse…God.' The fit of hysteria passes, but it takes its time. 'What's the state of play, mate?'

'Ian's with him. Just in case.'

'In case of what? In case he wakes up and steals the kid's skateboard? You did *check*, didn't you? I mean, we are definitely talking about an ex-copper, aren't we?'

'Of course I fucking checked! It was Ian's idea.' Roy sucks in air through his teeth. 'The boy's got potential in this field, Tom – from what I see, anyway. The old paranatural game, the lad's a natural.'

'I'm not sure I follow, mate. *What* was Ian's idea?'

'To stay with Kolko. Through the night.'

'Are you mental? You didn't agree, did you? Tell me you didn't.'

Appearing a tad more than formatively displeased by my interrogation, Roy slurps lager from his finger-smudged glass and shrugs his shoulders. 'The fuck not, Tom? The cunt's dead, if I need to remind you.'

'Yeah a bit louder, eh Roy?'

'Sorry.' Roy belches. 'Oooaah. Better out than in, I suppose. Unless you're a corpse.'

I sense that Roy is on the verge of our second act of this programme of hysteria, so I enlarge upon my views without further delay. To assist myself in the project I even put my glass down; I fold my hands over my knees.

'He might not be safe, Roy,' I tell him for starters. 'We don't know what Kolko's capable of, dead or alive. Why do you think he volunteered to stay there anyway?'

Roy's eyebrows beetle together. 'He didn't, Tom. We took him there in the boot.'

'Not *Kolko*. Why does *Ian* want to stay there overnight, with a dead bloke in a car?'

'He's a teenager! They wanna do stupid things! The dead's "in" right now, apparently: so he says. He even asked if he could have some friends over there for a cadaver party. I mean, the mind boggles, Tom, really it does. *Boggles.*'

'But you said no to *that.*'

'Yeah of course. We're not insured for one thing. Say one of them got adventurous with a bit of kit... fucking hell. The insurance premiums don't bear thinking about, Tom.'

'Nor does your spell in prison that would follow.'

'For what? *Ian's* insured, he works. If *he* lets his mates in then it's *his* prison sentence, mate. Anyway, I told him no. And I also told him if he goes against my wishes I'll reshape his testes for him. So he's on his own there... It's a bravery thing, innit?'

'Well I hope so. I still think we should get him out of there. Or at least stay with him.'

Roy shakes his head. 'Tom, he ain't going nowhere, son.'

'Maybe no. But I was thinking of it another way. What if there's a visitor?'

'Then he tells 'em we're done for the day, come back tomorrow.'

'I meant tonight... What do you think we should do with him?'

Roy finishes his pint. 'He's got sandwiches. He's got soup.'

'Not Ian! Kolko!'

I am close to laughing again, and this won't do. 'I mean, call me old-fashioned if you will, Roy, but you do agree we might have a tiny problem...' I lower my voice. '...with a dead man in your place of work.'

Roy twists his neck and looks into the fire. 'It's your round.'

11.

Naturally we return to Bible Street Cars. Apart from the fact that neither of us have anything better to do, there *is* nothing better to do.

The weather has taken a turn for the worse. Before, it was merely diabolical; now, as the cab spins and splashes us onto Stanbridge Road, there is a touch of the Biblical about this precipitation.

The cabbie says: 'I should be on danger money.'

Slow and steady wins the race. The vehicle inches along; the wipers beat momentary gaps in the water on the windscreen, but they're no more effective than unshielded cops at a riot.

It's not natural, I hear in the thwacking of the wipers. Yet it's warm in the back of the taxi; I experience that feeling I would have as a child, especially in the winter, gazing out of the bedroom window, with the rain outside a threat that couldn't touch me.

Rain assaults our taxi.

'I can't see a bloody thing, lads. I'm going to have to stop for a minute.'

'You can't,' says Roy. 'It'll fuck the engine.'

'Oh do you reckon?' the driver answers him. 'I *can't fucking see where I'm going.* It's gotta let up in a minute.'

'I'm a mechanic, mate,' Roy begins.

'Yeah I don't doubt it, but right now this is dangerous driving, all right? Don't know where I am's - no fucking landmarks. So mechanic or not, mate, you can take my advice or you're free to get on your toes.'

The taxi does not glide to a halt, there is insufficient acceleration behind it that would require the verb 'to glide'. It simply stops. Without the burr of the engine, the rain sounds louder than ever: so does the silence between the three men.

'Do I take it,' says Roy, his voice grand, 'that the journey so far is without charge?'

The driver sighs into his rearview. 'This one's definitely on the house. My good luck to you and all who sail in that fucker outside.'

'Are you thinking of walking,' I say to Roy, 'in *that* monstrosity?'

'In the absence of a cabbie with bollocks, mate, I see no viable alternative.'

The taxi-driver turns in his seat. Through the payment hole in the reinforced plastic he expresses his displeasure with Roy's disparaging dissert.

'You telling me I'm *wrong*?' he demands. 'You want me to drive in *that*?'

Despite everything, Roy sniggers. 'What happened to taxi-drivers calling you *sir*, Tom?'

'A different era,' I answer. 'The man's got a point.'

'Thank you! Voice-a reason!'

'We still have to *get* there,' Roy argues. 'How much money you got?' Roy asks me.

'…Change.'

'But how *much* change?'

'Do you want me to count?'

'Yes. And you–' to the driver '–can turn the meter off toot-fucking-suite, I tell you *that*.'

'It's off. I already said – this one's free. What are you suggesting?'

'We're going to buy your taxi for fifteen minutes,' Roy tells him. 'Just to get us there. I'll even give you *tea.*'

'I've told you…'

'*I'll* drive the bloody thing. It's only *rain*. We can do it. I'm worried about my lad at the garage, all right?'

'Your lad's there?' The driver remains twisted in his seat, seatbelt off.

No more than a glance at Roy's face is needed to tell me that Roy knows as well as I do that the driver has misunderstood the semantics: the driver thinks Roy means *son*.

'I shouldn't've left him there,' Roy continues. 'The babysitter didn't show up to collect him. With my wife a year in the grave…'

The driver shifts in his seat: now he's facing forward. The show of his indecision is a first night performance, exactly in the rearview mirror, framed beautifully. Exasperatedly he slams both hands on the wheel, his choice now made.

'Only life innit?' we catch from the back as he jerks the key in the ignition. 'Only *rain.*'

12.

Not without difficulty we turn onto the drive leading down to Bible Street Cars. The taxi is shaken like a tambourine. Every pothole in the gravel we find and we drain of water by heavy and noisy displacement. At laborious length we draw up to the garage, or as close to it as we can get with the other vehicles parked haphazardly on the forecourt. No one is required to state that there are too many cars present.

The driver tugs on the handbrake.

Is that *music* from within?

I expect Roy to be angry at Ian's disobedience, but Roy is as stunned as I am. It seems that it's me who needs to seize the reins.

'How much do we owe you?' I ask the driver.

'We're lucky to be alive if you ask me.'

'Then I owe you a favour.'

The driver snickers. 'Yeah you do. And twenty quid, mate.'

'Twenty *quid*? For a coupla-mile drive? That's outrageous!'

'Just pay the man, Tom,' Roy states calmly, pulling on the handle to open the door. He's suddenly all business.

Sure. I'll just pay the man – swiping cash from those unlimited barrels of fifty-pound notes I have stashed all over the countryside.

'I've got twelve pounds and some paracetamol,' I inform the cabbie.

'Then that'll have to do then.'

Rain sluices into the back of the vehicle through the door that Roy's left open. He's halfway across the yard, his head down, moving slowly against the downpour, into the gale.

'Roy, wait up!'

I stuff the money into the driver's dish in the Plexiglas window that separates us. I shuffle over and leave the cab by the same door.

I've never experienced rain like this. I thought I'd taken the worst the British climatic system can muster, but this is new – a ferocious quality, drumming the ground. Gravel dances at its spanking. Through the rain it's hard to breathe; as swiftly as my lungs will allow, I crabwalk around the parked cars, my feet frozen, the wind whistling in my nostrils, past my ears. The rain on my glasses, I see *dick*.

The main garage doors, through which cars are driven, are closed, I would imagine locked. The mansized door is wide open. I follow Roy through it.

The first body I see is that of Junior Mechanic Ian: Roy's apprentice, E. While I don't know if it's the first one *Roy's* seen, it is certainly the point at which he's stopped walking, though other sights are available for our scenetaking.

Ian is lying in a pool of blood that resembles oil; he is also lying in a pool of oil that resembles blood. Much of this blood has issued from Ian's mouth. A spanner has been forced into his mouth – its full length, sideways on – with such external pressure that he's lost teeth and had his gums torn open. A section of the spanner's metal can be seen jutting out of Ian's right cheek, where it's gone through like a hideous vast piercing.

'Fucking hell, E,' Roy mutters.

The music I heard from outside gets on my nerves. It's coming from Roy's old radio, and I walk over to turn it off. 'We're in danger, Roy.'

Roy doesn't hear me; his eyesight's transfixed by Ian, on the floor by a Mondeo. Partly *under* a Mondeo, Ian's right arm, from just above the elbow, has been crushed by the car's front tyre on the driver's side. There are scratches all over his hands; abrasions chase one another across his forehead, down his neck.

'Fuck they *done* to him, Tom?'

The rain outside remains consistent, as far as volume is concerned; it's amazing that I hear what I hear above this constant uniform clattermurmur.

But I *do* hear something.

'What's that?' I whisper to Roy. Bending down (my back creaking), I pick up a discarded screwdriver – for attack or defence I don't know. There is blood all over the handle; blood on the metal to its cross-tread point. For Ian is not the only victim of this evening's atrocities: far from it.

'What am I gonna tell his Mum?' Roy wails now.

'Keep your voice down!'

My grip on the screwdriver handle is slippery, and I understand that I've just provided my fingerprints for whoever investigates this scene.

Near Ian is another male of indeterminate age, indeterminate because his attacker has done a level-best job to remove his face.

Doing my best to ignore this victim and two others sprawled nearby (one of them a girl, face down on the bonnet of a Peugeot, her skirt bunched up around her waist, her bare buttocks for all to see; the other a boy wearing a tail formed from the hose of the airgun that has been embedded in his anus), I head over to Roy's office.

No one there.

But here comes the sound again; and my ears, if not attuned to the disruption exactly, are at least expecting a noise of some kind, and I'm led towards the source.

To find it I need to step over two dead bodies.

The sound is a whimper, pathetic and uncontrolled. The producer of this whimper is a boy, hiding almost under the boot of Roy's courtesy car. Pressed against the wall, and shaking.

There's a car between me and this sobbing mass; I have to bend down to see him, and even in this pose my view is far from perfect. He is the only one who has escaped the madness.

'You can come out now,' I tell him. 'They've all gone.' Instinct drives me to use the plural pronoun, surely one man on his own could not have done this.

The only movement the boy makes is a continuation of his trembling; and although I know he must need his time to panic, playback and reflect, I need him out here, to talk to him. As far as I know he's the only living witness to whatever happened.

'Come on, son,' I try. 'Time's ticking.'

The boy offers no additional motion. I'm not even certain he's heard me above the din of his shock. Then another possibility occurs, prompted by what I saw of Ian's mangled arm.

'Are you trapped under there?'

After a few seconds he answers.

'No.'

'Then let's get you out. You're safe now,' I add, hoping that my nose won't grow like Pinocchio's.

'Jesus *Christ*,' I hear behind me.

It's not Roy, it's the cab driver. For reasons of his own, presumably spurred on by a self-preservatory desire for personal safety, he has followed us into the garage.

'What the fuck?' I hear him say.

The boy beneath the courtesy car panics. 'Who's that?' he hisses.

Still bending over at the waist, I do my best to show the boy my empty hands, palms outward. 'It's fine.' I search for simplicity. 'He's a friend of ours. We're all friends here.'

I flick a look back towards the main garage doors. The driver stands a metre or so from Roy. The latter is still looking down at Ian's corpse…but how do we *know* it's a corpse?

'Roy!' I call. 'Roy-mate!'

'What is it, Tom?' he calls back, his voice diseased with sorrow, regret…

'You've got to check his vital signs!'

'Do what!' the driver spits back at me. 'I ain't going *near* him, mate!'

'I wasn't talking to you. Roy, will you listen to me, please?' I stand up straight but do not move from where I am near Roy's keybox, on the back wall of the building. I want the boy to be able to see my wet jeans and my drenched shoes; to let him know I'm still here.

'We're gonna have to work quickly,' I shout, but not in anger. 'Check his vital signs and call an ambulance.'

The cabbie interrupts me. 'You won't get an ambulance out in this weather, mate,' he replies, and I'm afraid I rather take umbrage at the tincture of overt glee in his proclamation. I point at the man and tell him he's out of order and that he's being a right royal pain in the arse. I don't know if he recognizes something in my face or even my words that suggests any further backchat would be pushing his luck, but I am grateful for the pressing-together of his lips (an exaggerated gesture of stroppy acquiescence) and for the fact that he doesn't answer me back.

'What's your name, mate?' I ask him. Now that he's here, of course, uninvited but present, we can use him.

'Wilson.'

'Good. I'm Tom, the man beside you is Roy, and this fella–'
This time I don't bend at the waist; I sink down onto my haunch-
es and I indicate to the boy under the courtesy car. '…is who?
What's your name, mate?' I even try smiling and give him a wink.

The boy answers but not with what I wanted him to answer.
'I thought you said you were friends,' he tells me.

'There are no flies on you, mate, are there? He's a driver –
a taxi-driver – he brought me here, with Roy. Now what's your
name?'

To my disappointment the boy resumes trembling and
shaking; I thought I had him there. Turning away from the boy I
call out: 'Wilson, check the other bodies, will you?'

'Are you on crack? I ain't going close-up to no *corpses*. I never even *seen* a dead body before, apart from me Nan. And she was
peaceful in bed, mate! Not like this!

'*Then get the fuck outside, you lazy cunt! We're trying to work!*'

'Woe…' says Wilson.

'Roy? *Move your arse, mate*. Now.'

'And you – I'm losing my patience with you, son. I asked
you nicely – what's your name. I've had a shit day you might say
and my temper's short at the best of times. I can help you or I
can *not* help you; but you have to know I've got a bad back – I've
been signed off work for months with it – and I'm not gonna keep
talking to you at ground level. So, for the very last time, what's
your *fucking name*?'

I twist the screwdriver that I've forgotten is still in my hand.
It's hard to believe that only about a minute has passed since Roy,
Wilson and I arrived, but I'm painfully aware of seconds ticking
away while the boy considers his identity. Eventually he answers:
'Wolfe. My name's Wolfe.'

…Something *familiar* about the name. I search the databanks. Wolfe, Wolfe…where have I heard that name before?

'The school bully?' I ask, almost incredulous. '*James's* bully?'

'…*Yes*. Never again,' he confesses.

'But what are *you* doing here?' I ask him.

'I came to watch,' Wolfe replies.

'Watch what?' As I rise to my feet, curious about this (no-doubt temporary) show of leadership and control which I seem to have at my disposal, I add, 'Forget that. Just come out right now or I'll give you *such* a hiding, Wolfe.'

One thing I've learned is that bullies are basically cowards – well, this one certainly is. One language they understand is that of the threat. Nevertheless relieved to hear him moving – the bluff has worked – I call to Roy, 'What's the story?'

'No pulse,' he calls back. 'I *shouldn't have left him, Tom*!'

'What about you, Wilson?'

'Same story, boss. Sorry.' I watch as Wilson's nose wrinkles – he is close to me now – and with an admixture of disgust and prudish respect on his face, he pulls gently at the girl victim's skirt, lowering the hem so that it covers her backside.

Wilson has earned himself as perspicuous a view of what happened here as have either Roy or myself. And as much as I wish he hadn't come in for shelter, it's not half as much as I imagine *he* wishes he hadn't entered Bible Street Cars.

While Wolfe gets himself to his feet, prissily brushing dust from his thighs and knees, I take two of the paracetamol I've carried in a front pocket, and I pop them into my mouth. Through the bitter chalky taste I say to the boy, who is nearly as tall as I am, 'Did you see this happen?'

He nods his head. Then he bows it; he chin spreads across the top of his chest.

'We're going into the office,' I tell him.

Another nod. 'But I don't want to look. Can I close my

eyes?' he asks.

'Close your eyes. Take my arm.' We start the slow walk that I know will feel long, even though it's only a matter of metres to Roy's room. 'Are you joining us?' I ask Wilson. Wordlessly and without a gesture he follows me and Wolfe as we shuffle along. Roy is at the office door, unlocking it. He sees the three of us in and then he joins us.

13.

I hand Wolfe a cup of tea. He takes a sip and winces. 'It's too sweet.'

'It's good for shock,' I tell him. 'Now, what happened?'

'Am I in trouble?' he asks.

'Well that depends what you say,' Roy answers – a comment that I don't think really does anyone any favours. I expect Wolfe to clam up, but he doesn't. He nods his head; he takes it literally; he sips more of his tea (and winces again).

'My brother was supposed to come but he's got man-flu. He didn't know I was listening to his phone calls, but I usually do. And I heard Ian say to Jack – that's my brother – there's a dead man on show. Free entry, just bring a bottle. But Jack says, I'm sick, I can't make it and I couldn't help myself, I said *Can I go? Can I go?*

Roy's brow is furrowed. 'What was so attractive for Christ's sake?'

'It doesn't matter, mate,' I answer on Wolfe's behalf. 'So you were having a party, simple as that?'

Wolfe nods his head. When the cup trembles in his hand he uses his other hand to steady the grip. He's reliving it now; we are making him relive it.

'I had to promise I wouldn't get on anyone's nerves. Jack said I wouldn't say boo to a goose so they let me come.'

Wilson stands closest to the door; he has declined the offer of a hot drink and now appears cocked and hairtriggered, ready to blow. 'But what *happened*?' he demands.

Looking into his tea, panning for solutions, Wolfe says, 'There were about eight of us in total. Some brought bottles but I don't think anyone drank anything – there wasn't time. It was all over in a few minutes…'

'*What* was?' Wilson asks.

'Wilson, please – let him speak, eh?'

Wilson nods his head; a resigned expression is what he tried for but I can detect his dread simply enough, and no doubt so can Roy.

'We could see the dead man, in the car at the back,' Wolfe resumes, 'but the other cars were in the way. A couple of the guys wanted to get closer, for a better view, so they climbed over the cars and knelt on the bonnet, just to see better.'

He sips his drink.

'Then one of them – I don't know his name – he started to scream.'

14.

One of them started to scream.

The panic spread at the speed of sound, and people were shouting, *What is it? What's wrong?*

The boys who had clambered onto the car now scrambled off it again, and quickly. Its metal was roasting hot, and all you could hear was swearing and a bit of sizzling.

Then *all* the cars heated up, the temperature passing from bumper to bumper, too fast for it to be natural.

The air was so hot – I thought one of the cars might blow. We were all backed away from the cars, up to your front doors, watching scared. And then a few said that's enough and they went back out into the rain. And then another load of panic went around, cuz my brother's mate Sammy said *He's moving*!

I don't know if he was or not. It was hard to see because − you know when it's hot and the air goes wavy? − it was like that out there. But t I didn't want to look like a pussy so I tried to front it out, thinking it can't be as bad as everyone's making out − because I've *seen* something supernatural. Something I can't explain…

Well, I could hear outside, they were having trouble getting their engines started. It just made the panic worse, somehow. Everyone was jumpy and a couple of people were screaming − not just Kathy, some of the guys, too…

Then there was all this confusion and some other people arrived, but not friends. I didn't hear any other cars pull up so they must've been parked outside all along, just waiting for the dead man to wake up.

There were three of them. One man and two women. And the man was a *big* man − overweight − I think about fifty or sixty − and one of the women was about the same age; but the other woman was much, much older. She was like my grandmother or something.

They were all holding guns − but they weren't bullet guns. They shot out… I don't know what to call it… like electrical pulses of some sort. They were *zapping* us! And everyone was going apeshit! Panicking! Running around like crazy bastards. It was like a war!

15.

'Did you see the dead man get out of the car?' Wilson wants to know − a man after my own heart, after all. He's taken the words right out of my mouth. I want to know if Wolfe recognized Kolko from his adventure by the side of the canal.

'No, I hid,' the boy answers. 'I couldn't get out the door because one of the women – the younger one – was guarding it; and she had the same look in her eye. But I don't know how they didn't see me, except someone turned all the lights off for a short time.'

Exhaling deeply, I mention something the boy said a few minutes earlier. 'But you think a few of them got away, you said.'

'I don't know. Either got away or were taken away. I don't know.'

'Okay, son,' Roy says softly. 'Wilson here's gonna look after you – aren't you, Wilson? – while Tom and me check outside in the yard, just in case. We'll be back in two shakes of a lamb's knob. Tom? Would you care to assist me?'

Leaving a distressed-looking boy and a more-than-mildly-fucked-off-looking taxi-driver, Roy and I slide over the wet floor – and we step into the tipping-down rain.

The air at least feels clean.

'What are we doing, Roy?'

'Checking the cars.'

'Okay. What are we checking the cars for, Roy?'

'For some poor cunt who made it out alive, that's checking for what. Or for anything else that seems out of the ordinary.'

I decide to let this one go. Taking another deep breath, I step out into the deluge, to my left – in other words, towards the far perimeters of Roy's kingdom. Behind me, Roy begins ferreting among the vehicles nearest the garage's main doors.

At first there's nothing, in Roy's description, *out of the ordinary* about the cars or the way they've been parked so haphazardly. After all, it had been galing like before the Flood when the funloving youngsters had arrived... However. However, there's something that catches my eye about one car in particular. Just one. A silver Punto with five year-old plates.

It's the only car with the driver's side door left open.

Why would anyone leave the door open in *this* weather?

Because they were running from some murdering fuckwits?

Yes, of course this is possible; but damn it if there's not something else – something that anchors me to the spot. It's a niggle I have... that I have seen this car before; and I know I'm not good with cars.

The number plate reads RO52 DXF.

Damn it, damn it.. where the hell have I seen this car before?

Hearing Roy's footsteps behind me, I spin around and stare into the man's muscular frown. 'What's that doing here?' he asks.

'I recognize it,' I tell him. 'I just can't place it.'

'It's Mrs A's Punto. Amelior Anderson's. But what's it doing *here*? I weren't looking at it; nor was Ian.'

Wolfe's words, both Roy and I heard them clearly enough. One of the women was old enough to be his grandmother.

'We can't be serious, can we, Tom?'

'She was here, mate. I don't know how much of what the boy said is spot-on accurate, but I think she was here.'

Understandably sceptical, Roy adds, 'But Mrs *Anderson* though...'

'I know, mate! I don't get it either... Do you recognize any of the other cars?'

'No, I can't say I do... Mrs A, though, are we suggesting seriously–'

'I don't *know* what we're suggesting seriously, apart from fucking pneumonia if we stay here much longer.' I turn to face him. Grief has shrunk him an inch or two. 'But that night we went to see her – and Kolko slit her throat, Roy. *He was there already*. The cunt was there! It wasn't a fucking *mind* trick he pulled on us, Roy, she was in on it, too! They *staged* it!'

'But why? We keep coming back to the whys of it, mate.'

'And I bet I know who else will be there, probably right at this minute... Stephen. The boy said a big bloke, fifties or sixties. I've got to ask you again, Roy. Did you and he fall out when you were in the nick? I mean, badly. Enough that he'd wait this long to fuck about with us for some sort of revenge.'

'Not that I know of.'

'Then it must be me they're after, Roy, and I can't tell you how scary that feels right now. *They* didn't know there'd be a lot of youths here, did they? They came here for us.'

'No. They didn't know you'd be here either. They came for me.'

'Let's get back inside. You're shivering.'

Approaching the threshold we see Wilson awaiting our return.

'Where's the boy?' Roy asks sternly.

'Cool your boots, man. He's in the khazi, and I can't say I blame the little sod. I thought I'd drive down to the end of the driveway and flash 'em down in case they can't find us properly in the rain.'

I'm confused. 'Flash who down?' I ask.

Wilson gives me a look like I've farted in bed. 'The police, of course.'

'Why are the police – Oh bollocks, guy, you didn't call 'em yet, did you?'

'No, I used mind control. Of course I fucking called 'em. I used the phone in your office. They're on their way.'

Roy flaps his arms, swinging anxiously, and sums it all up entirely adequately.

'Oh *fuck*,' is all he needs to say. He looks ready to punch Wilson, but instead of lashing out with violence he does so with words. 'Gimme your keys,' he orders.

'You've got to be…'

'I haven't *got to be* anything. Give me your keys and I was never here.'

'But *I* was!'

'You dropped off a fare. Someone stole your cab,' Roy continues in a lather, unable to settle on any one specific story. 'Go ahead and name me if you feel so disposed.'

I interrupt his ramblings. 'What are you thinking of?'

'Mrs A. Right now, Tom.'

Nodding my head, I address the driver. 'Give him your car keys, mate.'

'No way! I'm not insured to let anyone drive.'

Roy is swift. 'Fuck your insurance.'

'Yeah right. Because you seem totally emotionally stable at this moment.'

'Tom? Brain the cunt.'

'What?'

'You heard. Put a piece of fucking concrete through this twat's skull. I've had enough of being polite. I want his car.'

Wilson attempts to appeal to our collective commonsense. 'You've got a dozen cars here! Why do you want mine?'

'Are you a genius in disguise, mate?' Roy enquires. 'These cars are in a *garage*. This means there's *something wrong* with them. Now I won't ask you nicely again.'

'I'd give him your keys if I were you,' I say to Wilson. 'You can wait here for the razz: your choice. But we've got the people who did this to visit. And I do mean straight away.'

I can tell that the driver takes this seriously. This earnest consideration, at least, is something for which to be grateful. 'Say we stole it: Roy's right.'

'And look after the boy,' Roy adds, 'before he succumbs to a nervous breakdown or something… You're just going to have to trust us on this.'

I step past Wilson in the doorway. Blinkered in my vision, I stride past Ian's corpse and I enter the office, where the phone is located. While I flip through the heavy pages of Roy's address book, I sense the presence of the book's owner behind me.

'I'm looking for a number,' I explain.

'Well no shit,' says Wilson. '*Whose* number?'

'Whose number, Tom?' Roy also wants to know.

'Mrs Anderson's. For fuck's *sake*, Roy, where did you learn to write? In a *zoo*?'

16.

After long seconds she says, 'Hello?'

'Hello… This is Stephen,' I say to Amelior Anderson.

The line isn't a bad one but I begin to suspect that Amelior's silence is a direct result of telecommunications being affected by the weather. Yet I don't prompt the old girl. I do nothing but wait and wait.

'…Hello, Stephen,' is what Amelior gives me.

Is she gambling? Or does she really think I'm Stephen – or a man *named* Stephen, anyway, who happens to speak in an approximate accent?

'What do you want me to do with your Punto?' I ask her.

She hangs up.

But she didn't flinch at the mention of Stephen's name.

17.

As Roy and I leave in Wilson's taxi, sirens come looping closer. I drive as carefully as I can, and fortunately there's not much traffic on the roads.

'They'll be ready for us, Tom; you know that, don't you?'

'Yes. But not as ready as I am for them.'

We have reached the top end of town already; even moving as slowly as I am, the journey goes too fast. After a short wait at the lights, we are on the road that leads directly to Stoke Hammond, the wipers thudding with ineffective passion on the windscreen, the heater breathing out a continuous blast of oven-quality air.

'Should have called for Hannah,' I mention in passing.

'Why's that?'

'She knows fencing.'

'So? So do I, Tom. Did a lovely job at my ex's the other year–'

'Not fence *panelling*, you twat. I mean she's handy with a sword.'

'Christ. You think it's coming to that?'

I shrug my shoulders. 'Hasn't it already?' And Roy leaves the question unanswered.

Eventually he speaks again. We are passing The Globe on our right; the milestone after this will be The Grand Union, and then we'll be on Amelior's doorstep, no doubt with that wretched cat Nob hissing a fit in our direction.

'What do you think happened, Tom? Apart from the obvious.'

'I think it was Stephen and Amelior; I've no idea who the other woman was. They came looking for Kolko. Armed. It wouldn't at all surprise me if he was hiding from them. He didn't exactly kick and scream much, did he, or try to get out of the car?'

'No he didn't.'

'I think they wanted him back, mate. I think we helped him escape.'

'Maybe… There's something else seems worth mentioning, Tom. It's about them stun guns the kid mentioned.'

'I've been thinking about them as well,' I admit.

'We're not exactly tooled up when it comes to it.'

I point to the dashboard. 'Well I've got my trusty screwdriver.'

'Well *I* haven't!'

'You might not need anything. I'm not sure the electricity guns are anything but a figment of Wolfe's imagination. I mean, where would you buy one?'

'So what are you saying? How else did middle-aged killers and one dotty old bird overpower all those youths?'

'He wasn't lying to us, Roy. He believes what he saw as readily as I believed Stephen was with me on that boat in Iceland. We're creating our own fears.'

Roy sniffs loudly and says, 'Well, if it's all the same to you, Tom, I'd rather *stop* creating my own fears… Are you saying that boy's dad – James's dad – *didn't* come and see me and Ian? Because I know what I saw, Tom. I *talked* to the geezer!'

'I think you talked to yourself.'

'I shook his hand! I touched him!'

'They're in our heads, Roy. I don't know how – I especially don't know why – but they're not ghosts, they're not angels – they're certainly not *protectors* as we used to think. They're *stories*. *Our* stories. Stories we're telling ourselves. That's my opinion.'

'Okay, I'll buy that; but the question is, how do we close the book?'

'That's the tricky part. We're here,' I need not add, but I do.

Amelior Anderson's house appears no different from how it looked the other times I was here, blurred in the rain and the darkness. I tell a lie. There *is* one difference, a light is on behind the front room's curtains. Someone's home… Steaming in our damp clothes, Roy and I sit and wait. While the engine winds down I clean my spectacles on my shirt, stalling for time – they're going to get wet and smudgy again in about five seconds, as soon as we step out into the storm. I turn off the heater. Apart from rain on the roof there is silence.

'Come on, let's get it over with, Tom,' Roy says suddenly, and he opens his door and wriggles out.

Horses scream from the farm beyond the end of the road. I lock the car door. Roy is already halfway down Amelior's path, not waiting for backup. To catch him I have to jog around the vehicle and onto the old woman's property.

There is no need to knock or to demand entry.

The front door is already wide open.

Roy catches hold of my arm. 'Let's make a bargain,' he says.

'*Now?*'

'Let's promise ourselves we don't have to believe everything we see.'

'It's a deal,' I tell him with my fingers crossed.

III.

1.

It's not that Dorothy wants to be alone; it is more the case that she can't find anyone to be unalone with. She has already been across to Tom's door, but he didn't answer. Hannah's going straight to voicemail, Annette's phone just rings and rings, even at home (so where is Richard? Where are the boys? Have they all gone away on holiday?). Oh, and Sam's dead. And Dorothy cannot bring herself to call Patrick, though the temptation to do so is strong.

Where *is* everyone?

On and off, between stints at her desk with her fountain pen in her hand, she's thought of her defeat at the Tiddenfoot Centre the other night. She has tried to dilute the shame by referring to it as her-*and-Tom's* defeat, but this is a lazy bluff and nothing more. It was her own nightmare that had made her think they must rush to the centre; her own insistence that they had Annette to save.

Neither had been true; and yet she remains griefstricken in advance for Annette. She is certain that ill is planned for the woman, although whose plan this happens to be she is at just as much of a loss to answer as any of the group are. She should call the house, but *I won't call the house,* she has decided.

In addition to writing up what's occurred within the group, and some thoughts on what it all means (which she prints off and places in her handbag), Dorothy has engaged herself in some light research. The subject? Juvenile psychiatric detention centres in the area. The results? Slim pickings. Until she specifically contacts an institution named Chadwick Lodge, near Eaglestone,

Milton Keynes, she is confident that this will be the one were James is detained. Her phone call is met with a wall of professional curiosity-deterrence. Dorothy is informed that the institution is not at liberty to discuss individual patients.

'Fine; but can you just tell me if he's *there?*'

'I'm sorry. The institution is not at liberty to discuss individual–'

'Patients. I've got it. Thank you, anyway.'

Dorothy is about to hang up when the operator adds, 'Of course, you *could* put your request in writing, stating clearly your inquiry and your reason for making it.'

'I'll do that. Thanks. What's your email address?'

'I'd use a postage stamp if I were you,' the operator hints. 'It's more likely to get into the right hands.' She lowers her voice. 'We get a *lot* of spam here.'

Coupled, then, with her feeling of loneliness is the need to buy a book of stamps to use on the envelope that she has just written on; and it is these two factors that lead Dorothy out into the fresh air.

It's still raining. There is ice in the rain, too; the wind is a piledriving westerly, no prisoners taken. Very quickly Dorothy has folded up her new umbrella again; it will be of no use in a gale like this. And seeing as getting wet has become something of a new hobby, Dorothy does not so much as raise the raincoat's hood over her head.

There are no stamps for sale at the minimart on the corner: sold out. She will have to trudge up the road to the petrol station. Having done so, however, Dorothy is reluctant to stop walking; she needs the exercise. And on top of this reason, she has a yen to pop her head into the library again, to see what's going on. The last time she was in there she was dragged upstairs to view the story of her life, but there had also been all those copies of

Nutcracker Island on a display shelf.

What's there now?

Nothing odd. The library is not busy this close to the end of the working day; some children in school uniform are using the computers and typing almost as fast as she can herself. Not one of her books is on display for loan; not one of them ever is…

The urge to go upstairs is too potent to resist. Her lack of fear amazes her. As fast as her various aches and pains allow, Dorothy climbs the stairs. To Dorothy's disappointment, the theatre is in use; she'd hoped to sit alone in the stalls for ten minutes, let her mind chase and scurry with her thoughts. But it won't be today: from inside the theatre come sounds that can loosely be described as music.

The woman at the sales desk waves in that style that involves bunching the fist repeatedly. Although she appears to be looking at Dorothy, the latter checks over her shoulder; there's no one else behind her.

'Did you find him?' the saleswoman asks. Has Dorothy seen her before? The face is familiar. 'You were here the other day,' she reminds Dorothy, then she doubts herself. 'It *was* you, wasn't it? The day of the big rain?'

'Oh yes, I spoke to you,' Dorothy remembers.

'Not that *I* saw any of it, mind. They had me in the basement.'

Dorothy has no idea what this means, but she does know that she shared a dazed word with this lady after her autobiopic on the day of the deluge. This knowledge is sufficient to strike up a kind of conversation.

'I'm curious about the noise in there,' Dorothy says, referring to a freeform jazz recital of honking saxes, irregular drumbeats, the occasional crash of cymbals, and a few plangent scales from a pair of trumpets.

The employee smiles. 'I could sell you a ticket right now if you're keen.' She is quick to add, 'I'm joking. They're nowhere near ready yet, as you can hear.'

'What is it?'

'Some kids from Leighton Middle. Every year they do a cabaret afternoon for the old folks from the residential homes. A bit of big band. Bit of Dame Vera. Bit of magic. They're usually quite good; I always enjoy it. One of the perks of the job, I see everything for free. Well not for *free*. I chip into the charity box, of course.'

'Well of course,' says Dorothy. 'Do you think anyone would mind if I sat quietly and watched for a few minutes. You see, *I* used to do that: I played the violin. For the old folks.'

'You don't still play by any chance.'

'I'm afraid not.'

'Shame. I heard them talking yesterday, a couple of them, and they're shy a violin player for the Tchaikovsky. The boy who was playing it's got the mumps.'

Dorothy experiences a tingling sensation in her urethra. 'I used to play Tchaikovsky,' she says drily. '*Serenade for Strings*.'

'That's the one!' the saleswoman blurts.

'Small world,' she adds swiftly. 'I'm afraid I gave it all up when I was a girl.'

'...Go on in. It's dark in there anyway.'

Inside, the theatre is busy with more people, young and adult, than the noise heard from outside suggested. A teenaged soprano rides through her *doe-rah-mee*s. A little drummer boy tunes a snare. A few people look her way through the gloom, but only briefly; other grownups are in the audience, presumably parents or *au pairs*, and not all of them take a keen interest in their offspring's rehearsal. One, a few rows behind where Dorothy takes a seat, reads *The Standard*, the paper held up over his face, his leg stretched out into the aisle.

A teacher taps his music stand with a baton: a call to order. 'Falstaff,' he instructs his ten-strong orchestra. 'From the top, guys.'

The music transports her back to when she was these kids' approximate age. No, younger. Not only alone but lonely in a world of classical music; back to when she performed against her will, all calloused fingertips and anxiety. An ache in her wrist caused by needlessly energetic bowing. And Lord help her, the dimensionless, bottomless alternative timestream of pizzicato, which for Dorothy's immature and trembling hands had forever remained an alien, unbreakable code. She starts to sweat now, just to think of it. And the shoulder where she'd held her violin against her neck – the shoulder where she was shot, raped and pushed into a canal – begins burning with an immediate and complicated ache.

I don't want to be here, she decides. Without any room for doubt she knows that she played here, as a child; this was one of the venues that taunted her, enraged her. *It was here: where I dropped the violin. And Patrick and Amelior and Mum – they were sitting, sitting...*

They were sitting where Dorothy has chosen to sit this afternoon. Standing up, Dorothy stares simultaneously at the stage, at the youngsters giving Elgar their best shot, and also, with the perspective lent to her by the past, in the other direction, out into the rows of darkened faces. Patrick's *grin*. And the knowledge in her bowel that she would be punished and then, her lesson learned, she would be loved; but the two euphemisms equated – they were the same thing. The only variation was the *order* that things got done to her body.

Dorothy attempts to shake the memory. She moves into the aisle and hears the rude rustling of the man's newspaper. She turns to stare him down, and as she does so, as if he's interpreted her ill-will, he lowers the paper onto his lap.

2.

Fearful of apprehension at every step – a hand on her shoulder, her name called in such a way as to suggest that it's garnished with a strong exclamation mark – Dorothy strides along the High Street, making for the canal. Her limited ambition is to shake off any pursuers who might be interested. It takes every ounce of effort not to glance over her shoulder with every couple of strides.

Stepping foot onto the canal path, the overwhelming direction in Dorothy's mind is *left, left, turn left*. She can rejoin Grovebury Road much further up, and walk home from there. Surely no one will follow her so far without addressing her, or apprehending her. But now she discovers that there is a contradictory impulse at play: the one that says *right, right, turn right*. Turn north. *You'll find, if not the past, then at least the future*, she thinks.

She turns right, heading towards the The Globe, with the gravel her pacekeeper underfoot, counting out every stride. Within a few metres she has picked up the pace, almost as though she has a clue about what lies ahead. She strides on, sensing and seeking something, something more than the first of the pubs. Something more than an escape from any pursuer who happened to witness her disgrace in the library theatre.

She walks until she is certain that her feet must be blue with pinched skin, red-and-white with blisters. Such remote parts of her body that didn't hurt before the fall down the steps hurt now. She feels as though it was she who took a meaty punch.

'Good evening to you!' a man calls from far enough away that Dorothy is not confident about his identity. His elderly spaniel leads him along the path, towards Dorothy. 'We must stop meeting like this,' he goes on in a ho-ho-ho vein. 'People will talk!'

He is trying to be funny, but who the hell is he? At last Dorothy recognizes the man: he's the one who asked her if she was all right, here on this very path, though further back in the direction she's come from, on the evening of the film. She bids him a good evening, but she doesn't want to talk.

'Beware of the mad woman if you're walking much further,' he advises. And then to the dog, who sneezes at this moment: '*Bless* you, Pixie!'

'What mad woman?' Dorothy asks suspiciously.

'Threatening to throw herself in, she is. And what a potty mouth on her! Told me – bless you again, Pixie! – to eff you see kay off and mind my own business if you don't mind! Me! A respected pillar of the community! I was shocked at the language. I bet her parents never took her over one knee to give that bottom of hers a solid spank.'

'Oh they did a lot worse than that,' Dorothy replies.

'…Pardon?'

'…if it's who I think it is. How would you describe her?'

'Late thirties, I suppose. Athletic.'

'With streaks in her hair?'

'Why yes, now that you mention it – bless you thrice! – I take it you know her then,' the man adds.

'We've met,' Dorothy answers. 'I'd better go.'

3.

'Fancy meeting you here,' Dorothy says.

Annette turns to see who has spoken to her; then she goes back to looking at the water. The surface shivers in the wind; raindrops give it dimples. It's dark and it looks hostile.

'Why are you standing here?' Dorothy asks.

'There's nowhere to sit.'

'No, I know. I mean why *here?*'

'The same reason you are, I'd guess,' Annette answers. Quickly, without a pause, she adds, 'Do you think places have souls, Dolly? I've been thinking about that a lot. I think *this* place does. It's got a story to tell, this place. If you listen hard enough you can hear it…This is where my father tried to drown you, isn't it, Dolly?'

'Yes. Did Patrick tell you that himself?'

'No, not really. The canal told me. I read the water like I read a book.'

'Why haven't you been answering your phone, Annette? We've been worried.'

'Bit late for worry, I'm afraid.'

'Apparently you're going to throw yourself in,' says Dorothy, with deliberate sarcastic harshness. 'Because *that'll* solve all our problems, won't it?'

'You have no idea about my problems, Dolly.'

'Oh I think I do. I had a glimpse the other night, courtesy of your mother, I think.'

'I don't know what you're talking about.'

Dorothy explains the nightmare she received during the night she spent with Tom. 'And then we rushed to Tiddenfoot. Only to find it locked up for the night.'

'I was here. Right here, on this very spot, I believe. And your dream was close to the mark. I saw my past in the water, Dolly. And my future.'

'Which involves you joining it. Well what can I say? Think about your sons and Richard. They haven't won yet, Annette… Where *are* your sons and Richard, by the way?'

'They've gone to stay with his mother. Until I've sorted things out, quote unquote.' Annette laughs. 'I'm sure she'll be sick of them after the first year. And my name's Caitlin.'

'Excuse me?'

'My name's Caitlin. Not Annette. Tom was right all along. I did a terrible thing, Dolly.'

This is the first time that Annette (or Caitlin) has shown any emotion. Her sudden sob is sufficient to prompt an angry quack from a nearby duck.

Dorothy says, 'Why don't we walk on to the pub? Get out of the rain.'

'I'm not drinking anymore. I was drunk when I used that axe. An *axe*, Dolly – for God's sake! On my sons!

Dorothy realizes what else is different about Annette: the woman hasn't had a drink. She is confronting her grief sober, and Dorothy is not sure if this is sensible.

'How about a compromise?' Dorothy says. 'I'll treat you to a coffee. I've been walking a long time and I've just punched a man in the face, thinking he was Patrick.'

Arm in arm they walk on to The Globe.

4.

The Polish barmaid regards Annette with some suspicion. She has reached for a tall glass, which she'll fill with a triple vodka and top up with soda, when Dorothy says, 'Two black coffees, please. Sling a brandy in mine.'

They sit near the open fire, in front of which a shaggy dog with damp fur is sprawled in torpor. 'I hope we smell better than he does,' Dorothy says.

'I doubt we do.'

The dog lifts his head, acknowledging the insult, and then he returns to his nap.

'So were you serious before? You want me to call you Caitlin.'

The other woman shrugs. 'It's my name, it's what my mum

calls me. Annette was another identity, almost. It was a hiding place. You know, when things got…'

'Challenging?' Dorothy suggests.

'That'll do…I can't believe we're actually talking about this rationally. I was on the verge of killing myself an hour ago.'

'No you weren't…Thanks,' Dorothy adds to the still-suspicious barmaid who has brought them their refreshments. She puts the mugs down carefully, saying 'This one is the brandy' and withdraws.

'So then…Caitlin. You saw your past in the water. Was it whizzing past like I saw it in my dream?'

'Not whizzing. But moving.'

Annette falls silent and sips her coffee. Dorothy can guess what she is thinking, and to help her not to do so, she asks: 'Has Emil heard from James, by the way?'

'Not that he's told me. Then again, why would he tell me? I'm only his mother. Why do you ask?'

'A theory I have. And what about Sal?'

'What about her?'

'Have you heard from her at all?'

'She's dead, Dolly.'

'…*So*?'

'No I haven't. Nor do I expect to, particularly. The bond between us wasn't so strong, I wouldn't think I'd see her again. I think the bonds have to be strong.'

Dorothy nods her head. 'Which is why I'm surprised we haven't heard from Sam,' she says, 'unless Hannah has, of course.'

Annette looks startled. 'Sam? What are you telling me?'

'You don't know. You might need a splash of brandy in that, after all. I'm sorry to be the bearer, and all that, but Sam's not with us anymore. Hana killed her.'

The startled look on Annette's face shifts to fullblown shock.

She slumps in her chair, some of the strength vanished from her backbone. 'What did she do?' she asks quietly.

'She had sex with him, that's what she did. It's all caught on film.'

'With who? With Tom?'

'No, with *Hana*. What made you say Tom?'

'Oh, *Hana*. Not *our* Hannah. I thought you meant…'

'No. Although I think he's *our* Hana, too. I'm curious why you brought Tom into this.'

'Oh you know – it's crazy – but maybe a revenge thing. *I* don't know. She finds out he's sleeping with Sam as well and she goes berserk.'

Dorothy frowns. 'What do you mean *as well?*' she asks.

'As well as Hannah. As in Paddington.'

'Tom's not sleeping with Sam and Hannah, is he?'

'Well I don't know about Sam – that's what I was saying – but Hannah, definitely.'

Placing her mug back on the table, Dorothy says, 'I feel sick.'

'Why?'

'I didn't know. I had my suspicions.'

'I mean, why do you care? He slept with me as well, way back when. When I was mad.' She smiles. 'He got around, did Tom.'

'That's a different thing,' Dorothy answers stuffily. 'Are you sure I can't tempt you to a drink? I'm having one now, I've just decided. A double of something.'

Annette shakes her head. 'A scandalously overpriced fruit juice, please,' she orders.

A small queue has formed at the bar; this gives Dorothy some time to explore her emotions about Tom and her own burning sense of hypocrisy. While she knows that there are bigger fish to fry, she cannot help feeling betrayed. It is only a couple of minutes before she's served, but it feels like her hair is turning white.

'You're busy this evening,' Dorothy says to the Polish girl.

'Sure. We have two new ladies starting but they're both late. It's just me and Freda in the kitchen. Ice in the orange juice?'

'Please.'

'If we get busy I don't know what I'll do, I really don't.'

Dorothy pays for the two-drink order with a ten spot. Annette's predication of the juice being exorbitant has been proved correct. 'Well let's hope the rain keeps people indoors,' Dorothy says, palming her change into her purse.

'Oh is it raining again?' the Polish barmaid asks. 'It's worse here than Warsaw.'

'It's been raining all day,' Dorothy replies.

'Not here! I got here at ten this morning. Beautiful bright sunny morning! One of the days I *don't* miss Poland…Then I talked to one of the new staff who should be here by now, on the phone. She said she was looking up the weather back home on the Internet. It was hailstones.'

Dorothy smiles. 'Why was your new girl looking up the weather in Poland?' she asks.

'Oh sorry, I didn't say. The two new ladies both come from – I don't know if you know it – the Lubuski Region. It's on the German-Polish border, it's not very famous.'

'I know it,' Dorothy interrupts. At her core is a chill that no amount of coffee would be the equal of shifting. It's a good thing that she's switched to gin. 'I used to work there, many moons ago. Or I think I did.' She picks up the glasses, ready to return to the table. 'Tell me: these two new employees. Is one of them a black girl?'

The barmaid shrugs. 'I haven't met them; the manager interviewed them over the phone…Does it matter?'

'Not in itself. I think I might know them.' She turns away.

'Great,' she adds, this time to Annette. 'Now the barmaid thinks I'm a racist. Keep England for the English, and all that. She'll probably spit in our drinks next time.'

'I was thinking of a taxi after this. Did you wanna stay?' Annette asks.

'Well, I've got to see if it's the women I'm thinking of, haven't I?'

'I'm lost.'

Taking sips from her G&T, Dorothy explains what has just happened. Before Annette has a chance to say anything by way of reply, much less raise an objection to the simple plan of sitting put until the new staff arrive, Dorothy turns the topic back to Annette and says, 'Apart from the obvious, what are things *like* in your parents' house?'

'Honestly? They fuck,' Annette answers. 'And tell me if it's not bad enough to consider your parents having sex *anyway*; it's even worse if one of them's dead. It's like they're on honeymoon!' She rakes her hair with her fingernails, asking, 'Is it possible to forgive, Dolly, do you think?'

'For me or for you?'

'For anyone. I was speaking hypothetically.'

'Hypothetically I think it is. But for me it isn't – especially if you're referring to Patrick. Or Amelior. Or my mum. Or my rapists.'

'I'm trying to, Dorothy…' Annette's voice is low. '…I'm really trying to hate him. It's not as easy as you think when it's blood.'

'You did just hear me mention my mother, didn't you?'

'I did. But did you mean it?'

'Absolutely I meant it!' says Dorothy. 'She sold me into slav-

ery! And your dad needs psychiatric help! Until recently he came
swimming with me every now and then! I shudder to think what
he got out of *that*. At the *very least* he disturbed your childhood to
the extent that you felt murderous towards your own children.'

'I can't deny that; but he tried to make some sort of amends.
He made me forget – somehow. He gave me a new identity. And
you saw me as Annette, but that doesn't mean Caitlin was gone.
She wasn't gone. She killed her children. She went to prison. In
real life – or I should say, in Annette's life, even though I wasn't
even Annette then – Tom stopped me axeing my lovely boys. But
I can remember holding the axe, Dolly. Whether it was Caitlin
or Annette, it was still these hands. It was still my sons. It was still
jail.'

'Parallel existences,' Dorothy muses. 'Two alternative versions of the same story – or more – playing out at the same time.'

'In my case, two alternative personalities. Caitlin the de-
pressive – the child-killer, the Tom-stalker…Even more recently,
when I saw my past in the canal. I pretended to be Amelior Anderson's niece so I could steal her car from Roy's garage. Why? I
just gave it back! I didn't even damage it! It was *pointless*.'

'It was Kolko's fault as well,' Dorothy tells her, sipping her
drink. 'Let's not forget about him. He's been around us like ice
round a penguin. And even if he's not the magician we thought
he was, he's still got some tricks up his sleeve. He's *some* sort of…
facilitator. Or agent. And I think he's powerless without other
people's mischief. He *thrives* on it. Wouldn't surprise me, Annette,
if it was Kolko who put the ideas in your head, or at least some
of them. What else did you do?'

'How long have you got?' Annette answers sourly. '*Caitlin*
sent Tom a box of insects, just to annoy him. *Caitlin* took Roy's
apprentice a poisoned pizza, just to annoy Roy. *Caitlin* split up
from her husband for a while, and she and her boys rented the

house opposite the back of Tom's flat. So it was *Caitlin* who had sex with Tom. Not Annette. Not me. Which I only mention now because I saw how upset you were about him and Hannah.'

IV.

1.

Nob has grown in height and in bulk: the cat is now the size of an Alsatian, and he's not happy either. As we step in out of the rain, the cat opens his mouth wide and sprays spittle in our direction. Some of it lands on Roy's Doc Martens, but this is merely disgusting compared with the noise the animal makes – a desperate high-pitched whining – which is downright creepy and freezes the marrow in my bones.

Clearly the cat has been placed on guard, but I don't understand this if the front door is open. Do they want us to enter or not?

I don't know what thoughts bundle through Roy's head – he doesn't speak – but he acts much faster than I could ever dream of.

He kicks the cat square in the face. Then, as he steps back from the cat, preparing for the counterattack, we watch Nob shake his head and mewl pitifully. For an instant it seems as though there will be no retaliation – the guard cat arches his back and retreats – but then he gathers his strength and indignation into a fuzzy, muscular ball. With a horribly human squeal he launches its full weight into a leap in our direction.

As Roy raises his arms, I nudge the big man aside; I am ready. Time slows down. The cat flies into my path – our eyes meet, his mouth is wide open, front teeth dripping – and all I do is step slightly aside but leave my arms approximately where they were, both of my hands gripped around the screwdriver's handle.

When Nob begins his descent, his sternum clashes into the blade. In the fraction of a second I've got I thrust it deeper, I push on that screwdriver with all my might. A nasty sound – something like material ripping – is loud in my ears; but it's not as loud as the cat's screams.

'Close the door, Roy,' I say under my heavy breath. At my feet Nob writhes in pain; blood pours from the wound I've created. The possibly fatal wound.

Either Roy has not heard what I said or he's chosen to ignore me (or both). Is it bloodlust on his face? I don't think so, it's something sadder, more rueful. His expression says: *This was always going to happen*; and then he raises his booted right foot. Before I can say anything to stop his action, Roy has stamped down on Nob's head, either to finish the job or to put the animal out of his misery.

I turn away. I close the front door. Behind my back I hear Roy's second, third and fourth goes; the cat is not giving up without a fight. I wait. There's a terrible crunching of bones, and I remain in the same position, facing the door. I wait. Then the noises become quieter, apart from Roy's huffing and puffing. I can virtually count Nob's nine lives out, one by one. I examine the blood on my hands.

'It's dead,' Roy tells me. 'Where first?'

When I turn around to face the direction we'd first been in, I see a mangled cat by the staircase newel. A normal sized adult cat, not the dream-steroided monster that we countered upon our arrival.

'That's for Ian, you little bastard,' Roy mutters under his harsh breath.

'It's just a cat,' I mutter back, not intending to contradict or criticize Roy – merely making an observation. Bending at the waist, I examine the unfortunate creature.

'A victim of circumstance,' Roy tells me coldly. 'I need a weapon.' With which he makes a move, stepping over the feline casualty of war that we've co-killed and heading for a closed door at the end of the hallway.

I have to stay with him, I suppose, a decision I make in spite of the fact that there's a door on my left and one of those under-the-stairs cupboards to my right.

'Ready?'

I nod my head and try to tighten my grip on the screw-driver handle, slippery though it now is with cat blood.

Roy throws open the door.

I don't know what I expected but there's nothing out of place in Amelior's kitchen. The light is already on. I experience a twist of regret in my gut: its cause is the green plastic bowl of water on the floor near the door that leads (presumably) to the back garden, the bowl that Nob won't drink from anymore. But otherwise, nothing strikes me as odd about Amelior's kitchen, old-fashioned and clean as it is.

Roy tries a drawer. It's full of tea towels, a pair of oven gloves: no weapons. He closes it. Then he opens it again, and this time removes a pair of pink washing-up gloves, which, to my amazement, he begins to tug onto his fingers.

'Do you want a pair?' he asks me.

'I don't know what you're doing.'

'I'm not leaving any fingerprints, that's what I'm doing. I'm not going back inside, Tom, no matter what.'

Shaky and frazzled as I am, I know that Roy's got a point. The only crime we've committed, the front door having been open, is the killing of a pet. I skim through the database of tariffs that crimes call for, a database I picked up and half-learned in idle moments at work in the prison. I can't recall any of the prisoners there being in *solely* for animal cruelty, but I bet it would get you a year in a C-Cat.

So yes, I know that Roy's got a point; but I must admit, the reality of leaving behind fingerprints isn't high on my list of worries right now.

'Fuck the marigolds,' I tell him.

Rubbergloved-up, Roy wipes the handle of the draw-er whence they came, then he opens two more before he says 'Bingo' and rattles patiently for something hefty. He takes out a breadknife and invites me to make a choice with a highly-lilted 'Tom?', as though we are choosing from a variety of desserts.

'I'll stick with the screwdriver, thanks. Are you feeling all right, mate?'

'No. I feel peculiar… We should get a wriggle on.'

Leading the way, I do my best to tiptoe up the stairs. Behind me, Roy opens the door to what turns out to be an empty lounge. Although I want him to catch up with me – I'm halfway up the flight now – I don't want to say a word. My teeth chatter.

At the top of the flight is a small rectangular landing. The layout is not a million miles away from that of my mum's house, three bedrooms and a bathroom, but with all of the doors shut it's going to be a lucky dip gamble which is which.

I stop on the stair before the landing and test my senses. All I can hear is Roy moving closer up behind me; he seems to be un-der the impression that climbing slowly equals climbing silently. Unfortunately, for a big man like Roy there's no such concept as ascending a staircase silently. Further back from Roy's progress, I can still hear a muted sizzle of rainfall, but that's about it. There is nothing to hear from beyond the four doors.

And I think of Hannah.

2.

A man arrives in Hell and is offered a choice of damnations – offered this choice by the Devil.

This is Hannah's favourite joke.

Behind the first door is an eternity of fire; behind the sec-ond, an eternity of ice. So the man selects as his punishment the option of standing up to his thighs in excrement, upon choosing which he is told that the tea break is over and that the legions of the damned must resume their headstands.

The message I took from this (I know that Hannah has her own interpretation) was to be careful of outward appearances; circumstances are worse than how they present themselves. But *is* this the case? As far as I'm concerned, standing upside down in ordure for all time has still got to be better than being burnt or frozen over the same timespan.

I have four doors to choose from, four eternities from which to make a selection. Which makes me the damned mortal. I turn around and look down to gauge Roy's reactions, a few stairs below. My heart jolts.

For it is not Roy beneath me.

It is Stephen.

I can't draw in sufficient air; I am lost in my confusion, weighed down to the spot.

Lifting my legs is the greatest trial, but I must get away from Stephen. His presence is a horror to my heart… *Which door?* Which Hell is mine?

'Eeny-meeny,' Stephen chants quietly.

'Where's Roy?'

'Catch a Tommy by the toe,' he continues, regarding my boots.

Why don't I kick him in the face?

'Who's Roy?' he asks as an afterthought.

'I don't have to believe in you, Stephen,' I tell my uncle. 'We agreed.'

'Well *that's* convenient! How can you not believe in what you've just *named*, you arrogant prick? So which one's the magic door, eh, Tommy?'

'I don't know.'

'Well, innit about time you made an educated guess? Or would you like me to wipe your bum for you as well?'

'No I wouldn't. Never again, Stephen.'

To my surprise Stephen chuckles at this. Saints preserve us, he thinks I'm making a joke. He thinks I'm being ironic.

'But I do want you to answer a question. Did you kill a girl called Sabrina?'

Instantly, any sign of good humour evacuates Stephen's face, and what fills the vacuum is an outward appearance of such longsuffering weariness that in any other context I might have experienced sympathy.

'Was that her name?' Stephen looks down at my boots again, embarrassed. 'Yes I did, Tom. But I swear I never meant to. It was on Dunstable Downs. Do you want to see?'

Because I don't know what he's referring to I must look blank. Stephen adds by way of elucidation, 'It's there for you to see, if you want to. Just choose the door.'

'And what of the other doors?'

'I go back to my comment about wiping your bum,' says Stephen, and he takes one single step up the flight.

'No further.' I say this with gutsy assurance. 'Or I'll pick out your eyes with this thing.' And I brandish the screwdriver.

'Jesus. Well *go on* then. I haven't got all day, Tom. Unlike you.'

'And what's *that* supposed to mean?' I ask him.

'Haven't you been listening to the stories, Tom? You've got an eternity. Just *choose.*' Stephen smiles. 'Your destiny awaits,' he adds with deliberately OTT pomposity. 'Eeny meeny miney mo,' he says, and he begins his retreat down the staircase, one heavy tread at a time. Pause. Tread. His back is to me now; he is *ignoring* me!

I step up and try the handle of the door that would be the

bathroom in my mother's similar home layout.

It's the bathroom here, too. What's more, I consider using it. Apart from anything else, eternity is a long time to cross your legs needing a pee. But I'll have to hold it. I shut the bathroom door, and consider the other three. *Eeny meeny.*

I open the one in the middle and...

3.

...what I see is not a bedroom. It is nature. It's a scene comprising a slab of cardboard-coloured sky, which takes up fully three-quarters of my viewpoint. The remaining quarter is not the nightmare scene of mud-and-headstands that Hannah's favourite joke has led me to anticipate. In fact, there are no people present on the brown muddy ground that leads down and away from me.

I'm on the Downs.

Turning slightly to glance over my shoulder, I notice that the scenery is complete, there is no doorway through which to return to the landing. No glimpse of the landing itself. What I see instead, up above me on the steep slope, is an ice cream kiosk; and I wonder if James will be employed within, or is his father working there alone today? And what of stepfather Lenny?

Zombie-like, in a dreamdeep trance, I move forward, in the direction I faced when I walked over the threshold, down the slope. Sticky mud clings to my boots; a fresh breeze stings my earlobes. The light is fair but I don't know if this is sunrise or sunset. All I can do, it seems, is follow this slope down towards the fringe of trees and bushes that appear in such vigorous rude health that I'm convinced it must be summer.

This is what happened to Sabrina, I am sure of it.

The scary part is the shift in perspective. Not only do I sink in terms of the lie of the land, it takes me a few metres of committed downward stroll before I realize that I'm actually shrinking in height as well. I'm getting thinner. Smaller. I'm getting *younger*. My glasses clatter around and about my face, far too large in the frame, the prescription for the lenses entire decades too early and my eyesight blurred. After all, I am a boy, not a man, and I don't need glasses yet, apart from to read the blackboard at school. I remove my glasses and my vision swims into a better focus. I slip the glasses into the pocket…of my grey shorts. While I'm at it, I also pocket the screwdriver; I feel silly for carrying it at the moment.

I am still alone.

4.

While Tom was climbing the first of the stairs in Mrs Anderson's house, Roy nipped into what turned out to be the lounge. And he's still in there. He did not, as Tom believes, make a cursory check of the room and then follow Tom up the stairs. He did not even get out of the lounge. The door slammed shut.

Although he has tried the handle half a dozen times, Roy makes one last effort. It's still locked. Roy feels his blood pressure rising; he ignores the impulse he experiences to batter on the wood. It won't do anything, he is certain. Better to wait; but wait for what? Nervousness grabs hold of his consciousness. The next impulse he must fight is the one that suggests he pick up the television set and throw it through the front window. He could climb out to safety, albeit getting nicked and gashed by broken glass in the process. But what makes him think it's any safer outside?

Clutching the knife tightly, Roy surveys the room. An old sofa with an auburn antimacassar. A glass fronted cabinet stuffed with well-thumbed paperbacks and some porcelain cats. A shelf groaning under the weight of video cassettes…There's not much to see. So why have I been kept here?

The answer is surely obvious. To separate Roy from Tom. Roy fidgets on the spot, unable to decide what to do. He tries the door handle one final last time. It's still locked. He shivers as the result of displacement of air behind his back, something that turns into a form of static charge. Gasping, he turns quickly, lifting up the knife.

'Long time no see,' says the man by the closed curtains. 'Are you keeping well, Roy?'

Roy's mouth drops open but no words fall from it, only sounds. Dreamy gibberish.

'Has the cat got your tongue?' says Stephen.

'I don't have to believe in you,' Roy manages, a few seconds later.

Stephen smiles. 'Funnily enough, that's exactly what my bastard nephew is saying to me right now. On the staircase.'

'…What?'

'And I'll say to you what I'm saying to him. You can't disbelieve me once you've named me.'

'But I haven't *named you.'*

'In your mind you have. You said fuck me, it's Stephen again. *Or "Steve". You know, I never liked "Steve". It's always made me think of bodybuilders for some reason.*

Stephen gestures towards the knife in Roy's right hand. 'Is that for my benefit?' he asks.

Still standing by the door to the hallway, Roy experiences a pang of guilt. 'I don't know,' he admits. 'I didn't know what we'd find.'

'But it would be something you could tackle with a knife? How ambitious *of you!'*

Roy bristles at being the butt of Stephen's sarcasm. 'You've had a bit longer practising this than I have!'

'That goes without saying. But practising what *exactly?'*

Roy shakes his head; he lowers the weapon. 'Oh mate,*' he says sadly, 'what the hell have you got yourself* into?'

Is that really *what you want to ask?' Stephen replies. 'You have my undivided attention and* that's *at the top of your list?'*

'All right then,' Roy continues. 'Where's Tom right now?' Is he safe?'

'He's having a history lesson. I'm not sure about the second bit. That sort of depends on him, really.'

'Why did you kill Ian?'

'Who's Ian?'

'At the garage. What have those kids ever done to you?'

'Nothing. That's the whole point,' Stephen answers. 'No sweeter pain than the pain of the innocent.'

'Well I'm not innocent. Why do you wanna hurt me?' Roy demands. 'We were mates.'

'Who said I wanted to hurt you?'

'Then why have you locked the door? You want to hurt Tom?'

'I haven't locked anything, Roy. I thought I'd say hello, that's all. To my mate.'

'I don't believe you.'

'It's a free country.' Stephen smiles.

'No. You don't understand.' Roy takes a step towards his former cellmate; then another. 'I said: I don't believe you.'

The smile drains from Stephen's face… and then so does his face. Roy inhales and holds his breath; he concentrates as hard as he is able to. Stephen's head collapses; it topples in on itself like a crushed sandcastle. However, there is life in the apparition yet. With Roy no further away than one step, the hollow man makes a lunge at his tormentor. Flick-knife swift, Roy raises the knife… but there is nothing solid to puncture. Stephen passes through Roy like a gritty wind. The movement stings Roy's face, but it's nothing worse than that; it's like a group of shaving cuts.

Then Stephen is gone.

Shaken, Roy stands still for the better part of a minute. Eventually he remembers to exhale, his lungs squeaking. There is nothing but the room; nothing to wait around for. He wipes what he thinks is sweat from his forehead; his rubbergloved fingers carry a fresh skin of blood. The sight alarms him, so he bends at the waist and uses the television screen as a makeshift mirror. It is difficult to tell exactly in the black glass, but it appears that Stephen's *exit has cut his face all over. Mumbling something like 'Fuck it', he yanks the antimacassar off the sofa and presses it to his face as he would a flannel. His face is alive with pain and the material is spotty with blood; but none of the cuts appears deep.*

Again, he tries the door handle and the door opens. Stephen's apparition was to stall and slow Roy down (he thinks) – not to separate Roy and Tom for any great length of time. Roy hits the first stair at a brisk trot, and he ascends in seconds.

Four closed doors face him.

No; one of the doors is slightly ajar. Perhaps it was into this room that Tom ventured. Roy crosses the landing and uses the end of the knife to push the door wide. He peers inside and flicks on the light. It's such a relief to see Tom standing in the middle of the room with his back to the door that Roy neglects to feel worried that his friend is completely motionless and staring into space – and a second earlier, he was doing so in the dark.

'Tom,' Roy whispers, entering the room on mental tiptoes. 'Tom.'

There is no response. Acknowledging in passing that judging by the bags filled with balls of wool, the antiquated sewing machine, and the dozens of pairs of knitting needles in plastic sheaths, that this must be the room in which Amelior undertakes handicrafts, Roy moves in front of Tom and whispers his name with greater harshness. He is careful not to touch this breathing statue – he knows it can be dangerous to wake a sleepwalker, and this situation is the closest that comes to mind – but Roy is a heavy man and his movement to get into position makes the floorboards quiver. This reverberation, in turn, makes Tom shake, but a split second later, any enthusiasm Roy entertains that Tom's shaking is due to a possible waking-up has been crushed. The movement was involuntary.

'Tom-mate. Please,' says Roy, his voice becoming panicky. His eyes dart back to the door. Nothing there. Nothing on the landing. No sounds.

'Fuck it.' And Roy takes hold of Tom's shoulders and shakes him hard, breathing 'Tom! Tom, where are you?'

5.

Here I am and there I am.

It's me and I'm looking at myself: the chubby cheeks, the short trousers. The other me is standing by a dense copse, under the cover of sweltering leaves dropping odd drips of sweaty moisture. The other me sees me approach; my (or his) faces expresses gentle surprise. My (or my) face probably does, too.

What are we doing here? I ask the other me.

Uncle Stephen brought us. We're playing a game. I'm the guard.

Where are they?

In there, the other me answers, indicating the copse.

If I'm quick perhaps I can stop it; but how do you stop what has already happened?

What game are they planning? I ask.

Rapunzel and the Prince. He has to rescue her by climbing up her hair.

Feeling sick to the stomach, I pose another question. *Can I play with them as well?*

I'm the guard, the other me repeats matter-of-factly. *I can't let you in.*

From my pocket I pull the screwdriver. *Stephen's not the real Prince,* I tell my counterpart. *I am. And I have to kill the Beast…*

Uncle Stephen?

I nod my head and this makes the other me nod *his* head. Scratching my arms as I scuttle through a gap in the copse, I am fearful yet oddly confident, even if I do happen to be a prepubescent child wielding an electrician's tool.

The clearing into which I emerge is so small that it scarcely warrants the name. It's about the size of a king-sized bed. Lying on it, startlingly naked, is Sabrina. Stephen is on his feet, fully clothed, an expression of consternation pulsing on his face. Back and forth he paces, several times before he notices me, and I know that I'm too late, the Prince has not rescued Rapunzel by climbing up her long hair. The Prince has committed a foul deed.

It was an accident, Tom, Stephen tells me; but to a child there is nothing more worthy of distrust than an adult with panic on his features. *She stopped breathing.*

Even though it is dark in this hole, I can see the purple marks on Sabrina's throat and chest. Crossing over to where Stephen has stopped pacing, I jab the screwdriver out in a stabbing motion. I can smell the hatred on my own breath. The roar in my ears is louder than the drone of horseflies and wasps.

I am going to kill him. I know it.

On the other hand, Stephen has other ideas. Quickly, cleanly, efficiently, he twats the screwdriver from my grip with one flail of his right hand. With his left hand he slaps my face.

Control re-established, Stephen points a finger at my nose and says, *Listen, Tom. You can't tell anyone about this, do you understand?*

I can feel the child whose body I inhabit begin to nod his head; and although the adult me wants to stop this nod – I want to defy Stephen will all of my remaining breaths – I know that the child is stronger.

I nod my head.

Good boy, Stephen tells me. *Well this is what we're going to do, Tom. Are you listening? We're going to take her back to my van, and then we're going to go back to the building site where we're building the school for the handicapped kids, okay?*

Okay.

Good. And then I'm going to teach you how to forget all of this.

The child me is ready to nod my head again, but this time the adult me is faster. Although my voice is higher, my words are unmistakeably those of a grownup.

'Stephen?' I say. 'I know what you do with my mum. Your sister.'

He pauses before replying. '...You what?'

'You heard me, Stephen. You'll go to prison again when the authorities find out. Then they'll take me away and I'll be in care, and I won't be your bumboy any longer.'

Stephen hurls his bunched fist into the side of my head, and it knocks me off balance. With effort I manage to remain on my feet. The child me yearns for tears – apologetic, rueful, a spray of tears to be used as a plea for forgiveness – but for the moment I am still in charge.

This said, I'm not foolish. Unwilling to be clouted again, I stay out of Stephen's reach and carry on talking.

'My Dad used to tell me there were things he couldn't say to me – the worst things he'd ever seen.'

'Have you been eating the fucking mushrooms out here, Tom? You've gone loopy!'

'He was talking about you and Mum. He knew all about it,' I plough on. Keeping an eye on Stephen, I bend down and pick up the screwdriver from where it fell in the mud. And then, to fill Stephen's stunned silence, I pose the only question that remains.

'Am I your son, Stephen?'

But someone else has a question to ask. *Tom, where are you?* I hear, and it's not the other me waiting outside the copse, and it's not Stephen. It's certainly not Sabrina, whose skin is white and bruised. It's a man's voice, and I'm shaking as the words pierce me.

Wake up, Tom! Wake up, mate!

Shaking. A convulsive spasm. Vibrating…

6.

'…thought I'd lost you.'

'Where?' I begin to say, then the memory of Amelior's house crowds in.

Roy stops shaking me and takes his hands off my shoulders.

'Thank Christ for that,' he says. 'I thought you was a goner. Catatonic, you were.'

'He killed Sabrina,' I state simply, putting on the glasses that I seem to have removed at some point while in my trance. 'On Dunstable Downs.'

'Kolko?'

'No, Stephen…I was there.'

'Well, that's a lovely, heartwarming story, Tom, but don't you think we should make a move? I've got the fear.'

'The Downs didn't forget, Roy,' I explain carefully, knowing it's going to sound nuts. 'He made *me* forget, but he couldn't make the *Downs* forget.'

A blind man could sense Roy's confusion. It's got nothing to do with the lines on his face; it's like a wave of nervous energy, flowing between us. I know that he's aware that what I'm saying is important, but he's balancing this imperative against the instinct for self-preservation. He wants to leave.

'As far as we're concerned, this all started with the news of a murder on Dunstable Downs, right? But there wasn't one, we decided; it didn't happen. We thought it was Kolko, dicking around with our minds. And part of that might still be true. But it *did* happen, mate; it just didn't happen when we *thought* it happened. It happened more than twenty years ago. It was Sabrina. And *the Downs were keeping it secret!*'

Roy chews his lip. 'Something unlocked the secret,' he says.

'I think so. And everyone connected to the place was infected, if that's the right word. Annette was there with her lover and Kolko was there, spoiling for mischief, because *that's what he does*. It's his only function.'

Roy doesn't know what to do with this information. So Kolko replies on Roy's behalf.

'He's telling the truth,' Kolko says from the doorway onto

the landing.

7.

'That's a nice set of bruises you've got there,' Roy says to Kolko. 'Has someone given you a fucking good, well-deserved hiding? Oh yeah! I forget! It was us, Tom! Do they hurt?'

Kolko takes up much of the landing. He is dressed in a pair of jeans, a grey sweatshirt – which indicates to me, given the short amount of time that's elapsed since his Phoenix-from-the-flame act of getting out of the courtesy car at Bible Street, that he has changed his clothes, here on the premises. In turn, this suggests that he has sets of spare clothes, here on the premises. Kolko lives here, with Amelior Anderson. Indeed, his hair is still damp and combed back as if he has taken a shower.

'Yes, they hurt,' Kolko admits. 'So does my left kidney and so do my testicles.'

'Good,' I mutter.

'Do you want a few more,' Roy continues, 'or do you fancy feeding us a few morsels of information?'

A shrug of the shoulders. 'What would you like to know?' Kolko asks.

The question disarms me. Where should I start? Tensely turning the everpresent screwdriver in my right hand – deliberately providing Kolko with an eyeball of the same – I decide that there's no better place to begin than at the beginning.

'How did you know my mother?'

'I was investigating her. I was part of the unit detailed to look into rumours of impropriety involving children.'

'Wait a minute,' I interrupt 'You mean you really *are* a copper?'

'I was. A long time ago, mate; on the first rung of a ladder I had no heart to climb. A statement-taker; a fight break-er-upper; I never made it to the giddy heights of internal affairs, terrorism. My crowning glory was a football riot in Bury Park, after The Hatters lost a relegation-clincher. In fact, it was my actions during that that saved my bacon, in the end. They took my bravery into account – my bravery of all things! – when they heard the stories of my own misconduct, as they put it. Which was nothing they could prove, by the way. And I was offered a choice of walking away from the Force with a year's salary and the signed declaration, both ways, of no further repercussions, or I could stay on full pay until the claims against me had been investigated. The way I looked at it, it was a passport out of a job I hated; and better to leave then than take the risk of a prison sentence. So I left.'

'And what were the claims against you?' Roy wants to know.

Kolko gives me a look that says: *don't be naïve.* 'You know perfectly well what I'm talking about, Royvinder,' he says, airing a chuckle. 'By the way, the silly names were my idea,' he adds.

'You must be very proud,' says Roy.

Jutting out his chin, Kolko slips his hands in the tight tops of his jeans pockets – the pose is as artfully casual as his *ensemble* – and gives every indication of having missed the sarcasm. 'I suppose I *am* proud. We all are. But all good things swerve towards their inevitable end, eh lads? We can't go on forever; we're getting older now.'

A desire to tie up some biographical loose ends is still within me. 'You came to my house when I was a young man, do you remember? I was on a break from a teaching contract abroad. It was baking hot. I answered the door...'

For now, I slide the screwdriver into my front pocket.

'Yes, I remember.'

'You said Stephen had been discovered dead, and this was an hour or so after Mum thought she saw his ghost in the kitchen.

Or thought she saw *something*. I grabbed a saucepan and went around the house searching for an intruder.'

Kolko smiles. 'Yes, she told me about that, you brave little soldier. What were you gonna do if you found him? Boil him an egg to death?'

'It really was him in the house, wasn't it?' I say calmly – or as calmly as I can manage. 'Not his ghost; not a visitation, it was flesh and blood Stephen. And all of Mum's shock was a bluff. So who did they find? Who was the dead body in Wembley?'

Kolko nods his head. 'He was a vagrant, a bit loose in the head. We played with him for weeks. He was grateful for the whisky and the occasional chip. Let us do whatever we–'

'Okay, okay. I get the picture.'

It is now, when Roy breaks his vow of silence, that he points out a flaw in my deduction. He says, 'Tom, if your mother was lying, there needn't've been *anyone* there. It was all a lie – it was an act.'

'To knock me off-centre,' I approve. 'And then she went out – went out *shopping*. How out of character, we thought – my dad and I – for a woman to go out shopping in the afternoon when she rarely went anywhere in the afternoon, especially in heat like that day. It was planned.'

Kolko takes his hands from his pockets; he gives a brisk round of applause and flatters me with a 'Bravo!'

I am in no mood for appeasement; my muscles are tensed like the surface of a trampoline. 'Cut it out,' I tell him. 'Then you arrived and told my dad Stephen was dead. So it looked like it had been a ghost, but it wasn't: it was to throw us off the scent, wasn't it? And by "us" I mean me and I mean my dad. Because… because by then he knew, didn't he? – or at least suspected – what his *wife* was doing with her brother, and what the two of them had done to me, years earlier, and were still doing with God knows how many others, for all I know. Maybe Dad even knew about Sabrina. But if Stephen was *dead*, my dad could at least put some of those suspicions to bed, for the time being.'

'Your Mum can probably furnish you with more details.'

This prods me into an even more angry place of mind. 'I don't *need* my mother to furnish me with more details. Or anything else from now on, for that matter. What sort of mother tries to warp her son's memories?' I ask furiously. 'They'd already got away with it! I was an adult by then, for fuck's sake. And now we had a copper on board as well – to do what? To turn a blind eye? To misfile the odd piece of documentation?'

Kolko's face is as cold as stone. 'Something like that,' he answers.

'You're a credit to your profession,' Roy chips in. Before Kolko can retaliate, my friend also says, 'But what I don't understand is where *I* come into all this. What have *I* ever done to get involved, other than be Tom's mate. And Stephen's cellmate.'

Kolko sniffs. 'Pretty good credentials, wouldn't you say? Who better for when things became more… more *dramatic*? Than a shabby divorcee ex-jailbird who counts his ability to belch a tune as a redeeming feature. Face it, you prick: you're *fucking perfect.*'

I imagine I'll have to hold Roy back; for the last few sentences I have felt him straining, like a Doberman on a leash; and yet, on the contrary, Roy appears cowed by the insult. If I'm not mistaken, I sense him deflate.

He says, 'I'm really going *off* you, mate. What's to stop me driving you headfirst down them stairs, eh?'

Kolko shrugs. 'Your prison record? The certainty that you'll be doing some more time for what went on at your workplace?'

'What, that sham, do you mean?' Roy counters. 'It was all in our heads, mate!'

'I can assure you it wasn't,' Kolko replies, the smile growing back on his face. 'It was fun! Shame you had to miss it. You didn't even RSVP!' Kolko points a finger. 'And you scamps were the guests of honour!'

'We arrived fashionably late,' I tell him, and I also think of the cab driver, Wilson. 'With another witness. Who'll be able to testify that Roy was with me, in the taxi. So hard lines on that one.'

'Ah well. Nothing ventured,' Kolko says. 'Now. If the interview is over, time's time.'

'No, it isn't,' I reply. 'It isn't over. I want to know how you make us forget things.'

'Me?' Kolko lays the palm of his right hand on his chest, near the heart. 'Oh you flatter me, boys, really you do. But alas, no – I am little more, as you said yourself, Roy, than a minor player, *spoiling for mischief*. A technician, perhaps; what might be termed a *facilitator*. Or an irritant – I've heard that one before, and I rather like it, I must admit. *Irritant*. A nice ring to that, don't you think? But nothing too creative, I leave the bigger tricks to the bigger boys. And girls, of course. But we all make our mothers proud, in our own ways.'

The bigger boys and girls, I know, are Amelior and Stephen; but who else must be on this same list?

It is not a question on Roy's mind. 'What you showed the boy James – *that* seemed pretty creative,' he says.

'I was pleased with the fireworks message; and actually, the dancing boats wasn't bad either. Decent *tricks*, you see, but tricks all the same. Or maybe I shouldn't put myself down. I thought a rest in your comfortable car would do me a power of good, but I'm still exhausted… Anyway. I'm sure you lads have better things to be doing than chewing the fat…'

So many more questions swarm my brain, but I fear that

Kolko's right, our discussion draws to a close. To be replaced by what? I wonder. And I also find a space in my busy head to question why *now*. Why has Kolko chosen to divulge so much information *now*, when he's been so tight-lipped and aloof for so long?

He's afraid. He's afraid of what's waiting for me and Roy; and he wants to get out as soon as he can. Or he's making the whole thing up as he goes along.

As Kolko turns his back on us, Roy says, 'Whoa, there! You ain't going *nowhere*, sunshine,' and he tramps out onto the small landing, his knife raised. Instead of bounding down the stairs to a likely freedom, Kolko pauses at the head of the flight, an expression on his face that's part supercilious scowl, part relief.

'I don't think I can be of any more assistance, for now,' he says.

Roy happens to disagree. 'Yes you can,' he answers back, leaning over the banister so that his head, upper body, and above all, the knife, are blocking Kolko's descent. 'You're our insurance policy. Get back here!'

Kolko laughs. 'And you're going to do what exactly?' his voice a snarl. 'Walk me in first with your knife at my back? *Very* Musketeers, I must say! You silly cunt. *Do you think they give a fuck about me?*' he hisses in a whisper.

Roy is not perturbed. 'Well we're about to find out, aren't we? Coz Tom and I ain't going in *there* without a shield...'

'In where exactly?'

Roy jabs the knife at Kolko's face. It's the equivalent of a warning shot off to starboard. Holding up his hands, Kolko relents. 'Okay okay,' he mutters, and he takes the one step needed to get back onto the landing.

Roy orders him to turn around. 'Now I'm going to put this breadknife to your throat,' he explains. 'Just like you did to Mrs Anderson, in that pantomime you staged for me and Tom. Only this time, it's not gonna be fake blood or fake noises. It's going…'

And he stops talking.

'Roy?' I say, instantly scared. I don't want to be alone with this madman, true, but more immediately of concern is that my friend appears to have been paralysed by a stroke. Again I say, 'Roy?' – moving closer, just a wary step.

'He can't hear you,' Kolko answers, and he slips out of Roy's tight grip. To do so, he needs to manipulate Roy's knife-wielding right forearm away, and it is like a big boy playing with an over-sized Action Man. 'But he's safe enough. They want *you*, Tom; he doesn't matter much. So why don't you choose your door?'

Kolko steps back onto the stairs; he steps down two of them, looking up at me looking down on him from over the banister. What must I look like?

'Wait! Just one more, Kolko; please. I really need to know how the others fit in. Dorothy, Hannah…'

But Kolko shakes his head. 'That's too big a topic for right now, Tom,' he answers, almost sympathetically. 'That's another one you'll have to ask your mother about, I'm afraid.'

The comment incenses me. My voice raised and livid, I bark at my tormentor: '*Well that's very well, isn't it, but it's a bit inconvenient to speak to my mother right now!*'

Kolko frowns. His voice is level and steady, a little puzzled. 'Inconvenient why?' is his question, and as it transpires, his parting shot. 'She's in the next room.' And he nods at the next door along. 'She's been waiting for you for a long time,' he calls up the stairs.

V.

1.

Throughout the long afternoon, Hannah has remained at home, since viewing the film of Sam and Hana. She hasn't known what to do to occupy her mind. Her work on perioperative fasting is finished — she is awaiting comments from the project's commissioner — and there are no shifts to work at the leisure centre, as she had booked a week off as leave, believing that she would be in the sleep deprivation chamber for longer than she actually spent there. Left to her mind's devices, she has spent much of the afternoon replaying the conversation she had with Tom and Roy at Bible Street Cars, and she has picked at what she said there about her experiment, attempting to tease out latent meanings.

'She wrapped me in a blanket,' Hannah said, referring to Jill Kerrimuir. 'She seemed more embarrassed by my state of undress than I was. And more embarrassed by my state of mental health, of course.' Hannah laughed mannishly. 'She gave me a drink — hot chocolate. From a machine. It was too sweet and scalding, but I drank it in about three gulps. And then I asked her, when I could speak again — I said, "How long was I in there?" — expecting her to say four days, or something like that. Because… time warped in there, guys. But do you know what she said? She said, "Five hours, Hannah." Five *hours*, not days! Not even a day's work! If I wanted to, I could still be home in time for dinner and the evening news!'

'And were you?' Tom asked.

'No. I drove around for a long time — plus I got caught on the A5. But I didn't want to go straight home anyway. I needed to think… Because. Something happened to me in there, Tom. And fair enough, that was the whole point of going there in the first place – but… I flew right into the past, and I saw the passengers kill the thief. But *did* we?'

'It would explain *this*,' Roy answered, nodding at the screen. The screen was dark by now, but no clarification was required.

It is now. Clarification is required now, and urgently, Hannah believes. She has spent the last few hours, since dropping Tom off on Grovebury Road, in a numbed state of expectancy. Any second, she is certain, she will take a phone call, or worse, a personal appearance from the thief; and this time he'll do more than freeze her mind for the purposes of a crafty grope. And what happens when the body is discovered by a chambermaid, if it hasn't been already? What *then*?

And what do I tell Sam's ex-husband? He's bound to text or call.

He had sex with her, Hannah types, *and then he killed her. Why did he kill her? (And is that what he has in mind for me?) We offended him. (Or did we kill him?) He could've fucked us and proved his point that way. He didn't need to kill Sam. Oh Sam. You're always right and never wrong, are you? All you had to do was listen to me.*

Making the *tsch!* sound, Hannah touches the key for back-delete. She has all but scrubbed out all evidence of the last sentence, before she twigs that the only person she is likely to embarrass by leaving it in – by keeping the account honest – is herself. So, she types it out again, and then she sends it to Tom. When she logs off, the screen falls as dark as her window, at which she stares for long minutes, alternately pondering and panicking, crying, feeling outraged and guilty, while rain spots the glass and her desktop fan's river of cool air pushes her hair back.

She jumps when the doorbell rings.

By the time it rings a second trill, Hannah has only reached the hallway; someone is keen to speak to her. The muscles in Hannah's cheeks bunch as she grits her teeth together. She eyes the claw hammer that she's left on the phone table, momentarily picturing its weighty collision with the thief's frontal lobe…

Hannah unlocks and opens the front door.

It's not Hana. It's Toby.

'Can I come in?' he asks, sour-faced.

'That depends. Does Jill know you're here?'

'It was her idea.'

'Then I wouldn't want to disappoint her,' Hannah answers, unable to keep a note of bitterness from straying among her words.

Evidently much is on Toby's mind. Hannah recoils from the man's silence as he steps over the threshold. Scrupulously and customarily polite, it is not like Toby not to say thank you when invited in; nor is it his way to ignore the mat on which one wipes one's feet, especially on rainy evenings… but he ignores it now. In fact, Toby moves into Hannah's hall with the air about him of one who has lost an important thread; in doing so, he prints mucky feet on her carpet.

Hannah closes the door and says, 'What ails thee?' *And where's your silly hat, on a night like this?* she doesn't add. *You're prone to catch a cold.* Come to think of it, there's something else that Toby usually brings that he seems to have forgotten: a bottle of wine, usually an expensive one.

Toby has disregarded Hannah's question. 'Jill asked how you were,' he says, entering the kitchen.

'Are you going to sit down?' Two can play at the no-answer game. Mildly put out by Toby's head-in-air composure, but simultaneously grateful (she must admit) for the excuse that his presence provides to break her thoughts up with some conversation and as an excuse to sip some wine, Hannah busies herself with glasses, corkscrew and with a bottle from the fridge that she's denied herself draining all afternoon. She pours out a glass each and cannot play deaf to Toby's concern for a second longer – or Jill's.

'Tell her I'm fine,' Hannah lies, 'and thank her again for me, would you?'

Toby sips and nods his head. Although Hannah copies the former action, her second one is a tart wince that her ex fails to notice, with his attention captured by the table's surface. What on earth can be on the man's mind, so distracting that it's obscured the simple fact that she has served them both a sample of sweet vinegar posing as a white burgundy? It's what you get sometimes, buying cheap. But why hasn't Toby *noticed*? He sipped it as if it was water, when even Hannah's palate can tell that she's really pulled a rough one this time.

He sips again; and again, there is no discernible reaction – nothing on his face. An ugly feeling slides through Hannah; it is something she cannot name. It makes her sit upright, her posture perfect. She wants to believe that he's nervous about what he's about to say. Or do. She *wants* to believe that he's close to making a move on her again; that his head is in the air due to a potent dose of sexual tension.

Suddenly this possibility is not very pleasant either.

'I should ask: how's Jilly?' says Hannah, going some way to drowning her nerves with another swallow of sharp burgundy.

'Oh she's fine.'

'What's she up to tonight?'

'This and that. The usual.'

'I see.' A quantity has curdled inside Hannah; it's akin to admitting that you're in love, even if the relationship, for one reason or another, isn't suitable. This is fear. Disguised as a confused discomfort, it has sneaked up on Hannah. It's the real thing.

One more test.

'Do you like the wine? I took your advice and pushed the boat out. I hope you can taste the quality.'

Toby smiles. 'It's delicious, thank you.'

'Great. I won't be a second; I'm just going to the bathroom,' Hannah tells him, her jaws aching.

This isn't Toby. Doesn't matter what he looks like, it's not Toby.

That Jill might have overcome her aversion to the name 'Jilly' is possible; that Toby either missed or chose to overlook the slip – possible, too. But no man with more than a fondness for wine – no man with a knowledge of wine – would ever describe such a disinfectant as delicious.

It isn't Toby.

It isn't Toby at her kitchen table; and now it isn't Toby, chasing her from the room.

Hannah makes it down the hallway, to the front door; she even manages to open it half a metre. Then the left arm of the man behind her reaches over her shoulder, fingers splayed. He shoves the door closed.

Hannah spins on the spot. During the two seconds of the pursuit, she has readied herself for the reality of the true face behind Toby's mask; but no, it's still Toby....or is it? He hasn't changed his appearance into that of his true self, which must be Hana. But now – suddenly – he doesn't look quite like Toby either; or at least, this is a wicked grin that Hannah hasn't seen before, and wants never to witness again.

'What's the matter, babe?' he asks. 'Didn't you like our film?'

So it *is* the thief, beneath her ex-partner's makeup. It was only a residual doubt that stopped Hannah from kneeing his testicles flat, or jabbing her fingers into his eye sockets.

Belatedly, she attempts both of these strategies; but Hana's quick. Faster than she would have imagined. With snake hips he dodges her knee, and his left arm brushes her right arm from the air.

'Be honest. You loved it,' he says.

'No I didn't.'

'It made you *squirm*, Hannah. I bet you could've wrung your knickers out afterwards and doused a fire.'

'…Jesus.'

'Won't help you now.'

'What do you want?' Hannah asks, her back against the door, the hammer on the table within easy reach.

Having followed her line of sight, Hana sees the weapon too. He laughs. 'Is that for me? Oh you *shouldn't* have, really. I'm touched, babe, truly I am.'

He is a metre-and-a-half away. At such proximity it would be fifty-fifty, whether Hannah could raise her arm and swing before the thief got his arm in the way…

'Then try it,' Hana suggests.

Hannah pauses. 'No. I don't want to kill you.'

'Well *that's* bloody rich!' says Toby's mouth. '*Now* she tells me!'

It has taken a few sentences for the would-be victim to catch up; but now it occurs to Hannah that there remains something wrong with this scene. Even if she has no choice but to accept that Hana is speaking with Toby's vocal cords, there is a quality to the *style* of speech that sits strangely. Its rhythm; its vocabulary, perhaps. The answer flits in and out of Hannah's mental vision. What is it?

'It was a long time ago when we were on that bus,' Hannah explains slowly, 'and I'm not even sure I know what happened. But I *think* the passengers rebelled against you. I think they killed you.'

Hana waits. It takes a beat. Two beats. Then it's as if he's just heard the funniest quip in the history of the English language.

'Killed *me?*' Toby's face blurts, altering slightly, thinning with plant-growth speed. 'You think I'm *Hana?*'

'...Aren't you?' Hannah asks.

'Oh, you clumsy, dumb bitch, babe. I'm *Sam.*'

Part Three: Hannah/Enamel

The relief provided by the retreat is achieved at the cost of isolation, stagnation, and withdrawal, and some patients find such a state distressing.

John Steiner, *Psychic Retreats*

I sense in my blood the rotation of unexplorable universes.

Vladmir Nabokov, 'Gods'

I.

1.

'Some nights I wake up shrieking. I dream the wardens are holding me down and one of them wants to give me a lethal injection. But I'm shrieking as much from the fact that it's not true... *God*! I just want to *die*,' she says. 'Why's that seem such an unacceptable wish?'

After buying time with an eventful shrug, I eventually say, 'I don't know. Given the circumstances, I would've thought it a perfectly reasonable request.'

I wait a few seconds before asking: 'Why did you do it, Caitlin?'

'I had a bad day.'

'No, tell me. Why?'

'Oh Christ. What can I tell you?' She exhales. 'Tell me something, Tom' she says. 'Does your lady know you visit me in here?'

I know I've got one thing to say – I have come here today with one thing to say – but it sits, rotting in my chest. I don't want to discuss myself, not directly. The thing in my chest is a squatter; it's Stephen himself – it won't move. It feels ugly, and it's making my breath smell, like a heavy meal that refuses to leave my system.

'No,' I answer. 'I tell her I'm doing some research. Which I am, in a way.'

'I'm your work in progress, am I?'

'For now.'

'Meaning?'

I almost smile. 'You've changed since you came in here,' I

mention.

'Well fancy. Are you surprised?'

'No...'

'Changed in what way? I can't help it, I'm curious.'

'More bolshy.'

Caitlin laughs. 'More bolshy. That's good. That's a *right* laugh.' She sounds nasty. 'Let me tell you something, Tom: if you try the bolshy bit in here, there are ladies who like explaining to you exactly why you shouldn't bother.'

'Is it violent, then? Or is that a dumb question.'

'It's a dumb question,' Caitlin tells me.

'All right. I hope this next one's smarter...How come we're in your cell, Cait? Why aren't we in the Visits Hall?'

Caitlin regards her environment, as if the walls are something new and that she hasn't noticed them before. I see a flash of wary confusion cross her features.

'I don't know,' she admits after a few seconds.

'We were never here, Cait,' I tell her. 'It's time I forgot I was. And you did the same.'

She doesn't argue. Then again, she doesn't agree either.

'I am in a house,' I continue, 'where I don't know if you've ever been. It's the house your dad owned with his first wife. And some evil things happened here, Caitlin. But I have to face some of them, and this memory of you isn't helping. Don't take that badly.'

Caitlin's head has dropped forward. She is sitting on the edge of a narrow bed. Now I can see – for the first time since entering the room on the left of the landing – the décor and scenery. The cell has been constructed – and is in the process of being altered, as the seconds tick away – from what I know of prisons, based on my teaching work in one of them. Of course I never visited Caitlin in her own cell; how on earth would I know what it looked like? And yet, despite this truth, the cell forms itself around us, layer on layer, perfecting itself and making itself appear presentable. While Caitlin simply looks crestfallen.

'You're going away again, aren't you, Tom?' she asks me.

'Yes. And I can't take you with me. But you can take yourself – as Annette. You don't need to come back here anymore. You're not who you were then, and this was a story you avoided, Cait. We both did. It doesn't *matter* what we remember. Okay?'

Her face inches up and she raises her chin. 'You'll forget me,' she says flatly.

'And you'll forget me too,' I tell her. 'It's for the best. I don't belong in this room.'

She smiles a sad smile…and I float towards the cell door…

…in the same way that I float around the blocks sometimes – through the walls of our homes. I float, I spy, I snoop; and although I enjoy this peripatetic existence, it is not a voluntary action, the floating. It is something to relish during the hours of sleep. The path of sleep, it seems, is traced by an energetic gale which stretches the bones as it tugs the dreamer along. Elasticity proves essential, we are thinner than the molecules of paint, brick and steel through which we travel…

I dream a sub-dream of Kolko. In the sub-dream, at leisure, he has a piss in my empty fruit bowl and then starts to eat one of my books. It is a book that I don't even own. It is called *My Skin's Name is Stephen*.

'You're looking in the wrong place,' says Kolko, and pages fly from his mouth and turn into birds. Twittering, they circuit the room. 'He's got to be alive.'

I am sitting in my work chair. 'But he's dead,' I answer.

'Who says?'

'The policeman. The other policeman.'

'*What* other policeman?' Kolko demands; and his words

gush at me, knocking me sprawling against my wall. I cannot evaporate my way through; I cannot escape. The only thing I can do is stand and fight, which I do by saying:

"'I kept a diary," Stephen used to tell me. Now I know that that diary was me. *I* was the bearer of Stephen's secrets; his thoughts, words and deeds. It wasn't the *house*. It wasn't 47 Rosebank Gardens. It was me. It was always me...'

And then I am in another cell.

2.

It's a two-man cell – 'dual occupancy' in custodial lingo – and this time I am present as an observer, not a participant. It's the cell that Roy shared with Stephen.

Scarcely believably, the scene is touching. *Touching* of all things! The two men are reading together; they are practising their reading, taking turns and putting on silly voices for the dialogue. The book is a copy of *Nutcracker Island*, a paperback made into a hardback via the application of a laminated cover. A copy from the prison library, I suppose.

So, says Roy after a while, *out tomorrow then?*

Stephen keeps his counsel.

You must be excited, Roy tries again. It seems that reading aloud is permitted; individual thought leading to conversation is not.

Stephen keeps his counsel.

With a series of slaps to either knee, an improvised drum roll, Roy acknowledges defeat (and his cellmate's request for privacy) and he stands up to his full height, his previously curved spine cracking. Although there is no need to make an announcement as to his destination – there is only one place to go once he has left the side of his bed – he states clearly: *I need a tom;* and he takes the requisite two strides over to the saloon partition that separates the cell from the toilet stall.

I watch.

I watch the saloon door flap back into place; I watch Roy's ankles; then I watch the top of his tracksuit trousers smother his training shoes, then his regulation dark blue underwear, as he lowers his kecks. A tom is a tom tit; a tom tit is a shit. Fantastic. Am I here to spy on Roy as he evacuates his bowels?

No I'm not: for it is only now, with Roy behind the door, in his snug, that Stephen can speak. *I'm scared, mate, to tell you the truth,* he says, and I turn to face him. Still seated on the edge of his cot, with Dorothy's book in his hands, he stares at the floor, wondering how to make light of his confession.

'We used to do that a lot,' Roy says, to my left. Not the Roy in the prison cell cubicle, in his tracksuit: it is Roy as I left him on Amelior's landing, still damp from rainfall and still wearing a pair of pink washing-up gloves.

'I didn't hear you come in,' I tell him, and he smiles.

'Honey, I'm home,' he says.

'Do what a lot?' I ask him.

'Talk in the two different rooms…if you can call 'em that. One of us on the bed; the other one on the bog.'

'Do you remember this conversation?'

'I don't know. Let's listen.'

Prisoner Roy says, *What's there to be scared of, mate?* as he breaks wind.

I'm scared I'll go back to my old ways. It's like a disease, mate!

What old ways? You're in for a driving offence.

But I did worse. They just never caught me. Not yet.

Well, don't tell me; I don't want to know, Roy says quickly.

Stephen waits. Then he goes on: *By rights I should be on a different Wing...*

Now it is Prisoner Roy's turn to keep his counsel. The toilet flushes, and peeking under the door we see him reach for his underwear and trousers. A couple of seconds later, his face like thunder, he emerges (the saloon door flaps again), and he crosses over to the basin, saying, *What are you telling me, Steve?*

Stephen regards Roy with a mixture of sternness and cowardice. *I've been trying to tell you for months, mate. I didn't want to leave here with us lying to each other.*

Roy washes his hands slowly. The soap is no wider than a bookmark, and has been worn down to the shape of a maple leaf. *I'm not lying,* he tells his cellmate.

But I am! says Stephen.

'I remember this,' says Roy.

...I should be on Eagle Wing, by rights.

With the nonces?

That's right.

...I wish you hadn't told me. Roy brandishes what remains of the bar of soap in the same way that Kolko might show his badge when intending to enter a stranger's home. *I should wash your fucking mouth out,* he says.

'Fuck a lemming, I *remember* this,' Roy whispers.

Roy the Con moves to Stephen's cot. Halfheartedly prepared, Stephen raises his fists and warns: *Don't, mate.*

You filthy cunt, Roy tells him slowly and clearly.

Bafflingly, Stephen appears to find this amusing. *Worse than you?* is his question.

Well of course worse than me!

'He forces the soap into Stephen's mouth,' Roy mutters.

'...He?'

'I. *I* force the soap – to wash his mouth clean.'

With a sudden explosion of activity, Inmate Roy acts out this scene to his director's specifications. The fight is brief but believed-in; the energy spent can be felt – by me, at least.

'I can't watch this,' Roy tells me.

When the cell door opens it is with sufficient speed and force to impact me forwards, colliding as it does with my back. Momentarily the screw at the door appears puzzled, and checks the floor for obstructions to the door being opened as wide as it can be. Of course, there's nothing for the man to observe.

The fight has finished: it has ended as briskly as it began. Remaining on the edge of his bed, Stephen picks slivers of soap from his mouth; he does so with the sort of care that you might employ to tweezer glass shards from an animal's paw. Roy has stepped away from the incident, and stands by the toilet door, awaiting his punishment for the outburst.

Bullish, red-faced, packed to the seams inside a uniform that was once signed over to a smaller man, the officer critiques the scene with a shrewd experienced eye.

You hungry again, Meredith? he enquires of my uncle.

Yes, sir.

Well, don't be. What you doing to him? he asks Roy.

We were just exercising. Weren't we, Steve?

'We were just exercising,' Roy mumbles in sync with his earlier alter ego. Turning to the later version of the man, I notice tears on his cheeks.

Well, don't be, the officer reiterates. His voice softens slightly; he removes his hand from his hip, where his fingers toyed with the grip on his baton. *You're out tomorrow, Meredith,* he continues – *don't fuck it up for yourself now, whatever you do.* His pep talk completed, he is about the close the door; then another thought occurs. *Oh, and Meredith?*

Sir?

You've got bubbles on your chin: you look like you've given ten blowjobs in a row. Tidy yourself up before the chaplain comes round with his words of wisdom.

I've already seen him, sir.

Oh yeah? And what advice did he have for you, if you don't mind?

To stay out of trouble, sir.

Did he now, the genius? The screw is closing the door. *Well worth the fucking salary.*

The nasty chime caused by the metal door's slamming shut, it echoes itself out into oblivion within a second.

Alone at last, says Stephen, now leaning over the sink and spitting a grey lather of saliva and soap against the plughole.

Roy sits on his bed and constructs a steeple out of his outstretched fingers. In the time that follows his hands also become a swimming fish, a writhing bellydancer…anything, I infer, but potential murder weapons – or at least tools of retribution. Roy wants to keep those old hands of his occupied.

Stephen stands up straight but does not turn around; he addresses Roy via the medium of the chipped mirror over the sink.

I can make you forget, he says.

I shouldn't have anything to remember! You shouldn't've told me, Steve, Roy adds sadly. *Why did you have to* tell *me?*

'I don't want to hear this, Tom. I don't like it.'

'Do you remember what he tells you?'

'No; but I don't like it. Giving me the creeps.'

Personally, it's giving me hope, of all things. Can it be that I'm on the brink of eavesdropping on a confession, not of a crime but of a methodology? As Stephen and Roy face each other, both of them on their beds, leaning forward, their glowering frowns mirror images of one another, an imperfect symmetry is established, at least from my vantage point, back by the door.

'I'm leaving,' Roy tells me.

The two men are of similar build, in a similar pose and identical clothes. What I see is an atom that the truth might split; and I wonder what my friend sees.

'No I'm not,' he contradicts himself.

Roy charges over to his memory of Stephen, and hacks at his face with the breadknife. So sudden is the action that he has got a few gauges in before I can say anything.

'What are you *doing*?' I demand.

Roy has flailed and stabbed at empty air – his attack has had no more effect than if he's slashed at a projected image.

He accepts this, too.

'It's already *happened*,' I say.

'I was trying to stop it,' Roy replies. 'No Stephen, no nightmares. Our lives would've been different. We wouldn't be here in this house!'

Losing patience and nerve, I instruct Roy to hold his tongue and listen.

Have Stephen and other-Roy waited? We seem to have missed nothing; and now that he and I have concluded our brief argument, their ancient conversation begins again, with Stephen in low voice but audible.

3.

It's almost like there are two levels (*Stephen explains*). There's what you're doing for your own satisfaction; then there's something you're doing on behalf of something you don't even know the name of. A higher power. And it becomes like a duty: to do it worse, and then worse – to keep upping the ante, even though no one's told you to, not in so many words. It was something unspoken, but it was felt, mate, I promise you that. it was felt that… we had to keep doing *more*. More in number, more in…intensity. Coming here–

What?

Well *of course* I didn't tell the fucking chaplain! Can you imagine his views on confidentiality? *Straight* out the fucking window! And then what? The very best I could hope for is a transfer to a psychiatric unit of some description. All day in pajamas, on mood drugs. Or worse, I get assessed for me mental elf and I'm viewed to be taking the piss. Stalling. Rest of my sentence in solitary. Fuck that! Reassessment of external evidence. Then I'm doing ten more years, but amongst a bunch of fucking rapists and four-eyes.

I'm not explaining this very well, am I? It wasn't…it wasn't a *club*, Roy. It wasn't like earning your stripes – move up through the ranks. Nothing like that. I've tried to think of it in terms of gambling – raising the stakes with every bet – and there's a bit of truth to that one, I suppose, but it's not exactly spot-on either. No: the best I can do is keep coming back to what I said about a higher power, mate. Maybe God! It was something we *believed* in… but we couldn't even really discuss it. Not properly. It seemed like it was protecting us, Roy; and the worst we did, the greater the love we received. The more *favours* we received. Little abilities. If anything, it was like a religion. In a way, my crimes have been my salvation.

But now I'm frightened to go back to it. That lifestyle; that union. I mean, how much worse can I make it, just to snivel around for approval, for Christ's sake? *Murder*? Well I won't: I just *won't*, you hear me? I *refuse* to.

…What do you mean, who'm I trying to convince? I'm trying to convince *them*! The ones egging us on! The ones who want more and more from us, in exchange for their goodwill and charity. The ones who help us make people *forget*. Like I'll help *you* forget.

Don't be stupid. It's not about choice, mate. It's *recruitment*: I'm a recruiting sergeant, all right? I'm getting your name and contact details for our files. Even now – right now. God help me, I'm *working*… I've had the Return to Work workshops, and I thought: there's nothing you can teach me about making the best of my job prospects. Nothing! Because you don't know where I was, one; and two, you don't know where I'm going…

But I'm telling *you*, Roy. Whether you like it or not. And then I'll paint you over with amnesia and you won't give it all a second thought. You'll be one more soul in their army, that's all you'll be, mate. Sorry to call it like it is, but that's the truth. And one day, if they wanna use you for something, Roy, they will. You won't have a say, you won't have a chance to backchat; you'll feel a *pull*. Something you're at a loss to explain. Or even define. An urge. A something. And then the price of your amnesia – your debt, in other words – you have the privilege of paying that back.

So now you know.

I'll miss you, mate, and I'm sorry to have to do this, but it's like a vocation – get as many signed up as you can. You can think about what I've said, and it'll drip away from your memory, bit by bit…till there's nothing left but an echo.

Can you feel it? Already?

I shouldn't laugh, but you know what? I think they've been waiting for me to show you the way. They've been *waiting*, Roy…

4.

…*been waiting, Roy*, says Stephen.

'We need to go, Tom,' Roy tells me, his face as white as innocence and his brow both swollen and puckered – like an old familiar cushion. Sorry as I might feel for Roy – sympathy based on the weight of knowledge he's carried, unaware of the fact, all through the years, in much the same way as I have – I cannot trust that this is all there is to know, and for a few seconds more I continue to watch.

Roy looks up, towards the door. Does he see 'my' Roy? With the time that has passed between then and now, is it possible that a connection might be made? This is something I cannot answer. All I know is that Roy lies down – not one further word does he offer – and the process of amnesia is cultured, it would seem, as simply as that.

No pyrotechnics; no incantations. Not even an hallucination. Not even a hypnotist's subtle change of vocal tone! Just a promise; an assurance. *This is what will happen.* And lo, it came to pass...

'Come on, Tom.'

'...But that *can't* be it,' I complain into his vigilant frown.

He tugs at my fingers; the rubber gloves feel prophylactic and strange.

'Come *on*, Tom. Let's go...'

Stepping out onto the landing, I see that Roy remains *in absentia*, psychologically speaking, at least. Lights are on but there's nobody home, so where is he?

I remember how he reached me when I was on the Downs, simply by shaking my shoulders and repeating my name like a mantra. The thought occurs that I should do the same thing, or something similar.

Then I hear the sirens from beyond the walls.

II.

1.

Disappointingly, perhaps, but certainly not surprisingly, the black woman and the white woman arrive at The Globe with neither fuss nor fanfare; no herald of supercharged atmosphere announces their fresh presence. But for Dorothy it has always been the same, it's what they do, is it not? Using compound stealth, they sneak up on her, and strike when she least expects it. Indeed, now, as the hour strikes nine, with the fireplace dog having been claimed and led away by a geriatric owner some minutes earlier, Dorothy is not even facing in the right direction to see them enter the building, stepping in out of the rain and throttling a gallon of it from their umbrellas. Since the dog's departure, Dorothy has stared into the dwindling flames, urging herself to call it a night and phone for a taxi.

It is Annette who sees the two women. 'They're here,' she whispers.

Her back to the bar, and despite all the psychological preparation that she thinks she's completed, Dorothy freezes; her innards chill. Instead of giving warmth *to* her, the fire suddenly takes it away.

'Dolly? Did you hear me?' Annette says, louder this time.

'I heard you. What do they look like?'

'One black girl and one white girl, just like you said. They're talking to the barmaid, and she doesn't exactly appear impressed by their timekeeping, I must say!'

Dorothy swears under her breath. She opens her handbag for the sheet of paper that she printed off and stashed here earlier. As she does this, she notices the envelope that she addressed to Chadwick Lodge.

'I'll have to say this quickly,' Dorothy tells Annette. 'Do you see this? This is a script. And I know an actor's supposed to learn her lines, but I haven't learned mine yet. I only wrote them today.'

Annette shakes her head. 'I don't know what you're talking about, Dolly,' she says.

'You don't need to. Just don't let them take me anywhere, okay?'

'Take you…?'

'Anywhere, that's right.' And Dorothy stands up; with her script fluttering in her right hand, she marches over to the bar, her head full of righteous steam.

She is no further away than a metre, with an unrehearsed word of admonition leaving her lips, when she realizes that, for the second time in roughly as many hours, she has made a serious error of misidentification. Or rather, of non-identification: the fact is, she did not even check before embarking on her rampage over from the fireplace. True enough, the two women now in place behind the bar are the right creed and colour, but that's *it*; there is little else about their descriptions that would cause problems for a witness – for Dorothy! – asked to pick the original two women out of a police lineup. The black girl is too young and plump to be *Dorothy's* black girl; and the white girl is too old and thin.

It's not them.

2.

The canal path is close to invisible, its existence rubbed out by an eraser of rain.

'We'll have to go back and wait for a cab,' says Annette. 'We can't walk in this.'

'I'm not going back there,' Dorothy tells her. 'Ever.' To

prove what she's said, she lengthens her stride; she is angry, she doesn't wait for Annette to catch up. She walks quickly into the foul weather, head down and blowing off steam like a bull, even snorting. A one-woman stampede, the wall of rain her red rag to charge towards.

No one else is on the path – not until, fifteen minutes later, Dorothy is in sight of the canalside supermarket. Then she sees, up ahead, a human shape, dark in the downpour, silhouetted against light thrown out from the back of the shop. For Dorothy the vision is spiriting; it is heartening. It's good to know that there exist other people on tonight's planet. Sure enough, on the stroll between The Globe and here, there has been precious little evidence of the same. Suppressed illumination leaking out of a couple of moored boats; an occasional slurred voice from a proximate source, either real or via a radio. Not much else.

Whoever is taking his chances tonight, tempting fate, steps closer to the waterside. The supermarket's lights frame him easily, bending over the edge, and reaching for something.

What?

What could it be? Dorothy wonders, with every step delivering her close to the man – definitely a man now – whose voice can be heard, albeit faintly, above the heavens' growl. He is calling for help. *He has seen me. And Annette.*

'Help me, please! She can't swim!' the man calls.

Dorothy feels Annette as the latter brushes past her; Annette breaks into a sprint for the remaining ten metres, and as fast as she can, Dorothy follows.

'It's Pixie!' the man explains, his voice a shout of dismay and agitation. 'My dog! She's had a hip operation...'

Dorothy and Annette squint into the mess of water *above* the canal's surface – the rain tumbling down, ricocheting back up, the filthy mist astride a body of water both purple and black, a bad bruise – in search of the dog. But there's nothing to see.

'What happened?' Dorothy asks.

'We took shelter in Tesco,' the man answers; 'but it wasn't going to stop, so I had no choice. She broke away from me...the wind took her...she's old...Oh God! Oh God, *Pixie*! Where *are* you, girl!'

Annette points. 'There she is!'

The spaniel's head breaks the surface, though only briefly. The water is choppy and expects a sacrifice. Before the dog can make a sound the head sinks below again.

'Pixie, *swim*, girl! Swim to me!' the dog-owner implores the animal.

Annette unbuttons her coat.

'You can't mean it,' Dorothy says, estimating her friend's intentions.

'I can't do *nothing*. The poor thing!'

'The water'll be freezing!'

'Yeah. For her as well!' Annette drops her coat on the muddy verge. 'The dog's drowning, Dolly, and I'm a swimming teacher,' she explains. 'How could I live with myself if I didn't, eh? This one thing. Just this *one little thing* that isn't about me and what *I* want. This one thing: something selfless, Dolly. You can't possibly blame me for this.'

Dorothy waits. She sees tears in Annette's eyes; determination on her face.

'No, I don't blame you,' she says.

Barring the coat, Annette is fully dressed when she dives into the water. She has even kept her shoes on, and her entry produces a complicated splash.

Goodbye, Annette, Dorothy mouths. Then, disgustedly, she shakes her head. Where did *that* come from?

Long seconds pass. So surprised is Dorothy when the

dog-owner takes hold of her hand that she sighs and realizes that she has been holding her breath. Her lungs ache. *Come on, Annette!* she begs; but there is no sign of her friend. She squeezes the hand in hers; the man's fingers are rough and sopping wet.

Come ON! she pleads again.

The man is crying and Dorothy feels so useless that she could scream. Unbidden, thoughts occur to her: visions of what Annette must be seeing. Under the water it is as dark as Doomsday. Annette swims breast-stroke; she searches for the bottom. The water is syrupy with churned-up muck, and she is no longer certain in which direction she is moving. Her lungs sting with held breath; her eyes are on fire with the impurities in the water...

Pixie's owner squeezes Dorothy's hand.

'There!' says Dorothy; but she sees what Annette sees, she is looking through Annette's eyes. The dog is near the bottom of the canal, her four legs in spastic arrhythmia – trying to run but not moving, as one runs in an anxiety dream.

'Where?' the man demands.

Annette has spotted the spaniel, or has felt her way to her by fluke and the sense of touch. Beneath the water with her (Dorothy is holding her breath again), Dorothy watches helplessly as Annette gropes the dog and manages to get the animal in a kind of headlock.

'She's got her!'

'*Where?*' the man demands again. Frustrated by his inability to see what he should be able to see, he has taken to strengthening his grip on Dorothy's hand. He is all but wringing her fingers.

'They're coming up!' Dorothy resumes the commentary, yanking her hand away and stepping closer to the water's edge. Quite what good she believes she'll be able to offer she is uncertain of; all she knows is that she wants to offer assistance, and being as close to the canal as she can safely get seems like the best option available.

The dog's head breaks the surface; her eyes are closed.

'Pixie!'

Half a second later, Annette's crown shows through as well – then her face, filthy with gunk. Immediately she gasps for air; coughs and splutters. Her movements are ungainly as she struggles to bear the spaniel's mass and tread water at the same time.

The dog is not breathing.

Now kneeling on the soaked verge, near Annette's coat, the owner grabs hold of his pet's collar, and pulls. Dorothy bends at the waist to lend a hand. Each with one hand on the collar, they manage to pull Pixie out of the water: it's like yanking stubborn weeds, but after a short burst of violent exertion, she is there on the path, on her right side…but not breathing. Her eyes are closed. Rain falls onto her muzzle and floppy tongue.

There is nothing that Dorothy can do to help the spaniel – she is certain of this – and she turns her efforts to Annette, who is flapping in the water.

'Give me your hand!'

'I'm too heavy,' Annette replies and gulps. 'I'll pull you in!'

Dorothy is bent double once more. Although instinctively aware that Annette is right (she won't be strong enough to drag her out unaided: hell, it took two of them to rescue the *dog!*) she holds out both hands, anyway.

'Get a grip!'

The manoeuvre is clumsy, at best. Both pairs of hands are soaking wet, and they slide and slip away from one another like repulsing magnets. And then there is the matter of footwear to consider. Dorothy is all but *skating* by the side of the water.

Flustered and panic-stricken, Dorothy stands erect and scans the supermarket car park for someone – anyone! – who might be able to help. Yelling for assistance, she sees no one through the curtains of rain; and Pixie's owner is working on the dog, pummelling the bitch from teat to navel in a cackhanded effort to make her breathe and sick up what she's swallowed. No help there.

'Help me PLEASE!' Dorothy shouts. Surely someone in one of the boats will listen to her, and race to the emergency. *Surely…*

If her invocation is heard, however, there is no gallant knight abroad this evening. The only sounds are the dog-owner's entreaties – by turn, loving and then vicious – and of course the constant decibelage of the storm on the canal's surface. A whistle of wind, sometimes; or the sweeping noise of a car as it noses slowly over the bridge, its driver either recklessly thrill-seeking or determined to get home before the weather turns worse.

Annette attempts to lug herself out of the water; unfortunately, there is nothing to hold onto but wet grass and gravel, and her feet find no purchase on the bank. (Dorothy believes that she can feel mud as it oozes through Annette's shoes.) Try after try, Annette slips back into the canal, screaming wasteful curses.

'I'll get someone from the shop!' Dorothy decides. 'Must be *someone*.'

'Don't leave me!'

'I'll be back in two minutes! You need to go on a diet, love,' she adds.

'Shove it, Dolly…God, it's cold!'

'Keep kicking,' Dorothy calls from the path to the car park.

At the supermarket's front door she is met by a handful of congregants – all of them, to a man, to a woman, to a child, staring out at the downpour in apoplectic awe, as one might witness televised true-life violence. Such is the way that several of them move to the side to allow Dorothy entry, she is forcibly reminded of the large group that had met her in the library. Her pulse quickening, Dorothy even casts an eye out for the bad teeth of the villagers' salacious smiles – and for the idiot boy.

They're not here. These are shoppers, not daring to venture into the tempest. They carry plastic bags with the supermarket's name on, and the corporate logo

'My friend's in the canal,' says Dorothy, her words slurring with breathlessness. 'Can you help?'

'Your friend's *what*?' one young man asks.

'In the canal. She can't get out. Please.'

Two young men – one in a workman's fluorescent jacket, the other in a business suit – follow Dorothy back out into the rain; then overtake her and run around the building, towards the canal, from which direction a dog can be heard barking feebly.

By the time she arrives, in the rescuers' wake, it is a scene of great confusion. The spaniel is conscious, though she shakes uncontrollably and remains on her right side, not strong enough – or too dazed – to stand. Over and over, the owner repeats her name; weeping openly, he proffers either hand, left then right, which his pet licks with weary obedience. The dog has been covered over with Annette's coat.

There is no sign of Annette.

'Where is she?' Dorothy shouts.

'She went under. I'm so sorry,' the owner answers.

Decisively, in one quick movement, one of the young men ruins his suit by lying belly-down in the dirt, his upper torso leaning over the edge. With his head cocked to one side he trails his right arm in the brackish water, fondling for a hold on anything, stirring the whisked-up tide.

'Fuckin freezing,' he remarks.

Dorothy closes her eyes. She tries to look at what Annette is viewing, but there's only darkness. She needs a clue: anything!

But there is nothing to see; there is nothing for the young man to catch.

A net, Dorothy thinks. I need a net for Annette. The absurdity curdles her foul mood further; her lips tighten – she doesn't know why. The man in the fluorescent workcoat asks her (and not nicely) why she is smiling. 'I'm a bundle of nerves,' Dorothy tells him, not even certain if the comment answers his question.

Pixie barks; she tries to stand. Turning away from the be-suited fisherman, Dorothy watches the spaniel's progress instead. The bitch trembles and sneezes. '*Bless* you, Pixie!' the owner praises her; and Dorothy is visited by a notion of calmness and serenity, quite unlike anything that she has experienced in recent months. Once more she closes her eyes, and searches for Annette in her mind.

The water is cold against Dorothy's skin, but now there is no pain in her lungs. Why not? she wonders; but the solution is obvious: Annette does not need to hold her breath any longer. Does not need her lungs. The calmness and serenity – Dorothy is convinced – is her reaction to her friend's dying, shared with this very same friend. She is gone. She does not have to hurt any-more, either as Caitlin or Annette – or as her next incarnation, whoever this might turn out to be.

'Stop *smiling*, woman,' says the workman. 'It's giving me the creeps!'

'Sorry.'

And Dorothy has one further connected thought, one that astonishes her. In a hypothetical alternative universe – in an ex-istence in which she, Dorothy, arrived back at the canal to find Annette still alive – it was she, Dorothy, who would have lain down at the water's edge. It was she, Dorothy, who have placed a firm hand on Annette's head – and pushed her under: and An-nette would not have resisted. It is what she has always wanted, perhaps.

Dorothy takes some comfort from this.

She opens her eyes. Both men are now on their stomachs, angling for the biggest fish that this canal has ever boasted: the one that got away. From her handbag Dorothy takes her mobile phone; her fingers are numb and twitching, but there are only three numbers to press, and they are all the same number.

999.

Now that she's sure that Annette is dead, Dorothy can call for an ambulance.

III.

1.

'Fame at last!' Sam exclaims.

The discovery of Sam's body has made the local news. Someone's blabbed; something's leaked. It's enough for a short article on BBC Oxford: one of those segments that begin with an earnest simper and a sentence like 'Reports are coming in'… and ends with a clause like 'More on this story later.'

'Imagine what the interest'll be in that hotel,' Sam goes on in a ruminative manner.

'Interest?'

'Yeah. Ghostbusters, ghouls and Nazis: you know the type. They'll ask for the room where the woman was murdered…I should charge a commission! A finder's fee!'

'You're already wealthy,' Hannah tells her.

'Well I was. My earning potential is a little diminished now, you'd have to say.' Sam laughs. 'Do you think Mike'll still pay me his blood money?'

'I'll phone him and ask.'

'Oh?'

'He was in touch; he was worried about you, of all things. I kept his number…Come to think of it, why don't *you* call him?' Hannah asks. 'Give him something to *really* cut himself up over. Who knows? Maybe he'll kill himself and we can all be happy!'

'Oh, he's no use to me *dead*,' Sam objects.

Hannah pauses.

'That sentence doesn't strike you as ironic, does it?' she asks.

'Should it?'

'Think about it, Sam! What use are you to *me* dead?'

'Thanks a bundle.'

'I'm asking you!'

'You know, you're really not taking this as well as I expected, Han. I mean, I'm here to tell you about something wonderful,
and you're giving me a hardball game and a buncha lip!'

Hannah tuts. 'I'm so *insensitive*. So go on then: tell me. Tell
me something wonderful. Right after you tell me why you've tied
me up.'

2.

Her legs crossed beneath her, Hannah sits on the floor of
the room she works in. Her arms stretch around either side of
the front left leg of her heavy desk; her wrists are shackled together with a pair of pink handcuffs that have some jazzy white
fur on each bracelet. These restraints are made of cheap plastic
– they're a sex toy – and Hannah is sure that with a bit of effort
she can break free easily enough. Wouldn't even coax a sweat.
Indeed, when Sam had first presented these restraints, Hannah
had imagined it to be some kind of practical joke: she had asked
if it was her hen night so soon. But she'd gone along with what
Sam had in mind.

There'd been more than the element of surprise on Sam's
side. That shapeshifting gimmick, for openers. Sam has only
been dead for four days, and she has picked up some of her new
community's tricks already. Hannah remains impressed. There is
also the invisible presence, or at least existence, of Hana the thief
to consider; *that* guy's whys and wherefores; and Hannah, above
all, wants to understand. *Longs* to understand! So, if acquiescing
to Sam's will – to be loosely, pathetically incarcerated while the
two of them watch the local news on the monitor's screen, Hannah cricking her neck up at an awkward angle, which is going
to become uncomfortable soon – is how Hannah might *earn* this

understanding, then she will play along. Not for too much time, of course – she'll need to flee, eventually – but for enough time to learn the facts. She's a paid researcher, after all.

Sam is speaking.

'At first it hurt,' she says. 'As you might imagine…Do you mind if I turn this off now?'

The news has moved on to a story about an octogenarian lollipop lady, who has helped five generations of schoolchildren cross the road safely over the last fifty years and who is set to retire and is tipped to be rewarded in the Council's Honours' List.

'Be my guest,' Hannah answers wryly. Her eyesight skates across the carpet, and she judges parenthetically that the room could use a good Hoover. She shouldn't eat while she's working, there are biscuit crumbs mashed into the carpet's weave.

The room is quiet, and Sam continues.

'It wasn't just the pain of the attack, although that wasn't exactly a bowl of strawberries, babe–'

'Cherries.'

'What?'

'The phrase is a bowl of *cherries*. That strangulation killed more brain cells than you imagine,' says Hannah.

'Strawberries, cherries. The fact is, I actually felt my organs give out. Now *that* hurt; that really did. But he was with me, Han. I felt him with me, like a guide.'

'Holding your hand,' Hannah adds.

'Exactly!'

'And helping you across the road.'

'*Exactly*.

Hannah sniffs. 'He should get a job: be a lollipop lady. Why don't you tell him to *get a fucking job* and be a *lollipop lady*, Sam?'

The other woman shakes her head. 'You're nowhere near as graceful under pressure as I thought you'd be, babe.'

'You call this *pressure*?' Hannah bluffs. 'What on earth made you think of coming to me as Toby, by the way?'

'Why not? Friendly face…'

'That's debatable.'

'Can you imagine if I'd come as I am?'

'But why *Toby*? Why not Tom, for instance?'

'Is it Tom's practice to visit you late?' Sam asks.

'It's been known.'

Sam throws her arms up, saying, 'Hell, *I* don't know, Hannah! Gimme a break, why don't you! This is kind of new to me too, you know.'

She rises to her feet. Hannah is obliged to twist her neck up at a yet steeper angle – for the privilege of gazing at the underside of Sam's chin. It's not worth the effort. Better to sit and mope about the crummy nature of her workroom carpet, while Sam browses her shelves.

'Have you actually read all of these books?' Sam asks.

'No.'

'But you know roughly what each of them is about?'

'I suppose so. Roughly.'

'It's the same thing with me, though a slightly bigger scale. I know what's here… but I don't really know any of the specifics. Not yet.'

'Then why did you come back to me so soon?' Hannah asks. 'Why not wait?'

Sam looks down; their eyes meet and Sam smiles. 'Everyone loves bragging about their holiday. Oddly enough, I thought you might be pleased to see me.'

'So you came as Toby. Honestly, Sam, being murdered by that scumbag has certainly taken the keen edge off your commonsense.'

Sam's voice is low. 'He's not a scumbag, Hannah,' she says.

'Oh, he's watching us now, is he?' Hannah asks.

'I don't know.'

'Then why are you still protecting him?'

'I'm protecting *you*.'

'Well, I don't need your protection, Sam. Were the cuffs his idea as well?'

Throughout the interrogation, Hannah has kept both her words and her muscles tight: particularly the muscles in her arms. Once she has snapped the handcuffs, she wonders, how fast will she be able to spring to her feet? She won't be greased lightning, she knows, she's been crosslegged for some time and there's bound to be stiffness; but she possesses good aerobic and anaerobic strength. If she can combine her ascent with a punch to Sam's belly…there's a chance.

Haughtily Sam replies: 'The cuffs were *my* idea. Do you think he tells me what to do?'

'It looks that way, yes.'

'…Oh what do *you* know?' Sam's voice is candidly disgusted. 'Poor Hannah. We've waited for our saviour all these years, and now he's here you're too blind to see him, with your head in the clouds as usual.'

'My *saviour*?' Hannah repeats, in astonishment. 'Do you know what you sound like, Sam?'

'I sound like one of the fortunate,' Sam tells her.

'You sound like a huckster.' Hannah mulls over her options. A quick yank of her arms outwards, to break the link between the bracelets manually? Or roll backwards in a rowing action, the aim being to shatter the link on the desk leg? Would there be sufficient momentum? 'Like a carnival barker. I will you show you *the way*, ladies-gennermen. Oh, in return for your credit card number.'

Sam sits down at the desk again. 'Careful, Han.'

THE PARRY AND THE LUNGE

However, Hannah is not finished. Desperation has lent her authority.

'You've been sideswiped by supernatural forces we don't understand and never will...*babe*...and it's time you called their bluff. Or what's next? Riches everlasting? Get real, Sam. *Get a life*. Literally.'

Sam punches Hannah in the face, a right-handed blow, with not much *oopmph* behind it, but enough to shock the prisoner into a gasping grasp for additional words.

Further argument is not what Hannah requires. No, this warning-free assault from her former friend is what Hannah requires. Sniffing blood back into her left nostril, Hannah leans back with a jerk. The link between the cuffs snags on the desk leg: Hannah cannot recline any more. She heaves her arms – *row that boat!* – and muscles flex across her chest. With her legs now unfolded and bent at the knees, she digs her slippered heels into the carpet and tries to extend them, increasing the strain on the handcuffs' central link.

The desk shifts.

Against all of Hannah's expectations and mental calculations, the link does not ping open. She can scarcely believe her own eyes. Contrary to the odds, that small nugget of crappy plastic, instead of splitting and releasing Hannah, is *pulling the fucking desk away from the wall*.

'No...' Hannah bleats.

'*Yes*, babe,' Sam retorts, once more rising to her feet. In the second it takes Hannah to struggle on, Sam plucks two volumes of *The Medical Encyclopaedia* from their family of five on a high shelf. Each tome is hardbacked and heavy. Like a waiter showing off with two trays, Sam balances each volume on an upturned palm of her hand.

Hannah drags the desk a few more centimetres...but still

the handcuffs hold firm; there's no give. She screams in exasperation, then she spits away some blood that has dribbled from her top lip and into her mouth.

The handcuffs hold.

…and Sam attempts to clatter the two volumes together, in a motion that resembles the playing of marching band cymbals. What prevents the two books from making contact with one another is Hannah's head, between them.

The pain is fierce. When the volumes sandwich her head, Hannah is coerced into forsaking all immediate-future plans for physical exertion. She sags. The pain has caused immediate tinnitus, and as she sits almost motionless, her legs stretched out in front of her, hunchbacked by the necessity to have her arms out, she decides to listen closely to these inner-ear, inner-brain bells. In addition, the impact has birthed stars in the orbit behind her eyes. And why not? she asks herself. Right now is as good a time as any, Hannah believes, for some private, internal astronomy. After all, she has always enjoyed the skies.

Consciousness abandons her.

3.

It's not a dream. Yet it's not the place that she knows best either – it's not home.

Is it actually a place at all? she wonders. How about a state of mind?

Can a state of mind also be a place?

Hannah possesses no memory of the house in which she lives, but she knows that it exists. There *is* a house…only not in this new reality.

There is nothing in the wind – no resistance, no eddy – to suggest that Hannah is flying; but she is not still either. She moves through an absence of friction.

Above what?

It's not a desert, though it appears of a uniform quality for as far as her vision permits. It's not sand. It's not stone…It looks dry.

She descends.

It's *skin*. An eternity of skin.

Hannah descends closer: a violent, dizzying swoop. As she plummets through the atmosphere, she can feel the emanation of warmth from this skin, from this sleeping body. Whoever owns it, this flesh, is alive.

Closer!

And Hannah grasps a sense of her own insignificance; it is impossible to miss it or to misinterpret it. Not only has she never *been* so small, she has never *felt* so small either.

The deeper into the body's atmosphere she drops, the more the nature of the skin changes; and although she believes that she is still ten thousand miles from the solidity below – maybe more! – she is alarmed to see on the vast body great craters – millions of them – and individual hairs the size of skyscrapers. So the craters must be pores, she understands.

And closer!

4.

Hannah opens her eyes and releases a breath. It takes a few more breaths before her body has caught up with taking in the oxygen that it's lacked.

'How long was I out?' she asks.

'Half a minute? What did you see? Be honest.'

'…I don't know. Groggy,' Hannah answers. 'Was the beating absolutely necessary?'

Sam shrugs. '*What did you see?*'

As best she can, Hannah straightens her spine; in the workroom's limited space, the satisfying series of cracks that this adjustment produces sounds loud, and the only other sound is of whirring – the computer, on standby… Hannah rides a wave of nausea. It is so assertive (and yet so intoxicating) that it nudges her to the left, head and torso. It's a struggle to remain sitting upright. Although her nose has stopped bleeding, she tastes blood on her tongue, on her lips.

'Tell me!'

'I'm trying to find the words,' Hannah whispers. 'I was flying…'

'Yes?'

'…and I saw God. Swear to God, I saw…God. Or a part of Him.'

'Which part? Did you see his wang?' Sam asks in an exaggeratedly anxious tone.

Despite herself, Hannah smiles. 'I don't know which part. He was vast. I was tiny…I don't even know why I think it was God. It was a vision.'

'…You sound stoned.'

'I feel it! And I saw His wounds. There were flesh wounds all over His body, or what I saw of His body. Some were miniscule cuts; others were deeper gashes; and they opened and bled in front of me, then healed themselves up.'

More excited than ever, Sam leans closer; the chair squeaks. Her eyes are bright.

'Go on…'

'The wounds were *stories*, Sam.'

'Yes! Yes!' Sam claps her hands. 'That's exactly what Hana says!'

'But how could I have gotten so much in half a minute?' Hannah continues, her eyebrows pinching as she frowns. She tugs once more at the handcuffs, this time involuntarily. A spasm.

The bracelets have clawed purple grooves into her wrists; the sickness has yet to subside…but Hannah feels absurdly happy.

'Every scratch on His body was a story – an event. I saw a World War in a gash. I saw a Civil War in a paper cut…And I realized,' she continues slowly, 'these events are not unimportant to God. He accepts them! He takes them onto His own skin – if skin is the right word. And every time a wound is opened, the story it contains is retold; or maybe it's the other way round. The wounds don't heal! Not fully. They're sliced open, and they never recover in precisely the same way.'

Sam nods her head; her lips are thin with joy, with expectation.

Hannah asks, 'Will you take the cuffs off now?'

'No. When you've finished.'

'I've eaten my greens, Sam. I'm not going to run away.'

'It's not about that. Did you see anything about us and Hana?' Sam asks.

'Enough. Enough to know one thing, Sam: *there is no definitive story*. We didn't kill that man on that bus – but we didn't *not* kill him either…Same with the other passengers: they did and they didn't. Because *they're stories*. And they *change*. The wound alters and heals and splits open again.'

'Good. Good, tell me more,' says Sam.

'But He wants to heal every one of the trillion cuts on His skin, Sam – or worse than cuts – He wants them to heal. And so He's resting. He's wounded! He's been shot down in action, he's trying to recover…'

Hannah shakes her head. A few drops of blood fly from the end of her nose and land on the two volumes of *The Medical Encyclopaedia*, which Sam let fall onto the carpet as soon as she'd completed the swift attack.

'I can't believe I'm actually saying all this,' Hannah mutters, staring at the handcuffs, at the desk leg.

'Do you *trust* it? That's the important thing,' Sam tells her.

'It's hard not to, but it's just as hard to, as well. I don't know…'

'Then you've still got a lot to learn.'

Hannah waits. Her eyelids droop and flutter; maybe another blackout is on the way. She hopes it is; but for the moment she has one more thread to unravel. Choosing her vocabulary with caution, she says:

'God tries to help. Or whatever it is I'm calling God – He tries to help. Or *It* does. To heal the wounds, which will finish the stories, *our stories*. Once the wounds heal up, the stories dry to nothing – to less than sand – and then *no one will remember that tale again*. It's been cleaned; it's invisible, Sam. It's as though the damn thing never existed…

'So He gives us Evil and He gives us Goodness, the one as an aid for us to appreciate the other – though who's to say which is which? He gives us ghosts. He gives us a thief, and He gives that thief tricks – or powers – to monkey-wrench 'round in our minds. All to finish the fucking story!' Hannah sniggers. 'All of this for a spotless skin!'

For one last time, Sam praises Hannah's talent for comprehension with a nod of the head, and a breathed *Good*. 'So are you ready?' Sam asks calmly, standing up.

'For what?'

'You'll be able to tell your story, Han, don't worry about that. Very soon. To Dorothy, to Tom. You see, I know I *used* to be your diary, but they are now. I've lost that job – or the job lost me: I can't remember which one it was. It's not important, babe. I can't do it anymore – *that's* the important bit – but *someone* has to, don't they? Tell the whole story.'

'No, Sam! No, I'm *not* ready!' Hannah protests, her eyes

bulging with terror, and fixed for half a second on Sam's hands as they dart closer. '*No, Sam!*'

'Sshhh…'

Sam's hands fasten around Hannah's neck; they give a tentative squeeze, as if testing the resistance found here, and then something more potent and unignorable.

Hannah thrashes; she even tries to spit. Numb and tingly though her legs have become, there is life in them yet; and Hannah kicks madly, as if in a tantrum – or a seizure.

Sam's voice is steady, almost calm. 'Of course you're ready, babe,' she says. 'Or else, why would you let me put the cuffs on in the first place?'

'*No don't do it, Sam,*' Hannah gasps.

The grip tightens.

'*Please.*'

'Sshhh, babe,' Sam continues. 'We both know this story has to end *somewhere*.'

The link on the handcuffs finally breaks.

IV.

1.

The interview room is stuffy, but Dorothy doesn't mind. It is dry, that's the main thing; and the coffee she's been given is scalding and sweet.

WPC Webber is alert and considerate; a pretty young thing too, in Dorothy's modest opinion. But the poor girl hadn't expected this! She'd expected, no doubt, a lachrymose statement from Dorothy about how the accident happened, and how she and Annette came to be walking by the canal in the middle of another freak gale in the first place. However: Dorothy is a writer: she knows what makes a narrative tick.

So, Dorothy had started at the beginning.

Dorothy has been in the interview room for coming up to two hours, with WPC Webber as her scribe, her amanuensis. Efficiently, a digital recorder preserves their every word (and cough), but it's Dorothy who has spoken the most so far. A torrent of narrative! A tidal wave of tale! She and Webber are making this journey together, these two strangers, with Dorothy sipping her fifth or sixth coffee and taking infrequent comfort breaks but basically staying put, on a plastic blue chair that is the epitome of discomfort.

'What's the time, please, Officer?'

'Call me Donna. Nearly midnight, I'm afraid. Are you getting tired?'

'I was born tired,' Dorothy replies. 'I'd like to finish, if I may.'

'There's more?'

There is indeed. Much more; and Dorothy intends to sing

to the lot. 'Unless *you're* tired, of course,' Dorothy remembers her manners to enquire.

'No.' Webber smiles fleetingly. 'Or no more than usual. I was born tired, too.'

Off she goes again, Dorothy, unburdening herself of stories and comprehending with vulgar clarity that this is the one that she should have been writing all along: it would have been no different from making entries in a diary, or taking minutes. As she speaks she makes connections that she hasn't noticed before; and she does her best to keep her paragraphs clipped and short, fearful of losing her listener's attention.

At length, Dorothy sighs warmly and tastes coffee in the air. 'Which brings us up to speed, Donna,' she concludes. 'I'd like to thank you for hearing me out without giving me any reason to believe you can't wait to telephone the nearest funny farm...'

'Interview suspended at midnight-oh-four,' Officer Webber says for the tape's benefit. Then she presses Stop and says, 'I'll drive you home. Do you think you'll be okay?'

'I seriously doubt it...Actually I hope not. I mean, what sort of person would I be if I didn't get the shock sooner or later?'

'It'll come.'

Led by the officer, Dorothy is at the door that will take them back into the police station's lobby, which smells of the detergent that was used to mop up a worse-for-wear reveller's enthusiastic vomit earlier this evening. Webber has her fingers on the number pad, when they both hear:

'Donna!'

The speaker is a man in his mid-fifties. Salt-and-pepper closecrop; hornrim specs; white shirtsleeves, no jacket, black braces...He looks knackered.

'Guv?'

'Do you want to pull an OT?' he asks.

'Tonight?'

'Right now.'

Does this mean I've lost my ride home? Dorothy wonders. She supposes that OT equals an overtime shift.

'Sure,' Webber answers with a shrug.

'Good. You're on Ghoul Patrol.'

'Where?'

'Off Stanbridge Road. Mechanic place, called Bible Street Cars. Do you know it?'

Dorothy says, 'Oh Jesus' under her breath…but not quite under her breath *enough*. 'What's happened?'

The superior officer – impossible to rank with his jacket off – turns his attention to Dorothy. 'Do *you* know it?' he asks her.

'We've just been talking about it,' Webber informs her manager. 'Among other things.'

'I asked what's happened,' says Dorothy.

'I'm afraid it's murder, Missus…?'

'*Ms*. Anthony. Dorothy Anthony…Is the victim's name Roy?' she wants to know. Her thought is this: *It's one by one. Whatever it is, it's coming for all of us: One by one. First, Sam. Then Annette. Now Roy.*

'No. But that's a gentleman we'd very much like to help us with our enquiries, *Ms* Anthony. Do you know him well?'

'Fairly.'

Webber explains. 'We've just been talking about him, too.'

Perhaps it's the light in the office; perhaps not; but Dorothy is sure that she sees a glint in the woman's eye.

She's starting to believe me.

'It was Roy who incinerated the memory stick,' Dorothy adds clearly. 'The stick with the film on it of Samantha Twyfield being murdered in a hotel room. By an Arabic man named Hana. I don't know his surname,' she says to the senior officer, in precisely the same way that she did to Webber, about an hour earlier.

'What the hell do you know about *that*?' the supervisor asks. 'Sarge?'

'Samantha Twyfield was discovered dead this evening in a room at The King's Hotel,' the Sergeant continues, to Webber. 'She was strangled; possibly raped. She'd been there for four days, the room paid for upfront for a week and a DO NOT DISTURB sign on the door, so the maid hadn't been in.'

'Four *days*?' says Webber.

'We think. It's Buckinghamshire's case. But you're telling me there's a *film*?'

Dorothy nods her head. 'Well, there was. As I say, Roy burned it.'

'And why would he go and do a thing like that?' the Sergeant asks. 'Instead of showing it to us!'

'I don't know. He thought it was poisoning him, maybe,' Dorothy replies.

'Poison–' the Sergeant mutters. '…May I ask why you're here tonight, Ms Anthony?'

'My friend died in the canal.' Her voice is cold, to the point.

'Annette Bryant,' says Webber.

'No. It was *Caitlin* Bryant. It was Annette Harrison,' Dorothy corrects her. 'Though I don't know who she was when she died.'

The Sergeant is frowning. 'Honestly, I'm flummoxed,' he admits. 'I don't understand a bloody word of this.'

'Ms Anthony has given a full statement,' Webber interjects.

'Bit of bloody rain and I've got six dead bodies!' the Sergeant continues, as much to himself as to his small audience.

'There'll be more than that,' Dorothy tells him quietly.

'Pardon me?'

'Before all of this is over.'

'…Before all of *what* is over?'

'What I've told Donna.'

'Which is what exactly?' He shakes his head. 'Perhaps we'd better go back into the interview room, if you wouldn't mind,' he says.

'I'm very tired, Sergeant. Suddenly.'

The Sergeant smirks unkindly. 'Well, I'm sorry to hear that, but to be frank with you, Ms Anthony, I couldn't give a monkey's tail about your fatigue.'

'Something else,' Dorothy adds, almost as though she hasn't heard the rebuke. 'I'm suddenly very worried about my friend, Tom Lockington. I wasn't able to reach him earlier. Or Hannah Paddington.'

'…And who might they be, when they're at home?'

'Well, they're *not* at home, that's the point. Well, Hannah might be, I suppose; Tom wasn't…' Dorothy sighs; a yawn springs up from the depths. 'Hannah was the one who killed a thief in Cairo in the Nineties. With Sam. Sam Twyfield. Or so she believes. And Tom was the one who was raped by his uncle when he was a boy. He has a girlfriend called Sabrina who died when she was little.'

The Sergeant leaves a short pause. '…*What?*' he then asks, shaking his head. 'What say you we get this on the record, Ms Anthony?'

'It's already on the record,' Dorothy answers.

'Well, let's get it *more* on the record, then,' the Sergeant tells her firmly.

V.

1.

From below, in the hallway, I hear the sound of the front door opening – and Kolko's voice.

'I'm PC Simon Kolko, retired. Beds County Police.'

The other voice – the visitor's voice – I don't recognize.

'We've had reports of a disturbance, sir,' it says – a man's tones. 'May we come in?' Male, polite and above all certain of itself.

'Of course. The intruders are upstairs,' Kolko says with a level voice. 'And that's what they did to my mother's cat.'

Mother's cat? *Amelior?*

I am pinned to the spot, on the landing. I have seconds. *Decide!*

Movement in the hallway, at least two bodies entering the house. *Decide!*

On the other hand...decide what? There's no decision to make, is there? Not *really*. The first door I selected – the one on the right – took me onto the Dunstable Downs, and I'm not going there again. Why should I?

The second door – the one in the middle – is the one that Kolko reckons is hiding my mother; and while I didn't open it before (I lost my nerve) I have to now. My second choice of door was the one on the left: the one that transported me into Roy's memory of the cell.

Therefore, it's the middle door now; it stands to reason. It *has* to be.

Do it, Tom, Sabrina encourages me – right at the centre of my brain. *Do it for me!*

Roy's body is beside me, taking up the lion's share of the landing.

'Police!' an officer calls up the stairs. Strident treads on the first few. 'Stay where you are, son! And put your hands in the air!'

Where is Roy? Where did he go after the memory of the cell? He did not come back with me, so what memory is he lost in now?

'Forgive me, mate,' I say to the shell of a man next to me. 'You'd do the same…'

Roy's body is heavy, and with my left hand in his right armpit, and my right hand gripping his belt buckle, it is a job to manoeuvre the big man to the top of the stairs. We are face to face for the duration of this ludicrous fandango; his empty eyes reflect mine. What expression does he wear? It's hard to tell for sure, for the difference between our faces is that, while mine is covered in sweat, Roy's is covered in his own dried and congealing blood.

What was on his mind when Kolko froze him?

The first of three uniformed police officers – a man in his fifties, with a salt-and-pepper crewcut – is halfway up the flight.

'Don't do it, son,' he warns me.

Do it, Tom! says Sabrina. *I love you!*

It takes all of my strength, but my grasp – to armpit, to buckle – is confident, and facing up to a doomed situation lends us power – muscle power. Grunting volubly, I launch Roy's vacated body down the stairs. And although I'm not strong enough to get his toes much off the carpet, I have his bulk and I have gravity on my side.

Stiff but not plywood-rigid, Roy tumbles backwards down the staircase, his body consuming most of each tread's width. The lead copper has not expected this tactic. Although the officer is hardly a small man, Roy's mass strikes him like a rhino charging a Jeep.

I have bought myself a few more seconds. Taking anger as my compass, I venture forth, an explorer into uncharted terrain...and I open the middle door.

2.

It's just a room. No landscape, no vista; no compacted angles or sharp shadows. Neither the greenery of the outdoors nor the swollen greyness of a prison cell recollection. Just a room.

More specifically, however, it is *my* room: my bedroom, when I was growing up, or one of its iterations; and it is empty.

Empty of people, that is. The room is as busy as any kid's bedroom. A single bed with chocolate-coloured eiderdown; white furniture. Posters on the wall: footballers, tennis players, Showaddywaddy in their crepes and drapes...I must be about ten. Enid Blyton and *Star Wars* spinoffs on the bookshelves. A desk with a lamp; on the desk, a bicycle repair kit, some cassettes, a small tape recorder...

The mirror over the desk shows the now-me, the adult-me; even in a fantasy like this, there's no boy. Never was, not once it started happening – that's when a boy – or *this* boy – became something else. Not a man. Not even an individual unit, human or otherwise. From that moment, that first incident – I was a part of something evil and endless; a piece with a function, locked inside a construction built of desperation, fear, of anguish and inadequacy.

Remembering this is overpowering...The room stinks of boy and stalled air; it has a circulation problem, and it is a parody of innocence.

I want to shred it; to whittle it into kindling. To cremate this dead thing, once and for all. But memories don't burn. Memories are fireproof.

'Tom?'

My mother's voice, from the adjacent bedroom – from the room she shared with my dad, with my uncle – with who else?

Décor excepted, my mum's landing is nearly the same as Amelior's. For the moment the two landings have even meshed and overlapped. Peering over the banister I see three police officers, two men and one younger woman, on the stairs, moving animatedly in jerky spasms; they're as trapped as bluebottles, caught under an upturned pint glass, buzzing helplessly. These wraiths are also transparent, or nearly so, and colourless; I can see right through them, as I would through light mist, to where Roy's body lies motionless at the foot of the stairs. Roy is also drained of colour, and is of a questionable solidity.

'Tom?' my mother calls again.

I remove the screwdriver from my front pocket and knock on her bedroom door.

'Come in!'

What's the best I can hope for? *He woke up and it had all been a dream.* It won't happen. There's no difference between the dream and the live stuff anyway…Keeping hold of my breath, I enter; and the room is dim. Not fully dark, but dim enough to clumsify my vision. To either side of the bed's sideboard, one lamp burns on a stand.

The kingsize bed is full. From my perspective, from left to right, it is Amelior, Stephen…and Mum. As far as I can tell, with the sheets and blankets roughly at waist level, all three of them are naked…and no grown man should see his mother in the nod. I don't know where to look.

'Hello, Tom,' says my mother, and simultaneously Amelior says the same thing; but Stephen doesn't.

'*You* took your fucking time,' he tells me. 'What's that in your hand? Is it still that screwdriver?' He laughs.

'Yes. And I intend to use it,' I reply.

'About time you made yourself useful around here. How *old* are you, for fuck's sake!'

Although it's not a genuine question (it's undoubtedly an insult), it's a valuable point nonetheless. How old *am* I, for fuck's sake? Do they see me as a child – did I ever stop *being* a child, in their eyes? – or as an adult?

'I'm not here as a handyman, Stephen,' I say more clearly than I expected to. 'And it's not me who took my time. It's *you* who took my time. Speaking literally, that is.'

'Beautiful. Now we've brought up a smartarse,' says Stephen. 'That's *magic*, that is.'

'Oh let him be, Stephen. Don't you have a kiss for Mummy?'

My stomach rolls. 'You've got to be joking, Mum. How *could* you?'

'Want a kiss?'

'Oh stop it! You and your sick games…'

'They're not *games*, Tom.'

They're not games, Tom, I notice. Not: *They* weren't *games, Tom*…If I was under the spell of any delusion that this was all in the past – as unlikely and as unforgivable as even *that* would have been – this spell is shattered and decoded now, by my mother – through a simple matter of Freudian semantics.

'You're right. They were lives,' I tell her. 'Children's. And you stole them. All of you.'

Stephen has recovered some of his former bluster. 'To hell with this. Where's our breakfast, Tommy? I used to like it when you brought tea and toast. Afterwards.'

'How did you follow me to Iceland?' I ask.

'What do you mean, *how*? I *followed* you, boy! Cost an arm and a leg, too, I don't mind admitting.' His voice full of regret, he adds, 'I could have done more there. Shame.'

'More?'

'Yeah. I'm not gonna have another chance to eat puffin.'

My brain struggles. It takes me a moment before I realize that what Stephen has just said is not a cipher for something else. He's telling it point blank. He didn't get a chance to munch on a sea bird. Well, boo hoo. Neither did I.

'But you were fading out on me,' I say. 'Your picture kept fuzzing.'

'You saw what you wanted to see, Tommy. You're a coward. Always running away, weren't you, when you couldn't face up to what was real. I faded out? Well, that was your own doing. And your so-called dopey friends – they're just as bad. So don't blame *me*!'

'Who else should I blame? You made me think I was going mad!'

'Well, you are. You're in deep, son,' says Stephen. 'And it *is* a kind of madness, I suppose.' (My mother nods her head.) 'There's no way out. You have to keep doing more and more – and your reward is you're more and more protected. You can mess with minds so the people don't see what they don't want to see. Or what *you* don't want them to see.' Stephen shrugs his naked, hairy shoulders. 'That's part of the payment. Part of the *rules…*'

'Is that how you got away with Sabrina?'

He holds his hands up. 'I've already told you: the girl was an accident.'

'That's not what I asked. I asked you how you got away with it.'

Again, he shrugs. 'Friends in high places,' he replies. 'What can I say?'

'Meaning Kolko.'

'Simon helped, I admit. So did our *friends in high places*. Or are you simply not listening, Tommy-Boy?'

'Stephen, don't,' says my mother; but this enrages me further.

'Don't try to stand up for me *now*, Mum!'

'I'm your mother,' she complains. 'It's my job.'

There is so much I can say to this that I can't say anything. Words crowd around my vocal cords, like rubberneckers at a roadside car ding.

Do it, Tom! Sabrina urges me once more.

But do what? Assault three people, two of whom are nearly double my age, and one of whom, an old lady with watery dugs and an imbecile's grin, is much older?

Do *what* exactly?

'…I don't have to believe you, Stephen,' I say. 'I don't have to believe any of you.'

Stephen rolls his head on his neck. 'Don't start *that* one again…'

'I don't!'

At which point Amelior Anderson speaks for the first time, not counting her initial cordial greeting. 'You're one of us now, Tom,' she states quietly. 'We're getting old. We need someone to carry things on for us. For posterity…So why don't you come to bed and join us?'

VI.

1.

'I forgive you. I've brought you some fags.'

Dorothy stands in the rain outside Patrick's house, a carrier bag in her hand.

'Can I come in?'

Even for a man of a hundred and four years, Patrick appears shuffling and shoddy. 'It's nearly two o'clock in the morning,' he says.

'Were you in bed?'

'No. Well I was, but then I had bad dreams about Annette. They woke me up.'

Dorothy refuses to be drawn on the subject: not quite yet. 'Where's Justine?'

'Sleeping. So should you be!'

'Can I come in?' Dorothy asks again. 'This rain's not getting any better.'

Patrick's voice sounds suspicious when he asks: 'What's in the bag?'

'I told you: some of your favourite smokes. And two bottles of wine, one of each. For us. To say I forgive you.'

'Well all right, I suppose…Funny old night.' He stands aside.

'Hysterical.'

And Dorothy steps over the threshold.

2.

The next morning she wakes late. Justine's voice is in her head.

You've broken his heart, she informs Dorothy, over and over, until Dorothy twists away from the dreamy cobwebs and, rolling out of bed, pays attention.

You've broken his heart.

Dorothy is defiant. *Good. Let's hope it's the one thing he won't recover from. With luck he'll suffer – before and after he's a hundred and five.*

When she screams, the transmission is closed down. She doesn't know for how long, but the silence feels good. In fact, the scream itself feels good. After padding her way into the kitchen, Dorothy breaks up a banana and plugs in the blender. She churns together the banana chunks with a half-pint of low-fat milk and makes a smoothie. Feeling good.

Feeling…normal?

Not quite; but getting there – although she is well aware that she is currently somnambulating through a process of shock. When reality sets her down again – with a bump – there'll be emotional debts to pay; there'll be some psychological compensation due.

She knew that the poison wouldn't kill him, not a man who has lived as long as Patrick. On leaving the police station, she had declined WPC Webber's second offer of a lift home, preferring (she claimed) to walk, whatever the weather. To clear her head. But she had not walked directly home, she had gone via the minimart on her corner.

Revenge keeps you fit, she had realized, an epithet that she'd write down at some point, if she remembered the words. Certainly it was no easy activity to crush the painkillers with her pestle and mortar (while drinking a glass of the red wine that she'd bought). Then the *stirring* she'd been obliged to undertake! My! That powder had taken a while to dissolve, in a cup full of bleach. This solution she'd then transferred into the empty space in the bottle; and then – more exercise! – she had left the flat on foot, heading for Patrick's.

But she knew that the poison wouldn't kill him.

So she told him all about Annette's death.

As soon as he'd shown a few signs of sleepiness, Dorothy had laid in with the truth about his daughter, understanding that she might not have long before he slipped away into a healing snooze – or better still, a coma – but she'd also laid on thick the parts about which she was unsure. For what reason? To punish him: short and sweet.

And to make herself feel better about this day.

'Listen, Patrick,' she'd said, 'before Justine wakes up…'

She made Annette's death out to be entirely Patrick's responsibility, and his fault. For all Dorothy knows, this is indeed the case. 'You stupid, cruel man,' she taunted him. 'What made you think you could have them *both*? It's one or the other! You chose your dead wife, so your daughter had to die. My friend and your daughter. And she died *slowly*.'

He protested, of course. Patrick didn't want to hear.

Eventually, after a few minutes, so did his wife. Justine came down the stairs and gave Dorothy verbal hell – words in the air, also words in her head – but Dorothy maintained a tightlipped almost-silence (whimpering slightly at the pain in her skull)…and she slipped out of the house, tipsy and frightened, eager for her own sheets and a night that she was certain would not pass in sleepy bliss, but at least would *pass*.

And now? She feels good.

The banana smoothie is the best thing she's tasted in years.

3.

After trying Tom's front door buzzer and finding him not at home (or at least not answering his front door buzzer), Dorothy returns to her own flat and tries Hannah on the phone. Where is everybody? Hannah does not respond either. She does not call Roy, she is afraid of who will pick up the receiver and speak. Nor does Dorothy phone Annette, although she is perversely certain that Annette will find some way of speaking to her in the near future. For she did her best by Annette; she is confident that she has nothing to fear from Annette.

She calls Patrick.

'How's the patient?' she asks Justine.

'…You've got a lot of nerve,' Justine tells her.

'Yes I have, I suppose. It's rather surprised me as well; I didn't think I had it in me, but it's amazing what people will do in exceptional circumstances. I asked you how he is.'

'…Stable.'

'Upset?'

'Oh yes.'

'That's good,' says Dorothy. 'But you were never part of any of it, were you, Justine? I don't bear *you* any ill will. In fact, I feel sorry for you, having to come back to that greasespot you call a husband – and not even because *you* wanted to. Because *he* wanted you to! He wouldn't do you so much courtesy as to allow you to rest in peace. Well, he's made your bed, my dear, and now you have to lie in it. Forever, maybe.'

To Dorothy's surprise, Justine starts crying.

'I feel sorry for myself, too,' she manages to say.

Dorothy waits a few seconds. It alarms her to note how much she enjoys hearing other people weeping. She is certain that this is a fairly new development: surely new since the turn of the year.

'Do you mind if I read you something, Justine?'

'Read me…? No. I don't mind.'

'It's something I wrote yesterday. I wrote it for two women – one black woman and one white woman – who always go around as a pair. And have haunted me for a while now – for months, in fact. But I didn't see them yesterday. I'd *expected* to. They didn't come.'

Justine sniffs. Dorothy hears the brush of a tissue or a hanky against the mouthpiece as the other woman wipes her nose or dabs her eyes.

'Read what you want, Dorothy.'

'Thank you.' The piece of paper has been battered in her handbag, and is as curled and wrinkled as a sheet of ancient parchment. Although it slept on the storage heater overnight, the paper remains damp to the touch from where rain leaked into Dorothy's handbag. Between the thumb and middle of her left hand, Dorothy holds the script; and she reads: '"You used to make me fearful of everything, you two did. Everything I tried, everywhere I went, the two of you were in the back of my mind if you weren't there in person. Now I think that that was the whole point, your existence was to scare me sufficiently that I would question the grey areas in my past. You're my metaphors. So where have you been?

'"Girls – you don't mind if I call you girls, I hope; I'm not an old woman, far from it, but I'm old enough for you to be girls to me – I lived a precarious lifestyle until you two splashed your way into it. Precarious, not because of what I did but because of what I did not do. And what I did *not* do was care a hoot about my past. Because I didn't know that one existed that had been hidden from me. Hidden *from* me, hidden *by* me. And now I know that one can't live in ignorance. It's dangerous. So thank you, girls. I know what was done to me when I was a child, and I know that I was attacked on the border between Poland and Germany. And I survived it all. But the effort of keeping it so-called safe inside me was unravelling me, I can see that now. Concealing the truth is risky. I don't know if you two are the *actual* women that

I met on that hill with the face – I think not – but you're how I see those women, whether you're real or (as I say) metaphors. Perhaps you represent the women who fought over me when I was a child, too. That's something I've considered: the White Queen and the Black Queen, as it were. My mother and Amelior Anderson. Neither of whom are dark-skinned, as you know; but children paint their feelings in vivid colours. I'll work it out.'"

Dorothy coughs and clears her throat. 'Are you still there?'

'I'm still here, Dorothy.'

"'All I ask, ladies, is that you don't desert me. This request confounds the hell out of me, I confess, because all I used to wish for is that you'd disappear from my life like dust on the wind. But I miss you now; and I'm willing and eager to learn more from you from this moment onwards. And from Di, if that girl is appropri-ate – another metaphor, I am certain, though I don't know for what yet. But isn't that was life is for, ladies? To learn and to grow flabby with knowledge. To gorge and gorge? And what I learn I'll write, and what I write I'll learn – and share. Be my guides.'"

Justine leaves a space. 'Why are you telling me?' she asks.

'Oh, I don't know. I think I'm going to tell everyone. You can pass on the message, maybe. I'm going to make an appoint-ment with Dr Savros and I'm going to tell *him*. And then I'm go-ing to call my agent, Julia – and I'm not going to speak to Helen, I'm going to insist on speaking to Julia – and I'm going to tell her as well. Tell the world!'

'You need a rest, Dorothy,' says Justine.

'I'll rest when I'm dead,' Dorothy answers. When her fit of the giggles strikes, she is forced to put down the phone. She tries to sit it out, this fit of giggles; but it won't go away, so Dorothy moves about the flat, from room to room, doing nothing in par-ticular, or at least nothing urgent, simply hefting some laundry into the machine and filling the sink up with hot soapy water with which to do the washing-up. The fit of giggles erupts into gales of laughter. Gales! The laughter is like weather, filling the flat; bursting her open, and drenching her.

It takes her five minutes to calm down. Then she opens her address book at *D* for her entry for 'Doctor'. 'I'd like to make an appointment with Dr Savros, please,' she says.

Then she telephones Tom.

Still no answer.

Towards the close of the morning, with hunger roaming and prowling in her belly, Dorothy picks up the phone again and dials Julia's number. Anticipating that Helen will take the call (and steeling herself for the inevitable attritional pleasantries), Dorothy is pleasantly surprised when Julia says her own name in a business-like cadence.

'It's Dolly.'

'Dorothy! What a coincidence! I was just about to give *you* a ring.'

'Really?'

'You sound amazed.'

'I *am* amazed. First, no intercessionary squabble with your assistant, and now this. To what do I owe the honour?'

'Well, Helen's out to lunch with a client—' Julia begins.

'That's not what I meant, and you know it…A client?' Dorothy doubletakes. 'As in a writer client?'

'Yes. If you'd let me finish…'

'Ah, nostalgia. I remember when you used to take *me* out to lunch. As a client.'

'Well, that's why I was ringing: to invite *you* out to lunch, Dolly. As a client…We've had some interest.'

Dorothy blinks. 'In my book proposal?'

Julia chuckles. 'No, in your bra size, dear… So when can you catch a train? Tomorrow?'

'Uh…sorry, no; I've got a doctor's appointment tomorrow. How about the next day?'

'Nothing serious, I hope. The doctor.'

'It's nothing, Jules. How about the next day?'

Dorothy hears the tapping of keys. 'Can't do it,' Julia informs her. 'Tell you what. Let's put it back to Friday: a nice way to end the working week. What do you think?'

'Friday's fine…When you say *interest?*'

'Nothing firmed…but interest. A big publisher. No cowboys. Money per draft.'

Dorothy laughs. '…I'm a little bit stunned,' she admits.

'You sound it!' Julia remarks gleefully. 'Not often I make *L'Antionette* nearly speechless!'

'No, I suppose not.'

'So why were you calling?' Julia asks. 'It wasn't to chew me out about never inviting you out to lunch, so what was it?'

Smiling, Dorothy answers: 'It can wait till Friday. Believe it or not, I was going to read you something.'

'Yummy. An extract from the work in progress.'

The script that she wrote – the script whose purpose had been to provide notes for a lecture for the two women who once pursued her around town…can it be that this meagre chunk of virtually unparagraphed prose has a second function, a second life?

'Something like that,' says Dorothy.

'Good. You can read to me over a Singapore Sling. How far have you got?'

Julia means in the manuscript, of course, but the question draws out an extension to Dorothy's smile. 'It's mainly notes, but plenty of them.'

'Bring what you've got. Do you know how it ends at least?'

Dorothy sighs. 'I think so. Apart from a character called

Tom. I'm not sure where the hell *he's* got to.'

No sooner has Dorothy replaced the receiver than the phone rings. It must be Julia. She's forgotten something...*So answer it, Dorothy!* her mother breathes into her ear. *What are you waiting for? Cat got your tongue?*

The phone trills again.

Cold hands land heavily on Dorothy's shoulders; their fingers sink into her skin. She imagines that her wound – where she once held a violin, where a bullet once hit her, where a yokel hayseed idiot kid once tried to rape her – will flare up with its customary rosy agony. But there is no pain there, not right now; has it gone forever? The only pains that Dorothy feels are fresh ones, and they'll cease, by and by. Nothing that rest, recuperation and aspirins won't smudge out. They're not *mind* injuries; they're not abrasions of the memory.

'Ms Anthony? It's WPC Webber.'

Dorothy registers relief, it swims up through her body like mercury in a tube. She even sighs. 'Hello, Donna.'

'Hi. I'm ah...I'm making this call outside, on a private phone. I'm not in the office.'

'Oh?' A pretty young thing phoning me privately and on the sly, thinks Dorothy. Can my luck be *thrice* in?

'Do you know a man named Leo Cantaloni?' Donna asks. 'He was the business partner of James's stepfather Lenny. Also a former acquaintance of James's father, in the ice cream trade.'

'Oh, Leo. Yes. Well, I never knew his surname, and I've never met him...I've heard his name down the way. What about him?'

'I'm due a lunchbreak. Can we meet? I want to show you what he gave me.'

'What is it?' Dorothy asks.

'A letter. Written by James. Given to Leo – the man *swears*

– by James's dad. The one who happens to be dead. But after everything that's happened in the last twenty-four…'

'I'll meet you anywhere you want,' Dorothy tells her. 'Are you in uniform?'

'Yes, it's a normal workday. Kind of.'

'Perhaps not a pub then. How about the library? I'll meet you on the third floor, by the theatre. It's usually quiet up there until the matinees start. Oh, but Donna?'

'Yes?'

'You'll be filing the letter, won't you? It's evidence. So you'll be filing it.'

'Yes. I'll have to file it.

'But you're showing me because you believe me. Right or wrong?'

Webber's pause is long. 'I believe *something*,' she finally confesses; and then her voice is all business – as much as Julia's was, a few minutes earlier.

'Fine. Twenty minutes then,' Dorothy suggests. Once she has deposited the receiver once more, she sits peacefully for a while, contemplating a browse around the charity shops down by the post office, at the far end of the High Street. Some of them sell musical instruments. With a smile on her face, she wonders how much violins cost these days.

VII.

1.

If I leave my mother's room I will return to the landing at the top of Amelior's staircase, and the police are frozen halfway up the flight. There'll be nowhere to run. They will take me.

My other option is to stay here with these three recidivists.

What the hell do I do?

'If I stay, what happens?' I ask the trio.

Customarily angry, Stephen says, 'Well, don't do *us* any favours, you ungrateful little twat. Go out there and talk to the coppers if we're not to your refined palette.'

'Stephen, *please*,' says my mother.

'I mean, Jesus, he comes in here with a face like a smacked arse...'

My mother wants to answer my question.

'We have debts to repay, as we've told you. That's how we stay unnoticed, by and large. So you'll be expected to continue.'

It's hard to say the words that I require for clarification. 'With abuse.'

'Not necessarily,' Mum says brightly. 'There are other ways!'

'Of making mischief.'

'Yes, that's one way of putting it, Tom.'

'I won't do it.'

Turning my back on them, I stride for the door.

'Little *cunt*,' I have no choice but to hear Stephen bellow; then I hear the rustle of bedclothes as he clambers to his feet, but the door is open – and I'm back on the landing.

Amelior's landing.

Stepping back into the present triggers the dissolution of the charge that has kept the police in check, suspended between seconds on the staircase.

A female voice calls, 'Stop, Tom!' and I wonder how they know my name already.

Salt-and-Pepper Buzzcrop is almost at the top of the flight. His face is plum with spent energy and an inbuilt determination of rage.

Stephen is a metre or so behind me, wearing only etiolated Y-fronts.

I am trapped. Pincered-in. The Devil and the deep blue sea...

What's the best I can hope for from the law, as a perpetrator, as a felon?

Protection?

Don't make me laugh.

But what's my alternative? The remainder of my life in the keeping of a squad of perverts? How strong will I have to be? To resist them, I mean, with all of the spiritual back-up that they brag about. To resist them *forever*...

'Stay there!' I order the policeman at the head of the phalanx. I point the nib of the screwdriver at his eyes. He is a metre from me as well, at the most.

Said copper shows the palms of his hands. 'Let's not be hasty, son,' he advises.

'I'm not your son,' I tell him. Turning to Stephen, I add, 'Are *you*? Are you my father? Tell me straight, Stephen.'

Stephen shakes his head. 'No, boy. Your father's gone. He was a good man but he was weak. And he's long gone.'

'Then I can find him!' I realize.

A twitch at the top of the stairs.

'*I said don't move!*' I shout at the officer.

'All right, Tom,' he replies, still displaying the puff pastry of his palms. 'But why not put down the weapon, eh? Make it easier on yourself. On all of us. Eh?'

The Devil and the deep blue sea...

Which one do I choose, Sabrina?

Come to me! she answers.

Where? Where *are* you, Sab?

Fuck.

The answer is right beside me – the first door I chose, what seems to be thirty-odd years ago. The door on the right of the landing...the sewing room...

With a sharp, exact movement I fling open the door...

'Stay where you are, Tom!'

...as both the policeman and Stephen lunge at me in the same instant.

Crossing over the border, and into my memory of the Downs, I feel a hand on my coat collar, attempting to drag me back on to the landing. The coat's zip pinches at my throat. *Whose* hand? Who got me first?

I won't go back. Whose hand is unimportant.

In front of me is the vista. I stand at the crown of the hills, once again. A muted shriek leaving my mouth, I tug at the zip; it is strained with the pressure from behind, but it gives. The zip lowers. If I shrug off my wet coat, I'm free – at least for now.

I jerk the zip down – down to the bottom of its rungs. The tugging from behind does not desist, so as soon as the coat flies open – immediately it spreads its wings – the coat soars backwards...and I straggle forwards, just about maintaining my balance. I am scarcely in time to turn to see the coat vanish into thin air. Gone!

And now I'm on the Downs; it is peaceful for the moment, irrespective of my own haggard breathing. I bend over double and clutch hold of my knees. *Breathe.* And no one can chase me here, into my own memory. Can they? I hope not, anyway. *Breathe, Tom…*

I've bought myself some time.

That's my boy, Sabrina tells me. *Look on the bright side.*

2.

Approximately three-quarters of the way down the slope, I see someone up ahead, someone built like a fridge-freezer, with an aura of vagueness and *gassiness* about his body. Were it not for one peculiar detail about his attire, I might assume the walker to have been here all along – in my memory – but unnoticed and blotted out by sensory impressions of greater significance.

Then again, not many strollers on Dunstable Downs wear pink washing-up gloves.

I call: 'Roy! Roy-mate!'

Probably thirty metres ahead of and below me, the figure turns. Barring the rubber marigolds, from this distance the man could be Stephen – even Kolko. But it must be Roy – it's the gloves.

'Wait up!' I shout. Though the dirt on the slope is dry, loose and ultimately treacherous, I break into a trot, trying to reach my friend, the only friend I might have in this recollection. To see Roy again seems worth the discomfort that it causes my back.

'Tom!' Roy's face is a canvas of greedy relief.

We embrace. The hug is like great whales mating, with the added effect of robust backslaps. It is all I can do to stop myself kissing the man's lips.

'Have you seen yourself in a mirror lately?' I ask. 'I think you cut yourself shaving.'

'It's time to grow a fucking beard,' he replies. '*Fuck* it's good to see you, Tom.'

'Likewise. But how? You were never here: it's not your memory.'

'Now now. Let's not be pedantic.'

'Seriously. What do you think's going on?'

Roy looks up at the sky – a wooden colour, bark-like at this moment, amid regiments of cloud. 'Seriously, I don't know,' he admits. 'But you were never in the cell with me and Steve either and *you* made it in. I bet we didn't see it the same way, mind.'

I take this in. If the concept of logic is not helplessly *passé* by this juncture, then what Roy has suggested sounds logical. I work in a prison and so I know what a cell looks like. This doesn't mean I saw the *same* cell that Roy saw. It was just *a* cell, it was something that I constructed from informational nuggets snipped from conversations on the subject with this man. Similarly, here, Roy has no doubt built a picture of the Downs – he *knows* the Downs – based on chit-chat that we've shared. It doesn't mean that we are looking at the same thing.

Nor does this matter.

'Over there is where Stephen killed Sabrina,' I tell Roy.

He nods his head. 'I suppose we have to see. So I know what I'm dealing with, once and for all.'

'You sound like you're planning something.'

'Aren't you?'

'I'm only catching my breath, mate. That was close, in the house. I'm afraid I had to use you as a battering ram.' I explain how I threw him down the stairs, and to my delight he actually laughs.

'Being morbidly obese has *some* advantages then,' he says.

'It worked for me! So what are you planning?'

'Shall we walk? I need to stretch. I think I can feel bruises forming…where I landed on the stairs. Is that possible?'

We walk.

'When we left the prison cell – you and me, I mean – you went straight back to Amelior's house, didn't you. But I didn't. I went for a walk on the Wing. I followed that screw we saw – his name was Bennett, I think – and…I don't know what it was…I just couldn't bear the thought of going straight back, so I'm sorry about that, mate. I had a fear I'd go back into my body and I wouldn't be able to move. So I had a wander. And I suppose I could've just…like…floated through the doors at the end of every corridor, but I didn't. I waited while Bennett – if that was his name – took his keys out and unlocked it. As if he was chaperoning me personally! Like it was time for Visits or something. I saw people I haven't thought of in years. Friends, some of 'em. Or what pass for friends in the nick.'

'Your point being?'

'My point being…I could've *stayed* there, Tom.'

I'm confused. 'Why would you want to stay in prison?'

'Why did Stephen?'

'Because he wasn't ready to come out,' I reply. 'I hear it all the time from some of the lads in my classes at the YOI. When I set creative writing for some of the more able lads, I can guarantee I'll get at least one essay about how he's scared to go home. But *you* weren't.'

'No. No I wasn't, mate; but that don't mean I made a great success of it either, does it? I was out a few months after Stephen…'

'A business in London,' I remind him.

'Which was bloody hard work.'

'And now a business on Stanbridge Road,' I persevere. 'Why the hell would you want to stay *there*? I'm curious.'

'I thought I might be paralysed inside my own body, Tom. I could feel what Kolko did to me – and I was scared I might go back to that and be paraplegic for the rest of me days. Well, fuck that! I'll stay in the nick. Bide my time. Get out. Start again.'

'We can't live in our memories for ever, Roy.'

'Why not? *Old* people do.'

'We're not old!' I retort. 'Well you are a bit, but *I'm* not.'

'Cheeky cunt…Then it came to me, mate. If the rooms are choices we have to make, let them *be* choices. Surely it don't have to be for all time. You can change your mind…I had visions of following Bennett all the way out to the front gate. Following him home. It doesn't *all of it* have to be true, surely to God.'

'…Here we are.'

'Halt! Who goes there?' demands the boy who guards the entrance to the inner folds of the copse where Sabrina met her fate.

Roy laughs. 'Is that *you*? Oh mate, I love the shorts!'

'Oh right, you never did wear shorts, I suppose!'

'I did! I did! It takes me back to another generation, Tom.'

'It *is* another generation. Well, almost. I was only a wee nipper!'

'I can see that!' Roy replies, almost happily. Then his mood turns sombre. 'You guarded them, didn't you? he goes on. 'It's through them bushes.'

I nod my head. 'I didn't see it; but I saw the dead body. Sabrina's. She's been with me every step of the way, ever since. She's in my blood.'

'I said: *who goes there?*' the young boy version of me demands to know. He is slightly different on this visit; slightly chubbier, perhaps. It could be that I'm being more honest with myself and not pandering to the tendency that we all share: to soften the blow to our own feelings and rubbed-raw sensibilities. Furthermore, he – or I – holds up a long thin stick. In the boy's mind, this is a rifle – and he is on sentry duty. The gun is pointed our way.

Roy turns to me. 'Can't we stop him?' he asks sadly – sadly enough to suggest that this is a query for which he already has an answer.

'I tried. I was too late,' I tell him. 'I cussed him out but that was the best I managed.'

'Then we try again, Tom. Surely to God, we try *again*!' Roy's voice is suddenly passionate and full of pathos. 'However many times it *takes*, we try again. We *stop* the cunt doing what he does! We tell him his new fortune.'

'...In here?'

'In wherever, mate!'

'But it's already happened, Roy. I don't know how to *change* things.'

'Well, nor do I...*yet*. We've only just touched down on the runway; give it a chance...But if we can, mate – think about it! If we can actually change it in our memories...or *your* memory. It's gotta be a good thing, hasn't it?'

'I suppose so...'

'Because everything else will have to shuffle into a different shape,' Roy continues.

'Including us,' I tell him.

'Well, let's cross that bridge, eh, Tom? What do you say?' Roy casts his eyes about the immediate vicinity.

'What are you looking for?' I ask him.

'A gun.'

'A what?'

'A stick to use as a gun, like you've got. You weren't intending to batter your way past the poor little tyke, were you? How did you get in last time?'

'It was something about fairy tales. I was a Prince, I'm embarrassed to say.'

'So you should be.' Roy bends down and picks up a long stick, saying 'This'll do the trick' under his breath. 'You ain't no prince, Tom – no more than I am. And if your younger self wants to play War, we'll play War. Let's storm the castle!'

With a grin on my face I search for a stick of my own. Armed and dangerous, we approach the boy with my face on his smaller head.

'Put 'em in the air!' I tell him firmly.

The boy drops his rifle and raises his hands, a joyful expression on his face. He lets us pass and we stoop to crash through the greenery and the growth.

'Prepare yourself, mate,' I warn Roy. 'It's an ugly scene.'

'War is foul,' Roy says, a few steps ahead of me. 'But if we can't stop Stephen this time, it's just as well I see what really happened to give me some more rage for next time.'

'But what are we going to *do*, mate?' I ask pleadingly.

'What do any boys do when they're playing war? They pelt the enemy with fucking stones until the cunt surrenders. We'll deal with any further details later. You ready?'

Roy can't see me but I nod my head. 'Push on through, big man,' I tell him.

3.

Half an hour later, and we are back at the top of the Downs. Roy has wiped most of the vomit from his lips with clumps of torn-up grass. As a final gesture he spits into a wedge of daffodils.

Overhead, stately and regally slow, a glider feeds through the air. We watch this aircraft for a few seconds while considering our immediate options.

Soberly Roy asks, 'Do we have any money in your memory, Tom?'

I check. I have some shrapnel in my pockets. 'Only pennies and five pees,' I tell him. 'Why do you ask?'

'Fancied an ice cream, that's all. How much were ice creams back then?'

'I can't remember. I haven't got enough, anyway...What now?'

'It's *your* memory. Can you remember your way back home?'

'To Amelior's house? Already?'

Roy shakes his head. 'No, back to your home at the *time*.'

'It's a long walk. It's right on the other side of Dunstable. At least an hour.'

'Well, we walked to Stoke Hammond in the pissing rain and it didn't break our backs, mate. I'm sure we can manage a stroll on a pleasant summer's day like this. What do you think?'

Home. Back then...

'My father'll still be alive,' I realize. 'Oh my God, I can see Dad again!' Unexpected painful tears lurch up to and through my eyes and pour across the orbits.

'Perhaps you can warn Sabrina about strangers as well,' says Roy, doing his best to avoid the embarrassment of witnessing another man crying.

We start off down the steep road that leads up the Downs. At the bottom of the road, where it joins West Street, we turn right and past the pub with the windsock flapping high above its cringeworthy fake ramparts.

A woman I know well is waiting on the corner, near this pub. She is out of place, of course, she doesn't belong here...but it's good to see her, all the same. Especially as she appears, from the look on her face, to be in good spirits.

'Hello, Sabrina,' I say to her.

'Hello, Tom. It's a nice day for a walk. Mind if I join you?'

'Not at all,' I reply, well aware that I'm talking to her as if she's a stranger. She couldn't be less of a stranger if she tried. 'This is my friend Roy.'

Sabrina holds out her hand for the big man to shake. 'Delighted.'

After a nanosecond's hesitation, Roy shakes Sabrina's hand. 'Lovely to meet you, Sabrina,' he says. 'I've heard a lot about you.'

'All good, I hope.'

'Yes, darling. All good,' he replies.

We walk in the direction of town, through which we will pass, and if we choose to we will continue on down Luton Road, towards the house where my mother still lives.

'I don't know how long I've got, Tom,' Sabrina says suddenly. 'I might have to leave, but if I do you'll know I mean no offence.'

'I know…but stay as long as you can, won't you?' I say.

'Of course. But how about you? How long are you boys in town?' she asks.

Around me, details are filled in; colours sprout out of nowhere as my mind brings back the particulars: the buildings, the roads, even the cars. It is all coming back to me…or I'm coming back to it. I'm not sure which way round it is yet, but I'll learn.

Roy answers Sabrina's question on my behalf.

'As long as it takes, darling,' he says. 'As long as it takes.'

VIII.

1.

To Whom It May Concern:

My name is James and I am currently under 24-hour surveillance at a hospital for the criminally insane. This includes what is called a suicide watch. However, I do not display, from what I've overheard, any suicidal tendencies. I am not sure if this is a good or a bad thing (or for whom) and I refuse to ask. It's easier not to ask questions. Some people get angry.

I do not know what town I live in because again I won't ask, and no one has told me. It must be for my own benefit that I don't need to know. Wherever I am, I have been here ages. I try not to count the days. But I don't mind if I stay ages more. It's a nice place. It's warm and it's dry and meals arrive regularly. Whoever it is who prepares them generally remembers to not let the food groups touch. I like that. But I don't like semolina.

I do Arts and Crafts on a Monday morning and Spanish on Wednesday afternoons. I borrow science books from the library once a week, and one of the guards did an OU degree in Biology when she was thirty, so I like it when she works at night and I have someone to talk to and something to talk about.

There are no other children here. It's an adult hospital, usually, but I am an exceptional case. I like that as well.

The reason for this letter is to let you know that I am well. I am happy. I know that I will go on trial for murder. I am not afraid of this.

Mr Kolko said that he would make my father come back if I did some things that would make him proud. So I did them. And for a while I thought Mr Kolko had lied to me, but now that my father has been to see me, I know that he was telling the truth.

Dad can only see me rarely. You need special permission, and before long the authorities will catch on that he used to be not-alive. So Dad and I decided that I would write this letter, to let everyone know that not only I but Dad as well are doing fine.

When I see Dad next time (not counting when I see him in my sleep, they can't stop him visiting me in my dreams), he will try to smuggle this letter out of the hospital. Then he will photocopy it. Then he's going to ask Leo to find Tom and Hannah and Dorothy and Annette and Roy and give each of them – each of you! – a copy of it. Dad can't do it by himself because he has to hide; but Leo has accepted that Dad's come back, and he wants to help.

I want to give a copy to Mr Kolko as well. I want to say thank you and to show him that I remember my manners.

Yours faithfully,

James

P.S. I've asked Dad to tell Leo that if he can't find you in the phone book, the best bet might be the police station. I hope that's OK. I remember Tom's address, but I have not been to any of the other houses and I don't know where you live.

P.P.S. Thank you all for helping me get my father back safely from his travels. He has lots of interesting stories for me. Please could you ask Mr Kolko if he could help me get my mother back next. He can name his price. I regret killing her.

2.

Dorothy finishes reading the letter for the third time. Three times is the charm, and she lets the paper rest on her lap. She says, 'I see.'

'Do you?' asks WPC Webber. 'Because I certainly don't.'

'The boy's saying thank you.'

'Well I can work that out, Dorothy. I can read. But how do you explain it?'

'I don't need to give a third statement, do I?' she asks with a twinkle in her eye, thinking: *Three times is the charm; and as Roy used to say, three times is deeply personal.*

'Nobody's asking you to do that.' Webber smiles briefly.

Dorothy cocks her head. 'Then all I can do is refer you to my earlier explanation, of last night,' she answers, looking around. They are sitting in the empty theatre. The temperature is cool, the light subdued: there is not a film scheduled for another two hours.

'But it doesn't make sense!' the officer complains.

'That's true. Not to us, anyway. It does to James. It does to his dad...So Kolko was telling like it is all along. Who'd have thought?'

'I looked him up – Kolko, I mean – and he did serve: he was with the Force. And needless to say, perhaps, he gives a somewhat abbreviated version of the overall story from the one you gave us last night.' Webber sniffs. 'Far as *he's* concerned, Tom and Roy shoved past him at the door and forced their way into the house he shares with his mother: Amelior Anderson. The way he puts it, Tom was furious that his mother was having an affair with her brother and he wanted to sort the picture out... though he was mistaken, of course, in Kolko's opinion: about the affair...' Webber takes a deep breath. 'I must say,' she adds, 'he was convincing. Very convincing. Said he'd invited his old friends Stephen and Pam over to stay after they'd all had a few drinks.'

This is outrageous. 'They were naked, you said!'

'Yes, there is that. Kolko thinks it's odd – or he *claims* to think it's odd – himself; but he says they've been sleeping together, innocently, since they were kids. Even butt nekkid.'

'...Which is bullshit,' Dorothy adds.

'Probably. But the fact remains...Tom and Roy entered the house and they killed Mrs Anderson's cat. That's a fact. There's blood all over their clothes and hands. So we've got to do something about *that*.'

'When they wake up.'

Webber nods. 'When they wake up,' she agrees. 'But let me say something, Dorothy. Please don't doubt I'll be looking into this personally. Even if it's in my spare time. I know I'm still fairly fresh to the profession, but honestly, I've never seen anything like last night.'

'Could you go over it for me one more time?' Dorothy asks.

'There were three of us…'

'You went upstairs: you, your governor–'

'Sergeant Marcus. And one of my colleagues, PC Cooke… Stephen's on the landing in his Y-fronts. His mother's right behind him, completely in the altogether, but we didn't see what room she came out of – and even if it was Stephen's sister's room – or the room she was staying in for the night, I should say – there's no law against that either. The sister was still in bed in the spare room…or I should say, in Kolko's room.'

'The one she was sharing with her brother.'

'So you believe; I don't know. But possibly, yes…Mrs Anderson has two rooms with beds in them: one for her, Kolko says, and one for him. Only last night he gave his room up to the guests. Who happen to be brother and sister, and were in the nude.' Webber shrugs.

'And Tom was in the *sewing* room?'

'Yes. On his feet but completely catatonic. Breathing normally,' says Webber, 'but showing no recognition of sound or vision. No pupil dilation, no reaction to smelling salts. Nothing. And Roy was exactly the same: the lights were on…'

'…but nobody's home.' Dorothy fidgets with the letter in her hands. 'Can I see them?'

Webber nods her head. 'You'll have to call the hospital, but

I don't see why not.'

'Even though they're lead suspects in a case of cat butchery?'

'Not any more.'

Dorothy cocks her head again: a gesture of inquisitiveness.

'Just before I left to come here, Kolko phoned me.'

'Oh, don't tell me…'

'He's not pressing charges. A simple misunderstanding, was how he put it.'

'…The bastard.'

'Which is not to say that he's got away with anything, as I said.'

'I understand…but it still seems unfair.' Dorothy makes a decision. 'I'll catch a bus over to the L and D this afternoon. Right now, in fact. See if I can talk to Tom and Roy. Because I'm sure that now I've spoken to you they'll want to fill in any gaps that I might have left. *They'll* press charges, believe me.'

Webber's smile is faint and sympathetic.

Picking up on it, Dorothy adds, 'What? You don't think they'll be coming back?'

Webber waits a beat or two. 'If you want my honest opinion, not as an officer of the law but as a witness to something I can't explain, I think they're hiding,' she says. 'They're in a retreat. Catatonia is often the result of deep shock.'

Dorothy's smile is more pronounced than that of her interlocutor.

'They'll be back,' she says with confidence, standing up and showing signs of wanting to leave. 'I'd stake my life on it.'

WPC Webber also rises. 'I'm so glad you're a positive woman,' she says. 'Especially after everything…you know. But do me a favour, will you? Don't do anything to Patrick that I wouldn't do: that I wouldn't do *as an officer*. We'll get to him in due course, okay?'

Dorothy thinks about her visit to the old man of last night.

'I promise I won't do anything more,' she tells the police-woman.

Webber appears gratified. 'I'll be in touch. Thank you, Dorothy.'

'No, Donna – thank *you*.'

Together, they walk down the stairs in the auditorium, to-wards the exit with the green light over the door. Although Dor-othy's body aches, her mind feels fresh and clean.

Epilogue

Hannah's favourite joke is about Heaven.

A woman arrives at the Gates of Heaven…and there are no gates! There are no doors either: there is nothing to *choose* from. There is no one to greet her with silly questions.

It's the best joke ever because there is no trite punchline. She can wait in the feedline forever, with a gentle smile plucking at the corners of her mouth.

A relief from pain equals happiness, and a joke leads to happiness also, or should do. Is it not acceptable, then, that a joke is only a relief from pain (it doesn't have to be funny); and that a relief from pain is simply a joke?

Perhaps the logic is flawed, but Hannah likes the idea all the same. It feels good to be naïve. It feels good not to think, not to consider; it feels good not to have to make yet another wretch-ed choice.

If I'm wrong, I'm wrong, Hannah thinks, soaring high about a platform of cloud. All my choices can go to Hell!

Hannah laughs, or acknowledges a note of humour at any rate. A pile of warm wind collapses into and completely fills her beak. It's hard to breathe. She beats her wings; she dives down as close to the cloud as she dares – close enough to experience its icy tickle, but not so close that she penetrates the bank.

The carpet of cloud – rolling as far as the eye can see – is the sole barrier between *then* and *now*. And Hannah prefers *now*. She is not going back there; and she is not going back *then* either.

Then is not home anymore.

She will find the body. And then she'll describe what she's found.

David Mathew is the author *O My Days, Ventriloquists* and *Sick Dice* (Montag Press) and three more books are forthcoming from the same publisher after *The Parry and the Lunge.* His academic writing has been published as *Fragile Learning* and *The Care Factory;* a third volume has been commissioned. A keen traveller and researcher, David Mathew is also active in higher education and psychoanalysis.